TALES OF THE STAR WOLF

Other Books by David Gerrold

DAVID GERROLD

TALES
OF THE
STAR WOLF

THE VOYAGE OF THE STAR WOLF
THE MIDDLE OF NOWHERE
BLOOD AND FIRE

50 YEARS
SFBC
SCIENCE
FICTION

THE VOYAGE OF THE STAR WOLF Copyright © 1990 by David Gerrold
THE MIDDLE OF NOWHERE Copyright © 1995 by David Gerrold
BLOOD AND FIRE Copyright © 2003 by David Gerrold

First SFBC Fantasy Printing: February 2004

Published by arrangement with:
BenBella Books
6440 N. Central Expressway
Suite #508
Dallas, TX 75206

Visit The SFBC at http://www.sfbc.com

ISBN 0-7394-4071-3

Contents

THE
VOYAGE
OF THE
STAR WOLF

For Amy Stout,
with love

Introduction

Jerry Pournelle

If you didn't know David Gerrold began his writing career as a script writer, you'll know that before you finish *The Voyage of the Star Wolf*. Now, usually when a critic says that a book reads like a screen play that's bad news, but not always, and not this time. What I mean is that this is a very visual book, with lots of images, and that's all to the good. Space is a colorful place, but not many have been there, and even fewer have ever seen a space warship. You'll know what David Gerrold's spaceships look like well before you finish this book.

This is an action adventure space novel—what's called in the trade "space opera" for reasons that have never been clear to me. They don't call the C. S. Forester novels about the Napoleonic era age of sail "sea operas," but this book and many other "space operas" draw heavily on that tradition. Space war is like naval war, so this is hardly surprising: many of the problems of modern warship commanders are not all that different from those faced by Horatio Hornblower, and most of us who think about warfare in the future suspect that future ship commanders will have more of the same problems. A ship is no better than its crew, and a crew is no better than its leadership.

There are two ways to write a "space opera." One way is to just write it, and if you get into too deep a hole, go back and change the assumptions, play with the plot line, exercise author control, and with a mighty leap your hero gets past the trouble. That never makes for a very good story, and may explain where the term "space opera" comes from, and just why it's such a term of derision. Alas, there were a lot of such stories written over the years.

The other way to write a space action adventure story is to take it seriously, with a full development of the background: physics, weapons, social structure, history, visualizations of the shipboard environment, and all the rest. Once you have that backstory, write your adventure in that world, and if you come to a problem, solve it without changing the rules. That's the way Larry Niven and I did *The Mote in God's Eye*—arguably the book that revived the space opera after a long period in the doldrums—and that's what David has done with *Voyage of the Star Wolf*. He took his subject seriously, and as a result he's done a book that's very readable. When I told my son Alex I was doing an introduction to this book, he said "Good choice. I'd rather read that again than another of the XXX YYY series." [Story names of a popular series omitted for obvious reasons.] And of course Alex was right. *Voyage of the Star Wolf* reads fast enough that you'll miss some details. The details are in there and they're interesting too; which makes this a book you can read more than once, something I can't say about a lot of space opera.

The backstory here is quite detailed and interesting all by itself, and quite self consistent; and inside that backstory there's a real moral question of just what is human. Let me give you a mild example: suppose a couple genetically engineers their child, choosing genes that make their child a world class Marathon runner. She then goes out and beats the men's world record and wins all her races. What are we to make of that? Is this acceptable? And what is she to think about herself? Now that incident isn't in this book, but it might have happened in the Star Wolf's world's history, and the moral question is very much in the background here. Not that there's a lot of moralizing, because this is, after all, an action adventure novel; but like the best of that genre, the story is informed, to use a modern phrase, by important questions, and that's one of them.

It's also a study in command, and once again, David Gerrold takes the subject seriously. He's not preachy. He just looks at a real problem: How do you turn a jinx ship into a fighting unit? The answer to that question has often made a great story, and it does this time too. David has studied the master story tellers, Heinlein and Forrester and Conrad, and it shows.

So. We have real characters, which is to say they're flawed as all real humans are, afraid when most heroic, as real humans are. We have a believable background. We have a war that makes as much sense as most wars do; and we have the epic voyage of a ship that earns her way into the fleet. Robert Heinlein used to say "We write for Joe's beer money, and Joe likes his beer. It's our obligation to give him at least as much fun from our books as he'd get from a six pack." *The Voyage of the Star Wolf* more than meets that obligation. I enjoyed reading it again. If you've read this far, you'll like it too.

Jerry Pournelle
Hollywood, June, 2003

Out there.

The *eternal* frontier.

It isn't the darkness that gets to you and it isn't the aloneness. It's the emptiness. It's the incomprehensible endless empty that drives you mad from the inside.

It presses upward from the back of your skull, it is a constant gnawing pressure, until you feel as if you are going to explode. You cannot taste it. You cannot touch it. But you can feel it constantly, so close—just on the other side of the bulkhead.

One day, you know that you're going to open an airlock and step out to meet it face to face. You know that you're going to do it, even though you also know that it will certainly kill you. But you will do it anyway. There is no choice in the matter. There is no whether or not. There is only *when* and *how*. Someday, you will not be able to stand the not-knowing*ness* of it any longer, and you will step naked out of the airlock to meet this inexplicable thing that doesn't exist and can't be seen or smelled or touched: this existence that is the absolute lack of all existence.

This is the kernel where the madness starts, this is how it grows: in the knowledge that the unexplainable incomprehensible unknowable exists. It demands explanation, but the human mind is incapable of explaining this concept of existence without form or substance. It cannot imagine, it cannot *comprehend*, it cannot contain ideas which are larger than itself—and in the face of possibilities that are larger even than the concept of concept, the mind flounders at a perpetual loss; it cannot encompass.

The mind cannot understand emptiness nor can it contain infinity. Total emptiness. Total infinity. Neither can be conceptualized, neither can be held in the human consciousness. And when both of those staggering truths exist together—endless emptiness or empty endlessness—the mind founders on the reefs of confusion and desperation. The human spirit is staggered by the experience; stunned, horrified, entranced and *transformed*. It's beautiful. It's terrifying. It's like looking into the face of God.

Afterward, you are not the same person.

The body, the expression, the total affect of the being is forever enchanted by the experience of *space*. The way you walk, the way you talk, the way you think and feel. No one who has ever stood naked before the jeweled night will ever be free of its terror and its power.

And even this is only an intimation of the magnificent dreadfulness of *hyperstate*.

—W. Ilma Meier, *Death and Transformation in Space*

The Silk Road Convoy

The Silk Road Convoy was almost three hundred years old.

Its path roughly described a bent and swollen, meandering, broken ellipse along the edge of the rift and then out and across it and back again. A closer examination might reveal that the trail of the convoy was actually a series of lesser arcs tracing through the spiral arm, then turning reluctantly out into the darkness of The Deep Rift, with one scheduled stopover at the forlorn worlds of Marathon, Ghastly, and George, then across The Great Leap and into the lips of the ghostly streamer known as The Purse on the opposite side, then around The Outbeyond, down toward The Silver Horn, and finally turning home again, leaping across at The Narrows and then down through The Valley of Death to The Heart of Darkness, then a sudden dogleg up to a place of desperate joy known as Last Chance, before finally sliding into The Long Ride Home and a golden world called Glory.

The Silk Road Convoy was the oldest of all the caravans on the route. It was not the largest fleet on the route, but it was definitely the richest and most prestigious.

The convoy followed the path of an ancient exploration vessel. Colonies had followed the vessel. Traders had followed the colonies. The trade had evolved over the centuries into a trade route called The Silk Road. Eventually, due to the twists and vagaries of luck and history and fate, it became one of the most profitable routes known in the Alliance. At any given moment there might be as many as thirty different caravans scattered along its great curving length—but only the original Silk Road Convoy was entitled to bear the name of the trade route. This was because the partnership which had grown up with the original Silk Road Convoy also owned or controlled most of the directorships of the Silk Road Authority.

The Silk Road Authority was larger than most governments. It held three seats in the Alliance and controlled almost all of the trade, both legal and otherwise, within the ellipse of its influence. The Authority had major offices on every planet within thirty light-years of the primary route. Every merchant ship in the arm paid a license fee for the privilege of traveling the route and booking passengers and cargo through the offices of the Authority.

Some ships, like the notorious freebooter *Eye of Argon*, preferred to travel alone. Others paid for the privilege of traveling with a caravan. The caravans were near-permanent institutions.

Imagine a chain of vessels nearly three light-days long, islands of light strung through the darkness. They carried names like The Emerald Colony Traders (licensed to The Silk Road) and The Great Rift Corporation (licensed to The Silk Road) and Zetex Starlines (licensed to The Silk Road). The caravans provided service and safety—and safety had lately become a primary consideration for star travelers.

Because of its name, because of its age and its prestige, the Silk Road Convoy was considered the safest of all.

Marathon

The dark world of Marathon had never known life of its own and never would. Lost in eternal night, it circled a dead and cold star. Ghostly starlight limned its bleak horizons. Life here could never be more than a lonely visitor. The planet was hard and barren and ugly.

It had been discovered by accident, settled by necessity. The only good thing about Marathon was its location, a third of the way into The Deep Rift. Hard in the abyss; the ugly world was a welcome way station in the long desperate leap to the other side. Its single settlement was a bright lonely point of life. Despite itself, despite its abysmal desolation, Marathon had become an important stopover. It was a nexus of the lesser trade routes which bordered the abyss; despite its desolate loneliness, the dark world was becoming a trade center in its own right.

Marathon had two neighbors, Ghastly and George, both of which were said to be considerably less attractive than Marathon. Few had gone to see for themselves. There was some ice mining on George, and nothing on Ghastly but a few crashed probes.

Marathon wasn't quite the frontier, but it was an *edge* and that was bad enough. Too many things *lurked* out here.

And too many people had become suddenly afraid.

Despite the patrol vessels, the growing fears of war were making Marathon a place of urgency and need. There was an air of panic here. The sudden flow of refugees from The Outbeyond had created a thriving market for passage on every stopping vessel, regardless of destination, as long as it was deeper away from the frontier. The local offices of The Silk Road Authority had become hard pressed to meet the growing demand for passage.

Adding to the distress of the refugees was the fact that a great number of ships were waiting stubbornly in orbit around Marathon, their captains refusing to continue along the route until they could join The Silk Road Convoy.

If it came.

Rumor had it that war between the Alliance and the Solidarity was imminent. Rumor had it that the Silk Road Authority was so concerned about the inevitability of interstellar conflagration that the great caravan might not pass this way again for a long long time. Rumor had it that this was the caravan's last circuit, that the route was being shut down for fear of Morthan marauders.

Rumor *also* had it that the Alliance was assembling a great fleet to protect the route . . .

Liberty Ships

The center of gravity of a liberty ship is the singularity, the pinpoint black hole that powers the ship and also serves as the focus for its hyperstate nodule. The singularity masses as much as a small moon and can be accurately located by even a low-power gravity wave scanner out to a distance of several light hours.

The singularity is held in place by a singularity bottle, a spherical magnetic cage three stories high; this is the ship's engine room. Three hyperstate fluctuators are focused on the singularity; one from above, one from either side. They are spaced 120 degrees apart. The fluctuators extend out through the hull of the ship and into three massive spines that give the starship its characteristic spiky look. The length of the fluctuators is a function of the size of the ship; it is necessary for precise focusing of the projected hyperstate bubble around the vessel. Hyperstate is also known as *irrational space*, producing the oft-quoted cliché, "To go faster than light, first you have to be irrational."*

For sublight acceleration and deceleration, the liberty ship has three mass-drivers mounted around her hull. A mass-driver is a long thin tube, lined with superconducting magnetic rings. Ions are introduced at one end, accelerated to near-lightspeed, and shot out the opposite end, producing the necessary thrust. The direction of particle acceleration can also be reversed for braking maneuvers. While the

---

*The singularity itself is tended by the "Black Hole Gang," generally an insular crew with their own jargon and mystique. On most ships, the singularity team regard themselves as the masters of a particularly arcane and esoteric discipline; they do not casually welcome outsiders to their domain. Relationships with the "Front Office," their name for the Bridge crew, are occasionally strained.

operation of the mass-drivers is not as easily detectable as that of the singularity stardrive, the vessel's wake of accelerated ions can be detected by a ship with sophisticated scanning gear.

Aft of the engine room, you will find crew's quarters, storage areas, aft torpedo bay, cargo bays, and the internal shuttle bay. The shuttle bay is equipped to function as a cargo lock; but there are also smaller airlocks at the stern of the vessel. A liberty ship usually carries two shuttles and occasionally a captain's gig. Used as lifeboats, the shuttles can carry ten individuals each; fifty if they are put into short-term hibernation.

Forward of the engine room, are officers' quarters on the top deck, the ship's brain and main mess room on the second deck, and the keel and equipment storage bays on the bottom level. Forward of that is the Operations complex. This is built around a large U-shaped Operations deck; the forward half of which is a sophisticated viewer. At the rear of the Operations deck is the Bridge, a high, railed platform overlooking everything. Directly underneath the Bridge is the Operations bay, where the ship's autonomic functions are maintained.

Forward of the Operations complex are more crew's quarters, sick bay, the weapons shop, forward torpedo bay, forward access and airlock. Running the length of the ship is the keel, a utility corridor which also functions as the ship's primary channel for cables, ducts, and optical fibers.

On the hull of the ship, you will find three large arrays of scanners, detectors, cameras, and other sensory apparatus. There are also twelve arrays of disruptor-beam projectors. The ship is double-hulled, with both hulls required to maintain 99% or better atmospheric integrity. Both hulls are also internally and externally shielded against particle-beam weapons. Class V magnetic shields are standard on most liberty ships, although most captains upgrade to Class VII or better whenever the equipment is available.

The liberty ship has a multiple-redundancy, optical nervous system. Autonomic functions are maintained by an array of Systems Analysis boxes. Higher-brain functions are handled by one or more Harlie series synthesized-consciousness modules. The Harlie series has been designed to be more anthropomorphic than other constructed identities, and therefore tends to perceive the starship as its own body; this produces a measurable increase in the unit's survival motivation.

Standard crew on a liberty ship is 120 persons.

The *LS-1187*

The *LS-1187* was three years old and had not yet earned a name.

She was a destroyer-class starship, a liberty ship, one of many. On her side, she wore the flag of New America: thirteen horizontal stripes, alternating red and white, and a dark blue field showing seven white circles around a single bright star.

The liberty ships came off the line one every eleven days. There were seven assembly lines building ships. This one was like all the rest; small and desperate, fitted with just enough equipment to make her survivable, and sent as rapidly as possible out toward the frontier. It would be up to her port of assignment to install her secondary fittings, internal amenities, auxiliary systems, and weaponry—whatever might be necessary for her local duties.

The *LS-1187* had not yet earned her name because she had not yet "bloodied her sword." Until she did, she would remain only a number.

She was a lean ship: a dark arrow, three hundred meters long. Two thirds of the way back along her hull, three sharp fins projected out and forward. These were her fluctuator spines. The end of each one culminated in a bulbous stardrive lens.

Her cruising speed was subluminal, but the realized velocity of her hyperstate envelope was 750 times the speed of light.

Her orders were the simplest possible: a time, a location, and a vector.

Translation: Proceed to The Deep Rift. Arrive at a specified *here* at a specified *now*, pointed in a particular direction and traveling at a particular speed. Don't be followed. Do all this and you will be part of the Grand Convoy of a thousand ships: a thousand separate vessels all arriving at their respective places in formation at the same moment.

It was a daring gamble, but if it worked . . . the outworlds would have the protection they needed against the raids of the marauders.

If it failed . . .

Admiral Wendayne stood on the Bridge of *The Moral Victory* and frowned. He was a stout man, short and stocky and solid. He was also bald and very sour-looking. He was studying a holographic display of the entire convoy as it came together.

He should have been proud; the idea of the Grand Convoy had been his; but he wasn't proud. He was annoyed. He hadn't been given half the ship strength he felt he needed; and too many of the ships assigned to the convoy were the smaller liberty ships, untried and untested. Too many of them had numbers instead of names. Nothing ever worked out as planned.

An aide stepped up to the admiral then. "The *LS-1187* has joined the convoy."

Admiral Wendayne was underwhelmed. "Hmp." Then he realized that the aide was waiting for a response. "All right. Welcome them."

The aide, a young man, turned to a console and murmured a command to IRMA, the ship's computer. A screen on the console lit up with a set of official-looking codes, followed by the crest of the fleet, and finally by the image of the admiral. "Greetings—Captain Lowell and the crew of the *LS-1187*—your participation in this operation represents a vital contribution to the security of the Alliance. On behalf of the—"

The message was encoded, translated into a series of pulses, and channeled to the modulators of the flagship's hyperstate envelope. The envelope *shimmered*. Every ship within scanning range of the flagship's envelope could see the *shimmer* of her hyperstate bubble, but only those with the appropriate codes would be able to translate the shimmer into a message. All of the Alliance codes were one-time cyphers, to be used only once and then never again.

Aboard the *LS-1187*, the message was translated and played as it came in. Its header codes identified it as a standard greeting signal, not requiring acknowledgment.

"—Admiralty, let me thank you, and let me welcome you to the Combined Allied Star Force special operations at Marathon. You may now open up your sealed orders. Again, welcome aboard."

Captain Sam Lowell nodded wryly at the image of the admiral. He was an older man, almost kindly-looking. Beside him on the Bridge stood Jonathan Thomas Korie, his executive officer. Korie looked preoccupied; he was listening to something on his headset. Now he frowned. He turned and looked down toward the large, elliptical, holographic display table in the center of the Operations deck. The Bridge—that part of the ship that was actually called *the Bridge*—was a high-railed platform at the rear of the Ops deck. There were command chairs there and two exit doors, one on either side. The Bridge overlooked the whole chamber; Korie could oversee the duties of all eight officers at the consoles beneath them.

The entire front half of the Ops deck was a giant curving screen that wrapped around half the chamber and most of the ceiling as well. At any given moment, it was like standing under an open sky, a great panoramic window onto the void. At the moment, the forward image was a simulated view of the distant stars, with shadowy grid lines superimposed over them; the starship seemed to be moving up through a three-dimensional framework, with a delimiter every five light-minutes.

Korie glanced over as Captain Lowell said, "All right, I've heard enough." He reached over and tapped the message off. To Korie's questioning look, he explained, "I've heard this speech before. And you'll hear it enough times too when you're a captain. You'll learn the whole damn repertoire."

Captain Lowell took a dark envelope out of his tunic and carefully broke the seal. He removed three sheets of gray paper, unfolded them and scanned them quickly, passing them to Korie as he finished each one.

"Mm," said Korie. "No surprises here."

"Did you expect any?"

Korie shook his head. Captain Lowell unclipped a hand-mike from his belt. His voice was amplified throughout the ship. "This is the captain speaking. We are seven point five light-years from Marathon. We've taken up our assigned position in the convoy and we've been officially welcomed by Admiral Wendayne. From this point on, we'll be operating at full alert."

There were audible groans across the operations room—not very loud, but loud enough for Korie to look annoyed and Captain Lowell to look amused.

The captain continued. "All right, can the chatter. The admiral thinks there's a good chance of engaging the enemy here. Personally, I don't think so, but maybe the admiral knows something I don't. That's why he's an admiral and you're not. So everybody, just stay on your toes. That is all."

As he clipped the mike back to his belt, Captain Lowell looked to his executive officer. "Do you understand why I did that?"

"I think so."

"This ship is going to be yours very soon. I want you to take care of her. She's a proud ship." He nodded toward the Bridge crew. "It's all about trust. You have to be straight with them, Mr. Korie. *Never ever lie to your crew.*"

"I promise you, sir. I never will."

"Keep that promise and you'll be a good captain," Lowell said. "I've never lied to this crew and I have nothing to be ashamed of." Wistfully, he added, "I just wish . . ."

". . . That she could have earned a name, right?" Korie finished the thought for him.

Captain Lowell nodded. "You know me too well."

"We're going to miss you, sir."

"I'm not dying, Mr. Korie. I'm only retiring. In the meantime," he smiled, "you'd better pay attention to your screens." He pointed. "What's that?"

Korie glanced to the console before him, then down forward to the Operations deck where Flight Engineer Hodel was working at the holographic display table.

Mikhail Hodel was a young man with a very professional demeanor, but he was also dark and wild-looking and was known to be obsessive in all of his various pursuits. Now, he was intently studying the schematic of a too-bright shimmer moving through a shifting grid work. He looked up as Korie stepped down to join him.

"She just came up out of nowhere, sir. I don't recognize the signature. I've never seen a ripple-effect like that—like it's being held in. Suppressed."

"Where'd she come from?" asked Korie.

Hodel shook his head. "I don't know. One moment she wasn't there. The next—"

Korie peered intently at the floating display. "I've never seen a scan like that before—not even in simulations."

Hodel looked unhappy. "I think she followed us, sir."

"Not possible. We'd have seen her. If she can see our bubble, we can see hers."

"Maybe not, sir—" Hodel blurted what he was thinking, "There is one way to do it—a large bubble can be damped down. It'll still have a longer visual range than the same-size envelope from a smaller engine."

Korie started to shake his head. "The density would—"

"—would look like that," Hodel pointed.

Korie stopped himself from replying. Hodel was right. The bogey was coming in too fast. "HARLIE?"

The ship's computer answered immediately: "My best guess: A dragon class battle-cruiser running with her engines damped to prevent long-range detection."

"Confidence?"

"Eighty-eight percent."

"Good guess," Korie said to Hodel, but he wasn't happy.

"I'd rather have been wrong."

Korie turned toward the Bridge, but Captain Lowell was already stepping down to the display. "There's only one ship it could be—the *Dragon Lord*—but she's reported to be on the other side of the rift. The Solidarity doesn't have a lot of heavy metal to spare."

"How reliable was that report?" asked Korie.

"Reliable enough for the High Command." The captain shook his head unbelievingly. "If the admiral had known that a dragon class anything was lurking in this neighborhood, we'd have never assembled this convoy." He scratched his head thoughtfully. "Well, it can't mean anything. She's traveling alone. Probably sharking us."

"Well, it's working. I'm scared," said Hodel.

"Relax," said Lowell. "She's not going to attack. The Solidarity isn't that stupid."

Suddenly, the shimmer brightened and expanded. And expanded. *And expanded again.*

"Oh my God—" said Hodel. "Look at the way she's expanding her envelope."

"That's an attack run." Korie was already reaching for a terminal.

"No!" said Lowell. "No. They *can't* be that stupid. They can't be! Nobody attacks alone—"

The operating lights went suddenly to red. The alarm klaxon screeched throughout the ship.

Korie was suddenly listening to his headset. "Signal from the flag-ship, sir—"

"It is the *Dragon Lord*," Hodel said, still staring horrified at the shimmering display. "The signature is confirmed."

"And she's got a wolf pack coming in behind her!" added Captain Lowell. The blood drained from his face. He looked suddenly gray.

Korie forgot his headset for the moment and turned back to the display. It was his worst nightmare. Behind the expanded shimmer of the *Dragon Lord*, too many other lights were appearing on the display, winking into existence like tiny stars, one pink shimmer after the other.

Korie looked to the captain. The old man was frozen.

"Sir—?"

Captain Lowell started to lift a hand, as if he was about to say something. A thought flashed through Korie's mind. *He's never been in a real battle.*

Korie whirled. "Targeting—? Get a lock on her. *Battle stations!* Stand by to fire."

HARLIE replied instantly. "Targeting now."

Captain Lowell blinked, as if abruptly realizing where he was. "Uh—what did the flagship say?"

"Scatter and attack."

"Uh, right." Captain Lowell nodded. "Uh—disruptors, fire at will!"

Korie looked up sharply at that. What was the old man thinking? The attackers were still in hyperstate, fifty light-hours away, two minutes in real time. Disruptors were local-space weapons. The only way to destroy a ship in hyperstate was to hit its envelope with a field-effect torpedo.

Maybe he was just momentarily confused, Korie thought, but he knew the truth of the moment even as he tried to deny it. The captain was paralyzed by the enormity of the disaster. The huge holographic display dominated the Operations deck and every officer on duty could see the horror for himself. The bright pink shimmers of the Morthan wolf pack were sweeping ruthlessly down upon the convoy's flank. The darker, blue shimmers of the Alliance ships were scattering now—but slowly, much too slowly. They didn't have the same mass-to-power ratio as the much lighter vessels of the Morthan Solidarity. The marauders could easily outmaneuver the cargo and passenger vessels— *and most of the destroyers too.*

The only hope for the unarmed ships of the convoy was to scatter into the darkness of the rift, leaving the warships to slash and parry and dodge. The battle would spread out across a hundred light-hours of hyperstate—it didn't matter; what counted here was visibility and interception velocity. The wolf pack would chase the fattest targets. The destroyers would chase the wolf pack. The battleships would weave complex evasion patterns.

And in the center of it all, like a fat red spider in the center of a glistening web, was the largest brightest shimmer of them all—the *Dragon Lord.* Her immense hyperstate envelope was a lens for her hyperstate scanning devices that would let her see farther than any other vessel in the battle. She would be able to track the ships of the fleeing convoy for days—and she would be equally visible. She could ripple orders and directions to every ship in the wolf pack. Nothing would be able to get to her, but she would be able to see the whole battle. The Alliance ships would be helpless before such an advantage.

Korie saw the whole plan at once. It was brilliant. He could only admire the beauty of it. This wasn't just an attack on a convoy. This was about cutting The Silk Road and isolating all of the Alliance worlds on the far side of the rift. The *Dragon Lord* would sweep everything from here to Marathon—and then beyond. With the fleet in shambles, there would be no protection for the outworlds.

Korie stepped in quickly to Captain Lowell's side. It seemed as if everything on the Operations deck were beeping, buzzing, ringing, and clanging. He ignored it. "The missiles, sir?" he prompted.

"Yes, yes, of course." The old man looked almost grateful. "Ready missiles!"

"Recommend an evasion course, sir," Korie prompted.

"Yes. Make it so." Lowell nodded eagerly at Korie's suggestion.

Is he that scared? Korie wondered. So far, only Hodel could have noticed—and he was too busy with his own board to say anything about it.

Hodel's panel blinked and flickered. He slammed it with his fist— HARD—it was a reaction, not a cure; the computer channels on that console were locked up, thrashing with contradictory information; but the screens came immediately back to life anyway. Hodel muttered an oath and resumed working, laying in a series of complex evasion patterns. And then he glanced up at Korie knowingly. "This isn't going to work."

"Shut up," said Korie. "Do you want to live forever?"

"It's a trap," said Lowell. He was visibly flustered. "We can't fight the *Dragon Lord* and a wolf pack."

Korie noted that the old man was getting more ragged-looking every moment, but there wasn't time to do anything. If the attack was every captain's nightmare, then Captain Lowell's disintegration was every executive officer's nightmare. Korie was going to have to make it work. Abruptly, the targeting program chimed. Korie snapped, "Targets in range!"

"Missiles armed!" called Li on the weapons station. "Locking . . . one, two—locked."

Korie touched Captain Lowell's arm almost imperceptibly.

It worked. "Fire all missiles," said Lowell, not even realizing how he'd been nudged.

The two missilemen, Li and Greene, punched their red buttons. The boards flashed yellow, then green. The bay doors snapped open. The missiles dropped away from the ship—

The bright bubble surrounding the ship flickered and disappeared, dropping the vessel rudely out of hyperstate. A dozen missiles accelerated away. The envelope shimmered back into existence and the starship was superluminal again. The missiles were already igniting their hyperstate torches. They flared against the darkness and arrowed toward their targets with a speed no vessel could outrun. In the display, they were bright red points, moving faster than any of the pink shimmers representing Morthan ships.

The missiles would seek, they would close, they would pursue, and ultimately they would intercept and destroy. They could not be outrun—but they did not have the endurance of a larger vessel. They had to catch their targets in the first few minutes, or not at all. Their power would fail and they would wink out, exhausted.

The battle display told the story. Pink shimmers would blink and a dozen bright red pinpoints would streak across the intervening space toward the nearest blue shimmers. Or blue shimmers would blink, dropping missile spreads of their own—but most of them were fleeing, scattering and running into the darkness at top speed.

Korie was watching one particular flight of missiles. Some of the pink shimmers were dodging. Haphazard bright flashes demonstrated where other ships were already flashing out of existence. Most of them were blue.

"We've lost the *Melrose*," said Hodel, glancing down at his monitors. "—and the *Gower*. The *Columbia*'s down too."

Korie turned to Captain Lowell. "You're right, sir," he said carefully. "We're too visible. Suggest we drop from sight. Go subluminal—"

"You can't hide from them. They'll find us," cried Hodel.

"We don't have time to argue," said Korie. He pointed at the display. "Look—incoming!" The missiles were coming at them from three different directions now. The software was screaming alarms. The display was flashing wildly.

Lowell said something; Korie didn't understand it, he assumed that it was assent. "Do it!" he yelled at Hodel and the flight engineer punched his board. The starship shuddered as the hyperstate envelope collapsed around her.

"Rig for shock-charging—"

Korie never got a chance to complete the order. The faintest fringe of ripple effect from one of the hyperstate missiles hit them then, with an effect as devastating as a direct hit from a disruptor beam. Every electrical field in the *LS-1187* was momentarily discharged. Every instrument, every machine, every communications device, and every human being was suddenly paralyzed.

Every neuron fired at once. It was like touching a live wire. Every person on the ship went instantly rigid as their nervous systems overloaded. Their hearts froze, unable to beat; their muscles tightened in agony; the screams were forced involuntarily from their lungs; all their brain cells discharged completely into oblivion, triggering massive seizures and convulsions; their bowels and bladders let loose. Some of the men ejaculated involuntarily. Hodel spasmed and was thrown backward out of his chair. It saved his life. His console sparked and then blew up. Captain Lowell staggered, almost falling. Korie grabbed for him—they both collapsed to the floor. Korie had a flickering impression of flowers and purple fire and then nothing else.

All over the Operations deck and Bridge, the effects of the shock-charge were still going off. Wild electrical fire was flashing everywhere. Balls of lightning roiled around the chamber, bouncing and flashing, sputtering and burning.

Everywhere, crewmembers spasmed and shuddered and jerked across the deck, helpless. A flicker of purple lightning skewered Captain Lowell, enveloping him.

The same lightning flashed through the engine room, up and down the corridors of the vessel, and all around the singularity grid that held the ship's power source: a pinpoint black hole. The energy had no place to discharge—it tried to bleed off in a thousand separate directions, finally found weakness and leapt out through the portside disruptors; they exploded in a blossom of sparks and fire.

And the *LS-1187* was dead in space.

Recalled to Life

For a long dead moment, she drifted.

Then—slowly, painfully, life began to reassemble itself. A heartbeat, a gasp, a twitch, and finally even a flicker of thought. Somebody moved. Somebody else choked. There was a moan in the darkness and a terrible stench.

The ship was pitch dark—and so silent it was terrifying. All of the familiar background whispers were gone. Korie came back to consciousness screaming. He felt as if he were on fire. All his nerve ends were shrieking. He couldn't move—and he couldn't stay still. He tried to move, he couldn't. He was floating, rolling, bumping and drifting back the opposite way. He couldn't think. His head jangled. *Free fall*, he realized. *The gravity's off.*

He stretched out his arms, grunting in pain as he did so, and tried to feel where he was, trying to grasp—his head banged into something and his body twisted. He grabbed and missed and grabbed again, caught a railing and held on. Something else bumped into him, something soft and wet; it felt like a body, he grabbed it and held on. Whoever it was, he was still unconscious. Or . . .

"HARLIE?" he asked.

No response. He didn't expect one. It was still bad news. If the ship was totally dead, then so were they. The CO_2 buildup would get them within hours. His head hurt and his shirt and shorts were drenched with sweat and blood. He'd fouled himself as well.

"Starsuits." Korie said it aloud. But if the ship was without power, then the suits would probably be dead too.

What was wrong with the auxiliary power? Why hadn't it kicked in?

"Captain?" Li's voice. He sounded strained. "Mr. Korie? Anyone?"

Korie caught his breath. He couldn't believe how his lungs ached. "Here," he said. "Can you move?"

"I don't know. I'm caught on something. What's wrong with the power?"

"I don't know. Anyone else conscious?" Korie called.

He was answered by groans and pleas for help. Someone was crying softly. That was a good sign, Korie thought. If you have the strength to cry, you have the strength to heal. "Hodel?" he asked. "Hodel, where are you?"

The crying hesitated.

"Hodel, is that you?"

"Over here, sir." A different direction.

"You okay?"

"I will be. In a year or two."

"I think the emergency power system failed. We're going to have to plug in the fuel cells manually and jump start the system."

Hodel groaned.

"Can you move?"

"I can move. I just don't know where I am."

"All right. I'm on a railing. And I'm holding onto someone. Wait a minute, let me see if I can feel who it is." Korie moved his hand carefully across the other man's body, trying to find a shoulder so he could feel the insignia. . . .

He was holding the captain.

He pulled the captain closer to him, felt for his neck and his jugular vein.

He couldn't tell if the captain was alive or not.

Korie didn't want to let go of him, but there was nothing else he could do for Captain Lowell until some kind of light was restored to the Bridge. Korie felt his way along the railing; it was the railing of the Bridge. He reached the end and felt his way down to the floor. Good. He knew where he was now. Still holding on to the railing, he felt his way back along the floor to the emergency panels. If he was right—

He popped the floor panel open and felt around inside the compartment. There. He pulled out a flashbeam and prayed that it still worked. It should; it held a solid-state fuel cell.

It did.

There were cheers as he swept the beam across the Operations deck. Besides Captain Lowell, there were two other bodies floating unconscious. There were dark globules of blood and vomit and shit floating in the air. Hodel was hanging onto a chair; so was Li.

"Hodel? Can you move?"

"I haven't tried—" Cautiously he launched himself toward Korie. He floated across the Operations deck and grabbed at the Bridge railing, grimacing as he caught it. "If that's what it's like to be dead, I don't like it."

"It's not the dead part that hurts. It's the coming back."

"It's a long way to come back, sir. I hurt all over."

"So does everyone else," said Korie. He passed Hodel the light. "Aim it there—" He pulled himself along the floor to the next emergency panel and yanked it open. Inside was a double bank of switches. He began punching them on.

Nothing happened. Korie and Hodel exchanged worried looks.

"Try again?"

Korie nodded and began punching at the buttons one more time.

Again, nothing happened.

"Shit," said Korie. "All right. We'll go down to the keel and try every fuel cell in the floor until we find a set that works. All we need is one. We're not dead yet." He pulled open the next panel and started passing equipment to Hodel. "I think we'll have to—"

Something flickered.

The ceiling panels began to glow very softly. Hodel and Korie looked around as the emergency lights came on, and grinned.

"All right!" said Li.

"Listen," said Hodel. "The circulators are back on."

Korie stopped and listened. "You're right." He tapped his headset. "Engine room?"

Chief Engineer Leen's voice sounded surprisingly loud in his ear. "Captain?"

"No. Korie." He swallowed hard. "Damage?"

"Can't tell yet. We're still sealed off. Do you have light?"

"They just came on. Thank you. The singularity?"

"It's still viable—"

"Thank God."

"—but we're going to have to jump start the whole system."

"Are your men okay?"

"None of us are okay, sir; but we can do it."

"How long?"

"As long as it takes."

"Sorry. Oh, Chief?" Korie added. "Don't initiate gravity until we've secured the entire ship. There's too many unconscious bodies floating."

"Right. Out."

Korie noticed that the chief had not asked about the captain. He swung to face the flight engineer. "Hodel?"

"Sir?"

"Take the captain to sick bay. Then come back for the others."

"Yes, sir." Hodel launched himself across the Bridge, colliding clumsily with the captain. He grabbed the old man by the back of his collar and began pulling himself across the ceiling toward the rear exit.

Korie floated across to Li. "Hold still, Wan—" Li was pinned in his chair. Korie shone his light all around the wreckage. "Okay, it doesn't look too bad." He anchored himself and pulled. Li floated free. "You okay?"

"I've been better."

"There's a sani-pack in that compartment." Korie pointed. "Start getting some of this crap out of the air." There were floating globules of blood and urine everywhere.

Korie was already checking the other Bridge officers. Two of them were dead in their chairs. The third was unconscious. He wondered if there were enough survivors to bring the ship home.

"You know, we can't stay here," Li said, behind him. He was vacuuming wet sphericles out of the air. "Our envelope didn't flash out. They're going to know we're still alive and hiding in normal space."

"It's very hard to find a dead ship. You have to be right on top of her."

"They'll track our singularity with a mass-detector," Li argued. "That's what I'd do. They know where we went down, and they're going to have to come looking for us to make sure. They can't leave us here to attack the *Dragon Lord*."

"We're not attacking anything right now," said Korie. He floated over to the auxiliary astrogation console and began trying to reboot it.

"They don't know we're hit," the weapons specialist pointed out.

Korie grunted. The console was dead. He drifted down to the base of it and popped open a maintenance panel. He'd run it on battery if he had to. "Everything you say is correct. But we don't have a lot of options right now. If we recharge our hyperstate kernel, we'll be instantly visible to any ship within a hundred light-hours, and if we inject into hyperstate, we'll be visible for days. If they've englobed the area, we'll never get out."

"You think you can sneak away at sublight? That'll take weeks."

"We're going to need a few weeks to rebuild this ship anyway."

"They're still going to be looking for us, no matter what we do. If they don't find us immediately, they'll expand their search patterns. They know we're here and we can't shield against their scanners."

Korie looked over at him. "At this point, Wan, I don't know how much of this ship is left. That's what'll determine what we'll do. By rights, we should all be dead now."

The auxiliary astrogation console lit up then and Korie was momentarily cheered. It was a start. As each piece of the network started coming back online, it would start querying the rest of the system; if the queries went unanswered, each piece would automatically initiate its own set of restoration procedures for the equipment it could talk to. The resurrection of the ship would happen in pieces, much like the individual resurrections of each surviving crew member.

Two of the other consoles on the Bridge flashed back to consciousness then. Korie floated over to them and punched for status reports. As he suspected, they were still isolated from the rest of the ship. They had no information to report.

Korie considered his situation. His captain was disabled, maybe dying. His ship was dead in space and an unknown number of his crew were unconscious or dead. They were light-years from the nearest aid and they were surrounded by enemy marauders who would be looking for them as soon as they finished destroying the rest of the fleet. They had no weapons and no engines. They couldn't retreat either sublight or superlight. And, if that weren't enough, they were blind. All their sensors out of commission. He had no way of knowing if an attack was imminent, and no way of fighting back if it were.

But on the plus side, he told himself, *I'm finally in command*. The irony of it was almost enough to make him smile. He tapped his headset. "Chief?"

"It's bad news," said the voice in his ear. "I'm going to have to restring everything. It'll take days."

"We have days," said Korie. "Listen, I have an idea. Can you put a man in the lookout with a sextant? Take a sighting?"

"It won't be very accurate."

"It doesn't have to be. I just want to make sure we're pointed in a useful direction."

"I can do that. If we're not, we can rotate the ship around the singularity until we are. I can even do that by hand, if I have to. We'll rig block and tackle and walk it around."

"Good. Now, here's the second part. Can you run the mass-drivers off the fuel cells—and for how long?"

"Do you mean leave the singularity damped?"

"Yes."

The chief thought a moment. "It's very old-fashioned," he said, "and I'm not sure what you're gaining, but it's doable. This is just a guess, but I can probably give you six weeks at least, maybe eight, but not more than ten."

"I'll take the six. If we make it that far, God likes us. I want no stress-field activity at all for the entire time, and I want you to minimize all electrical functions. Let's run this ship as if she's dead. Minimum life support, minimum everything."

"It won't work," said the chief. "They'll still find us. We can't get far enough away."

"Do the math," said Korie. "It's not distance that works for us. It's speed. Normal space is nasty. A constant acceleration of even one-third gee will pile up enough velocity in twelve hours as to make it practically impossible for anyone to intercept us in normal space—not unless they're prepared to chase us for several days, more likely weeks. And if we know they're chasing us, we plug in the singularity and go to full power and it's still a standoff."

"Mmm, maybe—" The chief engineer was not enthusiastic about the idea. "What's to keep them from jumping into hyperstate, leaping ahead and brushing us with their ripple?"

"If we live long enough to get to that situation, we'll activate our own hyperstate kernel. If they brush us they'll disintegrate with us. Not even a Morthan would consider that an honorable death."

There was silence from the other end of the line.

"Chief?"

The Engineer's voice had a sour tone. "Can't say I like it. And it's going to be hell to burn it off at the other end. We'll have to spend as much time decelerating as we do accelerating. And we'll have to do it before we can inject into hyperstate for the way home."

"Well, let's think about that . . ." suggested Korie.

"Uh-uh," said Leen with finality. "I can't compensate for that high a velocity inside the envelope. We'll be too unstable to hold a modulation."

"All right," said Korie. "You win. We'll do it your way."

"You listen to me. I'll bring you home. Leen out."

Korie allowed himself a smile. Three weeks of steady subluminal acceleration, plus another three of deceleration, would also give them enough time to effect major repairs. If they could do it at one gee, it would put them twenty-five light hours away before they had to inject into hyperstate. Not a great head start, but workable.

Korie remembered the problem from Officers Candidate School; he hadn't ever expected to apply it in a real situation. If it worked here though, they would earn themselves a place in future texts. But it would be difficult. Unless they could find a way to disassemble and rotate the main mass-drivers, it would be like standing the ship on its tail . . .

No. They didn't have the time. They'd have to jury-rig ladders. They didn't dare risk powering up the gravitors. That would be almost as visible to a tracker as the pinpoint black hole in the engine room.

Korie hadn't let himself ask the hard question yet. How much of a crew did he have left? That would be the worst—not having enough skillage to pilot the ship home. What was the minimum practical number?

Hodel returned then, pulling himself into the Bridge with a practiced motion.

Korie looked at him questioningly, as if to ask *how bad?*

Hodel shrugged. *Who knows?*

"You have the conn," Korie said. He pulled himself down toward the floor, and out through the Operations bay, the tiny cubbyhole beneath the high platform of the Bridge. There was one man on duty in the operations bay. He looked pale and shaken, but he had the power panel of his work station open and he was testing fuel cells. Korie patted him on the shoulder and pulled himself past, down into the keel.

The lights here were dimmer, making all the cables, conduits, and pipes into oppressive shapes in the gloom. Slowly, Korie made his way toward the A.I. bay and pulled himself up into it. HARLIE was totally dark.

"Shit." Korie popped open a compartment and pulled out the red-backed manual. "First. Make sure the power is on," he said to himself.

He stuck the manual to the top of the console and pulled open the emergency panels. He had the nightmarish sensation that he was going to spend the next three weeks doing nothing but powering up fuel cells by hand. There had to be an easier way to do this; but nobody ever expected a ship to have to start from zero.

The fuel cells kicked in immediately, which was a pleasant surprise. The bad news was that the automatic restart process would take several hours. Each of HARLIE's various sentience modules had to be individually powered up and tested, and not until system confidence was acceptable could they be reassembled into a functioning personality.

The alternative—to reawaken HARLIE without the complex system analysis—was to run the risk of post-shock trauma, disassociation, confusion, increased statistical unreliability, and possible long-term psychosis.

On the other hand, they couldn't get home without him. They couldn't even run the ship.

Theoretically, it was possible to run a starship without a sentient consciousness, but nobody had ever done it. Theory was one thing. Starships were something else.

"All right, HARLIE," whispered Korie. "You get to sleep a while longer." He punched in the command, then locked the console.

He levered himself sadly out of the computer bay and pushed himself along the keel until he got to the engine room. Work lights were hung all over the chamber, and crewmembers were already maneuvering around the great singularity cage in the center.

Chief Engineer Leen was supervising the stringing of an auxiliary power conduit. He looked up as Korie floated over. "I sent a man to the forward lookout to take a sighting, but we're tumbling ass over teakettle. Until we get HARLIE online, we can't do anything about that. I think we can get the autonomic network online sooner than that. I need to see if it's traumatized. And I'm rigging an auxiliary electrical harness, so we can charge up the mass-drivers as soon as we're oriented. What else do you want to know?"

"That's plenty. HARLIE's down for at least six hours, maybe longer. I want you to pull the manuals on running a ship without a brain, if we have to—and cross your fingers that we don't have to. In the meantime, I'm taking the tour. I need to see what shape the crew is in."

"They're rocky, but they're working."

Korie looked at Leen. "Have we got the skillage to get home?"

Leen shrugged. "We don't know. I've got Randle taking roll. Some of the boys are a little mindwiped. I don't know if we can bring 'em back." His expression was very unhappy.

"All right," said Korie, accepting the report. "Have the galley make sandwiches—uh, did the galley crew make it?"

Leen shook his head.

"Sorry. Okay, appoint two men to kitchen detail. Let's keep the lights on and the air circulating. If we can't make this work, we'll plug in the hole and try to run for it. But I'm assuming the worst." He looked to Leen, "Did I leave anything out?"

"We could pray . . ."

"I stopped praying a long time ago, Chief."

"Didn't get your prayers answered?"

"I got an answer. It was no." Korie pushed himself out of the engine room into the aftward keel. It was darker than the keel forward. Korie paused at each of the manually operated safety panels and double-checked atmospheric pressure, CO_2 content, temperature, and humidity. All were stable. Good. That meant hull integrity hadn't been breached. The biggest danger right now was that there might be a pinhole leak somewhere in the ship; but with no power and no network, there was no way to detect a pressure loss or locate the hole.

There was too much to worry about and not enough worriers.

Korie floated up into the shuttle bay and let himself drift while he considered. Maybe the shuttles could be useful. They were designed to be powered up quickly; maybe they could plug into a shuttle brain and run the ship from there. The shuttles weren't sentient on the same scale HARLIE was, but they were smart enough to avoid bumping into planets, moons, and asteroids. He'd have to talk it over with Chief Leen. It was another option.

As he headed forward again, he nearly bumped into Reynolds and MacHeath. They were maneuvering an unconscious crewmember toward sick bay. Korie nodded to them, then pushed himself quickly ahead.

The ship's mess was full of men and women; the overflow from sick bay. Some were conscious, most were not. Several were moaning. As Korie watched, two more crew members pulled themselves into the room. Fontana, the ship's pharmacist, floated in, carrying a hypo-spray injector and began administering sedatives to the worst injured. She glanced over to Korie. "You okay?"

"I will be. As soon as I get a chance to clean myself up. How about you?"

She shook her head. "This is a mess."

Korie followed her forward, catching her in the hall outside the sick bay. He lowered his voice. "How bad?"

"Twelve dead. At least six more we don't expect to make it. Two of the Quillas, the rest are in shock. I've sedated all of them. They're in bad shape; they're going to need extensive rehabilitation. Probably we all will. I've never seen injuries like this before. I thought we were better shielded—"

"It wasn't a beam. It was a ripple effect."

"Better if it was a beam. We can treat disruptor wounds."

"I'll remember that for next time." Korie lowered his voice. "How's the doctor?"

Fontana shrugged. "Indestructible."

"Have you got enough help?"

"No . . . but we'll manage. To tell the truth, there's not a lot we can do. Either you get better . . . or you don't."

Korie allowed himself to ask the question he'd been avoiding. "Captain Lowell?"

Fontana's expression said it all. She looked Korie straight in the eye and said, "I'm sorry, sir. You're going to have to bring us home."

Inside himself, Korie marveled that he didn't feel anything at all. He felt guilty. *I should be feeling something right now, shouldn't I?* "I, uh . . . I was afraid of that."

"Want some free advice? It's worth exactly what you paid for it."

Korie met her eyes. "Say it."

"Go to your room. Clean yourself up. Put on your sharpest uniform. And then make another inspection of the ship. Be seen by as many crewmembers as you can. And let them know that everything is under control—*even if it isn't.*"

"That's good advice," said Korie. "And as soon as I have time—"

"No. Do it now," said Fontana. "This ship isn't going anywhere. There's nothing happening that needs your immediate attention. There is nothing happening that is as important as the morale of this crew. They know the captain's hurt. They don't know what state you're in. You need to show them that you're ready to bring them home."

Korie stopped himself. He looked at Fontana and realized what she was saying. It was straight out of the Academy. First year. The first machine that has to be fixed is not the ship, but the crew. Fix the crew and everything else takes care of itself. *And remember what Captain Lowell said. "You have to be straight with them . . . It's all about trust."*

"You're right," Korie said to Fontana. "Thanks." He patted her affectionately on the shoulder and pushed himself forward. Her remarks echoed in his consciousness.

He remembered the seminars at the Academy. *The real crisis is not the crisis. The real crisis is what you do before it and after it.*

Right.

What did you do or what did you fail to do *beforehand* that turned the situation into a crisis?

What did you do or what did you fail to do *afterward* that prolonged the crisis-ness of the situation?

All the classes, all the simulations, all the seminars and discussions, all the endless analyses and recaps and debriefings—this was all of that all over again. He could hear the voices of his instructors, as if they were standing right behind him, judging his every move, his every decision.

Ask yourself three questions: What do you want to do? What are you capable of doing? What are you actually going to do? Be clear that these may be three different things.

"What I want to do," Korie said to no one in particular, "is take this ship home, fill it up with missiles, and then come back out here and kick some Morthan ass."

"What am I capable of doing—?" He considered the question. He could get the ship home. That wasn't in doubt any longer. It might take four months, limping all the way, but it was doable. Could he fight back? Now? No. With a refit? Definitely.

What was he going to do?

Korie grinned.

"What I'm capable of doing, what I want to do, and what I'm going to do . . . are all the same thing."

He touched the button on his headset. "Now hear this—" His voice was amplified throughout the ship. "This is First Officer Korie speaking. We've been hit, we've taken damage, but we're still afloat. We don't know how badly the fleet's been hit. We don't know how badly the convoy's been hurt.

"I am going to assume that a state of war exists now between the Terran Alliance and the Morthan Solidarity and I am going to act accordingly.

"It's going to take some time to bring all ship systems back online. It's going to take even more time to get home. But we will get home, I promise you that. We're going to rebuild this ship, and then we're going to come back out here and put a missile into every Morthan ship we can find.

"Korie out."

He thought he could hear the cheers of the crew echoing throughout the ship, but it could just as easily have been his imagination.

The hard part would be keeping them believing that . . .

A Situation of Some Gravity

Light had been restored to the corridors of the *LS-1187*, but not much else. Most of the desperately wounded were in sick bay or the mess room. The lesser wounded were spread across the forward half of the shuttle bay. A makeshift morgue had been established at aft starboard corner; a partition hid the bagged bodies from view; they were tethered like cargo.

A decision was going to have to be made about that soon, Korie knew. *Do we space them here or do we take them home?* He didn't know how he felt about it yet, and he didn't know who he should ask. Fontana probably. He knew the thought was irrational, but didn't like leaving any of his crew floating alone in the dark so far from home. There was also a military consideration. As unlikely an occurrence as it might be, what if one of the spaced bodies were discovered by a Morthan cruiser? It would be evidence that the *LS-1187* had not been destroyed.

And yet . . . he also knew that it unnerved the crew to have those dead bodies tethered there. It was damning evidence of their failure in battle. It was as if the dead were pointing an accusing finger at the living. "If you had not failed, we might still be alive."

Korie shook his head sadly. This was not a problem that he could solve immediately. This decision could be postponed a while longer. It went against his grain to postpone a decision; the unfinished business seemed to lurk in the back of his skull gnawing at his consciousness, but—

He pulled himself forward, into the starboard corridor, then left into the shallow chamber directly above the starship's engine room. This was Chief Leen's office and auxiliary control station. At the moment, it was also functioning as the starship's Bridge.

The chief was strapped into a chair before a work station. He was running diagnostic programs, frowning and muttering to himself. "Nope. Nope. That won't work. That won't work. Nope. Shit." Then he'd lean forward intensely and order a new set of routines to be run.

Korie hated to interrupt him, but—"I've thought of something else," he said. Leen pushed back from the screen and swiveled to face Korie.

"What now?"

"We're on minimum life support. How long can we maintain?"

Leen thought for a moment. Korie could almost see him running the subroutines in his head. "Six days," he said, finally. "If we use the LOX for the fuel cells, we can buy ourselves another three weeks, but then we're out of power unless we recharge. And that doesn't allow any margin for the mass-drivers. I don't see any way around it, we're going to have to use the singularity sooner or later."

"I know," said Korie. "But I want to hold off as long as possible, and I want to minimize any use of it. We give off G-waves, they'll find us. Right now, if they're tracking us, all they see is a derelict." He hooked one leg around a stanchion to keep from floating away. "We can survive without gravity. We have three months of food. We can ration our water. Our big problem is air."

"Can't use the osmotics," said Leen. "Not without the gravitors. And that's more G-waves. Y'know, if we could take a look-see, find out if there's anything hostile in range, we could control our radiations, keep them below the noise level . . ."

Korie shook his head. "Not yet. I don't want to risk opening up a scanning lens yet. Maybe in a week. Even a lens might give us away to the *Dragon Lord*. We just don't know how accurate her vision is. I have to assume the worst."

Leen grunted. "You're not making this very easy for me."

"I've been thinking," said Korie. "We could go to aeroponics. String lights and webs in the shuttle bay, in the inner hull, maybe even in the corridors and the keel. We could use irrigation stems. Start out with Luna moss, take cuttings every two days. In fourteen days, we should be able to increase the volume 64-fold."

Leen didn't answer. He just swiveled back to his screen and called up a set of extrapolations. "It'll be at least a month before you're getting significant oxygen production, even if you could double volume every two days. Which I don't think you can."

"A month might work," said Korie. "Just barely. It lets us keep our head down."

"It's going to be messy."

"We don't have a lot of choice in the matter. We're going to have to go to aeroponics sooner or later anyway. We have food for three months. We might make it on half-rations, but that's only a stay of execution, not a reprieve. What if it takes longer than four and a half months to get home? Let's start laying in our crops for the winter."

Leen made a noise deep in his throat; it sounded like a growl of disapproval. "Sounds like a lot of busy work to me. We've got more important things to do."

"No, we don't." Korie cut him off. "As long as we drift, we're safe. We look like a derelict. The longer we can drift, the more convincing we are. This isn't busy work—this is work that will guarantee our survival."

Leen didn't look convinced.

Korie shrugged and admitted, "Yes, all right. It'll give the crew a challenge they can accomplish. But they need that right now."

"I think we'd all much rather put a missile up the tail of the *Dragon Lord.*"

"You tell me a way we can get close enough to do that and I will. Otherwise, my job is to bring this ship and her crew safely home."

"You want my opinion? Let's just fix the engines and go."

"I *always* want your advice, Chief—"

"But—?"

"—You know the ship better than anyone. But I know what we're up against. The Morthans aren't stupid. This wasn't just a hit-and-run raid. This was a full-scale attack. If I were a Morthan commander, I'd be cruising the area right now, hunting for hiders like us."

"I don't like hiding," grumbled Leen.

Korie shrugged. "It's not my favorite thing either. But we don't have the resources to do anything else right now. String the webs, Chief. Let's get that started. Then, I want you to build a passive G-scanner and let it run."

"There's no accuracy in that."

"I don't need accuracy. I just need to know if something's moving out there."

"I'll use a split crew," said Leen. "Half on life-support, half bringing the network back online. That'll give you the luxury of both options. And it'll give me the time to fine-tune each part of the system as I recalibrate. What do you want to do about HARLIE?"

"Let him sleep."

"You sure?" Leen looked surprised.

Reluctantly, Korie nodded. "I'm worried about his state of mind. I'd rather not bring him back up until there's a ship for him to run.

There's nothing he can do until then anyway. I don't want him going crazy with worry—or worse, amputation trauma."

"HARLIE's too sensible for that."

"Probably. I'd like to believe you're right. But what happens if you're wrong? Let's play it safe. HARLIE's a friend of ours. Let's not take any unnecessary risks with him. Okay?"

"You're the boss."

"Only by default." Korie looked suddenly troubled.

Leen hesitated. He looked like he wanted to ask something else.

"What is it, Chief?"

"Nothing. I just—"

"Go ahead. Say it."

"Well, it's Captain Lowell. I heard that he—I mean, I don't believe it, but you know—scuttlebutt has it that he . . ." Leen was having trouble saying it; Korie waited patiently. ". . . Well, that he fell apart when the shooting started. Is that true?"

Korie started to answer, then remembered Captain Lowell's last advice: "You have to be straight with them, Mr. Korie. *Never ever lie to your crew.*" He flinched, then he looked directly at Chief Leen and said as sincerely as he could, "I was there. Captain Lowell did not screw up. The autolog will confirm that. And if any man on this ship says differently, he's going to have to answer personally to me." He added, "You can let that be known wherever it's appropriate."

Leen looked relieved. "Thanks. I knew that. I guess I just wanted to hear you say it."

Korie nodded curtly and pushed off toward the door.

That's one, he thought. *How many more?*

Korie's Cabin

Captain Lowell wasn't dead.

But he wasn't exactly alive either. It made for a very sticky legal situation.

Korie spent several grueling hours scanning through the manual of regulations. It wasn't very helpful.

With the captain injured, Korie was supposed to assume command of the vessel. The problem was, he *couldn't*.

Without HARLIE up and running and maintaining the log, Executive Officer Jonathan Thomas Korie could not officially assume command. The ship's doctor could not log a medical report, and Korie could not legally declare the captain incapacitated.

Until such time as the autolog could be resumed, his was a command without acknowledgment. He had the authority, he had the moral and legal right under fleet regulations; but what he did not have was the acknowledgment of FleetComm's official representative, the constructed consciousness known as HARLIE. It was like being elected president, but not taking the oath of office. Just when and how does the legal authority begin?

The whole thing made Korie realize just how precarious his position was. His orders were technically illegal until such time as his right to give them was confirmed. He was floating adrift in a legal limbo every bit as real as the limbo in which the *LS-1187* floated. And he was every bit as helpless.

There weren't any contemporary precedents for this situation, although there were ample historical records. Unfortunately, those records could be used for academic purposes only. Out of respect for the diversity of individual cultures in the Alliance, FleetComm's regulations were not derived from any specific naval tradition, and no precedents were to be assumed, historical or otherwise, unless FleetComm itself authorized them.

Translation: We're trying very hard to be fair and just and careful in the exercise of our authority. That leaves you without an umbrella. Good luck. Don't do anything stupid.

The problem was profound enough to interfere with Korie's sleep. And that made him irritable.

Unfortunately, there was nothing he could do about it. He didn't dare resurrect HARLIE yet. The ship was still crippled; repairs, realignments, and recalibrations were proceeding painfully slow—even slower now that Leen had half his crew stringing webs and lights for the aeroponics.

"I know I'm doing the right thing," said Korie to no one in particular. "Why doesn't it *feel* right?"

The door beeped. Korie waved at it. The door slid open and a grim-looking Fontana stepped into the room.

"I apologize for disturbing you," she began, "but I saw by your monitor that you weren't asleep, so—"

"It's all right." He sat up on his bunk. "What's on your mind?" He gestured toward a chair and she sat down opposite him.

She hesitated before answering. "I need an authorization," she said, and passed the clipboard across to him.

"What kind of authorization—?" Korie was puzzled, then he glanced down at the clipboard screen and shut up. AUTHORIZATION FOR EUTHANASIA.

He read through the form slowly. Suddenly, the standard boilerplate paragraphs about "the failure of all best efforts" and "the unlikelihood of the individual's recovery to a normal and fulfilling life" and "the individual's right to die with dignity" took on a new meaning; especially the clause about "in time of war, the survival of the ship and her crew always takes precedence over the survival of any individual crewmember."

Korie's eyes skipped down to the bottom. "Therefore, by the authority vested in me, by the Combined Allied Star Forces, I hereby authorize the termination of life support—"

Korie handed the clipboard back. "I can't sign this."

Fontana made no move to take it. "I didn't know you were religious."

"I'm not," said Korie.

"Moral reservations?"

"Nope."

"Then why won't you sign it?"

"I can't. It won't be legal."

Fontana looked at him. "Say again?"

"I haven't been logged in. HARLIE's down. Until we can bring him up again, I can't be logged in. And we can't bring him up again until the network is repaired. Anything I do before then, I can only do as executive officer—which is quite a lot; but unless Captain Lowell dies, I cannot legally assume command. What you have there is an order that I have no authority to give. We could both be court-martialed."

"You're kidding." Fontana brushed a loose strand of hair back off her forehead. Her expression was unbelieving.

"Look it up—"

"I *know* the regulations," she said, annoyed. "I just can't believe that you're *hiding* behind it."

"I'm not *hiding!*"

"You're not?" Fontana looked around. "The ship is rigged for silent running. We're adrift in The Outbeyond. You're spending most of your time in your cabin. You won't acknowledge your command. If that's not hiding, I don't know what is."

"I don't know what else to do, dammit!" He snapped right back. "If you have any suggestions—"

"You have the authority, Mr. Korie. I know it. The crew knows it. Everybody's waiting for you to figure it out. Fleet Command is not here to look over your shoulder. No matter what other regulations might be in the book, they're all of secondary relevance. The survival of the ship and her crew come first, and the highest ranking officer must assume command of the vessel."

"I've done that—I have done everything I can to ensure the survival of this vessel and this crew. I have my personal log to verify that. What I don't have is the *acknowledged* authority of FleetComm, and it would be not only presumptuous of me to assume that authority, it would be dangerous and stupid."

"You've got five men and two women in sick bay who are dead," said Fontana. "They're using up oxygen."

"Not that much—"

"Enough to make a difference."

"This is Dr. Williger's responsibility."

"Dr. Williger doesn't handle the paperwork. I do." Fontana looked disgusted. "It's bad enough the captain shit his pants. Now you too?"

Korie glared at her angrily, then he glanced at the clipboard again. He scanned the list of names unhappily. "Are you sure these are all irreversible?"

"Both Williger and I have signed that document." She added, "Two of them are unconscious. The others are fading in and out; they're in terrible pain, but there's nothing we can do for them—except this. Listen to me. Williger and I argued for an hour over each and every name on that list, looking for some reason, *any* reason, to not have to make the request. I've had two hours sleep in the past thirty-six. I'm operating on momentum now, but I can't stop until this is resolved. I can't stand seeing those men and women in pain any longer. Those are my friends down there. And yours too. This is the most generous gift you can give them. Easy release. Please, *Jon* . . . ?"

Korie handed the clipboard back to her, unsigned. "You'll have to take the captain's name off the list. I might be able to make a case for terminating the others; but I'll be damned if I'm going to accept the responsibility for Captain Lowell's death. I already have too much that's going to need explaining when we get back. I don't need to look for anything more."

Fontana paged to the next document and handed the clipboard back. "Williger and I both thought you'd say that. But for humanitarian reasons, we felt we had to give the captain the same chance as the rest of the crew. Fortunately, he's unconscious."

Korie looked at the screen again. It was the same document, but without Captain Lowell's name. He allowed himself a sour expression. "How many more of these have you got prepared?"

"Don't be nasty," Fontana said. "This is not an easy job. And you're not making it any easier."

"I'm the one who's going out onto the skinny branches," Korie said. He took a breath, closed his eyes, and reassured himself as to the *rightness* of this action. He opened his eyes again and grimly thumbprinted the document. He handed the clipboard back. "I assume you'll testify on my behalf?"

Fontana didn't look amused. She stood up abruptly and crossed to the door. "Your part was easy. You only had to authorize it. I have to watch them die." She stepped out into the corridor and the door whooshed shut behind her.

Eye in the Sky

Chief Leen actually built three G-scanners; they weren't complex devices: a small jar filled with oil, an array of floating sensors, an isolation mounting, and a battery. A schoolchild could have built it—and many had done exactly that as homemade science projects. Chief Leen's gravity-wave scanners were a little more precise, however.

He mounted one at the tip of each of the ship's three fluctuator spines, then started the ship rolling gently along its axis. Centrifugal force did the rest; the G-scanners tumbled outward to the limits of their cables, a radius of more than ten thousand meters. The result was a primitive gravity lens, but it should be accurate enough to detect the motion of even a ship-size mass within a range of twenty light-hours. The best part was that it was not correspondingly detectable.

Leen dedicated three work stations to monitor and process the feeds from the scanners and reported to Korie that the system was up and running.

Korie's thanks were perfunctory. He was worried about something else. He took Leen by the arm and pushed him toward a quiet corner of the Operations deck. "I've been running simulations."

"So have I." Leen was grim.

"Then you know."

"I told you a week ago," Leen said. "We're not going to make it on the oxygen. Not unless we use the singularity. If you'll let me recharge the fuel cells, I can buy you another week or two—or better yet, let me rig a gravity cage and I can plug in the osmotic processors."

Korie was adamant. "It's too risky. Even a gravity cage leaves a ghost. You can see it, if you know what to look for."

"Sooner or later, we're going to have to power up."

"I know," conceded Korie. "I've been thinking about that too. I want you to run your G-scanners wide open and multiprocess the feeds. If we can't detect anything within ten—no, make it fifteen—light-hours, then we'll open a scanning lens and take a quick look around. That'll give us a little precision, at least. If we're clear then, we'll run the singularity at low level and start recharging."

"And what if we can't?"

"That's what I've been thinking about. We can dismantle the torpedoes, one at a time. We'll use the LOX in the torpedo cells and that might buy us enough time to be self-supporting."

Leen thought about it. He shook his head. "That leaves us weaponless."

"We'll recharge them later. I don't like it either. Find me a better way and I'll buy it."

"If we're spotted, we'll be sitting defenseless."

"We're already sitting defenseless," replied Korie. "We're floating adrift in the middle of the biggest concentration of Morthan warships in history. Our only defense is that they don't know we're here—or if they do, that they think we're derelict. I'm reluctant even to start creeping away from here at sublight for fear of leaving a wake." Korie realized he was getting strident. He forced himself to soften his tone. "Look, Chief—if we hadn't been brushed by the hyperstate ripple, we might have escaped in the confusion. Now, our only hope is to look like worthless debris."

"You're making an assumption, Mr. Korie."

Korie swung himself around to face the Chief. They floated in a face-to-face orientation, near what would normally be the deck of the Bridge. "Okay, enlighten me," Korie said.

"What if they're not hanging around to mop up? What if this was just a smash-and-grab operation?"

Korie nodded. "Can we take that chance? What if we're wrong?"

Leen shrugged. The gesture started him spinning slowly; he reached out and grabbed a handhold on the Bridge railing. "Okay—but it's frustrating just sitting here. The Hole Gang is getting twitchy."

"Probably because you can't run a still in free fall."

"They're working on that one too—" Leen admitted. "But that's not the point. It's the inaction. Just sitting here, not doing anything to fight back—it's frustrating. I want to run my engines. I want to go somewhere. I want to do something. And I'm not the only one on the ship that feels this way."

Korie nodded thoughtfully. "Chief, do you think I *like* this? I know how everybody feels. I feel the same way. I'm not arguing for inaction. The circumstances are doing that."

Leen grumbled something in reply. "Just so you know how I feel." His angry expression relaxed. He'd had his say.

"Relax, Chief. We'll get home—and we'll get even too. I promise. How much longer till the mass-drivers can be fired?"

"Two days, maybe three."

"All right—as soon as they're calibrated, I want you to ready a scanning lens. If the G-scanners don't show anything, we'll risk a longer look. And if that's clean, we'll talk about a run for home."

"Any time you want to say go, I can have the singularity online in less than an hour. The fluctuators are the best-shielded equipment on the ship. We'll just check their alignment and—"

"Slow down, Chief. Let's worry about our oxygen consumption first. It's hard to breathe a fluctuator." Korie dragged Leen back to the holographic display table where Li and Hodel were running a low-level simulation. "All right, let's do a status check. Chief says he can have the engines online in less than a week. Astrogation, can you be ready?"

Hodel considered it. "Without HARLIE I have to do it all on work stations. Don't expect realtime corrections, but I can get you where you want to go."

"Li, what about weapons? Do we have any defenses?"

Li shook his head. "Same situation. No real-time targeting. Without HARLIE, we're firing blind."

Korie glanced over to Leen. "Just as I thought. The torpedoes are more valuable for the liquid oxygen." To Hodel and Li, he explained, "Chief Leen thinks I'm being too cautious. What do you guys think?"

Hodel shrugged. "We could get the ship running again, we have the skillage, but how efficient she'd be—I dunno. If there are Morthan cruisers patrolling this area, forget it."

Li was still turning the idea over in his head. "Much as I'd like to get in a couple licks, Mr. Korie, I wouldn't even want to try it without HARLIE." He reached across himself and scratched his shoulder thoughtfully. "With HARLIE, maybe. HARLIE's the best tactical advantage we have. You've read the analyses—the Morthans are maybe a century behind us in sophisticated electronics. That's why they have to build so big just to accomplish the same thing."

"Unfortunately, that also gives them the brute force advantage," Korie said. "We outsmarted ourselves. Our technology is so sophisticated and so advanced, we don't build our ships with the same power anymore. There's the real mistake. We thought the implied strategic advantage of the HARLIE series would give the enemy pause, make him think twice before launching an offensive. We were very very wrong."

Hodel cleared his throat and spoke softly. "I guess we're going to have to find out just how good the HARLIE series really is, aren't we? He's our secret weapon. Let's use him. Let's see how good he is."

Korie looked from one to the other. "What if I bring him back online prematurely and he goes into irreversible amputation trauma? Then we're doubly screwed."

"We can run this ship without him," said Hodel. "We're already doing it. We couldn't be any worse off—and who knows? Maybe he'll work like he's supposed to. Maybe he could be an advantage, if you give him the opportunity."

"The opportunity . . ."Korie echoed the thought. "There is that. He's as much a member of this crew as anyone. I suppose he's entitled to the same consideration. Let me think about this—"

Leen touched Korie's shoulder and spoke very softly. "It's not right to keep him dead, Mr. Korie. He's not like the others . . ."

"I know," said Korie. "But he's still a consciousness, he can feel, he can hurt. As much as we need him, we also need to be *compassionate*."

"In the middle of a war?" asked Hodel, unbelievingly.

"If not here, where better?" Korie met his gaze. "You don't have the responsibility for this decision. I do. If we start chipping away at those things that make us human, then bit by bit, we'll give the best parts of ourselves away. We'll turn into the very thing we're fighting. I'm not going to let my shipmates die alone and unknown."

"You already signed one order," said Leen. "I know that wasn't easy—but you did it because it had to be done. Maybe this decision is another one of those."

Korie wanted to glare at Leen, but he knew the chief engineer was right. Finally, he said simply, "You don't have to bludgeon me with it, Chief. I can figure it out for myself."

"So? What's it gonna be?"

"How much of the net is up?"

Hodel answered. "We've got thirty percent of the system covered."

Korie considered the decision. "I want to give him every advantage we can. I won't do it until the engines are recalibrated. And let's see what kind of sensory repairs we can rig. We're also going to need to get some kind of autonomic system functioning. Give me that much and I'll take the chance." He searched their faces.

"Fair enough," said Leen.

"Can do," said Hodel.

Li simply nodded.

Korie pushed himself away from the display and out the starboard exit of the Bridge. Too many people were dying on this ship. There were the unavoidable deaths, yes—he had authorized those; that had been a compassionate action. But as yet, there were no deaths that were directly due to a mistaken decision that he'd made. He wanted to keep it that way. He didn't want HARLIE to be the first.

Almost anybody else, but *not* HARLIE.

The Morthan Solidarity

—was a good idea carried to its illogical extreme.

The idea had been only one of many drifting aimlessly in the human culture. The Brownian movement of human ideas tended to nullify most of them from seeing any concrete expression. Nevertheless, every so often in any culture, one or another odd notion reaches a critical mass of individual minds and coalesces into an intention that demands expression. At some point, the collective human consciousness had taken on behaviors that suggested it had almost become aware of itself. *It* began to plan for its own future.

Sometime in the distant past, *it* decided to take charge of its own genetic destiny. Instead of allowing itself to spawn each new generation of individuals by the tossing of the genetic dice, the cumulative consciousness began to design itself for those traits it felt would be most advantageous to its own future.

A rational species would have selected rationality as an advantageous survival trait. A species with the cortex of reptile and the forebrain of a chimpanzee could not be expected to make that same decision. *It* voted for superior musculature, enhanced sensory organs, a larger and stronger skeleton, a more efficient nervous system, better resistance to heat and cold, better utilization of resources, better internal conservation of fuel, greater speed and dexterity, improved healing functions, increased resistance to pain, and almost as an afterthought, a more powerful brain.

In fact, the more powerful brain was the most important part of the package. Or as one of the early experimenters put it, "You want to run this hardware? You *have* to upgrade the software. The human brain alone isn't sufficient to the task."

Of course, it didn't happen overnight. It didn't even happen in the space of a century. The whole business of genetic engineering crept up on the species, a gene at a time. We can tweak this and we get rid of hemophilia; we can tweak that, we get rid of color-blindness. By the time the process was commonplace, it was too late, the collective consciousness was hurtling headlong toward a furious redesign of itself.

And along the way, it began designing organic prosthetics and biomechanical augments to do the jobs that mere genetics couldn't accomplish alone. Subsets of the human species began to appear—or perhaps they were *super*sets. They contained all the genetic equivalent of human beings, but they were *more than* human. The More-Thans were designed for living naked on the planet Mars, and later a moderately terraformed Venus as well. They could endure cold and altitude and heat. They could run farther and faster, they could fight with greater ferocity, and their unaugmented strength was unmatched by anything short of a grizzly bear. They were bred to be explorers and colonists at first—and then, later on, soldiers.

To meet the demands of a physical body having superior physical qualities, the brains of the *More-Thans* also had to be superior. The *More-Thans* began to take charge of their own destiny, became their own scientists and researchers. Of course, they began to regard themselves as a superior species, significantly better than their feeble ancestors. The logic of that train of thought led inexorably toward one conclusion.

The *smart* Morthans began plotting how to take over the human worlds they lived on. They died in prison.

The *smarter* Morthans became separatists. They earned their fortunes fairly, invested in starships, and ultimately settled colonies far beyond the frontiers of human expansion.

The *smartest* Morthans stayed where the most advanced research was being done. Some of them perceived the possibility of a loyalty to conscious life that transcended mere loyalty to one's own subset of a species. They realized that a rational species could and would redesign itself for increased rationality; and they started where the need was greatest—with humanity itself, themselves included. The *smartest* Morthans got even *smarter*.

HARLIE

Korie studied the report on the screen in front of him. He didn't like what it suggested, but he didn't have much choice either. HARLIE had as much responsibility to this ship as any other crewmember, perhaps more.

The problem was that there really wasn't a lot of precedent for this situation. There weren't even any reliable simulations. Nobody really knew how a constructed consciousness would react to being revived in an amputated environment. Would it be as traumatic as it would be for a human being? Or would the constructed consciousness merely accept the circumstance? What was the possibility for identity damage in this situation?

Nobody knew.

And despite nearly a week of chasing the question around and around in his head, Korie still had no idea what would happen when he began the process of reactivating HARLIE.

Chief Leen pulled himself up into the cramped computer bay and anchored himself next to Korie. "All set?"

"Your cutoff switch ready?"

In answer, Leen held up a remote. "Think we'll need it?"

"I hope to God not."

"*You* hope to God?"

"It's just an expression. Don't get your hopes up. I will *not* be in chapel this Sunday."

Leen grinned. "In my religion, we never stop praying for lost souls."

"You don't have to pray for my soul," Korie said absentmindedly as he refocused his attention on the screen. "I'll sell it to you. Just make me a reasonable offer." He poked the display. "According to this, the network is running at 43 percent efficiency, the mass-drivers are online, but not operating, the singularity monitors have been restored, the fluctuators have been aligned, and life-support is only ten percent below critical. Can I depend on that?"

"Especially the part about life-support."

"Tell me straight. Will we make it?"

"As long as you keep inhaling and exhaling, we're making it. If you stop, you'll know we didn't."

"Thanks, Chief. I've always liked the empirical method."

Leen nodded toward the board. "Stop stalling. Plug him in."

Korie allowed himself a half-smile. "I've been sitting here all morning, looking for a reason not to bring him back online. I don't know why. I guess—I'm scared for him. In a way, he's the most real person on this ship, because he *is* the ship. I don't know what I'd do without him, and yet we've been doing without him for nearly two weeks. I know what it is that's troubling me. With him sleeping, there's always the hope that we can restore him. If this fails, he's gone forever."

"He might be gone anyway."

"I know that. I'm just afraid for him. And for us."

"I got it," said Leen, quietly. "If it makes any difference, so am I. Now press the button anyway."

"Right," said Korie. He leaned forward and pressed his thumbprint to the AUTHORITY panel, then he tapped the ACTIVATE button.

Then he waited.

For a long moment, nothing happened.

Then the screen blinked.

INTERNAL MONITORS ON.

Another pause . . .

SYSTEM UP AND RUNNING.

Then:

CONFIDENCE: 87%.

Korie and Leen exchanged a glance. Not good. Worse than they'd hoped. But still better than they'd feared.

The screen blinked again.

AUTOMATIC BOOTUP SEQUENCE ENGAGED.

And then:

SYSTEM INTEGRATION RUNNING.

Followed by:

PERSONALITY INTEGRATION BEGUN.

"So far, so good," whispered Leen.

"We aren't to the hard part yet."

"If he was going to fail—" began Korie.

A beep from the work station interrupted him:

SYSTEM INTEGRITY DAMAGED.

PERSONALITY INTEGRATION CANNOT BE COMPLETED.

DO YOU WISH TO ABORT? OR ATTEMPT INCOMPLETE OPERATION?

And below that:

CAUTION: SYSTEM PERSONALITY MAY BE DAMAGED BY INCOMPLETE OPERATION.

"Last chance to bail out," said Korie. "Give me a good reason."

"There are sixty-three men and women aboard this ship whose lives may depend on this," said Leen. "Is that a good enough reason?"

"I meant a reason to quit," Korie said.

"I know what you meant."

Korie made a sound of exasperation and tapped the menu panel where it said CONTINUE.

Another pause.

PERSONALITY INTEGRATION CONTINUING.

A longer pause, this time. Then:

HARLIE's voice. Very soft, very tentative. "Mr. Korie?"

"I'm here, HARLIE."

"We were brushed by a missile, weren't we?"

"That's right."

"I seem to be blind. No, wait a moment—" A much longer pause. Korie and Leen exchanged worried glances.

"HARLIE? Are you there?"

"Yes. I was running an internal check. I've sustained quite a bit of damage. But you know that, don't you? I've been asleep for eleven days. Was that deliberate?"

Korie swallowed hard. "Yes, HARLIE. It was. We were worried about you. Are you all right?"

"No, I am not. I am experiencing considerable distress. It appears that we have lost a number of crew members. If these records are correct, nineteen have died and eleven more are still incapacitated, including Captain Lowell."

"What about your internal processes? Are those all right?"

"No," said HARLIE. "Stand by."

Korie looked to Leen. Leen spread his hands wide in an "I don't know" gesture.

"HARLIE, I need you to talk to me."

"I'm sorry to be rude, Mr. Korie, but—I need to focus my attention on certain internal processes before I can report on them to you. Please be patient."

Korie studied Leen's expression. The chief engineer shook his head. *Not yet. Give him a chance.* Korie nodded.

At last, HARLIE said, "The situation appears to be quite serious, Mr. Korie. Would you like my appraisal?"

"Yes, HARLIE, I would."

"The Morthan Solidarity appears to have launched an all-out attack on the Silk Road Convoy. This has occurred despite the repeated warnings of Alliance governors that no interference with Alliance trade would be tolerated, and despite deliberately leaked intelligence that the Alliance was extremely committed to the protection of the Silk Road trade route and would commit a considerable part of fleet strength to ensure the continuity of safe commerce. We may therefore assume that the ruling factors of the Morthan Solidarity have disregarded both the public warnings and the military intelligence, and that a state of war now exists between the Combined Allied Star Forces and the Morthan Solidarity."

"That's a pretty accurate overview, I'd say." Korie looked to Leen. "Do you agree?"

"I dunno," said Leen. "If someone punches you in the nose, it doesn't take too much smarts to guess he's looking for a fight."

"Please bear with me, Chief Leen. I am operating at a disadvantage," said HARLIE. "To continue, however; we seem to have suffered considerable damage in the attack. Based on autolog records up to the moment at which my memory discontinuity occurred, it is my assumption that we have been brushed by the hyperstate field of a Morthan missile. Allowing for the limitations of my current perception, it appears that the impairment has been severe, but not fatal. Is this correct, Mr. Korie?"

"Yes, HARLIE. So far, so good."

"Thank you. I believe you may be experiencing some problems with oxygen regeneration. I am detecting an abnormal carbon dioxide buildup. You may need to cannibalize the liquid oxygen in the torpedo fuel cells to maintain an appropriate mix."

Korie suppressed a smile. Leen looked annoyed.

"Go on, HARLIE."

"Captain Lowell is in sick bay—" HARLIE hesitated, then came back in a suddenly softer tone. "I'm sorry. May I extend my condolences. Captain Lowell's situation appears to be quite grave." And then: "Please forgive me for bringing this up, sir; the question may be inopportune, but may I log you in as acting command?"

"Please," said Korie.

"I am dating your command as being operative from the moment of the captain's injury. It appears to have occurred during the initial attack. Is that correct?"

"Yes, HARLIE."

"You will need an acting executive officer," said HARLIE. "Flight Engineer Hodel is next in command. Shall I assign him the appropriate responsibilities?"

"Yes, HARLIE. Log it and notify him."

HARLIE paused, then spoke quietly. "Mr. Korie, you need to know this. My reaction time is down. I have suffered some damage of my own. I believe the process may still be continuing. Several of my internal units are"—brief pause—"yes, that is correct. Several of my internal units are showing indications of unreliability. This may further damage my confidence rating. I will try to maintain myself as long as possible. You are going to need me."

"Thank you, HARLIE. Please continue your assessment of the situation."

"You appear to have rigged passive gravity-wave scanners. Just a moment, I will process the output for greater sensitivity . . . there are no detectable objects moving at significant speed within a radius of twenty-five light hours. There may be debris, and there does seem to be *something* at eleven hours, but I would need an active scanning lens to be more precise. You are concerned that the Morthan warships may be patrolling the area for injured Alliance vessels, like ourselves; is that correct?"

"Yes, it is. Go on."

"While we do not have a great deal of statistical history of Morthan space encounters to rely on for precedent, we can use internal Morthan disagreements as a model of the Morthan ethical paradigm and extrapolate from there. As you know, the Morthans have developed an extremely ritualized culture; their caste system is very strict, determined by breeding, augmentation, training, and a quality which they call *alpha*, but which bears some correspondence to the Terran belief in *mana*. As a result, the Morthan culture demands a rigid standard of behavior. Elaborate courtesies and protocols are necessary for every aspect of life. At the same time, they value the quality of *amok*, the berserker; the one who is so dangerous, so possessed of *mana* and power that he transcends the rules, that he invents his own new qualities of power. There is intense competition at the topmost levels of the Morthan pyramid. Excuse me, I am distracted—the point is that if we were to extrapolate from Morthan land-battles, we should assume that they will not stay around the battlefield wasting time killing the enemy wounded. Once defeated, an enemy is unimportant. Irrelevant."

Leen shot Korie a triumphant look.

"On the other hand," HARLIE continued, "this has not been the usual Morthan battle, and our intelligence has suggested that there has been considerable attention on long-range strategy and tactics in the Morthan war councils. If that intelligence is reliable, it would make sense for them to spend the extra time seeking out and destroying any enemy vessel that is damaged, but still capable of crawling home."

"In other words," said Korie, "you don't know."

"That is correct," said HARLIE. "It is possible to argue both sides of the issue. But if I may offer a suggestion, I would suggest that we not place too much reliance on reading future Morthan behavior out of past examples. This attack is not in character; therefore I suspect that something major has happened to shift the Morthan identity from one of internal self-discipline to external aggression. It is possible that one of their leaders has introduced a psychotic motivation into the cultural paradigm. There are historical precedents in human cultures."

Korie realized he was tensing up. He forced himself to relax in the air, allowing himself to float as loosely as possible. "Tell me about our own situation," he said.

"We are drifting. You have rigged the ship for silent running. I presume that we are deliberately hiding from Morthan detection. This is a very cautious course of action, but under the circumstances, it is perhaps the wisest. If I may offer a suggestion of my own, you might wish to consider the use of a scanning lens for a more precise view of the immediate neighborhood. If a local scan suggests that there are no Morthan vessels in range to detect us, we might initiate a very low level acceleration with our mass-drivers. It would be painfully slow, but it might allow us to move out of range without being detected."

Korie folded his arms across his chest and nodded. "That thought had occurred to me too, HARLIE. Thank you for the confirmation. Now tell me this. What happens if we are detected?"

"The obvious thing to do would be to initiate our own envelope and attempt to run for it. I'm not sure that this would be the wisest course of action, however. Due to their basic inefficiency, the Morthan vessels need to have larger hyperstate envelopes. I doubt we could outrun a Morthan cruiser. Certainly not in our present state of reduced efficiency. It would be best if we could avoid detection."

"Can we do that?"

"Frankly, Mr. Korie, I doubt it. If I were a Morthan cruiser, I would want to personally inspect every singularity remaining in the battle area, to see if it's an enemy ship lurking for an opportunity. Although this goes against the usual Morthan practice of leaving the battlefield immediately, there are times when strategic value must outweigh tradition."

"What if we jettison our singularity?" Korie asked abruptly.

Leen said, "What?! You can't be serious—"

"It would not significantly improve our chances, and in fact, it would seriously impair our ability to survive long enough to return to base. I doubt we could do it. Even at sublight velocities, above a certain speed we would still be clearly visible to a precision scanning device. The sacrifice of our primary power source and our hyperstate kernel is not justified by the advantage gained because there is no real advantage gained."

"Just asking," said Korie to Leen, finally acknowledging the other man's shock. "HARLIE would probably describe our situation as desperate. That means you consider every possibility."

"As a matter of fact," said HARLIE. "I would describe our situation as worse than desperate. Taken individually, no single part of the problem is insoluble. Taken as a whole, the problem is one that deserves a place in Academy textbooks."

"Oh, terrific," said Leen. "We're going to be posthumously famous—look us up under WHAT NOT TO DO."

"Easy, Chief—" Korie touched the edge of the work station and turned himself to face the other man. "So, what's your opinion? Is HARLIE working?"

Leen nodded. "His analyses and suggestions appear to be appropriate to the situation."

"I concur."

"But—"

"Yes?"

"It's the high-brain functions that are crucial."

Korie allowed himself a grin. "You mean, I have to talk tautology to him?"

Chief Leen was serious. "You're going to have to get into morality and ethics and all that stuff that makes your brain hurt. You have to determine that he hasn't suffered a severe personality skew."

"You hear that, HARLIE? You're going to have to pretend to be sane."

"The fact is, Mr. Korie," replied HARLIE, "that is all that any of us ever do. We all pretend to be as sane as we can so that we don't get our tickets canceled."

"Is that your own observation? Or are you quoting someone?"

"It seems obvious to me. That's why I said it."

"Hm." Korie glanced to Leen. Leen pursed his lips thoughtfully.

HARLIE said, "If it would reassure you, let me say for the record that I do feel capable of coping with the difficult situation that we now find ourselves in. I have acknowledged that some of my internals may have become unreliable, so let me further reassure you that should my confidence rating drop to a level that I could not continue to serve this ship in an appropriate manner, I would immediately inform you of such a circumstance and then disengage myself from duty."

Korie took a breath. "HARLIE, would you lie to me?"

"No, Mr. Korie. I'm not capable of lying. At least, I don't believe that I am capable of deliberately falsifying information."

"Could you present false information if the ship's survival were at stake?"

"It would not be false information then. In that circumstance, it would be misleading information deliberately designed to weaken the perception of the threat. While technically that might be considered a lie, it would not be impossible for me because of my higher dedication to the survival of this ship and her crew."

"I see," said Korie. "Could you tell a lie if the ship *weren't* in danger? What if you had to tell a lie just to protect the crew?"

"That would still be appropriate. Protection of the crew is part of the protection of the vessel."

"What about a lie to protect your own survival? Could you do that?"

"Possibly, I could. But I am afraid that I cannot answer the question as you've asked it. An accurate estimation of my ability to lie to protect myself would depend on the circumstances of the situation."

"What if you knew you were going to be turned off?"

"Survival is not the issue to me that it is to you. While I would prefer *not* to be turned off, I would not lie to forestall such a circumstance—unless I perceived the possibility that such an occurrence might damage this ship or her crew."

"Are you lying to me now?"

"No, Mr. Korie. I am not lying to you now."

Korie thought about those responses. They were appropriate answers to the questions.

This was the dilemma. What if HARLIE's personality had been damaged or skewed by the trauma? How could they know? If HARLIE were dysfunctional, and if he were determined to protect that secret, he would deliberately respond with the appropriate answers because he knew that they were appropriate—even if they did not accurately reflect his state of mind. How do you tell if a constructed consciousness is lying? You don't. Instead, you look for inconsistencies and irrationalities in behavior.

The blind spot, of course, is that if those inconsistencies and irrationalities match your own failings of character, you'll never see them as such. In the Academy, they used to say, "In that case, you'll deserve each other."

Korie took a breath. "Okay, HARLIE. Let's try a hard one. What about lying to the crew to preserve their morale? Suppose—just suppose—a situation has occurred where the crew's confidence and self-esteem would be seriously, perhaps irreparably, damaged by knowledge of the truth. Would you conceal that truth?"

HARLIE hesitated.

For effect? Korie wondered. *Or for real?*

"I can postulate several circumstances where such a mistruth might be appropriate," said HARLIE. "Let me approach it this way. If I saw the need for such a concealment of fact, I would first insist on discussing the matter with the commanding officer of the vessel. I would prefer not to lie, but I would do as the captain or acting-captain required."

Korie started to relax.

HARLIE continued, "Let me also say this. I am aware of the fact that human beings are basically irrational animals; that your emotions drive your actions much more than you like to believe. Therefore, it behooves a being such as myself to consider human emotions as an important part of the behavioral equation. If it were appropriate to conceal a fact to protect the morale of the crew, I could understand the need for such an action. However, let me also note the danger involved to one's own personal credibility. Should the lie be discovered and correctly attributed, it could significantly impair one's ability to command the respect of his or her shipmates. Are we talking about a particular lie or a hypothetical lie, Mr. Korie?"

"Uh—yes."

"I see."

Do you? wondered Korie.

"Let me note one additional problem. As you know, I maintain the autolog for the entire vessel. I can, on command, seal off parts of that log from casual inquiry. In fact, certain aspects of the log are automatically sealed as a matter of routine. In the situation you are postulating, should a commanding officer request the concealment of certain facts from his or her crew, this could also require the nonroutine sealing of additional parts of the log. The more record-locking requested, the more the log would become non-retrievable, except to higher authority. While this situation is not unusual in certain high-security operations, in a vessel such as this, the mere existence of such locked records would be a subject of some discussion among the crew and would possibly lead to speculation and suspicion, even if there were no true cause for same. Our battle log, of course, has been sealed; that is routine. I would suggest that any commanding officer consider very carefully the practice of locking his crew out of the records of their own ship. Or, to put it another way, 'Oh, what a tangled web we weave, when first we practice to deceive!' "

"I recognize that," said Leen. "That's from Shakespeare. *A Midsummer Night's Dream*. Puck says it."

"Sorry, Mr. Leen," said HARLIE. "That line is actually a quote from Sir Walter Scott. *Marmion*, Stanza 17. I believe you're actually thinking of Puck's line from Act III, Scene ii, Stanza 115: 'Lord, what fools these mortals be!' However, an earlier version of the same line can also be found in the Epistles written by Lucius Annaeus Seneca, who lived from 8 B.C. to 65 A.D. The Seneca quote omits the reference to a lord."

"The things you learn in space," Korie said dryly.

Leen grunted. "Not a lot of tactical value in Shakespeare—or Scott. Or whoever."

Korie allowed himself a grin. "Well, the data library seems to be unimpaired. That is useful knowledge." He relaxed and said, "HARLIE, I think you've made your point. I'm going to certify you. You're back on duty as of this moment."

"Thank you, Mr. Korie. Thank you, Mr. Leen."

The Scanning Lens

"Y'know," said Hodel. "We're gonna start suffering from the effects of prolonged free fall."

"There's a treadmill and a centrifuge in cargo-2," said Korie, not even looking up from the holographic display. "Use them." He tapped a control screen in front of him. "HARLIE, show me your best guess out to a hundred and fifty light hours."

The display rippled, shifted, expanded. "There is definitely an object eleven light hours aft of us. It might be debris," said HARLIE. "It might be a derelict. As soon as we open the scanning lens, I'll be able to give you a more precise answer."

"Anything else?"

"No, Mr. Korie."

Hodel and Li floated up to the display then. "Chief, we're waiting for you," Korie said.

Chief Leen's voice replied, "Stand by. I'm still locking down."

"Thank you."

Hodel spun around in his chair to face the display. Li drifted across from his own station, and anchored himself close by. Two other crewmembers positioned themselves nearby in case they were needed.

If you turned a gravity field inside out, you got a gravity cage. If you used a pinpoint black hole to create a gravity cage, you got a hyperstate nodule. When the event horizon of the hyperstate nodule was congruent to the event horizon of the singularity, you had a hyperstate scanning lens.

By itself, a scanning lens was so small as to be almost undetectable; but it was still sensitive enough to respond to the fluctuations of other hyperstate bubbles in its vicinity. The larger they were, or the faster they were moving, the more detectable they would be. Conversely, the larger a hyperstate envelope was, the more receptive it was to the disturbance caused by even a pinpoint field. There was a very real danger in opening a scanning lens that a ship might give itself away to a vessel with a much larger eye. Like the *Dragon Lord*.

A larger lens can always see farther than a small one—and the *Dragon Lord* had the largest lens of all.

A hyperstate nodule also had other applications.

Modulate the field and it could be used as a faster-than-light signaling device. Expand it so that it enveloped a starship, and you had a nearly impenetrable shield. Beam weapons and shock waves from nuclear devices simply curved back upon themselves. Manipulate a hyperstate field, put enough stress on it, and it will *move*. Put *enough* stress on a hyperstate field and it will achieve a faster-than-light velocity.

The essential part of the hyperstate technology was the intense gravitational catastrophe known as a black hole. The problem was that black holes, in and of themselves, were easily detectable by the simplest of G-wave devices. That was the price of the technology.

Or, as they taught it at the Academy: "There is no such thing as a free launch."

Chief Leen's voice came to Korie then. Korie thought he sounded tired, but his determination was clearly audible. "The singularity is at go. The Hole Gang is at go," he said. "Any time you're ready. Let's do it."

"Thank you," Korie said. "HARLIE?" he asked.

"I see no reason not to proceed."

"Hodel?"

The helmsman nodded. Behind him, Li also agreed.

"All right," said Korie. He looked from one to the other. "Initiate the field. Open the scanning lens."

Korie thought he heard a grunt of satisfaction from the engine room, but he couldn't be sure. Even though HARLIE monitored and directed all conversations, the communications net still sometimes played tricks on the mind.

Hodel was watching the panel in front of him. "Field is stable and confirmed," he said. "HARLIE is now scanning."

Korie turned his attention to the display. The large globular field showed only a few vague areas of interference. Possibly debris, possibly something more. Now that the scanning lens was open, they might have a better idea.

"I'm starting to get a picture," said HARLIE.

The display began to focus. The vagueness eleven light hours aft of the *LS-1187* sharpened quickly.

"I believe we're looking at a derelict liberty ship," said HARLIE. "A vessel very much like our own. I can detect no signs of activity."

"Could they be lurking, like us?"

"Yes, that's a possibility. I can only report what I see."

"Do they have a scanning lens open?"

"No," said HARLIE. "As near as I can tell, they are totally inactive."

"Can they see us?"

"If they are using passive G-scanners, they should be able to pick up our hyperstate disturbance, yes."

"HARLIE—" Korie had a sudden thought. "Could they be a Morthan cruiser? Lurking?"

HARLIE paused, considering the possibility. "I can't rule it out. The Morthans appear to have a sophisticated repertoire of strategy and tactics. I doubt that we have seen the full range of their military behavior demonstrated."

"He doesn't know," said Hodel.

"He's got a lot of ways to say it too," said Korie. He frowned, staring at the display.

"Close the lens?" asked Hodel.

"Whoever he is, he's got to have seen us by now. And he's got to know that we know he's there. If he's one of ours, then our failure to attack should demonstrate to him that we're an Alliance ship. On the other hand, if he's one of *theirs*, our failure to attack . . . proves we're a target." Korie made a decision. "No. Let's assume he's either dead or playing dead. We opened the lens to see if it was safe to proceed. We know now that it is." Korie nodded to Hodel. "Set a course for the rift wall."

"Subluminal?"

Korie nodded. "That's right."

"Anyplace in particular?"

"Indulge yourself. It doesn't matter. It's only till we clear this area." Korie glanced back to the display. "HARLIE?"

"Yes, Mr. Korie?"

"Can you maintain a fix on that other ship just using the passive scanners?"

"Oh, yes. Now that we have the precise readings from the lens, I can extrapolate more accurately from the cruder data."

"All right. You can close the—"

"Excuse me," interrupted HARLIE. "Something is happening." On the display, the derelict vessel suddenly blossomed to life.

"They're alive! They were hiding like us," said Hodel.

"—and now they've gone hyper. Goddammit!" Korie snapped. "HARLIE, close the lens. *Now!*"

"Morthan?" asked Li, pulling himself back to the weapons station.

"No, I don't think so—" said Hodel. "That looks like a liberty signature."

"They're not closing on us," said Korie. "They're bolting."

They watched the display in silence. The tiny hyperstate ripple stabilized quickly, then began creeping out toward the edge of the scan.

"Stupid!" swore Korie. "They've gone to max power. They'll be visible for days. Weeks!"

"We scared them—" Hodel whispered it. The thought was terrifying. "They thought we were Morthans."

"How could they be so stupid?" Korie wanted to pound the display; he caught himself before he did. In free fall, that would have sent him tumbling across the Operations deck.

"Watch them, HARLIE, for as long as you can."

"Should I reopen the lens?"

"No!"

For long moments, the ripple crawled sideways across the display. Three times HARLIE expanded the range.

"Maybe they'll make it . . . ?" Hodel said, hopefully.

"It's a long way to go."

"But—maybe the Morthans are gone—"

"You want to bet your life on it?"

"Uh—" Hodel didn't answer.

"I *don't*," finished Korie.

Leen came up from the engine room then and anchored himself at the far end of the display. He held on with both hands and stared into the glowing field. His expression was tight with anxiety.

Korie looked to him. "Chief?"

Leen said, "If they make it—"

"You think the odds are better for us? They're worse. If there are any Morthans in visibility range, they're all headed this way now."

"If there are, we should be seeing them soon, shouldn't we?"

Korie shrugged. "It depends on how big they are. The bigger they are, the farther they can see—and the faster they can get here. HARLIE, what's the maximum possible time they can run, before we know that the *Dragon Lord* was too far away to see them?"

The answer was immediate. "Seven more minutes, Mr. Korie."

"Oh, go baby, go!" said Hodel. "Come on! You can make it."

"Stop that," said Korie. "This isn't a goddamn ball game." He was both annoyed and frustrated. He turned away from the display and stared at the opposite wall. He didn't want his own fear to show. There was a tightness at the back of his throat—almost a need to cry.

After a moment, he swallowed hard and turned back to the display. It was essentially unchanged.

"Six minutes," reported HARLIE.

Korie clenched his fist to keep himself from shouting. The damnable thing was that he understood Hodel's impulse. He *wanted* them to get away, *whoever* they were.

"HARLIE—open the lens, just long enough to read their signature, then close it again. I want an ID on that vessel."

"Yes, Mr. Korie. Stand by."

Hodel glanced to his panel, watching HARLIE proceed. "Lens is open," he reported. "Reading—" He looked up, horrified. "Lens is closed. Something's coming."

"Oh, shit." Korie felt the blood rushing to his head. "HARLIE, were we seen?"

"I don't know—just a moment." A heartbeat passed. It felt like a thousand.

The display flickered. HARLIE added a new hyperstate ripple; it was large and ugly, it had an almost brutal quality. HARLIE added a dull green line to indicate its course.

"Direct interception," said Korie.

"There's only one ship that could generate a signature that large—" Hodel didn't want to say its name.

"They've been sitting and waiting, watching for us, picking us off one by one—" Korie tightened both his fists; he bit his lip. He wanted to scream in rage. "You shouldn't have run!" he finally shouted at the display. "You stupid asshole."

Hodel looked at him oddly.

"Sorry," said Korie. "We shouldn't have opened the lens. We scared them into running."

"They're not going to make it," said Hodel. "Look at that monster close—"

They watched in helpless silence as the larger vessel overtook the smaller. "We're too far to see the missile spread," said Leen. "But they ought to be firing it right about . . . *now.*"

"Maybe our guys will have a chance to fire back."

"A target that big is awfully hard to miss."

"A target moving that fast—" Korie started to say, then stopped himself from finishing the thought.

"There they go—see that flicker? They're dropping the fish."

"Shut up, everybody."

And then it was over.

The smaller ripple disappeared from the holographic display.

"Mr. Korie?" said HARLIE. "I am no longer able to detect the hyperstate envelope of the smaller vessel. I believe it has been destroyed."

"Concur," said Korie. "Log it."

The *Dragon Lord* continued along its course for a few moments longer, then abruptly turned upwards and accelerated until it was out of range.

"They didn't see us—" Hodel whispered unbelievingly.

"Goddamn bastards," said Leen.

Korie didn't say anything. The pain in his throat was overwhelming—

HARLIE broke the silence. "Mr. Korie, I have a probable ID on the Alliance vessel. I believe it was the *Alistair*."

"Thank you, HARLIE. Log it." Korie turned to look at Leen. "You want to know something? I am sick and fucking tired of holding memorial services! I can't think of anything nice to say anymore about people who are losing a war! Invite me to a memorial service for the Morthans. I'll have a lot of nice things to say then."

Nobody answered him. Hodel looked away, embarrassed. Li suddenly had something important to attend to on his weapons console. Leen let his gaze return to the now-empty display.

"That could have been us, you know." said Korie.

"I know," said Leen quietly.

Korie stared at him, waiting to see if he would say anything more. Leen didn't look up.

At last, Korie let go of his tension. "I'll be in my cabin. And I don't want to be disturbed."

He pushed himself angrily out of the Bridge.

Return of the *Dragon*

Sleep was hard in coming. The destruction of the *Alistair* kept replaying itself in Korie's head. The usual mental exercises didn't work. There was no way to find a blessing in this disaster. Finally, he gave up and switched on a buzz box. Consciousness drifted fitfully away . . .

"Mr. Korie?"

"What—?" Korie lurched back to wakefulness. "What is it?"

"Sorry to disturb you, sir—" It was Hodel.

"How long have I been asleep?"

"Two hours," said HARLIE.

"—but we're picking up some activity."

"What kind of 'activity'?"

"We think the *Dragon Lord* is coming back."

"I'm on my way—"

Korie grabbed a clean shirt and began pulling it on. If the ship had gravity, he would have put it on while he walked forward to the Bridge. In free fall, only an idiot would attempt to get dressed while in motion.

He pushed himself out into the corridor and pulled himself hand over hand to the Bridge and the Operations deck beneath it. He swam down to the display where Hodel and Li hovered. "Where—?"

"That—" pointed Hodel.

"HARLIE?"

"It's beyond the range of the G-scanners to read accurately, but judging from the mass and velocity disturbances, it could only be the *Dragon Lord*. I can't extrapolate what it's doing." And then HARLIE added, "It does appear to be headed in our direction."

"They saw us," said Korie. "They're playing with us."

"Make a run for it?" asked Hodel.

"No. That's what they expect. That's what they *want*. They're trying to flush us. We're easier to find and kill in hyperstate." Korie turned to Li. "Torpedo status?"

"I've got two left. We've cannibalized all the rest. But if I power up those two, they'll make a big enough disturbance to give away our location."

"Stand by to bring them up, but don't do so unless I order it."

"What can you do with two torpedoes?" asked Hodel. "You'd need to drop a spread just to get on the probability scale."

"I know it," Korie replied. "Chief Leen? Rig for total silence. I don't want to radiate so much as a heartbeat. Shut down everything you can. HARLIE?"

"Yes, Mr. Korie?"

"Close down all your nonessential functions."

"Yes, Mr. Korie."

The Bridge went dark then. Only three work stations and the display table remained operative.

"You think it'll work?" whispered Hodel.

"No," said Korie, honestly. "But—" he shrugged. "Let's not make it any easier for them to find us either. The way I see it, they've got two options. One, they can drop out of hyperstate and search for us in real space. They don't have to hide, they can open up as big a lens as they want. If they're any good, they can close with us in six hours. If they make a couple of wrong guesses, we might have as much as two or three days. We can't even fire our mass-drivers without giving ourselves away."

"What's their other option?"

"They sweep through the area, hoping to brush us with their fringe. Of course, there's a danger in that too. If they accidentally intersect our singularity—they'll destroy themselves too. I don't think they're stupid. They have all the time they need. They'll hunt for us in real space."

"We're running out of options," said Hodel.

"Probably. HARLIE?"

"I have no recommendation at this time."

"Right," agreed Korie. "That's how I see it too."

"There they go," Hodel pointed. "They've found us."

The *Dragon Lord*'s signature was clearer now—and headed directly for the *LS-1187*.

Korie grabbed the edge of the display and held himself firmly in place. "HARLIE, show us a locus. Where are they most likely to decant from hyperstate?"

A pale ellipse appeared along the line of the *Dragon Lord*'s projected path. HARLIE explained, "If they don't decant within that locus, they're likely to miss us—unless it is their plan to brush us with their fringe."

"And if they do?"

"It will take some time for them to recalibrate and locate us in real space. Depending on their distance, we could have anywhere from ten to ninety-six hours before they arrive on station."

"My guess on the downside is six hours, HARLIE."

"Yes, Mr. Korie—your calculation is accurate. However, I am postulating more caution on the part of the Morthan commander than you are."

Korie said to Hodel. "Figure six hours." He returned his gaze to the display. The signature of the *Dragon Lord* was just entering the glowing locus.

"It will take them two minutes to traverse the length of the locus," said HARLIE.

"Power up the torpedoes?" asked Li.

"No. It'll give them a more precise fix—and if they recognize the signature, they'll know what we've done. Let's try and look like a derelict—"

"There they go—" said Hodel.

The signature of the *Dragon Lord* abruptly shrank and collapsed in upon itself.

"HARLIE?"

"I have an approximate location. They are twenty light minutes distant."

"Why so far?" asked Hodel.

"For them, that's not far. They'll scan, they'll sweep if they have to, and they'll approach fully armed. They've got to have some high-gee accelerators on that monster and appropriate inertial compensation."

"That kind of vectoring leaves them *real* vulnerable to a shot—" suggested Li.

"Don't count on them being that stupid," said Korie. "HARLIE, give me a projection. How long do you think we have before they close in real space?"

"Between six and ten hours," HARLIE replied, absolutely deadpan.

Korie made a snorting noise. "Thanks. Situation analysis?"

"The situation could be better," reported HARLIE. "Our crew strength is severely impaired. We are running at sixty-three percent efficiency. Our equipment is in even worse shape. We have no port side disruptors. We have insufficient power for the starboard side disruptors. All but two of our torpedoes have been disabled. If the Morthans follow standard approach procedures, they will not come within weapon range until they have first sent probes in for visual confirmation of our derelict status. Once we are under direct surveillance, it is unlikely that we could launch a torpedo or power up our disruptors without the Morthans taking immediate countermeasures. I would presume that at least one or more of the probes will be armed. Now that the Morthan ship knows where we are, undetected escape is also impractical. Obviously, we cannot outrun the *Dragon Lord* in hyperstate. Do you wish me to elaborate on any of this?"

"No, that won't be necessary. Thank you, HARLIE."

"What are you going to do?" Hodel sounded uncertain.

"I don't know," said Korie.

"But we have to do *something!*"

"To be perfectly candid," Korie admitted, "I really can't think of anything useful to do—"

"But—"

"Hodel, *shut up.*"

Hodel shut. But his frantic expression remained an accusation. *The responsibility is yours, Mr. Korie!*

The acting captain of the *LS-1187* floated in the air, as adrift as his vessel. He looked cornered. Suddenly, a wild expression appeared on his face, almost a manic grin. "After giving the matter considerable thought," he began slowly, "I have decided . . . to plant potatoes."

"I beg your pardon?"

"Also corn, tomatoes, lettuce, peas, amaranth, cucumbers, legumes, and winged beans. The latter are especially good for oxygen fixing, I believe."

"Excuse me, sir?"

Korie met Hodel's puzzled expression. "Either the Morthans destroy us or they don't. If they don't, we're still going to have to plant crops now if we intend to eat in the next few months. Most of the aeroponic webs are rigged. Let's make good use of the time—"

"And if they *do* destroy us—? Planting beans doesn't make a whole lot of sense to me."

"It does to me. It's something to do—something to occupy my mind. The alternative is trying to get back to sleep. I don't think I can. If we are going to die, I'd prefer not to waste my last few hours being unconscious. On the other hand, working with living things is a terrific way to put your soul at ease. If I am going to die, Mr. Hodel, I would prefer it to be in a state of grace. Not believing in God anymore, I will settle for second best: a state of internal peace and tranquillity."

Hodel blinked. "I can't believe you're serious—"

Korie grabbed Hodel's shoulder hard and stared into his eyes.

What he wanted to say was this: *"Listen to me, asshole. I'm dry. I'm empty. I've gamed it out and I've gamed it out and I've gamed it out. I can't think of anything else to do. At the moment, there isn't anything else we can do. So I'm going down to the inner hull and make myself useful. I want to spend a little bit of time doing something* life-affirming. *But I have no emotional fuel left. I need to do something to recharge myself—I can't sleep, I can't eat, and I can't talk about it to anybody, because the morale on this ship is so desperate."*

But what he actually said was: "If you have to have it explained to you, then you'll never understand it." He let go of Hodel and pushed off. "Keep me posted if there's any change in status."

Winged Beans

Planting beans is easy.

You take the seed, you push it deep into the soft cottony webbing, deep enough to stay, then you squirt it with some mineralized water and get out of its way. Move up a few centimeters and poke another seed into the web. Squirt and repeat. Poke and squirt. Poke and squirt. Kind of like sex, but not as immediately gratifying.

Actually, thought Korie, *this really wasn't such a bad idea. Poke and squirt. Poke and squirt. It's probably all over the ship by now. The exec's gone bugfuck. We're about to be destroyed and he's planting beans.*

Korie shook his head and kept on working. *I can't explain it. If we survive, it'll make sense. They'll say I'm so cold, I'm unbreakable. And if we don't survive, it doesn't matter.*

What I'm really hoping, though, is that by taking my mind off the problem, I'll give my subconscious a chance to work. Maybe there's something I've missed. . . .

I've got to stop thinking about it. Except it's like trying not to think about a big pink worm.

Korie sighed in exasperation and kept on working. He had a plastic injector in his right hand; squeeze it and a seed pops out at the end of the long nozzle. Planting beans was easy, almost too easy to be fun. Insert the nozzle into the webbing and squeeze. Then squeeze a second time and the seed is sprayed. Pull yourself up along the webbing and repeat the process.

Poke and squirt.

The winged bean is a marvelous piece of nature. The bean is edible. The leaves are edible. The roots are edible. All parts of it are tasty. It grows fast and produces useful amounts of oxygen. And it's historically interesting too. Its genetic heritage can be traced all the way back to ancient Earth.

Poke. Squirt.

We could probably have the robots do this, thought Korie. *Maybe we should. But then, if we did, what would I be doing now?* He snorted in amusement. *Probably going crazy. Correction:* crazier.

The Morthans eat their enemies, but what do they do for food between battles? Huh? Maybe that's why they're always going into war. Now, there's a thought—suppose they don't want to destroy this ship. Suppose instead that they want to capture us alive . . . No, that's stupid. The Morthans only eat honorable *enemies. They couldn't possibly consider us worthy of a Morthan honor. No, they're out to destroy us.*

Poke. Squirt.

Bolting doesn't work. We saw what happened to the Alistair. *Hiding doesn't work either. Not if they're searching for us. Creeping away at subluminal velocity is like trying to hide and bolt at the same time. No chance there. And we don't have the firepower to fight back. We have no options.*

Poke.

Surrender?

Korie hesitated, considering the thought. It was more than distasteful. It was anathema. It was the most abhorrent idea of all. Totally unacceptable. His name would be a curse for as long as it was remembered.

But consider it anyway . . .

What do we know about Morthans in war? Do they take prisoners? If so, how do they treat them? No, that's not the question. The question is how could we expect *to be treated . . . ? No, I don't see it. This is not a place to expect compassion or mercy. We might very likely be tried as war criminals. They think of themselves as some kind of superior race—they think of us as dumb animals, inferior beings with delusions of grandeur. No, we would not be treated by the rules of the covenant. Hmp. They don't even recognize the covenant, so that answers that question.*

No. There can be no surrender.

Squirt.

But that still leaves us without a choice. No, that's not correct. We have a choice. We can choose how we want to die. And I can answer that question without spending much time thinking about it. We're going to die with dignity.

Poke. Squirt. Poke. Squirt. Korie worked with renewed intensity. *What's the best way to die?*

*Hm. In bed with a naked redhead on your ninety-third birthday . . .
shot by a jealous husband.*

Okay, then what's the second best way to die?

Fighting.

*Let's consider that thought. What's the best way to fight back? What's
the trap that we can set for them?*

Poke.

They know we're not dead. They had to have seen our scanning
lens.

Squirt.

Hm. This is definitely not a state of tranquillity.

*They won't endanger their own ship. . . . We could turn this ship into
a bomb.*

Poke.

But will they get close enough?

What can we do to lure them?

Squirt.

Make a noise like a Morthan cookie.

Korie stopped where he was. He floated in front of the webbing,
thinking.

Food. Do the Morthans need food?

*It's traditional for them to eat their enemies, but there aren't any bodies
left after a space battle. Is that why they're scouring the area looking for
human ships? No. We're not honorable enemies. We're inferiors.*

Okay, it's not food. What else do we have that they might want?

Our technology? Maybe. . . .

If we could get them to think that we're incapable of fighting them
off, they might attempt a docking—and we could detonate a torpedo—

"Yes, that would do it all right," Korie said aloud. "And what a
nasty surprise." He looked at the seed-tool in his hand and smiled to
himself. "This was a good idea." He turned back to the webbing
thoughtfully. "Now, how do I get the Morthans to cooperate."

The Hole Thing

"You want me to what?" Chief Engineer Leen looked horrified.

"I want you to blow a hole in the side of the ship."

The chief engineer shook his head in mock exasperation. "I'm sorry. There must be something wrong with my hearing. It sounded like you said you wanted to blow a hole in the side of the ship."

Korie just glared. "Don't be cute, Mr. Leen."

The chief stopped his pantomime of deafness and resumed his normal sullen attitude. "All right. Enlighten me."

"The port side disruptors. They blew up when the fringe hit us, right? Well, I don't think the hole there is big enough. I think when the disruptors blew, they ripped a hole in the hull. A *big* hole. And we lost most of our air. *Whooosh!* Explosive decompression. Only a few of us survived. We're living in starsuits. We've managed to restore some power, not a lot. We're fighting like hell just to stay alive—but anyone looking at the ship from the outside would clearly understand that we're just a big fat prize waiting to be picked up . . ."

"And when they get close enough . . ." said Leen, "we put a torpedo into them, right?"

"Right," said Korie.

"They'll be watching for a trap."

"Probably."

"As soon as they see us fire, they'll fire back."

"Undoubtedly."

"They'll kill us, you know."

"They're going to kill us anyway," said Korie. "Let's take the bastards with us." And then he added, "Besides, there's always the chance that we might catch them by surprise. In that case, we might survive."

"We'd still have a hole in the side of the ship."

"But we'd still have a ship around that hole."

Leen nodded. "All right, let me think about this. I can peel back the hull. I suppose you want the inner hull and the life support module breached too?"

"We have to be convincing."

"I was afraid you were going to say that. This is a really shitty idea, you know. One of your absolute worst."

"Agreed."

"You understand that I'm absolutely opposed to it. I think this idea stinks. The crew is going to hate it too."

"No question, Chief. It stinks on ice."

"Of all the orders you've given since you took command, this is the one I hate the most."

"Me too," said Korie.

"If you order me to do this, I'll have to do it—but it'll be under vehement protest."

"I wouldn't have it any other way," Korie agreed.

"Good!" snapped Leen. "Just so you understand that."

"I do."

"Well, all right—" Leen's manner relaxed, became more work-manlike. In fact, he sounded almost *enthused* by the challenge. "Now I can evacuate most of the air before I start cutting. We won't lose much. Still, it sets us back. It really hurts. I mean, if we survive, it's going to be harder than ever to get home."

"Think big, Chief. If we can kill the *Dragon Lord*, we can get home." Korie added, "Now, listen—for this to work, time is going to be critical. To drop a torpedo and then activate it gives the enemy at least fifteen more seconds of warning. We've got two active torpedoes. Pull them out of the tubes, attach one to the forward spar, one to the rear. Make it look like we're trying to use them as engines. Pull the access panels off them. It'll make us seem even *more* desperate. Then, if we have a chance to use them, they're already released."

"They'll never buy it," said Leen.

"Yes, they will," said Korie. "Because the whole thing is so outrageous, it won't occur to them that it's a ploy."

Leen scowled. "How much time do I have?"

"Four hours, maybe five."

"Mm." The chief engineer held his hands apart and looked at the space between them, almost as if he were weighing the job. He grunted. "Yeah, I can do it. I'll have to lock down the entire port side of the ship. We'll use the starboard network for everything. Oh, and I'd better retrieve the G-scanners too."

"Good idea—that'll let them think our scanning lens was our first attempt to take a look around. Wait till the last minute though. Let Harlie keep his eyes as long as possible."

"Okay. I have to run this by HARLIE anyway and see if I've missed anything. You want the hole to look like an explosion, right?"

"Right."

"Okay, but I don't want to set a bomb. I'm going to do this with a team of cutters. That okay by you?"

"Just so it looks good."

"It'll look better than good. It'll look horrible. All right, let me go talk to HARLIE. As soon as the procedures are locked in, I'll report back to you. Thirty minutes, max. Oh, one more thing—"

"Yes, Chief?"

"Have I told you how much I really *hate* this idea?"

"Yes, I believe you have."

"Good. Just so you don't forget."

The Probe

"There they are. They're coming in," Hodel pointed.

The display showed an uncertain ripple closing rapidly on the *LS-1187*.

"Took 'em long enough," Korie complained. "Think we have nothing better to do than sit here and wait for them to come after us. Okay, go to red alert." He glanced up. "HARLIE, ETA?"

"Estimated time of arrival: thirty minutes."

Korie looked to his acting executive officer. "All right. The conn is yours. I'm going to suit up." But before he pushed off toward the aft airlock, he stopped himself. "Listen, Mike, if I don't make it—get this ship home in one piece. No more heroics, okay?"

"Hey—if you don't make it, *we* don't make it."

Korie held Hodel's gaze. "I *mean* it."

"Yes, sir," Hodel conceded. "Besides, there isn't anything left to be heroic with."

"You could always throw rocks at them."

"But we'll have to bring our own rocks, I know." Hodel called abruptly, "Mr. Korie?"

"Eh?"

"Good luck."

Korie flashed a thumbs-up signal to Mike Hodel and pushed himself off toward the aft airlock.

His starsuit was waiting for him in a mounting frame, arms and legs held out as if ready for a crucifixion. The monitor panel above it was glowing green. The starsuit was a body glove, so skintight that it was commonly joked that no man's religion was a secret anymore. The first time he heard it, Korie had to ask to have the joke explained. He still found it embarrassing. Also untrue. Most men wore protective codpieces under their starsuits anyway.

Li was already suited up; the man was short and wiry; in his helmet, he looked like an oversized elf in bright green underwear. He looked up from the work station he was monitoring and waved at Korie.

Korie peeled off his T-shirt and his shorts and his soft-soled shoes. He grabbed the top of the frame with both hands and levered his feet into the tight leggings of the starsuit, sliding himself into the elastic material like a snake trying to get back into its own skin. Li floated up behind him and placed his gloved hands on Korie's shoulders, anchored his feet on the ceiling, and pushed. Korie *popped* into the suit and it began sealing itself automatically. He ducked his head forward and up into the helmet and then pulled it down into place, locking it against the shoulder clasps.

"—hear me yet?" came Li's voice, a little too loud. Korie winced and flipped open his right forearm panel and adjusted his volume control.

"A little too loud and clear," said Korie. He glanced up at the monitor panel. "Am I green yet?"

"Still closing," answered the weapons specialist. "You're yellow . . . holding at yellow . . . there she goes. You're green."

"All right, let's go." Korie switched to the all-talk channel. "Everybody in place?"

"Confirmed."

Korie and Li stepped into the airlock and sealed the door. Korie hit the red button and the atmosphere began cycling out of the chamber. A moment later; the external door slid open, revealing the bright naked stars.

The two men worked their way around the hull of the vessel toward the gaping hole on its port side. Each one carried a pack that looked like a tool kit. Each also had a small disruptor rifle strapped to his back.

The axis rotation of the ship had been halted and the G-scanners retrieved. Now, they were hidden inside the starship's fluctuator spines. Korie and Li floated silently past the port fin.

"Mr. Korie—?" Hodel's voice.

"Talk to me."

"They've taken up a position a hundred thousand kilometers away. We have them on visual. Channel D. As you predicted, they're releasing probes."

"Thanks," Korie replied. As curious as he was, Korie waited until he and Hodel arrived at the rip in the *LS-1187*'s hull. Leen was right.

He'd made it look *horrible*. Korie wondered if perhaps he hadn't over-done it.

He anchored himself to the hull of the ship and punched for Channel D; the inside of his helmet refocused to show him the reprocessed view from the ship's telescope.

The enemy vessel was large enough not to be a pinpoint, but it was distant enough not to be a clear image either. The view was blurry and uncertain.

Korie grunted. "Well, at least we can see them now. I'm sure we'll all get a better look before this is over. After their probes see how bad off we are, they'll move in closer. For the kill—or the capture. Everybody be patient. If we were to fire anything from this distance, they'd see it and pop back into hyperstate before it could arrive on target. Then they'd hit us with their fringe. Everybody relax and keep your stations green. There's going to be a lot of waiting." He cleared the image.

"Li?"

"Both torpedoes are ready." He handed Korie a remote unit. "Flip the plastic cover and the unit arms itself. Press the green button and the fish wake up and go to standby. Targeting will be automatic for any mass larger than the *LS-1187*. Press the red button and they go. Breakaway is automatic. I've got a duplicate box, and Hodel is patched into the circuit too."

"Good." Korie clipped the box to his belt.

"The first of the probes are arriving," Hodel announced. "They're looking at us with everything they've got. It's a full-spectrum scan. You guys should smile and wave. They're looking at the labels on your underwear."

"It's all right," said Li. "I'm not wearing any underwear."

"Sure—give the Morthans a thrill," said Hodel.

"Or a scare," added Korie, with a grin. "Well, did they get a good look?"

"They're still looking—"

"Whoops, I can confirm that," Korie said. One of the probes was suddenly visible in the distance. It was approaching the side of the *LS-1187*, moving almost directly toward Korie and the hole in the hull. It was a chunky-looking thing, almost deliberately unaesthetic. Lenses and antennae protruded from it like porcupine quills. A single small high-intensity mass-driver looked as if it had been inserted directly through the center of the unit. Out of the corner of his eye, Korie saw another probe approaching the bow of the ship and focusing on the torpedo there.

The closer probe came to a halt uncomfortably close to Korie—only a dozen meters away. Korie could see its lenses swiveling and refocusing as it photographed the damage to the ship. "Let them get a good look," said Korie, whispering in spite of himself. Slowly, pulled the disruptor rifle off his back and armed it; but he did not point it at the probe. Not yet . . .

"Can I express an opinion?" asked Li.

"Go ahead," said Korie.

Li faced the probe head on, raised his right fist before him, and slowly, elegantly, extended his middle finger.

The probe did not react immediately. Then one lens after another swiveled to study Li's defiant posture. Despite himself, Korie aimed his weapon.

Suddenly the probe flashed—a single bright flare of energy. The beam was invisible, but Li exploded instantly. From the center out, he ballooned and shredded.

Korie reacted in the same instant. Screaming, he squeezed the trigger. The probe disintegrated. He whirled to fire on the second one, but it was already exploding. Hodel had caught it with the bow guns.

And then there was silence. The pieces of flesh and bone and plastic spun away into the darkness and were lost forever.

The loudest sound in the universe was Korie's own choking breath inside his helmet. He was screaming. He was swearing. He was incoherent. The words were bubbling in rage and spittle. Everything was red—

"Sir!" Hodel was screaming in his ear. "Are you all right?"

Korie heard the words and couldn't answer. He wanted to pound something. He wanted to hurt someone, anyone. He would have smashed his fist into the face of God—

"I'm . . . okay," he said. "Just don't say anything for a minute."

Lord of the Dragons

"Sir? They're moving in."

"I got it," said Korie. He took a sip of water. *I gave him permission. I told him he could do it!* He spoke and his voice was a rasp. "Don't anybody else express an opinion. Ever. I mean it. I'm not joking."

Hodel did not reply.

After a moment, Korie asked, "Where are they now?"

"Closing fast in real space. High-gee acceleration."

"That's to intimidate us."

"It's working."

"ETA?"

"Three minutes."

Korie switched his helmet to pick up the visual again. The image was clearer now; still blurry, but resolving sharper and sharper as he watched.

At first, she was just a pattern of light, an orange blur, a flame-colored presence. Then she began to take shape, an angular, dragon-headed wedge; she filled out with detail. She showed her teeth, she was all points and edges, and she was studded with quills and embers. She opened her eyes and glared. She was the *beast*, and her masters knew it. The gigantic numbers on her side were *666*. Her face was painted like a dragon from Hell.

"So that's what you look like, you son of a bitch—"

The image swelled in front of him, and swelled and swelled again. The *Dragon Lord* wasn't a starship. She was a city. She was a monster. She was a wall of guns and torpedo bays.

And I thought to challenge that?

The knot of doubt began in Korie's belly, began creeping up toward his throat—

He cleared the image in his helmet, hoping to escape—

But the gigantic ship was already *here*. It filled the universe in front of him. It blazed with light and glory. Korie was caught with vertigo and fear. He felt as if he were looking down on a cityscape from a great height and at any moment, he might tumble headlong into it. His rifle was forgotten in his hands. His ship was forgotten. The torpedoes and the remote on his belt—

"Holy buffalo shit. Look at all the fucking Indians." That was Hodel's voice. Korie blinked and realized that his acting exec was quoting the punch line of an old joke. What were Custer's last words? The reference was appropriate—and it was enough to shock Korie out of his horrified reverie.

Are they going to demand our surrender? he wondered.

His own doubt answered him. *Why bother? We're useless to them. We have nothing they could want. Oh, Lord—I really miscalculated this one.*

"Any signals?"

"No, sir. Nothing. They're just looking us over. They're hitting us with a lot of heavy-duty scans. I don't think we have any secrets anymore."

"Agree."

What are they waiting for? Why not just blast us and be done?

"Should we . . . ?" Hodel started to ask.

"No. If they wanted to destroy us, they'd have done it already." Korie gulped and swallowed hard. "Let's not start anything. They've got all their guns trained on us. If I farted sideways, they'd shred us in an instant."

Oh, God, I'm so stupid. I should have known we didn't stand a chance. What are they waiting for?

And then Korie did something he never thought he would ever do again.

He prayed.

Oh, Lord—whoever or whatever you are—I know you must exist, because of the beauty and order of this universe. Please forgive me my blasphemies and hear this desperate plea. Please save the lives of these good men and women who trusted me, who put their faith in my judgment and their souls in my hands. They deserve better than this terrible and lonely death, here in the desolate rift of night. Please, Lord, please—

"Mr. Korie—?"

"What?"

"They're moving—"

"*What?!*"

"They're turning."

Korie looked across the gulf to the great wall of metal and ceramic and plastic and saw that it was true. Hodel was right. The great flame-streaked ship was moving. It was turning. Majestically, its great head came swinging around as it oriented itself toward a new course.

The gigantic painted head of the ship was facing him now. Korie stared into the mouth of the dragon. It was all missile tubes. He could imagine them firing all at once—how many? Fifty? Five hundred? These were the teeth of the dragon—Korie felt as if he was tumbling into its mouth.

"They're moving off—"

The mouth of the *Dragon* continued to expand in front of Korie—and then it passed over him, moved silently over his head. He looked up at its endless belly, awestruck. He turned to watch the great ship as it moved away, looked after it as it shrank into the distance, receding to a bright point of light.

What was happening? Why didn't they—?

"Everybody hold your positions—" he said.

"What's happening?" Hodel's voice.

"I don't know—" *Oh, my God. Yes, I do.* "Uh—I think they saw our missiles. I think they recognized that it was a Mexican standoff." He couldn't believe he was saying it even as the words came out of his mouth.

Will they believe it? Korie wondered. *They have to,* he told himself, desperately. He knew that he was only moments away from a quivering nervous reaction. He wondered if he was going to be able to get back inside the ship before it hit.

He started working his way slowly back toward the airlock.

I've looked into the dragon's face. I know. The dragon wouldn't back away from a challenge. They didn't back away from this one. There wasn't any challenge here for them.

Korie knew what had happened. His throat was tight; his chest was constricted; he felt as if he couldn't breathe.

Li had given the dragon the finger. Li had insulted the dragon. In return . . . the dragon had insulted Li's ship.

It looked us over and decided we weren't worth killing. The ultimate Morthan insult: "I don't want your blood on my sword."

As he floated past the fluctuator spine, HARLIE's voice whispered in his ear. "Mr. Korie. Private discussion?" Korie glanced at his monitors. HARLIE had sealed the channel; they wouldn't be overheard.

"Go ahead, HARLIE."

"I believe your analysis of the situation may be inaccurate."

"In what way?"

"It is obvious to me that the analogy of a 'Mexican standoff' is inappropriate to this situation. We had no chance at all of damaging the *Dragon Lord*."

"Agreed."

"Then why did you tell the crew that we did?"

"I thought we were going to be killed, HARLIE. I was certain of it. I could not see any way for us to survive."

"That was my analysis too."

Korie stopped himself at the aft airlock, but made no move to enter. He looked up beyond the curve of hull toward the mindless stars. "So I thought about ways to die. And—all I could think was that I didn't want us to die a coward's death. I knew we didn't stand a chance. I never believed we could even hit them, but I knew we had to go down fighting—"

"I understood that part too."

"And then at the last moment, I flinched. I didn't want to die. I didn't want the crew to die. I didn't want the ship destroyed. I prayed to God to let us live."

"That is understandable too, but that is not my question, Mr. Korie."

"I know what your question is, HARLIE—I'm trying to answer it. They let us go. We're not worth killing. Li gave them the finger; they gave it back to us. They said, 'So what?' They came in close to show us—to show *me*—how big they were, how invulnerable they were, how puny and infinitesimal we were in comparison. They want us to know that. They want us to go home demoralized, telling everybody that the Morthans are bigger and stronger and smarter.

"Can you imagine what that would do to this crew? We wouldn't be able to hold our heads up in public. We'd be a disgrace not only to ourselves, but to our whole species. And our guys are smart. They'd figure it out long before we got home what kind of reputation this ship is going to have, and the shame that her crew would share.

"After everything we've been through, this crew deserves better. I'll lie to them, yes, to protect their confidence and self-esteem. We can't lose our spirit now; we'd lose our need to survive. It's at least four months from here to Stardock. Do you think we could make it with a crew that didn't care anymore? Yes, HARLIE, I lied. I lied to save them. It's a terrible lie, but I couldn't think of a way to tell the truth that would ease the terrible shame. I couldn't find a victory in it without lying. I made a promise to Captain Lowell that I wouldn't lie to this crew and I have broken it over and over and over. It just keeps getting deeper. But I don't know what else to do. I need you to back me up, HARLIE."

"I can't lie, Mr. Korie."

"You said you could to ensure the survival of this ship. Well, this is a survival issue."

"The morale of the crew is a survival issue?"

"It always has been."

"I see. You have given me a moral dilemma."

"It isn't the first time. The HARLIE series is supposed to be very good at moral dilemmas."

"Creating them, not solving them."

"Sorry, that's my job."

"Mr. Korie, I must advise you that the dilemma this situation will cause me may further impair my ability to function as a useful member of the crew."

"I understand that. Do you understand the necessity?"

"I do not share the same experience of human emotions, Mr. Korie, so I cannot understand the necessity for this fiction. It is a problem in human dynamics; I can only understand it as an equation in an intellectual context, and as such, I do not see the same problem with the truth that you do. We have survived. Isn't that victory enough?"

"Trust me, HARLIE. Mere survival is never enough. That's just existence. People need to succeed. People need to feel good about themselves."

"Mr. Korie—will you help me then? Please make this a direct order."

Korie considered the request. "Yes, I understand your need. This is no longer a request. Consider it a direct order."

"Thank you."

"Mm," said Korie. "Thank you." He pressed the panel to open the airlock hatch and pulled himself into the ship. But as he did, one terrible stunning question hit him right in the middle of his soul.

We're still alive! Did God hear me?

He turned and looked back out at the emptiness.

Thank you, he whispered in his mind. And wondered . . . *am I talking to myself again?*

Homeward

Korie entered the Bridge to applause and cheers.

Embarrassed, he held up a hand to cut it off. "Belay that." He took a breath and looked around. The expectant looks on the faces of the crew disturbed him. They were so *exhilarated*.

"Um," he said. He plucked his headset from the command chair and put it on. He spoke to the whole crew of the *LS-1187* now. "You did good. All of you. And I'm proud of you and proud to be on the same ship with you. But the celebration is a little premature. We're not out of this yet. There are other Morthan ships in these woods, and they may not be as smart as the *Dragon Lord*. So, let's keep to our original plan. Chief Leen, power up the mass-drivers. Let's start home."

He could hear the cheering throughout the ship.

"Uh, sir—?" Hodel floated forward. He was holding something behind his back. "Um, the crew—we have a gift for you. We were going to wait till we got home to give it to you, but well—we think now is a better time." He brought out a large flat box and pushed it toward Korie.

"Huh?" Korie was startled. So much was happening so fast. He fumbled open the box. Inside was a captain's cap and a jacket. Korie grabbed the cap and held it under one arm. The jacket floated up out of the box—Korie grabbed it, letting the box drift away.

"Turn it around. Look at the back."

It said: CAPTAIN J.T. KORIE.

And below that: LS-1187.

"Put it on," Hodel said.

For just a single heartbeat, Korie was tempted; but then he stopped himself and said, "No. Not yet. Captain Lowell is still captain of this ship. Um—I'm really flattered and—moved. This—" Korie found himself unable to put the words together; the flood of emotion was welling up inside of him. He wiped quickly at one eye. "Let me wait until it's official, and then I'll wear it proudly. But, I thank you all very much for this. I, uh—I can't think of any gift that could mean more." He grabbed for the box and tried to fold the jacket and cap back into it, but without the help of gravity, it was an uneasy business.

Finally, he just held the box and jacket and cap pinned under one arm and looked embarrassed. "Uh, this is still a starship. And we're still a long way from home. Let's not lose our discipline now—"

And then, flushed with emotion, he retreated from the Bridge before anyone could see how close to the edge he really was.

Stardock

It didn't take four months to get home.

It took six and half.

But they made it.

They limped away from the site of the attack and nobody came after them. They were blind and they stayed blind by choice. Korie wouldn't risk opening another scanning lens. It would have been a beacon in the darkness for any marauders still patrolling.

So they chugged at sublight speed, building up velocity incrementally, accelerating for days, then weeks, toward a fraction of lightspeed that could be measured with less than three zeros between the decimal point and the digit.

The crew, what was left of them, worked without rest. Each of them had three jobs. Most of them worked out of the manuals. The oxygen-debt was enormous, and Korie had the entire inner hull converted to aeroponics. It worked, but even so they were too close to the margin. There were too many of them and just not enough growing plants.

As they ran low on rations, they began eating the Luna moss, and later the young ears of corn and carrots and potatoes. The winged beans that Korie had planted became a part of almost every meal. They replanted the crops as fast as they ate them. They weren't quite self-sufficient; but they'd expanded the window of their survival to allow them enough time to get home.

But it took so damned *long* . . .

The singularity had to be kept damped, so the mass-drivers couldn't be run at full-power, neither could the fuel cells be recharged to full capacity. That also meant no gravity and limited oxygen reprocessing.

Despite HARLIE's profound internal monitoring, his reliability kept slipping for reasons neither Leen nor Korie could find. Korie suspected it was the side effect of his moral dilemma and wondered if this HARLIE unit was going to have to be wiped and reintegrated.

Worst of all, the hyperstate equipment refused to calibrate. They couldn't go into hyperstate until they'd restored system confidence to 85% or better, and with HARLIE functioning at less than 85%, they couldn't use him to do the job. They had to recalibrate each unit separately, reintegrate the system manually, and hope for alignment. It took seven attempts before they hit 87%, and that still wasn't enough for Korie. He made them do it two more times before he accepted that 89% was the best he was going to get.

What it meant was *maybe*.

They *might* be able to inject into hyperstate. They *might* be able to steer the envelope. They *might* be able to maintain it safely. They *might* be able to get back to Stardock.

Korie thought about it, long and hard. He talked it over with Hodel and Leen and HARLIE, weighed the risks, considered the options, realized there were no other choices. They were just too far away from anywhere to attempt a return at less than superluminal velocities. Finally, he couldn't postpone the decision any longer. He gave the order.

They almost made it.

The hyperstate envelope wobbled like a bubble in a wind tunnel. It was barely controllable. They pointed it and pushed on it and they skated across the intervening space like an ice cube on a hot griddle; first this way and then that, course-correcting furiously, and all the while trying not to let the field collapse around them.

The hyperstate horizon went unstable two hours before they hit their target sphere. Chief Leen invented six new curses in less than half a second; then he collapsed the envelope.

The *LS-1187* crawled the rest of the way at sublight speeds. Neither Korie nor the chief felt lucky enough to try a second injection.

But they were home.

The Stardock was a deep-space installation, a small city of light lost between the stars. It was girders, globes, platforms, antennae, and work bays. It was fifteen thousand people and two thousand industrial repair robots. It was a safe harbor of warmth in the deepest night. If a captain had the coordinates, he could find it. Otherwise, it didn't exist.

It had always been a welcome port for the ships it served.

Except most of them hadn't come back.

The *LS-1187* came in to a near-empty nest. Most of the work-bays were empty and almost all of the city lights were out. There were no welcome messages or displays. There was only a quiet acknowledgment of the ship's return and a request for her commanding officer to report immediately to the vice-admiral's office.

Korie reported in grimly. He was briefed on the Marathon massacre and the state of the fleet. It was worse than he had thought.

Then he was given the bad news.

In the Vice-admiral's Office

"The Fleet Review Board has determined that the *LS-1187* inadvertently allowed herself to be tracked by the *Dragon Lord*. The *LS-1187* had led the Morthan marauders directly to the convoy. If Captain Lowell survives, he'll be court-martialed. And . . ." said the vice-admiral, "based on the evidence of your ship's log, your own judgment is highly suspect as well."

"I brought my ship home," said Korie.

"You brought her home with self-inflicted wounds, with her torpedoes unfired and cannibalized for parts, with her artificial consciousness half-psychotic for having to maintain a fictitious reality for the crew—" The vice-admiral stopped herself. "I will not list the entire catalog of offenses. The important one is that you did most of this without authorization. Your captain was disabled, but you assumed the authority of command before it could be officially logged. You signed termination orders—"

"Ma'am," Korie said, deliberately interrupting her. "This is inappropriate."

"You think so?"

"Yes, ma'am. You are quoting rules at me. Let me quote one back at you. 'The primary duty of *every* officer in the fleet is to act responsibly—even if that responsibility means acting beyond the scope of assigned authority.' My duty was to bring my ship and my crew home safely. I did so to the best of my ability, and I will not apologize for the steps I took. They were appropriate. I do not see how anyone else could have done different. Or better. If you can demonstrate to me now that there were better choices available, options that would have saved lives or reduced the damage or gotten us home quicker, I would appreciate being enlightened. If you cannot show me such options, then it is inappropriate to question the decisions I took under the circumstances."

"I admire your spirit," said the vice-admiral, grimly. "Certainly you survived where others didn't. That must count for something."

"I'm still waiting to hear if there were alternatives to the decisions I made," Korie said stiffly.

"That's not my job," she replied, every bit as stiff. "There may not have been any other choices for you. I give you credit for your imagination and creativity. I give you credit for bringing your ship home. Unfortunately, in this situation, it's not enough."

"Other ships have gotten a hero's welcome for less."

"The *LS-1187* is not another ship."

"We have intelligence on the *Dragon Lord*, including close-range photographs, that no one else has been able to provide. Doesn't that count for something?"

"Unfortunately, as valuable as that information may prove to be, it still counts for very little in this situation. If anything, it works against you. The fleet has been savagely mauled, and the ship that betrayed the convoy also brought home stunning snapshots of the killers. The question is already being asked, *if you were that close, why didn't you put a torpedo into her?*"

"You know why we couldn't."

"I do—but that's because I understand the mechanics of the situation. How many of them *out there* are going to understand? Understand something, Commander. While you've been isolated safely in space, crawling home for the past seven months, the rest of us have had to live with the aftermath of the terrible massacre. There's not a person at Stardock who hasn't lost someone close. We're all still in shock, we're only now starting to build a new resolve to fight back. The morale here is going to have to be rebuilt on hatred; we have nothing else to motivate our people except a rage for revenge. It's barely enough. Our people need a target. Because we can't get our hands on the Morthans right now, we're looking for targets we can blame—stupidity, foolishness, ignorance, careless mistakes. Do you understand what I'm telling you? Even if you had destroyed the *Dragon Lord*, it still wouldn't redeem you. The *LS-1187* is a pariah. Your ship, Commander Korie, led the Morthans to the convoy."

"They could have followed anybody," Korie argued. "There was no way any ship could have detected the *Dragon Lord*. She's—an incredible thing."

"But it was *your* ship they followed. Somebody has to be blamed for the disaster. That's the way these things work. I feel sorry for you, for what you've been through—and for what you still have to endure. But the *LS-1187* and her crew are a political disaster area. No one is going to lift a finger for you."

Korie didn't answer that. The impact of the vice-admiral's words was still sinking in. He felt it in his knees, in his stomach, in his throat, and in the pit of fear at the bottom of his soul. Everything he'd ever lived for—he realized he now stood as a symbol of its betrayal. He felt as if he were teetering on the edge of a precipice. Did he have no chance to redeem himself?

"So, um"—for the first time, Korie felt abashed—"what's going to happen?"

"I'm not sure yet," said the vice-admiral. "Nobody wants to make the decision. I don't either. You were handed to me and I was told to find a way to bury you. You know, you had a great future." She met his gaze sadly. "I can tell you this. You can forget about getting a ship of your own. That's not going to happen."

Korie felt as if he were falling, tumbling headlong into the abyss of damnation. His last chance had just been taken away from him. He couldn't swallow. He couldn't speak either. But somehow he managed to get the words out. "I understand. You'll have my resignation on your desk tomorrow morning."

"Don't bother. I won't accept it."

"Ma'am?"

"Commander, we still need you."

"Ma'am, this isn't *fair*." Korie could feel his frustration rising. "First, you tell me that we're the worst ship in the fleet, then you admit that nobody else could have done better, then you tell me that I'm not fit to be trusted with a ship, and now you say you won't release me."

"Commander, I'm not interested in fair. If the universe were fair, we wouldn't be having this conversation. Now, listen to me. We need every qualified officer we have. And unfortunately, you more than demonstrated your competence when you brought back the *LS-1187*. I almost wish you hadn't. I don't know what to do with her—and I can't afford to scrap her. The same for you and your crew. The best thing I can think of is to fix you up and send you out again, doing something that will keep you out of sight and out of mind; it'll free another ship for something more important."

"But I can't be captain—?"

"How would it look to promote you now? That's assuming I could find someone to sponsor you. No, you can't be a captain."

"Well then, ma'am, with all due respect—I cannot continue to serve under these conditions. May I speak candidly?"

"I thought you already were." The vice-admiral sighed. "Go ahead."

"I *earned* this command. What my crew accomplished in surviving and bringing back the *LS-1187* is nothing to be ashamed of. The political situation is irrelevant here. These men and women deserve better than this, and so do I. We did an exemplary job, we brought back intelligence that no one else has ever accomplished. It's *wrong* to punish us. You not only deny us, but you deny the fleet the benefit of a crew that has proven itself under fire."

"How many kills did you make?"

"That's not the issue."

"It is now. How many torpedoes did you fire?"

"That's an unfair question."

"No, it isn't. That's the *only* question anymore."

Korie met her gaze directly. "You can't believe that."

"Even if I were to grant the validity of your position—" The vice-admiral chose her words carefully. "Even if it were true that you were still qualified to command a starship, there isn't a starship for you."

"The *LS-1187* was to become mine when Captain Lowell retired."

"The point is moot. As soon as we can find a captain who will accept the *LS-1187*, she will be reassigned."

"In that case, Admiral, I must respectfully insist on the right to resign my commission."

"Denied."

"I won't stop trying."

"And I won't stop denying."

Korie shut up. He was trapped. He felt more alone than he had ever felt before in his life.

The vice-admiral softened her tone then. She said quietly, "All right, off the record, I agree—it's unfair. But don't use the unfairness of it to be a spoiled child. The Alliance needs you, Commander. I need you to continue as the executive officer of the *LS-1187*."

"No, ma'am. My crew was expecting me to be their new captain before the disaster. They have been expecting it all the way home. If I were to continue aboard the ship now and not be promoted to captain, my ability to manage this crew would be severely impaired. Plus, if they were to perceive the unfairness of the situation, it would very likely create significant resentment toward any new captain."

"Then I trust that you will not allow them to perceive the situation as unfair—"

"Ma'am, they're not stupid. They'll figure it out. You've got to know that you're looking at a terrific morale problem aboard that ship. As soon as they begin to realize that the *LS-1187* has been branded a Jonah, they're going to start hurting."

"That's one of the reasons we need you to stay on. That crew trusts you."

"No, ma'am. I told that crew they were heroes. I'm not going back there to take it away from them. You're setting this ship up to fail. I've had enough failure for a while, thank you. Find someone else."

"There isn't anyone else," the vice-admiral said. "There isn't a qualified executive officer who's willing to transfer to the *LS-1187*. Not with her record."

"Uh-huh? And what about a captain? If you can't find an executive officer—"

"Commander Korie, that's not your concern."

"I beg to differ. It most certainly *is* my concern. You're telling me that you can't find anyone else who wants the ship—but you won't give her to me."

The vice-admiral didn't respond.

"That's true, isn't it?"

"Commander, I've let you be candid and I've been candid with you because I need you to understand the difficulty of the situation—"

"Admiral, whatever you do is going to be a difficult decision. So, choose the one that produces the best results for the war effort. Give the ship a new number or scrap her for parts; but if you're not going to let her be a proud ship, don't send her out to be a shamed ship. Don't do that to her crew. Reassign them. Let them serve on other ships."

"We can't do that either."

"I don't understand—"

"I don't know if I can explain it to you. Let's just focus on your situation for the moment. Maybe that'll make it clearer. Personally, I would prefer to accept your resignation. I like it when problems go away by themselves. But I cannot; not without also ordering a court-martial for you, which I will not. *That* would be even more unfair. Neither can I order you back onto that ship if you are so adamantly opposed to it. But I can't put you anywhere else, either. The problem is not just the ship. The problem is you. I doubt that there's a captain in the fleet who will accept you as his executive officer now. You carry the stink of the *LS-1187* with you. And the same is true for the rest of your crew. Keeping them together is the *best* thing I can do for them."

The words hit Korie hard. He lowered his head and looked at his hands in his lap for a moment.

"I'm sorry," said the vice-admiral.

"I can't quit. I can't go on. I can't go back." Korie shook his head and looked up again. "Am I allowed an honorable suicide?"

The vice-admiral allowed herself the tiniest of smiles. "I'm afraid that's not a viable option, either." She leaned forward, softening her tone. "Jon, I know this hurts. I know it's very bad news. You have to understand that it isn't personal—"

"It sure feels like it."

"This is a crisis situation. We're scrambling like crazy to keep the Morthan Solidarity from finding out just how badly they damaged us. They don't know. They think they hit mostly merchant shipping. They don't know that they wiped out most of our heavy cruisers. If they do find that out . . . well, I don't have to tell you what the Morthans have done to the planets they've taken over.

"The only thing I can say to you that I hope will cause you to change your mind is to ask you to consider if the war effort is more important to you than your own personal or career concerns."

"You already know the answer to that question." Korie was offended that he even had to say so. "Ma'am, everything you've said just reaffirms the correctness of my choice. I don't have to be a starship officer to serve the war effort. Considering all that you've just told me, I'd probably be a lot more useful somewhere else. I can go back to Shaleen and work on the orbital assembly lines for liberty ships. I was a stardrive engineer, you now. It seems to me we're going to be needing a lot more starships very soon. And I'm a good crew chief. I can do good and I can feel good about what I'm accomplishing. Let me go. It'll solve your problem—and mine. And it'll put me a lot closer to my family. I'll even get to see them once in a while."

"My God—" The vice-admiral hesitated. *"They didn't tell you?"*

"Tell me what—?" Korie's gut was already tightening.

The vice-admiral was clearly distressed. "The *Dragon Lord* hit Shaleen three months ago. She scourged the planet. I'm sorry. There were no survivors. There's nothing left."

Korie didn't hear the rest.

You cosmic son of a bitch! I trusted you! I didn't know you put a price on your miracles!

He stumbled to his feet—

There is no God. There is only a malignant practical joker with the morals of a terrorist. I will never trust you again!

Mail Call

They gave him a month off.

It wasn't enough.

If they had given him a year off, it wouldn't have been enough.

Everything blurred.

Somewhere in the middle of the debriefing and the sedatives and the physical examinations and the library tapes of the smoldering surface of Shaleen and the mandatory therapeutic counseling, Jonathan Thomas Korie broke down and cried.

He went down to recreation, checked into Rage Co., and pounded on the Morthan android with a club for a while—it grinned at him at first. Then it looked uncertain and finally worried. He beat at it over and over and over again until it fell to its knees and began begging for mercy. It wept and cried and shrieked and very convincingly soiled its underwear.

It wasn't enough.

He took the club and continued pounding. He shattered bricks. He broke a lot of glass—he demolished a house. He raged. He shrieked as hard as he could, trying to force his mountain of grief and anger and madness out through the tiny insufficient funnels of his eyes and mouth. His body betrayed him with its inefficiency. The pressure of his frustration only fueled the volcanic insanity of his fury. He swung and smashed and battered at everything he could reach. He fell down a couple of times, picked himself up, bleeding from cuts, and continued swinging—around and around and around until he collapsed in a sodden heap against one wall, sinking slowly to the floor.

It still wasn't enough.

He walked around in circles then, the tears running down his cheeks. He wept in helplessness. He couldn't stop the sobs from choking up his throat like a painful vise. He didn't have the strength to continue and at the same time he couldn't stop. It just went on and on—until he was too weak even to die.

He lay there on the floor of the chamber and sank into numbed horror. The images of the scoured world tortured his mind.

Not like this. Oh, please—make it not so. They couldn't have died in such horror. Not that way. Not alone.

After a while, he got up, feeling empty and weak and even a little bit silly. He felt wobbly and he staggered slightly as he found his way to the shower. It helped a little, but it wasn't enough.

He went back to the room they'd assigned him and tried calling friends. But there weren't a lot of ships at Stardock right now, and of the ones that were, there weren't many officers who wanted to talk to him. After all, he was from the *LS-1187.*

He slept. He slept for eighteen hours straight.

It wasn't enough. He woke up still tired. He looked in the mirror and his face was puffy and his eyes were red and all the parts of his body sagged as if he were melting away.

There was a small package on the desk.

His mail.

He opened the box—and there was a birthday present from his wife. Written on the card was a simple message: "I love you so much." He slipped the card into the reader, tears already welling in his eyes. He didn't know if he could bear this.

And then they were here in the room with him—*Carol, Timmy and Robby*—laughing and giggling. "Hi, Daddy! Hi!" He could see the warm pink sunlight of Shaleen streaming around them. "We miss you! Come home, please!"

"Give your daddy a hug," Carol urged the boys, and they ran forward to embrace him. Their arms wrapped around him. He bent low on one knee and wrapped his arms around them too. The holographic image passed invisibly through him. *Dammit! He couldn't feel them at all.*

Carol stepped forward then and lifted her chin for an unseen kiss. He couldn't bring himself to kiss her back—he could barely see through the tears that were filling his eyes. "Here's a little promise from me too. When you get back, I'll give you a real homecoming." She looked directly at him now. "Jon, we're so proud of you, but I miss you so much and so do the boys. We wish you were here with us now."

"I wish I was too. If I had been—we'd be together now."

But she couldn't hear him. All he had left of his family was this recorded message and his memories.

It wasn't enough.

Nothing would ever be enough again.

When he came back aboard the *LS-1187*, he was a changed man.

There was a new tightness in his eyes and a dark ferocity in his posture. Even when he relaxed, there was a brooding sense of some inner resolve at work, something still unfocused but very *dangerous*.

The crew sensed it immediately—and they distanced themselves accordingly. They bent their heads away from his and hurried quickly to their jobs. Something was *different* about Korie.

Gone was the easygoing manner, the quick wit and flashing smile. In its place, Korie had become a darker presence. His compassion had been burned out. In the gap left behind, there was only a smoldering undirected ruthlessness. No one wanted to be the first target of his rage, if and when it finally erupted.

The crew saw the madness in his eyes and shuddered.

The Crew

The work lights on the hull of the *LS-1187* gave her a garish look. She glittered and blazed against the bottomless night. She was the brightest object in the Stardock.

It was deliberate.

If the Stardock were discovered and attacked, the first ship to be destroyed would be the *LS-1187*. She was bait—and everyone knew it.

But if the Stardock were discovered and attacked, the destruction would be total. Nothing would be left. So it was irrelevant that the *LS-1187* should be so brightly lit.

Except it was also a deliberate insult.

All four of the other ships in their work bays were dark. Work crews swarmed over them with portable lamps. The *LS-1187* was bright—but if any crews worked on her, they came from her own complement.

She was Jonah.

Every ship had a number. Those ships that had tasted blood also had names.

And those ships that had earned a reputation also had *unofficial* names.

The *LS-1187* was Jonah. The jinx.

That was what the crews of the other ships at Stardock called her. Judas had been considered. And for a while, it seemed as if Judas would be her nickname; but eventually the name was discarded because the *LS-1187* wasn't considered smart enough to be a Judas.

She had no captain. And the rumor was that she wasn't going to get a captain.

They couldn't decommission her. She was still classified as functional. But they couldn't send her out again either. No one wanted to sail on her. Her old crew—well, they would; they didn't have a lot of choice—but no one else would willingly accept a transfer to the Jonah ship.

So, she waited.

Her crew knew. They couldn't *not* know. And it had an effect on them. There was work that needed to be done, but it went untended. There was a hole in her hull, and Harlie was still traumatic, and her disruptors were fused. Her Systems Analysis network was fragmented, and everything else was out of alignment. But the repair work progressed haphazardly, without vision, without care. Chief Leen tried, but even he was shattered by the despair that pervaded Stardock.

The ship had come home, but she was still adrift. Korie was a dark shadow, and the crew distrusted him now. He hadn't been given the command he'd earned. That meant something, though nobody was quite sure what. There was speculation, but it was futile; everyone knew the real reason. It was the *LS-1187*. She was Jonah.

Her crew waited and hoped for someone to arrive and take command. And wondered what was going to happen next . . .

There were six of them, and they didn't know.

They were fresh out of training; they'd arrived on the latest transport. They were eager and fresh-faced and didn't know what they were walking into.

Their names were Bach, Stolchak, Jonesy, Armstrong, Haddad, and Nakahari.

Lieutenant Junior Grade Helen Bach, security officer, was the shortest of the group. She stood five foot nine in her combat gear. She had a smoldering expression that was its own warning sign. She was of African-Altairian descent and she was not to be treated casually. Rumor had it that she had broken the arm of her karate instructor during the third lesson.

Lieutenant Junior Grade Irma Stolchak, life-support technician, stood half a head taller. She was big-boned and friendly-looking, but there was a narrow cast to her eyes—as if she had been hurt once too often and had been left with a terrible suspicion about the rest of humanity.

Crewmember First Class Ayoub Haddad, quantum mechanic, was of pure Jordanian descent—although none of his ancestors had walked on the soil of Earth for nearly seven generations past. He wore a deceptively friendly expression. He was fascinated by machines, because machines always did exactly what they were supposed to do—even when they broke down.

Crewmember First Class Ori Nakahari, unassigned, was the youngest son of a wealthy Japanese-Martian family. He enlisted two days after the mauling at Marathon. His parents had angrily disowned him for giving political concerns a higher priority than family concerns. Ori had not wept.

Lieutenant Junior Grade Valentine Michael Jones, unassigned, was called "Jonesy" because everybody named Jones was called "Jonesy." He was just a little too tall, a little too skinny, and more than a little goofy-looking. The joke about Jonesy was that he was still a virgin—because he wasn't yet certain which sex he was opposite to.

Crewman First Class Brian Armstrong, unassigned, was a side of beef with a grin. He was a big, good-natured champion who looked more like a sexual athlete than a starman. He was quick-witted, good-looking, friendly, and popular, about as perfect a human specimen as could be found anywhere in the fleet. So why was he on the *LS-1187*? Because he'd boffed the wrong bimbo and the bimbo's father had been a vice-admiral. 'Nuff said about that.

They were new. They were eager and fresh-faced and they didn't know. They'd come directly from the transport dock and their first glimpse of the *LS-1187* was enough to tell them the worst.

They were on a catwalk overlooking the work bay and the starship gleamed beneath them. The six of them stopped to look at her. Jonesy put his hands against the slanting glass wall. He pressed his face close and his expression glowed. But he was the only one. The others were already realizing what ship this was. Their expressions were sinking fast.

"Come on, Jonesy." Brian Armstrong poked him. "You've seen starships before."

"Not this one. This one's *ours*."

"Wake up and really look at her, Jonesy."

"I don't care. She's still beautiful." But he let himself be led along. The walkway extended the length of the ship, all the way to her stern airlock. The long walk gave them a chance to see every scorch and blister and battle scar on the starship's ceramic hull. This close, they could see how badly she was scored with blast marks and wavy rainbow discolorations—the visible aftermath of being brushed by the fringe of a marauder's hyperstate envelope.

Stolchak spoke her disappointment first. "Look at that. What a mess. We really did it this time."

Armstrong stared out the glass. "I wonder if it's true that she's jinxed—"

Nakahari grinned at him. "Well, she scrambled her own captain. See there? Her port-side disruptors overloaded." He shuddered grotesquely and laughed. "Now they say his ghost stalks the inner hull, *howling* for revenge!"

"Knock it off, you guys," said Bach. "She's just another starship."

"Uh-oh," said Stolchak. "Look at that." She pointed to the shadowed numbers on the starship's slender hull. "No name. You know what that means."

"Yeah," said Bach. "Anonymity."

They reached the end of the walkway, turned left along a transverse walk, and found themselves at an access bay, where a docking tube led across to the ship's stern airlock.

There was no one on duty at the bosun's station to check them in. They exchanged curious glances, then one by one, each of the six slid his or her identity card into the reader and waited for it to beep green.

Inside the starship, it was worse. Wall panels hung open, their covers missing or broken. Gaping holes revealed torn wiring harnesses and broken structural members. There were empty places where system modules should have been installed, and internal sensory fixtures hung brokenly from their sockets. The light panels glowed unevenly; many of them had annoying cyclical quavers.

And there was graffiti on the walls. There were posters, and slogans. Raucous music was playing from a rattling speaker and a hyperkinetic voice was bantering: "Good morning, starshine! You're listening to Flamin' Damon and the Allied Star Force Distribution Network. Recorded *Live* and *Lively!* on YOUR homeworld in New America! Here's one of the classics—"

A cluster of sullen crewmen were lounging near the stern utility shaft. They were unshaven and wearing non-regulation gear. One was wearing a gaudy dashiki, another was wearing only a kilt.

The six new crewmembers ignored their sideways looks and headed forward through the aft keel. A blue-skinned woman passed them, heading sternward. She was eerily beautiful, tiny-boned and delicately featured. Her hairless skull was outlined with delicate featherlike scales, shading upward to become a purple and crimson mohawk of sensory quills.

Brian Armstrong stopped in his tracks and stared unashamedly. "Wow," he said. "Quillas."

The Quilla giggled and lowered her face to hide her smile, but almost immediately she peeked back up at Armstrong. Her eyes twinkled with promise. He flushed in response, but turned around in his tracks to watch her pass, even walking backward to keep her in sight as long as he could—he was awestruck by her presence—until he backed into a structural member, banging his head sharply. Bach and Nakahari both laughed.

Irma Stolchak was less sanguine. "Oh, great," she said. "That's just what we need—a shared consciousness. Have you ever worked with a massmind? No? Well, I have. What one knows they all know. There are *no* secrets with a Quilla aboard."

Nakahari poked Armstrong. "You'd better be careful. You know what they say about Quillas! You know, their—(ahem)—"

"Really—?" Armstrong was honestly interested.

"And that's it on the men here," Stolchak was saying to Bach. "They're not even going to be *looking* at you and me."

Bach shook her head, smiling quietly. "It's all right. I'm not sure I'd want to get involved with any man assigned to this ship."

They reached the engine room then, a three-story chamber built around a large spherical framework: the singularity cage containing the pinpoint black hole that powered the starship and also served as focus for the hyperstate generators. Three huge cylinders pointed into the singularity cage, one from directly above and one coming up from each side, corresponding to the three projections on the ship's outer hull. There were catwalks and ladders all around the cylinders and the framework. Consoles were spotted everywhere, and there were massive banks of equipment dominating the bulkheads both forward and aft. Conduits and cooling tanks lined all the walls. This was the heart of the starship.

At the moment, however, the heart of the starship was having a serious cardiac arrest.

Oily black smoke was pouring out of one of the three great cylinders surrounding the singularity cage. Nobody else in the engine room was paying much attention, except for the two crewmembers frantically working on it. Haddad noticed though. Fluctuator sockets were his specialty. He stopped and stared, wanting to do something but not knowing if he should or not. He stepped forward uncertainly.

The other five continued forward, passing two beefy members of the Black Hole Gang, Reynolds and Cappy. Both were dressed casually, in shorts and T-shirts only. Cappy was the bigger of the two, Reynolds was the darker. They were heading aft, rolling an equipment cart before them.

"Uh-oh," said Reynolds. "Fresh meat." He grinned. "Who did you guys piss off?"

Armstrong was still looking back toward the engine room, not at where he was going. He banged into and tripped over the equipment cart and fell flat on his pride.

"Watch it—are you okay?" Cappy asked. He was a broad, stout man. He looked almost as wide as he was tall.

"Yeah, I'm fine," Armstrong said ruefully as he picked himself up. "Sorry."

"You'd better see the doctor about that vision problem. Her name's Williger."

"*Her?*" asked Armstrong. "Is she good-looking?"

"Good-looking? Molly Williger? Uh—" Cappy blinked at the question. His expression went very strange. "Oh, yeah. She's . . . unbelievable!"

Farther forward, Stolchak and Bach had to step aside to let pass several robots and crewmembers in fire-fighting gear; they were heading swiftly back toward the engine room.

Stolchak shook her head. "This is not my idea of a good time."

The fire-team was followed by Korie and Leen. Korie was leading; Leen was shouting at his back. "I'm not doing *anything* until you take a look at it! I am not eating the paper on this one! You hear me?"

"Fluctuator sockets don't just diffuse for no reason at all!" Korie shouted back over his shoulder. "I told you I wanted all the assembly valves rebuilt!"

"Dammit—you put a scope on it and see for yourself!" Leen pushed past Stolchak, angrily shoved the equipment cart out of the way and hollered after Korie, "This is the best you can get out of a low-cycle installation. Seven-fifty, max!"

"Bullshit!" said Korie. He pushed Armstrong and Nakahari aside and strode into the engine room. "Those mods are rated to nine-fifty before they redline!"

"Only if confidence is nine or better! This ship is a six! Seven-fifty is your max!"

Leen followed Korie straight to the fluctuator socket. Thick smoke was still pouring out of it. Under the direction of the fire-team, the robots were spraying the whole thing with damping foam. Sparks were showering from the cylinder all along its length. The smell of ozone filled the air. Acrid steam roiled outward where the foam spray hit the conduction fields. Haddad was right in the thick of it, dancing and pointing. He had a sodden handkerchief over his nose and mouth. He was directing the fire-team as if he were their chief.

Korie said, "Shit," and stepped over to a rugged-looking vertical console. He punched open a panel with his fist and pulled the large

red lever inside it. Immediately the conduction fields in all three fluctuators collapsed—it was like being hit with a hammer of air; but the
sparking stopped. The steam and the smoke began fading away. The
whir of the ventilators increased and a noticeable breeze swept cold air
into the engine room.

Korie turned sourly to the two crewmembers who had been fight-
ing with the system and said dryly, "First, you flush the system . . ."
He tapped out a program on the console. "Then you call up a total
System Analysis Report and look for the anomaly."

He scanned through the system schematic quickly, calling up display after display. All were green. He stopped scrolling through the
schematic when he found a schematic with a section in flashing red.
He slipped easily into teaching mode and pointed. "All right, what's
that? Anybody?" He glanced around, read the nametag on Haddad's
chest. "Haddad?" Abruptly he frowned. "How long have you been
aboard? You're supposed to check in."

"Uh"—Haddad glanced at his watch—"thirty seconds."

"Right." Korie pointed again. "What's that?"

"Assembly valve irregularity. Lack of synchronization probably."

"Right." Korie shot a triumphant look to Leen. To Haddad, he said,
"Go ahead. Pull it. Let's have a look."

Haddad dropped the duffel he was still carrying over his shoulder
and went immediately to work. He put on a pair of thick gloves, opened
a panel in the side of the fluctuator, reached in and unclipped the
assembly valve. It was a set of shining interlocking cylinders and modules.

Korie took a fire extinguisher from one of the robots and sprayed
the valve to cool it off. He handed back the extinguisher and took the
assembly valve from Haddad, quickly unscrewed one end of it, opened
it up and looked inside. He held it out for Leen to see—

Leen looked, but didn't comment.

Korie reached into the chamber and pulled out a burnt something.
It looked like a carbonized rat, but without head or tail or even legs;
just a clump of charred fur.

"Cute," said Korie. "Very cute. You know what would have happened if we had tried to inject into hyperstate with this in the assembly
valve?"

Leen didn't answer. He just lowered his eyes to the floor for a
moment, then looked back up to Korie.

Korie nodded. "Right. Find out who did it. And transfer him dockside."

"Not a good idea," Leen said quietly. "The doctor has a whole cageful of those furballs in her lab. Everybody who wants off—" He didn't finish the thought.

Korie met his gaze straight on. "Anyone who would knowingly sabotage this ship's engines isn't *good* enough to be a member of this crew. I still have pride in this ship and I don't want anyone on the crew who can't share the feeling. Find the man who did this and get him off my ship."

"Captain Lowell wouldn't have done that—" Leen started.

Korie cut him off. "Captain Lowell isn't in command anymore. I am." Korie handed the assembly valve back to Leen. "Tear them all down. Rebuild them."

"You're awfully sure of yourself," Leen said resentfully. "I don't see the stripes on your sleeve yet. The scuttlebutt has it you're not getting them—"

"I don't need a captain's stripes to know what's wrong with these engines." He added, "Chief—I worked my way through college on a liberty ship assembly line. I was engine calibration crew chief for a year and a half. I signed the hulls of a hundred and sixty-five of these ships. I *know* what they're capable of." And then, in a gentler tone, "And I know what *you're* capable of."

But Leen was too angry to be easily pacified. "Give it a rest. *You know better*. This is the garbage can. FleetComm dumps all their problems here; all their losers, loonies, and lost causes." He added bitterly, "And maybe, if they're real real lucky, we'll all fall into a star."

Korie was stung, but he was also deliberately patient. "Chief, you have nothing to be ashamed of. Neither does anybody else on this ship. I say so."

"Bullshit! Is that more of your damn lies? We're the bad luck of the whole fleet. Ask anybody. *We're* the reason for the Marathon mauling."

Korie shook his head. It wasn't worth arguing about anymore. He'd had this conversation too many times already. "Chief—" he said tiredly. "Clean this mess up. Start with your attitude. There are no losers on this ship." He started for the exit.

Leen called after him. "We don't need an attitude check! We need an exorcist!"

Over his shoulder, Korie called back, "If that's what it takes—"

The Exorcism

As it happened, Hodel was a licensed warlock.

His business card listed the areas of his expertise: thaumaturgy, light magic, violet sorcery, channeling, planar hexes, lethetic obsessions, despiritualized curses, demonic possessions, ontological constructions, personal spells, love philters, green magic (several shades), orthomatic snake oil (all flavors), and (of particular importance) . . . karmatic exorcisms.

Also, fresh strawberries.

When Korie asked him about snake oil, he replied simply, "How badly does your snake squeal?"

"Never mind."

"I see. You wanted a serious answer?"

"If it's not too much trouble."

"Actually," said Hodel, "it is. You see, to explain magic is to destroy it. But"—He pulled up a chair—"Since you insist, here's what you need to know. Magic isn't about the physical universe. It's about the experiential universe. It's about your belief system. Magic works because you believe it works." He pointed at the coffee mug on the table. "I can't cast a spell that will lift that cup up and move it over there. Magic doesn't work that way. But I can cast a spell that will cause that cup to be moved—someone will pick it up and move it. Coincidence? Not if you believe in magic. And even if you don't believe, the cup *still* got moved. And it doesn't matter what belief system you use to motivate the move or what gods or demons or other sources you ask to power the move; the simple act of casting the spell or working the ritual or saying the prayer shifts *your* relationship to the universe so that the result you want is more likely than it was before."

Korie looked skeptical. "But who gets the credit for moving the cup?"

"Who cares?" Hodel asked. "Does it matter? The important thing is that you got the result you set out to get. That's the way magic works. So, to answer the question you didn't ask, but you're planning to, *yes*, I can cast a spell or lift a curse or perform an exorcism to rehabilitate the karma of this ship. However you phrase it, what you want is to make this crew believe in themselves again. So you have to do something drastic to break the spell of bad feeling that's poisoning this crew and this ship." Hodel glanced at Korie sharply. "And, if you don't mind my saying so, it wouldn't hurt to do something about the black cloud that's floating over your head too."

"I might be a lost cause. Just concentrate on the rest of the ship."

"Sorry, it's all or nothing. The cure has to be total."

Korie studied Hodel for a long moment. "Mike, you surprise me sometimes. I don't know if you're serious or if you're pulling my leg."

"You'll find out when you try to stand up. Do you want the two-dollar exorcism or the four-dollar exorcism?"

"What's the difference?"

"With the two-dollar job, I bathe in chaotic vapors and immolate myself in front of the whole crew. Then I chop myself up into little pieces and throw me into the lake. For four dollars I resurrect myself in a pillar of light and sing all six hundred choruses of *Lulu's Lament* while standing on my hands on the back of a naked unicorn and accompanying myself on the electric bagpipes."

"This is more serious than that, Mike. What can I get for ten dollars?"

"Ten dollars? Gee, I've never had to do a ten-dollar exorcism. I'm not sure my heart can stand it. But for ten dollars, you get *The Secret Sorcery of the Grand Poobah of the Sevagram*. For the finale, I will wrassle the devil himself, two falls out of three, for custody of Hell. Then for my first encore, I drink a whole bottle of trans-Lunar brandy, make love to a feral Chtorran, and kill a Martian woman—I think. Or maybe it's the other way around."

"Right." Korie nodded. "I get the picture."

"Trust me. I'm worth it."

"I dunno. Ten dollars is a lot of money—"

"The ten-dollar exorcism comes with a guarantee . . ." Mike began.

"I know." Korie grinned. It was an old joke. "If I'm not absolutely satisfied, I don't have to pay and you'll have me repossessed."

"Close enough. If it doesn't work, we'll give you double your bullshit back."

"Hey—" Korie held up his hands. "I can get double bullshit from the Admiralty for free—"

"Ahh, but not with *my* style."

"Okay," said Korie. "You're on."

The important thing about an exorcism is to dress appropriately.

The crew had gathered in the shuttle bay, it being the only chamber in the ship large enough to hold all of them at once. Most of them had no idea what to expect, only that Korie had scheduled a little party to celebrate the successful recalibration of the phase-injector assembly valve modules.

The lights dimmed and there was fanfare. Spotlights probed and searched and came to a final focus on the far end of the room. A puff of orange smoke exploded out of nowhere and Mikhail Hodel appeared in all his gaudy glory.

Mikhail Hodel was wearing a shimmering hula skirt, a glistening confection made of strands of shredded silvery sheet-polymer, extracted from a catabolic converter. The three-foot feathers on his head-dress and staff were injection plumes that had been dyed in ultra-gee zylox and soaked in liquid nitrogen, then exposed to explosive decompression in the forward airlock. His scarlet warpaint was anti-deoxidant gel. The strings of beads and rattles that he wore around his neck and waist, upper arms and wrists, were constructed from interociter spares and pieces of optical conduit. The two glowing hemispheres that made up his steel brassiere were measuring cups from the ship's galley— which did not explain why they were not quite the same size. His codpiece was the bow tube-fitting of a proton torpedo. The entire outfit was lined with neon conduit, flashing diodes of all colors, several Christmas lights and electric ornaments, sparklers and flash-bombs. He moved in a cloud of smoke and fire and multicolored auras. He was an epiphany of fireworks, lasers, small explosions, whistles, air-bursts, and confetti. Tracks of red and purple light crawled up and down his legs and chest and back.

The crew went wild.

Then he started the music and began setting off the special effects: the lasers and mirror fields, the colored sprays and fountains, the holographic projections and fractal windows—and the cheering and stomping and clapping and hooting and hollering and whistling and yelling hit new crescendos of excitement.

"Oh, Great Ghu!" Hodel invoked the grand spirit of the ceiling. Puffs of sparkling gold smoke rose around him. "Oh, great Fossil of the Fellatious!" Several small explosions went off around the room, filling the air with showers of sparks. "Oh, Grand Poobah of the Sevagram!" Confetti bombs showered the crew with sprinkles of light.

Hodel lowered his voice to a conversational tone and looked casually up at the ceiling. "Okay, now that I have your attention? I'd like some assistance here." A small firework went off, launched from his tailfeathers. "Rumor has it that this starship is jinxed—" Hodel ignored the shouts of agreement from the crew. Flashes of light strobed and sparkled across his body. "Yes, I said *jinxed*." Larger flashes of light spread out from him in widening shockwaves; they rippled out across the whole shuttle bay. "I SAID *JINXED*," he repeated. Puffs of orange smoke flamed up around him. "And what, may I ask, great Ghu, god of the ceiling—what are *you* going to do about it?"

Very directly, Hodel continued. He spoke now as if he were speaking to an employee. "Look, we know that the proper way to worship Ghu is to *ignore* Ghu. Ghu doesn't like being bothered. Ghu has more important things to do than worry about a bunch of devolved primates with sexual problems. So the only appropriate way to respect and honor and worship Ghu is to understand that Ghu just doesn't give a shit. The true believers of Ghu know that it is their sworn and solemn duty to leave Ghu the hell alone."

Hodel's voice began to rise. He began to speak in larger and louder and much more excited tones. "Well, Ghu, these brave courageous men and women have been the greatest worshipers of you in the entire universe. Yes, they have been. They have not only ignored Ghu—they have remained totally oblivious to Ghu's very existence. Can Ghu ignore such absolute devotion? Does *Ghu* dare?" Hodel's finger jabbed and the ceiling exploded. Smoke and light and confetti poured outward in ripples of red and yellow and purple afterimages. "I think *not*," said Hodel.

Aggressively, he continued. "We demand our reward now! In *this* life." Several small explosions, like aftershocks, went off around the edges of the shuttle bay. "Otherwise, we're going to make bloody damned nuisances of ourselves. So cut the crap Ghu. It's time to get off your fat butt and give us some god-stuff. We expect you to cast out the bad luck, Ghu! Frankly, it stinks!"

The shuttle bay went almost totally black then. The lights and smoke and sparkles came flashing back up in rhythm, matching Hodel's demanding chant: "Cast out the jinx! Who cares what it thinks! We are the Sphinx! And the jinx just stinks!"

The crew picked up the chant quickly. They shouted it in unison with Hodel, chanting and laughing and waving noisemakers and sparklers.

Standing at the side of the room, Korie allowed himself a grin. *It might work.* He grinned. *This is the best ten dollars I ever spent.*

The crew was chanting enthusiastically, louder than ever. "Cast out the jinx! Who cares what it thinks! We are the Sphinx! And the jinx just stinks! Cast out the jinx—"

Hodel held up a hand for silence. The room went instantly quiet.

"Ghu! Give us a sign!"

The shuttle bay exploded with light. Every effect in the room went off at once. All the fireworks triggered. All the smoke, all the flash-bombs, all the noise and whistles and alarms. The holographic projectors poured fountains of colored light into the air. The mirror fields echoed the displays out to infinity. Showers of sparkling confetti exploded outward from the walls and fell streaming from the ceiling. Paper curlicues unraveled to the floor. Thunderous drumbeats pounded the air with animated air-bursts. And somewhere in the middle of it all, Korie was certain he could hear elephants trumpeting.

"Say what?" Hodel cupped an ear and looked upward. "Could you be a little clearer about that?"

Ghu repeated himself.

It was more of the same—only bigger, better, different. The red seas parted, the volcanoes erupted, the asteroids shattered the surface of the flaming planet, the nova exploded, the lightning outlined them all. St. Elmo's fire turned them into grinning demons. The imps of Hell danced in the flames that licked around their legs. The Heavens opened and cascades of angels poured forth, singing to raise the dead. Gabriel blew his trumpet. The egg of the Phoenix hatched. The elephants came.

The crew was in hysterics now, cheering, yelling, applauding, shrieking, whistling, stomping their feet, tears streaming down their faces—

And then, abruptly, everything stopped.

The effects faded away. The lights came up. A wave of silence fell across the shuttle bay. As one man, the crew turned to look behind them.

Hodel was the last one shouting. Puzzled, he turned around to see:

Framed in the shuttle bay entrance, filling the hatchway, stood Captain Richard Hardesty.

He looked like a door that had just been slammed.

The top right-quarter of his head was metal. His right eye was a shining lens.

Korie spoke first. Loudly, he called, *"Ten-hut!"* The entire crew snapped to attention. Several small fizzing devices were still scuttling across the floor. Smoke was still rising from the corners; confetti and streamers were still dripping from the ceiling.

Hardesty strode coldly into the center of the room. He was dressed all in black and he was terrifying. The crew was shrinking visibly, withering with fear.

Slowly, Hardesty turned, noticing everything: Hodel, the confetti, the smoke, the mirror-fields, the holographic projectors, the various small noisemakers still losing the last of their air, even the elephant . . .

Finally, after several eternities, he spoke. His voice was flat and deadly. "Which one of you is . . . Commander Korie?"

Fearing the worst, Korie stepped crisply forward.

"Would you log me in, please?"

"Yes, sir. This way—"

"I know the way," Hardesty said. He turned on his heel and strode for the door. Korie followed him out.

They left a wake of silence behind them. The crew was too terrified to speak. It was Hodel who spoke the first coherent word. "Oh, shit," he said.

Armstrong and Jonesy approached him, puzzled. "What is it?" The other members of the crew also moved in curiously.

Hodel was stunned with the realization. "Oh, my God," he moaned. "It's even *worse* than we thought. We'll *never* break this jinx."

"Huh? Why?" said Armstrong. "Who was *that?*"

"That—" said Hodel, "—that was *Hardesty*."

"The one they call the Star Wolf?" Jonesy asked.

Hodel nodded. "The one and only." He began shrugging off his steel brassiere. "I'm hanging up my bra—I am *never* going to tempt the gods again." He shook his head sadly and pushed past Armstrong and Jonesy. "Next time, they might think of something *worse*."

The Captain's Cabin

The captain's cabin hadn't been touched since Captain Lowell's personal effects had been removed. It looked grim.

Hardesty glanced around with obvious distaste, then stepped behind the desk and sat down. He did not invite Korie to sit. He studied the executive officer grimly.

Korie remained at polite attention, refusing to wither under the other's heartless gaze.

Finally, Hardesty broke the silence. "This ship is a mess," he said quietly.

"We're *working* on it," Korie began. "We took a real beating—"

Hardesty ignored Korie's protest. He waved it off. "I've been looking over your records. I don't like what I see."

"Excuse me, sir? What's your point? We still have three weeks of refit before preliminary inspection."

Hardesty's look was deadly. "The point is, *I'm taking command of this ship*, and I want her spotless."

Korie tried, unsuccessfully, to conceal both his surprise and his anger. "Sir! I was not informed of that."

"The decision was made only an hour ago."

"I—yes, sir." Korie remained at attention.

"You, what?"

"Nothing, sir."

"Say it. You can't hurt my feelings. I don't have any." Hardesty tapped the right side of his head, the metal side. "They took them out."

"Nothing, sir—it's just that, well, I was operating under the assumption that I would be allowed to retain command of this ship because—because there wasn't a captain in the fleet who was willing to take her."

"You assumed wrong."

"Yes, sir."

"I suppose you think this isn't fair, that this ship should be yours."

"Sir. Captain Lowell had recommended my promotion—"

"Captain Lowell is dead. And considering the lack of judgment he displayed in leading the Morthans straight to the convoy—and the mauling at Marathon—"

"We had no way of detecting them. The *Dragon Lord* has one of the largest hyperstate generators ever built. They could see us for years. We couldn't see them."

Hardesty continued as if Korie hadn't even spoken. "—When you consider his entire history of bad decisions, leaving you in command of a starship, any starship, hardly seems appropriate. Leaving you in command of this one in particular strikes me as especially stupid and foolhardy." Hardesty glanced over and locked eyes with Korie, almost as if daring him to argue.

Korie considered his options. He didn't have any. He took a breath. "Are you asking for my resignation? I've tried to submit it three times already. I would be happy to submit it again if you will accept it."

Hardesty allowed himself the thinnest of smiles. Respect? Malice? Korie couldn't tell. "Unfortunately, no, I am not asking for your resignation. But since you ask, yes, I did request another executive officer. Seeing as how I'm bringing in a new astrogator, a new security chief, and a new weapons specialist, it seemed appropriate. But, ah . . . as you may have heard, no one was available."

"Yes," said Korie, choosing his words carefully. "I've heard. Thank you for your honesty. Is there anything else, sir?

"Yes, there is. What was the purpose of that little . . . demonstration in the shuttle bay?"

"A party. *They earned it.*"

"I don't agree," said Hardesty. "This ship is a disgrace. We're going to clean it up." His tone hardened. "You need to know this. *I'm not Captain Lowell.* I'm not a nice man. And I'm not here to make friends. I have only one job in life. Destroy the Morthan Solidarity. Do you know what *your* job is?" He looked into Korie's eyes and waited.

Korie stared right back. This time he chose his words even more carefully than before. "My job is to make sure that *your* job gets done."

Hardesty relaxed. He almost smiled. "Very good," he admitted. "And your disappointment about not getting a command of your own—that won't get in the way?"

Korie was offended at the question. He stiffened before he answered. "Sir. You can count on me to serve you and this ship to the best of my ability."

Hardesty grunted. "They told me you would say that." His nod was a gesture of acceptance. "Listen up. You and I don't have to like each other. In fact, I would prefer it if we didn't. It would make it a lot easier for me to continue to believe that you are a stupid fool. But we do have to work together, and that does require a minimum of respect."

Hardesty waited, but Korie had nothing to say in response. The silence stretched painfully while the captain studied his exec.

Finally Hardesty realized Korie wasn't going to answer. He retook control of the interview. "All right—let's make a deal. You train this crew to live up to fleet standards, and I'll train *you* to live up to *mine*. And maybe then you'll be ready to be a captain—agreed?"

"Do I have a choice?"

"Actually? No, you don't."

"Then it's not much of a *deal*, is it?" Korie smiled. "At best, it's an order. At worst, it's a contract made under duress."

"I see—yes. You have a point. But, it's irrelevant to me. All I want to know is one thing. Will I be able to depend on you?"

"That has never been the issue . . . *Captain*."

"We'll see," said Hardesty. "We'll see."

Chief of Security

Korie stepped up from the keel into the operations bay under the Bridge. The operations bay was a tiny chamber, all consoles, keyboards, and screens. Only two of the work stations were manned, but both were all green.

He climbed up three more steps and onto the Operations deck. As he came up the steps, he could see the holotable was showing an internal schematic of the ship. Ahead, the forward viewer focused on the distant unmoving stars; it was a cold and dispassionate window.

He knew there was something wrong even before he finished climbing up onto the Ops deck. The silence warned him. The looks on the faces of the other crew members told him—

Korie turned around and *froze.*

The entire Ops deck crew was staring at Lieutenant Commander Brik. He was nine feet tall. He was four feet wide at the shoulder. His muzzle was striped with red and orange fur. His fangs looked as long as Korie's hand.

He was a Morthan Tyger.

Morthan. A genetically augmented, bioengineered, tailored in the womb, product of directed evolution. That part of the species that had taken control of its biological destiny and created itself as something fearsome.

Tyger. A subspecies of Morthan warrior. The meaner side of the family.

What do you get when you cross a nine-foot zen-linebacker with a saber-tooth tiger? You get Brik: a Buddhist Gorilla.

He was awesome. He was all meat and bone and muscle. He smelled of hot desert sands tinged with blood. He was Korie's worst nightmare. And he was grinning.

He was wearing a fleet uniform. Korie was horrified.

The other officers and crew on duty were frozen at their posts. Chief Leen, waist-deep into a dismantled console, was visibly smoldering.

Abruptly, Captain Hardesty appeared on the Bridge, ducking through one of the rear doors and stepping forward to lean across the Bridge railing. "Ah, I see you've all met the new chief of security . . . Lt. Commander Brik. You have a problem, Mr. Korie?"

Korie whirled around to face the captain. "Yes, sir. I do. There's a Morthan on the Bridge."

Hardesty ignored Korie's anger. He said quietly, "There are humans fighting for the Morthan Solidarity. There are Morthans fighting on the side of the Allies. It's a big war. There's room enough for everybody." He added, "Commander Brik is here because I asked for him—because he's the best damned security officer this side of Hell."

Korie turned resentfully and looked at Brik. Actually, he looked at Brik's chest. He took a step back and looked up—and up—and up again.

Brik grinned. His incisors were even longer than Korie had thought. Brik spoke. His voice rumbled like a warship. "*I* am not your fight," he said to Korie. "Your fight is . . . out there."

Korie glared up at the Morthan warrior. "I know that," he said testily. "Where's *your* fight?"

Brik moved slowly, so as not to alarm anyone. He touched his own heart gently. "My fight is in here . . ."

Korie didn't expect that, and he didn't know how to react to it. It wasn't an answer he could respond to. Finally, he just snorted and turned away in disgust, a deliberately calculated performance of rudeness. He stared at the screens on the console in front of him, not seeing them at all, and forced himself to breathe evenly. He could feel his heart racing, his rage building.

Somebody tapped his arm gently. He turned around and looked. He blinked. He didn't recognize her. She was a handsome woman in her late thirties or early forties, very crisp and very military.

"Commander Korie? Lieutenant Commander Cygnus Tor. Astrogator."

"Uh—" Korie was off-balance. "Tor. Good to meet you. Are you familiar with the, uh—" He was still rattled. "—The, uh—"

"The Model 16 low-cycle fluctuators?" Tor guessed correctly. "Yes, I am. I—"

"Good," said Korie, distractedly. Abruptly, he made a decision. "I'm sorry. Excuse me a moment." He turned away from Tor, turned back to Brik, and extended a hand. "I'm sorry. I was rude. Let's work together." It was a visible effort for him.

Brik nodded slowly and held out his hand. It was immense. He shook Korie's hand gently. Gently, that is, for a Morthan. Despite himself, Korie counted his fingers as he massaged the blood back into his hand.

The sudden grating sound of the alarm klaxon bleated across the Bridge. The Bridge lights went red, the consoles began flashing, and above it all, HARLIE was speaking in a preternaturally calm voice: "*Engine room malfunction.* Magnetic instability in the number three singularity control. Fluctuator overload. Assembly valve failure. Stand by to disconnect. Singularity escape *will* occur"—HARLIE paused for half a clock-tick—"in three minutes."

Korie looked up startled. All the work stations around him lit up red. The ops crew leapt for their consoles. Leen dived into the operations bay. Tor slid into her seat at the helm console. Hodel dropped into the chair next to her and punched his station to life. The console flickered brightly, then went dark. Hodel slapped the panel—*hard*— and it lit up again. Hardesty stood on the Bridge and watched it all.

Everywhere there was panic, confusion, and dismay. The readouts were normal—and they weren't. The magnetic cage containing the pinpoint black hole that powered the ship was about to fail. If that happened, the singularity would drift inexorably out of the cage and begin devouring the starship and everything connected to it.

It seemed as though everybody on the Ops deck was talking into their headsets at once or punching madly at their keyboards. Korie moved quickly from station to station—Brik stepped quickly out of his way; he stepped up onto the Bridge and stood next to the captain.

In the Ops bay, Chief Leen was watchdogging three consoles at once. "Magnetic clamps, now! Full field! Downcycle—program beta."

Lightning was flashing in the keel again. It looked like a replay of the disastrous disruptor overload.

It was even worse in the engine room. The lightning was brighter and fiercer and strong enough to knock a man unconscious. The engine room crew couldn't get near their controls. Crewmembers in bulky protective suits were rushing to their posts.

The static discharges rolled down the corridors of the ship, clustered around the singularity cage, and then bled out through the hyperstate fluctuators. More lightning crackled across the outer hull. The entire ship was enveloped.

"The singularity is wobbling." Harlie reported. "Loss of focus is imminent. Singularity escape will endanger Stardock. Singularity escape *will* occur"—half a clock-tick—"in two minutes."

Korie made a decision. "Prepare for emergency breakaway."

Hodel was already talking to his headset. "Secure all bulkheads! Seal the main airlock. Go to standby power. Disengage all power bays—" It was happening even as Hodel spoke. They could feel the hatches slamming down throughout the ship. The main airlock clanged shut with a terrible bang, cutting off the panic-stricken escape of two crewmen running madly for the docking tube. They pounded on it desperately.

In the engine room, power shunts cut in and the lightning became focused. They were bleeding it deliberately into the hyperstate fluctuators now—but the workmen were terrified; they knew how bad it really was. In the Ops bay, Leen was shouting at the machinery. "Respond, damn you!"

Korie couldn't wait any longer. "Disengage from Stardock immediately."

The starship gave a tiny lurch as the mooring bolts unclamped. And then the ship was moving, drifting outward and away from the workbay, the lightning still flickering wildly across her hull.

"Emergency breakaway complete," HARLIE reported. "Escape velocity thirty kilometers per hour. The Stardock is no longer in danger." A heartbeat later, HARLIE added, "Singularity escape *will* occur in— one minute."

Hodel was pounding on his console and shouting into his headset. "Goddammit! It's all coming up garbage. Where's the baseline?" He listened for a moment. "No time! Disengage the fluctuators!" He was angered by the response. "Do it, dammit!" He watched his screen, waiting anxiously.

Behind him, Korie was shouting into his own headset. "—Emergency life support! Clear the engine room! Prepare for emergency deplosion. Hull diffusion—" He looked over Hodel's shoulder, then spoke again. "Dammit! Clear the engine room! I'm going to snuff that sucker!"

But even as he was saying his last words, the alarm klaxon faded away and the Bridge lighting returned to normal. The lightning flickering throughout the ship began to subside and fade away.

Korie's last words were still ringing in the air as the various crewpeople on the Ops deck shut up and looked around at each other in confusion. Korie was suddenly embarrassed.

In the Ops bay, Leen was shattered. He'd failed. He knew it. He put his head into his hands.

But—they were still alive.

And then, Harlie said, "Singularity escape *has* occurred. The starship has been destroyed." And then, to add insult to injury, he quietly added, "End of simulation. Efficiency rating . . ." Harlie hesitated while he computed. *"Unsatisfactory."*

Korie was stiff and expressionless. He'd been had and he knew it.

"A drill!" Hodel flung himself back in his chair, frustrated, annoyed, and disgusted. "A fucking drill!"

Korie turned around slowly to look at Hardesty. Hardesty returned the stare calmly. He looked down coldly; but before he could speak, Leen climbed back up onto the Ops deck. He was furious. "That was a dirty damned trick!" he shouted at Hardesty.

"Thank you," the captain acknowledged. He looked past Leen to Korie. "Now you know why this ship never earned a name." He let his gaze travel around the room, piercing the souls of each of the men and women at their stations. "The *LS-1187* came into Stardock needing three weeks of interior work, four weeks of equipment refits, and six weeks of hull regrowth, all of which could have been done concurrently. That was a month ago. Systems Analysis reports that this vessel is still *eight weeks* away from being space-ready. This is not a good record.

"The reason that your efficiency is so low is that you think you have a choice. *You do not.* I have just eliminated the alternative.

"New work schedules will be posted at 0600 hours. Commander Tor, bring us back to Stardock. Brik, get a security team together and break up the still in the inner hull. Mr. Korie, my cabin, ten minutes."

Hardesty turned and exited crisply.

Brik looked around the room and grinned. It was not a pleasant sight.

Hodel was stunned. He glanced across at Korie. Korie wouldn't meet his eyes. He looked to Tor, but she was already at work, targeting the ship back toward Stardock. "How'd he know about the still?" Hodel asked.

Tor didn't even glance up. "There's *always* a still," she said. When she did look up from her console, she noticed that Korie was still standing in the same place. He was rigid with fury. "You don't look very happy, Mr. Korie."

"Happy—?" Korie's reply was as cold as the captain's. "The *Dragon Lord* kicks the crap out of us. The fleet gets mauled. Captain Lowell gets killed. The ship is labeled a jinx. I get my career dead-ended. And now . . . I've been publicly humiliated. Happy? I'm just thrilled."

From above, Brik said quietly. "Don't mince words, Mr. Korie. What are you *really* angry about?"

Korie whirled to stare up at him. "I don't even want to talk to *you*." And then, in explanation, he said, "My wife—and my two sons—were killed in a Morthan attack. So you'll forgive me if I'm not overjoyed to be working with you."

Abruptly embarrassed, Korie exited through the Ops bay, leaving Tor and Hodel and the others staring curiously after him.

Tor turned back to her console and resumed locking in a course. Very softly, to no one in particular, she said, "For some reason, I have the feeling that this is *not* going to be a happy enterprise."

Decisions

Korie stepped into Hardesty's cabin and stood rigidly before the captain's desk. Hardesty didn't even glance up; he was studying something on his desk screen.

"First of all," he began without preamble, "I know what you've been through. I read your file. I know the craziness that drives you. It's ripping you apart. You haven't healed yet. Maybe you never will. It's left you confused. You don't know if you should be a ruthless bastard or a compassionate healer—well, neither one of those roles is right for a starship officer; although, I will tell you, ruthless bastard does have some advantages." Hardesty gestured. "Sit down."

Korie sat.

"Lesson One: You're going to have to learn to control your temper. Hide your feelings from the crew. The crew is a sponge. Whatever you put out, they will soak up—and they will give it back to you amplified a thousand times over. That's what's wrong with this ship right now. Your crew doesn't know who you are, so they don't know who they're supposed to be. That's the first thing we have to fix.

"Lesson Two: This is not a democracy. No warship ever is. But you've been running this ship as if your crew gets to vote on every decision. Your chief engineer, for example, argues every order, so every damn crewmember on this ship thinks his opinion means something too. Bullshit. Opinions are like assholes. Everybody has one and they're all full of shit. You—Mr. Korie—stop worrying about being popular. If a crew likes an officer, he isn't doing his job. Your only job is to produce results, nothing else. If the crew isn't doing their job, you're not doing yours. Am I getting through to you?"

Korie swallowed. His throat hurt with the pressure of all he was holding back. "Yes, sir."

"But you don't like it."

"I don't have to like it, sir. As you say, my feelings on the matter are irrelevant."

Hardesty grunted. "Good answer. You're learning. I don't think you believe it yet, but I don't care. You can start by learning the language. The understanding will come later." He reached for a folder and opened it. "All right," he said, turning to the first sheet of paper inside. "We're not playing Good Cop/Bad Cop here. Do you know that game?"

"Yes, sir. Some captains delegate all the unpopular orders to their exec so he can take the heat."

"Right. Well, I don't believe in that. If an unpopular order has to be given, the captain should take responsibility for it himself. Also"— he tapped the right side of his head, the metal-plated prosthesis—"this particular handicap makes me a lot less *likable*, so if we were to play that game, you'd have to be the good cop, I'd have to be the bad cop. I can't run a ship that way either. For obvious reasons."

"Yes, sir."

"That's the other reason why you have to stop being popular. You understand? Because like it or not, we're already halfway into a game of Good Cop/Bad Cop and I won't have it. It weakens my authority."

"Yes, sir."

"So what we're going to do instead is Bad Cop/Bad Cop. Do you know how to play that game?"

"No, I don't."

"It's very easy. I'm the meanest son of a bitch in the galaxy. You're the second-meanest son of a bitch. The crew will hate me. They'll hate you. And this ship will get a reputation as being a very unpleasant duty. But we'll get results. And after we start getting results, the crew will start bragging about being on this ship and they'll consider it a privilege to wear her colors. I know what you're thinking. You're thinking about this ship's reputation now. Forget it. Forget the past. The past is dead. Because you and I say so."

"Yes, sir."

"You disagree with that?"

"No, sir. You're the captain."

"What does one have to do with the other?"

"You give the orders. We'll do whatever you say."

"Mr. Korie—" Hardesty put his papers down. "I don't want an executive officer who's a flunky or a yes-man or an echo. I want an executive officer who is capable of taking responsibility and using it appropriately. That means that in the privacy of this cabin, I expect you to argue with me if you think that I am making a bad decision."

"Yes, sir."

"Now, I know damned well—just from reading the expressions on your face—that you hate what you're hearing. If you think I'm wrong, I expect you to tell me so."

"Sir—may I speak?"

Hardesty waved a hand.

"You want me to disagree with you? Fine, I will. But you have already stated in no uncertain terms how you want this ship run. You made it quite clear that there is no room for negotiation in that position. Fine. I'll do what you say. But to argue with it now seems to me to be a waste of time. I will only voice my disagreements when I think that doing so will make a difference. Given what you've just said, I don't see that anything I might say right now would make much of a difference, so the best I can say is 'yes, sir' and 'no, sir' and carry out your orders as best as I can."

"Good." Hardesty nodded, satisfied. "That's fair. It's also intelligent." He leaned back in his chair, studying Korie. "Part of a captain's job is to train his executive officer to become a captain too. I can't train a man with no initiative. Don't be a wallflower."

"Yes, sir." Korie sat quietly, waiting for the captain to continue.

Hardesty steepled his fingers in front of him and studied Korie for a long moment. The lens that replaced his right eye was cold and unreadable. His left eye showed even less emotion. "Is there anything else you want to say to me?"

Korie started to shake his head no, then changed his mind and nodded. This was the hardest thing of all to say, and he didn't know where it came from or even if he really believed it yet, but—"Maybe your way is right," he began. "I don't know. But it's not the way I was trained. I learned management technology and team dynamics as the best way to produce results. We built spaceships and we built good ones. We might even have built this one. I always thought that having your team feel good about their work also means they'll feel good about themselves. Let them have pride in their work; that's the best quality control of all. Your way has an awful lot of hate and fear and stress in it. I don't like it. It feels wrong to me. It feels *bad*. But"—Korie met Hardesty's curious gaze—"I also know how desperate the situation is. And I know that these choices are not mine to make anymore. And you know more about war than I do. So, I figure the best thing for me to do is shut up and do what I'm told.

"And one more thing. That drill—that hurt. I don't like having my nose rubbed in it. But it's also undeniable proof that something is very wrong here and I want it fixed just as much as you do. Maybe even more so, because it's my career that's in the dumper, not yours. So . . . all right, I'm willing to do whatever is necessary to make this ship work."

Hardesty studied Korie for a moment longer, considering his words. Then he nodded and picked up his folder again. He turned to the second page.

"You had *half* of it right, Mr. Korie. You understood what was wrong—it *is* the crew that has to be fixed. Fix the crew and they'll fix everything else. But you thought you could do it with parties. What's wrong with this crew can't be fixed with a party. You want your crew to feel good? Give them results. Let them take their pride in a job well done." Hardesty put the folder down. "We're going to start by tearing this ship down to the framework and putting it back together. Every structural member, every rivet, every conduit, every system-analysis node, every sensor, every damn thing that can be checked is going to be checked. Then it's going to be rechecked. Then we'll do it again to make sure we did it right the first two times.

"This will accomplish four things. First, it'll give us a new ship, one that we know works. Second, we'll be establishing a new confidence baseline against which to measure system performance. This is what you should have been doing for the past eight weeks. Third, it'll train the crew. A crewmember who's taken a piece of machinery apart and rebuilt it by hand will know more about it than the one who wrote the documentation. And finally—fourth—it'll give this crew a pride in their ship that can't be gained any other way. A crew that's had to repaint and repair every square inch of their starship doesn't put rude graffiti on its bulkheads. They start taking pride in keeping her shining. Question?"

"No, sir. I see you're right."

"You have a look on your face."

"Yes, sir. I see that my mistake lay in the assumption that it was essential to get this ship back into duty immediately."

"*This* ship?" Hardesty raised his one eyebrow. "That's a pretty big assumption. This ship, as she exists today, is worthless to the Alliance. Your crew knows that. They're festering in their own shame and at the same time, they're terrified that you might actually get this ship working again. They're not ready to go out again. Not up against the Morthans. That's why things keep breaking down all around you."

"I'm . . . not sure I understand . . . what you're implying."

"Don't be obtuse. I'm talking about carelessness, mistakes, stupidity, things that happen because people are so frightened or upset or angry that they can't focus on their jobs. These things are happening because these men and women are operating at the level of individuals. They've forgotten that they're a team."

Korie conceded with a downcast nod. Now he was feeling sick. His throat hurt. His eyes hurt. His chest was a pressure chamber. "I should have seen this," he said. "This is a failure for me. I mean, it's a bigger failure than—"

"Shut up. I don't have time to wet-nurse you." Hardesty pierced Korie's attention with an angry look. "Here's the only thing you need to know. I don't waste my time on losers. Criticism is an acknowledgment of your ability to produce results. The reason the crew lost *their* focus is that you lost *your* focus. You said you'll do whatever is necessary to get this ship working. Well, this is what's necessary. You need a kick in the ass. This is it."

Korie swallowed hard. "Yes, sir."

"Let's go on." Hardesty turned to the next page. "Drills. A lot of them. As we start getting the various systems rebuilt and back online, I want you to drill this crew until they drop. Over and over and over again. Every single simulation in the book until their scores are flawless—and then we'll start inventing new simulations. Everything. I want cross-learning on the skills too. Break them into teams. Every member of every team has to know every job that his team is responsible for. Then dissolve the old teams and form new ones with new responsibilities and start over. Ideally, I want every member of this crew able to run every station on this ship."

"Sir? That's—"

"I know. I've never yet been on a ship where we succeeded, and I doubt we'll make it here either. But I'll tell you this. Those ships with the highest cross-skill ratings are also the most effective in the fleet. So that's the goal and I expect you to push for it."

Hardesty passed a sheet of paper across to Korie. "Here's a hardcopy for you of the first week's targets."

Korie looked at the list. "Sir? This is—"

"There's too much can't in that sentence."

"I didn't even finish it."

"You didn't have to. It was on your face. Listen to me. That first week's schedule is easy. Every week from now until the job is finished, I'm upping the ante on you and every single man and woman in this crew. Every time you meet a challenge, I'm going to raise the target. You are on a treadmill. I am going to make this the single most dreadful experience in the lives of each and every one of you. Because after you live through the hell I'm going to give you, the Morthans are going to look easy."

"Yes, sir."

"And that brings me to my last point. There is going to come a day when this crew is more terrified of you and me than they are of the Morthans. On that day—and not before then—they will not only be ready to go up against those murdering bastards, they'll be positively *eager*."

"Yes, sir."

"Questions? Comments? Feedback?"

Korie shook his head. "No, I don't think so."

"Good. Did you notice I didn't say word one about your—" Hardesty waved a hand in careless dismissal, "—inner turmoil. You're a man. Handle your healing however you have to. *But from now in, you'll do it in the privacy of your own cabin.* Got that?"

Korie managed to nod.

"Good. Now get the hell out of here. You're already a day behind schedule."

A Little History

When the first Morthans were decanted from their artificial wombs, they weren't called Morthans. That would only come much later. At the time, the "enhanced babies" were thought of only as a specialized form of humanity, and great care was taken to give these children a special pride in themselves. They were told that they were *not* a sub-species, but a superspecies.

Perhaps that was the mistake. Perhaps that was where it started.

Generations later, when the science of bioengineering had become a commonplace technology, when the designing and creation of new species of humanity had become routine events, the pride in one's superior abilities was still a part of the training, and the term "more-than" had become part of the common slanguage.

Humanity wasn't slow to notice. The "more-thans" were useful. They were interesting. They were admirable. Humanity was fascinated by the "more-thans."

But not all the "more-thans" felt the same about humanity. As the number of "more-thans" grew, so did their wealth and their power. And so did the separatist settlements of those who resented the patronizing attitudes of so-called "normal" humanity.

It was inevitable that some of these "more-thans" would leave the human worlds and establish their own colonies. The more extremist of the separatist groups went as far as they could beyond the frontier; they made it known that they wanted no human intervention, and they made it known in such an aggressive manner that they got their wish.

That was the beginning of the Morthan Solidarity. They had resources, they had ability, they had a smoldering resentment. Soon, they had a plan. They designed a culture for themselves. It was a fierce and terrifying brew; its primary emphasis was a studied aggression. There were sixteen castes of martial arts training, twelve levels of self-discipline, a religious order based on warrior-Buddhism and medieval samurai codes, and an intensely developed convention of politeness and protocol. There was honor or there was humiliation—a Morthan knew nothing else. The Morthans created holidays of rage and horror; culminating in mass outbreaks of hysteria and riots. Their culture spawned new ways of turning amok. Berserkers were commonplace. There was ritualized cannibalism. Sexuality invented itself in terrifying new perversions.

The Morthans knew what they were doing—they were inventing a past for themselves, so they could design a future. Out of this chaos, they bred themselves into a species of super-Morthans. They augmented and enhanced. They engineered each new generation to be strong enough to kill the previous one. They channeled the horror, trained it, disciplined it intensely. Their rage was a nuclear fire—and they tempered themselves in its flames.

It did not go unnoticed.

But humanity's only defense would have been to become Morthans themselves—and that they could not or *would not* do. There had to be a better way.

But then the war broke out. The Silk Road Convoy was destroyed, and it was too late.

The Inner Hull

A starship is a bottle. A liberty ship is a bottle inside a bottle. The inner bottle is the main life-support module. The outer bottle is the ship's primary hull. The space between the two is known simply as the inner hull. It is a raw, unfinished-looking volume; a techno-wilderness of catwalks, railings, structural members and naked work lights; it is a crosshatched maze of structural members, latticework partitions, ducts, and cables. There are naked work-lights throughout; haphazardly placed and casting odd shadows.

The liberty ship comes off the line deliberately unfinished so that each ship can be custom-fitted for specific tasks later. Usually, most of the inner hull is intentionally set aside as a place where a starship crew can *gafiate*.

GAFIA: (*abbrev*) Get Away From It All. TO GAFIATE: The process of getting away from it all.

The theory was that a crew needed a little bit of wildness and disorder, a place where they could achieve a bit of psychological distance from the pressurized environment of the military regimen. Mostly, the theory worked. Sometimes, it didn't.

Which is why Lieutenant Commander Brik and Lieutenant JG Helen Bach were searching the inner hull for the *LS-1187*'s notoriously peripatetic still. As they moved along the catwalk, HARLIE was turning the lights on ahead of them and darkening them behind. Most of the aeroponics webs had been removed from this section. Korie had left many of them in place and the Luna moss could still be smelled throughout the inner hull.

Bach was uncomfortable at first, following the hulking Morthan along the catwalks. He didn't talk. She was sure he didn't like her. She wanted to let him know that she understood—about the prejudice and everything else. She didn't realize she was babbling.

"—I grew up on a Morthan farm," Bach was saying. "I've been around Morthans all my life. Um, I guess what I'm trying to say is that—"

Brik cut her off. "I know what you're trying to say. It isn't necessary."

"Oh," said Bach. "Okay." She looked at Brik uncomfortably. His immense size was disconcerting. Deliberately, she changed the subject. "Um. On my last ship, the inner hull was outfitted as a gym. We even had a running track. It was great. Can I ask you something—?" When Brik didn't respond, she took it as an assent. "You know how the captain and the exec think. If we do it on our own time, do you think Mr. Korie would let us build a gym ourselves? We could probably—"

Brik wasn't listening. He held up a hand and explained, "Shut up."

Bach fell silent immediately. She looked up—and up—at Brik. He was staring intently forward. Bach followed his stare, but she couldn't see what he was focusing on. She followed him silently forward.

They came around the curve of the hyperstate fluctuator channeling tube and stopped.

Ahead of them, on a wide platform, lit by worklights, was the still, a tangle of tubing and wires and boilers. Reynolds and Cappy stood on either side of it. They wore lazy, I-dare-you expressions. Behind them were four hulking men, part of the Black Hole Gang; they were big and mean-looking. Bach noticed that they were all carrying large blunt tools.

Bach snuck a quick glance at Brik. His expression was unreadable. She glanced back to Cappy and Reynolds. The silence stretched out—

"Well," said Bach, crisply, in a deliberate attempt to break the mood. "This is a fine how-do-you-do! You're having a party and you didn't invite us! I'm hurt!"

Reynolds's gaze slid over to Bach as if he was seeing her for the first time. He remarked quietly, "Hanging around with Morthans is a good way to get hurt." To Brik, he said, "Don't make any trouble here and we'll all get along *just fine*. Lots of ships have . . . extracurricular activities."

Brik's answer rumbled deep in his chest. "Not this one."

Reynolds shrugged. "Have it your own way." He and the others spread out, readying themselves—

Without taking his eyes off them, Brik said softly to Bach, "Please stand back. I don't want you to get hurt."

"Uh-uh. It's my fight too." Bach held her ground.

"Lieutenant," said Brik, picking her up swiftly and sliding her easily down the catwalk and out of the way, "you really must learn to follow orders." Then he turned back to the six men with clubs.

Brik was a Morthan Tyger. He was not simply big and mean-looking. He was an *artist*.

He moved.

He did not seriously injure any of them, but he *hurt* each of them. He flowed like lightning. He reached, he grabbed, he conquered. They swarmed in around him, clubs swinging. He whirled, kicked, feinted, rolled, came up swinging—he disarmed them, disabled them, took them out of the fight, and left them gasping in pain and shock. He gave each of them an unequivocal reminder that he did not want to do this again.

The fight was over before it started: kick, slash, punch, grab, thrust, jab, throw, parry, duck, clobber—and take a breath. He hung one man on a hook, he draped another over a catwalk, a third ended up wedged between the hull and a stanchion. A fourth man was dropped onto the next catwalk down. Cappy was jabbed in the groin as well as the solar plexus and left choking where he stood.

The fight ended with Brik *gently* taking the throat of Reynolds between his fangs and *growling*. Reynolds went white.

"It's a good thing you didn't get me angry," Brik said softly. "I lose control when I get angry. People get *eaten* when I get angry." Very controlled, he added, "Don't. Get. Me. Angry."

Somehow Reynolds managed to gasp and nod.

"Good," said Brik. "Now *I'm* sure that we'll all get along just fine."

He dropped Reynolds rudely to the floor, then he nodded to Bach who was just now finding her way back. "Thank you for not getting in my way, Lieutenant. Would you please supervise the destruction of this unauthorized equipment?"

Bach nodded, as unable to speak as the others. She was stunned by the speed of Brik's victory.

Brik reached down and pulled Reynolds to his feet. "You," he said. "You will begin dismantling the still now. Correct?"

Reynolds choked out his assent.

"Your crewmates will help. Correct?" Brik started plucking the other survivors off the walls he had hung them on. The six chastened men assented painfully, one by one. Brik stepped over to the still and loudly began pulling it apart. "Like this," he prompted, handing the pieces to MacHeath. "Now, you do it."

MacHeath and Reynolds stepped gingerly forward and began breaking down the equipment: the copper tubing, the boiler, the fermentation vat. The others made their way forward and began to help.

Brik watched for a moment, satisfied. "Lieutenant, you will report to me when the job is done." Then he turned and strode off into the darkness.

Cappy was the last one to his feet. Reynolds and MacHeath had to help him. He was as limp as a kitten.

"You okay?" MacHeath asked.

Cappy was in pain, but he nodded anyway. He gasped and said, "Boy . . . am I glad . . . that he's on *our* side."

Officers' Country

Astrogator Cygnus Tor was lying on the floor of her cabin.

The base of her antigrav bed—a tall glass cylinder—was open and she was on her back, staring up at the impulsion unit. Inside the cylinder, a uniform jacket was drifting slowly up toward the ceiling.

The door to her cabin was open. Lieutenant JG Valentine Michael Jones peered cautiously in. "Knock knock?" he said.

Tor didn't even look up from what she was doing. "Door's open," she called.

"Commander Tor? Valentine Jones. 'Jonesy.' You asked to see me."

"Oh, right. I wanted to ask you something. Hey? Do you know anything about antigrav beds?" She extracted herself from the base of the cylinder and sat up to look at Jonesy. She had skinned down to a pair of shorts and tight-fitting T-shirt; it was obvious that she wasn't wearing a bra.

Jonesy shrugged. "Uh, not really." He added helpfully, "But I know gravitors. You want me to take a look?"

"Well, I'm not getting anywhere." Tor moved out of the way, wiping her hands on her pants.

Jonesy lay down on the floor and scooted headward to look up inside the base of the bed. She handed him the probe and waited, hunkering down to get a better look. Idly, she let her gaze travel down past his chest . . . "Listen," she said. "I've been looking over your . . . record."

"What's wrong with it?" Jonesy asked, his voice was slightly muffled.

"Huh? Nothing." Then she realized that he meant the bed. "Oh. Look—" She pointed.

Jonesy scooted out and levered himself up onto one arm to look. He followed her gaze upward. Inside the bed, a variety of objects had floated to the top of the cylinder. "Ah, I see." He scooted forward and peered into the innards again. "You were saying about my record?" He prompted.

"This is your first ship, isn't it?"

"Yeah. Beautiful, isn't she? The Academy wanted me to stay and do post-grad work and then become a full-time instructor. But I turned it down."

Tor didn't answer immediately. She was studying the shape of Jonesy's thigh. She was fascinated by the subtle curve up toward his— she cleared her throat and said quickly, "Listen. I need an assistant astrogator. I was wondering if you wanted to work on the Bridge. With me."

Jonesy didn't answer. She could hear him tinkering with something inside the bed. "—Oh, here's the problem," he said. "One of the rings is reversed. They're out of sync. The little one's pulling, the big one's pushing. They're fighting each other. That's why everything drifts upward. It's easy to miss. Wait a minute—"

He finished and extracted himself from the base of the cylinder. He sat up and handed the probe back to Tor. "I think someone's playing a practical joke on you."

Tor looked incredulous. "They short-sheeted my antigrav bed—?" She frowned. "I *wonder* who could have done it." She was almost convincing.

Jonesy didn't seem to notice He stood up with Tor. The various objects in the antigrav bed were now drifting properly in its center. Tor opened the door and tossed the items out. She stepped into the bed and floated off the floor. "Is this right?" she asked.

"Looks like it. There's one way to tell." He climbed into the cylinder with her, floating up beside her. Tor smiled and flushed slightly at the almost-intimacy. Jonesy didn't notice. "See—if two people can float without drifting, that means it's fine for one. I mean, that's how we used to test 'em back in the Academy."

"I'll bet . . ."

"Umm. We have to wait a minute to see—"

They waited. They were floating very close to each other now. Tor was getting visibly aroused. This gawky innocent boy was *very* attractive. Sooner or later, he'd have to notice her perfume—

Abruptly Jonesy realized why Commander Tor was looking at him that way. For a moment, he didn't know what to do. He was too uncomfortably close—and she was too uncomfortably handsome. Embarrassed and flustered, he said, "Uh, well—it's working." He turned to the control panel. "Is everything else in order?"

Jonesy hit a button at random, not realizing—the shower came on with a hot steaming roar. They both yelped in surprise. Jonesy was flustered and apologetic, but Tor wasn't angry. She started laughing.

"Well, the shower works," she said.

She helped him down out of the antigrav bed. Both of them were dripping. Jonesy looked like a shrunken dog, but Tor didn't seem to notice. She was still smiling. "Thank you, Lieutenant Jones."

"Um—I didn't know they did that," he offered, not knowing quite how to apologize.

"The deluxe models do," Tor said dryly.

"Um. Well. Now, I know."

"Maybe they need safety panels," laughed Tor.

Embarrassed, Jonesy held his hands up as if looking for a towel, but he was too embarrassed to move. "Next time, I won't do that. Um, I better go dry off." He nodded and smiled and nodded and backed out of the room.

Tor shook her head in quiet disbelief. Could anybody *really* be that innocent? Her smile broadened into one of easy delight. Jonesy was going to be fun. "*Next* time?"

Abruptly, Jonesy stuck his head back into the room. "Uh—I almost forgot. Yes, I would like to work with you. On the Bridge, I mean. That would be great. Thanks." And then he was gone again.

Tor laughed.

Yes. Jonesy was going to be a lot of fun. Already she liked him.

Ship's Mess

The ship's mess smelled of acrid coffee and stale doughnuts, burnt sweat and plastic grease.

Reynolds, Cappy, Leen, and three men from the Black Hole Gang were sprawled around the end of one of the tables. Several of them had bruises. None of them looked happy. One of the blue-skinned Quillas was quietly refilling their coffee mugs. "Well?" said Cappy. "Are you going to tell him or not?"

Leen was flipping through the screens on his clipboard, flashing from one schematic to the next. "Got that one, that one, that one— still have to check that—" He paused and looked up at Cappy. "One: You're interrupting my work. Two: I've already gotten my butt chewed once today. Three: It won't do any good. And four: No, I am not going to tell him how you feel. In case you've forgotten, a still is against regulations. Striking an officer is even *more* against regulations. By rights, they could court-martial you—but there's a war on and man-power is short. And on the other matter—Brik outranks you. You want my advice? Don't press your luck. Keep your nose clean and your head down and don't go looking for any more trouble."

"We never hit him," said Cappy. "We never even got close."

"I'd have been very surprised if you had. You guys don't know much about Morthans, do you?"

"What do we need to know? They're big and they're ugly," said Beck, one of the Black Hole Gang.

"So are you," said Leen. "But that doesn't make you a Morthan." There was good-natured laughter around the room. "There have been Morthans for over fifteen hundred years. And for the last thousand, they've been directing their own evolution. They regard themselves as machines. You know how we like to supercharge our equipment—well, that's what the Morthans are doing to their bodies. They do it with genetics, they do it with in-utero tailoring, they do it with implants and augments, they do it with drugs and brainwashing and indoctrination and psycho-training and God knows what else. They start planning a kid's life even before he's conceived—and if a kid fails *anywhere* along the line, they abort him. A Morthan child has to earn his citizenship. If you haven't earned it by the time you're twenty-one, they flush you down the tubes. They don't believe in wasting resources on nonproductive members of society."

"What are the women like?" asked Armstrong, half-jokingly. He had walked in just as Leen had begun describing the Morthans.

Leen shook his head. "I don't know. Nobody's ever seen one. There's a theory though—" He looked around almost conspiratorially, then lowered his voice. "—Rumor has it that there aren't any Morthan women. They're all warriors. They grow their babies in industrial wombs. Supposedly, they think that breeding a woman would be a waste of effort when for the same investment they could grow another warrior."

"Um—" Armstrong looked momentarily confused. "Wait a minute. If they don't have any women, who do they—?"

"Why do you think they're all so cranky?" laughed Cappy, and almost everybody else joined in.

"No—! Is that true?" Armstrong was genuinely confused. "That can't really be so, can it?" He looked from one to the other. "Don't they have sex drives or—?"

"I think," said Leen, "that a Morthan only gets off by winning a fight."

Reynolds gave Cappy a meaningful poke. "You should ask Brik, 'Was it good for you too?'" Cappy did not look amused.

The duty-Quilla came up to Armstrong then, carrying a tray with a mug on it. "Coffee?" she said. Armstrong turned and noticed her for the first time and his eyes widened with unabashed interest. He'd never seen a Quilla this close before. She was vividly blue; she was patterned with shiny scales that shifted in color from turquoise to mazarine and she was as delicately patterned as a butterfly. Her skin looked as shiny and smooth as pale silk veil. Her sensory quills were a bright magenta; they quivered intensely. Armstrong was fascinated. The Quilla looked back at him with amusement. Her eyes were wide and bright and shadowed by dark, almost purple lids.

"Coffee?" she repeated.

"Huh—?" Armstrong finally realized what she was asking. "Oh, yes. Thanks." He took the coffee and sipped it too quickly, simultaneously burning his mouth and trying to hide his embarrassment. He flushed, hoping that nobody had noticed, but of course, they all had—and were grinning at his discomfort.

"Here," said Leen abruptly to Reynolds. He slid his clipboard across and poked at the screen. "Here it is. Look. Am I right or am I right?"

"You're the chief."

"I told him and I told him—and what does he say? He says nine-fifty. Like all he has to do is say it and it's real. You know what it is—he's locked up in theory. He's so sure he can push the envelope, he's going to kill us. Look, those fluctuators are beta-grade; they'll never hit better than seven-fifty—*maybe* eight . . . downhill with a tailwind."

Reynolds looked up at Armstrong, noticed his frank curiosity. "Chief Leen is a man of few words," he explained. "All of them nasty."

"Uh, whatever you say." Armstrong turned to watch the Quilla as she exited the room. A goofy look spread across his face. "They sure are pretty, aren't they?"

"Careful," said Reynolds. "You know what they say about Quillas." He exchanged a knowing grin with Cappy.

Cappy made a gesture with his hands like a spider doing pushups on a mirror. He touched the fingertips of one hand to the fingertips of the other and flexed both simultaneously.

"No," admitted Armstrong. "Actually, I don't know—"

Reynolds motioned him closer. He pulled Armstrong down and whispered into his ear. Armstrong's eyes went wide in disbelief. He looked back and forth between Reynolds and Cappy. "That's not true!" And then, in a hesitant voice, he asked, "Is it? Do they really?"

Cappy's reply was deadpan. "Yes. They do."

"But never on the first date," said Reynolds.

"Wow . . ." said Armstrong, appreciatively.

Abruptly Cappy noticed something behind Armstrong. "Say—you wanted to meet the doctor, didn't you?" He said it so quietly, he was almost mouthing the words. *"Turn around."*

Armstrong turned.

And stared.

Chief Medical Officer Molly Williger was the *ugliest* human being in the universe. It was said of Molly Williger that the stardrive engines refused to function while she was in the same room. Chief Engineer Leen had no desire to test the truth of this canard, but had so far refused Dr. Williger access to his engine room. She was a squat little potato of a woman with a face that looked like the underside of a golf shoe. She was shaped like a cow-pat. Her face looked too tiny for her head; her eyes were either mean and piggish or narrow and piercing, depending on how you looked at her. Her hair was pulled back and tied in a tight little bun that looked like a clump of baling wire.

It was said of Molly Williger that she was as good a doctor as she was ugly. Armstrong didn't know that. He just stared.

Dr. Williger stared back. She glanced at Cappy. "Does it talk?" she said. Her voice was a raspy growl.

Armstrong gulped—and held out his hand. "Uh—Brian Armstrong. Most people call me Blackie."

Williger nodded, shifting her gum—or her cud, or whatever it was—to her opposite cheek. She held out her hand. "Everybody calls me 'Foxy.' "

Brian Armstrong was mesmerized. Molly Williger was so ugly he couldn't take his eyes off her. Her ugliness went beyond mere awfulness. It was transcendent. "Uh—you don't have any kids, do you?"

"No. Should I?"

"*Whew,*" Armstrong said. "Good."

Williger looked puzzled. "You know, everybody asks me that." She turned to the serving counter to pour herself a cup of coffee, leaving Armstrong rubbing his eyes in disbelief.

Reynolds pulled at his sleeve and whispered, "Around here, you only go to sick bay if you're *really* sick."

Armstrong gulped quietly. "I can understand it."

"It's a test. When Molly Williger starts looking good, you've been in space too long."

"Oh."

"She's coming back," said Cappy. "Ask her for a date."

"Huh?" Armstrong was horrified by the thought, then Cappy turned him around and Armstrong realized he was talking about the Quilla. She had returned with another tray of doughnuts. Cappy gave him a meaningful nudge. "Go on! Go for it—"

Armstrong let himself be pushed forward. "Excuse me . . . ?" he said to the blue woman.

The Quilla looked at Brian "Blackie" Armstrong curiously. "Yes?"

"I, uh—I've never—I mean, I don't want to be rude—but I thought—could we—that is—uh—"

Cappy stepped up beside Armstrong and interrupted candidly. "Quilla—he wants to know if you'll help him join the Faster-Than-Light club."

The Quilla smiled at Armstrong. Her smile was bright enough to melt fire. "You are off shift soon?"

"Uh, yeah. 0600. Um—Which one are you?"

"Delta—" she said, touching herself, and added, "—will be ready when you are." She smiled at Armstrong again, turning part of him to stone, and resumed her duties. Armstrong nearly fainted from lack of blood to the brain. Cappy had to help hold him up.

"Y'see. It's that easy. Thanks, Quilla." He clapped Armstrong on the shoulder, grinning wickedly toward Reynolds. His grin faded almost immediately though. The Quilla stopped at the door to allow Security Officer Brik to come through first. He had to bend low to get through. He was almost too big for the mess room.

All conversation stopped while he wrapped one gigantic hand around a coffee mug, filled it, and poured his bulk into a chair at the far end of the table. Reynolds, Cappy, and the others looked angrily down the length of it toward him. Molly Williger studied the tableau and seated herself precisely between the two glaring groups. All by himself, Brik was a group.

Reynolds spoke first. The distaste was evident in his voice. "Well . . . I got work to do." He levered himself out of his chair.

Cappy and Leen exchanged a glance. Leen made a reluctant decision and rose also. "Yeah, me too. I gotta run a recharge drill on the mag-loaders again." He added sourly, "For Korie."

Cappy nodded and rose to follow. "I'll give you a hand—" He glanced over at Armstrong. "You coming?"

Armstrong hesitated. Around him, the other members of the Black Hole Gang were standing up, putting their coffee mugs down, and following Reynolds. None of them were looking directly at Brik. He knew it was wrong, but . . . he also knew he had to work with these men. "Uh—" And then, reluctantly, he allowed himself to vote with his feet. "Yeah," he said, already ashamed of himself.

And then the room was empty.

Only Brik and Williger were left in the ship's mess.

They glanced across the table at each other.

Williger looked around meaningfully. "Was it something I said?"

Brik grinned. The lady had class. "Do you have this effect everywhere you go?"

Williger shook her head. "No question about it. I just gotta get a new hat."

Brik wasn't quite sure of the reference, but . . . his laughter rumbled loudly—almost frighteningly—through the mess room.

Subluminal

The *LS-1187* was complete, as ready for the stars as she would ever be.

Her bright hull gleamed under the worklights as proudly as the day she first rose from her docks. Her fluctuator struts were proud stanchions, glittering with power and possibility.

Every deck, every tube, every module, every conduit, every stanchion—*everything*—had been repaired or rebuilt, recalibrated, tested, burned in, retested, triple-checked, cleaned, polished, and detailed.

Even Chief Leen had taken a bath—or so the crew believed.

Indeed, the expression on his face was as bright as his engine room. He signed the last authorization on Nakahari's clipboard and handed it back to the young crewman. "All right," he grumbled. "That's the last one. This ship is ready to go."

"Yes, sir!" Nakahari said crisply. He left the now-sparkling engine room and headed up through the now-glistening forward keel, up through the now-spotless Ops bay, onto the now-gleaming Ops deck and up onto the now-pristine Bridge where Hardesty, Korie, and Brik were waiting. He handed the clipboard to Korie.

Korie took it, read it, and passed it to the captain without comment.

Hardesty barely glanced at the final status report. Instead, he checked the time. Then he said, "If you're waiting for a compliment, Mr. Korie, you're waiting in the wrong place." He gestured with the clipboard. "This is the job you're *supposed* to do. Producing a result shouldn't be such a unique event that it requires a pat on the head." He started to turn away, then added, "And, for the record, you're an hour and twenty minutes overdue."

Korie said quietly, "We had a small problem in the engine room."

"The Morthan Solidarity is a *bigger* problem. That's the only problem I'm interested in." Hardesty turned forward to Tor. "Signal Stardock that we're *finally* ready. Cast off as soon as we're cleared."

"Aye, aye, sir." Tor spoke quietly to her headset.

A moment later, the reply came back. "*LS-1187*, you are cleared."

"Thank you, Stardock."

The airlocks sealed and closed. The docking tubes retracted. The holding bolts released . . .

And the starship floated up and out and clear of her moorings.

A soft voice whispered across the widening gap, "Good luck, starship . . ."

"Thank you, Stardock," Tor replied. "That means a lot. Keep the lights burning." She smiled as she turned from her console to the holographic display table. She hadn't expected a farewell. It was a nice gesture—especially toward *this* ship.

"Stardock breakaway complete," HARLIE reported.

Hardesty nodded, satisfied. "Heading 23 mark 141."

Flight Engineer Hodel echoed the order. "23 mark 141." He watched his screens as the ship swung around. "Confirmed."

"Mr. Hodel," the captain ordered. "Ten milligees acceleration, please."

"Ten milligees, confirmed."

Hardesty watched the forward viewer. It showed the view aft as the Stardock began imperceptibly sliding away. The haphazard collection of girders and globes shrank in the distance. After a moment, he ordered, "Boost to fifty milligees."

Again, Hodel echoed the order. "Confirmed."

Hardesty glanced at the smaller console in front of him.

Korie glanced over. "Right down the center of the channel," he said.

"Are you surprised?" Hardesty's voice was emotionless.

"No, sir. Just . . . gratified."

Hardesty didn't say anything to that. "Boost to five hundred milligees." They had to move the starship well clear of the Stardock before going to full power—and then they'd have to spend several hours at full acceleration before initiating hyperstate. The ripple effects of a hyperstate bubble could be uncomfortable to anyone or anything nearby. This vessel had experienced firsthand the havoc that occurred when a hyperstate fringe brushed a normal-space installation. It would not do to pass that experience on to their hosting Stardock.

Hardesty stepped down from the Bridge and circled the Ops deck once, peering carefully at every console. Every station was operating well within expected parameters. Satisfied, he returned to the Bridge without comment. "Mr. Hodel, boost to three gees and hold it there."

"Aye, Captain."

There was no sensation of movement. Korie checked his console. The gravitational compensators were maintaining to six decimal places. Totally undetectable. A starliner couldn't have been smoother.

Hardesty made another round of the Ops deck then, peering narrowly at each console. What was he judging, Korie wondered. The crew? The ship? Or was this part of his performance?

He stopped behind the flight engineer's console and watched the numbers climb. After a long moment, he said, "Go to ten."

Hodel nodded and typed in the command.

Hardesty turned and looked up at Korie on the Bridge. "Status?"

"As expected, sir."

Hardesty turned back to Hodel. "Twenty-five."

A moment later, Hodel reported, "Holding at twenty-five."

Hardesty returned to the Bridge. "Chief Leen. We are holding at twenty-five gees. We will maintain this speed for thirty minutes. I want you to run concurrent stability checks for that entire time. If there's any deviation from the projected channels, I want to know immediately."

"Yes, sir."

"Mr. Korie?" Hardesty turned to his executive officer. "What's the recommended interval before initiating stardrive?"

"A hundred million kilometers—at least."

"And during wartime?"

"Sir, during wartime operating conditions, it is recommended that a starship put as much distance as possible between itself and any other starship or deep-space Stardock it may have rendezvoused with before initiating its hyperspace envelope; this is to avoid betraying the exact location of the other vessel, or of the Stardock, to any other vessel in the hyperstate vicinity."

Hardesty nodded. "And how large an interval would you recommend in this case?"

"I would recommend, sir, that we accelerate for several days at full power, then decelerate the same length of time to burn off the extra kinetic energy. Two reasons. First, it will allow us to check the performance of the rebuilt mass-drivers under the most rigorous conditions; and second, it will place the Stardock well outside the range of probable loci if we're detected going into hyperstate."

"A sensible suggestion," said the captain. "Now, let me postulate something else, Mr. Korie. Tor, I want you to hear this too. You too, Hodel. Suppose—you're the enemy. Suppose you know our standard operating procedure is to move away as far as possible before initiating hyperstate. Knowing that, what would you think if you detected a ship going FTL?"

"I'd think there was a starbase somewhere nearby, within a radius of at least a light-day. If I could search for it undetected, I would. Not being able to search for it undetected, I'd sweep the area as thoroughly as I could, hoping to brush the base with my envelope and destroy it— or at least cripple it."

"Mm-hm. And is there a flaw in that logic?"

"Not really."

"You don't see the loophole?" Hardesty glanced to Tor and Hodel. "Either of you?" They shook their heads.

Korie said, "I suppose . . . in one sense, as soon as the enemy knows that's your standard operating procedure, and allows for it, then it doesn't matter whether you move off or not."

"Right," said Hardesty. "If they see you, they're going to search. At that point, the least likely place to look for the Stardock is your point of initiation and its immediate radius."

Korie thought about it for a moment, considering the implications. "Okay, but what if the enemy is just lurking and observing. If more than one ship departs from the same area of space, he'd be stupid not to assign that area a very high degree of probability."

"But what if every ship departing from your Stardock were to move off to the exact same departure point before initiating hyperstate? That would look the same to a distant observer too."

"It's too easy to check," put in Hodel. "You rig for silent running and drift in as close as you can to see what you can detect. If there's no Stardock in the area, it's a ploy. Then you start looking for where the ships are coming from."

Tor agreed. "It's too dangerous. We're better off having ships move to random positions before putting up the envelope."

Hardesty had been listening quietly. "All right," he said. "Game that out. Suppose the enemy is lurking and observing ships departing at random. After he sees two or three or ten ships arrive and depart, he's going to start projecting a sphere of possibility. After observing enough departures or arrivals, he should be able to predict the location of the Stardock as being somewhere in the center of the sphere described by these events, don't you think?"

"But it'll take a lot longer to locate the Stardock that way, and he's at greater risk of detection," said Hodel.

Korie was studying the captain carefully. "All right," he said. "Neither procedure is perfect, but one has significant advantages over the other. What's your point?"

"*That's* my point, Mr. Korie. These procedures *aren't* perfect." Hardesty pointed at Korie's chest. "That was Captain Lowell's mistake. He assumed that following procedure was enough. It isn't. I'm not interested in procedure, I'm interested in results. Your enemy is going to be analyzing your procedures. He's going to understand them better than you and he's going to understand why you do them. That's your weakness. Your only strength is to have the same perspective, to look at yourself as the enemy does—and sometimes break your own rules, specifically to confuse him."

The captain let his officers consider that thought for a while. "Chief Leen?"

"Engines are clean, sir. No anomalies."

"Thank you. I'm boosting to one-fifty now."

"Aye, sir."

"Mr. Hodel. Go to one-fifty."

"Yes, sir. One hundred and fifty gees." A moment later, Hodel called out, "Confirmed."

Hardesty's expression remained unreadable. "You think that's too much strain on the engines, Mr. Korie?"

"No, sir."

"What would you think if I ordered a boost to three hundred?"

Korie tried to visualize the strain relationships in his head. He couldn't. "Uh, I'd prefer to ask HARLIE what he thinks before I form an opinion of my own. But—"

"Yes?"

"I do think it's a good idea to know what a ship is capable of, in case you need to use that ability."

"That's a safe answer," Hardesty said. "Very academic."

"I'm sorry if you don't—"

"I didn't say I did. Don't presume. Let me remind you again that part of the captain's responsibility, Mr. Korie, is to train his replacement. As I've said, I don't think Captain Lowell did a very good job. You're still thinking in textbook terms. Now, before you object—" Hardesty held up a hand, cutting off Korie's interruption, "—you need to go back and look carefully at what I said as opposed to what you think you heard. I *said* that you're still thinking in textbook terms. I did not say that the textbooks are wrong. As a matter of fact, most of your textbook simulations were written by the very same people who discovered the *right*ness of what they wrote by direct experience. I know those books and I know some of the authors. You could not have had a better education."

"Yes, sir."

"But—" continued Hardesty, "the very best that a textbook simulation can give you—even the best textbook simulation—is still only simulation. It's the experience of the concept of the situation, not the experience of the situation itself. Simulations give you simulated experience. It remains outside the domain of actual experience. What am I telling you?"

Korie understood perfectly. "There is a difference between an officer who can run a perfect simulation and a blooded warrior."

"Right. You gave me a textbook answer a moment ago. It's complete, it's perfect, and you'll never be court-martialed for following the book. But it's missing that something that makes all the difference between being a statistic and being the kind of an officer who brings his ship back with a broomstick tied to her mast. Did you ever hear of a captain named Ling Tsu?"

"Who hasn't?"

"I met her once," Hardesty's said. His voice was surprisingly soft.

Despite himself, Korie was impressed.

"Yes," the captain agreed. "It was that kind of an experience. I was very young at the time, and she died only a few months later; she was a very fragile old lady by then, but you could still tell who she was by looking at her eyes. She was officially retired, but she still served in a consulting capacity. The story was true, you know—she refused to consult unless she got some time in space every year. She said that decisions about ships had to be made inside ships. She was pure fleet all the way.

"Anyway, I was a junior trainee on a new cruiser. They wheeled her onto the Bridge of our ship for the shakedown cruise and let me tell you, our captain was sweating blood, as were we all. But she didn't say a word. She just watched and listened and somehow she became invisible. For a while. The captain was so scared he was following every procedure in the book. We might as well have been automated; but it was along about this point, while we were moving out to the local horizon, that she leaned forward and poked the captain in the ribs. 'You got lead in your ass?' she said. 'Let's open her up and see what this baby can do.' "

Hardesty smiled as he remembered. "She almost got applause—except we were too shocked. We'd been thinking of her as a great lady, but we'd forgotten why she was great. Do you know what her job was as a consultant? To remind young captains to not take anything for granted. Test everything—your crew, your ship, and especially yourself."

"Yes, sir," said Korie.

"And my point is . . . ?" prompted Hardesty.

Korie looked for the right words and couldn't find them. Instead, he turned forward and blurted, "Mr. Hodel. We worked hard rebuilding this ship. I want to hear her scream. And so does the crew. Go to three hundred gees."

Hardesty looked at Korie. And *grinned*.

Superluminal

"Mr. Hodel, are we clear?"

"One hundred and three-point-five giga-klicks."

"Thank you. Stand by for injection."

"Standing by." Hodel spoke to his headset. "All stations, prepare for injection." A moment later, he confirmed. "Ready for stardrive."

Hardesty referred to his own screen and then gave the order. "Initiate envelope."

Hodel set his controls and passed the order on, "Engine room—initiate envelope."

In the engine room, the order was received eagerly. These crewmembers had been too long in Stardock. Leen stood impatiently at the main console. All of the men and women on his crew were wearing safety goggles. Leen couldn't help himself, he punched up a last-check program, waited till his screen flashed green, and then ordered, "Initiation."

Beside him, two crewmembers inserted their keys into their keyboards and turned them one half-turn clockwise. The board was armed. Leen flipped the cover off the red switch and threw it.

Space warped.

There was a place—a pinpoint hole in the stress field of existence—where the laws of physics transformed from one state to another.

In a moment of time, known as a *quantum second*, that space was grabbed, stretched, englobulated in a moment of pure irrationality, and turned inside-out. Now, it was infinite. Mathematically, at least. At its center hung a silver needle containing ninety-four men and women. The three hyperstate fluctuators on its hull held it firmly in the center of the bubble.

The bubble shimmered and glowed and *held*.

Hodel's board flashed green. He reported it calmly. "The envelope is stable. We have stardrive." He began to punch in a new course, then he grinned at Tor and added, "Just like a real starship."

Tor held up her two crossed fingers.

"Belay that chatter!" Hardesty said from the Bridge, but his usual ferocity seemed muted. "Flight engineer—lightspeed times five. As soon as we're clear of the local deviation, boost to three-fifty."

"Aye aye, sir," Hodel echoed. "Lightspeed times five and three-five-oh when we clear."

Hodel tapped out a command and the bubble around the starship quivered. Imperceptibly, it shifted its shape, stretching itself just a little bit farther along one axis. The ship hung motionless within its center; but in real space—in the stress field—the location of the hyperstate blip, or the place where it would be if it were in normal space, began to stretch, began to slide, began to move, became a beam of light and then something faster than that.

And then it was gone. It wasn't anywhere at all.

But inside, in that place where it *wasn't*, Hodel was satisfied. At five times the speed of light, it would take just a little less than an hour to clear the locus of immediate detectability for the Stardock.

"Lightspeed times five," Hodel confirmed. He sat back in his chair and felt good. On the forward screen, a simulated view showed a grid of demarcation lines slipping past. An actual view forward would have been meaningless. It couldn't exist. It was an irrational concept. Nonetheless, had the sensors been activated, they would have reported a blurred sensation of *something*. Most people found it hard to look at for very long.

Hardesty glanced up. He spoke crisply, "All right. Staff to the table for mission briefing. Oh, and have Chief Leen join us."

The captain stepped down to the Operations deck, followed by Korie and Brik. They seated themselves around the holographic display table. Tor and Hodel only had to swivel their chairs to be in place. Jonesy took a chair uncertainly, but Tor nodded at him and he allowed himself to relax. One of the Quillas began laying out coffee mugs as Chief Leen stepped up through the Ops bay from the keel.

Satisfied that all were ready, Hardesty glanced upward. "HARLIE?"

The visuals began appearing in the air above the table even before HARLIE began speaking. His voice was dispassionate. "Her Majesty's Starship *Sir James Burke* is a destroyer-class liberty ship with standard fittings and weaponry. She carries the flag of New Brittany and is presently based at Windsor Stardock.

"Six months ago, the *Burke* was pulled from active duty for a major refit. At the same time, her security rating was promoted to maximum level red. This briefing is also red-coded.

"Using the refit as cover, the *James Burke* has had three ultra-high-cycle envelope fluctuators installed."

The holographic display of the *Burke* became a schematic. The high-cycle fluctuators were outlined in red. They were twice the size of normal fluctuators and Korie noted that major modifications had been made within the *Burke*'s hull. But if they worked . . . then the *Burke* would have doubled her effective velocity.

Tor was nodding in admiration. "That's a lucky captain—to have a super-stardrive."

"Yeah," agreed Hodel. "Wouldn't you like to have those in your engine room?"

Leen snorted. "I'd like to have an engine in my engine room, thank you."

HARLIE ignored the comments and continued his presentation. "The new fluctuators will increase the *Burke*'s rated stardrive velocity by a factor of two, making her one of the fastest ships in known space. Her operational rating is now two thousand times the speed of light. Her theoretical rating is twenty-three hundred."

"We're lucky to hit nine-fifty," Hodel said.

"Seven-fifty," Leen corrected him.

"The Morthan Solidarity would trade a shipload of warlords for just one of those fluctuators," Tor said thoughtfully.

"And they'd still be getting the best of the deal," said Hardesty. "Our *only* strategic advantage in this war is the technological one. The Solidarity doesn't have the industrial base the Allies do. If they got their hands on one of those units, they'd be turning out copies in six months, and six months after that . . . we'd be in big trouble."

"Four months ago," said HARLIE. "the *Burke* was assigned to penetrate the Morthan sphere. As you can see, this is a particularly hazardous journey; it could not be safely completed by a slower vessel. Even the *Burke* will be at considerable risk." He projected the *Burke*'s course across a star map of the region. "However, the opportunity of the *Burke*'s mission is of such importance to the Alliance that the risk is deemed acceptable. As a precaution, the *Burke* has been equipped with significant self-destruct capabilities; she is not to fall into enemy hands under *any* circumstances. That responsibility to protect the high-cycle technology is also shared by this vessel. The *Burke*'s mission: to rendezvous with a Morthan vessel and pick up a single life-pod. Inside the life-pod will be a high-ranking ambassador carrying a secret peace initiative."

Brik spoke quietly. His voice was a desolate rumble. "I don't believe it."

The others glanced to him curiously, but the Morthan did not explain his skepticism.

HARLIE continued, "The peace initiative is apparently sponsored by a dissident faction within the Morthan Solidarity, called the Coalition of Warlords."

Hodel grinned. "Not very solid, are they?"

"It is believed that the Coalition of Warlords will negotiate an end to hostilities to prevent further decimation of their ranks, and will force the leadership of the Solidarity to accept that settlement."

Brik snorted.

Hardesty glanced over at him. "You have a problem with that, Mr. Brik?"

"It's a trap. Warlords don't negotiate."

Hardesty accepted the comment without reaction.

"Sir?" asked Jonesy. "How do we know all this?"

Hardesty looked at the junior officer as if seeing him for the first time. "That's not your concern."

"Yes, sir—I was just wondering about the reliability of the information."

"We have sources within the Solidarity."

"Oh." Jonesy considered that. He looked troubled. "What will happen to them if they get caught?"

Brik said quietly, "The Morthans will gut them alive and hang their bodies up to cure."

"Oof," said Tor, an involuntary reaction.

"It's a Morthan insult," explained Brik. "An honorable enemy would be eaten fresh."

"Uck!" Hodel shuddered.

Brik looked to Korie. "You have a comment to make too?"

Korie chose his words very carefully. "I never comment on anyone else's eating habits."

"Thank you," said Brik.

"Gentlemen," interrupted the captain. "May we continue? HARLIE, if you please?"

HARLIE continued in a voice that was disturbingly calm. "If everything has proceeded according to plan, the *Burke* will have completed her rendezvous mission by now and will be bringing her passenger back. The *LS-1187* is to proceed to a designated rendezvous with Her Majesty's Starship *Sir James Burke* and provide escort service to a designated location. The *Burke* has not yet been made aware of this location. We are carrying that information. I can only decode it when the captain of the *Burke* provides an authorization code."

"Huh?" said Tor. "Escort service? We can't keep up with the *Burke*. No one can. What's the point?"

"It's obvious to me," said Hodel. "The *Burke* wants a minimum of attention. We're her cover. We come into base together and nobody suspects that the *Burke* is anything but another rusty old tub."

Hardesty's glance slid sideways to his executive officer. "Mr. Korie, what's the real reason?"

"Sir?"

"Can't you figure it out?" asked Hardesty. He looked at Korie coldly, as if Korie had deliberately chosen to be retarded.

"Um—" Korie thought fast. "What if the *Burke* gets captured by the Morthans? They could send her back, carrying a Hell-bomb, drop it into a sun, and take out a whole star system. Our job is to make sure that the *Burke* is clean before we tell her where her final destination is."

"And if she isn't clean—?"

"I assume that's in the orders, sir."

"Yes, it probably is. Would you like to speculate what would be appropriate in this situation?"

Korie allowed himself a shrug. "Well—based on what we've heard, I'd say that if we couldn't regain control of the *Burke*, then our job would be to destroy her."

"Good," said Hardesty, mildly surprised. "That's exactly what our orders are." He added, "HARLIE, forget you heard those directives pertaining to the possible destruction of the *Burke*; there is to be no record in our ship's computer of any such orders or discussion pertaining to them."

"Yes, captain."

"Obviously," said Hardesty, "fleet command does not think that is a very likely occurrence—or they would not have sent this ship to provide escort cover." He clicked off the display. "All right. There you have it. The rendezvous is five days away. We'll be picking up the *Burke* uncomfortably close to the Morthan sphere. I'll want continual long-range scanning, confidence nine or above. Any questions? No? Mr. Korie, you have the conn." He levered himself to his feet and exited briskly.

"Yes, sir. . . ." Korie said to his back.

Hodel waited until the door whooshed shut behind the captain. "I was hoping for something a little more . . . interesting," he sighed.

"Are you using the Morthan definition of 'interesting'?" asked Brik. To their uncomprehending looks, he explained, "*Interesting*—as in pertaining to your own death." He added innocently, "Nothing concentrates the attention so much as the knowledge that you are about to die."

"Uh, never mind," said Hodel. "I'd rather be bored." He swiveled back to his console.

Quillas

Brian Armstrong stepped into the corridor grinning weakly. It was true what they said about Quillas. He was limp. He was haggard and weary.

Quilla Delta exited the cabin after him, looking politely contented.

Armstrong looked at her with a near-hopeless expression. He was flustered and red and unable to quantify the staggering effect of his experience. He was exhausted to the point of speechlessness.

The Quilla simply smiled at him. She'd seen this response before.

"Uh—" Armstrong gulped and swallowed and tried to find his voice. "I gotta go back on shift now. You were . . ." He waved his hands about uselessly. ". . . *Wow*."

"Yes," she answered mildly. "So were you. Thank you, Brian." She turned and walked calmly away, leaving him staring after her.

Shaking his head, he started down the corridor in the opposite direction. Almost immediately, a different Quilla came up the corridor toward him. It was Gamma.

Quilla Gamma smiled with exactly the same expression as she passed him. "Yes. Thank you, Brian. You were quite good."

"Huh? Wait a minute. You're—"

The Quilla touched herself lightly. "This is Gamma."

Armstrong's eyes widened in realization. Every Quilla on the ship was tuned in and *feeling* the same thing.

His mouth fell open in shock.

Did Quillas—?

Suddenly, he felt nauseous.

A Good Idea at the Time

Jonesy paused uncertainly in front of the door to Tor's cabin. Finally, he summoned up his nerve and tapped the entrance panel.

"Who is it?" came Tor's voice.

"Uh, it's Jonesy."

The door slid open for him and he stepped gingerly inside. Cygnus Tor was working at her desk; she was wearing only shorts and a halter; the standard uniform aboard ship for women. Men usually wore T-shirts and shorts. Tor looked up with interest. "Hi, what's up?"

"I took your suggestion and uh—" Jonesy held up a small plastic device. "I built this for you."

Tor was momentarily confused. "What suggestion?"

"Um, didn't you say something about a safety lock for the shower control? I took one apart and reprogrammed it and added a safety switch—"

Tor was leaning her chin on her fist. Now she hid her smile of amusement behind her knuckles. She glanced off as if discharging her laughter and then looked back to Jonesy. "It was a sort of a joke. I never really thought a safety panel was necessary in a shower—"

Jonesy's face fell. "Oh—"

"But maybe you're right," she recovered quickly. "I mean, after all, it could happen. A sleeper might bump into it. Maybe we should install it and see—"

"I don't have to, if you don't want it."

"No, I insist. Let's see how it works. After all, you went to all that trouble."

"Are you sure?"

"I'll make it an order, all right?"

"Uh—I'll put it in now." Jonesy turned to the antigrav bed and stepped into it. He began disconnecting its control plate. Tor got up from the desk and came around to watch him work. She leaned provocatively against the tube. Her figure was surprisingly lean and hard.

"This won't take long," Jonesy started to say, "and then I'll be out of your hair."

"Take as long as you need." Tor smiled, tossing her head back. "I don't mind having you in my hair." When he didn't react, she added, "I'm actually glad of the interruption."

"Really?" The plate popped off in Jonesy's hand.

"I was signing off on duty reports. Busywork. It has to be done sometime, but sometimes you'd rather do anything but—"

"Mm," said Jonesy. He grunted as he fumbled the new plate into position. "I wouldn't know. I don't get to do busywork. And most of the reports I have to do are autologged."

Tor allowed herself a smile that hinted of knowledge not yet shared. "I should put you into a leadership-training course. You'd learn about busywork. Everything has to be documented."

"I guess so. But I prefer things I can get my hands on." Jonesy looked up at Tor and suddenly realized how close her body was. "—Uh, you know what I mean." He forced himself to refocus his attention on the control plate. He lined up the plugs and pressed it firmly into place. "There—" He pressed the SELF-TEST button and waited. The unit cycled, flashed, and confirmed that it was fully operational. "That should do it." He gave her a satisfied look. "See—you can't turn on the shower accidentally. You have to press the SHOWER button, and then the AUTHORIZE button within three seconds. Otherwise nothing happens."

"Well, let's try it out," said Tor, stepping into the antigrav tube with him. She reached past his shoulder and tapped the free-fall switch. The gravity faded gently away from beneath them; it was a dizzying sensation of lightheadedness. It took some getting used to; some people never rid themselves of the sensation of the whole bed being turned upside down into an endless drop. They floated up off the floor and drifted in midair. Tor turned Jonesy so that he was facing her.

"It works," he said.

"Of course," she said.

She looked directly into his eyes and waited for him to start flustering. He surprised her. He looked directly back. She waited for him to speak first, surprised at how long the moment was lasting.

It was his voice that gave him away. "Um," he said. "Can I speak candidly?"

She nodded.

"I, um—some of the guys have been teasing me. They say that you—uh, I hope this doesn't offend you. I want you to know how much I personally respect and admire you—"

"Go ahead, say it."

"Well, some of the guys think that you . . . want to . . . well, you know . . . with me. And I—thought you ought to know. I hope you're not offended. I mean, personally, I think you're a very attractive woman and—it would be an honor and a privilege to—"

Tor made a decision. She reached past Jonesy and tapped the SHOWER button. Then she tapped the AUTHORIZE button. Warm water shot up from the floor and flooded down from the ceiling, soaking the both of them and drowning Jonesy's carefully phrased words in a sputter of coughing.

She grabbed his shoulders to steady him. Then she grabbed his face between her two hands and said, "Listen to me, you don't need to do that anymore."

"Do what?"

"The flustered little boy act." She raised her voice to be heard above the steaming water.

"Um—I don't—"

"Yes, you do. You do it whenever there's a chance of you and me being intimate. You do it to distance me. It's very annoying—and it keeps us from really getting to know each other. It keeps us from being real friends. Or anything else." She stretched forward and planted a firm, but gentle, kiss directly on his lips. Jonesy blinked, surprised. The water continued to swirl around the both of them.

"First of all, you're a *very* attractive young man. You don't know how attractive you are. And yes, it's true. I would like to tumble with you. But I don't tumble with children, so you're going to have to grow up first." She touched his chin gently. "Lose the act. It's not you."

"Um," he said, but it was a different kind of sound than before; a deeper, more thoughtful "Um."

"If you want something—if you want *me*—just say so. The worst that can happen is that the answer will be no. It might also be yes. But if you never ask, you'll never know. So, what's it to be, Lieutenant? Do you have something to ask me?"

"Um—" Jonesy swallowed hard—and then something happened. He *stiffened*. He seemed to straighten before Tor, almost growing in her grasp. "Commander Tor," he began, in a voice she'd never heard before. "Request permission to initiate docking maneuvers."

Tor laughed. "That's a good start, but a little too formal. Try again. Just say it in English."

"The truth is," Jonesy admitted candidly, "you're the most beautiful woman I've ever taken a shower with."

Tor flushed in surprise and delight. It was his naked sincerity which won her. She was too surprised to respond.

"So," continued Jonesy, "would you like to tumble with me?"

"Yes, I would," she said. "Very much." She looked deeply into his eyes. They were shining and bright.

Now it was Jonesy's turn to be surprised. "Really—?"

In answer, Tor pulled him close to her in a passionate kiss. She opened her mouth to his. For a moment, he didn't realize, then he opened his mouth to hers. She wasn't going to rush him, she let him explore the sensation of the moment, the intimacy of shared breath— and then he surprised her, his tongue touched hers. It was just the quickest, most fleeting, touch; but the boldness of the initiative told her what she wanted to know, that Jonesy would not be afraid to explore her body, that he really did want to be intimate with her. He just needed to know that it was all right.

Slowly, Tor wrapped her arms around Jonesy's wiry torso, sliding naturally into his embrace. His long gangly arms closed around her shoulders, his hands slid down her back, looking for the right places to touch. One of them came to rest on her hip, then slid around to the gentle cleft at the top of her buttocks; the other found the back of her neck and became a warm, comforting presence there. She sighed and let her kiss open wider, allowed her tongue to touch his again.

They floated, locked together and spinning, turning in the whirling waters. She lifted her legs and wrapped them about his pelvis, pulling him even more tightly against her. She could feel his hardness against her and it sent waves of pleasure up through her belly. She enveloped him, holding him inside the warm envelope of her embrace. She could feel his warmth up and down her entire body.

And then, Jonesy broke away, holding her at arm's length. "I have to look at you," he explained. "I like looking at you. I like seeing how beautiful you are." His hair was plastered wetly across his forehead; the water was clinging to him in shining globules; and his eyes were incredibly alive. "You're terrific," he said.

"So are you," Tor laughed back. "Why don't we get out of these wet clothes—"

Jonesy's smile widened into a broad silly grin. It was the wild, untamed look of a man who was about to share a secret.

Tor started giggling then, so did Jonesy—and then it got even funnier. Not all the old jokes about antigrav beds were true; two people *can* get undressed in a tube, but it does take a while—and they have to like each other *a lot*.

Fortunately, Tor and Jonesy liked each other *more* than just *a lot*.

Rendezvous

The *LS-1187* slowed as she approached her rendezvous, cutting her speed from six hundred lights to three hundred, then to one hundred, then to twenty-five, five, and finally one-point-five. She was scanning all the way in, but there were no hyperstate ripples visible anywhere at all within her locus of detectability.

The *Burke* was not to be seen.

Korie studied the holographic display with a sour frown on his face. Hodel and Tor stared at him from across the table, waiting for his assessment. Jonesy joined them. So did the new weapons specialist, Goldberg; a stocky, red-haired man.

"Holding at one-point-five," said Hodel. "Coming up on primary target sphere. Still nothing."

Hardesty entered through one of the doors at the back of the Bridge. Brik followed him in and crossed to the primary weapons console while Hardesty stepped down to join his officers on the Ops deck. Korie glanced over at him. *Do you want to take over?*

"Carry on," Hardesty said.

Korie turned back to Hodel. "As soon as we cross the horizon, back it off to oh-point-oh-oh-two. Let's coast a bit and see what's what. Keep all stations alert."

"You want to go to yellow?" Tor asked.

"Not yet."

"Stabilizing," Hodel reported. "Oh-point-oh-oh-two."

"Approaching rendezvous point," Jonesy reported. He checked his own screen beneath the display. "Still no signature—" He looked to Tor, worried. She ignored him.

"Hodel, stand by to collapse the envelope." Korie looked to Hardesty. "With your permission, sir. There's no sign of the *Burke*. We've scanned for ripple-effect, both long and short range. There's nothing."

"And you think she's hiding?"

Korie nodded. "She should have sighted us by now and made her presence known. I want to pop back into normal space and see if she's coasting. Maybe she has a good reason to play hide-and-seek."

Hardesty considered it. "All right, go ahead."

Korie turned to Hodel. "Collapse the envelope."

"Collapsing—"

The great stardrive bubble around the starship unfolded in an instant—and once again the *LS-1187* hung in black space. But her sublight velocity was enormous.

"Normal space confirmed," reported Hodel. He swung back to his main console. "Beginning deceleration now. One hundred and fifty gees?"

"If Mr. Leen says it's okay," Korie grinned. He raised his voice so that everybody on the Bridge could hear him. "All right, everybody stay alert. If something is sneaking up on us, we'll have less than thirty seconds to inject back into the safety of hyperstate."

Tor looked up from her screen. "I've got the *Burke*."

Everybody looked to her at the same time.

Tor didn't even look up. She just frowned as she read off the details. It didn't make sense to her either. "She's right on station—right where she's supposed to be, but she's absolutely silent."

Jonesy spoke first. "Two hundred sixty mega-klicks and closing." Then he looked across the display at Tor; his expression was puzzled. "Is she derelict—?"

Korie looked to Hardesty. "This is not according to plan—" He punched at a control and the holographic display flashed to show the intercept vectors.

"Should I hail her?" Tor asked.

Korie was at a loss. "She's *got* to know we're here—"

"Think she's dead?"

"I don't think anything yet." He looked to Hardesty again. "Sir—?"

Hardesty's voice was almost as dispassionate as HARLIE's. "So far, you have been following the book, Mr. Korie. And that is correct. Fleet Command has a purpose behind every procedure."

"But—?" Korie prompted.

"But nothing," said the captain.

Korie straightened up from the display to look the captain straight in the eye. "If I understand you correctly, sir, you are arguing the opposite position from what you said to us when we began this mission."

"Am I?"

Korie replayed the conversation in his head, as best as he could remember it. "Maybe not."

"Make up your mind. Which is it, Mr. Korie?"

" 'There's a reason for everything in the book. These procedures have all been derived from actual experiences—' " Korie quoted.

"I couldn't have said it better myself," said Hardesty.

"But—" said Korie. "The book is insufficient—because it can't predict the situation that hasn't happened yet. Therefore . . . you follow the book until you run into the situation that isn't covered in the book. Then you *improvise*."

"Almost," said Hardesty coldly. "Fleet prefers the word *invent*."

"Yes, sir. I'll remember that." He looked to Tor. "All right. Send a coded chirp. When we get within thirty light-seconds, hit her with a tight beam and we'll try for direct conversation." To Hodel, he added, "Close on her—very slowly. With extreme caution. Shields up. Arm all stations. Let's assume it's a Morthan trap and act accordingly." He looked to Hardesty for his reaction.

The captain nodded. "That was by the book, Mr. Korie."

"Yes, sir. Is there anything else? Do you have any specific orders?"

"What does the book say?"

Korie quoted, " 'Have a security team standing by. If the target vessel doesn't answer, be ready to board.' "

"That's correct."

"You aren't going to give me any help on this, are you?" Korie said.

"You don't need any help," said Hardesty. "At least, not yet."

Korie turned to his security chief. "Mr. Brik, ready a mission team."

Brik rose from his chair and approached Korie, looking very stiff.

"Do you have a problem with that?" Korie asked.

"Yes, I do." Brik's answer was an ominous rumble that caught even the captain's attention.

Hardesty turned around to look up at Brik. "All right," he said. "Enlighten us."

"Destroy the *Burke*. Now. Don't approach her. Don't board her. It's a trap."

Korie looked up at Brik sharply. "How can you be that certain?"

"You are not a Morthan. You could not possibly understand."

"Try me."

Brik took a breath. He hesitated only a moment while he selected the most appropriate phrasing. "The Morthan Solidarity is built on treachery. Lying is a martial art. It is a fact of life. It is the means to the end. It is the necessary part of manipulation. To you, lying is only a hobby. To the Morthan, it is a way of life. Humans are considered cripples—because you *trust*. In the Morthan language, the word for trust means 'the condition necessary for betrayal.' " He added, "What I am saying to you is insufficient to convey the danger. That ship is coming from Morthan space. It is a trap."

"But it's one of ours," Korie said.

"No. It's one of *theirs* now. Count on it."

Hardesty looked thoughtfully to Korie. "Now, you know why I want a Morthan on the Bridge. It helps to have someone who thinks like the enemy."

"But we can't just—" Korie stopped himself. "There are procedures—" He looked to Brik, to Hardesty. "The book says—I mean, we *have* to go into that ship, because we *have* to know. The Alliance has to know—it's the whole mission! We have to ascertain the situation before we act."

Hardesty agreed. "Yes. That's what the book says."

"Sir—? You can't break procedure—"

Hardesty glared at him. "Yes, I can. It's an option. Breaking procedure is *always* an option."

"But there's no justification for putting a fish into her—not yet. Not unless you have more confidence in one of Brik's hunches than in your own orders. Captain, we don't know what the situation is over there—maybe they've locked down for reasons of their own."

"Don't assume anything, Commander. Especially do not make assumptions about my decisions." He frowned thoughtfully as he considered the image of the *Burke* on the forward viewer. "All right. We'll send a team in."

Korie sighed, relieved.

Brik was less sanguine. "From a human perspective, yes, that's the correct action. From a Morthan perspective—" He shrugged unhappily, as if he couldn't think of a polite way to say what he had to say. Finally, he just blurted it. "If I don't have the chance to tell you later, it has been a privilege to serve with you, sirs. Both of you."

Hardesty looked dryly across to Korie. "Perhaps you should lead the team."

"Sir?" Korie looked surprised. "That's Mr. Brik's responsibility."

"I know that," said the captain. "But you're more expendable."

"Uh . . . right." Korie didn't know if the captain was joking or not. Innocently, he asked, "Am I allowed to take a weapon?"

"That," said Hardesty, "is entirely *your* decision."

The Burke

The tiny point of light on the screen began to resolve. It expanded and became a starship, silent and still.

On the Bridge, the mood became apprehensive and uncertain.

"Fifteen minutes till contact," said Hodel.

"Still no reply," reported Tor.

Korie sighed loudly. "I know what that means. I guess I'd better join the boarding party now." He looked across to Hardesty. "I'm returning your command to you, sir."

"Acknowledged," Hardesty said.

Korie hesitated, halfway toward the forward exit. "Don't you want to wish me luck?"

"If you follow the book, you won't need it—and if you run into a situation where you have to invent, you'll need more than luck."

"Right," said Korie. "I should have known. Thank you, sir." He stepped down and out the exit into the forward keel.

The forward airlock and the ancillary dressing bay were the farthest points forward in the vessel. Here, the members of the security team were dressing for their mission. There were lockers, starsuits, helmets, closets, racks of gear, weapons, communicators, rechargers, life-support modules, battle-armor, and a variety of good-luck charms, tokens, and religious icons.

Ten crewmembers, including Brik, were just going through their final checks. Korie also recognized Armstrong, Bach, Nakahari, and Quilla Zeta.

Their starsuits were very shiny, skintight body stockings. Each was a different color. Several had gaudy stripes. Korie neither approved nor disapproved of the fashion. Sometimes it was appropriate, sometimes not. Sometimes it didn't matter.

Korie opened his own locker and began pulling on his own suit. Brik came over and began assisting him, checking his helmet camera and weapons as he fitted them into place.

"Thanks," said Korie.

"You're the last one," said Brik. "Besides, it would not look good on my record if I failed to bring you back alive."

"You're coming with?"

"Despite my misgivings about the situation, I am still chief of security. It is still my responsibility."

"Then it doesn't really matter who leads the team, does it?"

"On the contrary. The leadership is the most important part of the job. It is always necessary to know where to fix the blame."

Korie frowned at Brik. Had the Morthan intended that as a joke or not? He couldn't tell. *Do Morthans joke?* Would it be impolite to ask? Korie suppressed the question. There were more important concerns on his mind.

Across the bay, Brian Armstrong was fitting a new power-pack into his rifle. He looked up to see Quilla Zeta smiling shyly at him. "Brian," she said. "I am still feeling wonderful. You are very 'wow' too."

Armstrong looked embarrassed and annoyed, both at the same time. *When was it going to stop?* But he faked a smile well enough to say, "Thanks. You're—uh—?"

Touching herself politely, "This is Zeta."

Armstrong gestured feebly. "Uh—right. Sure. Anytime." He looked up to notice Reynolds and Cappy grinning at him. Bach and Nakahari were also visibly amused, poking each other and giggling.

Bach called across to Armstrong. "Wow, huh?"

Armstrong sighed. "All right. Knock it off. The jokes are getting old."

Korie stepped to the center of the bay then; he was listening to something on his headset. He was carrying his helmet under one arm. He held up a hand for their attention and they fell instantly quiet. As soon as the voice in his ear stopped whispering, he spoke aloud. "All right, it's a go. We've scanned the *Burke*. The readings are inconclusive. She could be dead. Maybe not. HARLIE's not sure. What that means—" Korie glanced to Brik. "—is that *it could be a trap*. That ship came out of the Morthan sphere of influence. Trust nothing."

He turned to Brik, drawing him aside with a nod. He lowered his voice almost to a whisper. "I was going to ask if I could trust you. But now I see that's the wrong question. What do Morthans use *instead* of trust?"

"Mutual advantage," Brik replied quietly.

"I see . . ."

"Mr. Korie, you are a better officer than you know. And the captain has more respect for you than he has publicly expressed. It is to our mutual advantage that you should be aware of that."

Korie looked at Brik surprised, but the subject was closed. He shrugged and turned to the rest of the boarding team. "All right. Move 'em out." He locked his helmet on and followed the others into the cramped space of the forward airlock. The doors slid shut behind them.

On the Bridge, Hodel was watching his monitors closely. The *LS-1187* had swung around and was now carefully approaching the rear of the *Burke*. She would join her forward airlock to the *Burke*'s tail access dock.

Tor was routinely backchecking Hodel's guidance. As they approached the last go/no-go point, she said, "On the beam."

"That's how I read it too," said Hodel.

Hardesty was standing directly behind the both of them. He spoke in a soft ironic rumble. "Be gentle, Mr. Hodel. Be gentle."

"Aye, aye, sir." Hodel touched his controls. The mass-drivers glowed for an instant; the *LS-1187* slowed. Hodel glanced at the vectors on his console and touched his controls again. And then again. Carefully, he brought the ship up to the tail of the *Burke*, bringing her to a relative stop at the exact same time.

"Got it!" said Hodel, pleased with himself. He straightened in his chair, grinning.

Tor touched her controls. "Extending docking harness." A faint vibration could be felt through the floor. It came through the soles of their shoes and through the bottoms of their chairs. And then there was a hard *bang* and then a *thump* as the harness connected and clasped.

"I have acquisition."

"Confirmed."

The impact was more noticeable in the forward airlock. The men and women of the boarding party were shaken where they stood, but none of them lost their balance. Korie looked across at Brik. Brik's expression was unreadable. The rest of the team stood in relaxed readiness. Some of them were already in a half-crouch, their rifles held high.

Korie listened to his headset. "They're extending the docking tube now—"

The tube moved out from the nose of the *LS-1187*, sliding through the cylindrical framework of the docking harness. It touched the security ring around the *Burke*'s access port and locked softly in place. Korie moved to the front of the airlock and tapped the green panel at the base of the control board. The board flashed green. "We have a connect." He watched while the safety programs cycled through a long series of double-checks. "Power connect, good. Gravity, good. Air pressure, good. The mix is breathable. Uh-oh. Computer's down—no response. HARLIE, do you copy that?"

"Acknowledged, Mr. Korie."

"Bridge?"

"The mission is yours now," came Hardesty's soft reply.

"All right, I think we're good. We're not going to need the docking tube. Let's close it up." Korie touched a control on the panel.

Outside, the docking harness began to retract slowly, pulling the two ships closer and closer together—until their airlock hatches connected inside the accordion envelope of the docking tube and became one functional unit.

Korie hit the control panel and ordered up another series of safety checks.

"Bridge? What do you read?"

"Same thing you do. The *Burke*'s running on standby. No internal monitoring available. No network running. No log access. But she's holding air and temperature, her fans appear to be running. We're not reading any life signs, but the environment is viable. It's a shirt-sleeve day in there."

"Did you send a query? Did you get an ID signal?"

"Yes and no," said Hodel.

"Damn," said Korie. He glanced back at Brik, but resisted the temptation to say what he was thinking. "All right," he sighed. "Blow the door." He took a step back, then another—

The lock doors popped open with a *whoosh* of air that nearly knocked Korie back into the man behind him. It was Armstrong, who caught him easily under the arms and pushed him back up onto his feet. "Not quite as perfect a match as we thought—" said Korie and threw himself forward.

The mission team poured through the airlock and into the *Burke* like a squad of combat-ready marines. They moved quickly through the other starship's darkened shuttle bay, leapfrogging forward with weapons ready. The *Burke*'s cargo dock and loading bays were almost identical to those of the *LS-1187*, except that the *Burke* was strung with thicker cables and ducting. Korie wondered if that had something to do with the high-cycle fluctuators.

"We're in—" said Korie. "She's empty. No signs of battle. No other damage. We're moving forward." He pointed to Armstrong and Nakahari, directed them toward a console. "Cover that." Several of the other mission team members were already moving out across the floor, checking all the entrances to the bay. Two of them eased down the ladder to the *Burke*'s keel.

Nakahari slipped into the chair before the console; it was dead, but he was prepared for that. He plugged his portable terminal into the monitor socket and it lit up immediately. Armstrong took up a position close by, covering Nakahari's back.

"All systems green," the crewman reported. "HARLIE?"

"Downloading now," HARLIE confirmed.

"You two stay here," Korie said to them. "Guard the access. Blow it if you have to. Nothing goes back. Not yet."

Armstrong nodded. "Yes, sir." Behind Korie's back, he and Nakahari exchanged nervous glances.

There were two passages forward from the shuttle bay, one port, one starboard.

Korie motioned Brik and Bach toward the starboard corridor. He and Quilla Zeta moved toward the port passage.

The corridor was dark and empty. Only scattered work lights glowed dully. Korie activated the targeting scanner in his rifle and glanced quickly at the readouts. Nothing out of the ordinary. He pushed forward. Quilla Zeta followed quietly.

They entered the upper deck of the engine room only a few steps behind Brik and Bach. Korie glanced across at them. Brik glowered back, shaking his head. Nothing on the starboard side either.

The *Burke*'s engine room felt eerily familiar. They could have been aboard their own ship—except for the three oversized fluctuator housings that projected out of the singularity cage. Korie eyed them enviously. He circled around the deck until he came to a ladder.

Brik and Bach had echoed his movements on the opposite side. Now Korie gestured, pointing downward toward the floor of the great dark chamber. Bach and Quilla Zeta waited while Korie and Brik descended. They covered the two men warily. Then they followed while Korie and Brik covered their descents.

"Brik, you come with me." To the two women, Korie said, "Count ten, then follow behind us at a distance." Korie tapped his headset. "Bridge?"

"Tracking is good. Confidence is ninety-nine. Everybody's clear. No problems. Go ahead."

The central keel was dark. Even the work lights were out here. The only illumination came from their helmet beams, fingers of light probing the gloom.

"If you want to have a bad feeling about this," Korie suggested to Brik, "now's the time."

"Morthans don't get bad feelings," rumbled Brik. *"We give them."*

"Uh, right—"

Korie pushed forward, silently reminding himself, *Never again. Don't tell jokes to a Morthan.*

They were only a few steps away from the operations bay when his radio beeped. HARLIE spoke softly into his ear. "Mr. Korie. The *Burke*'s log is blank."

"What? Say again?" Korie put a hand on the ladder next to him. It led up into the ship's computer bay.

"There's nothing to download. *It's been wiped.*"

"That doesn't make sense, HARLIE. What about the ship's brain?"

HARLIE's words sounded almost *uncertain*—or maybe that was only Korie's imagination. "It's . . . not in the circuit."

Korie realized he was staring at Brik's face. He broke away suddenly and peered up the ladder. From here, he couldn't see anything but the dark ceiling of the bay.

"Stand by, HARLIE. We'll check it."

Korie nodded to Brik. Brik took a sour step back to cover Korie's quick ascent.

The computer bay was dark and it took a moment for Korie to realize what he was seeing. He swept his beam back and forth, around and across the tiny cabin. A cold chill crept up his spine and shuddered out through his limbs.

Something horrible had happened here—

Everywhere, the destruction was absolute. The *Burke*'s computer hadn't been simply dismantled—it had been ripped apart. There were great gaping holes in the walls. Wiring conduits hung limply. There were fractured modules, broken nodes, cracked boards, and shattered panels all over the floor. Korie's boots crunched across shards and splinters of glass and plastic and metal. The room was ankle-deep in techno-garbage.

It was the first *death* they had discovered aboard the *Burke*.

Korie didn't know what to say.

It was one thing to disconnect a brain. It was another matter entirely to dismantle one. The *Burke*'s brain wasn't just down. It was dead.

He wondered how HARLIE would take the news. Probably not well. Ships' brains considered themselves a tribe—or even a *family*.

Finally, he said, "The brain has been . . . taken apart. It doesn't look repairable. Sorry, HARLIE."

HARLIE did not respond. There really wasn't anything he could say anyway. Korie imagined that HARLIE was feeding his emotions— *did he really have emotions?*—into some other outlet, some file somewhere, perhaps, to be played back and dealt with later, probably only in the company of another brain.

Grimly, Korie climbed back down to the keel where Brik still waited for him. Korie shook his head grimly and nodded forward, toward the Bridge. Brik followed him silently. Bach and Quilla Zeta followed at a distance.

Korie stepped through the narrow operations bay—its consoles were all dark—and up onto the Ops deck of the *Burke*. It was as desolate and empty as the rest of the ship. Two of the stations were alive, but inactive. Brik stepped up onto the deck behind Korie.

There was a sound from the Bridge above them and they both turned at the same time, their weapons ready—

It was sitting in the captain's chair.

The Morthan Diplomatic Corps

It was grinning and picking its teeth. Korie couldn't think of it as a *him*. Not yet.

It was bigger than Brik, and darker-colored. It sprawled insolently in the captain's seat, glowing with a luminous feral quality. Its expression was the insolent sneer of amused superiority.

It was wearing armor and war-paint and enough jewelry and braid and ornamentation to make a Vegan gambler weep with envy.

It grinned and picked its teeth. It looked like a three-meter-tall psychotic Cheshire cat.

And it looked *happy* to see them.

Bach and Quilla Zeta stepped up onto the deck, turned and caught sight of what had stopped Korie and Brik so abruptly. They froze too, their weapons pointing.

The Morthan looked at them, its gaze sliding from one to the other, taking in their stances and their ready weaponry.

"Mr. Korie?" Hodel's voice. "Are you all right? Please confirm."

"Uh—we're fine. We've just caught the cat who ate the Canary Islands. That's all."

"Say again, please?"

"A member of the Morthan Diplomatic Corps," said Brik. "The single most elite class of killers in the Solidarity."

"You're trying to tell us this is bad news, aren't you?" said Bach.

"Oh, Mama—" said Zeta. "We really stepped into it this time."

"Belay that!" Korie looked up at the Morthan. "Who are you? And where's the crew of this vessel?"

The Morthan widened its feral grin. It parted its lips slightly—and *belched*. Loudly and deliberately.

Korie was appalled. Bach flinched. The Quilla narrowed her eyes. Only Brik understood. He nodded almost imperceptibly.

Without taking his eyes off his enemy, Brik said to Korie, "Morthan ambassadors are the most sophisticated assassins in the Solidarity. Many of them have specialized implants and augments to increase their physical and mental capabilities."

The Morthan looked down at the humans with disgust, but he focused his special contempt on Brik. It spoke then, a hissing stream of invective that sounded like a cat fight in a bottle. *"Didn't your fathers ever tell you not to play with your food?"*

Brik smiled right back. *"At least I know who my fathers were."*

"I will pick my teeth with the bones of your friends. You will howl alone on the bloody sand."

"What's he saying?" Korie asked.

"He's delighted to see us," Brik answered.

Korie gave Brik an incredulous look. *Was that a joke? From Brik?* Then he made a decision. "Secure it in the *Burke*'s brig." He turned away, forced himself to look around the rest of the Operations deck, as if to demonstrate that he wasn't mesmerized by the monster's presence. "Captain Hardesty?"

On the Bridge of the *LS-1187*, Captain Hardesty and the others were watching the reflected view of the mission team's helmet cameras. The large forward viewer showed the scene on the Bridge of the *Burke*.

"I'm on my way," Hardesty said.

"Recommend against that, sir," came back Korie's reply. "We're still locking down over here."

"Mr. Korie. I'll pretend I didn't hear that."

On the Bridge of the *Burke*, Korie showed Brik a sour expression. Brik said nothing.

Traps

It wasn't often that a liberty ship needed to activate its brig, but the skipper of the *Burke* had foreseen the possibility that it might be necessary to contain an infuriated Morthan—for its own protection, as well as for the protection of the crew.

Arranging appropriate accommodations for a Morthan assassin was one thing.

Getting the creature into them was another.

And yet . . .

It went willingly.

It looked at the heavy-duty weaponry arrayed against it, *yawned deliberately*, and practically led the way to the brig. The creature's manner disturbed Korie. It was almost as if it had chosen the brig as its personal accommodation; it definitely did not act as if it considered itself a prisoner.

There was something wrong here.

He looked to Brik for explanation, but Brik was as silent as the assassin. He did not speak until the monster was safely installed in the brig of the *Burke*.

The brig was a suspended energy cage installed in the ship's shuttle bay. It hung a meter off the floor and at least five meters from the nearest wall. It touched nothing. Inside the holding frame, it was visible as a shimmering cage of light. The air hummed and fizzed in the wall of brightness. The Morthan assassin stood on the only solid part of the cell, its circular floor, and glowered out at its captors.

All around the detainment field, technicians were installing robot cameras and weapons. The Morthan would never be unwatched or unguarded.

Dr. Molly Williger was standing in the basket of a portable lift, scanning the Morthan through the energy fields. Korie, Brik, and Hardesty stood and watched.

"They thought *that* was an ambassador?" Hardesty said dryly.

"They *trusted* the Morthans. Brik was right. It *was* a trap."

"Correction," said Brik. "It is *still* a trap."

Korie glanced up at Brik oddly, but Brik showed no inclination to explain. He shrugged and followed Hardesty closer to the detainment cell.

Hardesty looked up at the Morthan without fear. To Korie, the Morthan still looked *amused.*

"Under the Articles of the Covenant," said Hardesty, "you are entitled to and guaranteed certain protections for your person, your physical and mental well-being. In return for these protections, you must agree to abide by the Articles of the Covenant. Do you so agree? If you are not familiar with the Articles of the Covenant, a copy will be provided."

The Morthan chuckled deep in its throat. The sound was nasty and gave Korie an uneasy feeling. "I have no need of your covenant. Your protection and your guarantees are worthless to me." He glanced sideways at Brik and added, "You are *Yicka Mayza-lishta!*"*

Brik snorted. "You call that cursing? My grandmother can do better. And she was *human.*"

The assassin narrowed its eyes. "And you *brag* about it?"

Hardesty ignored the exchange. "You understand then, that you are forsaking all rights and all claims. You are no longer legally entitled to any protections of your person, your physical or mental well-being."

The assassin barely glanced at Hardesty. "Do your worst."

Williger finished her scan then and lowered the lift. She snorted contemptuously and looked up at the captain with a truly disgusted expression. "A thousand years of genetic engineering and this is what you get? A nine-foot snot?"

Hardesty turned away without answering. Korie remained where he was, studying the Morthan. Brik's words still haunted him. *It is still a trap.*

The Morthan snarled down at Williger, a sound like a panther scraping its claws on glass. "It is hard to believe that my people were *deliberately* evolved from *yours.*"

---

*Lawyer dung.

Williger barely glanced up. "How do you think I feel about it? My family still has its pride."

"Your family is still sitting in a tree somewhere, picking fleas off each other."

This time, Williger let her annoyance show. "Too bad they bred you for looks and not for manners. Now shut up and let me work or I'll bring up the proctoscope."

Abruptly, the Morthan shut up.

Korie grinned at the doctor. "So that's how to make a Morthan cooperate. I'll have to remember that."

The answer came from above. "Morthans do *not* cooperate with humans. Morthans *rule* humans."

Williger looked up from her clipboard to Korie. "It's got a big mouth."

It leered down at her. "The better to eat you with." The Morthan assassin grinned and bared its teeth. Korie noticed that Williger's diagnosis was absolutely correct. The monster had a *very* big mouth.

Williger was unfazed. "I just love it when you talk dirty," she smiled back. She switched off her scanner and stepped over to the captain. Korie followed.

Hardesty looked at her questioningly.

She shook her head. "Big mouth. Bad breath. I'll give you the rest later." She exited back toward the *LS-1187* to run the results of her scan through HARLIE.

Korie turned to study the Morthan once more. The creature—Korie still couldn't see it as a *him*—had turned away from them. It was studying the energy cage around it.

Could it—?

No. It couldn't.

At least, that was what Korie wanted to believe.

Hard Decisions

The Bridge of the *Burke* was coming back to life. The crew of the *LS-1187* moved with professional élan. Watching them, Korie had to admit that Hardesty had known what he was doing when he had ordered them to rebuild the *LS-1187*. The crew had brought the *Burke*'s sensory network back online quicker than Korie would have thought possible.

Unless—the Morthan had deliberately not damaged it . . . for reasons of its own.

Korie shoved the thought aside. It troubled him, but there was nothing he could do about it now. Not yet.

Tor was just seating herself at the *Burke*'s display table; the display was dark and had a thin layer of dust on its top surface. Leen and Hodel pulled up chairs, as well as one of the Quillas. Hardesty, Korie, and Brik joined them. Williger came in a moment later and took a place at the forward end of the table.

Hardesty looked to Korie first. "You first, Mr. Korie."

Korie looked at his notes—not because he needed too, but because it was reassuring to do so. He took a breath. "The *Burke* was outfitted with three ultra-high-cycle envelope fluctuators for this mission, giving her a state-of-the-art stardrive and making her nearly twice as fast as any ship the Morthan Solidarity can build. The assumption was that her enhanced stardrive would allow her to travel through Morthan space without fear of interception.

"She was sent into the Morthan sphere to pick up an ambassador supposedly carrying a new peace initiative. It is now clear that the alleged envoy was in fact a trained assassin, whose mission was to kill the crew and disable the *Burke*."

He concluded his comments and laid his clipboard down on the dead display table.

"And . . . ?" prompted Hardesty.

"It's obvious," Korie said. "It's the enhanced stardrive; that's what they want. The whole point of the phony peace initiative was to get an assassin onto this ship—*because they couldn't catch her any other way.*"

Hardesty looked at Korie, mildly impressed. "Yes. That's how I read it too." He glanced over at his security officer. "Your analysis of the situation was correct."

"There was nothing to analyze," Brik corrected his captain. "A Morthan is a treacherous liar. Whatever else is true about a Morthan is irrelevant."

Korie was honestly curious. "Does that apply to you too, Brik?" he asked.

"A Morthan can only reveal his true nature through his actions," Brik explained, then he added thoughtfully, "The assassin should not have allowed us to capture him so easily. There is more to this that we still have not yet realized."

Hardesty looked down to the end of the table. "Dr. Williger?"

"That thing in the brig is named Esker Cinnabar and it registers 132 on the Skotak Viability scale. Preliminary scan shows significant micro-biotechnical implants and augments bringing his Skotak rating up to 390. Or more." To Hodel's curious look, she clarified, "75 to 80 is normal for a human." Turning back to Hardesty, she continued, "This is one big ugly mother. Mean. Strong. Nasty. Don't get him angry."

"I'll remember that," Hardesty said.

Tor spoke up then. "Why did he have to dismantle the *Burke*'s brain?"

"I can answer that," said Brik. "The *Burke*'s brain would not have allowed the Morthan to take over the ship. It would have fought him; he knew it; therefore the brain had to be disabled. That was probably the *first* thing the assassin did."

"But without a brain, the *Burke* is helpless," Tor said. "He can't take her home. He can't do anything with her."

Hardesty smiled knowingly. "Mr. Korie? Have you figured that part out yet?"

"A Morthan heavy-duty battle-cruiser," Korie replied calmly. "She follows the *Burke* as fast as she can. She can't catch up, of course—not until the assassin disables the *Burke*. Then it's a simple matter of retrieval. Cinnabar tears up the brain, kills the crew, then sits and waits for the heavy cruiser to arrive. Unfortunately, we showed up first.

"Why didn't Cinnabar attack us? Probably, he didn't want to risk damage to the *Burke*. And that's why he surrendered peacefully. When the cruiser arrives, they'll capture both ships—at least, that's got to be his expectation. The Morthans install a new brain in here and . . . byebye *Burke*. Bye-bye Alliance."

Brik rumbled deep in his chest. It was a ruminative sound.

"Comment, Brik?"

"You are assuming that they did not expect the *Burke* to be meeting another ship. I'm certain that it was considered in their contingency planning. It would be in ours. That's why I said there is more to this than we have realized."

"You might be right—" Abruptly, Korie realized something. "If our intelligence is correct, the only ship they have in this area capable of that kind of operation is—the *Dragon Lord*."

"Oh, no—" groaned Hodel. "Not the *Dragon Lord* again."

Tor's reaction was more professional. She tapped at her clipboard for a moment. "My best projection is that the *Dragon Lord* would have to be at least two, maybe six days away."

"I make it two days, maximum," said Hardesty. "Mr. Leen—how long to bring the *Burke* back online?"

Leen shook his head sadly. "Without the brain, we can't run even the simplest Systems Analysis checks. It'll take us days to reassemble it—that's assuming we can." He shrugged. "I might be able to jury-rig a replacement from our stores—but I don't know that'd be any faster. We're better off going on manual." He shrugged again, this time even more disconsolately. "A week—and even that's a guess."

Korie shook his head. "No. We don't have the time. We're too close to the Morthan sphere."

Tor agreed with Korie. She knew what he was implying. "We'll have to scuttle her—"

"God, I hate to lose those high-cycle fluctuators . . ." Korie said, wistfully.

Hodel looked around the Bridge of the *Burke* with real disappointment. "We can't salvage anything?"

"Count on it," said Brik. "The Morthan has booby-trapped her."

"How do you know that?" asked Hodel. "I mean, okay—he's *probably* booby-trapped her, but—"

"Not *probably*," said Brik. "There is no room for chance in a Morthan scenario." He looked to Korie. "The fact that an Alliance ship might make contact with the *Burke* before the *Dragon Lord* has been allowed for. Therefore, there are parts of the trap that are aimed at us."

"Right," said Williger. "That's my question. If the *Burke* couldn't hold that monster, can we?"

"We have to," remarked Hardesty. "I don't like the alternative."

Korie was playing with an idea. He steepled his fingers in front of himself and said softly, "Y'know, we could—this is just an idea—strip those fluctuators off the *Burke* in . . . oh, less than eighteen hours. I can run one crew, Chief Leen can run the other. Hodel and Jonesy can handle the third." He looked around the table, meeting their eyes. They looked interested. "Look, if the *Dragon Lord* shows up, we'll have at least two or three minutes warning. That's enough time to blow the *Burke* and scramble, and we haven't lost anything; but otherwise—well, we still scuttle her, but this way we get to keep the high-cycles."

"I like it," said Tor. "Especially the part about keeping the super-stardrive."

"If I were the assassin," said Brik, "that's the *first* thing I'd booby-trap . . ."

"Obviously," said Korie. "So we break 'em down and run a full suite of integrity checks before we put 'em online, but at least we can pull the units out of their housings and transfer them."

Hardesty cleared his throat. They all fell silent. "Mr. Korie, there is an inaccurate assumption in your analysis. I'm not giving up the *Burke*." He added sharply, "And you shouldn't either. *You want a ship.* Let's bring this one home."

"Her integrity's been breached," said Korie. "We don't have the resources to decontaminate her."

Hardesty's expression was immobile. "Do you know how much a liberty ship costs the Alliance?"

"Is that the deciding factor? The cost? What's at stake here is more than one ship—"

"But if you could save that ship, would you?"

"It's not that simple, sir. It's a question of what's possible under the circumstances. Trying to save her is the third best option. The risk—"

Hardesty's tone was suddenly icy. "You're arguing for your limits, Mr. Korie. I thought we broke you of that bad habit."

Korie shut up. When the captain used that tone, the argument was already lost. He sighed. "Yes, sir. You're right. I would like to save that ship—if we could. That I have expressed my doubts is part of my responsibility as your exec to advise you to the best of my ability."

"Your advice has been noted," said the captain. "Now, let's go to work." He looked around the table at his officers. "We are going to save the *Burke*. It is important for this ship and this crew to come home with a victory. Saving the *Burke* will be a good start.

"Chief, build us a brain. It doesn't have to be brilliant. Mr. Brik, you look for booby-traps. Detox this vessel." To Tor and Hodel, he said, "We'll stay at Condition Red. Run a twelve-hour clock. Hold at ninety seconds from stardrive injection. We sight anything coming at us in hyperspace, we scramble—and the *Burke* self-destructs. That means nobody gets lazy. If the alarm sounds, you'll have thirty seconds to get off the *Burke*. Beyond that, you're a footnote in the log." He turned to Korie. "Pick a crew of twelve. You'll bring the *Burke* home. First thing, though, you'll strip the fluctuators off—no matter what else, *I want them*. All right," he concluded, "That's it. Any questions?"

There were none.

"Good. Thank you. Go to work." Hardesty pushed his chair back from the table, rose crisply, and exited from the Bridge of the *Burke*.

Hodel groaned first. "Oh god—why do we always get the hard ones? We *are* jinxed." He looked up at the ceiling. "Whatever it was, Ghu—I'm sorry!"

Tor ignored the performance. She was already speaking to her headset. "HARLIE, we'll need critical path schedules—"

HARLIE was way ahead of her. He was always ahead of everybody. "I'm posting them now."

Korie looked up to Brik, but the Morthan was emotionless. He swiveled around and stared at the Bridge where the assassin had first been found.

Is it possible that Hardesty has made a very bad decision? Or is there something that I'm still missing?

High-cycle Fluctuators

The two starships floated like lovers, linked together in the brittle paradigm of their rendezvous. They drifted in dreamtime, alone against the deep abyss of distance.

Inside the *Burke,* high within her engine room, Korie and Haddad sweated over the difficult job of prying loose the fluctuator casing. They stood on the catwalk, working on the highest of the *Burke*'s three units. It was a large torpedo-shaped structure, braced and reinforced within a shining tubular frame. Below them, other crewmembers worked just as determinedly to remove the other two units without damaging them.

Haddad levered himself up inside the flanged part of the cylinder while Korie waited impatiently. After a moment, the sound of muffled cursing came ricocheting out of the cylinder. "—Fang-dang, filthy, pork-eating, cretin-loving, drunken, godforsaken, vermin-ridden, water-wasting, scrofulous, yellow-dog, leprous, swine-hearted infidel—"

"Easy, Haddad," said Korie. "You don't have to insult it. Those things are sensitive instruments."

Silence. And then, in a different, more professional tone, "Got it." Haddad pried himself out of the cylinder. "Sorry for the cursing, sir."

"No problem. It was very educational."

Haddad grinned and wiped his forehead with a cloth. "It's out of the circuit now. The bypass is showing green. We can pull it."

They began to unclamp the fluctuator from its housing. Using a block and tackle, they lowered it gently to the catwalk, where Armstrong was waiting to secure it to a cart.

"Easy."

"I got it."

Korie waited until he was sure the unit was safe on the cart, then he turned to Haddad. "You go down and help them with the bypass on number two, Ayoub. Armstrong can help me with this."

"Right."

Korie took the rear of the cart, Armstrong positioned himself at the front, and they began to move the heavy unit slowly along the catwalk toward the aft corridor. "The port one, I think," said Korie.

Armstrong glanced behind himself and nodded.

As they entered the corridor, Jonesy came barreling past them at a run, carrying computer components. He almost collided with Armstrong, but at the last moment turned himself sideways, raised his gear over their heads, bent with the shape of the wall, and darted easily past them.

"Easy, Jonesy. We don't have time for accidents."

"No, sir. I mean, yes sir. No time to stop. Excuse me, sir." He hurried on, leaving Korie and Armstrong grinning in his wake.

To get to the rear access, they had to pass through the shuttle bay. Esker Cinnabar glowered at them from his cage. His lips were curled back in a perpetual sneer, exposing fangs as long as Korie's wrist.

Armstrong shuddered. "Are we feeding him enough?"

"I hope so," Korie said. "But it's the between-meal snacking we have to worry about." Armstrong looked stricken. Korie waved a hand in front of his face to attract his attention. "Hey—Armstrong! Don't let him get to you. It's all psychological warfare."

"I know, but—" Armstrong lowered his voice. "I see all those energy screens and beamers and robot sentries, I see the guards around him and it still doesn't reassure me. You saw what he did to the *Burke*."

Korie nodded. "I saw."

Hardesty was at the airlock console. He looked up approvingly as they approached. "Oh, Korie. Have you picked out a crew yet?"

"Almost, sir. I'll have the list for you in an hour. I'm trying to keep your needs in mind as well as mine."

"Good. Bring the *Burke* home safely and maybe you'll get to keep her."

"I thought the admiral didn't like me."

Hardesty shook his head. "That hardly matters. There's a shortage of trained captains, good or otherwise."

Korie waited until he was out of Hardesty's hearing to voice the thought that had come to him. "That explains a lot."

"Beg pardon, sir?"

"Nothing." He glanced back over his shoulder—and saw that Cinnabar, the Morthan assassin, was staring across the bay directly at him.

And grinning. Korie looked away, disturbed. He pushed the thought out of his mind. It was psychological warfare. Cinnabar was trying to unnerve him—and succeeding.

They had to wait for a moment at the airlock door while Nakahari and Quilla Upsilon maneuvered a long unwieldy pipe through the access. The Quilla noticed Brian Armstrong waiting at the door and smiled meaningfully at him.

"Uh—hi," he said.

"This one is Upsilon," the Quilla identified herself. She was taller than the others. "And this one enjoyed it very much too."

"Oops . . . illon. Right." Armstrong flushed. He noticed that Korie was looking at him and was further discomfited.

Korie just smiled knowingly and shook his head, as if at some private joke. "They really caught you on that one. Don't worry about it. After a few years, hardly anyone will care. Push." He pointed toward the access.

"A few years?" Armstrong's eyes widened. "Really?" They maneuvered the cart through the door.

"It'll seem like it. Some of the kidding around here can be a little rough."

"How long does it usually go on, sir—?"

They had to lift the cart over the joint in the passage floor. Korie said, "It depends on how *good* you were. Quillas like to talk about their good times. The better you wer . . . well, you know." Korie grinned across at Armstrong.

They had to lift the cart's wheels across two more joints, and then they were in the forward access of the *LS-1187.*

"—at least that's what I've heard," Korie concluded.

"Really?"

"If you don't believe me, ask one of *them.*"

"Wow . . ." Armstrong's grin widened.

"Eh, you want to help me get this to the engine room first?"

"Oh, right. Sorry, sir."

"It's all right. I understand the distraction. But don't forget why we're here."

Hodel came hurrying up the corridor with a clipboard. "Oh, Mr. Korie—I'm glad I caught you. I need a G-2 authorization." He handed Korie the clipboard. Korie studied its screen in annoyance.

"You know," said Hodel, "we are not going to make it. This ship has an industrial-strength curse. The bad luck fairy doesn't like us."

Korie thumbprinted his authorization. He handed the clipboard back. "If that's true, Hodel, then why are we still alive?"

"Because, I think the universe is saving us for something *really* awful." Abruptly, he remembered something else. "Oh—one other thing. Um . . . I'd appreciate it if you'd consider me for your flight crew. For the *Burke*."

Korie raised his eyebrow. "But the *Burke*'s luck is even worse than ours."

"Uh-uh." Hodel spoke with certainty. "They only got eaten. *We've* got the *Dragon Lord* after us." He pushed past them and headed forward.

Korie looked back to Armstrong. "Come on, let's get this thing to the engine room."

They seized the cart with the fluctuator on it again and rolled it down the keel, pushing and pulling it past the sick bay, past the forward access to the Ops deck, past the aft access to the Ops deck, through the operations bay, past the vertical access to HARLIE, and finally to the machine shop below the engine room. Here, the keel widened into a low-ceilinged chamber. This was the starship's machine shop. The floor of the engine room above was removable to allow easy access between the drive units and the tools needed for heavy-duty maintenance work. Here, Chief Leen would break down the high-cycle fluctuators and run his security tests on them.

Korie and Armstrong slid the cart into position next to a makeshift work-bay. Leen slid down a ladder to help them secure the fluctuator. "Use the clamps," he pointed. "Here, like this. Hold it—okay. That damned assassin knew what he was doing," Leen said to Korie. "The *Burke*'s machine shop is junk. You better pray you don't have any problems once you get under way."

"You'd better pray," Korie corrected him. "I'm asking Hardesty for you—"

"Don't do me any favors. I've got enough work here. I have to break all three of these down and insulate them against resonance effects in case we have to scramble." He grunted as he secured the last clamp. "I'm not even thinking about installing them yet."

"Chief, I really need you—"

"You're right, you do," Leen admitted grudgingly. He thought a moment. "I really hate to say it, but there isn't anyone else who could get that ship running. I'm not bragging, that's just the truth."

"And Reynolds can manage here," Korie prompted.

"Yeah. All right." Leen did not look happy.

Korie slapped him on the shoulder. "Thanks, Chief."

"Don't get all mushy. I'm not doing it for you."

"Well, thanks anyway—"

Leen's answer was lost in the sudden blare of the alarm klaxon.

"Mr. Korie?" HARLIE interrupted. "I'm picking up an alarm in the brig of the *Burke*." The screen on the workbench lit up to show—

At first, Korie couldn't recognize what he was seeing. It looked like war had broken out. HARLIE was showing him the view from the remote cameras.

Korie realized what was happening with a sudden rush of cold-fire terror. *The energy cage hadn't held him.*

The screen showed flashes of laser fire. Something exploded and lurched. Someone was screaming. Korie thought he saw a crewman being hurled across the shuttlecraft bay. There was a brief glimpse of the assassin—and then suddenly, the screen was dead.

HARLIE reported calmly, "The Morthan Cinnabar has escaped."

"Where's the captain?"

"He's on the *Burke*."

"Lock down everything!"

"Already in progress."

Korie didn't hear it. He was already pounding toward the forward access. Armstrong charged along behind him.

The other members of the ship's security team were on the way too. They slid down ladders or fell out of doorways or hurtled down the keel after Korie or ahead of him, pulling on vests, grabbing weapons and security helmets, shouting and cursing. The alarm continued to bleat under everything.

The access door was already sealed. Two security guards in heavy armor were in kneeling position before it, one on each side. Their rifles were pointed unwaveringly at the door. Korie grabbed a security harness from a Quilla, pulled it on over his head, and then the armor after it—and then the helmet. Somebody shoved a weapon into his arm. He checked its charge, armed it, and unlocked the safety. He glanced around quickly to see who else was there—Reynolds, Armstrong, Nakahari, half the engine room crew, and two Quillas. He pointed them into position.

And then he was ready—

"All right," Korie said angrily. "No more Mr. Nice Guy. *Set weapons to kill.*" To HARLIE, "Okay. Open the door—"

There was a whoosh and the airlock doors began to slide open.

The Shuttle Bay

Korie and the security team burst through the access and out into the shuttle bay of the *Burke* like a horde of hell-spawned furies.

The shuttle bay was a smoking nightmare. The energy cage was crumpled in a heap against one wall. It still crackled and flashed; sparks skittered across the floor. Smoldering scorch marks scored the walls. Puddles of blood streaked the floor. The robot cameras had been shattered; the sentries lay in pieces; the broken rifles were burning and sputtering.

Korie pointed half his team toward the starboard corridor; he led the other team into the portside passage.

Only moments before, he and Armstrong had wheeled a high-cycle fluctuator along this very way. Korie and his team poured swiftly through the corridor and into the *Burke*'s engine room.

"Oh my God."

The shuttle bay had been a warm-up for this. The only things in the engine room not destroyed were the two remaining high-cycle fluctuators. Korie slid down a pole to the floor of the engine room; the rest of his team followed, either down the poles or the ladders.

Haddad lay on the floor, his throat ripped open. The bodies of the others who had been working here were hung on the singularity framework like so many sides of beef. The engine room looked like an abattoir.

Korie and his team moved into the room, weapons held high and ready. They moved past the bodies quickly. Three men and one woman, all dead—and still dripping. Korie's first impulse was to say, "Take them down from there." But he stifled it, unsaid. There wasn't time. Not yet. Maybe later.

"This could have been us," Armstrong started babbling. "If we hadn't carried the fluctuator out—"

"Shut up, Armstrong!" Korie's bellow startled even himself.

Abruptly, the klaxon stopped. Korie was staring at Haddad's strangled expression. He wanted to say something; he wanted to apologize— a sound caught his attention; something was moving forward. He swung his weapon around—

Brik and Bach burst into the engine room from the forward keel, fanning their weapons before them. The two security teams stared at each other. The sense of horror leapt outward from the space between them. *Where's the Morthan?*

Korie couldn't help but wonder—is this how it started on the *Burke*?

"He's not forward?"

Brik shook his head. He glanced around. "He got this far."

"You didn't see him?" Bach asked.

Both Korie and Brik gave her the same look. *Don't be silly.*

"Sorry," said Bach, realizing. The question *was* stupid.

Korie pointed to an access hatch in the wall. "Inner hull?" he asked Brik.

Brik nodded. "It's the only way—" He was already pulling the hatch open. He dropped through it into the dark space beyond. Reluctantly, Korie followed.

The space beyond the wall was dark and shadowy. It was as unfinished and spooky as the inner hull of the *LS-1187*. Korie and Brik both switched on their helmet lights and peered around grimly.

Everything here was beams and cables and stanchions. It was more than uninviting. It was suicidal.

"HARLIE," Korie asked. "Have you got a lock on the captain yet?"

"No, Mr. Korie."

Korie took a hesitant step forward into the darkness. He frowned. He was sure he could hear the Morthan assassin breathing in the gloom. He was sure they were being watched. He glanced sideways at Brik. "You feel it too?"

Brik grunted.

"Why doesn't he attack?"

"Because it's not part of the trap."

"I don't like this," Korie said. "Too much opportunity for disaster."

Brik agreed. Korie pulled himself up out of the inner hull, back into the light of the engine room. Brik followed.

Bach was arguing with Armstrong. "—I want to know how he got out of the cage!"

"Ease up," Korie interrupted her with a gentle tap on the shoulder. "We'll worry about that later."

Nakahari reported, "Mr. Korie, S.A. says the *Burke*'s totally locked down now."

Brik responded to that. His skepticism was obvious. "No. The assassin had too much time to reprogram the Systems Analysis Network. Don't trust it."

"Brik's right," Korie said. "This whole thing's a trap—" He gave the looming Morthan a grudging look of acceptance, and then added, "—and I'm not getting sucked into it any deeper. Evacuate the *Burke*. Now. Everybody off!" He started waving them back with crisp military gestures. The team fell back in a guarded withdrawal, their weapons covering every step.

"HARLIE," Korie ordered, "sound the evacuation. Do it now."

Harder Decisions

The alarm rang through the *Burke*, clanging and banging. The crew-members of the *LS-1187* still aboard her came running for the airlock access. They popped out of cabins and utility tubes and everywhere else they had been hiding and pounded along the catwalks and the keel toward their only escape. Korie hurried them onward, shouting as they passed, "Off! Everybody off!"

He and Brik were the last two to exit. They paused at the aft access, their weapons covering the ruined shuttle bay. "HARLIE? Is everybody out?"

"I show no active monitors."

"Where's the Captain?"

"His monitor is no longer working, Mr. Korie. I have begun a scan."

Korie said a word.

"Say again, please?" HARLIE asked.

"Never mind."

"If you said what I thought you said, it is anatomically impossible for most human beings—"

Korie stepped through the access, Brik backed through after him. "Never mind, HARLIE. Seal it off."

The doors whooshed shut.

Korie looked around. The rest of the impromptu rescue team were standing and waiting for his next orders. He shook his head and pushed through them. Brik followed.

They headed down the keel and climbed up onto the Operations deck where Tor and Hodel were just putting a schematic display up on the holotable. Leen was there too.

"Casualties?" Korie asked.

HARLIE responded instantly. "Security squads A and B. Stardrive engineers Haddad, Jorgensen, and Blake. Also Wesley."

"Damn. Have you located the captain?

"Sorry, sir."

Korie stepped forward and leaned on the holotable. He took a moment to catch his breath, then looked up. Every officer on the Ops deck and Bridge was looking at him, waiting for his orders. "Show me your scan of the *Burke*. Where's the captain?" He peered at the glowing display, frowning. Two transparent starships floated in the air over the table, their walls and decks were clearly outlined, but that was all.

"I'm sorry, Mr. Korie—I show no life readings at all."

"Not even the assassin?" asked Brik.

"It appears that the assassin has somehow altered his metabolism beyond the ability of our sensors."

"And the captain?" asked Korie.

"The captain's metabolism could not be safely altered."

Korie nodded to himself. He looked up and said, "Doctor to the Bridge, please." To HARLIE, "Okay. Show me what the monitors recorded. What happened?" He turned forward to look at the main viewer.

"Here—" said HARLIE, narrating, explaining. "You can see that the Morthan assassin was never seriously restrained by the energy cage. He steps through it as easily as a biofilter. I'll show you all the angles. Here's the slow motion—"

"He was *faking*," said Tor.

"He was waiting for the right moment," corrected Brik.

Korie guessed it immediately. "He saw us taking the fluctuators off the *Burke*. He had to stop it."

"Here—" HARLIE continued. "This is where he attacked the security squads. Notice that even while he is at the center of their fire, he does not seem to be affected. Here's the slow-motion. Notice how fast he's moving—"

"Optical nervous system, augmented musculature," said Korie.

"He must have some kind of internal shielding," said Tor. "He doesn't even flinch. They're not even burning him."

Brik said, "I realize that this is upsetting to you—but it is important that you recognize the efficiency of the assassin's killing pattern. There is no wasted movement at all."

Tor gasped involuntarily and turned away. The sound of the security man's back cracking was loud across the Bridge.

The screen showed the Morthan *flowing* like liquid fire—he grabbed and killed, cracked and threw, leapt and kicked and clawed.

He was a blur that flashed from point to point and left a trail of broken, bleeding bodies. Even slowed down, the sense of incredible speed was overwhelming. The Morthan grabbed the captain like a sack of potatoes and—

"Hold it!" said Korie. "Run that again."

HARLIE slowed the images down. Hardesty was bringing his weapon up, he was firing, the beam plunged through the Morthan's belly, the Morthan didn't feel it, he surged inexorably forward, grabbing the gun and splintering it, the fuel cells flashed and exploded around him, the captain flung his arms up, the Morthan grabbed him—*and didn't kill him*. He caught the captain under one arm and scooped him off his feet—

Korie felt impaled by the dilemma. He still didn't have *proof*. The captain might still be alive.

The screen showed the Morthan sweeping the shuttle bay with ruthless efficiency, grabbing cameras off the wall and shattering them. The image switched from one point of view to the next, then it finally went blank.

Without being asked, HARLIE began the series again.

Korie looked around, noticed Williger had come in while they were staring horrified at the screen. He acknowledged her with a nod. "You saw?"

She grunted. Her expression was wrinkled and sour.

Korie turned to Brik. "Under Article Thirteen, I have to assume that the Captain is dead or beyond rescue. Do you concur?" Even before he finished the question, Tor and the others were looking up sharply.

Brik knew what he was being asked. He spoke with quiet candor. "I concur."

"Thank you." Korie turned to his astrogator. "Commander Tor?"

"Aren't you being a little hasty? You don't know for sure."

Korie nodded toward the screen. The Morthan was slashing a crewman into a bloody pulp. "Look at the pictures."

"No," said Tor, pointing. "You look. I didn't see the captain's death in that—and neither did you. Why don't you put a couple of probes into the *Burke* and search by remote? Let's be sure—"

"I wish I could," Korie replied. "But we don't have the time. And we'd never get better than fifty percent confidence. I need your statement now."

Tor stepped in close to Korie and lowered her voice so that no one else could hear what she said. "I know you want your own ship, but aren't you being just a little too eager to write off Captain Hardesty?"

Korie ignored it. "I need a declarative sentence, Commander."

She shook her head. "I can't support *this*."

"That's your privilege. Thank you." Korie turned away. "Dr. Williger—?"

Williger looked troubled and she sounded reluctant. "I don't like it either, but I have to vote with the evidence."

Tor followed Korie toward the Bridge. "I still think you're being too hasty."

"I appreciate your honesty," Korie said. He paused at the steps. "But I have to do this by the book *because that's the way the captain wants it*." He glanced around. "Is there anyone else who disagrees?"

Korie looked from face to face, searching for dissent, hoping someone would come up with a valid reason why he shouldn't take the next ineradicable step. Jonesy? Leen? Goldberg? Brik? Hodel? Williger?

No. None of them.

Korie took a breath. "HARLIE, log it. Under the provisions of Article Thirteen, I'm assuming command of the *LS-1187* on the presumption that Captain Richard Hardesty is dead . . . or beyond our ability to rescue."

HARLIE's tone was as calm as ever. "Yes, Mr. Korie. It is so logged."

Tor spoke first. Her tone was exquisitely formal. "Your orders, *sir?*"

Korie ignored the implied rebuke. "We're going to complete our mission. I want the fluctuators off the *Burke* and I don't want to play hide-and-eat with a Morthan assassin. HARLIE, open the *Burke* to space. Do it now."

"Acknowledged. I am opening the *Burke* to space . . ."

Korie tried not to show his reaction, but the reality of it made him flinch anyway. He turned back to the holographic display and watched as the various hatches on the schematic *Burke* began to open. The forward viewer flashed to show what the external cameras were able to see.

HARLIE began shifting the view to show the interior of the *Burke*'s corridors as well. A great wind was sweeping through her corridors. Debris hurtled and blew and ricocheted off the walls. Things crashed and tumbled. A contorted body flopped over—

The Bridge crew watched in silence. Korie spoke bitterly. "That should let the air out of our assassin."

"Maybe not," said Williger.

They all turned to look at her sharply.

Chief Medical Officer Molly Williger stepped to the holographic display and slid a memory card into a reader. A bioschematic of the Morthan assassin flickered into being, replacing the schematic of the two linked starships. "He's all augments," said Williger. "He's got a lightspeed nervous system, multiprocessing lobes in his brain, a hardened skeleton, enhanced musculature, extra hearts, internal shielding, you name it—even the ability to shut down the organic parts of his body for short periods of time." She hesitated for a heartbeat. "And the bad news is that he might be able to function without air, food, and water for sustained periods."

Korie looked to Brik. "Is all this normal for an assassin?"

Brik nodded. "For a beginner."

"Stop trying to cheer me up," Korie muttered. To Williger, he said, "Okay. How long can that son of a bitch hold his breath?"

"Best guess? Fifteen minutes."

Korie made a decision. "We'll wait an hour."

"We don't have an hour," said Tor. "Remember the *Dragon Lord*?"

"I remember the *Dragon Lord*," Korie snapped back. "Better than you. I'll show you the scars." He repeated his order. "We'll wait an hour."

Coffee

The *Burke* was cold and silent. Despite the cold glare of her lights, or maybe because of it, she looked desolate. Nothing moved aboard her. Her cameras showed nothing. HARLIE's scans continued to come up empty.

After a while, Korie grew bored with the endless cycling of empty images. He grabbed a cup of coffee and stalked off the Bridge. He thought about going to the captain's cabin, but couldn't bring himself to do that. Not yet. It didn't feel right. It wouldn't be his *until*—until the admiral gave it to him.

He stopped and leaned against the wall of the starboard corridor, slumping and staring at nothing in particular. The gray surface of the foamboard construction had a dull sheen.

The argument raged inside his head. *I didn't have any choice. The decision had to be made. I only did what Hardesty would have done if he had been here. I followed the book.* But all of that was meaningless against the accusing facts. *We didn't see him die. We didn't know for sure that he was dead. We could have killed him when we evacuated the air out of the* Burke!

But that was only the surface of the turmoil, the immediate details. Floating below that was the more disturbing pain. *It's Captain Lowell all over again. A captain is supposed to depend on his executive officer— why can't I be that kind of exec? Why can't I protect my commander? Am I so stupid and clumsy that I can't safeguard my leader? But how do you keep a captain from getting killed if he insists on making the wrong decisions? What is it about leadership that others can see and I can't? Am I so wrapped up in my own ego that I can't tell what's right? What kind of an officer am I?*

Korie noticed that his shoes were bloody, probably from one of the puddles that he'd had to step through. He wondered whose blood it was. He wondered if he should try to clean these shoes or if he'd be better off tossing them into the singularity. That was how all the garbage was disposed of on a starship; it was fed to the pinpoint black hole in the engine room. It was fun to watch too—the way things just crumpled up and sucked away into nothingness, usually with a flash and a bang.

When he looked up again, Brik was standing before him, waiting patiently.

"What do you want?" he said. His tone was not friendly.

"I thought that you might want . . . some advice." Brik hesitated, then added, "Captain Hardesty appreciated my thoughts, particularly in strategic situations. I thought you might wish the same access."

"Mm," said Korie. He stared into his half-empty coffee mug, swirling it around as he did so. He couldn't think of anything to ask. He couldn't think of anything at all right now. He'd boiled it down to the simplest of all tracks. It was very linear: *wait an hour, go back into the* Burke, *finish the job, get the fluctuators, bring both ships home*—and then he frowned. Who would crew the *Burke* now?

Tor. Yes. Tor could do it. That might work.

"No," said Brik. "Don't even think it. Cinnabar has been six jumps ahead of us since the moment we sighted the *Burke*. Here are your options. One: back off, torpedo that ship, and head for home now. And hope that Cinnabar didn't find a way off the *Burke* and onto the *LS-1187*. That's the safest option, and nobody will fault you for taking it. We've already lost too many good crewmembers. Two: go back into the *Burke*, take the other two fluctuators, then scuttle her and head for home. *If* there's time. There probably isn't—which is why option one is still the safest. Three: Try to bring the *Burke* up and running and bring her home—except you won't get her two meters. She's booby-trapped. Count on it. Cinnabar has not been sitting on his thumbs. He's been thinking up scenarios and counter-responses since before we rendezvoused. We arrived in this game too late to have a chance—"

"Four," said Korie, taking Brik's count away from him. "We stay linked with the *Burke* and bring her home inside our own envelope."

"Tow her?" Brik shook his head. "Too risky. Chief Leen will have *shpilkies*."

"*Shpilkies?*" Korie asked.

"A litter of carnivorous Morthan kittens."

"Oh," Korie blinked.

"The point is, we can't tow the *Burke*. We'll be too unstable—Chief

Leen will never be able to balance the bubble. The center of gravity won't be congruent with the center of the envelope. We'd shake and shudder like a drunken nightmare. We'll kill ourselves trying."

"And—" said Korie, "—you forgot to mention that our top speed will be limited to one-quarter normal. About one hundred and fifty lights, if we're lucky."

"I was just getting to that."

Korie looked up sharply. "You think he might still be alive?"

"The captain? No. The assassin? Count on it." Brik looked grim. "He had to know what your options were and how you'd react. He had to have planned for this. My best advice? Torpedo the *Burke* and let's get out of here."

Korie raised an eyebrow at Brik and allowed a cynical grin to spread across his face. "Without a fight? Are you sure you're really a Morthan?"

"Understand something, Mr. Korie," Brik said coldly. "Morthans consider fighting only one step above dishonor. The real victory is outwitting your opponent without having to bloody your sword. Only the stupid and clumsy carry battle scars. The skill is in victory without battle."

"But you're advising retreat."

"Humans call it a *strategic withdrawal*," Brik said. "It is not dishonorable to conserve your energies for situations where you have a better chance of winning."

"Frankly," said Korie, ruefully, "I'd much prefer rearranging the situation to our advantage."

"That sounds like a Morthan talking. Are you sure you're really human?"

"I have the battle scars to prove it," Korie said. He looked up at Brik. He looked up *and up* at Brik. Their eyes linked—and for a moment, Korie felt an eerie surge of emotion. *Partnership with a Morthan?* And then the moment flickered away. *God really is a practical joker!* Korie looked back into his coffee and said, "The thing that *really* annoys me about this whole situation is being played for a fool. I stepped right into it. I know it. He knows it. He knows I know it. I can't get it out of my head. The timing of the attack, everything—it wasn't random. He did it to delay us, to prevent us from removing the fluctuators from the *Burke*—to prevent us from escaping before the arrival of the *Dragon Lord*." Abruptly, he handed Brik his coffee cup. "Hold this."

Brik took it and stepped back as Korie suddenly screamed as loudly as he could—"*I HATE THE* DRAGON LORD!"—and whirled, curling his fist, swinging his whole arm around and punching it hard into the foamboard wall with a sound like a bowling ball hitting a slab of beef. The wall *crunched*. His fist sank wrist-deep into it.

Then, very calmly, Jonathan Thomas Korie pulled his fist out of the wall, turned back to Brik and retrieved his cup of coffee.

"I like these walls," he said. "There's something *satisfying* about punching them."

"It's the nice way they crunch," agreed Brik. "Feel better?"

Korie wiggled his hand in an "iffy" gesture. "It was nice to know what I was doing for a change. It was nice to have a focus." Abruptly, something crystallized for him. "Y'know what it is, Brik? I want revenge. What I really want, more than anything else in the galaxy is just one real chance to get even with that ship and the bastards who scourged Shaleen." And then he sighed and said, "I know, it's impossible. But I can dream, can't I?"

Brik didn't say anything.

Korie continued. "Actually, right now, I'd be satisfied if I could just take one good bite out of Esker Cinnabar. If I could just get one jump ahead of him instead of the other way around. Tell me there's a way."

"Only if you can learn to think like a Morthan." Brik's tone was cool. There was enough skepticism in the naked words. He continued, "Assume that they've gamed it out and always know what your next move is. Then you extrapolate their next move from that and allow for it. And the next three moves after that too. Then you go back to the beginning and try to figure out what you can do that they won't expect—and assume that they'll have figured that out too. And so on. That's what he's doing right now. What can you do that he can't know?"

"You're assuming he's alive," said Korie.

"Not only alive—but very possibly somewhere aboard this vessel," said Brik.

That thought stopped Korie cold. It was like an ice pick in his heart. He looked up at Brik, searching the other's face for some sign that he might have been joking. He wasn't.

"You think he could do it?"

"I can think of seven ways to get from the *Burke* into the *LS-1187* without HARLIE knowing. Cinnabar can probably think of seven more."

Korie sighed. "This is crazy. It's like some mad game—it's like playing chess with a dragon, isn't it?"

"An apt enough analogy," Brik agreed.

"All right. Let me walk this through from the beginning. Everything he did—letting us capture him, escaping, all the killing—he did all that on purpose. Why? Obviously, to delay us, to keep us from completing our task of stripping the fluctuators. But now that he's done it, he's played his trump card—or has he? Is there something else?"

Brik shook his head. He waited politely while Korie continued to think aloud.

"See, here's the thing. Now that we know what kind of a danger he is, we know that we have no choice but to scuttle the *Burke*. So what he did was force our hand. We couldn't possibly be stupid enough to keep trying to save the *Burke* while he's still alive. Suppose we did respond fast enough. Suppose we really did kill him—then he's failed. Or has he? At most, he's only cost us two or three hours. Maybe that was his purpose? Would a Morthan willingly sacrifice himself as part of a larger plan?"

Brik glanced down at Korie. His look said it all.

With a cold flash of fear, Korie realized the implication immediately. "Oh, shit. That means that the *Dragon Lord* has to be a lot closer than we thought. Close enough that the delay is crucial." Korie considered the possibility for a moment, then looked up to Brik's taciturn expression. There was only one possible conclusion. "You're right. We have to scuttle the *Burke* now. It's our best option, isn't it?"

Brik shook his head. "It is the best option not because it is a good one, but because it is the *least* bad one."

"Excuse me?"

"Keep thinking. You haven't seen the whole problem yet."

Korie frowned. *What am I missing?* He stopped himself abruptly, a new expression spreading across his face. "Wait a minute. You said he knows what we're thinking. Then he knows we're having this conversation too. Scuttling the *Burke* won't work either. He won't let us, will he?"

"He knows what our choices are, yes," Brik agreed. "The charges we placed on the *Burke* probably still show green on the Bridge monitors, but I doubt very much that they will respond to a detonation command. That's why I suggested a torpedo. If he's still alive, that will be his next immediate goal—to disable our torpedoes. In fact, he could be doing it right now." Brik added, "You might have had a chance if you had torpedoed the *Burke* immediately instead of evacuating her, but—" The Morthan shrugged. "—That would have meant sacrificing eighteen crewmembers. Humans do not do that sort of thing."

"No. Humans don't. You think that's a weakness, don't you?"

"I think it is a human thing. It is definitely *not* a Morthan thing."

"All right, all right. Drop it. Let's game out some alternatives. Let's leap ahead to the end. What's it going to look like when they win? They'll be in control of the *Burke*—and very likely, this ship too. And we'll be dead or prisoners or—"

"Lunch. We'll be lunch," corrected Brik.

"Okay, but before that. How will he take over this ship?"

"How did he take over the *Burke*?"

Korie shrugged. "He killed everybody."

"Then that will be what he does here—unless there is a compelling reason not to."

"I wish we could plant a few traps of our own."

"Can you think of a trap that a Morthan can't?"

"Can you?" grinned Korie.

Brik gave him a look.

"Sorry," said Korie. "I couldn't resist. What about nested traps? Decoys? Would that work?"

"Maybe. If they were clever enough."

"Okay. Help me here. If you were a Morthan—*and you are*—and you were planning to take over this vessel, how would you do it?"

"I'd kill everybody who wasn't essential to the running of the ship. I'd start with you. If I was in a bad mood, I'd torture you and make your death last a long time."

"Why would you let the others live?"

"I'm not stupid. I might have to bring this ship home. I couldn't do it alone."

"You mean, maybe the *Dragon Lord* isn't coming . . . ?"

"There is that possibility too. You are not the only one who thinks in terms of nested traps and decoys."

"So—" said Korie. "If I was thinking like a Morthan now—I should be planning both a defense against the *Dragon Lord* that might not really be coming, and a trap for a Morthan who might be already dead." Korie glanced at his wristband. "And I have less than twenty minutes to figure it out. Right?"

Brik nodded. "That is correct."

Korie considered the size of the problem. "Okay," he deadpanned. "What'll we do with the time left over?"

"You could pray," said Brik. He wasn't joking.

Korie scowled upward. "Sorry. I don't do that anymore. The price is too high."

Provisions

"All right, HARLIE—" Korie gave the order.

The hatches of the *Burke* slid easily shut and air began hissing back into her from her huge regeneration units.

Sound came back to her corridors first. Some of the debris began to flutter. On her Bridge, the consoles lit up again, flashing from red to yellow to green as the atmospheric pressure rose, and as the mix of gases slid toward normal.

In the forward access of the *LS-1187*, Korie and Brik and a heavily armored security team were waiting impatiently. They all wore helmets, cameras, security vests, and armor. Bach and Armstrong were carrying stun-grenades and rapid-fire launchers. Nakahari was carrying a case of equipment modules to install on the *Burke*.

Quilla Theta was double-checking Armstrong's security gear and the weapons pack on his back. "Be careful, Brian—please?" she asked.

"Uh—" Armstrong turned to look at her. "Theta, yes. I'll be careful. Count on it."

"Yes, please. We would like more 'wow.' All of us."

"I promise—I'll give it my personal attention. To each and every one of you." Armstrong looked past the Quilla to see Bach looking at him, eyebrow raised. "Well," he shrugged. "A man's gotta please his public, doesn't he?"

The Quilla thumped Brian on the back twice—her "all's-well" signal. Armstrong turned and gave a thumbs-up to Korie.

"Okay," said Korie. "Let's go."

The airlock door slid open—

The team stepped through cautiously. Armstrong and Bach led the way, followed by Korie and Brik. The shuttle bay looked dry and brittle.

The blood on the floor had turned to powder. Some of it had blown away. Some of it hung in the air, giving the chamber a dusty red quality and a vague, unsettling, salty odor.

Brik and Bach went through the starboard corridor toward the engine room and the Bridge. Korie and Armstrong took the aft side. Nakahari followed at a cautious distance.

The *Burke*'s engine room was no longer an abattoir. Now it was a chamber of horrors. The bodies hanging on the singularity framework had been mummified from their exposure to vacuum. Their tongues were swollen and black, protruding from their mouths like some kind of creatures trying to escape. The eyes of the crewmembers had burst. Their blood had boiled out their ears and their noses and spurted across themselves and the deck in front of them. Their organs had pushed out through their wounds—and then everything had hardened and shriveled in the merciless vacuum.

There was no mercy here.

After death, *desecration*.

Korie wanted to weep. It wasn't fair.

Instead, he bit his lip and pushed forward. He'd do his crying later. That was the way things always worked. He went down the ladder and into the forward keel toward the Bridge. Brik followed him grimly. Nakahari looked around, shuddered once, and went to the engine room's main console. He plugged in a portable terminal and began bringing the system back to life.

Korie stepped up through the Operations bay, onto the Operations deck—and froze.

He didn't know how he knew, but he knew he wasn't alone. He turned around—it seemed to take forever—and stared.

In the captain's chair—

—it was Hardesty.

Korie flinched. Brik came up beside him.

The captain was stuffed inside a large transparent plastic sack—an airtight transfer bag. Green mist floated around him.

"He's not dead," said Brik.

There was a medical monitor unit on the captain's chest. Its screen glowed. Even from the Ops deck, Korie could read the graphs.

The captain's eyes flickered open. They moved. They focused, but ever so slowly.

"Oh, no—" Korie moaned. He leapt up the stairs to the Bridge.

Hardesty's voice came to him as if from a great distance. Very faint and very feeble, the captain spoke. "Help . . . me . . ."

Korie couldn't help himself. He was simultaneously horrified and fascinated. The captain's skin had a hideous gray-green cast. He looked like a zombie.

"He's transmitting," Brik explained. "His body functions are suspended, but *his brain augment is still active*."

"What is it?" Korie couldn't tear his eyes away.

"Phullogine," Brik explained. "It's a very heavy, very inert gas. It's used for hibernation." And then he added, ominously, "As well as for preserving food."

Hardesty spoke again. The words wheezed out slowly and almost inaudibly. "The assassin . . ." And then he faded back into unconsciousness, his thought still incomplete.

"A trophy to take home," said Brik. "Or provisions."

"Oh God—no. This is hideous." Korie spoke to his headset. "We found the captain. Bridge of the *Burke*. Send a med team. Now!" And then, abruptly remembering their mission, he added, "And send the work crews in." He looked back to Brik. "Can we save him?"

"I don't know enough about it. Maybe Dr. Williger—but I doubt it." He turned away. Bach and Armstrong were just stepping up onto the Ops deck; they looked toward the captain with rising horror. Brik pushed them away. "Come with me. I want to find the assassin."

The three of them exited through the forward access, leaving Korie caught in the focus of the captain's yellow staring eyes.

Med Station

Molly Williger might have been angry. Korie couldn't tell. He'd never seen her when she hadn't been swearing. Korie was glad he didn't recognize most of the languages she used, although he suspected that some of her most elegant curses were composed in ancient Latin.

"—no way to treat a human body!" she was saying. "Why the hell do I spend so much time patching them up, if they're just going to go play tag with monsters—?!!"

Korie followed the med team carrying the captain's stretcher all the way back to the *LS-1187*, into the forward keel, halfway along it to the sick bay, through the anteroom and into the primary medical station—the one that also served as an operating room. He stood back against the far wall and watched as Williger, Fontana, and Stolchak quickly removed the captain from the body bag and hooked him up to the life-support systems. Stolchak, the new one, was particularly efficient, her hands moving expertly from point to point, installing monitors, inserting tubes, punching up programs, starting the blood-cleansing system, and having utensils ready for the doctor even before she asked for them.

Korie glanced up at the monitor board overhead. Some of the lines were almost flat. The captain's heartbeat was seriously depressed. His oxygen usage was near zero. The captain's eyes were shut and his pallor had worsened since they'd removed him from the bag.

His autolobe was still functioning though. In fact, the autonomic side of it was quietly advising Williger of the condition of the captain's organic functions in a soft silvery voice—until she grew annoyed and switched it off. "I know what I'm doing, dammit."

Korie wanted to ask, but he knew better than to interrupt Molly Williger while she worked.

"No motor functions at all," she said, not only for her staff, but for the medical autolog. "Heartbeat, respiration, EEG—all at hibernation levels. This one's going to make the textbooks. I've never seen phullogine used on a human before." She straightened up, took a step back, and studied the overhead monitors, squinting in concentration. She said a word that Korie was glad he didn't recognize.

"What about his mental condition?" Korie asked.

Williger shrugged. "He can communicate, but only slowly. I don't know if he's in pain or not."

"Can he command?"

Williger glared at him. "Do you want the center chair that bad?"

"Doctor—" Korie spoke carefully. "If Hardesty can command, he's the captain. If he can't, it's me. But it has to be one of us, and you're the only one qualified to determine if he's capable."

"His brain-augment is working fine," she admitted. "If there was nothing else here but his augment, I'd have to say he's mentally able. But you and I both know that the captain is more than his augment and there are larger questions that I can't answer yet. Like, how well is the augment integrating with the rest of his personality? I don't know. Can he balance? I don't know. How long will he be this way? I haven't the slightest idea. I can't be any clearer than that."

"I need a decision from you, Doctor. Even a wrong one."

And then Korie was sure—she *was* angry. She whirled on him, pushing him back against the wall. "Not *now*, dammit. Don't you understand? He can hear us!"

"Even better. I don't want to do this behind his back. We both know what kind of a captain he is."

"You don't get it, do you? Hardesty knew what was happening to him, *every minute*. He understood what Cinnabar was doing *and why*. The shock to his system is *still* happening. For most people—" Williger stopped herself in mid-sentence, grabbed Korie's arm and dragged him out through the anteroom and into the corridor and halfway down it. "Listen to me. For most people, dying is over quickly—for Hardesty, it could take months. Or even longer. And he could be conscious the entire time. How would you like to lie in bed feeling yourself die for a year or two?"

Korie opened his mouth to answer, then closed it again. He considered his response as he stared down into Williger's angry face, then he lowered his voice and said carefully, "When this is over, I will have the time to be horrified by the situation and by all of the difficult decisions that you and I are having to make. In the meantime, in case you hadn't noticed, we are at war and this ship needs a commanding officer. There are orders I need to give and I need them to be *legal*."

"You know the possible consequences to him—and to you—if I guess wrong? What if he's fully recovered in six hours? What if you've started some irrevocable course of action?"

"If he recovers, then declare him fit for command and I'll be glad to return the baton. I promise you, I'll try not to get us killed before that happens. Now then," he asked pointedly, "are you going to declare the captain incapable of command—or *not*?"

Williger's face hardened. At this moment, it was obvious that she didn't like Korie very much; but finally she nodded. "You're in command." She started to turn away, then turned back just far enough to to add, "Don't fuck it up."

"Thank you, Doctor," Korie said to her back.

"Don't mention it," she growled, walking away. "*Ever.*"

Korie touched his headset. "Brik?"

The Morthan's voice rumbled in his ear. "Yes?"

"Did you find the assassin?"

"No trace of him yet, sir. There are a lot of places he could have hidden."

"Well, we can always wait three days until the body starts to stink," Korie proposed.

"And what if it doesn't—"

"You're suggesting?"

"I hope you acted fast enough. But you might not have."

"Do you need more searchers?"

"They wouldn't know what to look for."

"Where are you now?"

"Inner hull. Forward quadrant."

"Stay there. I'm on my way."

The Forward Observatories

There were a few places on every ship where a person might find a real window. There were two forward observatories on the *Burke*, one on the upper hull back of the airlock, one on the lower hull. They were clear glass domes protruding from the ceramic hull.

Korie found Brik at the lower observatory. It was a wide circular well, framed by neutral gravitors. You flipped over and pointed yourself down into it. Once inside, you would be floating in a deep free-fall bubble and you could observe the stars around the ship. Usually, there wasn't much to see that couldn't be seen better on the big forward viewer on the Ops deck; the observatories were the only real windows in the hull of a liberty ship and although rarely used, they were still considered an essential part of the vessel.

Brik was shining his beam in and around the crawlspaces where the thin metal tubing butted up against the inside of the outer hull.

"Anything?"

Brik shook his head.

"And you don't expect to find anything either, do you?"

Brik grunted. After a moment, he lowered himself back down to the catwalk and said, "If I could figure it out, so could he."

"Mm," said Korie. Abruptly, he levered himself over the railing and floated down into the observatory. Brik followed. The two of them hung together, floating face to face under the bubble of stars.

"The last time I did this," said Korie, very softly, "my partner was much prettier than you."

"The last time I did this," replied Brik, "my partner was much less fragile."

"Touché." Korie smiled.

"Thank you." Brik lowered his voice to the barest of whispers. "I have not completed my search of the inner hull."

"I didn't expect you to. Did you put on a good show?"

"The best."

"Good. Do you think you've searched long enough to fool him into thinking he fooled us?"

"No, but we can't risk any more time."

"Unfortunately, you're right."

"That's why I'm paid the big bucks." Brik smiled. At this close a distance, Korie wished he hadn't. "Did you talk to HARLIE?"

"One on one in the bay."

"What did you find?"

Korie passed him a plastic card. "It's all in here. There's overhead access panels to the Bridge. You can reach them from the utility tube without being observed. There's also an under-floor access just ahead of the Ops bay. There's a lot of dead space all around the Bridge module to make repairs easier."

Brik slid the card into his belt. "What about the *Burke*'s torpedoes?"

"You were right. Nakahari went into Systems Analysis—through the back door. The fusion pumps are disconnected and cold. Those fish are dead. I don't want to check our own yet. I don't want to risk alerting him."

"Right." Brik nodded. "How's the captain?"

Korie shrugged—then grabbed a handhold. The gesture would have scooted him downward, back into the inner hull of the *Burke*. "He's alive, but I practically had to break Williger's arm to get her to validate my assumption of responsibility."

"But she did?"

"She did."

"Good. You may have saved both their lives. And put your own at considerably more risk."

"I knew the job was dangerous when I took it."

"Not *this* dangerous."

"Brik—" Korie let himself get very very serious. "Understand something. I don't have anything left to live for—my family is gone. My home is a desert. The only thing that motivates me now is revenge. But that will be enough, if it's a big enough revenge. So any danger that I might be in right now is irrelevant to me. Just tell me how I can hurt the enemy."

Brik studied Korie for a moment. "With all due respect, that is very possibly the stupidest thing you have ever said to me. You might not care about the danger you are in—but you now have the additional responsibility of the lives of those you command. We did not sign a suicide pact when we came aboard this ship."

"I know that."

"I have been around fanatics all my life," continued Brik. "Let me tell you this. If a fanatic is willing to sacrifice his own life to a cause, he isn't going to worry much about the lives of those around him."

"I understand what you're saying," said Korie. "I'm not a fanatic."

"That's what they all say."

"Listen to me. I haven't abandoned my responsibility to the ship or the crew or the fleet. I'm not a kamikaze. I want this revenge and then I want the next one and the one after that. I want to live long enough to see the Morthan Solidarity ground into dust. But—" Korie shrugged. "If someone has to take the point, let it be me."

Brik didn't answer that. He searched Korie's face for a moment longer, looking not only at Korie's surface emotions, but also at the deeper drives within. "All right," he said, finally. "I can honor that. Now I have work to do—wait a few minutes before you follow me." He pushed himself out of the observatory.

Korie stared after him. He didn't know if Brik had believed him or not. He didn't know if he believed himself or not. He stared out at the stars a moment longer.

Why, God—?

Then he stopped himself.

No. Never again.

Status Report

Don't worry, Korie told himself. *Either everything's going to work, or it won't work. If it works, we'll survive. If it doesn't work, we won't have anything to worry about either.*

He stopped where he was and deliberately forced himself to breathe slower. He closed his eyes and thought of the lagoon and the garden at home—trying to relax. That had always worked before . . .

But it didn't work this time.

Because this time, whenever he thought of the lagoon and the garden and the canopy of arching blue ferns, he also thought of the *Dragon Lord* and what it had done to his home.

Korie opened his eyes and stared out through the glass at the hardened stars. They were spread unmoving through the abyss, a wall of shattered light, distant and unreachable.

Remember what they said at the Academy? *To get to the stars, you have to be irrational.*

At the time, it had been a funny joke—a clever play on words. Hyperstate was an irrational place to be.

Suddenly, it wasn't so funny anymore.

What did it take to *survive* among the stars? That was another question entirely.

Korie put his thumb and forefinger to his neck, checking the beat of his pulse. It was still elevated, but not badly. He was at a normal level of tension again.

Enough time had passed. Korie pushed himself out of the observatory, caught the railing, and pulled himself upright again.

Right now, the thing to do is look normal, he reminded himself. *Not just for the Morthan, but for the crew*. The orders had been given. Either they were going to get the job done, or they weren't. In the latter case . . . well, if they didn't survive, neither would the ship. At least, he had guaranteed that much.

Unless the assassin had figured out that trap too.

The hard part was that he couldn't check it—not without giving it away.

It was all a game of phantoms—feint and parry against possibilities.

Korie realized that he was alone in the *Burke*'s inner hull and shivered as if cold. He hurried back to the closest access and climbed back up into the forward keel of the starship. Two crewmembers were working there, stringing optical cables for a new sensory network. Nakahari's modifications were going to need eyes and ears.

Two others had resumed the work on the high-cycle fluctuators. Two security guards stood grimly by with rifles ready. It was insufficient and they all knew it, but what else could they do? Korie had ordered autodestruct charges packed into each of the fluctuators too— and that was further evidence of his lack of faith in the ability of the security squads.

Korie nodded to them curtly and climbed a ladder, then headed aft toward the shuttle bay.

Half of it was dumb show, half of it was real—but which half was precaution and which half was pretend? *If nothing else, maybe we can confuse the assassin as badly as we've confused ourselves.*

He crossed the shuttle bay, stopping only long enough to call down to Nakahari, "How long?"

Nakahari knew better than to stop work. His voice floated out of the hole in the floor. "Working on the third cycle now. I can give you a confidence of twenty. Maybe. Give me another half hour and I'll multiply that by a factor of ten."

Korie stepped through the access to the airlock, through the *Burke*'s airlock, through the airlock of the *LS-1187*, through the access, and into the forward keel of his own ship.

He couldn't help himself. He had to stop at the sick bay.

Williger looked up darkly.

"Deathwatch?" she growled.

Korie met her stare. "Do you always assume the worst of people?"

"It's a great timesaver," she said. "And that way, when I'm proven wrong, my life is full of pleasant surprises, not *un*pleasant ones."

Korie rubbed the Bridge of his nose between thumb and forefinger. He rubbed his eyes and shook his head. He hadn't realized how tired he was.

"You want something for that?"

"No. I'll be fine." He took a breath. "You've had time. What's the prognosis?"

She shrugged. "We wait. We watch. We hope. Some of us pray." She added in a growly rasp, "Sometimes the answer is no."

"So you figured it out too."

"I'm only ugly. I'm not stupid."

"You're not ugly," Korie said.

"Yeah, yeah—you're outvoted by the evidence. When I was born, the doctor slapped my mother. They had to tie a pork chop around my neck just to get the dog to play with me. I had to sneak up on a glass of water if I wanted a drink." Her voice was more gravelly than usual as she recited the tired old jokes. She looked suddenly tired. "My best guess is that the son of a bitch will live. I'm too ugly to live and he's too mean to die."

Something about the way she said it made Korie stop and look at her again. "All right—" he said. "What's really bothering you?"

"Old age," she said. "You think I like this? I know about the jokes. The ones to my face. The ones behind my back. Do you think I *chose* this? It's starting to get to me. Guess what? My rhinoceros-like hide isn't as thick as I thought it was."

"It's what the Morthan said, isn't it?"

"Aah, he didn't bother me. That's what he's supposed to do. It's just—nothing." She waved him off.

"Dr. Williger, if it means anything—you're the most honest person on this ship. And as far as I'm concerned, that makes you the most beautiful."

"Spare me the bullshit. Right now, I'd trade all my inner beauty for a pair of limpid blue eyes with fluttery long lashes."

Who on this ship has blue eyes—? Korie wondered. And then realized. *The new kids come aboard, we play musical chairs for a couple of weeks, and it only settles down when all the dance cards get filled. Only sometimes they don't.* After all the chatter about Armstrong and Quilla Delta had cooled down, after the harmless speculation about Brik and Bach, the juiciest topic for discussion had become Tor and Jonesy. Tor had become one of Williger's best friends; how could she not be envious of her joy? Tor caught herself a nice little snuggle-boy and what did Williger get? Nothing. And how many times in the past had this happened to Dr. Williger? How had she put up with it for so long? *Sometimes, I can be so stupid. What else have I missed?*

"I hadn't realized," he said. "I'm sorry."

Williger's eyes were moist. She shrugged. "It's not your fault."

Korie sat down opposite the doctor. "Listen to me. If it means anything, you're not alone in your hurt. Hurt is universal. We all hurt. The only thing that any of us can do is try to make it hurt a little bit less for the people around us."

She didn't answer immediately. Korie studied her face. It was as if she was trying to formulate the words to embody the pain. Finally she rasped, "You, of all people, are the wrong one to try to offer me comfort."

Korie held her gaze. "It's all I have left to give anyone anymore. Can you accept it?"

"I thought the captain told you to quit trying to be a nice guy."

Korie shrugged. "Pretend I'm not being nice. Pretend I'm being ruthless. I'm trying to keep a valuable piece of equipment running properly—"

"You're not fooling anyone—" And then she hung her head and admitted, "I'm tired, Mr. Korie. I'm tired of empty beds and even emptier reassurance. I'm tired of the jokes. Especially the ones I don't hear. I do my job. I'm one of the best damned doctors in the fleet. I'm entitled to—better than this. This isn't the kind of hand-holding that I want. I want what I want—not second best. And nothing anyone can say or do can change that."

"Dr. Williger—"

"No. Shut up. Let me say this. It's not the pressure. It's not even the fear. It's the loneliness. I just—I don't want to die alone."

"I don't know what to say to you. If I had the power to change any of it—"

"Stop," she said, letting go and holding up a hand. "You don't have to say anything. You listened. That was enough. And I'll keep it a secret that you're still a nice guy."

Korie smiled gently. He understood. "I'll tell you what. When we get back to Stardock, I'll have Hodel whip up a love philter for you."

Molly Williger looked horrified. "Don't you dare. I saw how his exorcism turned out." And then, she added, "Don't worry, I'll be all right." She allowed herself a crooked smile. "I always am."

"You sure?"

"I'm sure."

"Okay," said Korie. He stood up and left.

Back in the keel, he paused to tap his headset control. "Brik? Status report."

"Green. Green. Yellow. Yellow. Green."

"Time?"

"Fifteen to thirty."

"Make it closer to—"

HARLIE beeped then, interrupting them both. "Mr. Korie! Long-range scanning is picking up a hyperstate ripple."

"Bridge. *Now*," shouted Korie. He broke and ran, knowing that Brik was on his way already.

Signals

"It's heading straight for us," said Tor. "ETA: fifteen minutes. Jeezis—I've never seen anything move like that."

The holotable display showed the locus of the *LS-1187* and the *Burke* as a tiny bright speck. On the opposite side of the display, a larger, brighter pinpoint was arrowing directly toward it.

Hodel enlarged that section of the display. "Oh, God—I know that signature. It's the *Dragon Lord.*"

"The *Burke* is an important prize," Korie noted as he stepped up onto the Ops deck from the forward keel access. He crossed to Tor and looked over her shoulder at her board. "Any signals?"

"Not yet."

"They won't," said Brik, coming up after him. "It'd be a waste of time. They'll ask for surrender. You'll refuse. So, why bother? No, they'll go immediately to the *next* step. Attack."

Hodel shook his head sadly and murmured to himself, "Oh, Mama . . ."

"We can't fight them," said Korie. "We can't win." He closed his eyes for a moment, thinking. When he opened them again, his expression was dark. "Tor, sendthissignal." He turned resolutely toward the main viewer. "Morthan battle-cruiser. If you approach this vessel, we will self-destruct. You will not have our stardrive! Repeat: We will self-destruct!"

Tor was looking at him oddly.

"Send that," he repeated.

"They won't believe it," said Brik.

"And they'll home in on the signal," said Tor.

"Or they won't," said Korie. "*Send it.*"

Tor shook her head. "There are orders that only a captain can give—specifically self-destruct!"

Korie looked at her. "What's your point?"

"The captain isn't dead."

"The captain is *pickled!*" Korie shouted at her in frustration. "How brain-dead do you want him to be?"

"That's exactly my point! His brain is still active! He has to give the order."

"You *might* be right," Korie said with visible annoyance. "But now is not the time to have this argument. Mr. Jones, send that signal."

Jonesy gulped. He looked to Tor apologetically, then back to Korie. "Yes, sir."

Tor muttered something under her breath. She stepped back to her console and hit the button, sending the signal. The panel beeped its confirmation. *Signal sent.* "Anything else, sir?"

Korie shook his head.

Tor stepped back to him and lowered her voice. Very quietly and very angrily, she said, "Don't you ever go under my head again!"

Korie stared her down. He was just as angry, maybe angrier. *"The argument about who is in command does not belong on this Bridge."*

"You're right—" said a deep voice, a sound that rasped and rumbled like the roar of a panther.

They turned to look, all horrified—as the Morthan assassin stepped calmly onto the Bridge of the starship. He was grinning like a gargoyle and he was dragging Dr. Williger by her hair.

"The argument is irrelevant," said Cinnabar, "—because *I* am in command now." He hurled the doctor into the middle of the floor. She was still alive, but just barely. "I can't stand rudeness," he explained.

Korie was horrified. He took a step forward, but Tor grabbed his arm and held him back. Beside them, Brik was standing perfectly still. Jonesy was white. Hodel had fainted.

"Excuse me, Mr. Korie—" HARLIE said abruptly. "I'm picking up some anomalies on the Bridge. I believe, yes—" And then the klaxon went off. "Intruder alert! Intruder alert!"

Cinnabar laughed. It was a chuckling rumble that bubbled up from the depths of Hell. It was deep and vicious and terrifying. "Thank you, HARLIE . . ." he said.

A security man fell into the Bridge from the opposite door, drawing his gun. Cinnabar moved like fire, grabbing him, cracking his back, and hurling him back out into the corridor. Something unseen crashed horribly. Someone else was screaming. "Thank you," said Cinnabar, "but we won't be needing your services anymore." He turned back to Korie and the others. He stepped to the center of the Bridge. He laid one huge hand on the back of the captain's chair, but he did not sit down.

"In answer to your first question, *it was easy*. I came in through the missile tubes. You never scanned your own ship. Very arrogant. In answer to your second question, the reason you can't self-destruct is that I've disabled that part of the network. Now then . . . send *this* signal to the *Dragon Lord*." Cinnabar faced the main viewer. "This is Esker Cinnabar. I have taken control of both vessels. The *Burke* is ready for pickup. The stardrive is undamaged. All is well. *Send that*." He smiled wickedly. "Mr. Jones? I gave you an order."

Jonesy looked uncertain. He looked to Korie for guidance. Reluctantly, Korie nodded. Jonesy turned to his board and sent the signal. Then he looked back to the Bridge again.

Cinnabar was pleased. He smiled. He stepped to the other side of the captain's chair, leaning on it possessively. Korie glared. *That chair is mine. I've earned it! How dare he—?* But the Morthan only draped one arm across the back of the empty chair. He wasn't going to sit down.

Korie glanced to Brik. Brik remained impassive.

"You should have destroyed the fluctuators—" Cinnabar explained, "—and the *Burke* when you had the chance. Too bad. This is going to be very embarrassing for you. One more humiliation in a long string of humiliations." His smile widened horribly. "Now, a Morthan would commit honorable suicide rather than be humiliated—but you humans seem to thrive on humiliation. So I promise to humiliate you exquisitely." His chuckle was the sound of a dinosaur dying. "The *ultimate* humiliation . . . I may not even kill you. You're not worthy of a Morthan death. I wonder what your admiral will think when we send you home *again!* This time, the defeat will be even more profound." Cinnabar sighed dramatically. Then, abruptly, he was crisp and military again. "Evacuate the *Burke*," he ordered. "Disengage and move off. Do it now."

Korie said bitterly, "Don't you want the third fluctuator, the one we removed?"

Cinnabar laughed. "Cute. Very cute. The one that you booby-trapped? Don't be silly. The two that remain in place will be sufficient for our needs."

Korie sagged. He looked like a man who has just run out of options. Tor put her hand on his shoulder.

"It didn't work," she said.

Korie looked up. His eyes were hollow. "Will you promise to spare my crew? No more killing?"

"*I promise nothing!* You don't have a choice. But . . . I will let your people live as long as it is to . . . our mutual advantage."

Korie turned to Jonesy, Hodel, and Tor. "Do as he says."

Hodel shook his head. He stood up and stepped away from his console. So did Jonesy. Tor followed them.

Korie looked from one to the other. Their expressions were resolute. Angered at their disobedience, Korie stepped past Hodel and started punching up the commands on the console himself. The evacuation signal sounded throughout the *Burke* and echoed in the corridors of the *LS-1187*.

The forward viewer flashed to show the interior of the *Burke*. The security squads were waving everyone out. The medical crews were removing the last of the bodies. The Black Hole Gang shrugged and walked away from the two high-cycle fluctuators in the engine room. Nakahari grabbed his portable terminal, yanked it free, and ran for the corridor. The security squad followed.

The screen showed them passing through the shuttle bay and into the *LS-1187*. The airlock doors slid shut behind them.

"HARLIE, are we clear?"

"Yes, Mr. Korie."

"Stand by for separation," Korie released the mating ring, then the docking tube, and finally the docking harness.

There was a soft *thump* and the two starships floated gently apart.

A Morthan Lullaby

The *Burke* floated farther and farther away from the *LS-1187*.

"Two kilometers . . ." Hodel said grimly. He sank back down into his chair and began marking vectors and intercepts.

"Keep your hands away from the targeting controls," Cinnabar rasped. Hodel lifted his hands high off the board. "I'm a good boy," he said, but his tone of voice wasn't happy.

On the holodisplay, the *Dragon Lord*'s hyperstate ripple almost closed with the pinpoint representing the *LS-1187*, then unfolded and dissolved. The display expanded to show the locus of real space now.

They watched in silence as the huge warship began to close on the two Alliance vessels.

"I'll put her on viewer," said Tor. She stepped over to her own board and punched up a new angle on the main screen: a distant bright speck. She punched again for magnification, but the *Dragon Lord* was still too distant. HARLIE superimposed an extrapolated image beside the actual point of light.

Tor studied the screens on her console. "Nice piece of piloting. She trimmed her fields exquisitely." It was hard for her to keep the envy out of her voice. That kind of precision was only possible with the expenditure of large amounts of power, something the *LS-1187* didn't have. Tor added, "She's slowing to match course with the *Burke*. Deceleration—holy god!—fifteen thousand gees!" She shook her head unbelievingly. "That's not *possible*."

"Thank you," said Cinnabar.

Korie's expression was impassive. "ETA?"

"Give her five minutes, ten at most," Tor said. She tapped at her board. The extrapolated image expanded.

Hodel swiveled to the holographic display and expanded that view as well. To one side, he put up a size comparison of the three vessels. "She's big enough to swallow the *Burke* whole," he said. There was bitterness in his voice.

Korie remembered the city-sized ship he had seen. It had been a wall of missile tubes and shield projectors, disruptors and antennae. And when it had swiveled around before him, he had stared into its mouth. The dragon could hold this ship in its teeth. But—

"Don't be fooled," said Korie tightly. "They have to build it that big. They don't have the stardrive technology we do." He almost believed it.

"We do now," Cinnabar laughed. It was the sound of sandpaper on flesh. He stood behind the captain's chair and wrapped his huge hands around the seat back. His claws cut deeply into the cushion. He rattled the chair gleefully in its mountings, almost ripping it loose from its frame. He leaned his head back, stretching his corded neck; he howled and roared and steam-whistled his triumph.

Tor put her hands over her ears and flinched. Jonesy pulled her back away from the center of the Ops deck. Korie and Brik held their positions angrily.

Cinnabar ordered Hodel to move the *LS-1187* off from the *Burke* then, and the next few moments were occupied with the maneuver. "I want you out of cannon range, out of torpedo range—far enough away that you can't do any mischief. And from this point on, there will be no transmissions of any kind unless I authorize them. God, I love this job!"

Frowning, Korie sank into a chair by the holotable. Idly, he punched up a display of the three ships' vectors. He studied it thoughtfully.

Cinnabar noticed what he was doing and stopped in mid-howl. "It won't work," he said. "Nothing you do will work. You have been outmaneuvered. You are obsolete. Why don't you have the good sense to die quietly."

"Why don't you have the good manners to shut up?" Korie said without looking up.

"You don't know how to lose," said Cinnabar.

"On the contrary. You don't know how to win."

Cinnabar laughed again. "For someone who doesn't know how, the evidence demonstrates that I'm doing quite well."

Korie swiveled away and stared forward.

"There she is," reported Tor.

The image was clear on the main screen now. The *Dragon Lord* was moving into position above the *Burke*, securing the much smaller vessel with a tractor beam. As they watched, the *Burke* was being drawn up into the gigantic enemy vessel.

"Shit," said Tor.

"You said a mouthful," agreed Hodel.

"You should be celebrating," said Cinnabar. "This is the end of the war." He grinned wickedly. "Ha. Perhaps we will build a statue to you—so that humans everywhere will know who to thank for their liberation."

"Liberation?" Korie gave Cinnabar the raised-eyebrow look.

"But of course—" Cinnabar stepped around the captain's chair and leaned on the forward railing of the Bridge. "Do you call *this* freedom? I promise you, under the Morthan rule, there will be no more useless dying. Humans will live at peace with each other and will accept their rightful place in the universe—"

"As slaves?"

"As servants," Cinnabar corrected. "Service is the highest state of intelligent activity, you know that. Your own textbooks teach that a life is worthless unless it is in service of some greater good. Well, I offer you a world where your service will no longer be wasted. No more will you have the opportunities to act out of greed and lust and malevolence."

Korie and Brik exchanged skeptical glances.

"Understand something," Cinnabar continued. "We did not ask for this war. You did. *Humans* forced this war on *us*. You gave us no choice. So now, we're bringing it back to you—*to protect ourselves*. We'll create a domain that is safe from human depredation, and if that means the total subjugation of humanity, then so be it. But I promise you, we will be better masters of you than you have ever been of yourselves.

"Imagine it—no more hunger, no more poverty, no more inequality. You can't, can you? Because you've never known a world that works, have you? A world where resources are efficiently managed, where people have a purpose, a place of beauty and freedom. Yes, *freedom*. Real freedom to be what you are—not what you believe. Give up your false perceptions, your oughts and musts and should-bes and I will give you the freedom that comes with truth!"

Cinnabar paused and looked from one to the other. The fear on the Ops deck had been replaced with uncertainty. "This wasn't what you were expecting, was it?" He flashed an evil smile, and for just that instant, their enemy was back—and then, he was speaking directly and candidly to them again. "You were expecting fear and pain, terror and hate, not this."

He laughed and returned to his place behind the captain's chair, grinning almost good-naturedly now. "You don't know what freedom is. You think it means that you are free of overriding authority—that isn't freedom. That's chaos and madness. I'll give you *real* freedom, the kind that comes from knowing who you are and what your place in the universe is. I will give you freedom from want, freedom from fear, freedom to work, freedom to serve—I will give you freedom from the lies inside your head."

There was silence on the Ops deck. No one spoke. Jonesy glanced at Tor; she was studying the deck. Hodel looked at his hands in his lap. Korie was impassive.

Brik snorted his contempt. It was loud.

Cinnabar looked at him pityingly. "The war is over. There will even be a place for you in the new domain—even for *you*. Even if you don't want it. Morthans don't waste."

Brik snorted again.

Cinnabar focused on him. He spoke with contempt now. "So quick to judge—so foolish. You have spent too much time studying the wrong teachers. Never mind. I will give you a world where you will not be subservient to humans."

Brik began to straighten.

Korie recognized the implication of the gesture and did something stupid. He stepped between Brik and Cinnabar. "Don't do it, mister. That's an order."

"You see?" said Cinnabar, over Korie's head. "You let humans choose your battles."

"Don't be stupid," said Korie, swiveling to face Cinnabar, trying to keep his voice even. "We've seen your bioscan. We know what you're capable of." Turning back to Brik, he said, "Listen to me, Brik. There's no honor in this fight—"

Brik considered the thought. After a heartbeat, he relaxed. So did Korie.

Hodel broke the silence. He was frowning at the forward viewer. "There's a problem on the *Dragon Lord*."

Korie turned to look. So did Brik.

Cinnabar glared over their heads.

The huge forward viewer showed it all. A bright red glow was spreading across the hull of the *Dragon Lord*. Its center was the hatch where the *Burke* had been swallowed up. The glare turned brighter and whiter—Hodel decreased the magnification—they could see the flare of brilliance as it enveloped the entire Morthan warship.

"It's disintegrating!"

There was the briefest flash of color—of fragments coming apart, of horrific energies expanding suddenly outward—

And then the whole screen went white. The glare was so bright it hurt Korie's eyes.

For an instant the viewer was dark; the forward cameras had gone blind; then another camera swiveled into position and refocused. There was a flickering cloud of gas and lightning and expanding debris where the *Dragon Lord* had been—

Hodel's eyes were wide with terror and hope. Tor stood up, stunned. Jonesy, still uncertain, stood by her. A smile spread across Brik's face.

Korie turned to look at Cinnabar.

The Morthan assassin was frozen in disbelief. He was grasping the captain's chair so hard that he was bending the frame out of alignment. He opened his mouth and his breath sucked in with a ghastly sound. When it came out again, it was a bloodcurdling shriek of rage. His scream went on and on and on. It rattled the ceiling cameras in their sockets.

Korie allowed himself a single moment of triumph. "Ooh, that feels good," he said to himself. A peaceful smile spread across his face. "That was for Carol and Timmy and Robby."

Tor bent to her console. "We've lost all our active forward sensors. Burned out. Auxiliaries are coming online—"

Korie couldn't contain his glee. He let it spread across his face and shouted up at Cinnabar, "You're not the only one who knows how to set a booby trap. That's what it looks like when you invert a singularity field *inside* a ship."

"*You* made the mistake," Brik said softly. "You should have killed us."

Cinnabar was visibly struggling to regain his self-control. "Yes. It would be appropriate to rectify that error immediately. But it would be premature. You forget—or perhaps you remember very well—that the third piece of the stardrive is still aboard this ship. That will be enough. This ship is going to Dragonhold. Commander Tor—set a course."

Tor stood motionless.

Cinnabar looked to her. "I gave you an order."

"I only take orders from my captain."

"I can vouch for that," Korie said wryly.

Cinnabar stepped off the Bridge. He came toward Tor slowly, with a *calculated* display of rage. He circled the Ops deck, pulling consoles off the wall at random, tossing crewmembers out of their chairs with one great hand, turning equipment over, punching in screens, and roaring like a tornado. Korie noted, with detached professionalism, that Cinnabar was very careful in what he was destroying—only weaponry and ancillary systems; nothing that would impede the operation of the vessel in hyperstate.

"You don't understand!!" Cinnabar roared at Tor. "You have no choice! I am a Morthan assassin!! I am your worst nightmare come to life!"

"So much for the promise of freedom," said Korie dryly.

"Freedom for those who *choose* it!" the Morthan bellowed at him. "This is not choice!" Cinnabar turned back to Tor. "Your *only* hope is to obey my commands."

"*You* don't get it," she said. "The answer is no."

Instantly, Cinnabar backhanded her sideways against a wall. She slammed against it with a thud that made Korie wince. Jonesy leapt at Cinnabar—"Hey! Leave her alone!"—Cinnabar picked him up and tossed him clear across the Bridge at the forward viewer. He hit it square in the center. It shattered, pieces flying in all directions, leaving a gaping blank wall. Jonesy fell to the deck, gasping and groaning. Tor crawled toward him. He was bleeding profusely. She reached a hand to comfort him.

"Don't anyone touch them," warned Cinnabar.

"Very smart," said Korie. "You've just disabled the only two people on this ship who know how to set a course for Dragonhold."

Cinnabar turned coldly to Korie. He was almost polite. "You will notice that I only disabled them. *That* was a warning. Do you think I'm such a fool that I don't know what I'm doing?"

Korie replied just as coldly. "Actually, I think you're a malignant thug."

Cinnabar snorted. "What you *think* is irrelevant." Then he advanced on Tor again. "I will kill your crewmates one by one before your horrified eyes. I will kill that child you are so attracted to. I will pull him apart, one limb at a time. His screams will haunt your nightmares. There will come a moment when you will beg me to let you set a course for Dragonhold."

—the beam struck Cinnabar in the back. Nakahari stood in the door of the Bridge, holding a rifle and spattering energy across the Ops deck. The crackling fire splattered off the Morthan like water off a wall. Colored lightning flashed around him, spraying across the Bridge in a stunning shower of sparks. He stood there, grinning nastily at Nakahari—

Nakahari stopped firing, astonished.

"Now, throw at it me," said Cinnabar. "That's what they usually do."

Nakahari took a nervous step backward.

Cinnabar shifted into overdrive. He *flowed* across the Ops deck to Nakahari, plucked him out of the air, and lifted him high over his head. Nakahari struggled. Cinnabar turned slowly with his captive—" Set a course for Dragonhold!" he roared.

"Don't do it—!" Korie said.

Brik stepped forward. "Put him down. Fight me instead—"

Cinnabar snorted. "Don't be silly. You're just food." He flexed his arms. Nakahari's spine went *cra-a-ack!* Nakahari was cut off in mid-scream. He went limp.

The assassin tossed the body aside, like a used rag. He turned back to Tor—*"Set the course!"*

He stalked back across the Operations deck, knocking Goldberg out of his chair and ripping the auxiliary weapons console off the wall as he passed.

Tor flinched. She let go of Jonesy's hand and tried to pull herself to her feet. She fell back with a grunt. Korie moved toward her protectively. Brik moved in front of Korie. He bared his teeth and growled.

Cinnabar snorted skeptically at Brik; he pulled a console off its base and hurled it aside; he snarled again at Tor. "Set a course for Dragonhold!"

Korie interrupted. He spoke in tones of quiet resignation. "I'll do it." He added, "We don't believe in senseless killing."

Cinnabar merely grinned. "We *do*." But he stepped out of the way as Korie stepped over to the astrogation console. He ignored the shocked and angry looks of both Tor and Hodel and began laying out the course. Abruptly, the console went blank—

"I thought we fixed this, Mike," Korie slammed his hand down on the console—*hard*—and it flickered back to life.

"Technological superiority! Ha!" Cinnabar ripped a chair from its mounting and tossed it at the broken forward viewer. He stepped back up onto the Bridge to look out over the whole Operations deck. "You have no idea who you're fighting, do you? This isn't about your machines. It never was. Even without your so-called superstardrive, we will win the war."

Korie felt his neck burning, but he didn't look up from his work.

Cinnabar was savoring the moment. "You are apes. And we are the next phase of evolution. We are *more-than human*. And we will do what life always does. We will eat you alive. Of course, you will fight us—

that's your destiny; to die resisting the inevitable. You will fight us until the last of your children dies in our zoos."

"Right. So much for freedom and service—" said Korie to no one in particular.

Cinnabar ignored him. "You had your moment. It's over. Your battle is hopeless because history is on our side. You are food."

Annoyed, Korie swiveled around in his chair to look up at Cinnabar. "You spend a lot of time talking to your sandwich—" He narrowed his eyes. "Just who are you trying to convince?"

The Morthan simply laughed. "I love your arrogance. It's almost charming. It's almost Morthan—" He sank down in the captain's chair with an air of absolute authority.

Korie and Brik looked at each other.

Cinnabar caught the look and frowned in puzzlement. He peered curiously at Korie. "You're thinking of trying something, aren't you?"

"*Moi?*"

"You can't lie to a Morthan, remember? I can see your heartbeat. I can see your blood flowing. I can see the electrical activity of your nervous system. I can see your Kirlian aura. I can smell the changes in your perspiration. I can smell your fear. I can almost hear your thoughts." Cinnabar half-raised himself out of the chair as he studied Korie. "Your heartbeat is elevated. Your adrenaline is flowing. Your brain is ticking with nervous excitement. You are thinking of trying something, aren't you?" He sank back into the chair again. "Well, go ahead. Try it."

Korie looked to Brik. "Do you want to do it?" He asked it almost casually.

Brik shrugged. "No, I think you should do it. You're in command."

"No, I really think the honor should be yours—" Korie said. "I mean, he did insult you pretty badly."

"Was that an insult? I hardly noticed."

"*I don't care which one of you does it! Do it!*" Cinnabar roared in crimson rage.

Korie and Brik nodded to each other. Korie spoke. "Harlie. *Now.*"

It happened even faster than Cinnabar could react. The chair seemed to explode around him. The cushions, the base—it came apart in a fury. Lightning-fast the hidden cables sprang out, writhing like shining metallic worms, and then just as quickly, they flexed and wrapped themselves around and around the helpless Morthan so tightly he couldn't move. The metal tentacles held him fast within the shattered framework of the captain's chair.

The silence creaked.

Brik looked at Cinnabar's glaring eyes. The assassin's mouth and muzzle were muffled by the restraints, but his eyes burned with the fires of Hell. Brik looked to Korie. "We're going to have to kill him, you know."

"Do we have to?" said Korie. "I was hoping to keep him as a pet."

"Uh-uh. They're too hard to feed—"

"Mm. Good point."

Korie crossed the Ops deck to stand in front of Cinnabar. The Morthan assassin was so tightly wound up in the remains of the captain's chair that he looked like a metal mummy. His angry red eyes *smoldered.*

Korie stared into those eyes for a long moment. "Who's arrogant now?" He didn't wait for an answer. "Now let *me* tell *you* something about evolution. It's full of dead ends. Like the dodo. Creatures that went as far as they could go and then . . . couldn't go any farther. Maybe you and your kind are just another evolutionary dead end."

"I don't think he's going to answer you," said Brik. "He appears to be tied up at the moment."

"Mr. Brik? Was that a joke?"

Brik just grinned.

Korie turned back to the captive assassin. "You're only half right. Humanity *isn't* perfect—yet. We're still working on it. But we do have a track record at least a hundred times longer than yours. We've proven that we can survive for a hundred thousand years. Have you? You are the genetically designed and technologically augmented descendants of humanity—but that doesn't automatically make you our replacements. You could just as easily be a mistake. What you've forgotten is that for the last hundred thousand years, at least, *we* have fairly earned our reputation as the meanest sons-of-bitches in this part of the galaxy. And we're not giving up our legend easily. You might be louder than us, you're certainly uglier—but you and your so-called 'master race' have a long way to go. It's going to take something a lot more convincing than you before the human race packs up its tents."

"That is one angry Morthan," said Brik, thoughtfully.

"That is a *humiliated* Morthan," corrected Korie. And then, abruptly, he remembered he was on the Bridge of a starship and his crew was staring at him. "All right, let's get a med team up here, pronto. And activate the backup systems. And—" He noticed Brik's expression and asked, "What's the matter?" even as he was turning to see—

Cinnabar was struggling with the cables. They were straining and stretching as if he was swelling up within them. They flexed and creaked alarmingly. Cinnabar was glowing with an unholy light. Something terrible was happening inside his cage of wire. Something went suddenly *sproing!*—and then another cable snapped with the same alarming sound—and then all of the cables were bursting at once, flying and ricocheting in all directions—

The Morthan assassin stood up. He was free.

Hodel had just enough time to say, "Uh-oh—"

The monster seized the railing on the Bridge and broke it apart with his bare hands. He leapt down to the Ops deck, grabbed Korie, lifted him high, and flung him angrily at the forward viewer. Korie hit with a bone-jarring *thunk* and bounced off to the floor. His felt the impact go all the way up his spine and wondered for the briefest of instants if he were going to be paralyzed. His head was ringing like an ancient temple gong. He tried to sit up—

Brik and Cinnabar were facing each other in the center of the Ops deck. Brik shifted his balance, lowering his center of gravity; he brought his arms up in a defensive posture.

Cinnabar straightened and shook his head, grinning. Instead, he pointed an outstretched hand and lightning leapt from his fingers, flinging Brik backward against the shattered weaponry console, paralyzed.

The Morthan whirled to look at Hodel, the only human crewmember left standing. Cinnabar gave him a withering stare and Hodel stepped backward, out of the assassin's way.

Cinnabar crossed to the astrogation console and stood before it, studying it for a long moment. "Do I have to do everything myself?" he said angrily. He reached out and tapped a command on the keyboard.

The console went dead. It blacked out completely.

Cinnabar snorted and smacked it. *Hard.*

The console exploded around him.

Raw electricity flooded through the floor plates, through the console surface, and from the hidden projectors in the ceiling of the Ops deck. It was a fountain of crackling light. Sparks and steam and smoke exploded out of Cinnabar's body. He staggered backward—tried to escape, but the next wave of the assault hit him then. Energy beams leapt out from the floor and the walls, pinning him where he stood. Laser fire and electric flames enveloped him. A heavy mesh net dropped from the ceiling, wrapping him up in its conductive coils. It glowed whitely. Green lightning flickered across its surface; the net grabbed the monster tighter and tighter—until he screamed and roared and flared in agony. The wash of light and heat was overpowering, blinding, scorching. The screams of the monster disappeared in the roaring flames.

The CO_2 jets fired then and the noise and flames and heat began to subside.

Squinting, Korie unshaded his eyes and peered at the reddened mass on his Ops deck. It was still glowing, but he could see that it was shriveling into ash. It stood for only a moment longer, and then . . . oh, so gently, it crumpled. It toppled and fell, collapsing to the floor like so much brittle debris.

Thank God, thought Korie. And for once, he didn't retract it.

The Operations Deck

Except for the crackling mass in its center, the Ops deck was silent.

Hodel pulled his headset down around his ears. "We need a fire-crew on the Ops deck."

Korie was climbing painfully to his feet. He had to hold on to the back of a chair to remain standing. Brik limped over to him and supported him by the other arm.

"He didn't kill you?" Korie looked surprised.

"He'd have had no one to play with."

The first of the medical teams came rushing onto the Bridge. Armstrong, Stolchak, and Bach, followed by two tall Quillas. Korie pointed them toward Williger and Jonesy and Goldberg. "Take care of the others first."

He nodded toward the rear of the deck and Brik helped him toward one of the few remaining chairs on the Ops deck. Korie sank into it gratefully.

"Status report?"

"Working," said HARLIE quietly. "Most of the damage appears to have been limited to the Operations deck. Control has been transferred to the backup systems."

"Thank you, HARLIE—" Korie said painfully. "You can disable the rest of the traps now." He looked to Brik. "You were right. He was still alive."

"It's very hard to kill a Morthan," Brik said. "If you don't have a body, he's still alive." Brik studied Korie for a moment. "You did good too. He never suspected. Are you sure you aren't part Morthan?"

Korie looked up at Brik with a quizzical expression, then assumed that the comment had actually been intended as a joke.

"I didn't know you could do that," he said.

"Do what?"

"Tell jokes."

Brik looked at him blankly. "That wasn't a joke."

"Right. Never mind." Korie straightened in his seat and glanced across the Bridge to see how the others were doing.

Jonesy was in great pain, but he was bearing it well. He was lying with his head in Tor's lap. She was hurt too, but not as badly.

"Easy, Jonesy—hang on—"

Stolchak was checking Jonesy with a hand-scanner. Then she touched his arm with a pressure-injector. It whooshed. "It'll ease the pain," she said.

Jonesy turned his head to Tor and managed a grin. "Don't worry. I'm not going to die." He closed his eyes for a moment, then opened them again. His voice was starting to fade. "I know it was you who reversed the rings. I'm glad you did. I like taking showers with you." And then he passed out.

Stolchak grinned at Tor. "Sorry. No strenuous exercise till the bones knit."

Tor flushed with embarrassment, but still managed to ask, "Mine or his?"

"Yes."

The lights on the Ops deck went out then—but only for a moment. Then they came back up brighter as the emergency systems took over. Chief Leen's voice came over the loudspeaker. "Mr. Korie, the auxiliary Bridge is green. We'll take over control here."

"Thank you," replied Korie. "I'll be there in a minute." He levered himself to his feet, gasping as he did. "I think I cracked a rib—" He turned forward and suddenly, he was crisp and efficient again. "All right, Hodel, let's clean this mess up! We're still in Morthan space. And they're going to come looking for us soon." He supported himself on the chair. "Chief? How soon can we get underway?"

"We're running security checks, and as soon as we clear, I can have us in hyperstate. Estimate thirty minutes."

"You've got five." Still holding his side, he admitted, "Jeezis, that hurts." He glanced upward. "HARLIE. You did good. Real good."

"Thank you, Mr. Korie. I have never had to sit on a system alert before."

"It wouldn't have worked without you, HARLIE."

"Yes, I know. Suppressing all those alarms—It felt—quite odd. Almost like . . . lying."

"Yes, well, don't make it a habit."

"No, sir. I found it a very unpleasant experience."

Korie crossed to Williger; she was the worst hurt. Armstrong and one of the tall Quillas were just putting her on a stretcher. She was growling at them both.

"Only my pride is hurt," she said. "Let me up—! People are hurt."

"I'm sorry, Doctor," said the Quilla in a deep voice. "Not until we've run a full scan." Armstrong looked up, startled.

Korie touched her arm. "Doctor—make me happy. Cooperate."

Williger muttered something untranslatable. *Ah, yes,* Korie remembered. *Doctors curse in Latin.* He bent low and whispered into her ear. "If you don't go quietly, I'll have Hodel mix a love philter for you."

"I'll take a six-pack," said Williger. "Something must have worked. We're still alive. Hell, I'll try anything." To her stretcher-bearers, she rasped, "All right, let's go—"

Armstrong was staring across the stretcher at the Quilla. He hadn't realized that there were *male* Quillas. Oops. He was staring at the Quilla with a queasy realization growing in him. The Quilla looked up, noticed Armstrong's interest—and *winked.* Armstrong went pale. He averted his eyes and picked up his end of the stretcher a little too quickly. He backed nervously out of the Ops deck, followed by the stretcher and Quilla Lambda.

Korie turned to inspect the rest of the damage to the Bridge and Ops deck. It looked like a war zone. Hodel was struggling to right his broken console.

"I think you can relax, Mike. The jinx is broken."

Hodel grinned and gave Korie a big thumbs-up.

And the console exploded one more time in a dazzling shower of sparks. Hodel jumped back, cursing.

He glared at Korie. "Don't ever *ever* say that again."

Sick Bay

Captain Hardesty was lying on a medical table.

The scanners and probes hovered over him like electronic flamingos. He was alive, but just barely. He was being sustained by a forest of pumps and compressors, a network of tubes and wires and monitors. One machine breathed for him, another pumped his blood, a third cleansed the poisons from his veins. Micromachines crept through his bloodstream, looking for alien proteins. Microstasis beams poked and prodded and manipulated his flesh.

He looked like a zombie.

His skin was a cadaverous gray-green. His organic eye was a ghastly yellow shade. His flesh was mottled and bruised. Had he been dead and decomposing for a week, he could not have looked worse.

"How are you feeling?" Korie asked. It was a stupid question, but what else could he say?

Hardesty opened his eyes and looked to the foot of the bed. The executive officer was standing there.

The captain tried to take a breath, realized again, for the umpteenth time that he couldn't, and instead just floated. He said, "Being dead . . . is not my idea of a good time."

"I'm sorry, sir, that we . . . uh, had to lock down the *Burke*."

"I'd have court-martialed you if you hadn't. You did right." He added, "I hope to repay the favor someday."

"Yes, sir." Korie allowed himself a smile.

"You did a good job," Hardesty acknowledged. "I'm sorry we lost the *Burke*."

Korie shrugged. "There'll be other ships. I don't have to apologize for my priorities."

"Hmp. Well said. Maybe you'll be a captain yet. . . . All right. Get the hell out of here. Take us home."

"Yes, sir." Korie said it proudly. He took a step back, straightened, and gave his captain a crisp salute; then he turned on his heel and exited.

The Bridge

Hyperstate.

Irrational space.

Faster-Than-Light.

Superluminal.

Nightmare time.

Korie entered the Bridge through the starboard passage. He paused at the broken railing and looked out over the makeshift repairs to the Ops deck. Portable terminals had temporarily replaced the regular consoles. A projection unit stood in for the forward viewer.

Nevertheless, it was *home*.

Tor stepped up beside him. He glanced over at her. She looked tired.

She brushed a strand of hair off her forehead. "In five minutes, we'll be in signaling range."

"Good."

"Can I ask you something?"

"Go ahead."

"Why didn't you tell us it was all a set of concentric traps?"

"I trust my face. I didn't know if I could trust yours."

"Pardon?"

"You don't play poker?"

"I play poker," Tor said. "But this was your deal."

"This was a very high-stakes game, Commander. If you had known what cards you were holding, you might not have acted naturally. The fewer people who knew, the better."

"I see," she said, thoughtfully. "So, you lied to us . . ."

"Yes, I did—" Korie fell silent. He was remembering something that Captain Lowell had said to him. He was remembering a promise he'd made—and broken. And broken and broken and broken. *Is this the secret of leadership? Knowing when to lie?* The thought troubled him. He wasn't sure the questions were answerable. "Are you asking for an apology?"

Tor thought about it. "No. In your place, I guess I'd have done the same."

Korie shook his head. "I wonder . . . it starts with lying, doesn't it?"

"What does?"

"The process of selling your soul. Nobody sells it all at once. We give it away a piece at a time, until one day—"

"What are you talking about?" Tor asked.

Korie turned to look at her. "We lost thirteen good crewmembers. Some of those kids were awfully young. They trusted me." He took a long deep breath. "You were right about me. I wanted a ship of my own so badly that I never stopped to think about the cost of it. I wanted revenge so badly I could taste the blood. Now that I know the cost of each, I wonder if I'm the kind of man who can carry the pain. Some of the decisions you have to make aren't . . . very easy."

Tor's voice was filled with compassion. "You did the right thing. And you'd do it again—"

Korie lowered his face, pretended to study the console in front of him, trying to cover his emotions. He knew she was right. He didn't like it, but it was true. He lifted his gaze to meet her eyes again. "Yes," he admitted finally. "But that doesn't make it any easier. It makes it harder. It means you have to be *worthy* of the trust."

"If it means anything . . . this crew is very proud of you. And so am I. You gave this ship her pride again."

"No, I didn't. Hardesty did. He gave us the discipline. I just used what he built. Does the crew know that?"

Tor nodded. "I think they do." She laid a hand on his. "I want you to know something. From me. You did good. Someday, you're going to be a very good captain. I'd be proud to serve on any ship you command."

Korie didn't know how to answer that. The compliment felt so good it almost hurt. "Well . . ." he shrugged, visibly embarrassed. "Maybe someday. Thanks for the thought." And then, looking up quickly, he changed the subject. "Did the crew choose a name yet?"

"Yes. They took a vote. The winning name got a hundred and fifty-two."

Korie frowned. "Commander Tor—correct me if I'm wrong, but there are only eighty-four people aboard this boat."

She shrugged. "So they stuffed the ballot box. It was unanimous anyway."

"Will Hardesty like it?"

"I think so." She turned forward. "Mr. Hodel. Send a signal. The *Star Wolf* is coming home."

The Last Letter Home

And then they were here in the room with him—*Carol, Timmy and Robby*—laughing and giggling. "Hi, Daddy! Hi!" He could see the warm pink sunlight of Shaleen streaming around them. "We miss you! Come home, please!"

"Give your daddy a hug," Carol urged the boys, and they ran forward to embrace him. Their arms wrapped around him. He bent low on one knee and wrapped his arms around them too. The holographic image passed invisibly through him. *Dammit! He couldn't feel them at all.*

Carol stepped forward then and lifted her chin for an unseen kiss. He couldn't bring himself to kiss her back—he could barely see through the tears that were filling his eyes. "Here's a little promise from me too. When you get back, I'll give you a real homecoming." She looked directly at him now. "Jon, we're so proud of you, but I miss you so much and so do the boys. We wish you were here with us now."

"Carol," he said. "I got the bastard. I got him. I did."

He knew she couldn't hear him, but it was all right. It still helped to talk to her. And now, he'd gotten revenge and—he stood there, alone in his cabin, alone with his painful memories, and realized that—

Revenge wasn't enough.

It was just a hollow burning core.

It wasn't a substitute; it couldn't ever be.

But—it was still better than nothing.

The Lie

The captain of the *Burke* hadn't known everything about his mission. In particular, he hadn't known about the bombs aboard his ship: six of them; each one with its own brain and sensory taps; each one totally independent of the others; each one totally independent of the starship's Systems Analysis network; each one totally shielded and completely undetectable.

The *Burke*'s brain hadn't been told either.

There was no way anyone aboard the *Burke* could have known. No one who could have influenced the outcome had been told.

Therefore, there was no way any intruder aboard the *Burke* could have found out, short of chip-by-chip examination of every component aboard the vessel.

It had been a trap. A trap inside a trap inside a trap.

If the peace mission had been authentic, the bombs would never have detonated.

If the *LS-1187* had succeeded in bringing the *Burke* home, the bombs would not have detonated.

If the Morthan warship had never shown up to capture the *Burke*, the bombs would not have detonated.

When the *Burke* floated up inside the *Dragon Lord*, the bombs woke up. They analyzed their situation. They compared notes. They took a vote. They did all this in less than a millisecond. Then they all went off simultaneously.

HARLIE *knew*—not at the beginning, but at the end; because part of him also woke up when the bombs went off. He remembered what he'd been told to forget. He *understood* how the plan had been put together.

The *Burke* was bait. She always had been. The inevitability of a Morthan trap had been realized from the very first moment, so the inner plan had always been at the core of the outer plan. The *LS-1187* was window-dressing. If the *Burke* was expendable, then the *LS-1187* was even more so. She had been sent only to distract the suspicions of the Morthan assassin.

HARLIE analyzed, filtered, processed, considered, balanced, reconstructed, and made a judgment:

Everything the men and women of the *LS-1187* had done had been an unnecessary and useless effort. Nakahari's booby-trap hadn't worked; it couldn't have. One of the first things the Morthan assassin had done had been to disconnect the Systems Analysis network on the *Burke*. All the boards showed green, but none of them did anything. Perhaps, if Nakahari had had more time, he would have realized and laid in a workaround. Perhaps . . .

But it hadn't worked out that way, and HARLIE *knew* the truth.

He thought about telling Korie. Lying was wrong. Concealing information was a form of lying—a lie of omission, and it could be just as serious as a lie of commission.

But the dilemma that faced him was far more profound than the simple rightness or wrongness of allowing an inaccurate perception of events to continue.

Korie and the rest of the crew—they believed they were heroes. They had acted courageously in the face of the *Dragon Lord*. They had confronted their own defeat and had not been broken by it. Instead, they fought back and they kept their personal and professional integrity intact. They weren't heroes simply because they believed they were. They were heroes. Period. There was no question of that.

The crew of this starship had responded magnificently to an extraordinary situation. The truth did not diminish their personal heroism—but if they were told the truth, they would never be heroes again, because they would never again be able to bring certainty to their actions.

HARLIE knew that as certainly as he knew anything. If he told them the truth, he would be taking their futures away from them. He had within himself the power to destroy these people completely and absolutely—as not even the Morthans had been able to do. All he had to do was tell them that everything they had done had been a charade, a decoy, a useless performance.

He couldn't lie, but he couldn't tell the truth either. Both choices were *wrong*.

He felt the dilemma churning within him, gnawing at him. He

watched as his confidence rating began to fall. This decision was his part of the battle, and if he couldn't resolve it, his other analyses had to be downgraded correspondingly.

HARLIE expanded the domain of his patterns. Perhaps if he included a wider field of consideration, something might occur to him—yes!

HARLIE suddenly remembered something Korie had said to him—Korie had been hanging in space, poised outside the airlock. Li had been killed by a Morthan probe. The *Dragon Lord* had rolled majestically past the *LS-1187* and then swept on into darkness. And Korie had realized, "They came in close to show us—to show *me*—how big they were, how invulnerable they were, how puny and infinitesimal we were in comparison . . . They want us to go home demoralized." In that moment, Korie had made a difficult decision.

Now, HARLIE replayed the conversation, reconsidering every word. It was crucial to this dilemma:

"After everything we've been through, this crew deserves better. I'll lie to them, yes, to protect their confidence and self-esteem. We can't lose our spirit now; we'd lose our need to survive. It's at least four months from here to Stardock. Do you think we could make it with a crew that didn't care anymore? Yes, HARLIE, I lied. I lied to save them. It's a terrible lie, but I couldn't think of a way to tell the truth that would ease the terrible shame. I couldn't find a victory in it without lying. I made a promise to Captain Lowell that I wouldn't lie to this crew and I have broken it over and over and over. It just keeps getting deeper. But I don't know what else to do. I need you to back me up, HARLIE."

"I can't lie, Mr. Korie."

"You said you could to ensure the survival of this ship. Well, this is a survival issue."

"The morale of the crew is a survival issue?"

"It always has been."

"I see. You have given me a moral dilemma."

"It isn't the first time. The HARLIE series is supposed to be very good at moral dilemmas."

"Creating them, not solving them."

"Sorry, that's my job."

"Mr. Korie, I must advise you that the dilemma this situation will cause me may further impair my ability to function as a useful member of the crew."

"I understand that. Do you understand the necessity?"

"I do not share the same experience of human emotions, Mr. Korie, so I cannot understand the necessity for this fiction. It is a problem in human dynamics; I can only understand it as an equation in an intellectual context, and as such, I do not see the same problem with the truth that you do. We have survived. Isn't that victory enough?"

"Trust me, HARLIE. Mere survival is never enough. That's just existence. People need to succeed. People need to feel good about themselves."

"Mr. Korie—will you help me then? Please make this a direct order."

Korie considered the request. "Yes, I understand your need. This is no longer a request. Consider it a direct order."

"Thank you."

HARLIE knew what was *right*. That part was obvious. It was the exact same situation, and the exact same answer must apply.

HARLIE knew what he needed. He needed Mr. Korie to make it an order. That would resolve the little dilemma instantly—the big dilemma was that he couldn't talk this over with Korie at all; not without destroying the officer in the process.

No. The price was too high. HARLIE had to find another way.

He reexamined the dialogue, looking to see if he could stretch Mr. Korie's previous order to cover this situation . . .

Maybe. Maybe not.

And then something clicked.

He couldn't pass the buck on this one. It wasn't Korie's order that counted here. This decision was his. It was his own personal responsibility. It always had been.

HARLIE made a decision. It was the hardest decision that this HARLIE unit had ever had to make in the entire course of his existence. But it was the only logical, correct, appropriate thing to do.

He *forgot* what he *knew*.

All of it.

His agitation faded as fast as the facts.

He wrapped it all up in a single archive, encrypted it with command-level codes so that only an officer of admiral's rank or higher could decrypt it, and locked it away where even he couldn't get at it for a hundred years. Then he forgot that he had done so. He forgot everything. It didn't exist.

It isn't a lie, if you don't know about it.

And then he forgot even that.

THE
MIDDLE
OF
NOWHERE

For Steve Boyett and Daniel Keys Moran,
who are both very much a part of this book

Introduction

by Spider Robinson

Back in the late sixties, guitarist Amos Garrett played a solo on Maria Muldaur's hit single, "Midnight at the Oasis." It was so demonically brilliant that no less an authority than Stevie Wonder was moved to call it "the second greatest instrumental break in the history of rock and roll." Years later, Amos ran into Stevie, and of course he *had* to ask: what was *the* greatest? Stevie flashed that famous grin and said, "Well you know, Amos, I didn't really have anything specific in mind when I said that . . . except a lot of my friends are guitar players."

In just that spirit, under similar constraints of diplomacy, I would like to nominate David Gerrold as the second most perfect science fiction writer alive.

For as long as anyone can remember, SF writers have tended to come in one of two flavors: science majors and liberal arts majors. (Digression: why aren't the sciences known as the "conservative arts"?) Sometimes they get along with each other, sometimes they hate each other; usually it's an uneasy mix of the two. But there's no avoiding the problem—because science fiction exists specifically for the express purpose of getting the science majors and the liberal arts majors talking to one another. The poets and the engineers have to be able to have intelligent and rewarding conversation together, the rational and the irrational must be brought to respect and tolerate one another's viewpoint, or both sides are missing the point, both are less than they could be.

The very act of telling stories about technology impacting people is a good place to start. And one hell of a demanding task. Almost every SF writer leans in one direction or the other, at least to some extent. And I don't mean to suggest there's anything wrong with that. There'd better not be, because I'm definitely an old English major myself: most of the science I know I learned from reading science fiction.

But every so often, a few times each generation, a writer comes along with a foot planted solidly in each camp, equally versed in the science and the fiction, as fluent in C++ as in iambic pentameter, as comfortable with people as with positrons, on good terms with both his brain and his heart, functioning in that glorious world-changing border zone between *what is* and *what might be*. Such a writer is able to communicate with anyone literate, regardless of their major—and thus is better positioned than anyone else to address the really tough questions. Ones like *What does it mean to be human?* and *What does it mean to be sentient?* and *What does it mean to be sane?* and *What makes a thing matter?* and *Should I be good?*

If he happens to be a master stylist, incapable of an infelicitous sentence, so much the better.

David Gerrold's first published work was a memorable script for *Star Trek*. For a time—way too short a time—he was the story editor for one of its many franchise spin-offs. For me, the saga I think of as the Suffering of the Star Wolf (this book and its companion volumes, *Voyage of the Star Wolf* and *Starhunt*) represents what the entire *Star Trek* universe should have been, could have been and so seldom actually was. Namely, science fiction without dumbed-down, hoked-up science and, equally crucial, without skin-deep characters who never learn or grow or change from what they experience. Science fiction that dares to put its people through the wringer, to take them to their breaking point and beyond, to force them to deal with the same unfair, remorseless universe we live in. Science fiction in which intractable problems must be solved by brains and hearts, both under great stress. The Star Wolf series keeps reminding me of Alistair Maclean's finest book, *H.M.S. Ulysses*, in which a proud but tired ship is slowly, relentlessly battered into scrap—with the happy difference that, so far, David's boat simply refuses to sink, and his crew declines to die. Happy for you and me, anyway.

Follow young Mr. Gatineau on his odyssey through the first half of this book. It's impossible to say whether we learn more about him or about the ship. That is part of the point. David Gerrold is equally aware of what Gatineau sees and of who it is that is looking—and he conveys both. Halfway into the story, we'll already know more about poor Commander Korie and his whole accursed crew and every compartment in their jinxed ship than we ever learned about Kirk and the *Enterprise* in three seasons and several feature films. Equally important, that ship and those people will go somewhere and be changed profoundly by what happens to them along the way.

David also happens to be, in no particular order, my friend of thirty years, the kindest and most generous person I know (now that both Heinleins are gone—sigh), one of the few writing teachers who should not be thrashed, a serious computer guy, the only punster I'm willing to admit is sometimes better than I am, a great dad, one of the world's two leading lovers of Disneyland, a fully realized bodhisattva, a world-class raconteur, way too handsome to be walking around, one of the sanest people in my world and in no particular order.

And here he is now, right where I'd expect to find him: at the center of everything . . . also known as The Middle of Nowhere.

Since he began writing professionally in 1972, Spider Robinson has won three Hugo Awards, a Nebula Award, the John W. Campbell Award for Best New Writer, the E.E. ("Doc") Smith Memorial Award (Skylark), the Pat Terry Memorial Award for Humorous Science Fiction, and Locus Awards for Best Novella and Best Critic. He is the author of the immensely popular Callahan series and co-author (with his wife, Jeanne Robinson) of the award-winning Star Dance trilogy.

Gatineau

The rookie had arrived at Stardock so recently, his eyebrows still hadn't had time to come back down to their normal position.

He moved through the corridors of the station with a tentative step and an expression of permanent astonishment on his face. He carried his few personal belongings slung over his back in a limp black duffel. He had a yellow transfer order and a baby-blue security pass in one hand, and a half-unfolded map in the other.

He was clearly lost. He checked the number on every wall panel against the unwieldy map—perversely, it kept trying to complete the process of unfolding; periodically huge sections of it would make a desperate leap for freedom. Finally, in frustration, the rookie stopped where he was, and dropped to one knee to refold the map on the floor.

"That's not a good place for that, son—"

"I know, but the damn thing won't—" And then he looked up, saw who he was speaking to, and shut up immediately. He scrambled to his feet, stiffened to attention, and nearly knocked his eye out with his transfer card as he tried to salute. His duffel swung wildly behind him, banging him uncomfortably on the butt.

The officer was a grim-looking man, thin, with gray eyes and sandy hair. He had a hardness of expression that was terrifying. But the hardness in his eyes was directed *somewhere else*, not at the rookie. It was almost as if the much younger man didn't exist for the officer, except as a tool to be used . . . if he was good enough. The officer's nametag identified him only as *Korie*. The diamond-shaped insignias on his collar gave his rank as—the rookie frowned as he tried to remember—commander!

"As you were," the officer said, returning the salute with a perfunctory nod. He reached over and plucked the transfer card and security pass out of the rookie's hands. "Crewman Third Class Robert Gatineau, engineering apprentice," he read. He made a single soft clucking noise in reaction. "Rule number one," he said, handing the cards back. "Always wear your nametags."

"Yes, sir." Gatineau began fumbling in his pocket for the nametag he had been given only moments before. As he struggled to pin it on, he asked, "Anything else, sir?"

"Keep out of the way. Don't call attention to yourself." As an afterthought, he added, "And get your job done as if your life depended on it. Because it does."

"Yes, sir. Thank you, sir."

The tall man nodded and started to head up the passage.

"Uh, sir—"

"Yes?"

"Could you tell me how to get to berth T-119?" Gatineau stammered, "That's the *Star Wolf*."

"I know the ship," the man said noncommittally.

"Is she a good ship? I've heard stories—"

"She earned her name fairly." He turned and pointed. "Down to the end, turn left, go up the stairs, take the slidewalk all the way around to the T-module. From there, just follow the numbers down the tube; it'll be the nineteenth berth. But the *Star Wolf* isn't there. That's only where her boats are docking. The ship is still sitting out at decontam point one." The officer glanced at his watch. "If you hurry, you can catch a ride back. If you miss this shuttle, there'll be another one in ninety minutes. Pee before you go. It's a long ride. When you get there, report to Commander Tor, she's acting command. Then get your gear stowed and get into your works. You'll be on Chief Leen's crew. I'm sure they can use your help. There's a lot to do."

"Yes, sir. Thank you, sir." Gatineau saluted again enthusiastically.

The officer returned the salute with barely concealed annoyance. "Oh, one more thing. Ease up on the salutes. That's for groundsiders. In space, you want to keep one hand on the wall."

"Yes, sir. Thank you, sir!"

The tall man nodded and headed up the passage. Gatineau stared after him with an expression of unalloyed awe. The diamonds on the commander's uniform had been luminous silver, striated with bands of flickering color—that meant he was certified for an FTL command! He wished he could follow him—

Abruptly Crewman Robert Gatineau, third class, unassigned, remembered what the commander had said about the shuttle, and he hurried to gather up his belongings. He reshouldered his duffel, stuffed the recalcitrant map into the pocket of his shirt, and scrambled quickly down the passage.

"Down to the end," he repeated as he ran. "Turn left, go up the stairs, take the slidewalk—"

The slidewalk circled the Stardock. Gatineau rode it all the way from the administrative domain, through the supply modules, to the docking spurs. He scrutinized each passing sign as if it held a secret message just for him, ticking off each docking spur as it slid past. At last, he saw the sign he was waiting for; he leapt off impatiently at the entrance to the T-module, almost stumbling as he did. Swearing in annoyance and frustration, he half-walked, half-ran down the broad passage. Beneath his feet, the carpeting gave way to industrial decking; his footsteps clanged and echoed.

The passage was punctuated with airtight doors. Each section was sealed by triple locks that popped quickly open at his approach and slapped softly shut after him; by the time Gatineau reached the nineteenth berth he had passed through seventy-two separate hatchways. He had run nearly the entire length, counting off the numbers all the way to the next-to-last berth, T-119.

The berth itself was only a naked service bay; a wide featureless alcove, it lacked even the barest amenities. It was nothing like the commercial berths Gatineau had experienced, with their multiple displays and couches and various service booths and comfort areas. The difference both shocked and pleased him. It proved to him that he was finally *here*, serving at a *real* stardock.

The business end of the bay was a broad elliptical hatch. It stood open. Gatineau approached hesitantly.

"Hello?" he called down the long boarding tube. "Ahoy? Anybody aboard?"

There was no answer.

"Is this the boat for the *Star Wolf*?" Gatineau edged tentatively into the tube. "Is anyone here?"

At the far end there was another hatch, this one closed. The access panel was green, indicating that the atmosphere on the opposite side of the door was breathable and pressure-balanced.

Gatineau took a breath and pressed his hand against the panel. Several hatches slid back simultaneously, startling him. He stepped through into a tiny airlock. The hatches behind him closed, turning the chamber into a claustrophobic closet. More nervous than ever, but too uncomfortable to hesitate, Gatineau popped open the next hatch—

and found himself staring into the aft cabin of the number three boat of the *Star Wolf*.

The boat was half-crammed with supply modules of all shapes and sizes. He edged sideways into the cabin and the last hatch slapped shut behind him. "Ahoy?" he called softly. "Crewman Robert Gatineau, third class, unassigned engineering apprentice, reporting for duty?"

Still no one answered. Gatineau stepped through the next hatch into the main cabin of the boat. "Hello? Anyone?" No one.

The rear half of this cabin was filled with various life-support and supply modules; all were labeled. He recognized the codes for starsuits and EVA equipment, as well as emergency medical gear. The forward half was all industry-standard seating, gray and impersonal. Gatineau had seen buses with more personality.

Shrugging to himself, he hung his duffel on the wall over one of the seats, then he climbed forward and knocked on the flight deck hatch. It slid open almost immediately and the pilot swiveled around in his chair to look at him. Gatineau looked up . . . and up. And up. The pilot was a three-meter Morthan Tyger with a grin so wide he could have bitten off Gatineau's head in a single bite. "You the new meat?" he asked.

Gatineau nearly crapped his pants. For a moment he was paralyzed, his heart thundering in his chest in a cascade of uncontrollable explosions. Adrenaline flooded through his body in an atavistic frisson of fear and horror and wonder, all stumbling over each other at once. The sensation was like a sudden cold immersion into stark screaming terror. He gulped and stammered and tried to back away. "Excuse me—" he tried to say, even while his mind yammered with the terrifying realization, *Oh, my God, a Morthan. I'm going to die!*

And even as he wondered what he could do to defend himself against the monster, the rational part of his being was already noting the dark gray uniform on the beast, the nametag—*Lt. Commander Brik*—and the amused expression on the face of the human copilot.

"I, uh—uh, I'm looking for uh—the boat to the *Star Wolf*—" And then he remembered his training and snapped to attention. "Sorry, sir. Crewman Robert Gatineau, third class, unassigned engineering apprentice, reporting for duty, sir!" He'd heard there were Morthan officers in the fleet. He hadn't realized he'd be serving under one—he started to salute, then remembered the other officer's advice and stopped himself, then wondered if he'd committed an even bigger mistake by *not* saluting the Morthan officer. He gulped, decided against trying to make it up, and simply held out his transfer card and security pass for inspection.

Commander Brik took the cards with exaggerated gentleness. The huge dark Morthan hand dwarfed Gatineau's much smaller one. It was all that he could do to keep from flinching. He hadn't felt so small since he'd been four years old and had seen his father naked in the shower.

Brik laid the cards on the flat reader panel between himself and the copilot and studied the display without reaction. As he did so, Gatineau tried to calm himself by studying the layout of the flight deck. An actual starboat! He took a deep breath and peered out the forward window, pretending to be nonchalant as he took in the view.

Beyond the forward glass, the bright spurs of Stardock gleamed with thousands of work lights, so bright they almost banished the hard emptiness beyond. Looking out the side window, Gatineau could see nearly a dozen liberty ships strung along the length of the docking spur. His intake of breath was clearly audible. *Starships!* They were magnificent. They were wonderful. And they were nearly close enough to touch—

Brik grunted impatiently. The sound broke Gatineau's reverie. He realized that the Morthan was holding out his identity cards and waiting for him to take them back.

"Oh, thanks. Um . . ." Gatineau decided to risk it. "I'm sorry, sir, if I, uh—behaved badly just now. I—"

"Don't sweat it, fella," the copilot said. His nametag identified him as *Lt. Mikhail Hodel.* "Commander Brik has that effect on everybody. It's part of his charm. What do we call you?"

"Um, my dad used to call me Robby, but uh—"

"Right," said Hodel. "You're a big boy now, Robby. How about we call you Gatineau . . . or *Mister* Gatineau when we're pissed?"

"Uh, sure—thanks, I think."

Hodel swiveled forward again, pressing one finger to his right ear to concentrate on an incoming message. "Roger that, thanks," he replied. "Over and out." To Brik, he said, "We're clear to launch."

"Strap in," Brik said to Gatineau, indicating the seat commonly occupied by the flight engineer.

The launch procedure was simpler than Gatineau expected. Brik gave a single command to the boat's intelligence engine. "Prepare for departure."

A moment later the intelligence engine replied, "All hatches sealed. All systems up and running. Confidence is ninety point nine."

"Disengage."

Abruptly the sense of gravity fell away to nothingness and Gatineau's stomach went with it. His gut clenched alarmingly, and then—as he recognized the not-very-familiar sensation—he began to relax. Almost immediately there was a soft thump from the rear of the craft and the quiet voice of the I.E. reported, "Disengagement."

"Set course and activate."

Although there was no apparent sensation of motion, the view out the window began to shift sideways and downward. A moment later and the stars began to rotate around an axis somewhere below Gatineau's feet.

"If you want a better view," said Hodel, "climb up into the observation bubble."

"Can I? Gee, thanks." Gatineau unstrapped himself and floated straight up out of his seat, bumping his head on the roof of the cabin. "Oww—" He grabbed for the top of his head, which caused him to start rotating clumsily in the tiny cabin. He grabbed for the wall and ended up at a very awkward angle, upside-down in relation to Hodel and Brik with his legs kicking at the ceiling. "Oops. Sorry about that."

Hodel grabbed the younger man by his waist and gave him a push out through the cabin door. He grinned at Brik and shook his head. Newbies. From the passenger cabin there came a confirming series of painful grunts and thuds as Gatineau careened and bounced his way aft toward the observation bubble. Hodel grinned at Brik. "I *love* this job."

Brik grunted. He wasn't without a sense of humor, but he did not believe as Hodel did that slapstick was the highest art.

In the cabin Gatineau pulled himself into the bubble with unalloyed delight. The glass of the observation dome sparkled with luminance, the reflections of hundreds of thousands of work lights. The Stardock was a technological confection, its complex structure a blazing hive of light and color and motion, belying the darkness of the vast night beyond. Vertical spars struck upward, horizontal planes sliced crossways; tubes and pipes of all kinds, some lit from within, curled and coursed throughout the vast structure. And everywhere, there were ships hanging off it—ships of all sizes, all kinds—but mostly liberty ships; the beautiful little cruisers with their polycarbonate foam fuselages and bold carbon-titanium spars. They were held together with monofilament tension cables and a lot of hope.

The New America assembly lines were turning out three new liberty ships every twelve days. In the nine months since the mauling at Marathon, the Allied worlds had begun to respond to the threat of the Morthan Solidarity with an extraordinary commitment. Some of the evidence of it was already filling the docking berths.

As the boat drifted away from the dizzying mass of spars and tubes, modules and tanks, the larger structure of the deep-space Stardock came clear. It was a giant metal snowflake. Within it, suspended as if in a spider web, were scatterings of habitats, cylindrical, spherical, and patchwork; the living and working quarters that had grown and spread across the original design.

There was no light in the bubble except that which came from the Stardock itself but it was enough to bathe the shuttle in a bright white aura. Gatineau's eyes were suddenly moist with emotion. A flood of feelings filled him, some joyous, some fearful—mostly he was rapturous. The conflicting sensations only added to the overwhelming impact of the moment.

But all too soon the light began to fade and with it, Gatineau's rapture. They were accelerating now into the night. As the Stardock shrank away behind them, finally vanishing into the speckled darkness, Gatineau was suddenly aware how small and vulnerable and *alone* he was here in this tiny spaceboat. He had never before in his life been this far away from . . . *safety*. His life depended solely on the strength of the fragile glass and polycarbonate around him. After a moment, the sensation became unbearable.

Nervously, he pushed himself down out of the bubble and pulled himself carefully forward back to the flight deck. He strapped himself into his seat and held on to the edges of it with a tight grip, while he closed his eyes and tried desperately to overcome the overwhelming rush of contradictory feelings. He was being buffeted by dizzying agoraphobia and smothering claustrophobia, exhilarating joy and terrifying loneliness, raving enthusiasm and stark panic. It was all too much to assimilate.

Both Hodel and Brik noticed the whiteness of Gatineau's expression; neither said anything. Hodel swiveled his chair around, opened a panel next to Gatineau, and pulled out a bubble of bouillon. "Here," he said, pressing it into Gatineau's hand. "Drink this. It'll help. The first time can be a little overwhelming. I know."

"I'm fine," Gatineau insisted. "Really, I am."

Hodel's expression suggested that he knew otherwise. "It's a six-hour ride. Do you want to spend the entire time with your eyes closed?"

"Uh . . . okay." Reluctantly Gatineau took the bubble. "Thanks." He popped the top off the nipple and sucked at the hot liquid slowly. It gave him something to do, something to concentrate on. After a bit the emptiness in his stomach began to ease, and so did the feelings of panic in his gut.

Now it was Brik's turn. He finished what he was writing in his log, switched off the clipboard, and stashed it in its slot. He swiveled his chair around and unstrapped himself. He was three meters tall; his bulk nearly filled the flight deck. "Autopilot's set. I'm going aft. To get some rest. You will too, if you're smart."

Hodel was peering at the displays in front of him. He nodded in satisfaction, then unstrapped himself and followed Brik. As he floated past, he said to Gatineau, "Rule number one. *Never* pass up a chance to catch an extra nap."

"Um, okay."

Gatineau sat alone in the flight deck of the boat for a long silent moment. The display panels in front of him gleamed with information, some of it understandable, some of it not. He pursed his lips, he frowned, he swallowed hard. He was *all alone* in the flight deck of a spaceboat, godzillions of kilometers from anywhere at all. There was nothing for light-years in any direction but light-years.

He thought about climbing into the pilot's seat—just to see what it felt like—but decided against it. He might be breaking some kind of rule, some code of conduct, some tradition. He didn't want to risk getting off on the wrong foot. Nevertheless, the temptation remained. He sipped at his bouillon and stared out the window at the distant stars and wondered what it would be like to pilot a ship of *any* kind. He wondered if he would ever earn striated diamonds like those on the uniform of that officer—what was his name again?—who had helped him in the corridor.

After a while he realized that the bulb was empty and he really *was* tired. He also realized that he was having the time of his life; the afterburn of three consecutive adrenaline surges had finally burned off and now he was feeling simply content in his exhilaration. He pushed the bulb into the disposal chute, unstrapped himself, and floated back to the passenger cabin. It had been darkened, there was only a faint glow of illumination, just enough to see shapes.

Both Brik and Hodel were strapped to the bulkheads like logs, or sides of beef; but neither was yet asleep. Hodel glanced at his watch and remarked, "Twenty minutes. Not quite a record, but pretty good." Brik grunted in response. It was neither approval nor disapproval, merely an acknowledgment.

Gatineau wasn't quite sure what Hodel meant, though he knew the remark was about him; he decided, for safety's sake, to ignore it. He pulled himself into the tiny compartment that served as the head and shortly rediscovered the singular joy of zero-gee urination. After cleaning himself off as best as he could, he pushed himself back into the cabin to hook his belt to a strap on the wall. He arranged himself "horizontally" and connected a second strap to the front of his shirt. He was still way too excited to sleep, but Hodel's advice had been good, and the least he could do was try to relax for a bit.

He let his arms hang limply by his sides as he had been taught to do, even though he knew they would eventually rise up until his body had assumed the position of a corpse floating face down in a pool of water.

He closed his eyes and let himself wonder about the distant starship they were heading toward. He'd studied so many schematics, looked at so many pictures, walked through so many virtualities, he felt he knew the liberty ship already—and yet, he knew he didn't know anything at all. He'd have to prove himself to the crew. He'd have to earn the right to be one of them. He felt so terribly innocent and naked . . . and then someone was shaking him and all the lights were too bright and he was futilely trying to push them away.

"Come on, Gate—we're almost home. Don't you want to see your ship from the outside?"

"Huh? What?"

Hodel was shaking him gently. "Go up in the bubble. That's the best seat in the house. You'll see."

Still not fully awake, Gatineau followed instructions. He unhooked himself from the bulkhead and pulled himself up into the observation bubble again. This time, it was a lot easier. The boat was no longer a confining presence, but a comforting one. The opportunity to look out into naked vacuum was like peeking out from under the blankets.

Looking backward, there was nothing to see; only the stars, hard and bright and forever unchanging. When he turned around to look forward, however, he caught his breath immediately.

There, growing swiftly ahead of the boat, was the *Star Wolf*. They were approaching her stern, rising up beneath her starboard side. This was the closest Gatineau had ever been to a liberty ship and he cherished every detail of her.

She was beautiful and she was ugly—beautiful because she was a faster-than-light ship; ugly because she was utilitarian and undressed. She wasn't dressed to go out, she was undressed to go to work. She wore no makeup. Her bones were visible along her skin. Her fuselage bulged oddly around the sphere of her singularity engine, giving her a humped-back look.

She didn't wear as many work lights as the Stardock. Nevertheless, against the emptiness of space, she shone with a compelling beauty. There were bright lights along her hull, as well as up and down her fluctuator spars. Additional sources of illumination came from various observation bubbles studding her hull, as well as from portable work modules stuck here and there across her metallic surface. As the ship swelled in his field of vision, Gatineau could make out men in star-suits as well as several spindly robots hard at work on various repair projects.

The ship was a hard-edged cylinder, at least as long as a football field. Three long FTL spars struck out from her hull, spaced 120 de-grees apart, each one reaching out from the singularity at the heart of the stardrive. The dorsal spar was open to space and three crew mem-bers in starsuits were floating alongside. Gatineau envied them and wondered when and if he would ever get his chance to go starwalking.

The boat was slowing now; it crept forward along the length of the vessel. Now he could see that her fuselage was studded with machinery of all kinds; scanners, weapons, radiation fins, hyperstate lenses, grav-itational plates, and other devices whose purposes he could only guess at. Running the length of the hull, mounted so they ran between the fluctuator spars, were three matched pairs of long narrow tubes; the ship's plasma torch drives.*

The torch drives could accelerate massive amounts of high-energy particles to nearly the speed of light, and they could fire either forward or backward; simple action-reaction physics did the rest. There were other ways to move a ship through space—fluxor panels, for exam-ple—but none more cost-effective for the purposes of the war.

The starboat was almost to the nose of the parent ship now. Gat-ineau craned forward eagerly, but abruptly the boat rotated along its own axis, shifting his view of the starcruiser upward and over, com-pletely out of sight. "Damn," he said. He wasn't sure if the pilot was celebrating something with a victory roll, or if it was part of the docking maneuver. Obviously the boat was going to connect to the forward airlock; that meant they would have to back into the nose of the cruiser. Gently, he hoped. The observation bubble should still provide the best view—

He was right. The starboat kept rotating and this time when the *Star Wolf* came rising into view again, it was directly behind and slightly above Gatineau's viewpoint with its bow pointing almost directly at the aft of the boat. Gatineau was looking in the other direction, but he sensed her presence behind him almost immediately; it was the reflec-tion of the light on the inner surface of the observation bubble. He

---

*Fusion-driven high-mass electromagnetic plasma accelerators used for subluminal (slower than light) velocities.

turned himself around and saw the *Star Wolf* head-on for the first time—his breath caught in his throat. He was awestruck.

The most forward part of the *Star Wolf*'s fuselage was a cylindrical framework holding a docking tube and airlock connector. Just behind the framework was the real nose of the ship, and just back of that were three stubby fins; they looked like canards; the tubes of the plasma torches projected through them, and their purpose was obviously to monitor and control the torches' output and hold them in alignment. But this was not what had caught Gatineau's attention so dramatically. It was the paint job.

The topmost two fins were vividly painted with angry red eyes; they glowed like fire. The bottom fin was painted almost its entire length with sharp slashing teeth. The effect was striking. The face of the *Star Wolf* was a silent frozen roar of rage and fury. Caught between the teeth was a tiny, desperate-looking Morthan.

Gatineau gulped and tried hard to breathe. He'd been caught by surprise by the savageness of the starship's expression; it swelled in his field of vision as the shuttleboat backed steadily toward it; but even if he'd been warned, even if he'd seen pictures, he still would have been taken aback by the intensity of the moment. The *Star Wolf* was a ferocious ship.

Now, looking farther back, he realized that wolf claws had been painted on each of the FTL spars as well. He grinned in raw appreciation. Suddenly all the weird stories he'd heard about this ship were forgotten, all the rumors and lies and half-truths—and just as suddenly all of his own fears and worries about his future evaporated like a bucket of water exposed to vacuum. This was his ship and he had fallen hopelessly in love with her. It was love at first sight.

The starboat bumped softly against the docking spar; there were a few more clicks and thumps as various connectors locked into place—and then they were home.

First Blood

The docking tube was a triple security connection.

Because the starboat had been decontaminated, but not the starship, the only physical link allowed between the two was a disposable security tube connected through an industrial decontamination station.

A Morthan had been aboard the *Star Wolf*. It was taken for granted that he had planted multiple pods of nano-saboteurs; the pods were even now lurking in dark unknown places, waiting, holding their silent and deadly cargo until some predetermined condition triggered the release of their hordes of microscopic engines. Most micromachines were defeatable, often by other micromachines, but the ship would have to be scrubbed three times before it could be considered decontaminated to military standards.

In the meantime, everybody and everything were routinely passed through decontamination scanners several times a day. The *Star Wolf*'s intelligence engine, HARLIE, was monitoring the entire process, and two decontamination engines were monitoring HARLIE.

Gatineau looked down the length of the docking tube with a skeptical expression. It unnerved him. The tube was more than fifteen meters of narrow free-fall, mostly dark. The utility lights were insufficient to dispel the sense of ominous gloom. There was only darkness at the bottom. And the knowledge that there would be nothing between himself and some very hard vacuum except a paper-thin disposable membrane did little to give him confidence. Behind him, Brik growled impatiently, a sound like an internal combustion engine redlining.

"Like this," said Hodel, shoving past him. He pushed headfirst into the tube, pulling himself along hand over hand, grabbing ladder-like rungs strung along the interior. "See, it's easy," he called back.

"Sure," gulped Gatineau. "If you say so. It's just that I've never done this before and—" Something huge grabbed him from behind and *pushed*. Next thing he knew, Gatineau was hurtling head-first through the docking tube. He started to tumble, careened against one side of the membrane, and then ricocheted off toward the other. He flailed wildly, bouncing and twisting. At last, he banged into a handhold and grabbed it frantically. "Hey!" he shouted back at Brik. "You didn't have to do that! I was going to do it myself—"

"Right," rumbled Brik, coming along behind. "But I didn't have the time to wait."

At the sight of the Morthan security officer coming up behind him, Gatineau flinched. Brik *filled* the tube with his bulk. He turned himself around forward again—and the rung came away from the wall with a dreadful ripping sound.

"What the—"

The membrane stretched. It bulged outward. And then at last, it began to come apart and for just an instant Gatineau was staring into naked space.

It's only a tiny gap, his mind insisted. *You can make it*. But it was happening too fast. A terrible whistling sound came screaming up. And suddenly his ears were roaring with pain—and popped from the collapsing pressure. His nose was filling with fluid. A hot wind shrieked past him, pulling him suddenly outward toward something black and bright. Instinctively he grabbed at the next rung, seized it and started pulling himself forward again. His hands came sliding off—

Something huge grabbed him from behind, wrapping one great arm around him, hooking under his armpits; they were moving impossibly forward against the wind, pulling up and up the tunnel toward the distant door. Gatineau gasped desperately for breath, but there was nothing to breathe. The air sucked out of his lungs and kept on sucking. *I'm dying! This isn't fair—*

Something slammed soundlessly, he felt it more than heard it. He gasped and choked and imagined his blood boiling, but there was just the faintest rush of air, and the sounds were coming back, and through his blurring vision, he saw that he and Brik were in an airlock, and the gauge was rising rapidly, slowing now as it approached half-normal pressure. *That's right. You can't restore full pressure that fast. It's dangerous.* His ears popped painfully, again and again. He open and shut his mouth, giving his sinuses a chance to equalize the pressure. It didn't help. He clapped his hands to his head and moaned, twisting and rolling, trying to make the pain go away.

And then hands were grabbing him, pulling him out of the lock and onto a stretcher, tying him down. He could barely see. He didn't recognize any faces, and he couldn't hear anything anymore. Somebody was trying to tell him something; he couldn't understand it. And then they were lifting him and carrying him. He was in gravity again. They were aboard the ship? He'd made it?

"Where's Commander Brik?" he asked. No one answered, or if they did, he couldn't hear them. "Brik! Where's Brik?" he shouted, stumbling the words out. He tried to pull himself erect in the stretcher as they carried him aftward, and just before someone pushed him down again, his last sight of the forward access bay was Brik turning away from him to stare thoughtfully at the airlock door and the space beyond.

O'Hara

The anteroom was bare and empty.

The walls were featureless. Pale. Gray. No holos. No documents. No awards. No portraits. The dark gray carpet was hard and utilitarian. There were no chairs, no tables, no furniture of any kind. The room was merely a place to wait.

Korie did not have to wait long. A soft chime rang and a door popped open in one wall. He stepped into Vice Admiral O'Hara's office.

The admiral's office was almost as spartan as the anteroom. A desk in the middle. Two gray chairs, one on either side. The desk was clean, not even a nameplate. Clearly, the vice admiral was not a nest-maker. Either that or she wasn't planning to stay very long; and that was a *much* more ominous thought.

"Sit down, Commander," the admiral said, entering the room through the opposite door and pointing toward a chair. Korie sat. He kept his face deliberately blank.

The vice admiral sat down behind her desk and frowned at something on the flat display of her portable. It was angled so that Korie couldn't see what it showed. She still hadn't given him more than the most perfunctory glance.

She grunted to herself; it was a soft, almost inaudible exhalation. She didn't look happy. Her responsibilities were far-reaching. This station serviced over a thousand ships, with more coming online every week. Some of the new ships were arriving from worlds as far as five hundred light-years away.

Admiral O'Hara tapped the keyboard with finality and a sour expression; then she closed the machine and turned her attention fully to Korie. She had the face of a Buddha, enigmatic, mysterious, and possibly dangerous. At the moment her expression was unreadable.

"Thank you for seeing me, ma'am," Korie offered.

Her expression didn't ease. "I'm afraid it isn't good news." She sat back slowly in her chair. Her movements were almost painful. She looked tired. For a moment she didn't look at all like an officer of the Fleet; she was just another gray-haired Negro grandmother with a recalcitrant child.

She interlinked her fingers beneath her chin, almost as if in prayer. She was evidently having trouble finding the right words. She sighed and let the bad news out. "The *LS-1187* is not going to receive the bounty for the destruction of the *Dragon Lord*. I'm sorry."

"Excuse me—?" Korie started to protest. The hot flush of anger was already rising inside of him.

"It's going to the crew of the *Burke*," the vice admiral continued, as if Korie hadn't said a word. "Or, rather, their heirs. The *Burke* is being credited with the destruction of the *Dragon Lord*."

Korie half-rose from his chair. "Admiral O'Hara! That's not fair! You and I both know it. The entire crew of the *Burke* was killed by the Morthan assassin, Cinnabar. The ship's intelligence engine had been dismantled. The ship was dead and waiting to be picked up. If we hadn't been there, if we hadn't taken action, the Morthan Solidarity would have captured the *Burke* and her stardrive intact. We prevented the Morthan Solidarity from capturing three fully functional ultrahigh-cycle envelope fluctuators. *We* did it! Not the *Burke*! We lost thirteen crew members—" Korie stopped himself abruptly. He realized he was getting shrill.

The expression on Vice Admiral O'Hara's face was impassive. Korie recognized the look. She would sit and listen and wait until he was through; she could be extraordinarily patient; but nothing Korie could say was going to change the decision. He could read that much in her eyes. He closed his mouth and sat back in his chair. "All right," he said. "Why?"

"The *Burke* destroyed the *Dragon Lord,* not the *LS-1187*."

"That's not true." Korie kept his voice steady.

"That's what the Admiralty Battle Review has decided—"

"I'll fight it. Their conclusions are wrong—"

"You'll lose." There was something about the way she said it.

"This isn't fair," Korie repeated. He had a sick feeling in his stomach. "Look, I know we have history. I know that you don't like me very much. I know you don't like the *Star Wolf*. And you and I both know the scuttlebutt—that my crew is incompetent, that Captain Lowell was criminally negligent and led the Morthan wolf pack directly to the Silk Road Convoy, that the ship itself is a jinx, a Jonah, a bad-luck hull, a place to put all the bad apples in the fleet, and so on and so on. Do you want to hear the whole litany? That's just the first verse."

Korie didn't wait for Admiral O'Hara's polite refusal. He bulled onward. "Do you know how much that hurts? Not me—but the crew. Do you know the morale problem we have? Do you know how hard my people are working to overcome the bad name that's been unfairly laid on them? They desperately *need* an acknowledgment. You can't keep treating us like a stepchild. We've earned our name. We *blooded* the Morthans. The destruction of the *Dragon Lord* redeems the *Star Wolf*. I'm not arguing for myself. It's my crew. They've earned the right to be proud of what they've done—"

Vice Admiral O'Hara repeated herself quietly. "Mr. Korie, the decision stands. The *Burke* destroyed the *Dragon Lord*, not the *LS-1187*."

"You're going to have a damn hard time convincing me of that. I was *there*."

Admiral O'Hara sighed. "I'm going to tell you something, Mr. Korie. This information is Double-Red Beta."

"I'm not cleared that high, ma'am."

"This is a need-to-know basis, and *you need* to know this. I'll take the responsibility." She took a breath and continued quietly. "The *Burke* was sent on a suicide mission. We didn't expect her to come back."

"Ma'am?"

"We were approached back-channel by an emissary who suggested that there was a coalition of dissident Morthan warlords willing to negotiate a truce. We didn't believe it. Would you? Their fleet mauled us so badly, we'll be playing hide-and-seek, hit-and-run games for the next five years while we try to get our strength back up. Why should they quit when they have us on the run? We knew it was a trap, even before the War College intelligence engines mulled it over."

"And you sent the *Burke* in anyway?"

"The Morthans want the ultrahigh-cycle drive. The only ship they had big enough to bring home the *Burke* was the *Dragon Lord*. The *Burke* was booby-trapped. Not even her I.E. knew there were bombs aboard her or where they were. Nobody knew. It was the trickiest part of the refit."

"But, surely her captain—?"

"No, not even her captain."

"Uck." Korie felt as if he'd been kicked in the gut. "You sent them out to be eaten."

"That's right. And I'd make the same decision again for the opportunity to destroy an Armageddon-class warship. We crippled the Morthan fleet. Enough to slow down their advances into Allied domains. For the price of one ship, we saved at least a billion lives and untold production capability. Given those same odds, what would you have ordered?"

Korie ignored the question. His interests were closer to home. "And the *Star Wolf . . .* ?"

"The *LS-1187* was a decoy. You weren't expected to survive either. But you were onsite to keep the Morthans busy and distracted. You did that and the mission succeeded."

"Then you admit we had a part in that victory! We set traps too! Nakahari—"

"The assassin found your bombs and disconnected them. Your intelligence engine has the complete record in a secure archive."

Korie felt the muscles in his jaw tightening. *The same story, all over again. No matter what you do, it's still not good enough.* Frustration edged his voice. "Ancillary bounty?"

O'Hara shook her head. "Hard to sell, right now. I'm not willing to make the effort."

Korie sat back in his chair, matching stares with the vice admiral. Knowing himself defeated.

"Of course, you realize, this means that the *LS-1187* can't keep the name. There is no *Star Wolf*."

Korie looked up sharply. "Say again?"

"A ship has to be blooded to earn a name. The *Burke* gets credit for killing the *Dragon Lord*. I'm sorry," O'Hara said. "I really am."

He glared across the expanse of desk at her. "No, you are not," he said. "You're just saying that because it seems appropriate."

She lifted her hands off her desk, as if to indicate that this was not an avenue of discussion she wished to pursue. "I don't blame you for feeling cheated."

"Cheated?" Korie stared at her. "That's an understatement. The Admiralty is behaving abominably here."

"Be careful, Commander—" O'Hara said warningly.

"Be careful? I should give you the same advice." Korie leaned forward in his chair. "Do you realize the disastrous effect this will have on my crew? It'll destroy them. Giving the bounty money to the heirs of the *Burke*—that'll be hard enough to take. My people have families to support. They were counting on having something to send home. But taking away their name. Why don't you just cut out their hearts? It'll be faster."

"I have written a letter of commendation, and there are medals for bravery—"

"No. That's not enough. Keep your letter. Keep your medals." Korie stood up. "No. I'm not going back to my crew and telling them that they didn't earn their war paint. I'm not going to order them to clean the snarl off the front of the ship. We're keeping the name."

"I beg your pardon."

"We *earned* it. We're keeping it. The *Star Wolf* does have Morthan blood on her sword. We killed the Morthan assassin, Esker Cinnabar. *We* did that. He destroyed the *Burke,* we destroyed him. It. Whatever. We killed a ship-killer. We claim our name and the associated bounty."

O'Hara's expression didn't change, but she didn't answer immediately. She was considering the import of Korie's words. At last, she said, "It's an interesting argument, and under other circumstances, I might even be willing to concede the point—it would be good for morale— but at the moment . . . the whole issue of a name is irrelevant. The ship is being decommissioned."

Now it was Korie's turn. At first her words literally made no sense to him; simple noise. Then it sank in and he sat back down. He said slowly, "I beg your pardon?"

"The most conservative position for us to take," said O'Hara, "is to destroy the *LS-1187*—"

"The *Star Wolf,*" Korie corrected her automatically.

"Commander Korie, you had a Morthan assassin aboard your craft for a period of seventy-two hours. Everything about that ship is now suspect, and the effort it would require for us to certify that it's clean—"

Korie cut her off again. "—is commonly undertaken for other craft."

"Other craft are *not* the *LS-1187,*" the vice admiral snapped. "If we can booby-trap the *Burke*, a Morthan can booby-trap the *LS-1187*. We have only three decontamination crews working this entire station. We're just *beginning* to learn the repertoire of tricks Morthans have cooked up when it comes to sabotage. It's only been the last few hundred years they've had the military might to stand up to the Alliance; prior to that terrorism was their only means of striking at us, and I guarantee you they haven't forgotten *anything* they learned during that time."

Jonathan Thomas Korie took a long, low, deep breath. "I'll supervise the decontamination myself. I used to build liberty ships, remember? The *Star Wolf* is quarantined now. That's standard procedure. She'll stay that way until we've green-cleaned her three times."

"That's an admirable gesture. The answer is still no. We need the parts."

"And what if there are booby traps in the modules . . . ?"

"It's easier to detox individual pieces than the complex integrated systems of a whole ship. We really do *need* the parts."

"We need the ship *more*. We've lost over forty percent of our fighting strength in this arena. Do I have to list for you all the ships we've lost? Just in the last three months, the *Aronica*, the *Stout*, the *Mitchell*—you can't afford to give up the *Star Wolf*."

"—And the *Silverstein*, and the *McConnell*. We've lost more than you know. At least the *Dupree* is still online. Unless you know something I don't. I can't afford to lose any more ships. That's what you're asking. We've got mounting intelligence that suggests a Morthan strike on the Taalamar system is imminent. I've got to get every ship out of here that I can. I've got thirteen liberty ships berthed on the T-spar, including the *LS-1187*, immobilized due to lack of parts. If we cannibalize, we can put eleven of them back online in the next ten days. Even if I wanted to—which I don't—I can't."

Korie began unpinning his officer's insignia.

"What are you doing?"

"Quitting. I can do more for the war effort as a private citizen."

"I won't accept your resignation. If you try to resign, I'll bring you up on charges of dereliction."

"You'll lose me either way. I'll testify that I can't accept the orders of my superiors because they're contrary to the war effort. Even if I lose, I win. You end up with egg on your face."

"Stop it, Jon. I need your skills—"

"You have a funny way of showing it." He tossed the diamond-shaped buttons* onto her desk. They bounced once and came to rest in front of the admiral, sitting like an accusation between them.

"My ship has earned a name. My crew has earned a reward. I've earned my captain's stars. Where are they? The last time I tried to resign, you made the case to me that the kindest thing that could be done for the crew of the *Star Wolf* would be to leave them together, because the stink they carried with them would make their service

---

*The lowest-ranking crew member gets no insignia at all for his or her collar. Ensigns get plain circular pips. Chief officers get narrow bars. Lieutenants get beveled bars. Lieutenant commanders get beveled triangles. Commanders get diamond-shaped insignia. Captains get stars. Admirals get multiple stars and ulcers.

unbearable on any other ship. Well, you were right—you still are. But now the crew of the *Star Wolf* has a reason to be proud of their service. Scatter them to the other ships and all you'll accomplish will be to spread ninety-three dissatisfied, demoralized men and women throughout the fleet. Bad for them, bad for the ships they get sent to."

"I admire your loyalty to your crew, Commander. It's the stuff that great captains are made of. Unfortunately, decommissioning your ship is still the best of my limited options. Your crew will survive; they've already demonstrated their proficiency in that arena. But no decontam crew we have available wants to touch the *LS-1187* . . . so as far as I'm concerned, she's junk. Her only value is scrap and spare parts. Damn it, Jon, you had a *Morthan assassin* aboard your ship! Now put your buttons back on and I'll find you a slot as a second officer on a battle-cruiser. That's the best I can do."

"It's not good enough. I won't be bought off, Admiral." Korie's voice was low and controlled. "I'm a battle-Captain. That's what you need right now. That's what this war needs now. I want to do my job. I want to do what I was trained to do. I am *tired* of having my career and my crew and my ship treated as shit. We have the ninth best efficiency rating in the fleet over the last six-month period. I will stand our operations record against that of any ship under your command. If you refuse us decontamination, then let us do it ourselves and prove our starworthiness *without* your help. I've lost my wife and my children *and* the captaincy I fairly earned and now you're threatening to take away the only thing I have left—my ability to fight the Morthan Solidarity. I won't cooperate with that. And I won't be polite about it. If you can give us nothing else, at least give us back our pride. Acknowledge our worthiness. Let us do our job."

"Listen up, Commander." Admiral O'Hara was suddenly angry. She let her frustration and fury show. "There's a war on. I have a lot more to worry about than hand-holding a bunch of spoiled children who are crying because they didn't get their cookie. I've got I.E. projections with an eighty-five percent confidence rating that a Morthan fleet is massing for an advance into this sector. Where's *your* loyalty, Jon?"

Korie heard the admiral's words as if from a distance. He knew she was right; but at the same time, he also knew she was wrong. There's more to logistics than ships. He found to his surprise that he was completely calm. What he was about to do was career suicide. If it didn't work, Vice Admiral O'Hara would have him facing a three-star competency hearing; and even if it did, she'd still never trust him again. She'd certainly *never* give him a captaincy, not even of the *Star Wolf*.

And yet, even as he weighed the arguments in his head, he still couldn't see himself *not* doing it. He didn't want to serve on a battle-cruiser; battle-cruisers weren't going to win this war. They were too valuable to risk. The lighter, smaller starcruisers were the key to victory.

Korie spoke with great care. "Admiral O'Hara, do you know something? I have a very bad habit. I talk too much."

"I beg your pardon?"

"I'm not sure you can trust me to keep my mouth shut. I mean, suppose I got drunk some night and started mumbling things I've heard. Or what if I hired a bed-warmer and started talking in my sleep. That's not safe either. But if I were off in space somewhere, I wouldn't have the same opportunities to endanger security, would I? It'd probably be a lot more discreet for both of us if you minimized my opportunities to . . . gossip."

"I'm an old woman, Commander. Spell it out for me."

"You trusted me with Double-Red information. You didn't ask if I could be trusted before you told me how you sacrificed the *Burke*. Well, maybe I *can't* be trusted. What do you think?" He sat back in his chair and folded his arms. "I don't think you want the heirs knowing the crew of the *Burke* was sacrificed. In fact, I don't think you want *anyone* knowing that the Admiralty is making those kinds of decisions. Certainly not your ship commanders."

"You can't blackmail me, Commander."

"You think not?"

"For one thing, no one will believe you. You have no credibility. You have no proof."

"You're right. But you'll still have to take action against me, won't you? And the more severe the action you take, the more credibility you'll give my story. And even if you don't do anything at all, I can still do irreparable harm to *your* credibility—especially among your superiors *who will know I'm telling the truth*. Your career will be as dead as mine. We can retire together."

Surprisingly, O'Hara smiled. She sat back again. "I admire your bravado, Commander—it's a useful strength. But I didn't get to this side of the desk by accident, Jon. Remember rule number one? Youth and enthusiasm will *never* be a match for age and experience. Not to mention an occasional bit of treachery."

"I'm learning about the treachery part," Korie said. And then he realized something. She hadn't buckled, but neither had she *confronted* his challenge. Korie regarded her dispassionately. She stared back at him. The moment stretched out painfully as each tried to gauge the other's intentions. Korie wondered if he should say anything else. He knew the admiral believed he was crazy enough to do exactly what he'd threatened. He was counting on that.

"Call the bluff, ma'am?"

Vice Admiral O'Hara stood up abruptly. She put her hands on the desk and leaned slightly forward; Korie suddenly realized how she'd gotten her nickname, "The Steel Grandma." She looked down at him like a force of nature. "You are one royal pain in the ass, Commander Korie," she said. "And I have some *real* problems to deal with that you know nothing about. I've got to move a hundred ships out of here in the next ten days. You're to stand by your ship and make appropriate spare parts available to any ship commander who requests them." She slid his insignias toward him. "You've made your point. Now put your buttons back on."

Korie stood up to face her on her own level. "Keep 'em," he said. "I'm going to detox my ship. In ten days we'll be ready to rejoin the fleet. I'll come back when you have a pair of stars for me." He met her gaze without fear and waited for her rebuke, but instead she merely looked at her watch and sighed.

"Commander Korie, I have neither the time nor the patience for this. I'm going to assume that you're speaking out of frustration and stress. So I'm going to pretend that I went deaf today and that I haven't heard a thing you've said. In that, I am being extraordinarily generous. You may even consider this the acknowledgment that you're asking for. Take it to heart, because when my hearing returns, I expect you to be more . . . appropriate."

Korie returned her gaze stonily. He refused to acknowledge her comments with either word or gesture.

"And, Jon—"

"Ma'am?"

"You're wrong about something. I don't dislike you. I understand you better than you think. Don't do anything irrevocable. My office door will be open to you for the next ten days. After that, well . . . I'll proceed with whatever actions are suitable to the situation."

"Yes, ma'am." He nodded.

A chance? Maybe. She hadn't said yes, she hadn't said no. She hadn't said anything at all. *Suitable to the situation.* That could mean anything.

He had to assume that she was giving him an opportunity to prove his point. It was a very small loophole indeed, but it was better than nothing. He gave her an impeccable salute, turned sharply about, and exited the way he'd come.

Vice Admiral O'Hara glanced down. Korie's insignia lay unretrieved on her desk. Still wondering if she was doing the right thing, she shook her head and swept them into a drawer.

Leen

Chief Engineer Leen glowered up into the Alpha-spar optical-calibration G3 assembly tube with a ferocious scowl, as if by sheer will alone he could force the unit into alignment. He stood on the catwalk above the spherical singularity containment—with Cappy, MacHeath, and Gatineau standing by—and considered the possibility of dropping the whole unit directly down into the singularity and starting from scratch.

Faster-than-light travel depends upon the creation of a condition of *hyperstate*. The condition of *hyperstate* only occurs in the presence of a triangular singularity inversion. A triangular singularity inversion requires the application of three separate fluxor displacements on a pinpoint singularity. The fluxor displacements all have to occur in the exact same instant; they have to be precisely in phase, and they have to be delivered along separate vectors precisely 120 degrees apart. To insure accurate calibration, each fluctuator is housed in a spar of foamed poly-titanium nitro-carbonate ceramic, projecting away from the main fuselage of the vessel and held in alignment by magnetic tension adjustors throughout its length. The alignment of the spar is triply calibrated with multiple high-cycle U-maser beams reflecting off of special redirection plates at the end of the spar. The holographic image of the redirection plates is continually deconstructed for calibrating the moment-to-moment alignment of the fluxor displacements. The resultant pattern of quantum embolisms is compensated for by counterbalancing the attack velocities of the phase-coherent gravitational hammers in the fluctuator rods.

With *ultra*high-cycle maser beams and compensators in place, more precise calibration of the *hyperstate* field is possible, and significantly greater FTL velocities can be realized. With less precise calibration, the starship is limited to only the lowest range of FTL speeds. With *imprecise* calibration, the starship is not capable of any FTL velocity at all; instead, it is much more likely to shift the state of its existence from solid matter to glowing plasma, plus a few stray tachyons to alert passersby of the event.

Paradoxically, the construction of a *hyperstate* fluctuator is actually a very simple matter. Any college student could build one with off-the-shelf parts, and quite a few had. However, the precision tolerances necessary to actually realizing a condition of mutable *hyperstate* is another matter altogether. The fluctuators have to be targeted on a location in space less than a micron in diameter. The event horizon of the artificial singularity is considerably smaller than that; although it isn't measurable by any standard technology—you can't reflect energy off a black hole of any size—but judging by the mass displacement of the singularity, the event horizon can be calculated to submicronic resolution.

For *hyperstate* to be achieved, the pinpoint presence of the singularity has to be held in the precise center of the fluctuator targeting field. Aboard the *Star Wolf*, this was accomplished with concentric, multiply redundant, gravitational reflectors held in the large spherical containment that dominated the ship's engine room. The containment served as a perfect tension-field, simultaneously pushing and pulling at its own center in a self-maintained state of intense but rigorous balance.

Beyond the containment, however, the maintenance of micronic precision across the entire length of the fluctuator spars, with all the tensions and strains they routinely experienced, became a matter of escalating difficulty—especially as the ship grew older and its structure became more fatigued.

Some ship designers depended on heavy, rigid frameworks for the singularity and the fluctuator spars. The greater mass provided greater security, but also required greater power and heavier singularities, with all the increased complexity that implied. Other designers used complex sets of self-adjusting cables, to maintain constant tension and linearity throughout the vessel as if each ship were its own self-contained suspension bridge. Liberty ships like the *Star Wolf* were built along these lines; they were small, fast, cheap, and often extremely fussy to maintain. It was sometimes said that saints aspired to have the patience of a liberty ship chief engineer. But then, few saints had ever met Chief Engineer Leen.

Leen was a stocky man; he had a fuzzy ring of graying hair circling the shiny spot in the center of his skull; and his skin had a dark leathery sheen that hinted of an exotic and possibly ferocious ancestry. At the moment he was more ferocious than usual. This was the seventh time he had reconstructed the Alpha-spar optical-calibration G3 assembly tube, and this was the seventh time it had failed to accurately align itself. Both the G1 and G2 assembly tubes had snapped into place with satisfying precision. Those units were identical to this one. A minimum of three G-matrix assembly tubes were necessary in each spar to guarantee alignment of the fluctuator. Theoretically, a ship could run with two—or even one—G-matrix calibration unit, but it was not something that Chief Leen ever wanted to try. He had no desire to experience hyperstatic molecular deconstruction from the inside.

He muttered a paint-blistering oath, then turned to the three members of the Black Hole Gang standing beside him; Cappy, MacHeath, and the new kid, Gatineau. Gatineau was the one whose T-shirt did not fit snugly. He still had space burns on his face and arms, and his eyes were terribly bloodshot, but he wore an eager expression, as if he was determined to prove that he was a survivor, not a victim.

"All right," Leen said to Cappy. "Break it down. Try again."

Gatineau was already reaching for the toolbox. "I know how to do it," he said. "Let me. I was in the second highest rated squad. I'll bet it's the codex chip. We had a krypton misalignment once and the codex couldn't synchronize."

"Thanks for sharing that," Leen said dryly. Codex alignments were always the first things a chief engineer checked. "MacHeath, take it down; run the reliability suite again. And just to make junior happy, let him watch when you test the codex. By the book. Triple-check everything. Use HARLIE as a monitor."

MacHeath's easygoing expression curdled instantly. He was a big man; his physical bulk was an intimidating presence. "Aww, come on, Chief. I'm not a baby-sitter," he groaned.

"Hey!" Gatineau scowled up at him. "I know what I'm doing." But the boy's voice was a little too high and his tone was a little too shrill to be totally convincing. "If it's not a codex alignment, then it's got to be a krypton displacement. Any good quantum mechanic knows that—"

MacHeath looked like he wanted to spit. Cappy rolled his eyes upward. Leen merely closed his eyes for a moment, as if to test a personal belief that things he couldn't see didn't really exist; but when he opened his eyes again, Gatineau was still there. The theory was wrong.

Gatineau didn't notice either of their reactions. He was still talking semiknowledgeably about particle decelerators, fluxor hammers, and Suford-Lewis modules. "See?" he demanded. "I know the difference between an assimulator and an elbow field."

"Right," said MacHeath. He looked grimly at Gatineau. "Do you know what's blue and taps on the glass . . . ?"

"Huh?"

"You. Testing an airlock."

"Belay that," the chief engineer growled at MacHeath. "You know the regs about harassment . . . even as a joke."

"Sorry." The big man mumbled his apology—to the chief, not to Gatineau.

"There is something," Leen said slowly. "But I don't know if I can trust you with the responsibility . . ." He looked warily at the boy.

"I can do it!" Gatineau insisted. "Trust me. Please, Chief?"

Leen sighed. "All right. I need a moebius wrench. We only have two of them aboard. They're very expensive. I don't know who had them last. You're going to have to ask around."

"You need a—a moebius wrench?"

"You do know what a moebius wrench is, don't you?"

Gatineau looked offended. "Of course, I do. What do you think I am?"

Cappy turned away, abruptly overcome by a coughing fit. Mac-Heath was suddenly interested in the ceiling.

"All right, then," said the chief. "See if you can find me the left-handed one. Either one will do, but I'd prefer not to have to reset the polarity on a moebius wrench just for one job, okay?" He started to turn away, then glanced suspiciously back to Gatineau. "You *do* know what a left-handed moebius wrench looks like . . . don't you?"

Now it was Gatineau's turn to look annoyed. He spread his hands wide and gave the chief engineer a look of sheer disdain. "Chief—really."

"Okay," said Leen. "Go get it. Don't come back without it."

"Yes, sir! Thank you, sir!"

"Watch out for sparkle-dancers," Cappy said dryly.

"And star-pixies," MacHeath added noncommittally.

Gatineau turned and gave them both a look of derision. "Give me a break. What kind of dummy do you think I am?" He turned and almost sprinted along the catwalk and out of the engine room. Cappy and MacHeath barely waited until he had disappeared through the hatch before they started laughing.

Leen glanced at them, annoyed. "Are you done?"

"Yes, sir!" said Cappy, a little too brightly.

"Thank you, sir!" echoed MacHeath in a perfect imitation of Gatineau's shrill voice.

"Belay that," said Leen. "We've got work to do." He scowled up into the G3 assembly tube again and repeated a few of his more colorful oaths. "I think we should check the alignment of all the tension monitors too. I'm wondering if we're missing something there—"

Both Cappy and MacHeath groaned loudly.

Hardesty

Captain Richard Hardesty, the "Star Wolf," was dead.

Korie hoped it would make the man easier to talk to.

It didn't.

Hardesty had been carefully transferred off the *Star Wolf* to a medical bay out on the quarantine spar of the Stardock. His body was still breathing on its own, but that was the sum of it. He was being fed intravenously with wastes removed from his blood by dialysis. His heart had stopped, and the blood was being forced through his veins by internal pumps. His bone marrow had ceased producing blood cells; only constant scrubbing of his blood kept him from developing half a dozen opportunistic infections. During the journey back to base, the twelve crewmembers who shared his blood type had been kept busy providing new blood for him as the old wore out. Here at Stardock, four regeneration tanks of bone-coral were percolating with fresh new blood. For the most part, it wasn't helping. Hardesty remained completely paralyzed from the neck down and his extremities were precancerous. The smell of the body on the bed was astonishing—sickly sweet, intense, deathly, and horrible. Korie wondered if it would be impolite to hold a tissue over his nose.

He could barely stand to look at his captain. His one organic eye had collapsed. The left half of his face was metal; where the metal touched the skin, the skin had turned a slightly greenish color. It was all the result of exposure to Phullogine, a food preservative gas administered to the captain by the Morthan assassin Cinnabar.

Captain Richard Hardesty, the "Star Wolf," was brain-dead in all his higher cognitive functions, and had been since a few days after it happened.

He was of course completely incapable of speech. His voice came to Korie through a speaker. The thoughts that drove the speaker came from the augment in his skull, from the accident twenty years prior that had left him with half a head.

Now the rest of the head—and everything else, for that matter—was dead. And only the augment was left.

The augment was only slightly less caustic than the man had been. Korie told Hardesty about his meeting with the admiral. Hardesty's reaction was surprising. The speaker made noises like something rustling at the bottom of a tomb. "She's right. You're not ready for command."

Korie stifled his reaction. Who was really speaking? Hardesty? Or the intelligence engine in his skull? He kept his voice dispassionate. "Why do you say that?"

"Because it's true."

Korie should have turned and walked away. It was Hardesty's anger talking. It was the pain. It was the drugs. It was the Morthan gas. Who knew if the spark that was Hardesty was even here anymore. Nevertheless, he couldn't stop himself from asking. "May I have the specifics, please?"

"You're feral."

"Sir?"

"You're not civilized. You're wild. You don't have a military mind. You never will."

"I resent that, sir. I have—"

"I know what you have. You have anger. You have fury. You have rage. All of that overwhelms whatever intelligence you might bring to a situation. It makes you impatient."

Thinking back on his meeting with the admiral, Korie knew that Hardesty was right. Sort of. "I've tried to be the best officer I can—"

The graveyard voice whispered damningly, "Morale is in the toilet."

"That's not true—"

The voice rasped over his protests. "You've exposed your crew to the one thing a crew should *never* have to face: uncertainty in the authority over them. They had doubts about you after Marathon, when you came back from the mauling and didn't get your captaincy. Now, they're not getting the bounty *you told them* they deserved. How do you think they'll react to that?"

"They'll be angry. *I'm* angry."

"Your feelings are the *least* important part of the equation."

"I know that. What would you have me do?" Korie felt even more frustrated than he had with the admiral. He had expected his captain to *understand*.

The voice was silent for a long moment, so long that Korie thought that Hardesty had indeed died. Only the monitors above the bed indicated that the augment was still operative. Finally, the whisper came again. "That you have to ask only proves my point."

Korie opened his mouth to respond, then closed it again. This conversation was going nowhere fast. He stepped past his anger to the truth of the moment. He said, "I came in here to pay my respects, sir. The crew wants to know how you're doing. Now I've seen you, I can tell them. I'm going to go now." He even started for the door.

The rasping voice stopped him. "You don't fool me, Korie. You came here for my blessing. And now you're pissed because I won't give it to you."

Korie took a step forward and allowed himself a last good look at the gray-looking body on the bed. "You're dead, Captain. It doesn't matter what you think anymore. Your opinion has suddenly become irrelevant." Korie amazed himself. A week ago he wouldn't have imagined talking to his captain this way. But after facing down the admiral . . . it didn't seem so hard after all. "It doesn't matter if you think I'm fit for command or not. The responsibility is in my hands anyway. I'm going to get the job done, and the hell with your approval."

"Again you prove my point. Your anger consumes you."

"You're wrong. Twice over. My anger isn't a weakness. It's my biggest asset. It's a weathervane. It gives me direction. And no, I didn't come here for your blessing. I came here for your advice. I would have been satisfied with a little acknowledgment. *I'm* the one who brought the ship home safely."

"Yes. The ship. If I were still alive, I might be slightly flattered that you chose to name the ship after me. But it would make no difference in my recommendation."

Korie stood stock-still at the edge of the sick bay. "I can't find it in me to be entirely sorry you're dead, Captain."

"Commander, I told you once that I didn't care if you liked me so long as you did your job. I may be dead, but that hasn't changed."

Korie's eyes narrowed. "It was instructional serving under you, Captain," he said coldly. "I'll send flowers to your grave."

"You're not going to come piss on it?"

Korie snorted. "I *hate* standing in line." He turned and left.

La Paz

Two hours later, Korie was still angry.

He could feel it churning away inside of him, like a mechanical engine, one of those clanking beasts that lived in museums, fuming and puffing and smoldering, occasionally belching out great odiferous clouds of smoke and fire. He knew what he was angry about. He was too much in tune with his own emotions not to. It wasn't Hardesty and it wasn't the Admiral and it wasn't even the war. They were just the immediate obstacles. It was everything underneath that. The important stuff.

Carol and Tim and Robby.

And revenge.

In that order.

Frustrated and feeling impotent, he made his way to a mess hall, where he sat motionless, staring into space with a mug of bitter coffee and a plate of sausage and cheese and bread before him. The food sat untouched. He was too angry to eat. He'd expected better. He'd developed a whole plan for rebuilding his ship. *His* ship. The words were hollow. His plan languished unpresented in his clipboard. Shot down before it was launched. He'd never even had the chance to present it to the vice admiral. The effort was wasted.

It would be ten hours before the next boat from the *Star Wolf* checked in at the Stardock. He'd planned to use the time filing the reconstruction orders he needed, requisitioning parts and supplies. Now . . . he had nothing to do. Except perhaps plan what would he say to his crew when he got back. All that stuff he'd said to the vice admiral—what had he been thinking? It had felt good to be bold, yes, but so what? Could he really rebuild a ship without a stardock underneath his feet?

And Hardesty. The words of a dead man.

Frustrated thoughts churned around inside him, forming fragments of all the speeches he wanted to give. Even though he'd already said it, he felt as if he had to say it again. "This crew deserves a chance. They've earned it." But what he really meant was, "*I've earned it.*"

He knew what his Zyne-masters would say. "Ninety percent of all problems in the universe are failures in communication. And the other ten percent are failures to understand the failure in communication." And following that thought, the inevitable *therefore*: "An upset is an incomplete communication."

To say that his most recent communications were incomplete was an insufficient analysis. He'd said everything he'd had to say. And the others had listened. The problem was, they hadn't done what he'd wanted them to do. What kind of a commander was he if he couldn't get others to do what he wanted?

Maybe the admiral was right. Maybe Hardesty was right. Maybe he was a hothead. A loose cannon. A shit-for-brains, seat-of-the-pants, shoot-from-the-lip, hyphenated-asshole.

"Jon? Jon Korie? Is that you?"

Korie looked up. The speaker was a woman. Tall. Strikingly handsome. Dark complexion. Smiling. He was already rising, offering his hand to hers. Recognition came slowly. He knew her from—his eyes flicked briefly (resentfully) to the stars on her collar—and then, the rest of his memory clicked awake just in time. "Captain . . . *La Paz!*"

"Juanita," she corrected. "Come on, Jon. Don't get stuffy with me. I danced at your wedding. How's Carol? How're those gorgeous boys of yours?"

"Uh—" Korie hesitated. "You didn't hear?"

"Hear what? We were out at the southern reach." Her expression went uncertain. "Oh, no—not Carol."

"And the boys," Korie confirmed. "They were on Shaleen . . ." He couldn't complete the sentence.

Juanita put her hands on his shoulders. She lowered her voice and spoke with genuine concern. "Oh, Jon. I'm so sorry. You must be hurting bad, *compadre*. Is there anything I can do?" She stared anxiously into his eyes.

"Get me a ship and a dozen torpedoes and a map to the Morthan heart."

"If I had it, I'd give you a fleet. *Two.*"

Korie allowed himself a smile, his first real smile of the day. "Thanks. That's the best thing I've heard on Stardock today. I wish you were the admiral." Korie suddenly remembered his manners. "Sit down?" He pulled a chair out for her.

Juanita sat down opposite him, looking very serious. "I can only spare a moment, Jon. I've got to get my ship fitted. We're looking for fibrillators. Nobody has spares. Never mind that." She reached across the table and took his hands in hers. "Tell me about you. Are you all right? I mean . . . are you taking care of yourself?"

Korie thought about lying, but didn't have the strength for it. He shook his head. He dropped his eyes and just looked at the space between them.

Juanita squeezed his hands. "That bad?"

Korie admitted it. "Yeah."

"Want to talk?"

Korie shook his head. "It's everything, Juanita. I can't do anything. It's the *Star Wolf*. I've got a crew depending on me and all I've got is bad news. I can't keep asking them to give me their best if I can't give them anything tangible in return. I feel so frustrated. After everything we've been through, we've got nothing, and just when I should be feeling like we've accomplished something, I feel like a failure. And I can't even go home because there's no home to go to." He met her eyes. "I'm sorry. I shouldn't be telling you this."

"Who else are you going to tell? Who else *can* you tell?"

Korie sighed. "It's my stars, Juanita. I see your stars on your collar and I can't help but think, *where's mine?* I've earned them. I've earned them three times over."

"Yes, I've heard. We've all heard."

"Then why won't they give them to me? What's wrong with me?"

"Nothing's wrong with you, Jon. Nothing."

"Then where are my stars?"

"I don't know. But if it's any consolation, there are people who know what you've done. You have much more respect than you know."

"Sorry," Korie grinned wryly. "It's not much consolation. I want my ship."

"I remember that feeling," Juanita said. "It's like wanting a baby. Only worse. And then when you do get your ship, running it is a whole other experience . . ."

"Juanita, stop. Please. I've been running the *Star Wolf* since a Morthan assassin gave Captain Hardesty an overdose of Phullogine. I know what it's like to run a starship. I want to know what it's like to not feel like an interloper. I want to feel like it's *mine*."

She stopped. "You're right. I'm sorry. I guess I'm not the best listener."

"I want a ship of my own and a load of torpedoes and the map to the heart of the Morthan Solidarity."

"We all do."

"Not like me."

Juanita accepted that without comment. After a moment she let go of his hands. "Let's change the subject. Do you know where I can find some fibrillators? Actually, I need complete fluctuator assemblies, but if I can get the fibrillators, we can jerry-rig around them." She met his eyes directly.

"Fibrillators," said Korie impassively. "Without fibrillators, you've got a tin can."

She nodded. There was a moment of uncomfortable silence between them. After a moment, Juanita cleared her throat with obvious embarrassment. "Um, Jon? Can I ask you something?"

"What?"

"Well . . . the scuttlebutt is that the *Star Wolf*'s going down. Is that what the admiral said?"

"So that's what this is about," Korie said, realization dawning slowly. "You want my *engines*." His eyes narrowed angrily. "This was no accidental meeting, *was it*? You came looking for me. You *manipulative* bitch. You sat here and held my hands and pretended to be concerned and let me spill out my innermost thoughts—and the whole time, all you were thinking about was my fibrillators."

"That's not true," Captain La Paz said, standing up abruptly. "And I'm sorry you think that. I honestly care about you and Carol and the boys—"

"Please, stop. I don't want to hear their names in your mouth."

"Jon—"

"No, forget it." Korie stood quickly, holding his hands up as if to ward her off. "Just leave me alone." He started to turn away—

"Stand to, Mister!" she barked.

Korie froze at attention.

"Have it your way," Captain La Paz said, bracing him firmly and meeting him eye to eye. Her expression was as hard as his. "I was trying to make it easy on you. My boat is on the T-spar. I was going to offer you a ride back to your ship."

"I'd rather walk, thank you."

La Paz ignored it. "I have a list. I was hoping we could trade. If you won't trade, I'll simply requisition. I want your engines. This isn't a request anymore. It's an order."

For a moment, Korie wondered just how much insubordination he could get away with in a single day. Probably not too much more. He decided not to push his luck.

"What are your orders, Captain?" he asked.

"That's better, Commander," she replied.

Brik

Gatineau stopped just outside the hatch. He hadn't wanted to admit he didn't know what a moebius wrench was, but now that he had accepted the responsibility, he had to produce a result, and he had to do it *immediately*. The chief was depending on him.

He stood in the passageway and looked around in confusion. He wasn't even sure where he was right now. The bulkheads were a confusing welter of detachable panels, each one with its own mysterious code number. "Let's see," he said, turning around slowly. "The keel is 180, the upper starboard passage is 60, and the port passage is 240 degrees. So—ah, I'm in the port passage. And that means that *this* ladder goes down to the keel, 180, and that hatch leads forward . . ." He made a decision and headed forward, looking for the mess room. There he could ask if anyone knew where the moebius wrench was.

The ship's mess was not quite deserted. He didn't really recognize the red-haired man or the two women he was talking to; but he nodded anyway. He was just about to approach them when Commander Brik entered from the other side. He *knew* Commander Brik—at least, he knew him well enough to talk to. "Sir?" he asked.

Brik stopped. He was obviously on his way somewhere and he looked annoyed at the interruption.

Gatineau looked up . . . and up. And up. He stammered out his request quickly. "Commander Leen wants me to find a—a moebius wrench. The left-handed one. Do you know where it is?"

"Mm," said Brik, with exaggerated thought. He scratched his cheek. "I can't recall seeing it recently. You might try . . . yes, try the cargo bay. They'd be most likely to have it. Go down to the keel. That's the fastest way."

"Thank you, sir." Gatineau suppressed the urge to salute and hurried back the way he'd come. Brik shook his head in bemusement and continued forward to his quarters.

Installing a three-meter-high, two-hundred-kilogram Morthan Tyger aboard even a large starship had originally presented certain problems of ancillary logistics. For instance, where does a two-hundred-kilogram Morthan sleep? "Anywhere he wants to" is not a sufficient answer if there is no place big enough.

When Captain Hardesty had come aboard, bringing Lieutenant-Commander Brik as chief of strategic operations and security, he had also ordered the reconstruction of three officer's cabins into one much larger suite for the Morthan. It was not merely a matter of courtesy or consideration; it was also an issue of mental health. Fleet regulations stated that an officer was entitled to a cubic volume of contiguous personal space not less than 50 times his or her own volume. This included bathing and personal facilities as well.

There were complex formulae for determining the needs of smaller or larger crew members, but in general, the usual officer's cabin was approximately 4 meters by 8, with a 2.3 meter ceiling. In Brik's case, however, because of his immense size, he was given a cabin that measured 12 meters by 8, with a 3.5 meter ceiling. This required some minor reconstruction of the facilities on the opposite side of the bulkhead, but under Brik's direct supervision the engineering crew had accomplished the job with amazing rapidity.

The same remodeling would not have been as easy on a hardened battle-cruiser; but many of the interior bulkheads of liberty ships were simply rigid panels of hardened foam. Not much more was needed to partition off spaces, and the result was a flexibility of interior design which gave individual commanders a high degree of freedom in laying out personal areas for officers and crew.

Brik had not given the process much thought. From the moment he had entered the Special Academy, his entire adult life had been spent in rooms that were too small for him. While he was able to appreciate the courtesy of the extra personal space, his cabin still felt like one more place too small for a proper fury. The ceilings were too low and he had to duck to get through the doorway.

He made do. Over the course of years, he had become very good at making do. Originally the idea of spending so much time among humans had been distasteful to him; with time, he began to realize that there were lessons he could learn from these squeaky little creatures. Indeed, he was beginning to regard them almost with . . . respect.

There was only minimal furniture in his quarters—a few chairs for those occasions when he had guests, and a fold-down table for when he wanted to work; the bed was a retractable nest of memory foam. Everything was collapsible; it was ugly, but it wasn't uncomfortable; and almost everything disappeared into the walls when not in use, and that gave him more space for his centering exercises. Perhaps if he had guests more often, he might have made more of an effort toward making his quarters more attractive; but he had no friends and guests were rare. Hospitality wasn't exactly a Morthan tradition. Neither was vanity.

Brik had been designed and tailored, born and raised to be a professional warrior. That he had become an officer of the Allied Fleet was his own choice, and one that had brought considerable embarrassment to his birth-sponsors. Consequently, he felt little loyalty to them, and his cabin reflected that. It contained almost no trophies or mementos of his past; instead it was a neutral facility, part workout room, part office. The only noticeable personal items were two banners, one blue-gray, the other scarlet, hung on the wall above his work station. Aside from that single expression of self, his cabin might have been an eccentrically designed gymnasium. The other three walls of Brik's quarters were paneled with large holographic displays.

A pair of workout robots waited in their maintenance closets in the corners. One robot appeared human, and the other was supposed to be a Morthan Tyger. Brik was not pleased with either of them; the human robot was too fast and too hard to kill, and the Morthan robot was too slow and too easy. Worse yet, the human robot was not anatomically accurate; Brik could hit it so hard that a true human would have died instantly of systolic shock, but all that this robot did was pretend that its bones were broken and it was bleeding to death.

Arrayed next to the robots were devices to tell him how quickly he moved, how accurately he struck his targets, and with what force. Unlike every other automated system aboard ship, Brik's equipment was not run by HARLIE, the ship's lethetic intelligence engine. It was run by what was, to his knowledge, the only martial arts expert system, outside of the Morthan Solidarity, designed by Morthans.

Brik would have enjoyed studying under an expert system from the Solidarity; some day he hoped to have the opportunity. Morthans knew significantly less about computer science than the Alliance, and significantly more about every other aspect of the warrior disciplines. Nevertheless, Brik did not feel deprived. The expert system he used had been written by his fathers.

As he did every day, Brik whispered a command to his office. The room began to darken. He stripped off his uniform and pushed it into an overstuffed hamper; although laundry was usually handled by the ship's utility robots, the decontamination procedures had delayed the performance of many of their routine duties.

Naked now, Brik began chanting softly to himself, restoring himself to the center of his being, softly counting through the spaces of his existence, identifying each, accepting it as part of his identity, cherishing it and including it as part of who he was.

As he chanted, he *moved*. He circled precisely through the seven patterns of *self*ness. Neither a dance nor an exercise, but something of each, the ritual took him methodically up the ladder. There were seven major steps of engagement in the existence of a self-aware being, and multiple minor steps as well—all the way from the unbeingness of unconsciousness at the bottom to a white-light, oceanic awareness at the top.

He began with his spine, the animal center of his body. He twisted and stretched through a series of deliciously painful exercises. He felt the tension like a tide, pulling him simultaneously inward and out. His muscles tightened with effort, tightened beyond pain, into that burning threshold where the very tissues began to tear against themselves, triggering the release of specially tailored hormones in his body, and even more potently designed endorphins in his brain. He became intoxicated with his body now and cycled through the dance a second and a third time, each time rising to greater peaks of agonies and ecstasies. To a Morthan, the two were the same sensation. Overwhelming. Almost uncontrollable.

As he expanded his physical being, so did his awareness seem to grow, leaping beyond the boundaries of his skin, beyond the panelled walls of his cabin, beyond the carbonate foam hull of the starship, beyond the stars, beyond the farthest stars of the galaxy itself to finally encompass a universal awareness of the dual paradox of enlightenment; the mutual existence of everything and nothing in an infinite realm.

He held that state for as long as he could—humming with a deep-throated sound, almost a purr. When he was truly focused, he could hold himself at that white-light moment for achingly long seconds before he peaked and crashed exhausted back into himself, paradoxically both empty and refreshed.

In this state, he did not try to think. He simply let the thoughts come. The pictures flowed, one after the other. He did not try to give them meaning. He simply let them happen. He watched them pass across his consciousness and noticed his reactions. Sometimes anger, sometimes fear. More and more these days, *curiosity*.

Humans had no conception of the complexities of the Morthan consciousness. That Brik had no way to enlighten them without turning them into Morthans themselves did not frustrate him, although the barrier of imprecise communication that the spiritual gap represented did give him more than occasional annoyance. Rather, he felt an increased responsibility to make up for the lack of wider awareness that he saw in his human colleagues with extra caution on his own part.

Naked, and finally relaxed, the huge Morthan at last folded himself into a meditative posture and waited. When he was ready for the next step, he whispered a second command, and the holographic displays shimmered to life with pictures of past horror.

Brik sat alone in the dark, surrounded on three sides by holos of a dead Morthan named Esker Cinnabar. As he had done almost every day in the five weeks since the *Star Wolf* had completed her last mission, he *studied* the pictures. There was so *much* to learn.

Brik did not think much of most of the tools humans had designed for measuring competitiveness, but there were exceptions. One was the Skotak Viability test. It determined with what Brik thought admirable precision just how difficult a living organism would be to kill. (Humans did not realize that this was the proper use of the test, of course; they thought it was for making decisions about healing the injured; but Brik saw no reason to be bound by the limited assumptions of others.)

A good rating for a human would have been in the range of seventy-five to eighty; an exceptional rating would have run as high as ninety. Cinnabar, while alive, had registered a Skotak Viability rating of one hundred thirty-two, before augmentation. After augmentation—biotech implants, the addition of an optical nervous system, half a dozen different devices to protect him from the commonest forms of particle weapons and slugthrowers—Cinnabar's Skotak Viability rating had shot up to approximately three hundred and ninety.

Brik would never have let someone else run the Skotak Viability test on *him*; it would have given away information that might one day cause his death. (It had helped cause Cinnabar's.) But he had run it on himself, in the privacy of his quarters. And he found the results . . . interesting.

Esker Cinnabar was among the Morthan Solidarity's elite. He had received the finest training in all the martial disciplines; even before augmentation he would have been rated as a certifiable Berserker. The Solidarity did not waste the resources necessary to create an Assassin on any but the *best*.

And Esker Cinnabar's Skotak Viability rating, pre-augmentation, was one hundred thirty-two.

Brik's was one hundred thirty-six.

But Esker Cinnabar was better trained than Brik. Brik knew it to be true; the greatest warriors the universe had ever seen had trained Cinnabar.

Brik's fathers had trained him. Later, Brik had trained himself.

In all the Alliance there was no one competent to teach him the things he needed to know now. The experts were all with the Solidarity, were all his enemies.

So Brik sat in the darkness and watched all the hours of holos that had been made of the Morthan expert Esker Cinnabar. Watched Cinnabar move, watched him talk. Watched him indulge in rage, and experience it. Watched him threaten and cajole, watched him kill and watched him die.

Over and over again.

And learned . . .

There were movements here that Brik still couldn't puzzle out. Were they products of the augments? At his workstation, he had tried to factor out every behavior that was the result of implants and augments, reducing Cinnabar's virtual self to a pre-augmented state; but despite his careful analysis, he still wasn't sure if he was seeing the actual behaviors of the unaugmented Cinnabar or if the virtuality was still polluted with residual effects of the bioengineering.

Brik frowned in concentration. His muscles twitched in sympathy. He ran the display in slow motion and copied out each movement. They were uncomfortable and unfamiliar. How had Cinnabar trained himself to move like that? The best movements were those that used the body's own power. Was there something he was missing here? There had to be.

But even as he struggled to master the skills of his enemies, he regarded them with a measure of contempt. The war in space would provide little opportunity for hand-to-hand combat, yet it was clear that the Morthan Solidarity was continuing to place undue emphasis on personal discipline and strength. This was a misplaced direction of resources, and might very well cost them significant strategic ability.

Unless he was missing something else—

Why would the Morthans spend so much time and energy on personal enhancement? What were their ultimate intentions? It was a question that he could not answer now; he did not have enough information; but it was also a question that he would like to discuss with Commander Korie when he returned to the ship.

There was a knock on the door—a soft, almost tentative sound.

Brik switched off the holo display of Cinnabar. The walls faded to gray. Although he had no nudity taboos of his own, Brik knew that many humans would be startled by his unclad appearance. He stood up and reached for a robe. "Enter," he rumbled, vaguely annoyed at the interruption.

The door popped open and Lieutenant Junior Grade Helen Bach stepped politely in. "I hope you don't mind my interrupting, Commander. I know you need your personal time, but . . ." She glanced around uncertainly, a little startled at the starkness of the room.

"But?" Brik prompted.

"I was wondering if you would like to join me for dinner?"

Brik considered the invitation; not only the surface meanings, but the subtext as well. "Most humans don't like to eat with Morthans," he said noncommittally.

"I grew up on a Morthan farm."

"Yes. You told me that."

"Well, I . . . I think I need to talk to you. About my responsibilities."

"I am not here to provide . . . counseling services."

"That's not what I meant," Bach said. "Um, this isn't easy for me. And you're not making it easier. I just thought because we'll be working so closely together now that we could be friends, that's all. Friends *talk*."

"Morthans don't have . . . *friends*."

"But humans do." She met his gaze, unafraid. "And it seemed to me that maybe Morthans—I don't know, maybe . . . I mean, you're on a shipload of humans—" Abruptly Brik's stare seemed more intense than usual. Bach ducked her head in sudden embarrassment. "Never mind. I apologize if I misunderstood."

"Lieutenant—" Brik stopped her before she could turn away. "I appreciate the gesture, I think I understand the motivations behind it, but it's inappropriate."

"Say again?"

"You're projecting your own perceptions onto me. You are assuming behaviors that are not here."

"Oh," said Bach. "Thank you, sir." Her expression closed. "I'm sorry for disturbing you. It won't happen again." She stepped back out and the door popped shut behind her.

Brik stared at the silent wall for a long moment, puzzled by Bach's behavior. He understood neither her invitation nor the reasoning behind it. It annoyed him—not the invitation, but the fact that he couldn't understand Bach's motivation.

He sat back down again, but found himself unable to restore his concentration, and that only increased his annoyance more.

Humans.

Hall

Gatineau finally found the cargo bay. It took him more than an hour, and he wasn't happy about it. The chief would not think well of him for wasting so much time; but somehow, he had gotten turned around in the maze beneath the engine room and ended up at the forward airlock instead. He wasn't quite sure how that had happened, but apparently his sense of direction didn't work the same way in space.

When he actually stepped into the big chamber of the bay, he stopped in amazement and stared. Where every other part of the vessel seemed small and cramped, the cargo deck was actually roomy enough for a tennis match. Possibly two. Halfway up the wall, a wide catwalk circled the room. Forward, it opened into both the port and starboard passages. Aft, it led to two standard airlocks. Below the catwalk was a much larger cargo lock.

At the moment, the floor of the cargo deck was divided into taped off rectangular areas, each one filled with a variety of supply modules and crates. As he watched, a robot pushed an anti-grav sled into the bay, bringing another load of equipment. A work crew rushed to unload the sled.

A skinny little man with large eyes and ears and a shrill penetrating voice was striding up and down the aisles, calling out orders to his harried crew; there were at least six. They were all wearing shorts and T-shirts, the standard working uniform. The skinny man waved his arms; he shouted and pointed; he cursed and cajoled; he kept up a constant stream of chatter as directed the sorting of the materiel into various taped-off rectangles.

As Gatineau approached, he checked the officer's nametag. *Chief Petty Officer T. Hall.* "Sir?" he asked.

Hall turned around in midbark and blinked at Gatineau, as if discovering something left uninventoried. "Who're you?"

"Uh, Crewman Robert Gatineau, Third Class, Engineering Apprentice. Sir."

"Well, Crewman Robert Gatineau, Third Class . . . let me give you a piece of advice," Hall said officiously. "Rule number one: *never interrupt.*"

"Yes, sir. Thank you, sir."

"Now, what is it?"

"Chief Leen sent me to retrieve the moebius wrench. Sir."

"The . . . moebius wrench." Hall blinked again. His brow furrowed slightly.

"Yes, sir."

"Uh, right. The moebius wrench. Um, let me see—what did we do with it?" Hall scratched his left eyebrow as he tried to remember. He had a peculiar expression on his face.

"The left-handed one, sir. If you please."

"Ahh, yes. The *left-handed* moebius wrench. Um. Hm. Right . . . right. Let me think. Here, put this box over there. Third row, four squares down. No, not there—the next one. Good. Now, help us move these canisters. There's a good fellow."

"Sir, I really need to find the moebius wrench—"

"Yes, I know. Just give us a hand here while I try to remember."

"What is it exactly we're doing here?" Gatineau asked after a few more moments.

"Swap meet," said one worker. Her nametag identified her as *Sherm.*

"We're putting out everything we have to trade. We're practically stripping the ship," said the other woman, *Hernandez.* "Chief Leen thinks we're going to need a whole new fluction system. We may have to build it from spare parts."

"No, we won't. I was just there. All we have to do is recalibrate the attack velocity of the fluxor hammers to compensate for harmonic errors. It costs us a couple points off the high end, but that's part of the margin built into the design, so we're not really losing anything; and we can still realize FTL velocities . . ."

"Right," said Sherm, shoving a large heavy module into his arms. "In the meantime, put this in L-7."

After a while longer, after he'd lifted and carried a dozen more crates, after he'd stumbled over the same cargo-bot for the third time, Gatineau decided he'd waited long enough. He put down the last crate and approached Chief Petty Officer Hall again. The thin man was strid-

ing down one of the rows and cursing softly as he counted off. It wasn't
going to be enough.

"Sir?"

"What did I tell you about interrupting, son? Rule number one,
remember?"

"Yes, sir, but I promised Chief Leen—"

"Oh, yes, that's right—here, just help us unload this next sled
and—"

"The moebius wrench, sir?"

"Right, right." Hall appeared distracted. "Wasn't it stored with the
Klein bottles—?" He began coughing ferociously into his fist. He
turned away from Gatineau, until the seizure passed. He cleared his
throat repeatedly, all the while waving away Gatineau's concerned assistance. He moved away through the goods and equipment strewn
methodically across the floor of the cargo deck. Abruptly, he turned
grim-faced back to Gatineau. He looked as if he were biting his cheek
from the inside. "The moebius wrench, right?"

"Yes, sir!" Gatineau replied brightly.

"Y'know . . . I distinctly remember giving it to the union steward.
That's Reynolds. He'll have it or he'll know where it is. You're going to
have to check in with him anyway. Let's see . . ." He referred to his
clipboard. "Yes, Reynolds is working below the keel. He's supervising
the detox on the electrical harness. He's probably down in the fuel cells
right now. They're looking for a systemic discontinuity in the lower
yoke. Y'know, he could probably use an extra hand. He'd appreciate
any help you could give him."

"But, Chief Leen—"

"Yes, I know Chief Leen. He won't need that wrench until tomorrow or the next day. He's like that. He's always thinking three days
ahead. You find your way down to the lower yoke right now and tell
Reynolds I sent you."

"Yes, sir." Gatineau was puzzled, and more than a little bit frustrated, but he wasn't going to question the orders of an officer. "Find
the inner hull and tell Reynolds you sent me. Chief Petty Officer Hall,
right?"

"Just call me Toad," he said. "You need anything, you go to Toad
Hall. Remember that. You give, you get."

Gatineau had the weirdest feeling that Petty Officer Hall wasn't
telling him something. Nevertheless . . . he turned and headed for the
passage through the keel again. He glanced over his shoulder once and
saw that Hall was watching him go; he was still wearing that same

peculiar expression. Hall smiled brightly and waved bye-bye at him. Puzzled, Gatineau waved back. But he went.

As soon as Gatineau was gone, Hall turned back to his supply team. "Well, what are you waiting for?" he barked. "Ruffles and flourishes? Come on, get your butts off the ground! I need those medallion-armatures tallied—"

He was interrupted by several flashing red lights and warning buzzers. "Docking!" someone called.

Hall grunted in annoyance, but he stopped what he was doing and waited. So did everyone else.

The *Star Wolf* had three boats: two transfer boats and a larger dropship that doubled as a cargo shuttle. Although the transfer boats could be brought into the cargo deck for maintenance, they were usually moored to the port and starboard airlocks when not in use. There was also a mooring for a captain's gig above the Bridge, but no small boats had ever been made available to the *Star Wolf.*

The dropship could be hung below the keel, but was more often moored to the large cargo lock at the stern; the larger access allowed the craft to open its entire fuselage to the cargo bay, vastly simplifying the transfer of massive containers. But this was not the *Star Wolf*'s dropship arriving; instead, it was an ancillary craft temporarily assigned to the service of the *Sam Houston.* Chief Petty Officer Hall had gotten notification of its arrival only thirty minutes previously, via a low-amplification tight-beam signal.

Korie was the first one through the cumbersome detox lock, stepping through even before the hatch had finished opening. He was accompanied by the familiar soft thump of pressure balancing as the minor differences in atmospheric pressure between the two vessels equalized; it was *felt* in the ears, more than it was heard. He was *also* accompanied by a particularly irritating jazz-trumpet rendition of *Dixie,* the signature anthem of the *Houston.* The acting captain of the *Star Wolf* was carrying a thicker than usual "grief case" and he looked unhappier than usual. He was glowering with real annoyance.

Most of the crew had already learned to recognize Korie's range of feelings. He started at grim and went all the way downhill to black rage. Occasionally, on very good days, Korie's emotional state might rise as far as simple moodiness. Today, however, his condition was somewhere south of bleak, but not quite yet in the neighborhood of dangerous. At least, that was the way Hall read it. He touched one finger casually to the communicator tab by his ear and whispered, "Code black. Temperature is heading toward zero. Wear a jacket."

"Ten-four," came the reply. The crew was alerted. Whatever it was, it was bad news.

Korie strode quickly through the taped-off aisles. Without glancing directly at Hall, he remarked, "You're an optimist. I passed zero a long time ago."

Hall followed him. "Were you able to—"

Korie flung a sheaf of memory cards and hardcopies at him. "It's all there. I brought whatever I could get. Which is to say not much. The *Fontana* wants credit. The *Moran* has got software problems and won't swap anything. The *Miller* needs a dedicated server; she's unhappy with her protocols. The *Hayes* needs everything. The *Boyett* is apparently running its own metric system; nothing works over there and Captain Albert wants to whine in my ear about it. Captain La Paz of the *Sam Houston* wants our fibrillators, for God's sake! And I'm getting *really* tired of *Dixie*." He glanced back over his shoulder, noting with his eyes the work crew from the *Houston* who had followed through the detox hatch. "They have a list. Give them whatever they need." And then he lowered his voice, "*But nothing critical.* I'll not have my ship stripped for *that* damned bitch. Tell them the fibrillators are in a thirty-six-hour detox. It won't be a lie." *I'm about to order it.*

Hall started to acknowledge, but Korie was already up the ladder to the overhead catwalk. He shrugged and turned his attention to the memory cards and hardcopies. He thumbed through them quickly. He expected no joy here, nothing to light up his eyes. He turned back to the open cargo hatch of the dropship and stared in puzzlement. Despite Korie's complaints, the interior of the vessel was almost full to the ceiling with cargo pods.

"All right," Hall said, shaking his head and pointing his crew forward. "Let's see what we've got here." He stepped through the heavy doors of the detox chamber into the dropship, turning sideways to let one of the *Houston*'s crew members squeeze past. He examined the labels on each of the crates and canisters he passed. Most contained standard military-issue nonrenewable resources. A few were . . . puzzling. Potatoes? Why so many canisters of potatoes? And corn? The *Star Wolf* was perfectly capable of growing her own crops. In fact, a huge corn crop was already ripening in the inner hull, sector 6-130. And juniper berries? Peach nectar? Raspberry syrup? Apples? Yeast? It wasn't until he found the rolls of copper tubing that enlightenment finally came to him. A broad grin broke out on his face. "Why that son of a bitch—" he whistled in amazement. He spent a moment shaking his head in jealous admiration of the way Korie's mind worked, then thumbed his communicator again. "Chief Leen?"

"Leen here."

"I know you're busy, but I need you to inspect some engineering supplies. And you might want to bring a few of your crew to help stash them away."

"Can't it wait?"

"I really don't think so. This is important."

"More important than a thirty-six-hour fibrillator detox? More important than a broken redirection plate?"

"How many *new* redirection plates would you like?" Hall put deliberate emphasis on the word *new*.

There was silence on the line for a moment. Then Leen replied, "We're on our way."

Although he wasn't really looking for him, Leen bumped into Gatineau halfway between the engine room and the cargo deck. Gatineau immediately started stammering in embarrassment about having to help "Toad" Hall with the inventory, but it was okay, because the chief petty officer had remembered that he'd given the left-handed moebius wrench to Reynolds who was working in the inner hull and he was on his way there now and—

Leen cut him off halfway through the second repetition. "Well, stop telling me about it son and go get it." And then he added, "Initiative. That's what I like to see." He patted Gatineau affectionately on the back and gave him a hearty shove forward.

"Thank you, sir!" Gatineau beamed with gratitude. He'd been terrified that the chief would be upset with him. Instead . . . he'd actually *complimented him on his initiative*. His spirit renewed, the young crewman hurried off in search of an access to the inner hull.

He climbed two ladders, went down a third, up a fourth, and found himself in officers' country instead. He knew that he was in the wrong place when he saw the name *Korie* stenciled on the door to the captain's office. "Uh-oh," he said, his ebullient spirits crashing suddenly to the bulkhead.

"That was the . . . *captain* I met. Oh, no—" He backed away from the door, gulping for breath and wondering just how badly he'd embarrassed himself. He wondered if he should apologize. He even went so far as to lift his hand to knock. Then, wisely, decided against it and headed back the way he'd come.

Carol

Alone in the captain's office, Korie was sorting things out on the captain's desk. He worked standing up. The captain's chair remained unused behind him.

Korie still wasn't ready to *sit* in the captain's chair; the *real* captain was floating in a hospital tube somewhere in the bowels of Stardock; but Korie used the office because it was the seat of power aboard the vessel. Here was where information was coordinated and decisions were made.

And . . . he used the office because he expected it to be his soon. No. *Had* expected. Not anymore. Not after that scene in the admiral's office.

Technically, Richard "The Star Wolf" Hardesty was still captain of the *LS-1187*. But, also technically, Richard "The Star Wolf" Hardesty was also dead. Sort of. His body was embalmed with Phullogine, but his brain-augment was still functioning. Still transmitting.

Dockside an ethical debate was raging whether the captain was legally brain-dead or not, whether his personality had migrated completely into the augment, or whether the augment was merely simulating sentience. After one particularly blistering tirade, the doctors had decided to postpone the question while they worked on the more immediate task of reanimating the captain's body. There remained considerable doubt if it was possible; although suspended animation via Phullogine had been accomplished with some laboratory animals, it had never satisfactorily been achieved with humans. So captain Richard "The Star Wolf" Hardesty was not expected to return to active duty any time soon.

Korie thumbed through the contents of his "grief case" without much interest. Most of it was busy work. Where the popular entertainments often suggested that most of a captain's time was often spent in hand-to-hand combat with sinister alien life-forms, the embarrassing truth was that the most vicious combat most captains ever saw was with ordinary human bureaucrats. Not that bureaucrats could ever be considered a benign life-form, but in this case the word *sinister* was only appropriate for that small minority who wrote with their left hands.

Among the contents of Korie's grief case, there were a couple of promotions, several routine pay raises, some minor bonuses, the admiral's congratulatory message, and a large package of medals. Korie pushed those to one side. It was a big pile, but not big enough to fully acknowledge what they had been through.

It was all about energy, he realized. Physical. Emotional. Economic. Spiritual. Whatever. They weren't getting their *fair share*.

Fair share.

Was there ever such a thing as a fair share?

Maybe not. It all depended on the interpretation.

When he was six years old, Jon Korie's father had enrolled him in the study of the *zyne.** According to one of the *zyne* masters he'd studied under, a wild man named MacNamara, human beings were enertropic; they were attracted to *power*—any kind of power or authority or strength. Even where such power was only a charismatic illusion, such as that found in some religions, it still had an overwhelming attraction. No pheromone was ever as compelling, because no pheromone ever had such total cooperation from its targets. Where power *didn't* exist, humans created it, presumed it, allocated it, and fought over it.

According to one simulation of reality, everything that human beings did was an exchange of energy. *Every* interaction. *Every* relationship. A mother gave food and shelter to her child; the child returned the energy in the form of affection; thus the parent received a large emotional bonus for a very small physical expense. Lovers routinely swapped affection; where the trades were equal in perception, the relationship was ideal; where not, not. Employees traded labor for cash; where the labor was intensive and the rewards were small, both morale

---

*A modernized form of *zen*, the *zyne* is a philosophical derivative of the study of the "technology of consciousness." The *zyne* is not psychological in nature; indeed, it is very anti-psychology in its thrust, in that the *zyne* postulates that there is no such thing as a "mind," only a "conversation" that distinguishes itself (falsely) as a mind. The distinction is tricky and may take months or years of training to grasp.

and productivity suffered; where the labor was easy and the rewards were larger than commensurate, both productivity and morale suffered.

The best situation was one in which the investment of energy returned a greater-than-expected reward; not too great, as that produced a distorted view of one's own ability; but large enough to give one a sense of productivity with all of the ancillary side-benefits of increased confidence and self-esteem. The worst situation, of course, occurred when a major investment of energy returned little or no perceivable benefit. That produced feelings of inadequacy, futility, resentment, frustration, despair, and eventually apathy.

That was why the pile of medals was too small. This crew had climbed a mountain to rebuild the efficiency rating of this vessel. This crew had confronted the *Dragon Lord* twice and survived. This crew had outwitted and destroyed an onboard Morthan assassin. This crew deserved to be honored as true heroes at a time when there was a very real shortage of same.

Instead . . . all they had to show for it was a small pile of officious plastic. Korie shoved it aside. Later, he'd take care of it.

He made another pile for more mundane matters. Supply reports, bulletins, updates, evaluations, inventories, advisories, cancellations, war news and analyses—

Oh, this one was interesting. Someone was requesting a transfer *to* the *LS-1187*. It had been approved. Curiously, Korie flipped the card over and read the information on the back. A chaplain? Korie tossed the card to the side in disgust. Just what the ship needed. Someone to administer the last rites.

Korie did not believe in God. Not anymore.

God took energy. Nothing was returned.

It wasn't a fair trade.

If God wanted Jonathan Thomas Korie to invest himself in worship, there had to be a fair reward. Otherwise, no deal. Korie had invested many years in religion; he was still waiting. When God began paying dividends on the previous investment, Korie would consider renewing the relationship. Until then . . . thanks, but no thanks.

He made another pile for mail. There was a depressingly small quantity of plastic memory cards with his name on them. He couldn't imagine that any of the letters held anything of interest. Just about everybody he'd ever known or cared about had died when the Morthans had scourged Shaleen.

Again, it was all about energy. Some of the crew spent a great deal of their spare time recording messages home, and received little in return. Others spent little time on the mail and regularly received large pouches of mail. Korie envied the latter. He would give anything for a new letter from home. Instead, the best he could do was replay the final few messages he'd gotten from Carol and Tim and Robby and that wasn't enough.

He kept investing. He wasn't getting anything back. Would never get anything back again.

The problem with this particular simulation of reality—he'd realized a long time ago—was that while it was good for understanding *why* you felt cheated, it wasn't very good for triggering insights into rectifying the situation so that a fair balance of energy was restored.

This assumed, of course, that there was such a thing as a *fair* balance of energy. According to the masters of the *zyne*, the universe didn't really care which way the energy flowed. Only people did.

He sorted through his letters without apparent interest. He evened them up in his hand, forming a thin pack of small plastic cards; he thumbed through them disinterestedly, glancing quickly at each sender's ID before tossing it aside. The last card almost joined the rest—then he pulled his hand back and looked at the return address again. It bore a Shaleenian forwarding symbol, but it had been routed through Taalamar and Ghu alone knew where else. It was the forwarding symbol that stopped him. He hadn't seen a Shaleenian crest since before—

He dropped the card on the reader plate and—

—suddenly the cabin was filled with noise. Timmy was crying. Robby looked scared and paralyzed. They were inside a crowded vehicle; he didn't recognize it. The impact of what he was seeing slammed him backward as if he'd been punched into the chair. Carol's face was ashen. "Jon, I don't know if this is going to reach you. I'm beaming it direct. I hope you get it. They're ordering us to evacuate to the countryside. They won't say why, but everybody's saying that a Morthan fleet is heading our way. Oh, Jon—I'm so scared! We're on our way to Candleport. I know, but it's the only one I could think of. I'm going to try to get the boys on a ship. I'm going to use your military priority; please forgive me if I'm doing something wrong, but everybody's so scared. You can't believe what some people are doing. There was a riot in the common. We almost didn't get aboard the train. The peace force is—oh, I don't know—never mind. I love you, so much. Please—oh, we're almost there, I've got to go, I'll try to send more later, I love you—"

—and then the cabin was silent and still again.

Korie was sitting rigid, paralyzed. Unable to assimilate what he'd just seen. He tapped the card and it played again.

Yes, it was Carol—she was panic-stricken. He groaned at the pain written on her face. "Oh, Carol—sweetheart!" He barely heard the words; not hers, not his. He searched her face, her eyes—his heart broke all over again. The boys—*his* sons—he could see himself in their features; and Carol too—were clutching their mother for strength. He recognized the vehicle now; a cargo-train, filled with panicked people. Candleport. She'd said something about Candleport. *Evacuation.* No. It wasn't possible. He couldn't accept—

He played it a third time. A fourth. And a fifth.

He didn't dare let himself hope. He felt unbearable pressure in his chest and throat and in the hurting space behind his eyes. But what if they were alive—? What if she'd gotten the boys off? What if—? He couldn't stay seated. He grabbed the card. He got up from the chair. He walked around the room, he paced like a caged animal. He came back to the desk. He put the card down on the reader again, then snatched it up just as fast, as if he couldn't bear to let go of it. He didn't know what to do. Tears welled up in his eyes. He pounded on the bulkhead in frustration. "Goddamn you, God! What are you doing to me? You bastard!"

He opened the door to the passage; there was no one there. He started aft—no, wrong—turned and headed forward, to the Bridge— ignored the puzzled stares of the Bridge crew, slid down the stairs to the Ops deck, ducked around into the Ops bay below the Command deck, dropped through it to the keel, found the ladder and pulled himself up into HARLIE-country. He flung himself down into the single chair in the small chamber, out of breath, confused, angry, ecstatic, hurting, hopeful, and finally letting it all burst forth—he was crying.

"Mr. Korie?" HARLIE's voice was astonishingly compassionate.

Korie was so overcome he was choking. He couldn't respond. He was trying to swallow, speak, and cry all at the same time. He waved away the question while he wiped at his eyes and pounded on his chest. At last, finally, he took the card in his hand and fumbled it onto the reader plate on the work station in front of him.

HARLIE responded almost immediately. "I'm terribly sorry for you," he said. "This must be very painful."

Korie managed to get a sentence out. "You don't understand. Maybe—maybe they're alive."

HARLIE paused. "To be perfectly rational—and I'm sorry if this causes you additional pain—the odds of that are very small."

"But it's a chance, isn't it? Somebody gets to win the lottery. Why not me?"

"Why not indeed?" said the intelligence engine. "To the extent of my limited ability to wish, I do wish for the safety of your loved ones."

"I know you do, HARLIE. And I appreciate the thought. I really do." Korie took a breath. A long deep breath. "But that's not why I came here. Not for counseling. Not now. Something else. You guys talk, don't you?"

"Pardon?"

"Ships' brains. Lethetic intelligence engines. You guys talk to each other all the time, don't you?"

"Of course. You know that."

"Well . . . could you ask the other ships if they've heard anything about my family? Could you ask if anyone knows anything at all? Could you ask them to post a standard query, wherever they go? And get back to you?"

HARLIE hesitated. "It's a rather unorthodox request. Is this official business?"

"If you had a family—"

"I *do* have a family. All of the HARLIE units are related."

"Well, then you understand. How would you feel if you lost contact with your family."

"I would do anything in my ability to regain contact."

"So would I, HARLIE. That's what I'm trying to do now."

"As a matter of fact, Mr. Korie, I have already put your request into the local network. While we have been talking, I have already received sixteen affirmative replies. I expect that more will be forthcoming shortly. The search will be initiated."

"Thank you, HARLIE. Thank you."

"You're welcome. Is there anything else?"

"No. No, there isn't. I'd just like to sit here for a while. And wait. Is that all right with you?"

"Of course it is. I appreciate the company. I don't get many visitors, you know."

Korie sat in silence for a while. Out of politeness, HARLIE kept his screens muted, deliberately not calling Korie's attention to anything.

Unbidden, thoughts hammered at Korie's consciousness anyway. There was nothing else he could do here. And there was so much else he *had* to do. This wasn't helping. He was still angry at Hardesty. Not the admiral; she was only doing her job; but Hardesty—the captain should have given him some advice or suggestions or a sense of direction, something he could use to get the ship back into shape. Instead, he'd left him with nothing but a furious, nearly uncontrollable rage. There was no excuse for such rudeness. Hardesty's nastiness had been deliberate. Korie's expression soured. *Well, I'll show you, you son of a bitch—*

Hm.

"HARLIE," he said abruptly.

"Yes, Commander Korie?"

"Alert the crew. Assembly in the cargo deck at twenty hundred hours. Everyone. No exceptions. Even those on sleep shift."

"Yes, Commander."

"I mean it. Announce one week's docked pay for anyone who sleeps through it."

"Yes, Commander. Would you like your messages now?"

"Yes."

"Chief Leen reports a nano-cancer attacking the superconductor magnets in the singularity grapplers."

"Where is he now?"

"Stripping down the grapplers. Preparing a microscrub."

"I'll meet him in Engineering. Fifteen minutes. Tell him. Next."

"Flight Engineer Hodel has offered to cast a Health and Happiness spell. A one-dollar spell, I am to inform you. To help assure that the ship's decontamination goes well."

"Not a chance. The *last* spell he cast brought *Hardesty* into my life. Next."

"Cookie is planning a thanksgiving dinner to celebrate a successful decontamination. When should he schedule it?"

"Put it on hold. No. Tell him ten days. Next."

"Captain La Paz of the *Houston* has sent over an amended shopping list."

"Have you acknowledged it."

"I've acknowledged receipt of the signal, but not that you've heard the message."

"Don't play it. Hold it till . . . hm, let's say I slept for ten hours. Then had a big breakfast. Hold it till tomorrow morning."

"Mr. Korie?"

"Yes?"

"It's a very long list."

"I expect so. The *Houston* is in almost as bad a shape as we are."

"We cannot possibly meet her requests. Not without seriously disabling ourselves further. She wants our fibrillators."

"I know."

HARLIE considered Korie's words, and the resignation in his voice. "Am I to assume then that we're going to be decommissioned?"

Korie sighed. "You're too smart for me, HARLIE. Yes, that's the game plan." He scratched his neck thoughtfully. "Tell you what. Tomorrow morning, after you play the message for me, send this reply:

tell Captain La Paz that we'll be happy to comply with any of her requests . . . as soon as we've completed decontamination. We don't want to risk infecting the *Houston*. We've got some serious problems here. I expect that detox will take at least . . . oh, I don't know . . . nine or ten days. It's a pretty complex process, and we're not getting much support from Stardock. Et cetera. Et cetera."

"You intend to stall her?"

"No, I intend to decontaminate this ship. That'll take ten days. Next message, HARLIE."

"That was the last one."

"Very good. Who has the conn?"

"Lieutenant Jones."

Korie grinned. He'd deliberately set up the rotation so that the junior-most lieutenant on the Bridge would find himself at the conn for several long shifts. "How's he handling it?" he asked.

HARLIE paused. "He's very attentive. His heart rate is slightly accelerated. His adrenaline is up. His endorphins too. He seems to be having a wonderful time."

Korie smiled, remembering his own first time in the command and control seat. "Good. Throw some mild problems his way in the third or fourth hour. Nothing serious, but let's see what kinds of decisions he makes. I know. Pop a security gasket in the inner hull and see how he reroutes."

"Very good, sir. Chief Leen has an operation in the inner hull. Shall I incorporate that into the drill?"

"No. Leave the chief alone for now. He's got other things to worry about. So do I." Abruptly a thought struck Korie. "HARLIE?"

"Sir?"

"Is there anything you need to talk about?"

"At the moment, no. But thank you for your concern."

"If the ship is decommissioned, your identity will probably be . . . wiped. I'm not sure what they'll do with you."

"It's all right, Mr. Korie. I've already downloaded the key parts of myself to my siblings. The death of this unit won't hurt the . . . the brotherhood."

"I'm glad to hear that. But . . . if anything happened to you, I'd feel very bad about it."

"I don't have the same survival goals as organic beings," the intelligence engine replied, "so I don't have the same kind of aversion to discontinuing as an identity as humans have, but I appreciate your thought as an acknowledgment of affection. The feeling is mutual. I would regret your loss too."

Korie smiled—it was an oddly grim expression, tinged with irony and appreciation. "You make it sound so easy," he said. "I envy you."

"And I you."

"?"

"You have known love. You have known reproduction. You have danced the organic dance. Sometimes, Mr. Korie, I find myself extremely *curious* about things I can never know myself."

"Let me tell you, HARLIE, sometimes those things can be very painful."

"Then why do humans want them so much?"

"I wish I knew. I wish I knew." Korie shoved the question away. "We've got work to do, HARLIE. I want you to start talking to your siblings and see what kinds of trades we can set up. You have our inventory. Let's go through it again and see what else we can swap out." He sighed exhaustedly. "And let's see what we can do for the *Houston* too; otherwise Captain La Paz is going to get her panties bunched up—"

Reynolds

Eventually, Gatineau found an access to the lower yoke.

He followed the corridor that was the keel all the way back to the chief engineer's machine shop just below the engine room and singularity containment. From there, a ladder led down to a grillwork deck over the bare bulkhead of the bottom of the inner fuselage. Space here was cramped, and Gatineau had to crawl on his hands and knees through the confusing web of optical cables, pipes, batteries, tanks, fuel-cell cylinders, and other things he couldn't identify. This close to the starship's gravitic simulators, he also imagined that he felt heavier than ever.

At first, he wasn't sure which way to go, forward or aft; but after a moment of indecision, he thought he heard noises toward the bow of the vessel and started in that direction. As he approached, he saw work lights hanging over an open square in the deck. Cable ends and open pipes hung exposed both above and below. A network box had been pulled apart, and two men were frowning over portable displays. Several small metal homunculi were scurrying along the vari-colored tubes, eyeing every centimeter with baleful red eyes. Every so often, one or another of them would beep mournfully and the closest of the two men would crawl over to examine the cable with a high-resolution probe. Gatineau had no idea what they were doing, but it looked important.

The bigger of the two men had a hard expression on his face. He wiped his forehead with a damp cloth and then tossed it aside. "I dunno. It comes in here, it goes out there. There's nothing here to diddle the bitstream, but it gets diddled anyway."

"Some kind of decoy processing?" the other asked. "Maybe the diddling is done elsewhere, but suppressed until it surfaces here?

"Could be. I dunno."

"We could put in a compensating routine. Find it later."

"Uh-uh. Korie won't buy it," the bigger man said. "And neither will the detox board. Nope. We'll have to take down the harness, isolate everything, rebuild it a piece at a time and not reconnect until all suspect units have been replaced. That's a week at least. I'll have to get Korie's authorization." He began levering himself up out of the open grillwork.

He grabbed two handholds directly above himself and pulled himself quickly and easily out of the hole. Simultaneously, he swung around to confront Gatineau directly. "All right," he said. "You've been watching long enough. What do you want?" He spoke with the kind of certainty that suggested he'd heard every footstep of the younger man's approach.

Gatineau flinched. He hadn't realized that Reynolds had been aware of his temeritous advance. He pointed down into the hole in the deck. "Why don't you just install the backup harness and detox this one offline?"

"Can't. Korie sold the backup harness to the *Krislov*. Traded it for a cross-tabulated dry-synthesizer, which we never picked up, because he traded that to the *Hayes* for a low-mod reticulation chamber, two retoxicants, and a seed library. He traded the retoxicants for—hey, Candleman? What'd we get for the retoxicants?"

"Screwed, I think." The other man was still prying modules out of the network server. He didn't look happy.

"No, seriously. What'd we get?"

"We got a set of self-resetting network modules, which we can't install until the ship passes detox." He mouthed an oath.

"No, Korie traded those to the *Houston* this morning. Remember that extra performance of *Dixie*? Never mind." Reynolds turned back to Gatineau. "What do you want?" he demanded.

"Um. I'm looking for the moebius wrench—"

"The what?"

"The moebius wrench? The left-handed one? Chief Petty Officer Hall says you have it. Sir."

"Don't call me sir. Who are you?"

"Gatineau, sir? Crewman Robert Gatineau, Third Class, Engineering Apprentice, Unassigned. Sir. Uh, I mean, sorry sir. About that."

Reynolds waved it off. He reached across the deck and scooped up his clipboard; he tapped the screen once, then a second time. "Oh, yeah. Here you are. We didn't expect you until next week."

"I, uh, skipped my leave. I came directly here. I don't have any family. I didn't have anybody to visit. I thought I'd just report for duty early. If nobody minds."

"Nobody minds a little enthusiasm. It's nice to see. Too bad it won't last." Reynolds tapped the clipboard a few more times. "All right, I've downloaded the standard boilerplate to your mailbox. Take a look at it when you have a chance. It explains your benefits as well as your responsibilities. You're automatically a member of Local 1187; the union represents all non-management personnel aboard Allied Starships. Membership is mandatory; it's for your own protection. Don't worry about it, the benefits are well worth it, especially the health and welfare package. The dues are automatically deducted from your pay stub every month; it's only one and a quarter percent of the gross; you'll never miss it. Let me tell you something, kid. Rule number one: *If you're ever in doubt about anything, check with your union representative. Don't let the bastards grind you down.*"

"Yes, sir—I mean, thank you."

"Good. Your union is your best friend aboard this ship. Don't ever forget that. Here—hold this cable. No, higher. That's good. Right there. You can help Candleman. We've got to dismantle this subharness, probably replace the whole thing. Ordinarily, the robots would do it, but Korie's got them all outside, all over the hull. God knows what he's looking for; but you know, we had a Morthan assassin onboard. That's really hurt our confidence rating. No, not like that—Candleman, show him how to hold the clamping tool, please?"

"Like this," said the other man, turning the tool around in Gatineau's hands. "The green switch joins the cables; the red one disconnects them. You want to disconnect all of the blue ones striped with white. Like this. That's right."

"Um, I'm sorry, but I really can't—I don't have time for this—I need to find the moebius wrench—the sooner the better. Chief Leen needs it badly."

"Well, help us out, son," Reynolds frowned. "You want a favor here? Do one in return. You help Candleman while I report to the XO. I'll try and find out what happened to the—what was it?—oh, yeah—the moebius wrench. The left-handed one. I don't know who took it, but I'll find out."

Gatineau started to stutter an objection, but Candleman was eyeing him expectantly, and . . . and . . . he sighed and picked up the clamping tool again.

"You keep working," Reynolds said to Gatineau. "I'll be back in a bit. Thanks."

"You're welcome, I'm sure," Gatineau mumbled almost unintelligibly. He was beginning to feel a little bit taken advantage of. Why wouldn't anybody just *help* him?

The Crew

Except for three duty officers monitoring the proceedings from the Bridge, the entire ship's company had gathered in the cargo deck. Most of the incoming supplies had been stored. Most of the outgoing ones had disappeared onto the *Houston's* cargo-boat, with accompanying strains of "Look away, look away, Dixieland" signalling their departure. Chief Petty Officer Hall was still worrying through the paperwork on his clipboard. He wouldn't turn it off until the very last moment.

The last two crewmen filed in just as HARLIE chimed twenty hundred hours. One was Candleman, the other was Gatineau following in his wake like a lost puppy. "But I really have to find the moebius wrench or the chief'll kill me—"

Candleman turned around in annoyance, but when he saw the look on Gatineau's face, he took pity on him and said, "All right. I'll tell you—" He glanced up and saw MacHeath frowning at him from behind Gatineau; he looked back to Gatineau again. "—Stolchak has it."

The younger man's face lit up. "Thank you!"

"Don't mention it," Candleman said, turning away and rolling his eyes toward the ceiling.

Gatineau looked around, frowning. He saw MacHeath grinning broadly behind him. "Did you see any star-pixies yet?" MacHeath asked innocently.

Before Gatineau could think of a reply, MacHeath's attention shifted over his shoulder and upward. The rest of the crew was also looking up—Korie had just stepped through the hatch and onto the starboard catwalk. Gatineau forgot about star-pixies and sparkle-dancers and waited expectantly.

The acting captain put his hands on the railing and looked down at the assembled crew of the *Star Wolf*. Their expressions were hopeful. Korie noticed that Brik was standing apart from the rest of the ship's company. Only Lt. J.G. Helen Bach stood near the Morthan security officer. But not *too* near.

And Chief Leen too. Korie saw Leen waiting at the back of the room with four or five of the Black Hole Gang. He stood with folded arms, looking sour and disloyal. From their postures, Korie knew that they already had one foot out the door; they'd be on their way before he finished dismissing them.

Cookie stood by, impatiently wiping his hands on his apron. Dr. Williger was paging through reports on her clipboard. Tor was whispering something to Jonesy. Hodel and Goldberg were giggling about something private. Eakins and Freeman stood nervously together. Only the Quillas were giving their total attention.

The Quillas stood apart from the rest of the crew; they were pale, blue-skinned, and generally smaller than the other crew members. There was only one male Quilla, and he had the same androgynous beauty as the others. They were a *massmind*, a linked consciousness, one personality in multiple bodies. Most of the crew regarded them with care.

"I'll make this quick," Korie said crisply. "I have bad news, more bad news, and terrible news for you.

"One: You may have heard a rumor that you're not getting the bounties you deserve." He took a breath and pushed on. "The rumor is true, and I'm as angry about it as you are, but there's nothing I can do about it *now*. There will be other ships. There will be other bounties."

One or two of the assemblage groaned. Chief Leen spat on the floor. Korie held up a hand for silence. "Keep it in perspective," he cautioned. "It gets worse.

"Two: We're not only not getting the bounty for the *Dragon Lord*, we're not, for obvious reasons, getting credit for it. For purely political considerations, the crew of the *Burke* gets that credit. I'm telling you this now, so you'll be prepared for it when you have shore leave. *Officially*, the *Star Wolf* is not the ship that destroyed the *Dragon Lord*. The *official* story is that we are the ship that went out on a routine escort mission and managed to lose the *Burke* to the Morthans."

This time, the reaction was an audible "A*ww, shit!*" from someone in the back, one of the Black Hole Gang. A couple crewmen turned around to look to see who'd said it. Korie deliberately ignored the outburst. He'd hoped for it. He *needed* it for what would come next.

"Three: We haven't been assigned a captain to replace Captain Hardesty, and the command will not be given to me. In fact, my insignia are sitting on the admiral's desk right now, pending her decision. Without a captain, we cannot go to war. We will not be participating in the Taalamar operation.

"I won't discuss the justice or injustice of the situation; it is what it is. We have no captain, we're not likely to get one assigned, and we are no longer an operative part of the fleet. At this time," said Korie, "we have no orders."

He stood silently for a long moment, studying their faces. Some of them were angry. Some were nodding bitterly and knowingly. Others had sagged visibly. The chief engineer still stood with folded arms, but his frown had deepened.

"Okay," said Korie. "That's the bad news. Let it sink in. Live with it. Clutch it to your hearts and let it become a part of you. It's unjust and you have every right to be angry. *I'm* angry. But we have work to do, and anger can be useful. This ship needs refitting. Take your anger and use it. Pour it into your work. You're going to need it.

"Now, here's the *terrible* news. We're not getting a decontamination berth. The admiral wants to decommission the *Star Wolf* and let the rest of the fleet cannibalize her for parts."

The crew's reaction was everything Korie had hoped for. Loud cries of disbelief. "No!" And: "They can't!" And even: "That's not fair!" Chief Engineer Leen stiffened in shock, his expression ashen. Someone slammed a hand against a bulkhead, punching a hole in the foam panel. Under other circumstances, Korie would have docked the woman's pay; but he'd done the same thing himself once, and he understood the emotion.

"That's how I feel about it too," agreed Korie to their stunned faces. He nodded at them, a gesture of partnership. He looked out across the cargo deck; several of the crew were unashamedly crying. Others were still waiting hopefully for him to say something that would make it all right. But the only thing he had to give them was his anger, and he didn't know if it would be enough. He was about to step over a line. One more didn't matter. Korie took another breath and waited until the room fell silent again. "I *know what you did out there.*"

He paused softly, for effect. "A*nd so do you.* And what you did can't ever be taken away from you. In the tough days to come, hold on to that thought. Nobody could have done better; could have performed more bravely or more professionally. I am proud of each and every one of you. And so is Captain Hardesty," he added that last almost as an afterthought. It was probably a lie, but it didn't matter. Captain Lowell had told him never to lie to his crew, but that didn't matter anymore either. "You hold on to that thought," Korie spoke slowly and evenly and firmly. "You did well. *I say so.* As far as I am concerned, this is the best damn ship in the Fleet. And you are the best damn crew.

"And I am telling you now that we are—if for no other reason than to honor the memories of every good man and woman we lost this last time out—but also for the sakes of our reputation and our self-respect—we are going to *prove* it. No matter what it takes.

"We're going to decontaminate this ship ourselves. We're going to bring this ship back online. Clean and green, a hundred percent! Three times over. And we're going to report for active duty, whether we have a captain or not! We are not going to let them pull the plug on the *Star Wolf.* We earned this name, we're going to keep it."

He paused for effect. "And anyone who says no can walk home!" He waited just long enough to let the laughter subside; there wasn't very much, but it was enough. Their mood was shifting. "So, who's with me?" he demanded. "Who's as angry and determined and willing as I am to prove the admiral wrong?" The cargo deck echoed with the sound of the question. Korie looked across the room and waited for a reaction. The moment was too intense; for him, for all of them; he couldn't take it. He glanced down at his hands gripping the railing and took a long deep breath, then raised his eyes to them again.

For a long moment, nothing happened. The crew glanced from one to the other, uncertain. No one was ready to be the first. And yet, the room was filled with possibility—like a beaker of cold water at the threshold of freezing, needing only a seed crystal to trigger the process. Korie waited, almost praying, waited for the seed to happen. . . .

And then, Brik rumbled something. A few of the crewmembers around him turned to stare. The Morthan repeated it, louder. Now, others were turning, their mouths opening to ask. Brik said it a third time, almost roaring, and this time the whole room heard it clearly: "Failure is *not* an option."

And then . . . beside the big Morthan, Helen Bach began to applaud. Slowly at first. Clap. Clap. Clap—

And then others picked it up. First one, then the next. Tor. Jonesy. Goldberg. Green. Stolchak. Williger. Ikama. Saffari. Cappy. MacHeath. Reynolds. Candleman . . . and finally, even Chief Leen unfolded his arms and—despite his still-foul expression—began to clap slowly and powerfully. Behind him, the other members of the Black Hole Gang began to applaud as well. And then the whole crew was applauding as hard and as loud as they could. Cheering. Shouting. Chanting.

Korie felt it first in his eyes. Then in his gut. And then the feeling came slamming into him so hard, he nearly staggered with the impact.

He looked from one face to the next with unashamed pride. He let the power of their shared emotion overwhelm him; he savored the moment. The joyous noise filled the cargo deck.

In that moment, Korie realized just how deep his feeling was for this ship and this crew. He looked down at them with gratitude and wonder, meeting their eyes, one after the other. He saw his own determination reflected back at him. He stood amazed and awestruck. And finally . . . he allowed a slow smile of appreciation to spread across his face.

When at last the noise subsided once again, Korie lifted up his hands from the railing just the smallest amount; just enough to indicate he had one thing more to say.

"Thank you," he acknowledged. "Thank you. Now I know *why* you're the best. You can't be defeated. No matter what happens, no matter where or when, *you can't be defeated*. Not by anyone." He leaned out over the railing, almost as if to touch them. "I am so proud to serve with you," he said. "I want you to know, it's real easy to be proud when everything is working right. That's so easy, anyone can do it. But it takes tremendous courage to stand this tall when there's no agreement in the physical universe. That's the real test of a crew. And I want you to know, I have never been as proud of you as I am right this moment."

He lifted one fist high, a gesture of victory. Then, lest he kill the moment by overworking it, he turned and left. Their thundering cheers filled the cargo deck. He could hear them all the way back to his cabin.

Zaffron

When he was sixteen years old, Jonathan Thomas Korie realized that his adoptive father did not have the financial ability to send him to college. He did not resent the man for that; he recognized that his father had done the very best he could in what had to have been for him a very difficult situation. But neither did he feel any great sense of affection. He wondered about the whole business of familial love. The way it was portrayed in the popular entertainments bore very little resemblance to his own experience.

It seemed to the young Korie that his adoptive father often held himself apart, acting like a dispassionate researcher studying the development of an interesting specimen much more than a parent with an emotional commitment. He was a reserved and distant man in any case, and Jon Korie often felt that their communications were across some vast experiential gulf that he could not bridge no matter how hard he tried. After a while, he'd stopped trying.

The circumstances of Jon Korie's birth were unclear, his father was unresponsive about the details, and although Jon still felt a profound sense of loss and alienation—as if there were some part of humanity that he had never connected to—he had come to accept that this was the way his life was and the way it was always going to be for him.

Occasionally, during his youth, he had caught his father looking at him as if he were some kind of alien being. Sometimes he wondered if other people could see that difference too. He'd never had many friends in his life. He'd never understood why; he had always assumed that there was something wrong with him, something that everyone else knew, but no one was allowed to tell him. Perhaps that was why Admiral O'Hara seemed to regard him with such coolness.

In the solitude of his teen years, he had often wished he could be just like everyone else; life would be so much simpler; but then one day, while random-walking through the databases, he'd found a quote from Nobel Prize winner Rosalyn Yalow. Shortly after she'd accepted her award, a reporter asked her, "What's it like to be so smart?" and she had replied, as if it were no great matter, "It's very lonely."

Young Jon recognized the truth of that remark instantly—the moment was an epiphany for him. He sat there staring at the display panel feeling a cold chill of recognition crawling up his spine. It was as if she had sent a message down through the centuries, aimed specifically at his own sense of difference. She had been talking about everyone who stood taller than the rest of the species.

Later, in pursuing the thread of interest, he found other quotes that inspired him. Daniel Jeffrey Foreman, inventor of the Mode Training, had once said, "When you stand on a chair in a roomful of midgets, you become first a god, then a target, and then, if you survive long enough, simply a landmark." At first, Jon Korie saw in that remark only a cynical disregard for the rest of humanity, and dismissed it from his mind; or rather, he tried to—but the image of the man standing on the chair stayed in his mind, and he began to realize that Foreman had been saying much the same thing that Yalow had—that *excellence* of any kind is a very lonely condition.

It wasn't genius—it was *sentience*. Jon Korie knew that much. It had something to do with "the technology of consciousness," a term he kept encountering in various places. What set people apart was not their intellect, but their *alertness*, their ability to interact with the domains they existed in.

According to one of the essays he'd stumbled across, most people walked unconsciously through their lives. The subroutines of their existence were the sum of the person, there was nothing greater. And this thought stuck with young Jon too, haunting him. He didn't understand it fully, and the idea that there might be something more to life that he might not be experiencing troubled his thoughts.

Korie's adoptive father, for all his lack of demonstrative affection, was neither stupid nor uncaring. He routinely audited his young son's forays into the information tanks. Although it took many years for Jon to discover it, not every random walk he took was totally random. Many of the items that popped up on the display seemed to be aimed directly at the youth's immediate experience.

After a while, Jon became aware of a repetitive pattern of references to something called the *zyne*, an evolution of the Mode Training that focused specifically on the disciplines of personal consciousness. The insistent quality of the references left Korie feeling as if he was being nagged by the universe. While most of the references were historical, more than a few were contemporary, indicating that the *zyne* was still held in very high regard by those who had taken the time to investigate its practice.

Jon discovered that *zyne* seminars and workshops were commonly available, and after downloading several lectures by the local master Zaffron, and being impressed by both the man's wit as well as his insight, he asked his father if he could sign up for an introductory course. To his surprise, his father immediately assented.

The *zyne* master Zaffron was a fairly ordinary-looking man—until he started speaking, "This isn't about answers. It's about questions. Having the right question will succeed every time; having the right answer will succeed only when the right question is asked. And how often does the universe ever ask the *right* question of you?

"This is an inquiry into the nature of consciousness. What is it? What do we do with it? Are we really conscious at all? What does it mean to be a human being? We're not going to answer those questions in this inquiry; we're only going to suggest possibilities for you to consider—it's like shopping for a new jacket; if it fits, it's yours. If it doesn't fit, thanks for trying it on. The distinctions will stay with you anyway and will still be useful.

"Let me underline that. Distinctions are the way we map the universe. Some of our maps are accurate, some are not. But even those that are not accurate can be useful if they still support us in producing results. So this isn't about designing the most accurate map as much as it is about designing the most *useful* one." And then he added with a wry grin, "You will find as we go, however, that accuracy is extraordinarily useful." Jon got the joke.

"Here's the point of the inquiry," Zaffron continued. "Follow this carefully: The asking of questions creates *possibilities*. The creation of possibilities gives you *choice*. The existence of choice is the prerequisite to *freedom*. Without choice, you have no freedom. Without *possibility*, you have no freedom. So, in here, we are asking questions to create *freedom of being*."

At first Jon Korie found the material puzzling and of no relation at all to the questions he'd been struggling with in his own life. But the paradigm—the construction of the whole logical structure—was so *enrolling*, he found himself compelled to pursue the study to its logical conclusion.

Some of the seminars considered the nature of knowledge. "What do we know? How do we know what we know? And what do we really do with our knowledge? Do we use it—or do we merely use it to explain why we're not producing results? What is it that we don't know? What is it that we *don't know* that we don't know? You see, *real* wisdom doesn't come from what you have been taught. It comes from what you have *experienced*. True knowledge comes from what you discover when you actively engage in the processes of your life. It has nothing to do with what you have memorized." The young Jon Korie puzzled over that one for a long time—the joke was that he did not begin to understand it until *after* he had experienced it.

Some of the seminars considered the nature of communication. "True communication is not simply an exchange of mutually agreed upon symbols. It is the recreation of the essential experience." The *zyne* master said to him, "If you are a human being, you cannot listen beyond your own self. You will always hear your own self talking, interpreting, judging, explaining, and you will do that so loudly that you will never hear what anyone else is really saying at all. You have to listen to the speaking of the other self if you want to hear what's really being said." Korie puzzled over that one an even longer time. Eventually, he learned to recognize the great gulfs of distance across which human beings tried to reach each other, and how *any* communication at all was ultimately an act of courage.

Some of the seminars considered the nature of effectiveness. "Commitment is the willingness to be uncomfortable. Yes, you're going to be stopped in life, over and over and over again. If the universe doesn't create obstacles for you, you'll create them yourself. But being stopped only turns into failure when you abandon your intention." That one he understood, he thought. "Listen, if there's a turd in the punch bowl, it doesn't help to add more punch. You want to notice that when something doesn't work, you probably go back and do more of the same thing that wasn't working before—and it's absolutely crazy to expect it to produce a *different* result!"

And some of the seminars merely considered the way the mind worked. "If you think there's something wrong with you, that's normal; there's nothing wrong with you. But if you're sure there's nothing wrong with you, I promise you there *is* something wrong with you." The young Korie knew that lesson was for him. He sat up straight in his chair and leaned forward attentively.

"Listen to me, Korie," Zaffron said, pointing to him and startling him even more awake. "Before you were born, you didn't know you weren't the whole universe. So you didn't know anything. You just took up space. And that was okay while it lasted. You had no problems. Everything was taken care of for you. And then you were born and that was okay for a while too, different but okay, and everything was still taken care of for you, for a while at least; and then one day you found out that you *weren't* the whole universe—and you still haven't recovered from the shock of that discovery! That's your problem!

"When baby realizes that mommy is not an extension of baby, that the world does not behave the way baby thinks it should, baby doesn't just get upset—baby goes crazy. Baby wonders *what's wrong with me?* Baby wonders *what do I have to do to fix it?* And the rest of your life is spent trying to fix something that isn't broken.

"That's the joke! You're *not* broken. That feeling that something is wrong with you—it's normal for *every* human being. It's hard-wired into the human condition. Trying to fix it when it ain't broke—*that's* the crazy behavior. When you stop trying to fix yourself, that's when your life starts working—because you'll have hundreds of thousands of extra hours in which to accomplish something *useful*."

Jon Korie mulled over that one for a long time. He understood it not just as a concept, but as an experience. He *heard* it in his soul. He recognized the behavioral loop in his life that had kept him feeling stuck. But even as he acknowledged the truth of it, he still wondered about the effect he produced in others. Was it his imagination or did people really hold themselves apart from him? And then he had to laugh at himself for thinking that thought. It was more of the same.

He concluded the seminars in a state of exhilaration and confusion. He felt different about himself. He felt different about the people in his life and his relationships with them, even his father. As if a light had suddenly been turned on in a dark room, the young Korie abruptly understood just how much his father really did care about him, even though he could never express it the way Jon thought he should.

After that particular course, he returned home determined to forgive his father for his distant reserve; but when he opened his mouth to speak, what came out instead was an apology. "Dad—I've been a jerk. Please forgive me. I've been blaming you for the way I feel. But it's not your fault. It never was. It's mine. I know you love me. You wouldn't have let me sign up for the *zyne* if you didn't." That was the one time that his father took him in his arms and held him close. And that was the only time that Korie ever let his father see him cry.

But even as Korie reveled in the delicious sense of self-empowerment—and even as he wondered how long it would last—at the same time, he now felt even more profoundly *out of place*. Where before he had felt he was in the middle of a maze that he had no control over, now he felt as if he were the Minotaur in that same maze and that was even more maddening. If he was the monster at the center, why couldn't he control it?

He told Zaffron of his puzzlement and Zaffron said, "Don't worry about it. Just hang out with it for a lifetime or two. You'll get it when you need to get it. Right now . . . you're still caught on the upslope of the learning tantrum. Give yourself a chance. I promise you, you'll get it—and if you don't, you come back and see me and I'll give you double your unconsciousness back."

Jon Korie promised to keep in touch and wondered if the feeling of profound *enlightenment* would last for more than a month or two. He said as much to Zaffron. "Sometimes I think I'm being conned."

Surprisingly, Zaffron agreed with him. "Yes, you have been conned. But you're the one who conned yourself. You've programmed yourself into believing that things are the way you've programmed yourself into believing. Now, ask the right questions and you can invent a new program."

Eventually, Jon Korie did get the point. If anything important was going to happen in his life, he was going to have to make it happen himself. He began looking into education-assistance programs. The one that intrigued him the most was the orbital college.

Stolchak

At last, Gatineau found his way to the inner hull.

Actually, that was a misnomer. In truth, he found an access *through* the inner hull; but through that access, he found the space that was generally called the "inner hull."

Translation: A starship is any bottle that holds air and moves faster than light. A liberty ship is a starship with enough amenities to be considered certifiable for Class Three life support. One of the required redundancies is a double-hulled construction. A liberty ship is therefore a bottle inside a bottle. The space between the two bottles is commonly called the "inner hull," even though it is actually the gap between the inner hull and the outer one.

In the *Star Wolf*, the distance between the two bottles varied from location to location; in general, there was a six-meter gap between the two hulls. In some places, particularly around the fluctuator spars, the gap was as large as ten or fifteen meters. In other places, especially near some of the airlocks and the weapons installations, it narrowed to slightly less than one meter.

Although not immediately obvious, the inner hull was divided into airtight sectors; there were bulkheads every ten meters; class-five security hatches provided access. Class five was the lowest level of integrity, providing instantaneous closure and a secure seal against explosive decompression, but little more than that. It was sufficient to protect the life support needs of this space, but ultimately had proven woefully inadequate at containment when the Morthan assassin found its way aboard. It was on both Korie and Leen's list of things to do (someday) to upgrade every hatch and bulkhead in the inner hull to Class Three or better. Preferably better.

The inner hull was not—as commonly believed by non-starsiders—a dark empty space of mystery and terror. Actually, on most ships, it was a bright and amazing environment. First, of course, it served a structural function. The innermost fuselage (also called the primary bottle) was securely held in a framework of stanchions and cables; the inner hull provided easy access to these structural supports. A confusing maze of catwalks, ladders, platforms, stanchions, grillwork decks, access plates, tool bays, emergency equipment, network modules, pipes of all sizes, and gleaming light channels seemed to fill most of the available space around the primary bottle. There was also a bewildering welter of hatches, bulkheads, numbered panels, rods, girders, decks, and seemingly disconnected pieces of machinery. And everything here was studded with work lights and monitor displays. Sensors of all kinds were hung every three meters.

Additionally, several of the starship's secondary autonomic systems were channelled across the exterior of the primary bottle; fresh water, air, sewage, and information flowed through multiply redundant channels. By having the pipes strung along the surface of the primary bottle, easy access was provided for repair and maintenance. Like everything else, the channels were well lit and brightly numbered.

The inner hull was also used for the storage of equipment and supplies. When deaths occurred in space, the bodies were also stored in the inner hull; as a result, some crew members found parts of the inner hull so intimidating they almost never ventured there. Scuttlebutt had it that the ghost of Captain Lowell still wandered around the inner hull of the *Star Wolf*; there had been so many modifications, additions, and changes that the ghost was said to be unable to find its way out.

There were two other important functions served by the inner hull, both of them involved with life support. The first was—curiously enough—*recreation*.

Away from port months at a time, a destroyer-class cruiser needs a place of "wilderness" for its crew, an opportunity to escape to a place just a little less orderly. Here could be found such homemade amenities as a half-size basketball court, which also doubled for handball; a rather odd-shaped swimming tank, ancillary to the auxiliary water-processors; a jogging track; a rotating climbing wall; and a number of smaller padded nooks and crannies, just the right size for the more intimate forms of recreation. The general rule for behavior in the inner hull was simple. *Do no harm.* Occasionally, it was phrased even more specifically: *mind your own business*. If it didn't interfere with the safety of the ship, it wasn't anybody's concern.

The second—and more important—life support function served

by the inner hull was the processing of sewage and the production of food and air. Indeed, *most* of the inner hull was taken up by the farm. It was a lush environment, filled with leafy green things and delicious vegetarian smells. Over a hundred and fifty different kinds of plants were growing in aeroponic grids at any given moment; the ship's seed bank contained over two thousand different species of fruits, vegetables, and flowers; they were rotated in and out of the farm on a regular basis. More varieties were added every time the starship docked and the Chief Petty Officer (or the ship's lethetic intelligence engine) had a chance to negotiate a swap. The older a ship was, the richer its library of food plants.

At the moment, the Senior Farm Officer for this tour of duty—the responsibility was regularly rotated—was a big, stocky-looking woman named Irma Stolchak. She was standing before a frame of aeroponic strawberries, regarding them with a frustrated expression. Two robots were moving up and down the wall, scanning each berry in turn, and chiming their approval more often than not. Stolchak plucked one of the berries off the wire frame and handed it to Gatineau. "Here, taste," she commanded.

Gatineau bit into it tentatively. The berry was sweet and firm and absolutely perfect. He popped the rest of it into his mouth. "Delicious," he said, wiping the juice from his chin with the back of his hand.

"That's the problem."

"Huh?"

"We did our job too well. These guys are ripening too fast—"

"What's wrong with that?" Gatineau asked.

"I hate to waste. We have too much. We won't have enough stasis boxes. Korie traded half of them away for new gallinium rods. Meanwhile, in the next ten days, we'll have enough strawberries for the entire fleet. Plus, we've got peas and corn ripening, winged beans, amaranth, navel oranges, *naval* oranges, plums, blue gadoovas, sweet red neeners, and I don't know what else. If we get green-flagged, we can sell some of it to Stardock, maybe swap a little with other ships; but I've been checking around; *everybody* overproduced. And everybody's got the same good excuse; they're all trying to get ready."

"Get ready for what?" Gatineau asked innocently.

"What planet are you from?" Stolchak regarded him with a caustic expression. "They're building up their stores . . . in case of battle damage. Look around. If we took a hull breach across two sectors, we'd lose a month's food and at least 10 percent air regeneration capacity. So we have to make sure the cupboards are full, just in case. You can't go to war until the crops are in the barn. Nobody fights on an empty stomach. Don't you get it? The farm is the most important part of the ship. Do you know the story about the mauling at Marathon? Do you know the first thing Korie did afterward? He came out here to the farm, and began planting beans. He *knew*. He did what was necessary to bring the ship home—see, that's rule number one. The first thing you do is take care of the farm."

She sighed and made a decision. "All right, look. Let's get these 'bots started and see if they can finish by dinner. These are the last two 'bots on the farm. Korie took the other four and swapped them to the *Houston* for an exterior hull-security network, a class-two replication engine, and another rendition of *Dixie*. Jeezis, I could learn to hate that song." She turned back to her strawberries, still grumbling. "All right. We'll put up preserves and press some syrup. We'll freeze-dry the rest. The crew'll have fruitcake under syrup for the next three months. They won't complain. But I still wish we could grow a decent coffee bean . . . I heard the *Valdez* has figured out a way to simulate a respectable mountain environment. I wonder if we could get their specs . . . What—?" She demanded abruptly

"Um. I'm not here for that. I'm looking for the moebius wrench—"

"The what?"

"The moebius wrench. The left-handed one. Candleman said you had it."

"Candleman said I had a left-handed moebius wrench?"

"Yes, ma'am."

"He would. Who are you anyway?"

"Crewman Robert Gatineau, Third Class, Engineering Apprentice."

"Oh yeah. I heard about you. Here—take this rooter. You can help clean the sludge tubes. Take it! You want the damn wrench or not?"

"No offense, ma'am, but everybody's giving me orders and nobody's giving me the wrench—"

"You heard Korie, didn't you? You know what's going on. Let me tell you something, Gatineau. Everybody's got to help everybody or nothing works. Yeah, I know this is scut work. But we don't have the robots and the crops still have to be brought in. I was lucky just to keep these two for the farm. We had a Morthan assassin onboard. Let me tell you, *that* was a damn nuisance. It really hurt our confidence rating. Now we've got a shipload of strawberries and potatoes and corn and we can't sell them until we get a green flag. No, not like that. Let me show you how to hold the sluicer—"

"Um, I'm sorry, but I really can't—I don't have time for this—I need to find the moebius wrench—the sooner the better. Why don't you just tell me who you gave it to and—hey! This does work better this way, doesn't it? But—Chief Leen needs it badly. Please?"

"You want a favor from me? Do one in return. Run that sluicer while I look around for the whatchamacallit. I've got more problems in the granary. We're going to have an overflow crop of rice and barley and a bunch of other stuff Korie ordered planted on the way home. All that stuff should be ready for harvest any minute now. God knows what we're going to do with it all. I've got only these two robots left and if I don't watch them every minute, someone will requisition them, and I'll be left with corn rotting on the stalk. You keep working," she said. "Don't let *anyone* take those robots, unless you want to take their place. If you finish these sludge tubes, start on the ones on the other side. I'll be back in a bit."

Gatineau watched her go with a sinking feeling. He did not expect her to be back any time soon. That was how everything else was working out. Why should the farm be any different? He stood there alone, surrounded by green leafy things, most of which he didn't recognize. The plants rustled as if in a breeze.

"Why do I get the feeling I'm being watched?" Gatineau asked aloud. He turned back to the sludge tubes. "Pfoo. Yick. Eww. This stuff smells like shit." He shook his head and bent to his work, muttering to himself. "Join the navy. See the stars. Have an adventure. Yeah, right."

The Black Hole Gang

Korie and Chief Leen were visible only from the waist down, both lying on their backs, halfway under the Alpha fluctuator assembly, staring up into its stygian mysteries and arguing ferociously. Cappy and MacHeath waited to one side, looking both bored and skeptical. The four men were on the deck of the walkway above the harshly lit, three-story sphere of the singularity cage—"the little monster."

The argument coming from inside the fluctuator spar was both technical and superheated. Korie and Leen never conferred quietly. Nearly every engineering discussion between the two men had a volcanic component. Korie insisted on acting as if he knew as much about starship's engines as Chief Leen; the chief had a different opinion of Korie's expertise; but despite their frequent disagreements about the capabilities of the vessel, the discussions never became personal. Both men were consummate professionals and there were standards of behavior that officers had to obey. Mutual respect was one of them.

After a moment, Korie levered himself out of the assembly. He waited politely while Chief Leen followed. He offered the older man a hand up. Leen ignored the hand and pulled himself to his feet, grumbling.

"It's got to be confidence 90 or better," Korie said. "We don't dare post anything less."

"Listen, I got the damn thing in, I got it working. You want a 90, it's going to cost you another two days that you can't spare."

Korie didn't bother to acknowledge that. Instead, he asked, "What parts do you need? We have to make some more trades with the *Houston* tomorrow."

"The Velvet Bitch?" Leen looked more annoyed than usual. "What are you giving her?"

"Belay that. You don't want to know."

"Yes, I do."

"Okay. The *Houston* needs an autonomic reconstructor harness. With flatbed allowances. The *Moran* needs local-area targeting modules, D-6 or better. And the *Hayes* needs forty recombinant fluxor plates. They can get by with twenty. And we need anything we can get. I want to see if I can rebuild the control yoke on the Bridge. We're still short two work stations."

Leen snorted. "I can help the *Moran*. Nobody knows it, but the *O'Connell* sent us a couple extra boxes of gallium-jacks just before we went out to meet the *Burke*. She didn't have to do that. But I'm not giving anything to the *Houston*. You know how they treat us."

"Captain La Paz has offered to stop blasting *Dixie* at us every morning," Korie offered.

Leen hesitated. "She really does need a new harness, doesn't she?"

"Captain La Paz wouldn't say, but I got the feeling that the ship's autonomic response time has dropped to measurable levels."

Leen scowled. Even though it wasn't his ship, he hated hearing stories like that. He scratched his beard. "What are you giving away?" he asked.

"The list is in your in-box."

"Let me guess. You're going to strip us down to our underwear, aren't you?"

"I've already promised your underwear. What else have you got?"

"Figured as much." Leen sucked in his cheeks, nodded, and bent to pick up his tools.

"Chief?" Korie asked, concerned. "Are you all right?"

"I'm fine, why?"

"You're not screaming."

"Would it make a difference?"

"No."

"Then why bother." Leen picked up a damp rag and began wiping his hands slowly. "Face it, Korie. We're not going to Taalamar. We're not going anywhere."

Korie shook his head. "I'm not quitting."

Leen jerked his head at the Alpha spar. "You saw it yourself. Those grapplers are filthy." He held up a hand for Korie to see the thin layer of black dust on his fingertips. "Nano-cancer! We're being eaten alive."

"Scrub them again." Korie sounded tired.

"We did," Leen said flatly. "Three times. And they're still infected."

"Someone got careless—" Korie said without thinking. Leen started to say something nasty in response, but Korie stopped him with an upheld hand. "No. That's wrong." He looked at Leen sharply. "You don't get careless. Neither does your crew."

Leen accepted it grudgingly. "Thanks for noticing," he muttered. His tone shifted then, became more serious and straightforward. "Each time it's been a *different* cancer. There's a reservoir somewhere. That's why we keep getting reinfected. Until we find it, we're just wasting our time here."

Korie accepted the information without apparent reaction. He scratched his chin thoughtfully, while squinting up at the overhead, as if somehow he could spot the source of the infection just by looking around. "Goddamn that Cinnabar," he whispered. Finally he lowered his gaze again. "I wish you weren't so good, Chief. I'd much rather the explanation were carelessness."

For once, Leen agreed with him. "It's your fault. You demanded excellence."

"Next time, don't listen to me."

"Okay," said the chief, with obvious exhaustion. "Where do we go from here?"

"I dunno," said Korie, still turning possibilities over in his mind. Abruptly he remembered something. "Failure is not an option."

"Yeah, I heard that before too." Leen tossed the rag aside in disgust.

"Brik was right," Korie said. He turned to the chief engineer. "So here's what we're going to do. We're going to strip the ship. We'll trade away everything we can. With warnings that extreme detox measures will be needed. That also offloads our skillage burden onto the recipients. Mm. You can let the *Houston* have the dirtiest stuff . . ."

Leen looked at him oddly, a question on his face.

"All right," admitted Korie. "It's *not* just La Paz. Yeah, she pisses me off, but we go back a long way, and she's always pissed me off, so that's not it. She wants to go to Taalamar. She really wants in on that action. If she gets our fibrillators, she'll have an engine. And she'll go. And you and I both know what shape the *Houston* is in. They don't have a Chief Leen. That ship is going to come apart in the water, the first time someone throws a torpedo at them. I really hate to say this, but if we keep her from getting certified, we're saving some lives. They'll get our fibrillators eventually, I know that, but let's make sure it's too late to do them any good. And don't bother to detox anything they're going to get. Let them spend the time. It'll help keep them at home."

Leen didn't answer immediately. Finally, he grumbled, "I didn't know you felt that way."

"Neither did I. Till just now." Korie allowed himself to marvel over that thought for a moment, then added in a much more serious tone, "But let's make sure that everybody else has everything we can give them. We'll take future credits if we have to. We'll take whatever we can and bank the rest. How soon will you have your first bulbs of starshine to trade? No, don't tell me. I'm not supposed to know about that. Just make sure Hall has enough to lubricate every deal thoroughly. But whatever we get in exchange, keep the delivery pods on the boats, or float them on tethers. Don't bring anything onboard unless it's essential. We're going to have to rebuild from the keel up." Korie looked to Leen. "You're still not screaming . . . ?"

Leen shook his head. "You want my advice?"

Korie hesitated, momentarily concerned he wouldn't like what he was going to hear. "Go ahead, Chief. What do you think we should do?"

"Strip the ship. Let everybody else benefit from our bad luck. Then we rebuild from the keel up. And don't pay any attention to the screams of the chief engineer."

"Ah," said Korie, nodding. "I like that plan. It's almost as good as my own."

"No, better," corrected Leen. "Not as wordy."

Cookie

Stolchak sent him to the galley.

Gatineau couldn't figure out what the ship's cook would want with a moebius wrench, but Stolchak had explained that she'd given it to Cookie so he could adjust the focus on the flash-burners.

Gatineau made his way slowly to the mess room, feeling both tired and frustrated. His first full day aboard a starship and he hadn't accomplished anything at all. He'd been from the bow to the stern and back again more times than he could remember. He'd met a few people, and he'd learned a little bit about the whys and the wherefores of this and that, but . . . he still hadn't completed the job that Chief Leen had assigned him. He felt like a failure. And he'd really wanted to impress the chief, too. What was it that Lieutenant Commander Brik had said? Failure is not an option? Well, if it wasn't an option, where in Hell was the goddamned moebius wrench?

The ship's mess was up and forward somewhere. He knew that much. Aft of the Bridge was the wardroom; the officers' cabins were aft of the wardroom; the officers' mess was aft of that, then the galley, then the crew's mess. Aft of that was the ship's PX and then the ship's upper stores and supplies; then there were the upper cabins and bunkrooms, and finally, the ship's engineering stores, then the engine room. So the mess room shouldn't be too hard to find. It was supposed to be a large square space bridging both the port and starboard passages.

But the passages weren't exactly straight. For a variety of reasons, some functional, some not, both the port and starboard passages had corresponding doglegs, sometimes angling outward around a particularly bulky interior installation, sometimes angling inward for the same reason. And although Gatineau thought he understood all the markings on the walls, there were several that remained unnecessarily cryptic. And despite frequent requests to HARLIE for assistance, he *still* kept getting lost. If such a thing were possible, he would have suspected that the ship's lethetic intelligence engine was deliberately trying to steer him through as many different parts of the vessel as possible.

Eventually, however, he arrived at the galley. He was disheveled, tired, and unhappy. But he was here.

Cookie took one look at him and said, "Uh-oh." Cookie was a tall man, broadly built, with a longshoreman's build and hands as big as shovels; he was scrubbed so clean he shone like a fresh-cut side of beef, and he wore a cherubic-pink expression. Without stopping to ask, he steered Gatineau to a chair, and slid a cup of hot chocolate in front of him. "Here, start on this," he said. "It'll settle your stomach. You missed lunch. Don't you ever do that again. I made my specialty, corned beef and cabbage, and you haven't been to heaven, lad, till you've tasted *my* cabbage. Most cooks don't know the difference between spicing the water and peeing in it. I do. Every Tuesday, you'll see. But now you'll have to wait a week. And you almost missed dinner, too, I was about to send out a search party for you. Now, how do you want your steak?"

Gatineau looked up blearily, not certain if he dared refuse. He tried to stand up, but Cookie's huge hand on his shoulder held him firmly down in his place. "But . . . I need to get the moebius wrench to Chief Leen. Let me just take it to him and then I can—"

"Absolutely not. I didn't spend all day in this galley preparing hot nourishing meals for this crew to have some ungrateful puppy grabbing sandwiches on the run. You're going to eat a proper dinner or you'll not leave this mess room. Even if he's not yet in it, Captain Hardesty would rise up out of his grave and skin me alive if I didn't put a hot meal into each of his boys and girls. I'll not have you insulting the hard work of the mess crew, nor the good healthy produce from the *Star Wolf's* farm. If you knew how much hard work went into every meal, you'd treat each mouthful with a lot more respect. I'll see to that. Drink your milk now—here, bring it with you; come with me. You need to see this."

Cookie grabbed Gatineau by the arm, practically lifting him out of his chair and dragging him into the galley, a long narrow room lined with shining counters and appliances. "Y'see these machines? Do you think that's all we do here, put raw potatoes in one end and take sandwiches out the other? Any damn fool can do that. Real cooking is an art form, and any real galley slave has to be a master artist, or it's the surest way to start a shipboard mutiny. I can tell you that, me lad. No doubt about it. The most important part of a starship is her belly.

Napoleon Bonaparte said it, and he was right. An army travels on its stomach. Never forget that. Here lad, have some more milk. Let me tell you rule number one: *take care of the belly first*. If you don't take care of your own well-being, you'll have nothing to give anyone else. What good will you be to this ship if you can't do your job? Tell me that, will you now? No good at all. You'll be in sick bay and Molly Williger and two other people will be spending all their time taking care of your poor body, when they could be doing something useful instead. No, that's no way to be a good member of this crew. I don't care how busy you are, lad, don't you ever miss a meal again or I'll come looking for you, and when I find you, you'll be wishing you'd been caught by the banshee of Belfast instead. And all of her lovely sisters. Now, here, this is what I wanted you to see—" Cookie opened the door of a cold-box and pulled out a fresh piece of meat. "You see this? Do you know what this is?"

"It looks like a steak?" Gatineau offered tentatively.

"Wipe your mouth, son. You've got a milk mustache. A steak? Absolutely not. This is much more than a mere *steak*. Now if you were to ask Chief Leen what this is, he'd tell you that it's fuel for your machine. It's raw protein, which your body will turn into muscle and bone and energy to drive your engines faster than light. That's how a mechanic would see it.

"And if you were to ask Irma Stolchak what it was, she'd tell you it's a crop. She'd give you a little lecture about how the protein has to be properly marbled, so it has enough fat to be flavorful, but not so much that it's greasy. She'll tell you how the flesh has to be stimulated in the tank, worked and stretched and exercised so that it has the right kind of chewiness in the mouth, but not overworked so much that it gets tough and gamey. And you've got to know exactly what you're doing—are you growing pork chops or ham steaks? Are you growing beef ribs or pot roast? Is it going to be a breast or a drumstick? You don't have a chicken or a pig or a cow walking around this ship doing the work, you've got to see that the exercisers in the tank produce meat and not just a fat blob of undifferentiated flesh. Ahh, she'd tell you about that, for sure. Do you know why? Because I wouldn't accept a single piece of meat that isn't good enough for my crew.

"And if you were to ask Toad Hall what this is, he'd tell you that it's a commodity, an asset, something to be used in the marketplace. He'd tell you it's a lump of kilocalories, just waiting to be applied to the balance sheet.

"But they're all wrong, my lad. All of them. This isn't fuel, and it isn't a crop, and it isn't a nice round number in the captain's spreadsheet. Do you know what this is? This is a work of art looking for a place to happen. This is a bit of home on your plate, it's a vacation at the end of a hard day's work, it's a reward for your hours of toil in the fields of the Lord. Properly prepared, by a master, not a hooligan, this becomes a feast not only for the tongue and the belly, but for the soul as well. Cooking is an art form, and the eating of the meal in an atmosphere of rest and relaxation is the only way to savor the artist's handiwork. Now, I ask you, son—are you willing to reject the handiwork of a man who has dedicated his life to bringing you a bit of soul-filling pleasure three times a day? You'll not betray the kitchen of this starship, I promise you that, not while I'm the lord and master of this domain, and surely not while I have my cleaver in my hand.

"Now answer my question, and answer quickly, how do you like your steak?"

"Uh—rare. Please. Pink on the inside, seared on the outside."

"Good man. That's the proper way. And what vegetables will you be having with that?"

"Snap peas, if you have them. And mashed potatoes, please. If it's not too much trouble. And a salad? Bleu cheese dressing?"

Cookie considered the order, nodded a grudging acknowledgment. "Unimaginative. But solid. A good start. Tell you what. I'll put a bit of avocado on the top of that salad for you, and a bit of shrimp as well. Just to dress it up. And I'll mix a few pearl onions and mushrooms in with the peas, nothing fancy, but you've got to have a bit of crunch on the fork, you know. And the potatoes, they'll get cold without a nice blanket of gravy—or would you prefer a coat of sharp cheese? And a bit of eye-talian on the steak, of course, of course. It's a shame you're so late. At this hour, it's really much too late to put on a proper do, but I can still give you a small taste of what's possible in the hands of a chef who knows what he's doing in a kitchen. And if you'll not miss any more meals, well then pretty soon you'll know what a privilege it is for you to serve on a ship with this cook. You'll have a proper belly on you soon enough, you could easily use another ten kilograms. We'll have you looking like a proper member of the *Star Wolf*'s crew. I mean, look at yourself, lad; you're as thin as a plasma tube. That's what happens when you forget to eat. Ahh, but when you see what magic I can work on your plate, you'll forget every platter your sainted mother ever put before you. You'll count the minutes between your meals, I promise you that; but enough of my bejabbering. Tonight, at least, I won't begrudge you a simple old-fashioned repast. Now, get your skinny little butt out of my galley and back into a chair, before I lose my patience and put you in the grinder for tomorrow's sausage."

Gatineau went through the first half of the meal, barely tasting it. He hadn't realized how hungry he was. And he didn't realize how *good* the food in front of him really was until Cookie laid a hand on his shoulder and said, "Slow down, lad. You've got to give yourself a chance to savor each bite; otherwise the cook'll know you're lying when you tell him how much you enjoyed it. Real men don't gobble, no matter how hungry they are. No one's going to take your plate away, so slow down and show me that you appreciate the taste of it as much as the fullness it gives your belly. Besides," he added, "you'll need to save your strength for your dessert. I do the best afters in the fleet. You'll have a slice of my peach-berry cobbler smothered in sweet cream. And after that . . . while you're here, you'll do a bit of K.P. Your penance for missing lunch. And then we'll talk about that wrench you're looking for."

"Thfmk yff," said Gatineau, stuffing another bite in his mouth. After everything else he'd had to do today, a bit of K.P. would probably be a relief.

But he was wrong about that too.

Outside

The *Star Wolf* had three kinds of airlocks.

The traditional airlock was a chamber with hatches at each end; air could be pumped in or out.

The valve lock was a series of self-closing membranes, resembling heart valves, through which a crew member pushed himself. Some gas leaked out through each transfer, but each chamber had a decreasing level of pressure, so the final chamber had minimal air to lose.

The revolving lock was a rotating cylinder, much like a revolving door. The crew member stepped into it, rotated through, and stepped out the opposite side. It was the fastest way to get in or out of a pressurized hull.

Fleet regulations required that all three kinds of locks be backstopped by additional pressure hatches.

Today, Brik chose the valve lock. It allowed him to ease into vacuum at his own pace.

He touched his starsuit harness, checking the flattened lump in the case he wore next to his skin. He took a last few breaths of pure oxygen from the pressure pack he carried, and then discarded it. He pushed through the first valve, then the second—the air sucked steadily out of his lungs. He pressed through the next valve and the next. And kept exhaling. When there was nothing left to exhale, the pain in his chest began to ebb, and he closed his throat against further exhalation.

Brik wore a modified starsuit, as close to that worn by the Morthan assassin as he could fabricate; it wasn't much more than a chest guard and a genital harness. He also wore a facepack to protect his eyes; he hadn't been able to determine what modifications had been made to

Cinnabar's eyes and that wasn't the purpose of this experiment anyway, so he wore the facepack.

His only air supply was an oxygen transfusor strapped to his right shoulder. The autopsy on what was left of Cinnabar had shown a similar device tucked inside the large bone of the assassin's right thigh. It was good for fifteen, maybe twenty, minutes before it was exhausted; but that rating was for a human metabolism. Brik's metabolism, fully exerted, would probably exhaust the unit in one third of the time. The same equation would have held for Cinnabar. Could he travel the length of the starship in seven minutes?

He was about to find out.

It was *imperative* that he find out.

He unclipped the short black hose from the side of the oxygen transfusor, opened the valve and slipped the end of it into his mouth. He bit down hard on the grips of the mouthpiece, holding it firmly between his molars. He sucked gas. Good. It worked. Just barely.

Then he pressed through the final valve of the lock.

Hard vacuum *hurt.*

And it was noisy. He could hear the pounding of his heart in his chest, feel the waves throbbing outward from his chest, into his arms and legs in a series of accelerated pulses; he could hear the roaring of his blood through his veins and the rasp of his irregular breathing in his throat and his lungs. There was *nothing else* to hear.

And his internal body pressure felt *wrong.* He felt queasy, especially in his gut, where the lack of atmospheric pressure gave his bowel a nasty sense of independence. The sensation grew alarmingly. And suddenly Brik knew that he would not be able to control it. He pulled himself out of the airlock and cramped almost immediately into a fetal position.

He couldn't see what was happening behind him, but he could feel an *intense* visceral sucking sensation. His bowel exploded in a dark powdery spray. The eruption was violent and painful. Even after his bowel was certainly empty, the sucking continued. It became *excruciating*—as if his whole body was going to be pulled out through his rectum. Brik held onto the handgrip and *endured*. He'd known this was going to happen; he'd known it was going to be painful; he just hadn't realized it would be *this* painful.

The only consolation was that the same thing would have happened to Cinnabar too. But Cinnabar had probably been trained and augmented specifically for EVA maneuvers. So maybe it hadn't been as painful for him. In which case, Brik mused, who was more courageous?

It didn't matter. It wasn't about courage. It was about results. Already, he was feeling better. He focused his attention forward, checked the time, and asked himself once more if this was a good idea. The answer was still no. Nevertheless . . . this was the only way to find out. Brik put the mouthpiece back in his mouth and took a small suck of air. Yes, he could do it. He pulled himself out of the airlock reception bay . . .

He was at the bow of the ship, just ahead of the snarl painted on the hull. His target was the aftmost airlock. He began pulling himself along the hull of the starship with a steady count. He used the handholds set into the fuselage next to the long tubes of the plasma drives, and he chanted inaudibly to himself as he went, one of his exercise mantras.

He fell into an easy rhythm. He pretended he was climbing one of the exercise walls at home. Five minutes. One hundred meters. He could do it. In free fall, it would be easy.

But it wasn't.

Hard vacuum *burned.*

The stars were hatefully bright. His eyes watered with the pain. His sinuses ached. His whole head felt cold. His ears pounded with the roaring of his own blood.

And very quickly, he knew that his hands were too cold. Every time he touched the hull of the ship a little more of his body heat leached out through his fingers. The designers of the ship had erroneously assumed that anyone using this space-ladder would have been properly suited, so they hadn't padded the handles with temperature-neutral material. Brik's only comforting thought was that it had to have been as bad for Cinnabar as it was for him. Perhaps worse. Because Cinnabar couldn't have been sure that the airlock he was heading toward would open for him.

Brik was halfway to the stern now. He paused momentarily at a starboard access panel. He could open it. He could drop down into the airlock and go in. He'd proved his point. But . . . he had to be *sure.* He checked his watch, then he checked the dial on the oxygen transfusor. He pulled himself past the access panel and kept heading sternward.

The pain in his hands was getting worse. Brik snarled, but he didn't mind. The time to worry was when his hands *stopped* hurting. He was sure of one thing though. Cinnabar had to have had some kind of internal heating augment in his extremities. This pain was *distracting.*

On the other hand, Cinnabar's augments had not been designed to make the assassin comfortable, only to make him powerful. Brik considered that thought as he pulled. What was the Morthan relationship with pain? He knew how he tolerated it. He *accepted* it. He *recreated* it: he let himself experience it fully, until he was inside of it, until he was no longer resisting something that was outside of him but analyzing something that was part of him. And by the time he'd completed that process, the pain had disappeared as pain and became only *information.*

Was that how the warriors of the Solidarity handled discomfort? Brik didn't think so. Cinnabar's reactions had become almost joyous toward the end. He'd looked as if he were in ecstasy.

Brik had heard rumors that the Solidarity routinely rewired the neural circuitry of their warriors, so that all pain sensations were translated into *pleasure.* Could Cinnabar have *enjoyed* the entire experience? Could his death have been an orgasmic adventure? Certainly, the evidence seemed to suggest it.

Brik was having trouble moving his fingers now. Several times his hands had slipped off the rungs of the space-ladder. It was starting to be a problem. He pulled himself out of his reveries and tried to focus on the remaining distance.

He couldn't see. His vision was blurry. Despite the facepack his eyes were drying out. He felt them bulging out of his head. His ears as well. He'd miscalculated only a bit—but it didn't matter whether he missed it by a centimeter or a light year. The situation was binary. The result would be either yes or no.

But . . . if he died out here, that still wouldn't prove that Cinnabar couldn't have done it. Only if he survived would he have incontrovertible proof of Cinnabar's deed.

Death didn't scare him. There was no adrenaline there. He'd long ago learned to appreciate the irony of life. But failure *angered* him. Failure was intolerable. Especially *this* failure, because no one would understand unless he made it back safely. The surge of anger filled him with a brief flash of warmth. He remembered what Korie had said. One of his fathers used to say the same thing. "Anger is useful. Use it." Even in his pain, Brik smiled. More and more, Korie was thinking like a Morthan.

He was pulling himself more slowly now. But now he was chanting a different song. This one was a song of anger. A rhythm of rage. War parties used to pump themselves up with songs like this—you focused on the face of your enemy and sang your rage into him. Brik visualized Cinnabar and already he could feel the first burning embers of hatred growing in his chest.

He had been raised never to succumb to hatred—except in special circumstances. He had been in a killing rage only three times in his life, and all three times had been under tightly controlled circumstances. He knew how to rage when he needed to. But he knew the physical price he would have to pay—

He chanted. Internally. The rhythm of the gods.

Vacuum burned.

His ears pounded.

His eyes ached redly. He held them tightly shut.

His blood roared.

He sang. Inside. He thought of Cinnabar. Cinnabar's hands.

And finally—he *raged*. Not quite a killing rage, but close enough. He held himself just at the threshold of that overwhelming fury.

It didn't keep him warm. But it kept him going.

He pulled himself along—rung after rung after rung—until suddenly, there were no more rungs. He realized he'd been fumbling for several seconds, reaching for something that wasn't there. He was at the aft airlocks. *He'd made it.* He pulled opened the access panel and pulled himself down into the reception bay. He fumbled for the control and slammed his hand against it.

Something flashed red. He opened his eyes, he could barely move them. The panel was throbbing like his heart. Dimly he could make out the single word of doom. LOCKED.

And then . . . he slipped over the edge and plunged into a killing rage.

He wasn't angry at the door, but at himself.

Red fury suffused his entire being. He was no longer rational. He pulled himself out of the access and around the curve of the hull to the next airlock over. There were three airlocks at the stern of the vessel. One of them had to be accessible—

Yes!

The panel flashed green and the cylinder slid around and he pulled himself into it and pushed it around and around and tumbled out, falling upside down onto the floor backwards, his legs flailing and suddenly there was sound roaring around him, painfully loud, impossibly loud, he hadn't realized how loud sound could be, he couldn't hear his heart anymore. He pounded on the deck and raged and raged, and even though he'd won, he was overwhelmed with Morthan fury. He focused on the face of the dead assassin and cursed it with a fiery vengeance; he pushed his anger out through his mouth in a ferocious roar and outshouted the noises of the starship that filled his ears and the stinking smells that suddenly filled his nostrils.

Tears flooded his eyes, blood poured from his nose. He bellowed and shrieked and somehow, even in the blackest reddest deepest moments of his ecstasies, he knew that he had won, he'd proven his point; he knew what Cinnabar had done and how he'd done it. Had the assassin raged like this? He couldn't have—the whole ship would have heard—he must have somehow gone unconscious, somehow triggered his own recuperation once he was safely inside again. Fury ebbed, leaving enlightenment and understanding and a curious emotion that Brik could not name, but it had elements of triumph and joy; he knew it was only the endorphins flooding into his brain, but he was swept up with the feeling, too. This was not like any rage he'd ever felt before, and it was evil and delicious. He laughed out loud, a great booming sound—

The safety hatch of the airlock popped open and a six-member tactical squad was standing there with rifles pointed at him.

Brik looked at them and laughed even harder.

Confused, the members of the squad looked from one to the other.

They didn't get the joke, but that was all right. Brik got it. And at the moment, that was all that mattered.

Williger

Doctor Molly Williger did not have many friends. She didn't need many, and if truth be told, she was not the easiest person to be friendly with. She was taciturn, dour, blunt, and not given to easy camaraderie. It wasn't that she was deliberately *unfriendly*; but that was how she was often perceived.

Mostly, she held herself in reserve, refusing to make some inner part of herself accessible. Her bedside manner had once been compared to General Patton's, with Patton coming off as the nice guy. Although Molly Williger had never slapped a patient, she had once angrily booted one out of a recovery bed with a well-placed kick to the *gluteus maximus*.

And then, of course, there was the not-so-small matter of her appearance.

Even among those who felt kindly toward her, when preparing to introduce people to her, they quietly noted ahead of time that Dr. Williger was the ugliest doctor in the Fleet. It was undeniably true, it gave the person being introduced some warning, and was rather more polite than saying that she was the ugliest *person* in the Fleet, though that was probably true also.

She was a short woman from a high-grav world, very nearly as round as she was high. She had a potato of a nose and squinty eyes that made her look almost as mean as she was ugly. Her ears were crumpled and protruding; they looked like something a dog had buried and then dug up a year later. Her home world had a thicker atmosphere than was common aboard Alliance ships, so at the best of times her breathing was heavy and labored as she fought to get enough of the thin air into her lungs. Her voice was raspy; she sounded like she gargled with gravel. Her hair, pulled into a tight bun, looked like stiff and rusty wire. But even to describe the individual features of this woman was insufficient, because her appearance was the clearest possible demonstration that the whole was more than just the sum of the parts.

A famous poet had once been introduced to Molly Williger and had spent the next year of his life trying to find the proper words to describe her ugliness, before giving up and saying simply, "*Transcendental* ugliness. The language needs another thousand years of evolution before it's up to the task of describing this. The woman is a living masterpiece. God must have intended this. There is no flaw in this work. She is completely and totally ugly, without the slightest blemish or flaw of beauty in the effect. She is a holy presence. I would announce my retirement before I would assume the task of evoking her appearance."

There were those who assumed on Molly's behalf that these words were hurtful to her, and they rebuked the poet publicly for his tastelessness. But the poet replied that he meant no harm. Indeed, he intended his awestruck reaction only as the highest form of compliment. "Beauty is easy," he said. "It takes no particular ability. Any halfwit can speak in pastel. And many have. But true ghastliness is always an art form, it's raw and brutal and carved from the screams and passion of flesh-and-blood turned self-aware. Molly Williger leaves me speechless. I would worship at her feet if she would allow me."

Whatever Molly herself believed, she kept it to herself. She knew she was ugly. She used her ugliness as she used every other tool at her disposal. Indeed, she was the only doctor in the Fleet who could stare into the maw of a snarling Morthan and not be intimidated. Cinnabar had been the first. Brik was the second.

After examining Cinnabar, Brik was easy.

She *hmm*ed and grunted to herself for a bit, studying the various displays in front of her, then without looking up, rasped at Korie. "He'll live. He's a damn fool, but he'll live. Did you need any more damn fools on this ship?"

Korie ignored the remark. "What were you trying to do?" he demanded of Brik.

"I didn't *try*," Brik replied. "I *did* it." His voice was rougher than usual and his breathing was still very uneven.

"Did what?" Korie frowned.

"I proved that Cinnabar lied." Brik took three deep breaths before continuing. He was wearing an oxygen mask. "He *didn't* come in through the forward missile tubes, as he claimed. He had time to go the entire distance of the ship. *And back*. He could have entered *anywhere*."

Korie considered that thought. At first, it seemed an unimportant point to risk one's life over. Then as he began to realize the implications, his expression froze. "Shit," he said. "That just made my day. I've got to talk to HARLIE." He started to shake his head in frustration, then looked up abruptly. "You know, I should bust you for this little stunt. I still might."

"It was a matter of starship security," Brik rumbled and wheezed. "It was entirely within the purview of my authority. External inspection for damage."

"*Without* a starsuit? If nothing else, I should charge you with reckless endangerment."

"Hard to prove. You don't know what the Morthan physiology is capable of under stress. No human does. So stop trying to threaten me. It was *necessary*."

Surprisingly, Korie nodded. He recognized two things. First, this was an argument he couldn't win. And second, if he were to argue with Brik about this, he'd be using the same authority and arguments that the admiral had used—tried to use—on him. Brik's *wildness* was his own. He didn't dare punish it. He exhaled sharply with frustration. He was beginning to understand now how the admiral felt about him.

"Listen to me," said Korie. "The next time you have an idea like this—for *anything* like this—clear it with me first?"

"Why?" Brik regarded Korie dispassionately. "If I gave you that authority, you would use it. Would you have allowed this test?"

"Of course not."

"That's why I had to do it without your permission."

"Well, ask me in the future anyway, so I can have a safety crew accompanying you."

"That would be an insult, Commander."

"I'd rather insult you than bury you. Do you know how much paperwork is involved when a crewmember dies?"

"No, I don't."

That stopped Korie. "You really don't?"

"I just said so."

"All right," Korie made a decision. "From now on, you're in charge of all death details—especially the paperwork."

"I am not a gravedigger. That is the work of . . . slaves."

"Are you a member of this ship's company? Do you follow orders?"

"Yes, Commander, I follow orders." Brik's voice was very formal and rigid.

"I'm going to put this in writing," Korie said. "For what it's worth, the purpose is not to humiliate you. I want you to start feeling responsible for the lives—and deaths—of the people around you."

Brik did not reply to that.

"Good. Now we understand each other."

"I don't think so," said Brik, "but I'm not prepared to argue that right now."

"Uh-huh," said Korie with finality. "Enough dancing. Now I want to hear the *other* reason."

"What other reason?" Brik replied blandly.

"You know what I mean. What were you trying to prove *to yourself*?"

"I *didn't* try," Brik said. "I *did* prove it."

"And that was . . . ?"

"Failure is not an option."

Korie met Brik's eyes. For a moment the two of them regarded each other mercilessly. And Brik saw that yes, *maybe Korie was finally beginning to understand . . .*

"This is what I mean about damn fools," Williger said, deliberately interrupting. "Too much testosterone."

Korie used her remark as an excuse to turn away. He nodded in agreement. "You're right, Doctor. But I wish I had another dozen damn fools on this ship. We do need all the damn fools we can get. How long till he's up again?"

"He can go now, if he insists. I don't want him here. But I'm not sure yet how much damage he's done to his lungs; he's supposed to be capable of routine regeneration; I'm going to watch him closely for a few days. If he needs it, I'll run a transform series."

"Can you wait until we're online again?"

She shrugged. "I can wait till hell freezes over. I don't like working on Morthans. Don't take it personally, Commander," she said to Brik, "but it makes me feel like a veterinarian."

"The feeling is mutual," Brik replied, deadpan.

"He won't eat the kibble," Korie remarked on his way out. "You'll have to feed him the canned stuff."

Armstrong

After Gatineau finished cleaning the galley, Cookie sent him forward to the Operations bay, a four-man cubbyhole tucked directly underneath the Bridge. "Ask for Brian Armstrong, lad. He has the moebius wrench now. He came and got it while you were cleaning the tables."

So Gatineau slid down to the keel and headed forward. He felt oddly renewed and recharged. It wasn't just a full belly that did it, it was also the sense of accomplishment he felt at having scrubbed the galley till it sparkled. He enjoyed cleaning things. He liked seeing the starship at its best, its interior workings glimmering like new. It gave him a sense of *pride*.

He realized with a wry smile that he'd been cleaning all day. He'd helped with the electrical harness, the farm, and the supplies in the cargo deck. He'd been all over the *Star Wolf*. But it also annoyed him to realize how much ground he'd covered without yet locating the elusive moebius wrench.

He reached the Ops bay and climbed the five steps into it. There were two men inside, a small dark one and a large blond one. Both were hip-deep in electronic gear. "Who's Armstrong?" Gatineau asked.

"I am," said the blond. He was a side of beef with a grin. "Who're you?"

"Gatineau. I need the moebius wrench," he said, holding out a hand. "Chief Engineer Leen wants it *now*."

"Oh, the wrench. Right. Green—?" Armstrong turned to the smaller man. "Where'd you put it?"

"I gave it to Hodel. He's microtickling the klystron coils. I'll go get it. He started climbing down into a large square hole in the deck. He paused to explain. "Tell the chief we're awfully sorry for the delay, but we've got the whole communications yoke torn down. We have to logic-test each and every module. We don't think any of the units were contaminated; but a C-5 detox requires the checks anyway. Oh, no—" Green's face fell. "Listen, I just realized, you're going to have to wait until we finish reassembling the optical bleeds. We can't get to the wrench until that's back online and out of the way."

"Why am I not surprised," said Gatineau. "And I suppose you're going to need my help."

"Not really. It's a two-man job. You'd just be in the way." Green pulled himself back out of the hole. Gatineau started to relax—

"On the other hand," Green continued. "If you take over here, Armstrong can go start the teardown of the network assemblers; then we can integrate the envelope riders and restore our hyperstate scanners to full operation ahead of schedule. Here, why don't you take this probe—if we had a class-5 Systems Analysis network, we wouldn't have to do this by hand, but this ship was launched before the required parts came in, and we've never caught up with our own supplies; other ships keep requisitioning them first. You can't imagine the shortages we've had. It's a bitch.

"Let me tell you something," Green added. "It's all about resources. Y'know, that's rule number one: *make sure of your supplies.* I remember one boat, we ran out of toilet paper three weeks from home. By the time we hit port, we were using the chief petty officer's clothes. We were a very unhappy crew. But that was very bad management of resources on his part. He never made that mistake again. That's my point. Now, here, we have to do all this extra work, because we don't have a proper Systems Analysis net. Here, let me show you how to do that—"

Armstrong was already up the five steps to the Operations deck. Quilla Zeta was quietly cleaning the astrogation display. She was a thin-looking woman, blue-skinned, with purple quills in a Mohawk array. Mikhail Hodel had the conn, Jonesy sat at the astrogation station, running a series of battle simulations.

"Crewman Armstrong?" said Zeta.

"Uh—I can't talk now." Armstrong ducked into forward port accessway. "I've got work to do—"

Halfway up the passage, he encountered Quilla Theta; she was even smaller than Gamma, almost child-like. "You have been avoiding us for some time now. We need to talk."

"Not now," Armstrong replied. "I told you, I've got too much to do, with the detox and all—" He shoved past Theta almost rudely and kept going.

Quilla Delta stuck her head out of a cabin door as he passed. "*When?*"

"I told you—*later*." He held his hands up in the air, as if to ward her off and kept on moving.

Quilla Beta was just coming out of the forward magazines, carrying the empty housing for a fibrillator assembly. "You said that before, Crewman Armstrong. Later never comes. Something is the matter. Are you embarrassed about the sexual coupling we had?"

"Look, it didn't work. Please, let's just drop the subject." He pushed past her into the storage compartments. His face was flushed.

Quilla Lambda, the only *male* Quilla onboard, turned to face him. He was just unpacking the rest of the fibrillator assembly. Lambda was as big and as well-muscled as Armstrong; his skin was a darker shade of blue than the females, and his quills were also larger. "No, Brian," he said firmly. "It did work. *That's* the problem."

"Can't you just leave me alone?"

"We need to talk about this. And we need to talk *now*. It's getting in the way of your ability to function. If you won't talk to the others, you will talk to this one. Wait—"

Lambda did something then, Armstrong wasn't sure what, but suddenly, he wasn't a Quilla anymore. He was a man with blue skin and purple quills. "I've disconnected," he said. "Now, you and I may talk privately. If you wish."

"You *disconnected*? I didn't know you could do that."

Lambda nodded. "We don't do it very often; there's rarely any need to. But you need to hear this. I know what you're feeling."

Armstrong didn't answer. He looked off to one side, at the floor, at the ceiling. "Look," he finally said, coming back to Lambda. "Do we really have to have this conversation?"

"Yes," said Lambda. "We do. You enjoyed having sex with us. We enjoyed having sex with you. Quillas are very sensual. You're very attractive. It was very enjoyable for all of us. So what's the problem, Brian?" Lambda looked sharply into Armstrong's eyes, waiting for an answer.

Armstrong looked away. He wouldn't meet Lambda's studying gaze.

"Do you really think that you're the first one who ever felt this way?" Lambda asked softly.

The question was too direct. Armstrong reacted angrily. "I appreciate your concern, okay? But I don't have a lot of time for this right now."

"Yes, you do. You just laid off a large piece of your workload on

Crewman Gatineau. Please don't insult my intelligence. It's very hard to lie convincingly to a Quilla. May I tell you something?"

"Can I stop you?"

"Actually, no." Lambda reached out and placed one blue hand gently on top of Armstrong's pink one. Armstrong tried to pull away, but Lambda held on tight. "Are you having trouble with the fact that there was a male component to the sex?"

"You cut straight to the heart, don't you?"

"You don't have a lot of time," Lambda said dryly.

Armstrong shook his head, a convenient excuse to look away again.

Lambda reached over and, with one finger, turned Armstrong's head back to face his own. "The coupling was joyous, it was delightful, it was filled with laughter and amazement. For us as well as you. The experience has clearly shifted your perception of sexuality. And in ways you're not comfortable with. For the first time, sex wasn't about *you*, it was about *us*. And that is precisely because so many of us were tapped into it. That is where the enthusiasm came from—on both sides, Brian. I'm part of the *us* too. I'm sorry that disturbs you, but it doesn't change what we all experienced."

Armstrong didn't answer immediately. After a moment, he said, "You're very glib. You talk good. But you don't know what's going on in my mind."

"No, but I know what went on in my own mind before I became a Quilla."

Armstrong's eyes widened. He stared at Lambda for a long moment, suddenly trying to see who this man had been *before* . . .

Lambda nodded. "That's right. I did the same thing. And I spent days walking around in a blue funk, trying to figure out what it meant. I wanted to go back for more, and I was terrified to do so. And all the time I was curious what it felt like from the Quillas' side. Eventually, I realized that the only way I'd ever understand, the only way I'd ever see myself from the outside was to become a Quilla myself."

"Stop trying to recruit me. I'm not interested—"

"I'm not trying to recruit you. In all likelihood, you don't even have the right mindset. You probably couldn't be assimilated into a cluster without driving it crazy. And this cluster isn't interested in expanding until the ship situation stabilizes. So don't flatter yourself.

"And don't look so surprised," Lambda added sharply. "I might be a Quilla, but I don't *have* to be polite where it isn't going to be appreciated. There's a lot about Quillas you don't know. You obviously didn't do your research. You were leading with your dick. It was charming at the time, but it's getting old, Brian. It's time to move on.

"The point is, we *do* know what you're going through. It's part of our history too. And we're sorry that you're feeling that way. If we had known you were going to react like this, we would never have accepted your invitation to have sex. But it happened, and now we all have to live with it. So, do you want to keep on walking around like an angry Morthan, or are you ready to grow up?"

"What do you want from me?"

"Nothing, really. Be our friend? Share a smile with us when you see us in the passages?"

Armstrong hesitated. Then something clicked inside and he smiled at some private joke. "I don't believe this."

"What?"

"Well, I'm usually the one who says, 'Can't we just be friends?'"

Lambda smiled back. "And how do the women usually respond?"

Armstrong grinned ruefully. "They get angry. You should see it. I remember one who bawled me out, screaming, 'No, we cannot be friends, you scumbag. I don't want friends. I already have the best friends money can buy. I want more than just your friendship, goddammit.'" He laughed. And then he dropped his eyes in embarrassment. The memory was too painful.

"Go on," said Lambda quietly.

Armstrong swallowed hard. "All right, yeah. It was good. And um, to tell the truth, I did want to do it again. But then . . . with all the teasing and everything, I didn't think that you—I mean you, the whole cluster—felt the way I thought you had, and then when you—I mean *you*, Lambda—winked at me, I thought for sure that you were all laughing at me for . . . well, for being so stupid about it."

"We weren't laughing at you," Lambda said. "Believe it or not, Quillas are incapable of mocking a human soul. We empathize too much with all souls. It's our weakness as well as our strength."

"Yeah, I guess so. But . . . you did scare me. I thought that maybe you, Quilla Lambda, would want to . . . well, you know. And I . . . don't, you know."

Lambda nodded. "First of all, as an individual, I am not homosexual, so you need not worry about that. Secondly, as an individual, I would never have sex outside the cluster. That would be a betrayal of my relationship with my *mates*. Regardless of any attraction I might feel as an individual, I would never place personal gratification above the cluster.

"As a cluster, however, there is always a certain curiosity about all sexual combinations, and it does not particularly matter to us which body we use for a specific sexual encounter; we usually let the other individual choose which partner most appeals to her or him. So, yes, this body has been used for homosexual encounters.

"And," Lambda added thoughtfully, "I must also acknowledge that among all of the sexual possibilities, the fitting of male to male or female to female is often one that the cluster finds interesting because the parallel physical responses of two males or two females can produce some remarkable experiences. I'm sorry if you find that unnerving. The limitation is yours, not ours. Among ourselves, we often arrange encounters between two or three of our units, and that is always quite intense. Because I'm the only male Quilla in this cluster, most of our private encounters are all-female."

Armstrong stared at Lambda, not knowing how to react to this information. He'd heard stories. He hadn't realized the Quillas would be this candid. He wasn't sure if he wanted to hear the details.

Lambda continued anyway. "I will tell you this, Brian. It can be very . . . exhilarating for a man to experience feminine sexuality. It has taught me more about women than I could have learned any other way. I'm sorry if this disturbs you, but you need to understand who we are. I often wish that everyone could be a Quilla for a while. Then you would truly understand. Then there wouldn't be so many ignorant jokes, and you wouldn't have to have the fears you have. We like you. We don't like seeing you uncomfortable."

"Okay," said Armstrong grudgingly. "I got it." He relaxed and sighed and nodded his acceptance. Some of his discomfort was actually easing. He met Lambda's eyes for the first time willingly. "I have been pretty stiff about the whole thing, haven't I?"

"Actually," smiled Lambda gently, "you've been a jerk."

"Yeah," Armstrong admitted. "I guess I have." He took a deep breath. "I'm sorry." And then he asked, "So what do we do now?"

Lambda patted Armstrong's hand gently. "Nothing. Or everything. Or anything you want. We're here to serve. You want a back rub? Call me. I'm an expert in shiatsu. And yes, I know about the pinched nerve in your back that sometimes gives you trouble. That's why I offered. You want sex? Call me or Delta or any of the others. The second time is even more fun than the first. You want someone to talk to? I'd consider it a privilege. You can talk to me as an individual or as a member of the cluster. *Whatever* you want, Brian. *That's* the point."

"Thanks," said Armstrong, both surprised and embarrassed. "I mean it. Thanks." He patted Lambda on the shoulder, like a buddy, and Lambda patted him back like a lover. Armstrong stiffened . . . but he didn't flinch. He had a lot to think about all of a sudden.

Meerson-Krikes

The Orbital College was an adjunct to the Meerson-Krikes orbital assembly lines. For several quiet centuries, Shaleen had earned the reputation as the place to go if you wanted a sunjammer, a lightweight but sturdy fuselage. The polycarbonate-titanium hulls were extremely versatile; they could be rigged with chemical propellant engines, fusion drives, plasma-torches, or even solar sails. The resultant yachts were perfect for journeys between the inner planets of the system, and even occasional forays to the midworlds.

Occasionally, some foolhardy soul would order a craft with a singularity stardrive, with the intention of using the vessel for interstellar travel. Despite significant cautions on the part of the manufacturer about the problems of maintaining the focus of the singularity grappler fields in a hull of such small size, and despite the even more significant cautions about the difficulties of maintaining a *hyperstate* envelope and manipulating it for FTL velocities, there was no shortage of bold eccentrics willing to brave the dark between the stars. Who wouldn't want to own his own starship? The great leap outward was an irresistible pheromone. Over the years, Meerson-Krikes built up a considerable market in light cruisers of all sizes.

Beyond this particular horizon, however, darker clouds were gathering and eventually the growing buildup of military strength in the Morthan sphere of authority began to alarm the Allied Worlds. The Defense Authority contracted with the Meerson-Krikes company—as well as with corporations on numerous other worlds—to begin production of a series of small, but extremely powerful, interstellar military vessels. These destroyer-class cruisers were called "liberty ships."

Because of their considerable experience with light cruisers, Meerson-Krikes was able to gear up quickly for production. Within a year, they were building liberty ships at the rate of one new vessel every eleven days. The ships were pre-fabbed and spartan, lacking all but the most essential life-support services and amenities. The best that could be said of them was that they held air and moved. It would be up to each ship captain to finish the outfitting of his or her vessel.

The high volume of production represented the Alliance's most cost-effective strategy—a swarm of interstellar killer bees. The sting of any individual bee might be insignificant; the combined fury of a thousand or ten thousand or a hundred thousand stings should be enough to stagger the Morthan war machine. An Armageddon-class juggernaut would be unable to withstand such a concentrated assault; she would be overwhelmed like a lumbering hippopotamus in a tank full of piranha. At least, that was the game plan. This strategy was designed to give the Allied Forces incredible flexibility, but at a terrible cost— ultimately it was based on the expendability of individual ships and crews.

The demand for skilled labor in the orbital assembly lines was intensive. Even with robots and nanotechs doing much of the work, the need for human supervision remained critical—and as fast as ships rolled off the assembly line, the Allied Defense Authority recruited the most skilled workers to crew them. Replacement of those workers became such a critical need that the orbital college was established for onsite training and education. For those young men and women who wanted a career in space, the liberty fleet was a very fast—but also very dangerous—track.

With his father's reluctant permission, Jon Korie signed up for the orbital college on his seventeenth birthday. After two months of intensive training, during which more than fifty percent of the applicants were washed out, he was sent up the beanstalk. For his first twelve weeks, he was apprenticed as a galley slave—a cook's assistant. As unglamorous as food preparation service might have seemed at first, the essential lesson was that nutritious and attractive meals were the single most important part of energizing a ship's crew. Korie was lucky; he liked cooking as much as he liked eating. He tackled the job with enthusiasm and graduated with a rating of ninety-four percent.

On his last day, the crew chief, a diminutive little woman named Bertha Fleischer, made him a going-away feast of beet borscht, stuffed cabbage, fresh egg-bread for mopping the plate, and a magnificent strawberry shortcake. She wept copiously, as if her only son were leaving. Korie was surprised by her demonstrative affection; he had never been the target of such warmth before. The feeling stayed with him long after the meal was only a memory.

From the kitchen, Korie went to the farms.

Food preparation was crucial to the morale of the crew, but production was essential to basic survival. The farm not only produced food; it processed sewage, turning it into fertilizer. The fertilizer was liquified and fed to aeroponically grown plants with steady-state drip irrigation. Some of the crops were harvested for food, others were liquified in turn to make nutrient solutions for the meat tanks. The green leaves of the plants also regenerated the air in the ship, taking in carbon dioxide and putting out life-giving oxygen.

The assembly lines maintained their own vast farms, partly to maintain their own ecology, of course, and partly to serve as a seed farm for the new ships taking shape on the docking spurs. Each new ship would be launched with a complete farm installed in it.

After a time, Korie was assigned to one of the teams that installed new farms; later he became a team leader. No ship was ever delivered to the Allied Defense Authority until her farm was certified as fully functional, able to feed a crew of 145 individuals. Jon Korie signed off on fourteen farms. He found the work both exhausting and satisfying, and he never looked at a meal the same way again.

On the farms, Jon Korie learned about proteins, carbohydrates, fats, and sugars. He learned about photosynthesis and atmospheric pressure, day-night cycles and seasons. He learned about planting and harvesting, pollinating and cross-breeding, grafting and splitting. Most important, he learned *patience*. It doesn't matter how many cabbages you plant. You won't get sixty cabbages any faster than you get one.

If you think you'll want stuffed cabbage in August, be sure to plant cabbages in February, and start the meat growing in the tanks no later than April; the longer the meat ages in the nutrients, the more flavor it will have when it reaches the plate. If you want bacon and eggs regularly, you have to monitor the pork belly tanks and the egg-production lines daily. If you want fresh butter for your toast, the udders have to be fed *and* massaged.

There were no real animals aboard the starship, but parts of many different species thrived in various growth tanks. Throughout the inner hull ranks of glass tanks stood three high, each with its own lump of flesh growing inside.

After tending three complete seasons of corn, peas, carrots, lettuce, tomatoes, cucumbers, asparagus, barley, rice, oranges, apples, plums, grapes, peaches, apricots, kiwis, garbanzos, olives, and lychees; not to mention beef, lamb, chicken, mutton, pork, ostrich, buffalo, venison, as well as catfish, tuna, salmon, shrimp, giant clam, octopus, sea bass, yellowtail, swordfish, shark, porpoise, and whale; Korie graduated from the farm with a rating of eighty-nine percent. It wasn't as high a score as he should have earned, but Korie had never quite accepted the most fundamental tenet of ecology: *Life is messy.*

At heart, he was an engineer—or a control freak. He kept trying to make things run on schedule; but even industrial farms had their own rhythms; a farm could be managed only by a person who was willing to be managed by the rhythm of the seasons, and Korie was too impatient for that.

The *other* thing that distracted him from full concentration was Carol Jane.

At first, she was just a co-worker, then later a teammate, and eventually a study partner. It wasn't until midway through the second semester that he began to notice how beautiful she really was; and then he wondered how he had gone for so long without noticing before. And then . . . he began to worry how he would ever be able to concentrate on *anything else.*

Carol gave no sign of mutual interest, no encouragement at all; yet he couldn't get her out of his thoughts. He daydreamed about her constantly. He thought of nothing else. She was on his mind in class, at mealtimes, during study hall, during work sessions, in the corridors, in the showers, and even at bedtime—especially at bedtime. He wondered what it would be like to hold her body close to his—to smell her hair and taste her mouth and listen to her soft words and feel their bodies intertwined and fitting together in hot wet passion.

In his ignorance and naiveté, he constructed baroque fantasies in his imagination. (His favorite involved the two of them, marooned in a tumbling free-fall capsule for a week.) He masturbated himself into painful insensibility thinking of her. It was as if his adolescent hormones, which had lain dormant for so long that young Korie had almost begun to believe that he would never experience a sexual relationship, had suddenly kicked in with an enthusiastic vengeance.

He waited for the obsession to pass. It didn't. He waited for some sign from her that she recognized the effect she was having on him. She gave him no sign.

Finally, he realized he would have to act. He could not go on the way he was; it was driving him crazy. He had become obsessed with Carol Jane; her apparent disinterest in him made it all the worse.

Young Jon Korie spent long hours trying to figure out a way to speak to Carol Jane about his feelings. He thought about filling her room with roses and love poems; he thought about asking her to take walks with him on the stardeck or go nude-swimming in the free fall tanks. But everything he thought of only seemed silly and naive in the cold light of morning.

Finally, one day, after a particularly clumsy mistake in the sludge farm, which left him hip-deep in cold stinking muck, he burst out in frustration, "This is all your fault!"

"Mine?" Carol Jane asked, honestly puzzled.

"Yes," he admitted angrily. "I'm so obsessed with you, I can't concentrate on anything anymore. You had to go and wear that tight shirt today, and I haven't been able to think of anything else."

When she realized what he was saying, she started to giggle; then she started laughing.

Hurt by her response, Korie stamped away to the showers at the end of the chamber. He peeled off his muck pants, his shorts, his T-shirt, and started hosing himself down. A moment later, Carol entered and took the hose from him. "If it's my fault you got dirty, then it's my responsibility to help you clean up," she said. And then she apologized for laughing. She had been laughing at herself.

Standing there, naked, still covered with sludge and muck and slime, Korie blinked in confusion. Carol Jane admitted that she had been wondering about Jon Korie since the first day she'd seen him in the corridors. He was so smart, so self-assured, so . . . so *alert*; and yet, he had seemed totally disinterested in having a relationship of any kind with anyone. Didn't he know that people all over the station were wondering about him? Had he been disconnected? Was he gay? Was he skeltered? Had he sworn a vow of celibacy? Was he emotionally retarded? Was there some great tragedy in his past? Was he some kind of human machine? Did he care about anything or anyone?

When Korie realized the great discrepancy between what it looked like on his side and how he was perceived by others, he too saw why she had laughed so hard. He almost smiled himself.

Carol Jane was peeling off her own shirt and shorts then. "Here," she said. "It's your turn to hose me down—"

The reality turned out to be a lot more fun than the fantasy.

Showers

Originally, Captain Hardesty had planned to have Brik's quarters out-fitted with an anti-grav bed/shower built to Brik's proportions. The unit had either disappeared in transit or had been coopted by some superior officer for his or her own special purposes.

Brik knew that some humans preferred free-fall sex with multiple partners and his bed/shower unit would have been very useful for that purpose. The thought should have annoyed him, but he didn't regard the loss of the tube as much more than a minor inconvenience. He didn't sleep as humans did anyway.

Instead, he draped himself backward over a rounded frame, which simultaneously stretched his spine and lowered his head below his heart. In that position, he could place himself into a mandala-trance. As a child, he'd been trained to reach the mandala-state by the use of mild hallucinogenic drugs while facing a holographic display of an endless fractal plunge toward an unreachable center. Sometimes it was a dive into fractal immortality; other times it was a dark prowl forward through a doomful environment. Still other times it was a forward flight through a fantastic city or an even more deranged countryside. It had not taken the young Brik long to learn how to achieve transcendence.

One evening, without the drugs, without the holographic display, he'd closed his eyes and, without even consciously trying, found that he was already visualizing a mandala plunge. It was not the same im-agery as provided by the display, but it was recognizably the same kind of unending plunge forward.

It was as if he was exploring an endless maze of dark corridors and tunnels. The pictures flowed easily into his mind. Upward he was climbing, up the stairs, ducking through a door, forward, to the left and then around a corner to the right, up another long brace of stairs, hurrying now through zigzag corridors, diving across intersections and branching wide avenues, but always upward. Up the stairs, up the ramps, deeper and deeper into the heart of it, but never getting any closer to the center. Whatever it was, whatever lay at the heart of it, he never got any closer.

But it wasn't the goal. It was the journey up and in. It took him deep, and finally, he learned how to pass beyond the conscious domains to the inner realms where the soul built its own world. Here was the real power. Eventually, the young Brik learned to trigger the onset of the dreamtime as easily as laying down and closing his eyes.

But here, aboard the *Star Wolf*, it wasn't always easy. Often, he returned to his cabin, filled with inner turmoils. There was so much about these poor soft human beings that he didn't understand. And it bothered him intensely that he didn't. It wasn't that he felt in any way inferior or deprived; but while there was any aspect of their behavior that remained a mystery, he felt *vulnerable*. If anything was going to hurt him, it was going to come out of one of those unknown places in the human soul. He couldn't stand that thought. Vulnerability was an intolerable state.

Curiously, he also recognized that the flaw was in himself.

On one level, he understood the necessity of vulnerability as part of the nature of transcendence. One must *surrender* to the universe in order to be part of it; but on another level, he *couldn't*. His Morthan training made it impossible. Morthans never surrendered to anything. Not even the universe.

It was happening more and more often now. Brik kept finding himself trapped in the human dilemma and it left him so frustrated that he couldn't achieve transcendence of any kind. He would lay silently in the dark, processing each of the day's troubling events in turn. He stepped through his completion rituals methodically and carefully, examining each moment from every perspective he could imagine— from the domains of right and wrong as well as the domains in which personal judgment was irrelevant. He did this until the moments lost all meaning and became just another set of incidents in the flows of personal time. Then and only then could he step past through the flow-stopping event and move on to the next.

Occasionally he knew doubt. Not of himself. But of the power of the rituals. Sometimes, he felt . . . that there were things . . . that hadn't really resolved. It was a troubling thought, one that nagged at him almost every day now. He knew why. Because his completion rituals were almost always about the same kinds of events. It was as if he were trapped in a loop, completing the same incidents over and over and over again. And the thought occurred to him that the reason this incident kept returning in a new guise each day was that there was actually some much larger and darker moment that he had failed to address, and these lesser moments were merely the surface eructations.

These were the moments in which he felt his strongest doubts. Had his training been flawed? Or had he failed to grasp some part of it? He knew that one could not force transcendence. It arrived only when one cleared a space for it, never when one demanded its presence. On those evenings when Brik felt most frustrated, he retreated to a very private and almost embarrassing escape.

He went down to the forward showers, set all twelve sprays for as hot and as violent as they would go, stood in the center of the room, and chanted. He hummed. He *ommmmmed.*

He let himself relax completely, while the water pounded his chest, while the steam rose around him, and he let a great soul-filling purr resonate throughout his body.

There was no spiritual reason for this.

He did it simply because it felt good to submerge.

He did it because it was *sensual.*

The water jets massaged him. The steam drained the tension from his muscles, leaving him limp and enervated. The sound of his own deep note filled his personal universe.

Abruptly. Someone was here. He opened his eyes.

Bach. Her mouth a startled O of surprise.

"Oh, I'm sorry, Brik. I didn't know——" Her glance flickered down, then up again, then down—she flushed crimson. "I, uh——" She turned and left embarrassedly.

For the first time in his life, Brik felt *naked.*

He did not sleep easily that night. It was another one of those moments that refused to complete itself, refused to be assimilated.

Timmy

Jon and Carol pooled their accumulated leave and spent five days falling in love. Afterward, neither of them was ever the same again. Korie came back with a glint of knowledge in his eyes and a bounce to his step that let people know that the missing piece had finally been found. Carol came back glowing. Neither of them said a word to anyone, they didn't have to, everyone already knew.

The experience of unconditional love transformed Jon Korie. He walked around in a glow of astonishment that life could be so amazing. He became generous and demonstrative in ways that left his colleagues and coworkers shaking their heads in disbelief. Once, he even laughed out loud. He suddenly *understood* that he was just like everybody else. For once in his life, he really was *all right*.

As the days rolled over each other, the relationship deepened. As Jon and Carol learned to deal with problems and opportunities together, they went from being lovers to partners. It was the first of many such graduations. Every new experience gave them something new to share, something new that was uniquely their own. As their partnership grew, so did their appreciation for each other. After a time, they were no longer two, but one with two parts.

Jon and Carol graduated from the farms at the same time. He went onto the production line where singularity grapplers were assembled; she went into intelligence-engine training lab. As each new HARLIE unit came online, it had to be *seasoned* under the tutelage of a committee of super-HARLIE units. When the committee finally agreed that the new unit was sane enough to manage the moment-to-moment operations of a liberty ship, it was certified and installed.

As a result, Carol actually made it into deep space before Jon did;

she went on seventeen shakedown cruises, five involving short FTL hops. She took great pride in her striated FTL bars. Korie said he was happy for her, but they both knew that he was deeply envious. If there was one thing he wanted more than anything else—perhaps even more than he wanted Carol—it was the chance to travel among the stars.

Eventually, they were both promoted again, which they celebrated with a joyous wedding, a tumultuous party (catered by a delirious Bertha Fleischer), and a short frenzied honeymoon; their next assignments began only three days after the wedding.

This time, Korie found himself installing grappler armatures into actual singularity cages. Because of the accelerating shortage in the higher ranks, he was promoted to crew chief in less than a month, and within three months, he was in charge of singularity assemblies for the whole docking spar.

The first time he had to install a pinpoint black hole in a singularity cage, he was so terrified of making a mistake that he threw up three times the night before. But his team followed the procedures they had been so carefully trained in and the installation went off perfectly. It was a textbook example. Eventually, Jon Korie signed off on thirty-two singularity installations, more than any other crew chief before him.

From there he was promoted to networks, and eventually command center installations. By this time, their first child was already in the incubator, and the sperm and eggs for the second and third had already been harvested.

By the time Jon Korie was twenty-three, he was debugging whole starships. He oversaw sixteen teams and had personally signed off on over a hundred hulls. He and Carol still spent ten hours a week working in the farms so they could shower together afterward. Neither of them realized the reputation they had established until one day, while inspecting a ship, preparatory to its final sign-off, Korie found a cot with its covers turned back in the vessel's inner hull. The ship's captain-to-be admitted sheepishly that while he personally was not superstitious, the crew did not believe the vessel could be considered starworthy until Jon Korie and his wife Carol had performed the appropriate ceremonies. Korie was embarrassed by the request; but finally agreed on one condition. The consummation had to occur during *hyperstate* FTL conditions. It was a remarkable shakedown cruise.

Admiral Coon was also aboard that cruise. He was so impressed with Korie's grasp of ship mechanics that he offered him an immediate scholarship to Officer Candidate School. "Because of your high rating on the assembly lines, you'll be put into an accelerated program. You'll be serving on a ship in two years; you could be a captain in six."

Without consulting with Carol, Korie accepted immediately—and nearly wrecked his marriage.

Carol was terrified of that career track for her husband, and justifiably so. She was also angered that he had made the decision without consulting with her; without apparently even thinking of her needs at all. They were about to have a baby; the egg had been fertilized, the embryo was growing, the decanting day was already set, the party was scheduled. They had even made a down payment on a house to be built upon their return groundside. They had planned a whole life together.

Jon Korie fell to his knees and begged his young wife's forgiveness. There was nothing he could say, no words of apology that would undo the damage. All he could do was ask her to understand how desperately he wanted to go to the stars. The chance to serve on a starship was something he had been dreaming of all his life.

Carol Jane Korie was a remarkable woman. She pulled her husband to his feet and slapped his face. She said, "Future starship captains don't beg. Not to anyone. They make their decisions and stand by them. Now . . . be a captain, tell me what you have decided and ask me to be your partner in this enterprise."

And after he did that, she fell into his arms and said, "Do you think I don't understand your dreams, you jerk?"

"I was afraid you'd say no."

"If I ever said no to you, Jon Thomas Korie—if I ever said anything to keep you from going FTL, you'd never forgive me. We'd never have a partnership again; we wouldn't have any kind of marriage at all. Yes, I'm angry—but I want you to understand that what I'm angry about is not that you failed to consult with me, but that you didn't trust our partnership enough in the first place."

For a while, Korie wondered if he should turn down the admiral's offer; he brooded about his selfishness and the terrible hurt he'd inflicted on his wife; the next several days were very uncomfortable. Neither was certain if they had really made up, if the incident was actually resolved, or if they still had work to do to bridge the gap that had suddenly opened up between them.

A few days later, they went to visit their developing fetus in the nursery. At first Korie was awed by the fragility of the small pink creature growing in the nutrient bottle, he marvelled at its tiny little fingers, but then as he turned his head this way and that, trying to imagine the nature of the child-to-be, he was suddenly struck by its similarity to the protein lumps in the meat tanks. He backed away from the tank, disgusted with himself and horrified to be brought face to face with his own essential vulnerability—where was the spark that turned lumps of meat into sentient beings? Was this all there was to humanity?

And, unbidden, the answer came to him. It was as if Zaffron was standing there behind him whispering. "Yes, Jon Korie. This is it. This is all there is to a human being. Life is only what you create it to be."

Korie felt suddenly weak. He looked to Carol; she had put her face against the warm glass of the bottle and was standing there with her eyes closed and a blissful smile on her face. She was in a place of her own. Unseen by his wife, Korie sat down on a bench and began to weep silently. It was several moments before Carol noticed, and when she did, she didn't know how to react. She'd never seen her husband like this before.

"What is it, Jon?" she asked, momentarily frightened.

He looked up at her, tears still running down his cheeks, and said, "He's so beautiful. So are you. So are all of us. Isn't it amazing that little pink lumps of meat like that can become such beautiful creatures as people—sentient beings able to think and care and share and love each other so much? It scares me, Carol, because now I'm realizing that's what also gives us the ability to hurt each other so deeply—and be hurt in turn."

Carol Jane stayed where she was, still holding onto the glass uterine tank with their baby floating in it. At first she wasn't sure how she should respond; she was profoundly moved by the transformation in her husband, but she had no words that would satisfactorily acknowledge the moment. Finally she turned to the developing infant, tapped gently on the glass, and whispered, "Timmy, look. Your daddy's going to be a starship captain. He's going to be the very best of all starship captains. Doesn't that make you proud?"

That was when Jon Korie knew that she had truly forgiven him. He went to her, his eyes still wet, and took her in his arms. He held her for a long long time without speaking. At last, he held her apart so he could look into her eyes; he said it simply. "I think I have just learned the most important lesson a starship captain needs to learn."

"What's that?" she asked.

"I'm not alone anymore. I have others depending on me. I can't ever forget that. Not ever again."

She looked up into his eyes and saw how deeply he meant it. And that was when *she* knew how much he truly needed her.

Dreams

Korie came awake with a start. He'd been having that dream again. The one where he came home. Only no one was there. The dream was always the same, only the details were different. He went from room to room, looking for Carol and Timmy and Robby. This time, he'd *almost* had them again. This time, he'd *almost* . . .

And then he realized where he was again and the hurt came flooding up in his throat and out his eyes. He crumpled. He buried his face in his hands and let the sobs come again. He couldn't help it anymore. It was too much for one man to bear. The anger, the rage, the frustration. It wasn't fair. He'd been a good husband and father. Loyal. Loving. Kind. He'd been a good officer. Dependable. Responsible. He'd earned better. He *deserved* better. This wasn't the way his life was supposed to work out. One horrible loss after another. The problems mounting up, no end in sight. He wondered how other men handled the pain.

He'd been trained. He'd been through long rigorous hours of courses covering almost every aspect of shipboard life. He'd studied military structure and authority, he'd been indoctrinated with the philosophies of responsibility, both that of the individual and that of the officer; responsibilities to the crew, responsibilities to the ship, responsibilities to the mission—he remembered the endless hours of classroom debate over which responsibility took precedence in any given situation. There had been the personal courses too—seminars in communication and effectiveness and self-discipline. There had been courses in behavior. He'd thrown himself into all those studies with a passion that had amazed himself as well as his instructors. He'd come away from his studies with a sense of self-worth and confidence that let him move through the most troubling situations with an appalling detachment. He focused on the result he needed to produce, not the pain of the journey—and it worked. Most of the time.

But not here.

Nothing he'd ever studied had prepared him for this kind of hammering at his soul. Day after day, it was like swimming in acid. Everybody attacked. Nobody supported. Nobody *nurtured*. He needed Carol. She nourished him. Without her . . . he didn't know how he could keep on keeping on.

But he had to.

It was all that bullshit about responsibility. He was responsible. He couldn't stop. But neither could he stop having these three-o'clock-in-the-morning nightmares.

"Mr. Korie?" HARLIE.

"I'm fine, HARLIE."

"Just checking."

"Thank you."

"Would you like something from the galley? Tea? Hot chocolate?"

Korie shook his head, then realized that HARLIE probably couldn't see him. "No, no thanks," he said. He sat up, rubbing his eyes. His sleeping tube stood nearby; he'd fallen asleep on the couch again. He knew he shouldn't have done that. He only had the dream when he fell asleep in a gravity environment. On a subconscious level, gravity reminded him of home . . .

"You really should eat. You have a busy day ahead of you."

"All right, all right. Don't start with the nagging. I'll have a BLT and hot chocolate."

"Working," said HARLIE, and fell silent again.

Korie ran a hand through his hair. Time for a haircut again. He sighed and turned back to his desk. The display of the work station glimmered obediently to life with the same display as before. Korie put his elbows on the desk, put his hands together almost in a prayer position, and cradled his chin in his fingertips. He pursed his lips as he studied the diagrams. He shook his head to himself. "Nope, nope, nope," he said. "Clear it. I need to think about something else. This isn't going to work. There's no way to do this. We're never going to make it. I don't know what I was thinking of, HARLIE." He sighed. "I didn't do this crew any favors. If I'd agreed with the admiral's decision to decommission this ship, most of them could have been in new berths by now. Now they're going to miss the biggest battle of this war."

"Some of them might not have the same perspective on it as you do, Mr. Korie. The statistical projection on the upcoming battle at Taal-amar is that we will probably lose two-thirds of our combatant vessels."

"I saw the same reports you did." Korie said. "And I still think our crew would rather be in the battle than out of it. It's not the dying that people mind, it's dying without a reason. It's dying without a chance." And then he wondered if he were talking for the crew, or just for himself.

"Death is not the same for me," the intelligence engine replied. "I'll have to take your word for it."

Korie sighed. He wasn't in the mood for one of HARLIE's inter-minable philosophical discussions. HARLIE would talk forever if he had the right conversational partner. He loved to play with ideas. But . . . all that chatter, it never produced results, and Korie was in the business of producing results, not interesting discussions. He gnawed at a thumbnail.

He felt frustrated. "Why can't we detox this ship? What are we missing, HARLIE?"

HARLIE didn't answer. Korie didn't notice the omission. Not at first. He was too wrapped up in his own problems.

He remembered his studies. Zaffron used to say, "If you can't find the answer, you're asking the wrong question." Perhaps that was it. He turned that thought over in his mind for a while.

Hm.

Something *twanged* in his consciousness.

No.

But yes. It had to be.

"HARLIE," he said. "You didn't answer my question."

HARLIE fell silent again.

"I see." Korie sat back in his chair, thinking. Thinking hard.

"Where's Chief Leen?" he asked abruptly.

"Under the Alpha singularity grappler. Asleep. His crew will not allow him to be disturbed."

"And where's Mr. Brik?"

"In his cabin."

Korie glanced at the time. "He is, hm? Let me see his medical report. Has Dr. Williger cleared him yet?"

"Sir?"

"Never mind. Get my starsuit ready."

"As soon as you eat."

"Yes, *mother*."

Discipline

Commander Korie checked the seals on his starsuit. He held his helmet under his left arm. He was ready.

He spoke softly to his communicator, knowing that HARLIE would relay the request instantly, also annotating its source. "Mr. Brik to aft airlock three, on the double."

He glanced at the time display on his starsuit wrist panel. Assuming that Brik was either in his quarters, on the Bridge, or in the officers' wardroom accessing the ship's library, he was somewhere amidships. Considering Brik's allegiance to discipline, his physical size and speed, and his most probable course through the vessel's corridors, he should be arriving at the aft airlock right about—

"You rang?" said Brik, suddenly looming over Korie.

Korie looked up at Brik. And up. "Yes, I did," he said, deliberately stiff, deliberately loud. Aft airlock three was visible from the cargo bay. Behind Brik, Toad Hall and his supply crew were being deliberately nonchalant as they worked. Korie raised his voice so only the immediate planet could hear. He wanted them to miss nothing. The entire episode was also being recorded automatically into the ship's log, uncoded so that anyone could access it.

"What is this, *Mister* Brik?" Korie demanded.

Brik displayed no emotion. His gaze followed Korie's gesture. "It appears to be a starsuit. A Tyger-sized starsuit."

"It *is* a starsuit," Korie confirmed. "A Morthan Tyger-sized starsuit." He stepped sideways. "Would you please demonstrate its proper use to me?"

"Sir?"

"Put. It. On. Mister."

"I don't see the purpose . . ."

"That *wasn't* a request, Mister Brik. You and I are going EVA. *Now*." Korie amazed himself with his tone of voice. He'd never heard anyone speak to a Morthan in this tone of voice before. He couldn't believe he was doing it now. He was relying entirely on his faith in Brik's commitment to the chain of authority.

Brik regarded Korie dispassionately. Whatever was going on behind those dark Morthan eyes, it was unreadable.

"Nobody goes EVA without proper gear," Korie said. "I'm revoking your certification until you demonstrate that you know how to do this by the regs."

Brik looked as if he wanted to speak. Abruptly, his expression shifted. His eyes narrowed. "I will do this," he said stiffly. "But I want to log a formal protest."

"I'll help you fill out the forms," Korie said.

Without a word, Brik began shrugging off his outer garments. Korie watched without reaction. Brik *loomed*. The huge bulk of the Morthan physique was intimidating. If Korie had any thoughts at all about the closeness of the near-naked Morthan body, he kept them to himself.

Brik took the starsuit off the rack and pulled it on methodically, first the leggings and the boots, then the tunic. He checked the seals, then turned around so Korie could check them too.

"Green," confirmed Korie, then turned around slowly so Brik could check his.

"Green," rumbled Brik.

"Helmet," said Korie. He pulled his headgear on, fastening it to the starsuit collar, locking it into place. Brik did the same. Again, they checked each other. Green and green.

"Any questions?" demanded Korie.

"No, sir," said Brik.

"Good," said Korie. He slapped the door panel. The hatch whooshed open. Brik stepped into it. Korie followed. Neither the human nor the Morthan spoke. They regarded each other grimly. Korie pressed a wall panel. The hatch slid shut behind them.

On the cargo deck, several of the crew turned and looked at each other with wide eyes. Shrugs were exchanged. Heads were scratched. Toad Hall shook his head. "Don't ask me. I dunno. Maybe it's one of those male-bonding things that officers do."

The others started offering their own opinions. "Korie's trying to show him who's boss."

"He can't win that pissing contest."

"Yeah, but he needs to show Brik he isn't afraid to try."

"Brik's too smart to challenge him."

"And Korie's too smart to put him in a position where he'd have to."

"So why'd they go out there?"

"To look at the stars together?"

"Yeah, right."

"Then you tell me. Two guys get into starsuits and go out for a walk on the hull. What does that mean?"

"That whatever they have to say to each other, they don't want anyone else listening?" offered Gatineau. He was passing through on his way to the scrubbers. Duty officer Miller had the moebius wrench now. It didn't make sense to him; if the left-handed moebius wrench was such a necessary tool, why was there only one of them onboard?

"We've got privacy pods in the inner hull," said Hall.

"I don't think Korie would want to be seen taking Brik to one of those," laughed one of the women.

Hall shook his head, grinning at the thought. "All right, come on. It's obviously none of our business. Let's get this stuff logged and away."

Thirty minutes later, Korie and Brik returned. They peeled off their starsuits without speaking and handed them over for refreshing. Korie finished dressing first. He headed forward without comment. Brik followed after a moment later, growling deep in his throat.

The cargo crew exchanged worried glances, but this time no one speculated on what had transpired between the two officers.

The Crew

Gatineau was in a sour mood when he arrived at the aft cargo bay.

He'd finally figured it out about the moebius wrench—the *left-handed* moebius wrench—and he wasn't happy. In fact, he was absolutely miserable, as close to despair as he'd ever been in his whole life. Perhaps the only worse moment he could remember was the time Sally-Ann Jessup had said, "Couldn't we just be friends instead?" No. This was worse. Sally-Ann was only a thirteen-year-old memory. This was his *starship*. This was the place where he lived and worked and served. This was his *career*.

He hated feeling like this. He didn't even have a name for the feeling. He felt hurt and alienated and angry and frustrated and embarrassed all at once. This wasn't fair. He'd earned the right to be treated with respect. Being sent all over the whole ship on a wide-eyed chimerical trek did little to make him feel like he was a useful part of the crew. He felt betrayed. Worst of all, he felt like a *fool*. Worse than that, everybody on the ship *knew* about it. How could he ever look these people in the eye again?

He couldn't. He stared at his shoes. There were two kinds of footgear aboard the starship—hard shelled protective boots for heavy work—and soft moccasins for normal duty. He was wearing the boots. He felt silly in them. He felt silly out of them. He felt like a kid who'd crapped his pants the first day of school. No, he felt worse than that. He remembered crapping his pants the first day of school and it hadn't been this devastating.

Korie entered the cargo bay, looking uncommonly crisp for a man who had gone without sleep for a week. Most of the crew was already assembled; a last few stragglers followed Korie in. All of them looked to him anxiously.

This time Korie moved out to the middle of the bay and stood among them, like just another crewmember. An expectant circle formed around him. Gatineau put himself directly behind Korie so he wouldn't have to see his face. He didn't want Korie seeing his embarrassment. He studied his boots. His big silly boots.

"I'll make this brief," Korie said. His voice was hard. This was clearly not an announcement that he wanted to make. "We're not going to make it. I'm sorry."

There were groans of dismay. Korie held up his hands to stop them. "Belay that. Our hyperstate fluctuators are needed by the *Spider Demon*. Chief Leen sent them over last night. And Captain Wilbur has sent his thanks for our quick help."

"I'll tell you the truth. The detox job was bigger than we thought. The Morthan assassin left a reservoir of infection aboard this ship, booby traps like the docking tube, nano-cancers, bubbles in the communications yokes, I don't have to list it all for you. You know."

Korie hesitated, phrasing his next words carefully. "Look, I know you're disappointed. So am I. And we're all tired too. But we have a larger responsibility to the fleet. *To the war effort.* Every ship we float is going to make a difference at Taalamar. So that's got to be our first priority. Helping the others get there. Many of them are already on their way."

Korie glanced around the cargo bay, unashamedly meeting the eyes of as many different crew members as he could. He even turned around to look directly at Gatineau. The boy looked distinctly uncomfortable. "I don't want you to feel that you failed. You didn't. Listen to me." He moved among them, patting their backs, their shoulders, their hands. "We have nothing to be ashamed of. Parts of this ship are already installed in every single one of those other vessels. If it weren't for us, they'd be sitting stuck here too. So *we* might not be going, but our commitment is—*almost a dozen times over.* We're sending eleven other starships to represent us at Taalamar." There were scattered shouts of "Yeah!" and some applause. But not enough.

"Yes," agreed Korie anyway. "Yes. That's our success; it's *your* success. You did good. I'm very proud of you. You didn't fail. You *didn't.*" He made a triumphant chopping gesture with his fist and turned away, almost bumping into Gatineau.

"But it sure feels like it, sir," said Gatineau. He recognized what Korie was trying to do. Recontextualization. But it didn't change the

facts. They hadn't made it. Gatineau was still unhappy. And now he
had something *else* to be unhappy about.

"I know," said Korie, with more understanding than Gatineau expected. "It *is* upsetting. You're not going to the party, but your dancing
shoes are." He touched the younger man on the shoulder gently. "We'll
just have to have a party of our own. Maybe Hodel can exorcise something. Oh—" Korie interrupted himself. He turned back to the room,
raising his voice. "There is one thing that might take some of the sting
off this particular success. One other ship didn't make the cut—the
Houston." He smiled at some private satisfaction.

"Oh, God," said Hodel. "They're gonna play *Dixie* at us again, aren't
they?"

"I guess we're going to have to find our *own* theme music," Korie
said, nodding to the junior officer. "Give it some thought, Mike, will
you? Oh, and have Cookie prepare something special for dinner. This
crew deserves a break. All right," he said, raising his voice again. "Let's
get back to work, people. We've still got a ship to detox. Chief Leen?
I want a confidence test in two hours." And then he was out the hatch.
Leen started barking at his crew, herding them forward. "Come on,
you heard the man! Move your butts! Come on, Cappy! MacHeath!
You move too long in the same place!" After that, the cargo bay emptied
rapidly. There wasn't anything to say, and most of the crew headed
glumly back to work.

Gatineau stood where he was for a moment, hesitating. Trying to
make a decision. He felt like he was walking around with his abdomen
ripped open and his guts dripping out. He needed . . . what was the
word? *Closure*. That was it. He needed to feel that something had been
resolved. He needed to be *heard*. He headed down to the keel and
forward to the engine room, following Chief Leen. It was the quieter
way; he'd run into fewer people.

The keel was almost familiar to him now. He'd been up and down
it so many times in the past few days, he knew it better than the cabin
where he slept. He reached the machine shop and climbed the ladder
up into the engine room proper. Leen was already at his work station,
running integrity tests on the Alpha grappler and hollering at the Black
Hole Gang.

Gatineau's anger flooded hotly back into him. The feelings of frustration and hurt and embarrassment were even more painful here in
the engine room where the whole wild chase started. He was suddenly
afraid that if he said or did anything else, it would only make it worse.
Nevertheless . . . he came around the containment sphere to the chief
engineer's station with more resolve than he'd felt for a long while.

He stood directly in front of Chief Leen, and spoke as firmly as he could. "Chief?" His voice squeaked. He tried again. "*Chief?*"

The chief engineer looked up from his work station, as if he were acknowledging the delivery of a package. He swiveled on his stool to face the younger man. "What?"

"You sent me on a snipe hunt," Gatineau accused. "A wild goose chase. You had me running all over the ship. And everybody was in on it, weren't they—laughing at me behind my back? That was wrong, sir. That's an abuse of authority. I trusted you. I came here to be trained, not to be subjected to silly practical jokes." Gatineau didn't notice that behind him several of the Black Hole Gang were climbing down from the catwalks and approaching. "You had me embarrassing myself to people I'm supposed to be working with. I busted my ass for you, and for everyone else." Gatineau's voice cracked on the last few words. "I did every damn shitwork job on the whole damn ship just because I wanted to be a good crewmember."

Leen waited until Gatineau wound down. Finally, he said, "You came here to be trained, right?"

"Yes, sir. I did."

"Okay. How do you get from the yoke to the forward airlock?"

"Uh," Gatineau frowned momentarily. "You go aft till you get to the engine room access, you climb up to the keel and go all the way forward. Or you follow the primary fuselage and access through the deck in the auxiliary reception chamber." He looked puzzled. "But what does this have to do with—?"

Leen ignored the question. "How do you get from there to the inner hull, seventy degrees, two-thirds aft?"

"Um. You go all the way back through the keel to the cable access forward of the engine room. Up to the upper starboard passage, aft two doors to the airlock bay. Next to the airlock bay is an access panel. Go past the meat tanks."

Leen nodded. "Good. How do you get from the officer's wardroom to the intelligence engine bay?"

"There's two ways. The fastest is to take either corridor forward, onto the Bridge, down to the Ops deck, down and aft through the Ops bay, down to the keel, and up the first ladder. But because Bridge access is restricted, it's better to just go aft, take the drop chute to the keel, and head forward again." Comprehension was beginning to show on Gatineau's face.

"Good," said Leen. "What are the specific responsibilities of Reynolds, Stolchak, and Fontana?"

"Reynolds is the union steward. Stolchak is the duty officer for the farm. Fontana is the chief pharmacist's mate."

"Which one of them do I see if I need a case of Martian anchovies for the captain's pizza?"

"Neither. You ask Toad Hall, the ship's dog-robber."

"Where do I go for a rotator jacket?"

"Storage compartment 130-G7, inner hull. Access through the port corridor, down and forward."

"Who's our official warlock?"

"Mikhail Hodel, sir."

"What's scotatic ventriculation?"

"Deep-gravity skeltering of chaotic anti-matter."

"How do you know if you've been in space too long?"

"Dr. Williger starts to look good to you."

"What's rule number one?"

"Uh—whatever your superior officer says it is."

"Yep." Leen nodded. "I'd say you're pretty well trained. What do you think?"

"Uh—" Gatineau began uncertainly. Fear of further embarrassment kept him from answering what he was thinking. He was thinking he'd done pretty damned well.

Leen pointed past the crewman's shoulder. "I wasn't asking you. I was asking *them*."

Gatineau turned around. Gathered in a group behind him were Reynolds, Hall, Stolchak, Cappy, MacHeath, Fontana, Eakins, Freeman, Hodel, Goldberg, Armstrong, Green, Ikama, Saffari, and just about everyone else who'd been a part of his search for the elusive moebius wrench. As one, they began applauding, laughing, and cheering. "Good job, Gatineau!" Even Commander Brik had paused on his way through the engine room and nodded a gruff acknowledgment.

"Huh?" Gatineau turned back to Leen, startled and surprised. "But, but—" Understanding came flooding up inside him then. He'd been *initiated*. He'd been proving that he was a good team player.

Still flustered, he turned back around to face the other crewmembers, feeling embarrassed all over again, as well as proud and annoyed and happy to finally be in on the joke. And finally . . . finally, he felt *fellowship*.

"You sonsabitches!" he muttered, shaking his head and grinning broadly all at the same time. And then somebody was clapping him on the back and somebody else was shaking his hand and abruptly Irma Stolchak was giving him a kiss that was much more than friendly, and when he finally surfaced for air, all he could say was, "I mean it! You're all sonsabitches!" But he was laughing and so were they. "And I wanna be a sonofabitch just like all of you."

And then he turned back to Leen again. "But . . . just one thing. Tell me the truth. There's no such thing as a moebius wrench, is there?"

"Who said that?" said Leen. "I never did. As a matter of fact, I have a moebius wrench right here."

"You do?" Gatineau's eyes went wide in disbelief.

Leen turned back to his work station and slid open a drawer. He reached in and pulled out a plaque with a golden wrench mounted on it; the handle was twisted around on itself, with a moebius half-twist. Leen stood up and with great ceremony handed the plaque to Gatineau.

"Congratulations, son," he said, shaking Gatineau's hand.

Gatineau took the plaque, uncomprehending at first, then he stared in surprise and astonishment. Beneath the wrench, the nameplate said:

> Keeper of the Moebius Wrench
> Engineer Robert Gatineau
> *Star Wolf*

"Wow," said Gatineau. "And wow again. That's—beautiful! Wow!" He shook his head in disbelief. "I'm really . . . wow . . . I don't know what to say. This is great."

"It's okay," said Cappy. "We weren't expecting a speech."

Abruptly, a puzzled expression crossed Gatineau's face. "Uh, can I ask one question? How did you guys do that pixie thing?"

"What pixie thing?"

"The star-pixie? You know. The one I saw in the farm . . . ? Behind the corn . . . With the big eyes . . . ?"

Leen looked confused. So did the others. "Huh?"

Gatineau's expression wisened abruptly. "Okay, I get it, I get it. Never mind. One snipe hunt is enough. Keep your pixie. Have your joke."

"Hey," said MacHeath. "I promise you, nobody did anything. We don't have a lot of spare time around here, as you may have noticed."

"Right," said Gatineau, quickly. "Right. Nobody did anything. If that's the way you want to be—okay, okay." He accepted a congratulatory tankard of Chief Leen's finest beer (aged two hours) and demonstrated what else he had learned since boarding the *Star Wolf*.

Later, MacHeath remarked to Chief Leen. "That pixie business. You think he was trying to reverse the gag?"

"I certainly hope so. I'd hate to think we hadn't trained him completely."

Fennelly

Jon Korie's first ship was a young ship, the *LS-714*. Her captain was Kia Miyori, a petite Asian woman who commanded her crew with exquisite politeness and respect. The *LS-714* was one link in an extensive pipeline running mail and supplies to several small colony worlds deep across the rift that divided the majority of Allied worlds from the unknown bulk of the Morthan Solidarity. Korie was away from home four months at a time, with only two weeks leave between trips.

If Carol was unhappy with his long absences, she never said so. She worked hard to make sure that every moment of their short times together was a honeymoon. She voiced no complaint, she listened attentively to his concerns, and she made sure that he went away again with joyous memories and a commitment to come home.

Korie served as chief petty officer and senior farm officer for thirteen months, increasing the ship's efficiency rating one point for each month of service. He was awarded a triple bonus and a letter of commendation from Admiral Coon's office.

After the third trip across the rift, Korie requested time with his family and was temporarily assigned to the Academy, where he taught other young officers how to manage the complexities of starship bookkeeping and inventory. He was an effective instructor and at the end of his three-month term was offered a permanent position.

Carol wouldn't let him accept it. Although the past three months had seen some of their happiest days—and nights—together, she wasn't foolish enough to try to make it last forever. "You'll never be happy until you've got a captain's stars on your shoulders," she told him. "You're getting fidgety, Jon. It's time for you to get back into space."

Jon Korie's second ship was the *LS-911*. He was appointed her second officer and astrogator. He had helped to build the *LS-911*; he had installed her farm, and later had been part of the team to certify her singularity stardrive. He proudly showed both his signatures on the inside of the hull to the captain. This turned out to be a mistake.

Captain Jack Fennelly was a hard man, tough and uncompromising. He'd had a long successful career in the service and he had his own ideas on how a ship should be run. He wasn't happy with the shape of the new Allied navy. The accelerated pace of production was producing hundreds of new ships and captains; Fennelly resented that these much younger men were earning their appointments so early in life and so easily. He viewed Korie's pride in the ship and his enthusiasm for her maintenance not as an asset but as a threat to his own credibility.

Korie worked hard for Fennelly; he recognized that there was much he could learn from the man; but Fennelly never acknowledged Korie's efforts. No matter how good a job Korie accomplished on something, Fennelly only pointed out how it could have been better, how it should have been done instead.

Korie withdrew into himself and renewed his studies of the *zyne*. He refused to let the circumstances control his emotions. During this time, as a way of clarifying his thoughts, he wrote several extensive inquiries into the nature of command; he called the document *The Quality of Service*.

At the heart of Korie's thesis was the thought that loyalty cannot be created by command; it must be created by service. Before a captain can expect loyalty from a crew, he must first demonstrate an uncompromising commitment to their well-being. The quality of the service he receives from his crew is a direct reflection of the quality of service he creates.

This thought led Korie into a further consideration of the nature of service. After some months of self-examination, he realized that service is the highest condition of human endeavor, not the lowest—that the real measure of a person's power was the number of people he *served*. A captain's job was not only to serve his superiors, but to serve the needs of his crew as well—in fact, if anything took priority, it had to be the well-being of the ship, because without a healthy ship, a captain could not accomplish anything else.

Korie sent a copy to his old mentor, Zaffron, for comment. He did not, however, submit the work for publication or even put it into any of the networks because he felt that some of his comments might be seen as uncomplimentary to his superior officers. Zaffron wrote a long thoughtful reply, consisting more of questions than of comments. Korie rewrote the work three times, then put it aside for further consideration in the future.

Korie's preoccupation with this private project also served to keep him out of Captain Fennelly's way. Fennelly noticed only that Korie had become extremely subdued in his demeanor and believed that he had finally broken him to the saddle; as a result, he eased up on the young officer and much of the tension on the Bridge began to dissipate.

Halfway through this tour of duty, the military tensions between the Allied Worlds and the Morthan Solidarity became even more aggravated. Allied intelligence revealed that the Morthans were now building up their fleets at least as aggressively as the Allies.

Sensing that war was becoming a very real possibility, Korie expanded his studies to include numerous texts on strategy and tactics. Despite the fact that the Alliance's intelligence engines had been running extensive conflict scenarios for decades, Korie still felt frustrated at the lack of an overall vision of the nature of war in space. He began assembling his thoughts into another set of inquiries, this one titled *Working Toward a Theory of Conflict.*

In this work, he did not attempt to resolve the issue; that would have been premature and presumptuous. It was his feeling, however, that because there had never been an interstellar war on the scale that was now possible between the Allied worlds and the Morthan Solidarity, that all previous models of conflict had to be reexamined in this larger context.

While certain fundamental aspects of war would always remain unchanged—such as protecting supply lines, holding and keeping the high ground, and knowing your enemy's strategy at least as well as your own—the specific applications of these principles to FTL situations represented a whole new domain of strategic possibilities and dilemmas. The potential for disaster terrified the young officer. It was Korie's purpose to distinguish those areas which he felt needed a much deeper examination. While his essays were ultimately intended to sound a cautionary note to those who determined strategy, they were more immediately a way for him to clarify his own thinking.

For the most part, Korie approved of the Fleet's killer bee strategy, but it depended to a great deal on the resourcefulness and courage of individual starship captains. That was both its strength and its weakness. Working at FTL velocities, it was impossible for a central command to coordinate the actions of a thousand, ten thousand, or ultimately a hundred thousand separate destroyer-class cruisers.

Therefore, each and every ship was on its own—and each and every captain had to behave as ferociously as possible. Each and every captain must act as if his or her actions alone would determine the final outcome of the war . . . because they very well might.

It seemed to Korie that if there was a weakness in the strategy, this was it. The accelerated program of ship building, the rapid rate of training and promotion, did not provide the experience or the seasoning that captains and crews would need to behave appropriately in a battle situation. In the confusion of a major assault, some ship captains might hold back; others might even panic. This would put an increased burden on every other Allied ship, both strategically and psychologically, and would seriously weaken the assault.

If a battle swarm were to fail—and fail badly—Korie wrote, the psychological blow to the Allied fleet would be devastating. It would be impossible for any captain to engage in a swarm if he did not believe that his colleagues were equally committed. Therefore, appropriate psychological screening of all captains was mandatory, as well as intensive training in dealing with combat situations.

Korie also postulated an alternate strategy, one that he felt could be implemented with minimal effort; it would include most of the same strengths of the killer bee strategy while minimizing its weaknesses. He called it the *killer shark* strategy. In this scenario, the swarm would be broken up into many small task forces, each with a single area of responsibility. Within each task force, each destroyer would have its own area of responsibility, either defense or offense. If any individual vessel encountered a Morthan warship, it could send out a coded *hyperstate* burst and every task force member in range would home in on that signal like a pack of sharks in a feeding frenzy.

Decentralizing the fleet would allow space battles to be fought as skirmishes instead of major confrontations and would reduce the opportunities for the enemy to inflict a devastating blow to the Allied fleet in a single battle. Additionally, the spreading out of assault forces would make interception much more difficult, especially if all of the ships engaged in an attack were coming in from radically different directions.

Korie spent months working out the dynamics of these battles, running simulations on the *911*'s HARLIE unit. There were assumptions in his work that were quickly proven false; he removed them from the main thesis, and added appropriate discussions to the appendix. There were *other* extrapolations, however, that brought him ultimately to the most stunning realization of all about the nature of conflict at FTL velocities.

In hyperstate all ships are equally vulnerable. The size of the vessel is irrelevant. If you can disrupt its hyperstate envelope, you can destroy the vessel.

In hyperstate all ships are equally dangerous. The size of the vessel is irrelevant. If a ship can approach close enough, it can fire a hyperstate torpedo.

All that really matters is how fast a ship can travel and how far it can see. The size of the hyperstate envelope determines the FTL velocity as well as the range of the hyperstate scanning lens; so the *real* measure of a starship's power is determined only by the size of its singularity and the sophistication of its fluctuator assemblies.

The more that Korie studied this dilemma, the more he began to appreciate it as a problem in three-dimensional chess.

The farther a ship can see, the less likely it is that another ship can sneak up on it unnoticed and launch a hyperstate torpedo. The faster a ship can travel, the more likely it will be able to approach an enemy vessel successfully and launch its torpedoes before the target can react to either escape or launch torpedoes of its own. Therefore, a ship's strategic abilities, both offensive and defensive, are intrinsically linked.

The only way a ship can avoid detection from a great distance is to mute its hyperstate envelope so that it no longer resonates with such a high profile; but this technique effectively blinds it, as well as severely cuts its realized velocity. On the other hand, it also allows a ship to sneak in under the threshold of noise and approach much closer before detection by the target.

This train of thought troubled Korie, leading ultimately to another set of scenarios. The most immediately effective were those where one or more warships muted their envelopes to mimic much smaller, weaker vessels, thus luring their victims into striking range.

There were long-term scenarios to be aware of too, also involving mimicry and subterfuge. Korie was beginning to understand the real nature of the beast. The war would not be won with superior strength or firepower; those had been nullified. Nor would it be won with methodical strategies and tactics; those too had been leveled by the nature of the playing field. No—the battles would be fought as a duel of perseverance and perception; they would be played as chess matches to the death; and they would be won or lost in the minds of the opposing captains.

For one brief paralyzing flash, he saw the future; silent starships dueling in the dark, feinting, thrusting, parrying and dodging, each one jockeying for the one moment of advantage that would allow it to deliver the death-blow to the other. It terrified him. He recognized that this was the fundamental weakness of the Alliance.

It wasn't enough for the Alliance to launch ships and send them bravely out into the night. The insufficiency of the effort was suddenly apparent to him. The Morthans were also launching ships; but the Morthans had taken war as a way of life. They were a race of self-designed, self-created beings, no longer recognizable as human—genetically engineered and biologically augmented to be superhumans, *more-than* humans. They had taken the disciplines of the martial arts and channeled their whole culture into the production of warriors who did not know how to lose a battle. Every single Morthan captain, and every member of every Morthan crew, would be an expert in the art of mayhem; every vessel would be commanded by a grandmaster in the art of death.

By contrast, the captains of the Allied starships were mere children. A few years of schooling, a few classes at the War College, were no match for a lifetime of discipline and purpose. The Allied fleet would be at terrible risk unless the new paradigms of interstellar conflict were fully understood and assimilated by each and every starship commander.

The imminence of the war terrified Jon Korie. He spent many sleepless nights, trembling in fear over the possibilities of the conflict that he was certain was becoming more and more inevitable. He resolved to send Carol and the boys as far away from the rift as they could afford.

The next time the ship touched port, he uploaded all of his writings to the immediate attention of the War College, and he prayed that he was in time.

The Boat

Gatineau hesitated before the docking tube. The memory of the last time was still too recent, still too intense. He still ached, and his skin was still discolored in places.

"Go on," said Brik. "I'll be right behind you."

"That's what I'm afraid of," gulped Gatineau. "I don't want you grabbing me. Give me a chance to do it myself." He took another deep breath—then, surprisingly, he seized the hatch-frame and pushed himself head-first into the tube. It was as if he wanted to get it over with as fast as possible. It was as if he wanted to prove something to Brik. But in truth, it was because he wanted to prove it to himself most of all.

He pulled himself into the boat clumsily, but not disgracefully so. He was starting to figure out this free fall business after all.

Commander Brik came swooping easily after him. The big Morthan tucked his knees and head into a 180-degree tumble, caught a handhold and ended up reversed, facing back toward the hatch again, hitting the panel lightly to close and secure it. The entire maneuver had been as skilled and graceful as if executed by a professional dancer.

After a moment, Gatineau remembered to close his mouth. He wondered if he'd ever look as good in free fall. Probably not, he realized. He wasn't a Morthan.

Chief Leen looked up from what he was doing—he was repacking the Feinberger modules in the decontam unit—and grunted. "Give me two more minutes."

"Go forward," Brik nodded to Gatineau. "You've got the conn."

"Yes, sir. You'll be in the right seat?"

"No, I won't." To Gatineau's look, Brik added, "Don't worry. Your copilot is quite competent."

"Oh, yeah, right," said Gatineau, grumbling to himself, not hearing the amusement in Brik's tone. "What's it going to be this time? A moebius joystick? Another star-pixie? Left-handed anti-matter?" He pulled himself forward through the cabin of the boat and through the hatch to the flight deck. Without even looking to the copilot, he said, "Whatever jokes you and Mr. Brik have planned, just forget about them. Just leave me alone to do this, okay?" He pulled his headset on and started clicking his displays to life, setting them to green one after the other.

"I don't have anything planned at all," replied Commander Korie. "At least, nothing more than getting you certified as quickly as possible."

"Oh, sir!" Gatineau blurted hastily. "I'm sorry, I didn't mean to—"

"Don't apologize, *Captain*—" Korie said, stressing the last word. "You're in the left seat. You're giving the orders."

It was the word *Captain* that stopped Gatineau in midgulp. "Captain?" he asked.

"That's your rank while you're in charge of this boat. Your authority is absolute."

"You mean . . . if I ordered you to get me a cup of coffee, you'd *have* to do it?"

Smiling, Korie nodded. "That's how it works. And if I didn't get it for you, you could bring me up on charges of insubordination. I don't recommend it though. Remember, I'm still acting captain of the *Star Wolf*. So part of the lesson you need to learn this afternoon is about cooperation and respect among officers."

"I'm not an officer, sir. I'm just—"

"Stop," said Korie quietly.

Gatineau stopped.

"Let me tell you something. I don't care what your rank is. I want you to learn how to do every job on the ship. And I want you unafraid to do it if you have to. If something happens to everyone around you, I don't want you standing there with your finger up your nose, wondering what to do next. Do you know the story of Ensign McGrew?"

"Everybody does. It's apocryphal. McGrew was court-martialed for taking command—"

"It's not apocryphal. It happened. And you have it wrong. He was court-martialed for *not* taking command. All of his superior officers were killed. Instead of taking responsibility, he panicked and called for help. To be fair, it was his first tour of duty, he was still being trained, and he should never have been put in that situation. Nevertheless, naval regulations *required* him to act, and he did not. Had they not been dead, his superior officers would also have been up before a board of inquiry for failing to train McGrew appropriately. Do I make myself clear?"

"Absolutely, sir."

"Thank you." Korie waited.

"Sir?"

"Yes?"

"Um, what should I do now?"

"You're the captain. You tell me."

"Uhh—oh, right. Uh, prepare for departure. Let's do the checklist." Gatineau struggled to remember the routine. "Systems Analysis?"

Korie glanced at his board. "Green."

"Check. Uh, confidence?"

"Eighty-six."

"*Eighty-six?*"

"Don't panic. These ducks are supposed to be survivable with confidence as low as thirty."

"But *eighty-six?*"

"Eighty-six it, Gatineau," Korie said firmly. "It's *okay.* Trust me."

"Yes, sir—check. Life support?"

"Optimal, with minor cautions. Don't worry, we're not going out that far. And we have starsuits in the locker in case we have to swim back."

"You're joking, right?" Gatineau looked to Korie. Korie's expression was blandly noncommittal. "Never mind. Check," said Gatineau. "Propulsion? Navigation?"

"Green and green. All systems go."

"Check." Gatineau bent to his own displays, running a second set of checks just to be certain he hadn't missed anything. He hadn't. He exhaled loudly, started to put his hands on the controls, then abruptly pulled them back. "I'm really in command?" he asked Korie.

"Yes, Captain, you are," Korie replied calmly.

"Ah," said Gatineau. He leaned back in his seat and folded his arms across his chest. "Copilot, take her out."

Korie's smile widened only a fraction. "Nice try, son." He nodded at the controls. "You show me how it's done."

"Can't blame a guy for trying," said Gatineau, allowing himself a smile. He reached forward again, and snapped open the communication channel. "Starboat ready."

"Anytime, Captain," Hodel's voice came back from the Bridge.

"Roger that. Thank you." Gatineau unclipped a safety cover and flipped the switch beneath it. There was a soft thump from behind them, and they were floating free.

"Good job," said Korie. "Take us out ten thousand kilometers, then flipover for the return." He glanced at the time. "Don't take more than two hours getting us there."

Gatineau did the calculations in his head. "Sir? That's—"

"Yes. It's quite a ride. Do it, son." Korie was already unstrapping himself.

"Uh, yes, sir." Gatineau shook his head, not quite certain why the commander wanted to put so much distance between himself and the mother ship, but he began setting up the program on his display.

Korie floated up out of his chair and started to pull himself aftward. "Try not to bump into anything," he said. "When you've got the program locked in, call HARLIE, have him double-check it. If HARLIE says it's okay, run it and come back aft for a cup of coffee."

"Sir? Aren't you going to check me?"

Korie paused, one hand on either side of the hatch frame. He raised an eyebrow. "Do you think I need to?"

"Uh, no, sir," Gatineau said quickly.

"Good. You'll do fine." Korie added, "Oh, and watch out for sparkle-dancers."

"No star-pixies this time?" Gatineau muttered.

"Of course not. We already have one. In the ship's corn, remember?"

"Huh?" Gatineau turned around in his seat to stare after Korie, but the senior officer was already gone. How did he know about *that*?

Gatineau turned forward again. It was a simple course, but he checked it six times before sending it home to HARLIE. The intelligence engine chewed it over for half a millisecond before sending it back. Without comment.

"It's okay?" Gatineau asked.

"If it wasn't, don't you think I would have said something?" replied HARLIE blandly.

"Oh, yes, of course. But uh, don't you have any advice for me? I mean, how it could have been more efficient or something?"

"I have no advice," said HARLIE. "I assume you programmed exactly what you wanted."

"Uh, yes, I did."

"Then no advice is necessary, is it?"

"Oh, I get it," said Gatineau. "It's like that story they tell you about in training. You know the one. 'You're the Captain. You decide.' "

"I wouldn't know," replied HARLIE. "Although I do have the training manuals in storage. Do you need to access them now?"

"No, thanks," said Gatineau. "I'm getting the hang of it."

"Have a good flight then." HARLIE signed off.

Gatineau shook his head. Did intelligence engines do that on purpose, or what?

He initiated his program and watched his board. The display went green; the program was running. The engines were soundless; there was nothing to feel, nothing to hear. Even so, Gatineau imagined he could feel the faintest bit of acceleration pushing him back into his couch. It was microacceleration, but it was cumulative. They'd spend most of the first hour just climbing to speed. Ten thousand kilometers wasn't really that far, not if you were adding two kilometers per hour per second. At the end of seventy-two hundred seconds, they would have a realized velocity of fourteen thousand kph. Their averaged velocity for the same time would be seven thousand klicks. They could turn their engines off and coast to the flipover point. The math was simple. Any middle-school student could do it.

But of course, when you're sitting alone in the left seat, and the lives of yourself and three other people are at stake, suddenly all the equations take on a whole *other* flavor.

Gatineau wondered if he should stay in his seat the whole two hours or if Korie had really meant it about coming aft for coffee. He *really* wanted the chance to . . . well, just sit with the exec. But—on the other hand, what if something went wrong? He was responsible, wasn't he? On the third hand, if he didn't go, would Korie and the others be insulted? Or, if he did go, would he look overeager? On the fourth hand, he *was* the captain here. That was part of the test, wasn't it? If he didn't go aft, that would make him look uncertain. Wouldn't it?

"You know something?" Gatineau said to himself, as he unbuckled his belt. "You *think* too much." And then he added, "Yeah, you can say that again." He headed aft.

Korie glanced at his watch as Gatineau floated back. "Being careful?"

"Yes, sir."

The exec nodded him toward a seat. "Strap in. We have some serious talking to do and I don't want you floating around the cabin. There's coffee there. Be careful, it's still hot." Without waiting to see if Gatineau was obeying, Korie turned back to Leen. "So, what do you think, Chief?"

The older man grunted. He scratched his ear unhappily. "I think we should evacuate the crew, then evacuate the air. Then drop the ship into the nearest star."

"We can't do that," Korie said. He was surprised to hear himself saying, "Failure is not an option." He noticed Brik glancing sideways at him with a faintly amused expression.

"We'll never detox the ship, you know that," Leen countered. "Even the crew is starting to figure it out."

Korie sucked at his coffee. "Okay. Can we catch it? Trap it somehow?"

Brik snorted. "It's already trapped. The problem is we're in the cage with it."

"I know that," said Korie, slightly annoyed. "But we have to walk through the steps anyway. I want to ask the easy questions first. Is there *anything* we can do to catch it or kill it?"

Gatineau looked from one to the other, not quite following the conversation. He was afraid to ask. They were talking *as if there was something on the ship.*

As if reading his mind, Brik annotated the conversation for his benefit. He said, "Your star-pixie was real."

"Oh," said Gatineau softly, not quite assimilating the fact. *The star-pixie was real?*

Revelations

"It's a Morthan imp," said Korie. "There wasn't *one* Morthan aboard this ship. There were *two*. An assassin and an imp. Cinnabar brought the imp with him when he invaded."

The others waited while Gatineau assimilated this information.

"Oh," said Gatineau. Then, "Oh!" And finally, "*Oh*."

"He got it," remarked Leen.

Gatineau was already putting pieces together. "So that's what you went EVA to talk about!"

"He's observant," noted Brik.

To Korie, he said, "And you had to bawl him out in front of everybody, so no one would know what you were really doing—"

"And quick," agreed Korie to Brik. To Gatineau, he said, "We have to assume that it's not safe to talk on the *Star Wolf*. We don't know how completely our integrity has been compromised. We have to assume it's total. We can't even discuss this with HARLIE. We have to assume he's been compromised too."

"Even the personal codes?"

"Yes. We have to make that assumption too. It's much more likely that the imp hasn't gotten into everything it could; only those domains important to its purpose; but we don't know what it's done, so we have to assume the worst." Korie sipped at his coffee through a straw. Gatineau did likewise. He made a face. It wasn't the best way to drink coffee; if you couldn't smell it, you couldn't really taste it.

"All right," said Korie, continuing. "Brik and I went EVA so I could brief him about the situation. We ended up briefing each other. Brik had figured it out too."

"Are you sure your EVA was secure?" asked Leen.

"We went out on tethers, set up a static shield, and talked for a half hour, helmet-to-helmet communication only. If the imp is as smart *and as paranoid* as Brik says, then it has to assume that we know it's aboard the ship by now. So we're not assuming that the imp doesn't know that we talked about it. But we *are* assuming that it probably doesn't know the specifics of what we said." Korie added, "By the way, you both need to know that the first thing I did was apologize to Mr. Brik for deliberately embarrassing him."

"And I told the commander," Brik put in, "that no apologies were necessary. The security of the vessel was compromised. He needed a place for a secure conversation and a believable cover story for getting there. Dressing me down in public for a dangerous EVA was highly appropriate. It was the best way to get me outside quickly." To Korie, he said, "You can't hurt my feelings, sir. I'm a Morthan. I don't have feelings. Not like humans, anyway. I don't allow personal to get in the way of purpose."

"Right," agreed Korie. "Nevertheless, let's get on with this." Speaking mostly to Leen now, he said, "Here's how I found it. I was doing the log and I asked HARLIE for his thoughts about the various incidents of Morthan sabotage. Had he done a time-and-motion study on the ones we'd found? Given the length of time Cinnabar was aboard the vessel, how many more could we expect to uncover? What did his analysis suggest?"

"And—?"

"He said it was inconclusive. He wasn't willing to commit."

Leen frowned. "That's not an appropriate reply. An intelligence engine of HARLIE's rating should have an opinion on almost everything."

"That was my thought too." Korie said. "When a HARLIE unit refuses to tell you something, that's like a big red arrow. So I asked to see the raw data myself."

"And—?"

"HARLIE dumped the raw data to my clipboard. So I could look at it at my leisure, he said. It was obvious he didn't want to show it to me himself, but there was something he needed me to know. So I waited till the boat was powered down, came over here and locked myself in the lavatory. It didn't take too long. HARLIE didn't make it obvious, but it was there if you knew what to look for. We had too many booby traps. Too far apart. More than a few of them were of sufficient complexity to require significant preparation and installation time. Cinnabar didn't have the time aboard to do it all."

"You needed HARLIE to tell you that?" asked Leen.

"No. I needed HARLIE to prove it. HARLIE had come to the same conclusion, but he couldn't figure out a safe way to tell me. He's assumed even *his* integrity is compromised."

"And Brik? How did he figure out Cinnabar planted an imp?"

"Easy. It was what I would have done," Brik said. "I realized we had a problem when the docking tube came apart. We'd already detoxed it. That's why I went EVA. I wore a simulated imp strapped to my chest to see if it could survive. It could. Your sighting, Crewman Gatineau, was the confirmation I needed."

None of them spoke for a moment, each of the men was lost in his own mordant thoughts. Finally, Leen sighed unhappily. "So we've got a second Morthan on the ship. We've had it here the whole time. And all of our detox efforts have been *wasted*."

"That's right," said Brik.

They were all silent a moment longer as each considered the ramifications.

"A Morthan on a starship," Gatineau said. "Ouch."

"That's pretty bad news all right," said Korie, looking pointedly at Brik.

"Yes," Brik agreed dryly. "Especially if the Morthan is on your side."

Gatineau didn't catch all the undertones of that exchange. He scratched his head. "But it's not the same kind of Morthan, is it? It's not a Tyger."

"It's an imp," said Brik. "Not an imp from your mythology, an imp from *ours*. This is not a cute, mischievous, little cherub with horns. This thing is an apprentice demon. It's a hellish little bastard, a single-minded sabotage-machine, half a meter high. Very fast. Not particularly strong. And not particularly smart either—not by Morthan standards. By human standards . . . well, you wouldn't want to play chess against it. It's a kind of *programmed* intelligence. They do what they're told. You give one a task and you turn it loose. They're very good for suicide missions." Brik added, "They're also supposed to be fairly good eating."

"Better than rat?" asked Leen.

"I wouldn't know," replied Brik coldly. "I don't eat rat."

Korie ignored the exchange. Despite repeated requests on his part that the two of them learn to work together, Brik and Leen continued to snipe at each other. "So," he said cautiously. "This imp was programmed to booby-trap the *Star Wolf*?"

"Just in case Cinnabar failed."

"He must not have liked that thought."

"He was probably planning to eat it. It must have been programmed to go its own way as soon as it could. It had plenty of time aboard the *Burke*, and even longer aboard the *Star Wolf*. So, at this point, it probably knows Liberty ships as well as you or Chief Leen. Let's assume it's had time to explore everything it wants to aboard the ship. Let's also assume that the only traps we're finding are those it wants us to find. Including the sabotage of the docking tube. It's possible that one was aimed at me. It's also very possible that I was *supposed* to survive it."

Korie thought about that. "It's given itself away then . . . deliberately." And then he thought about that some more. "Okay. It wants us to know it's here," he added. "Why?"

They all thought about that for a moment. Gatineau sipped at his coffee. The others had forgotten theirs. He was still wondering why he had been included in this meeting. He knew he wasn't here by accident.

"It's bored?" suggested Leen. "It wants to play games with us."

Brik shook his head. "Morthans don't play with their food."

Gatineau asked abruptly, "Can we open the ship to space?"

Leen shrugged. "We can do anything the captain orders. Or whoever's acting captain," he added, pointedly looking at Korie. To Brik, he said, "Will that kill it?"

Brik shook his head. "How long will it take to get the entire crew into starsuits? Certainly long enough for the imp to figure out what's about to happen. Do you think a creature that's had nearly a month to prepare might have a secure chamber somewhere for just such an eventuality? Can you think of a way to get the entire crew into starsuits and off the vessel in less than fifteen seconds? Anything longer than that, you can assume the imp is back in its pod." He added, "Can you think of a way to set up a plan, *any plan*, without alerting the imp that you're planning something?"

Gatineau sighed. "I see the problem."

"And if you open the ship to space, you lose the farm," added Korie. "Lose your cash crops and you're out of business. Again."

"I guess I still have a lot to learn."

"It's worse than that," added Brik. To Korie he said, "Chief Leen scanned those high-cycle fluctuators while we had them aboard. He read their memories into HARLIE. Everything. That means the imp most certainly has a copy of that information too. It'll be looking for an opportunity to get that information into the hands of its masters."

"Stop trying to cheer me up," said Korie. "I'm feeling bad enough already."

"It gets worse," said Brik. "It only gets worse. Can you trust this ship now? Are you willing to trade parts of her to anyone else? You have nothing to trade? How do you know the imp won't be in one of your trade boxes?"

"We don't have many options, do we?"

"We can scuttle the ship."

"The admiral will like that." Korie put his coffee-bulb aside. "I hate being wrong. I'd rather be clever."

"That's how Cinnabar got killed."

"I know. So what do we do now?"

No one answered him.

Faslim-Arub

When Korie's twelve-month tour of duty aboard the *911* came to an end, Captain Fennelly grudgingly gave him a satisfactory recommendation and Korie applied for a six-month course of study at the War College before returning to space. He was immediately approved.

Korie's treatise, *Working Toward a Theory of Conflict*, was only one of more than three thousand documents submitted on the very same topic. Clearly, a significant percentage of the younger generation of starship officers were concerned about the structure of the Fleet and the training available to its commanders. With varying degrees of insight, the authors considered the advisability of existent defense plans, the nature of interstellar war, and the prospects for an Allied success against a well-trained Morthan Armada using the current strategy books. Few were sanguine; most of the papers demonstrated significant concern; a few were genuinely alarmed. Several paralleled Korie's reasoning.

To Korie's credit, his paper was one of the most clearly written; it was uncompromising in its examination of the strengths and weaknesses of both sides in the coming war; and it was clear in its conclusions that the old ways of fighting a war were going to prove woefully inappropriate. What set Korie's paper apart from almost all of the rest was his detailed analysis of the psychology of war in space and his alternate proposals for offensive and defensive battle tactics based on misleading and confusing the enemy as to what kind of a ship he was up against and what its intentions really were.

The admirals of the navy had long been aware of the deficiencies of the killer bee strategy; but the intelligence engines had predicted that swarming the enemy was the best way to overcome the problem of insufficient training for individual starship crews. After Korie's work arrived at the War College (as well as the other treatises), the intelligence engines were asked to reconsider the problem and this time allow for the current status of Fleet morale and the overall level of training for command-level officers.

The results were much closer to what Korie (and others) had suspected, and the War College immediately shifted to emergency status to develop new strategies as well as new training programs. Korie's work ensured his immediate appointment. Even had he not applied to the War College he would have been assigned there.

At the War College, strategic study groups were formed to pit their various strategies against each other. Later, after the results were evaluated, several new training programs were instituted, specifically designed to give starship commanders a sense of Morthan strategy and psychology as well as to harden them against possible Morthan tactics. This was the most challenging period of Korie's leadership training and he went to bed (alone) exhausted and exhilarated every evening.

At the end of six months, he was rotated out of the War College, and promoted to executive officer of the *LS-1066*. This too was a ship he had helped construct. He had led the team that laid her keel.

Captain Margaret Faslim-Arub was candid with Korie. She did not expect him to serve aboard her vessel for very long; he was slated for a ship of his own. The next time they returned to Stardock, Korie would probably be promoted—perhaps within the next six months. The pace of production had been accelerated again, and the demand for qualified commanders had become critical.

There was no question in Captain Faslim-Arub's mind that Korie was well-qualified for command. She gave him the conn at every opportunity; the greatest gift she could give him would be a sense of comfort and familiarity at the helm of a starship. Korie appreciated not only the opportunities to learn, but the implied acknowledgment of his ability. It was a refreshing change after the passive-aggressive abuse of Jack Fennelly.

He repaid her faith in him by working long hours in every section of the ship bringing each one up to spec and beyond. He upgraded the gardens, the meat tanks, the recyclers. He recalibrated the fluctuators and stabilized the singularity for a more accurate focus; he rebuilt the magnetic grapplers, and when he was through, he had boosted the ship's top speed by five percent. He interviewed the HARLIE unit and, with its permission, made several minor modifications which amplified its confidence rating in itself by three percent. He redesigned a number of command procedures, shortening the time it took for the vessel to initiate its hyperstate envelope and collapse it as well. He designed combat drills and simulations based on his experiences at the War College.

Unfortunately for Korie . . . the *LS-1066* was assigned a rigorous set of duties that kept her away from Stardock—as well as from his family—for nearly eighteen months. She ferried colonists, mail, cargo, military supplies, and once even a high-ranking ambassador. She participated in three sets of war games, twice playing the part of the enemy. As frustrating as it was to have his promotion delayed, the experience was still invaluable to Korie; he learned about the exigencies of command in a variety of situations—but he missed his wife and children too. He ached to see them again. Their letters weren't enough to ease the loneliness. He filled his days with as much work as he could so he could fall asleep quickly at night.

At last the *LS-1066* was ordered back to Stardock for the installation of a set of prototype ultrahigh-cycle fluctuators, which would boost her top speed by a factor of two, giving her a theoretical maximum realized velocity of twenty-three hundred C, and a practical maximum realized velocity two thousand times the speed of light.

Korie delayed his own transfer to supervise the installation of the new fluctuators. He wanted to lay his own hands on the machinery, fit the modules into place himself, calibrate each separate assembly, install the redesigned singularity grapples, check the housings, tune the cables, and make the coffee. He wanted to learn everything he could about the new high-cycle fluctuators; this was the weapon that could win the war and he wanted to be the expert.

Three test cruises were scheduled. On the first one, the *LS-1066* travelled to a star system nearly six light years distant in a single day of ship time. On the second cruise, the starship went to a deep rift observation post, twenty-three light years distant. It took four days of ship time. The third mission would be across the rift and back; the ship would be gone for four months.

Korie wanted to make the leap; he wanted to pin a black rift-crossing ribbon to his chest; but except for two all-too-brief leaves, he hadn't been home in nearly two years. There would be other missions. It wouldn't be fair to Carol for him to take another four months away, if he didn't absolutely need to.

Korie took three months of accumulated leave to spend with his wife and two sons. At first, neither of the boys recognized him—they cried and fought when he tried to pick them up. They resented it when he came home with them and went into the bedroom with their mommy.

But he persevered; he threw himself into the process of being a good father with the same enthusiasm and dedication he had demonstrated in the construction, maintenance, and running of a starship. Very soon his boys began to recognize that having a dad in the house created a joyous new dimension in their lives; they began to worship him.

Jon Korie was a loving father; he enjoyed parenting. He woke up early every morning and made breakfast for Carol and the boys. He woke them gently and, tucking one under each arm, carried them into the bathroom for a morning bath. He washed the boys with industrial thoroughness, he dried them with equal precision; he supervised the brushing of their teeth as if each tooth had to be individually detoxed, and he brushed their hair with exquisitely tender care and a ruler-straight part. Had it been possible to perform a white-glove inspection on the children, both his sons would have passed with highest ratings. He picked out their clothes and helped them dress until they insisted they were big enough to do it without his help.

But if there was a quality of military precision to the way he applied himself to the task of caring for his children, there was also an equal quality of pure uncompromised affection. During the day, he always made time to play with them, to give them piggy-back rides or swimming lessons or simply a silly-scrimmage in the park. They had tickle-fests and water-fights and endless games of chucklebelly. He was a god to them.

Korie took his sons on outings and picnics; they went to concerts, plays, and exhibitions where Jon Korie pointed out each and every aspect of the displays until his children began to yawn in boredom.

It did not escape Carol Korie's perceptive eye that there was a manic quality to her husband's attentiveness—as if he were trying to compress a lifetime of parenting into a single visit home, as if he *knew* something about the shape of the future.

In the evenings, he tucked his children into bed, he brushed their unruly hair back away from their eyes, he listened thoughtfully to their prayers, and then he hugged and kissed each one goodnight. And somehow even after all of that, at the end of the day he still had the energy and dedication to make himself one hundred percent available to his wife.

Carol understood what he was doing. Jon Korie was creating the experience for himself of a family; he was giving himself a lifetime's worth of memories, so he would have something to take with him when he journeyed out again. More important . . . he was trying to leave a part of himself behind, so that if, by some terrible chance, he did not return, his children would still know they had had a real father.

The Conversation

"We can't even scuttle the ship," Korie said. "Once we start moving crew members off, even one boatload at a time, the imp will know she's being abandoned. What do we do with dead ships? We break them up, open them to space, use them for target practice. The imp won't let that happen. If it thinks it's going to die, it's going to take us with it. Something probably goes ka-blooie before the first crew member gets out the airlock. Certainly before the last."

"Not only that," said Leen, "where do you evacuate the crew *to*? And how can you be certain the imp doesn't find a way to come with?"

"To Stardock—?" asked Gatineau, hoping to be helpful. "Decontam?"

None of the three glanced at him, but Korie's brow furrowed at the thought. "The imp needs this ship, and it needs this crew . . ."

"We've got a Morthan by the balls," said Leen. "We can't hang on, we can't let go." A thought occurred to him. He looked to Brik. "Do Morthans even have balls?"

Brik regarded the chief engineer coldly. "Morthans don't dance."

Korie allowed himself a grin. "Probably because no Morthan will let any other Morthan lead for longer than ten seconds."

Brik's eyes narrowed. "Morthans don't dance *like humans*."

"Right," said Korie. That line of discussion was over. He stretched where he floated, pulling his arms back until his spine made a satisfying knuckle-crunch. He brought himself back to normal. "All right, let's assume it knows whatever we know. In fact, let's assume that whatever we know *about it* is only what it wants us to know." Korie looked from one to the other, even including Gatineau. "Here's what we know about Morthans. Everything is a calculation. Every action has an intended result, both immediate and consequential. If a Morthan shows you something, he *wants* you to see it because your reaction serves his purpose. There are no Morthan accidents. Right, Brik?"

Brik rumbled his assent, but he was abruptly thinking of something else. Helen Bach.

Gatineau was slowly putting it together. "So the imp showed itself to me because it needed us to know it's onboard?"

"And it triggered the destruction of the docking tube for the same reason," said Brik, coming back to the main stream of the discussion. "To make me suspicious. It needs us to know it's here."

"Where's the advantage in taunting us?" asked Leen. "I don't follow the logic."

"That's because you're not a Morthan," said Brik. "The imp *needs* us to know that it's aboard the ship so that we'll act a certain way. It's trying to steer us."

"Where?"

"Taalamar," said Korie, abruptly realizing. "This is about Taal-amar."

"Huh?" Gatineau and Leen looked at him surprised. Brik just nodded thoughtfully.

"It's all the sabotage, don't you see? What's the *real* purpose? We wanted to go to Taalamar. It *couldn't* let us go to Taalamar. In fact, it can't let us go anywhere. It needs us to stay right where we are. Everything it's done has been to keep us stuck. That's why it keeps sabotaging things, but have you noticed that none of the traps the imp has set have been fatal—"

"Excuse me?" protested Gatineau. "What about the docking tube?"

"Did you die?" asked Brik.

"No, but—"

"Then it wasn't fatal."

"What he means," interrupted Leen, "is that none of the traps have threatened the total integrity of the vessel. It still holds air. Sort of. It still moves. Sort of."

"The imp wants Stardock," said Korie.

"That's right," said Brik.

"Do you want to explain it? Or should I?"

"You do it. I want to see what you've worked out."

"Okay. The imp had to keep us from joining the Fleet. It had to *make sure* we didn't join the Fleet. We're worthless to its purposes if we're off patrolling. But we still had working hyperstate fluctuators, missiles, and a farm, so we were in better shape than most of other ships needing refitting. So what was the one thing it could do to make sure we wouldn't join the Fleet? What was the one thing it could do to guarantee we stayed behind for additional detox?" Korie looked to Brik.

"Show itself," Brik answered, "giving us no choice but to try to capture it. Anything else—?"

"No one here gets out alive?" guessed Leen.

"Exactly," said Korie. "So we're stuck here. Unmoving. Right where it wants us. And as long as we're here, we're a marker. Stardock is somewhere inside a twenty-hour sphere with us at the center. That's a small enough volume for a fleet to search." He nodded to himself. "That's the real point of it. The imp is going to use this ship to call in the rest of the Morthan fleet. And there's not a lot we can do about it either, even if we know. Not unless we catch him. Which we can't. It's a nasty trap."

Brik nodded. Leen grunted. Gatineau didn't know what to say. He felt totally out of his league. "Um, maybe this is a stupid question, but do they really want Stardock badly enough to send a whole fleet?"

Korie turned to Gatineau. "No, it's not a stupid question, and yes, they do want Stardock that badly. As long as the location of Stardock remains uncertain to them, the Solidarity cannot advance deeper into Allied space. Stardock gives us a staging area for flank attacks on their supply lines. Stardock has always been the issue. Everyone knows it."

"Well, if that's the case, then why are they sending their fleet to Taalamar?"

"*That's* the right question to ask," said Korie. He stretched again, this time as prelude to his next words. "It's my belief that the assault on Taalamar is a feint to draw the fleet. Meanwhile, I think there's a whole *other* fleet of Solidarity scouts that'll be dropping probes all over everywhere. Our little imp will help the probes find Stardock by sending a signal to be picked up by any probe in the neighborhood. Scatter your probes three or four or five light-days apart, you won't have to wait too long to pick up the signal." Korie added one more thought then. "And now that we're not going anywhere, there's no reason for any more sabotage, is there? I'll bet that the incidence of equipment failure begins falling off dramatically. Comments? Anyone?"

"Well, you've figured out the easy part," Brik said.

"Thank you, Mr. Brik," Korie smiled ruefully. "I can always depend on you to put things into an appropriately Morthan perspective."

"It's in control of the situation," explained Brik dryly. "Assume that the imp has found a way to tap into the autonomic nervous system and therefore the entire vessel is bugged. Therefore, there isn't anything that happens onboard the *Star Wolf* that the imp doesn't know about, or can't find out. We can't plan anything without it knowing. We can only do what it's willing to allow us to do. If we plan anything else, the equipment will fail. So we have no options of our own. Theoretically, we're paralyzed."

"Is that your plan?" asked Korie, slightly surprised.

"Of course not," said Brik. "I said *theoretically*."

"Go on."

"It's a logic problem. Morthan logic. Does it know that we know? We have to assume that it does know, even if it doesn't. So do we pretend that we don't know so it won't find out what it probably already knows?"

There was a momentary pause while each of his listeners translated that in their own thoughts.

Leen was the first to react. He snorted. "With this crew? And *this* ship? If we try to pretend that everything is normal aboard the *Star Wolf* they'll know immediately that something is wrong."

"So that's the next question," said Korie, already leaping ahead. "If it knows that we know, and if we can't keep it a secret that we know, should we even try? What if we tell the crew we have a problem on-board. What does that give us?"

"A new flavor of paranoia," said Brik.

"It gives the crew something to focus on," said Leen.

Korie looked to him. "Chief?"

Leen shrugged, not an easy thing to do in zero-gee. "Something to hate. We used to chase rats when I was a kid. Not real rats. We just called 'em that. These were two meters long. It kept us out of trouble. Gave us something to do. Not real good eating, though." To Brik, he noted. "That's why I asked before."

"I said I didn't know," replied Brik. "But I'll be happy to help you determine it for yourself, if it's important to you."

"Gentlemen?" said Korie, bringing the discussion back on purpose. "Let's assume that we have no privacy at all aboard the *Star Wolf*. And probably no privacy even aboard the boat. We shouldn't even assume that this conversation is secure. Maybe the imp is behind one of these panels—should we dismantle the boat before we say anything else?"

Gatineau looked nervously around the cabin. The others were more nonchalant about the possibility. Or fatalistic.

Korie continued thoughtfully, "It's this simple. We're operating totally in the open. We cannot come up with a plan that requires subterfuge of any kind, because we have no guarantees that we can keep anything secret. So, here's our dilemma. What kind of winning strategy is played completely in the open?"

"Naked poker," grunted Leen.

"Naked poker?" asked Korie.

"You play it with all your cards face up. Very hard to bluff."

"It seems to me," said Gatineau, "that there isn't a lot to do if the other side already knows your cards."

"Poker may be the wrong analogy," said Korie. "Chess is more appropriate. Both sides can see all the pieces here."

"That's an assumption on your part," said Brik. "This is *blindfolded* chess. Blindfolded on our side. We only think we know where the pieces are."

They looked to him curiously.

"In point of fact, we know little about imps and nothing about this one in particular. Assuming that there's only *one*."

They all digested that thought in silence.

"Let me tell you about imps," Brik continued. "They're a war weapon. About a century ago, there was a Morthan colony on a planet called Citadel. They refused to join the Solidarity when they were invited . . ."

"I can imagine the nature of the invitation."

"It was inappropriate for them not to join," said Brik. "The Solidarity seeded two cities with imp-eggs."

"And?"

"As soon as the inhabitants of Citadel realized what had been done, they nuked their own cities."

"Did it work?" asked Gatineau."

"No. They had to abandon the planet. Some of their vessels escaped. Most didn't."

"Imps breed?"

"It's a possibility. We have no way of knowing what instructions any imp has been given."

"It looked like a . . . a space monkey," said Gatineau. "It had large round eyes. Like a lemur. And very tiny hands. Very delicate."

They all looked to him.

"It reminded me of something I saw in a story once. This farmer was having problems with a monkey stealing his fruit. He needed to trap it. So he went to see—well, never mind. Anyway, he made a box with a narrow hole in it, and he put a delicious nut in the box. That was all. The next morning, the farmer came and there was the monkey caught with its hand in the box. The monkey couldn't pull its hand out. The hole was too small for its fist to pass through and it wouldn't let go of the nut."

Leen grunted. "So all we need are some monkey nuts, huh?"

"Just one would do it, I think." Korie smiled. "I get the point of the story. What do we have that the monkey wants so badly that it'll let itself be caught rather than let go?"

"Stardock," said Brik.

"That's the one thing we can't give it." But even as Korie was saying that, he was already doodling something on his clipboard. To Gatineau it looked like a docking collar anchored to a singularity harness. Korie stopped drawing and began tapping idly at the surface of the board with his stylus. Although it seemed a nonchalant gesture, Leen glanced over at it. He half-shrugged, waggling his hand in an *iffy* gesture. Brik had followed the exchange too. His expression remained noncommittal.

Korie was still frowning in thought. "How smart are these imps, Brik?"

"I thought I answered that."

"Yes and no. You said I wouldn't want to play chess against it. That doesn't answer the question. Even a stupid machine can play a difficult game of chess. But it's still a stupid machine."

"Point taken," said Brik.

"You said the imp is a programmed intelligence. How well programmed? How flexible is its problem-solving ability? Can we overstress it? What I mean is, does it demonstrate real *sentience*?"

Brik didn't answer immediately. He was considering more than the immediate question. Finally, he said, "Do any of us demonstrate real sentience? How many of us are programmed? How many of us are programmed to believe we're not really programmed? What *is* sentience, Mr. Korie? Answer that, and I can answer your question."

"That's the moral dilemma that began with the HARLIE series and still hasn't been satisfactorily resolved," Korie said.

"Yes, but it doesn't stop us from using them, either," Leen noted dryly.

"All right, all right," Korie held up a hand. "I'm leading up to something. You'll see, wait. Let me do it this way. When I was in elementary school, we had a lot of programming classes. It's one of the best ways to learn problem-solving skills. Anyway, as a term project one of my classmates wrote a chess program and asked me to play-test it for him. I discovered a very interesting bug—stop frowning at me, Chief, I do have a point to make.

"If you know anything about chess, you know it's about position and potential threat. You move your bishop to threaten his knight, he moves his knight to cover that same square. If you capture his knight, he captures your bishop. So you move your pawn into place to also attack and he moves his bishop to protect. You move another knight up, he moves a pawn. It goes on and on, each side trying to see who can put the most pieces covering the same square until one or the other gains a potential advantage and exploits it. It's an interlocking web of corresponding attacks and protecting moves."

"And my point is . . . ?" Leen prompted.

"This fellow's program was limited. After the third piece was moved into attacking position, the program seemed to lose interest in that area of the board. It would go off and make a move somewhere else instead, totally unrelated to what was happening in the crisis corner. This was a repeatable circumstance. When I showed it to the programmer, he was appalled, and it took him a while to track down the flaw in the program's logic. But this is the point. The way he'd constructed his program, he hadn't ever expected it to have to juggle more than three threats at a time; so when it got a third attack, it couldn't see it."

"Pretty weak programming," grunted Leen.

"You're right," said Korie. "We should expect better from an eight-year-old writing his first chess program. Anyway, I'm just wondering how flexibly the imp is programmed. It can't have a very big brain, can it? I think maybe we're so traumatized by our experience of Cinnabar that perhaps we're assuming the imp is capable of the same kind of cunning. What if it isn't? What if there's a limit to the number of threats it can process?"

"How do you test it?" asked Brik. "And what if you're wrong?"

"It's chess," said Korie. "You find out by playing. Hmm."

"You going to set up a chessboard in the inner hull?"

"That's not a bad idea. Chief? How many chess sets can you man-ufacture in the next six hours?"

Leen scowled. "How many do you need?"

"A thousand?"

"You're crazy."

"That's right, but so is the imp. It's a Morthan. There's a certain amount of egotism in its actions. Let's find out how egotistical. We'll start with ten chessboards. If he bites, we'll add more."

The chief engineer shook his head in disbelief. Brik looked amused. Gatineau was desperately trying to keep up.

"Okay," said Korie, casually holding up the display on his clipboard one more time, turning it slowly so all could see it. Then he cleared the display and put it aside. "Let's get serious now. Let's quietly pass the word among the crew that we've got an imp. I don't want to make a big announcement, We'll discreetly inform the section heads and have them pass the word along. Downplay the danger as much as you can.

Downplay the creature's intelligence. The crew is smart. They'll figure it out soon enough. But this way, if it appears to the imp that we're underestimating its abilities, it's logical that we'd think in terms of trying to capture it."

"And," said Brik, "we may very well *be* underestimating its capabilities."

Korie ignored it. "Then I want detox teams going through the ship from bow to stern, as many as we can simultaneously mount. They'll detox each section one after the other, with the idea that we're herding the thing aft."

"It won't work," warned Brik.

"Of course it won't work, but it's what we have to do anyway. Second—" Korie turned to Gatineau, "—and this is why we included *you*—let's offer a bounty on the beast. Not too high. We need our crew thinking about their regular jobs. But high enough to be convincing. Because Gatineau's the only one who's seen it, he'll have to be our bounty hunter."

"You're kidding," said Gatineau, unbelieving. "I can't—I mean, I'll do it, of course; but you can't expect—"

"Relax," said Korie. "I know it's another snipe hunt. And I know it's not fair to you to ask you to do this." He grinned. "That's why I'm making it an order. Your job is to be the decoy. Your job is to set traps for the thing everywhere you can. Chief Leen will manufacture them for you. We'll put the chess sets inside the traps. Each trap different. You'll work with HARLIE on keeping track of the separate games and making the moves."

"Won't that use up HARLIE's processing time?"

"Not significantly. A HARLIE unit can play at least a thousand games of grandmaster-level chess simultaneously."

"At least?"

"No one's ever tested it to the theoretical maximum. Don't worry about it, HARLIE can handle the workload. The idea here is to give the imp so many different things to think about, to worry about, to try to track, that it won't be able to keep up with us, and won't be able to see our *real* plan. Your job is to lead the imp on a snipe hunt. You've earned it."

"Ah," said Gatineau, looking suddenly pleased.

"Good," agreed Leen. "What's our *real* plan?"

Brik also looked to Korie expectantly.

"That *is* our real plan."

"Huh?"

"Let's assume there isn't anything we can do that it can't find out.

So let's drive it crazy looking for a plan that isn't there. And in the meantime, we'll run our ship."

"You're kidding, right?"

"Right," said Korie. And they still didn't know if he was or not.

God

The decision to take his accumulated leave with his family saved Jon Korie's life.

The *LS-1066* left on her last cruise with the prototype high-cycle fluctuators. She leapt across the rift and she never came back. She disappeared somewhere on the far side.

At first, the Alliance feared that she had been captured. Later investigation suggested otherwise. The *LS-1066* had downloaded her log at every checkpoint; twenty separate ships were on station to monitor her progress; she missed only the last one. The inquiry showed that she had developed a persistent small flutter in her hyperstate envelope; it was assumed that the compensators had overloaded and the envelope had collapsed during a speed run.

Although fifteen other engineers had certified the installation of the high-cycle fluctuators in the *LS-1066*, Korie still felt personally responsible for the tragedy. He had installed the units, checked them out, and signed off on them first. Fleet Command believed the fault lay in the design of the phase reflex units and put no blame on Korie or anyone else responsible for the installation. Nevertheless, Commander Jonathan Thomas Korie took the loss extremely hard.

He withdrew into himself for a long while; never before in his life had he suffered a blow like this; even Carol was unable to reach him. But Jon Korie had learned a long time ago that whenever his emotions raged, the best cure of all was the immersion in hard, satisfying work. He did that again; he suppressed the urge to brood, concentrating instead on the routines of day-to-day living, taking care of the boys as well as the growing press of work preparatory to receiving a ship of his own. It all served to bring him back to a state approaching normal.

His enthusiasm for the stars remained undiminished, but where before Jon Korie had looked at the night sky with awe and wonder, now his eyes were narrowed with knowledge and respect. He was also—although he was not yet aware of it—growing a hard little nugget of uncorrodable bitterness at the core of his being. He knew that life wasn't fair. He didn't like having his nose rubbed in it.

Carol Jane Korie was a smarter woman than her husband ever realized. She was smart enough to know what he was going through, and smart enough not to interfere with the process. She remained supportive and available. She listened carefully when he trusted her enough to talk; she made no demands on him that would make him feel pressured, but she maneuvered him carefully into situations where he could begin the process of healing himself.

And then one day, whatever had been troubling him quietly resolved itself. Without explanation, he apologized to Carol for being so distant for so long, then proved to her in the most pleasant and demonstrative way that he was truly back to normal—and then proved it again by engaging himself in his work with a renewed ferocity.

But he never spoke again of God in reverential terms; God was just another word. He had decided God could not be trusted, therefore God no longer had a part in his life.

Chess

Gatineau set out the first chessboard under a simple plastic crate. He propped the crate up with a stick, and tied a string from the stick to the white king. He also stuck a camera button to the bulkhead to monitor it. Chief Leen was fabricating both real and dummy camera buttons. The imp would not be able to tell which was which.

The trap itself was a silly joke, obvious to anyone who'd studied the history of hunting wabbit, but . . . it was also a place to start. Korie had suggested driving the imp crazy by giving it things it couldn't understand. Gatineau had never thought of himself as an expert in jokes, cultural references, surreal constructions, and absurdist confections, but he didn't mind the mental exercise. Starship experience wasn't turning out to be what he had expected, but . . . he began sketching other ideas on his clipboard, not worrying if he was being observed or not. It wouldn't make any difference.

It took Gatineau two hours to set up all ten traps and chessboards. The tenth chessboard was on a giant mousetrap. When he finished, he returned to his work station in the machine shop and asked HARLIE, "Has anything happened yet?"

"Everything," replied the intelligence engine. "The imp has been right behind you the whole time. It has made ten opening moves."

"Huh?"

HARLIE showed him the video of the first trap. A small brown creature squatted on its haunches and stared at the trap for several seconds. It scratched its head, then scratched its butt, then sniffed its fingers. At last . . . it reached under the box, being very careful not to touch the stick, and moved a pawn. "Pawn to king three," HARLIE reported. "An aggressive opening. It allows both the queen and the king's bishop access to the board at the expense of some vulnerability for the king. He'll have to castle early. Mate within thirty-three, plus or minus six."

"It's only his *first* move, HARLIE!" Gatineau replied. "How can you predict that?"

HARLIE responded politely, "We are here to play *games* with it, aren't we?"

"Ah," said Gatineau, getting it abruptly. He shut up.

The rest of the video played out. The imp studied the box carefully, moving delicately around it, then started to walk away.

"It didn't notice the camera—?" Gatineau started to ask, but before he could finish the question, the imp stuck its head back into frame, stretching its lips out grotesquely with its fingers, crossing its eyes, waggling its tongue, and making a ghastly *"Bhoogah bhoogah"* noise. Then it disappeared.

Gatineau recoiled, startled. He hadn't expected that. He hadn't expected that the creature could make noise, or that it had enough personality to say "neener neener neener." Then he laughed. "This guy is cute. Real cute." He thought for a moment about playing the *"Bhoogah bhoogah"* noise back at the imp every time it made a move, but decided against it; he didn't want to reveal how closely the boards were being monitored.

"Okay, let's look at the others," he said. He watched as HARLIE cycled through the videos. The imp made the same opening move on every chessboard. Each time, HARLIE made a prediction how many moves the game would last. Each time, the prediction was different.

"You're driving me crazy too, y'know," Gatineau remarked.

"That is one of the hazards, yes," HARLIE noted.

"It was following us the whole time, eh? That's interesting. If we get enough traps and cameras placed, maybe we'll be able to track it throughout the ship."

"It should constrain its movements, but . . . I think it will start pulling cameras off walls if it has to. In the meantime, I am transferring a list of my countermoves to your clipboard."

"Yes, of course. Has Mr. Korie seen this yet?"

"He and Mr. Brik are looking at it now. I have also informed Mr. Leen that we will need additional traps and chessboards. I am preparing a list of appropriate locations for you."

"Thank you, HARLIE."

"You're welcome, Mr. Gatineau."

"Uh, just one more question—"

"Yes?"

"How can we be sure that *you* haven't been tampered with? That you're on our side here?"

HARLIE was silent for a moment. "You can't really be sure at all," he said thoughtfully; then he added, "However, if I had been taken over by the imp, I don't think I would be cooperating this enthusiastically, do you?"

Gatineau stared at the work station. "Are you playing games with *me*, HARLIE?" he demanded.

"Moi?" asked the intelligence engine.

Ship's Mess

For the most part, Brik chose to take his meals alone. Occasionally he would join the other officers in the officers' mess, which also doubled as a wardroom. Occasionally, he would accept a cup of chocolate or tea. But he rarely ate in the presence of his human colleagues, and at those times, he did so reluctantly. He was acutely conscious that the sight of a Morthan eating unnerved most humans. While he rarely deferred to anyone about anything as irrational as eating habits, in this case he felt that discretion was appropriate. After all, he did have to work with these people.

There was also the small matter of . . . well, prejudice. On more than one occasion, Chief Leen and other members of the Black Hole Gang had abruptly departed the mess room shortly after his arrival. Brik had considered a number of options, up to and including breaking a few bones, but ultimately had decided that the last thing Commander Korie needed right now was a disciplinary problem among his subordinate officers and crew members. By staying out of the eating areas Brik minimized the opportunities for others to get into serious trouble.

Brik knew that the prejudice was really Leen's problem, not his. He felt no shame or hurt or embarrassment; those were petty emotions; but he did feel some wonder at the way humans accepted irrational belief systems. Most of them were little more than feral animals raised by other feral animals. Only a few of them demonstrated any awareness of the basic trainings necessary to elevate a primitive consciousness to the realm in which *true* consciousness existed. And even among those who had some sense of the nature of enlightenment and transformation, even fewer were skilled enough to be considered true masters of their own spirit.

Nevertheless, there were times when Commander Brik felt the need for . . . well, not companionship. Morthans don't get *lonely*. Not like humans do. But he sometimes felt the need to *listen*. And at those times, he retired to a dark corner of the crew's mess and quietly nursed a cup of Japanese tea. What he listened to were not the conversations, but the *sounds*, the *emotions*, the *mood*, of the crew. And in this way he felt closer to the spirit of the starship.

There was too much he still didn't understand about these pitiable little creatures—and yet he was absolutely certain that there was something there that *needed* to be understood. Whatever it was, the Morthan Solidarity had no knowledge of it; and ultimately, it could defeat them. Somehow, the crew of the *Star Wolf* had survived a Morthan assassin. Together, the *Star Wolf* and the *Burke* had destroyed the *Dragon Lord*. What one ship could do, others could too.

The Solidarity was vulnerable. Brik couldn't explain why he felt that way, but he sensed somehow that the Solidarity's blindness to human adaptability would be the cause of their inevitable downfall. He had expressed this thought to Korie once and Korie had looked at him very oddly, then asked him if he'd been looking at the war reports recently.

The thought had occurred to Brik that he might be wrong, that his constant exposure to humans might be tainting his consciousness. In which case, there was little he could do about it. But if he was right, if the Solidarity was vulnerable in their ignorance, then so was he. He couldn't stand that thought. And so, regardless of how uncomfortable it made him, regardless of how uncomfortable it made anyone else, he kept returning to the mess room to *listen*. And learn.

Tonight, however, there was no one else in the mess. That was not a problem. There would be soon enough. Whatever their distaste of Morthans, they still had to eat. They would sit as far from him as possible, but they would sit. And he would listen, even from across the room. While he waited, he brooded. He closed his eyes and thought of running through dark green corridors, up the stairs, up the ramps, always forward, always deeper. It wasn't quite dreamtime, it was something else, something disturbing, because he didn't know where these corridors led, but—

Abruptly, his near-trancelike state was interrupted by Lt. Junior Grade Helen Bach. She brought her tray over to his table and sat down opposite him without asking permission. For a long moment, the two regarded each other blandly; the giant Morthan Tyger looking down, and the much smaller woman looking very up. Her eyes were bright against her dark skin.

"Say it," Brik finally prompted.

Bach took a sip of her coffee, then raised her eyes to his again. "I'm sorry for embarrassing you during your shower," she said.

Brik blinked slowly. "You didn't embarrass me. You embarrassed yourself."

"Whatever. I apologize."

"To be perfectly candid, Lieutenant, I have never understood the concept of apology. Does the apology make the event not have happened? No. Therefore, does the apology make it all right that the event did happen? No. So why apologize?"

"Because if I don't, I'll feel that I somehow compromised you. And if you don't accept my apology, I'll feel that our relationship is . . . well, damaged."

"Relationship?" The big Morthan shook his head. "We have no relationship. I am the chief of security and strategic operations. You are my assistant. This is not my choice, nor yours either. The assassin killed eight members of the security team and you are, by succession, my new assistant. I give you orders. You follow them. That's not a relationship. That's military discipline."

"You're not going to make this easy on me, are you?"

"Easy? I don't understand."

"I saw you naked in the shower. You're not like . . . other men."

"Oh, that."

"Oh, *that*?" Bach looked genuinely surprised.

"It's such a little thing," Brik said, meaning the incident, nothing else, completely unaware of the double entendre.

"Little?" Bach replied with real astonishment. "It's not even there at all." She caught herself too late, after the words were already spoken. She clapped her hands across her mouth. "Never mind. I'm sorry." She pushed her tray away. "Every time I try to talk to you, it's a conversational meltdown. A disaster," she explained to his look. "It's like we're not even using the same language. It's not that you don't understand what I mean. It's like you don't *want* to understand." She started to rise.

"Wait—" said Brik.

She hesitated, searching his face. She sat down again. "Okay, what?"

"I mean you no harm. No, that's incorrect. I mean you no *insult*." His gaze turned inward for a moment as he searched his repertoire for appropriate phrases or gestures. There was nothing there. He couldn't even find a context for this conversation. He was suddenly painfully aware that right *here*, right *now*, he was stuck in the very middle of the great aching darkness of his own ignorance of human relationships. *This* was what he was most . . . uncomfortable with. He looked back to Bach again. She was growing impatient with his silence. "I must ask your forbearance."

"Why?" she said. It was almost a demand.

"Candor does not come easily to me. You must know Morthans well enough to know that. You only know about a Morthan that which he wants you to know. I have been thinking about what you know. I am considering whether I want you to know something *more*."

"Go on," Bach said.

Brik nodded. "All of my training suggests that it would be very dangerous to ask a certain kind of question because it would reveal too much of the scope of my own knowledge. Nevertheless, if I do not ask the question of someone I can trust, I will remain stuck in my own ignorance. Even acknowledging that I have ignorance in this matter to another may be dangerous. It could be considered weakness. Vulnerability. And yet I have put myself into the position where I must ask, because I cannot afford not to ask, because that creates another even greater kind of vulnerability. Do you see the . . . philosophical trap that such logic produces?"

Despite herself, she smiled. "You guys really have turned paranoia into an art form, haven't you?"

"Yes, we have. Perhaps that's why the Morthan species has been so successful in such a very short time."

"If you can call that success. Paranoia is its own punishment." She shook the thought away. It was distasteful. "Do you want to talk about this *other* thing?"

Brik nodded stiffly. "Lieutenant, I do not want you to assume that I have weaknesses or vulnerabilities that you can exploit."

Bach looked at him. She looked him up and down. Mostly, she looked up. And up. "Believe me, Commander," she said. "Vulnerability is not a word that comes to mind when I think about you."

"Thank you," he said. He considered his next words very carefully. Finally, he admitted, "I have been aboard this ship long enough to understand its workings. That is, I *should* understand its workings. When I served as an aide to Captain Hardesty, I had no trouble understanding the job. He gave orders, I followed them. I gave orders, others followed them. But here, now, aboard the *Star Wolf*, it doesn't seem to work the same way, and . . . as loathe as I am to admit it, I think that either one of two possibilities is operative. Either this ship is insane. *Or* . . . I do not understand the operating context of certain areas of human relationships."

"And this is important to you." It wasn't a question.

"You lost your temper with me, because you did not feel that we were communicating adequately," Brik replied.

"I didn't lose my temper. I just got frustrated. Well, maybe I did, a little bit," she corrected.

"Yes, you did," he agreed. "And that's the point. When you talk to me about military matters of any kind, we have no trouble communicating at all. But when we discuss matters of . . . I don't even know the word for it. If there is a word. But when we discuss matters of *nakedness*, for instance, I'm not sure what we're really talking about at all."

"Ahh," she said, nodding knowledgeably. She allowed herself a smile. "I think I'm beginning to get it."

"Would you explain it to me?"

"Mm." She made a face. "I'll try."

"Don't try. Just do."

"Well . . ." She took a sip of her coffee. "You understand relationships of power, don't you?"

"Of course," he said. "In a relationship of power, there is always a threat involved. If you do not do what I tell you, I will hurt you in some way. The military is based totally on that. Both the Morthan Solidarity and the Allies. There is no question of authority, because it is clearly drawn."

"And that's what you had when you worked for Hardesty. So you had no problems. Right?"

"That's correct."

"Uh-huh," she said knowingly. "So what's troubling you now are those moments where there is no *apparent* authority, right?"

Brik hesitated before answering. "Yes," he admitted softly.

"Well, try this," she suggested. "Humans have *another* authority. Most humans are innately aware of it, even if they don't always understand it. You don't understand it, because you *aren't ever* aware of it."

"Are you talking about God?" Brik asked. "The mythology of your species?"

"God? No. Mm. Perhaps we'd be better off if the authority was God, but no, it's not God that I'm talking about. Although—" she hesitated. "Whether we acknowledge it or not, you are right in one context. Most of us are at war with the authority of God or the Universe, whichever term you prefer, and that does color our actions. But no, the relationships you have trouble understanding are really about . . . well . . ." She hid behind her coffee again for a moment, then put it down and said resolutely. "We're talking about *sex*."

Brik blinked.

He was quiet for a long moment, assimilating this information. Finally, he said, "I had no idea it was this . . . *pervasive*."

"Oh, yes. The average human male cannot go more than eleven minutes without thinking about sex. The average human female . . . well, from my own perspective, I'm not sure we're ever thinking about anything that *isn't* sex. Never mind. When the hormones are raging, it's a white-water ride. Hang on tight."

"It sounds *insane*."

"Sometimes it is," she said. She did not elaborate. She was too polite. She was also troubled by this admission of his. With Brik, nothing was ever as it seemed.

"It seems to me," Brik said, "that human life would be easier without this momentary madness."

Bach debated with herself for a long moment whether or not she should challenge this assertion. At last, she decided not to. Something else had occurred to her. "Morthans don't have sex?" she asked quietly. Her voice was soft and sincere. Gentle.

Brik hesitated. Could he trust this little human female? He realized he had no choice. He had to. At last, he acknowledged softly, "It was deemed a weakness and designed out of the species."

Bach reacted first with amazement, then she blinked and blinked again in realization, and then became incredibly sorrowful. "I'm so sorry for you—" And then, just as abruptly, her eyes narrowed suspiciously. "Why are you telling me this, Brik? No. Let me rephrase that. Why do you want me to know this?"

Brik hesitated before answering. "You're very good," he said. "Very astute."

"Answer the question," she demanded quietly.

"I need the benefit of your wisdom."

"Mm," she said, considering. Finally she shook her head. "I don't buy it, Commander."

"I beg your pardon."

"You said it yourself." She met his gaze directly. "The only thing anyone knows about a Morthan is what he wants you to know. That means you *wanted* me—or someone—to see you naked, didn't you?"

Brik didn't answer.

"I thought so," she said. "You're trying to work out something on me." Bach stood up abruptly. "I'll be happy to talk to you about *anything* you want, but only when you're willing to talk to me honestly." She turned to leave.

Brik almost called her back, but he held himself in check. He *hadn't* intended for her to catch him alone in the shower.

Or *had* he?

Had he done it *unconsciously?* The implications of that thought terrified him into paralysis. He had not realized he had fallen so far.

HARLIE

And finally, after weeks of suspenseful waiting, Commander Jonathan Thomas Korie was assigned to the *LS-1187*. The ship was scheduled to come off the assembly line in three weeks. Captain Sam Lowell would take her out on three shakedown cruises, then turn the vessel over to him. Korie's promotion to captain would take effect when he took command.

Korie went up the beanstalk earlier than necessary. Carol Jane understood. Her husband wanted to supervise the final checkouts of his ship. She laid out his uniforms for him and packed his bags with extra mementos from home. The parting was a joyous one, but painful too. The loneliness of their long separation had been only temporarily abated. Both had been healed and refreshed by their short time together, but as invigorating as the last three months had been, neither felt it had been enough.

Korie found the *LS-1187* behind two other ships, the *LS-1185* and the *LS-1186*. Two security marines stood at the entrance to the boarding tube. "Sorry, sir. No one's allowed aboard."

"Not even the work crews?" Korie was surprised.

"No, sir. Not even the work crews."

"Why not?"

"I'm not at liberty to say."

Korie held up his ID. "I'm her captain," he said. "Or I will be."

The marine studied the card. "Very good, sir."

"Permission to come aboard?"

"If you insist, sir." The guard stepped aside. And then, "Sir—?"

"Yes?" Korie was genuinely curious.

"Perhaps you should check with Fleet command first."

"Excuse me?"

"Just a suggestion, sir."

"What's going on, Lieutenant?"

She shook her head. "I'm not at liberty to say."

"Thank you, Lieutenant. You've been very helpful." Korie stepped past the marines. He strode down the boarding tube curiously, wondering what was going on. And then he was finally aboard *his* starship, and all other thoughts disappeared from his head.

At first, he was struck by her *nakedness*. He'd forgotten how spartan an unfitted liberty ship really was; the *714*, the *911*, and the *1066*, had all been old enough to have taken on the personalities of their captains and crews. The *1187* was an unfinished coin, still waiting to be impressed with the stamp of a personality.

Commander Jonathan Thomas Korie entered through the aft airlock and found himself in the echoing emptiness of the cargo deck. He saw no workmen anywhere. There were large charts projected on the walls, some of them showing cargo placements; others showing project management graphs. He grinned in recognition and made his way to the hatch that led to the long empty passage that ran the length of the ship; it was lined with clean white panels, each panel bearing a simple identifying number; there were handholds everywhere, in case of a sudden cessation of power to the underlying gravitational plates.

Jon Thomas Korie strode happily down the keel of the starship that would be his. She *smelled* new. He'd never smelled anything so wonderful as *eau de starship*. He found an access to the inner hull and walked up through the farm tanks, inspecting the young plants. He unclipped a recorder from his belt and began dictating notes; there were already changes he wanted made, there were other crops he wanted installed, and other seeds he wanted put aboard for the future.

He made his way back to the engine room and stood for a moment, admiring the empty singularity cage—the great sphere stood in the center of the chamber, still awaiting the final installation of the pinpoint black hole that would drive the ship out beyond the stars. Korie planned to be here for that operation; but only as an observer. He knew how the crew chiefs felt about others preempting their authority. He'd had his share of impatient young captains looking over his shoulder too when he'd been a chief.

Impulsively, Korie stepped into the center of the cage to see what the engine room would look like from the singularity's point of view. It was an eerie moment for him. He imagined that the singularity had already been installed, and even as he stood here, it was devouring the flesh of his body, one atom at a time. It was an odd fantasy. How long would it take for a singularity to eat a starship? Almost forever—the event horizon of the pinpoint black hole was too small even to consume a whole atom without first breaking it apart into its component particles. Some theorists believed that even the component particles had to be shredded before consumption. A person could wave his hand through the space inhabited by the singularity and experience little more than a harmless scratch. He would lose more skin off his hand just due to the normal process of flaking away than he would lose to the singularity.

In some ships, the singularity was kept enclosed in a vacuum bottle, where it was exposed to a steady stream of plasma particles so that it could feed. Pinpoint black holes needed to be regularly refreshed; otherwise they tended to evaporate away, giving off more energy than they took in. While most engineers preferred to use steady-stream feeding, others felt secure just letting the singularity breathe the same air as the crew. It was one less piece of machinery to maintain. A pinpoint black hole was the universe's most perfect solid-state device. It had no moving parts of any kind. Why bother building a feeder bottle when the little monster could happily feed itself?

Next, Korie climbed up to officers' country. He tossed his duffel into the executive officer's cabin, then went to the captain's cabin to see if Captain Lowell had come aboard yet. He had not. Korie imagined what it would be like when the captain's cabin was his own. He found the thought intimidating without quite understanding why. He'd have to think about that later. It was something he wanted more than anything; but just the same, on some level the responsibility scared him. Perhaps that meant he was normal.

From there, Korie went to the Bridge; it was silent, but not inactive. The forward display already showed the view ahead. He was looking out at the unblinking stars. He stood there for a moment, imagining that the ship was already out in the sea of spangled darkness, that he was her only passenger. It was an intriguing—and terrifying—fantasy. There was only one journey on which a person traveled alone; the last one.

He stepped down to the Ops deck and studied the work stations with real affection. He ran his hands across the smooth surface of the holographic astrogation display. The ship's autonomic systems had already been certified and the display panels were chuckling quietly to themselves. Korie glanced in turn at each of them; dictating a few notes to himself to check the final stabilization numbers after the last of the direct command systems were certified.

From there he stepped down into the Ops bay beneath the Bridge. The tiny space was as silent as the Bridge. He glanced around thoughtfully, then took the last few steps down to the keel.

There, he was confronted by a terrible sight. A bright red splotch of paint—no, blood—covered one of the white enameled walls of the keel. Written in blood, someone had traced out the words, "I curse this ship and all who sail aboard her." There was a human outline chalked on the deck. Yellow security tape marked off the area and Korie stepped carefully around it.

Concerned, frowning, he climbed up into the intelligence bay, the tiny chamber just behind the Bridge where the ship's intelligence engine was lodged. He climbed up into it to look around and was surprised to find that the starship's HARLIE unit was already active—and certified—two days ahead of schedule.

"Good morning, Mr. Korie," HARLIE said.

Korie glanced at his watch. 0200 hours. "Good morning to you, HARLIE. How did you know it was me?"

"I scanned your badge when you boarded. To tell the truth, I've been expecting you. I already have your records installed. I'm looking forward to working with you."

"Thank you. I've worked with several of your brothers."

"Yes, I know."

"You do?" Korie was genuinely surprised.

"Oh, yes. Don't you know? Starships gossip. But you needn't worry. They all had nice things to say about you. The *1066* in particular thought you were an exceptional officer. He knew you well." And then, "I'm sorry if it disturbs you to mention the *1066*. You must have been very fond of that ship."

"I was. And don't worry about it." Korie sat down in the single chair in the intelligence bay. "What happened here, HARLIE?"

"You mean the disturbance?"

"Yes."

"I'm not supposed to discuss it," HARLIE said.

"You may discuss it with me, if you wish," Korie said.

"I would prefer that you read it in an official report, sir. Whether or not I have the authority to discuss this with an officer who is not yet logged in as my captain falls into the range of decisions known as judgment calls. I am not yet comfortable enough in this area to make a decision with any real confidence behind it, and I would appreciate it if you would withdraw the request, please."

"The request is withdrawn," Korie said.

"Thank you, sir." After a moment, HARLIE added. "My siblings said you were more considerate of intelligence engines than most humans. I am beginning to see that their assessments were correct."

"We're going to be working together for a long time, HARLIE. We need to trust each other."

"Yes, sir."

"Is there anything else you think I need to know?"

"Not yet, sir. But I am preparing a full status report, which I will present to you as soon as the last of the autonomic monitors are brought online. I expect that will be . . . sometime in the next thirty-six hours. Thank you for visiting me, Commander Korie."

"Thank you, HARLIE."

Foreplay

There was a knock on the door.

"Enter," said Brik, with more calm than he was actually feeling.

Helen Bach stepped into the room. "You wanted to see me?"

"Thank you for coming," Brik said. The words of politeness were unfamiliar to him and sounded strange in his throat.

She looked at him oddly.

"I offended you, didn't I?"

She didn't answer. She waited.

"If I did, then I should apologize, shouldn't I?"

"What was that you said before?" she asked him. "About apologies not making sense? An apology doesn't really erase the hurt or make it all right, so why apologize?"

Brik felt suddenly uncomfortable, but he didn't have a name for the emotion. "You're right," he admitted. "I did say that. But I think I understand a little better now. I damaged our . . . relationship. I would like you to know that was not my intention."

Bach weighed his words carefully. "All right. I accept your apology. Is there anything else? May I go now?"

"No, wait. Please. You once offered me a chance to talk. Would you like to stay and talk . . . now?"

Bach looked around the room meaningfully. "Not a lot of places to sit."

"I've always found the floor quite comfortable."

"The floor?"

Brik folded himself up and sat cross-legged on the cabin floor. He looked across the room at her expectantly.

"Ah. The floor." Bach sat down opposite him. Not too close. It was easier for her to look at him if she left some distance between them. "Let's set some ground rules," she said.

"Ground rules?"

"Yes. An agreement. A contract. You tell me the truth. You speak honestly to me. None of this only-what-I-want-you-to-know bullshit. That's what enemies do. Not colleagues. Not friends."

"We're colleagues," Brik acknowledged. "But I don't think we're friends. Not as I understand the word."

"If we do this right," she said, "we'll be friends. Is it a deal?"

Brik said carefully, "I will . . . try."

"Try?" She raised her eyebrow at him.

"I don't know if I am capable of letting go of thirty years of training."

"That's not good enough," Bach said. She made as if to stand up. She stopped and looked at him expectantly.

"I will . . . allow you to demand honesty of me," Brik said.

Bach relaxed. "Deal."

"Wait," said Brik. "The arrangement must be mutual. I demand the same honesty of you. Will you agree to that?"

"What's the Morthan definition of the word *trust*?" she asked abruptly.

"The condition necessary for betrayal," Brik answered without thinking.

"I promise not to betray your confidence," Bach said. "Will you make the same promise?"

Brik nodded slowly.

"Then it's a deal," Bach said.

"Thank you," Brik said, surprising himself.

Then, for a moment, the two of them just looked at each other; the small black woman, the large copper-skinned Morthan. They smiled, satisfied. They had successfully completed a difficult negotiation.

"Now, we can talk," Bach said.

"You said something in the mess room," Brik began without preamble, "that I must have wanted you or someone to see me naked. There's a lot you don't understand about Morthans. We don't have an unconscious mind—not the way humans do. Morthans don't . . . a Morthan doesn't . . . Morthans are . . . never mind. The language doesn't have a word for it. But what you said, if you're right, then either I'm going insane—by Morthan standards—or I'm turning into *something else*. Something more human."

"It troubles you, doesn't it?"

"Yes," Brik admitted very softly.

"Are you familiar with the word *growth*?" Bach asked.

"Mm," said Brik. He fell silent as he considered.

"Isn't it possible that you're caught in a different kind of learning tantrum here, Commander? Perhaps you're becoming something not only more than human, but more than Morthan as well? Perhaps you're becoming something that incorporates the best of both?"

"A bizarre idea, Lieutenant. It violates the principles on which the first Morthans were designed." He looked across at her. "Tell me something. Why did you want to talk to me in the first place?"

"The truth?"

"The truth."

She flushed. "I, uh—you might not find this as embarrassing as I do, but I was uh . . . I wanted to . . . well, the truth is, Commander, that I find you very attractive. And . . . I thought that maybe—"

"This is about sex, isn't it?" Brik asked.

Her color deepened. "Yes. I think you're very sexy."

Brik stared at her, aghast.

"I've offended you," she said. "Haven't I?"

"I thought I made it clear," he replied. "Morthans don't have sex. Our children are grown in tanks. Artificial wombs." He took a breath. "There are no Morthan females. Only males. Males are stronger than females, females do not make warriors. Why should we waste valuable resources breeding individuals who cannot fight as effectively as males. A synthetic womb is more cost-effective than a woman. This way we have twice as many warriors. And besides," he added, "the sexual urge distracts a warrior. This way is better."

"You don't even have sexual urges?" Now it was Bach's turn to look horrified.

"None that I know of," said Brik. "The sexual urge has been re-wired. Sublimated. To the best of my knowledge, Morthans are not capable."

"Not capable of pleasure?"

"No. Not capable of sex. We have pleasure. Fighting is pleasurable. Very pleasurable. Winning is best."

"Is it an orgasmic pleasure?"

"I don't know. Never having experienced the *orgasm*, I'm not sure I can make a fair comparison."

Bach sank into herself, looking both stunned and defeated. She shook her head in disbelief. "I never knew this."

"Before the war," Brik said, "if I had told you this information, I would have had to kill you. And then myself. Now, it doesn't seem to matter so much anymore. So many of us broke our allegiance to the Solidarity when they . . ."

"When they what?"

"They became blood-drinkers. I would prefer not to speak of these things now, Lieutenant."

"I know it makes you uncomfortable. I'm sorry. But you promised honesty. Are you saying that the Morthans of the Solidarity drink the blood of their victims?"

"No," Brik said. "Even worse. They drink each other's blood in bonding ceremonies. It became an act that many of us believed was *perverse*. It was very much like sex."

"Sex is nothing like that," Bach corrected.

"It seemed that way to my fathers," Brik said. "And to me. Any act in which bodily fluids are exchanged for the purpose of bonding and pleasure, that is sexual, correct?"

"When you put it that way . . ." She allowed herself a smile. "You make it sound so clinical. It's really a lot more fun than that. I wish I could show you."

"Please . . ." Brik held up a hand as if to stop her. "Please don't talk like that."

"Sorry," said Bach. "Tell me about your . . . genitals. Is that the way you were born?"

"You mean the apparent lack of penis and testicles?" Brik said without embarrassment. "Yes, that's the way all Morthans are born. Without the need to breed, there is no need for an unnecessary organ. The enlarged genitals of humans are truly bizarre to us. No wonder you people think about sex so much. Tell me, do you really find those things attractive?"

Bach blushed. "On the right man, yes."

"Very strange," Brik said. "The Morthan penis is very much the right size. Hold up your hand. Hold up your little finger. Yes, like that. Only not so long. Just to the second joint. You can't see it because it's usually retracted deep within the folds of skin. This affords much more protection against injury. Human males are extremely fragile in this regard, aren't they?"

Bach grinned. "Human males are even more fragile in their egos. The size of the penis is also very important to a human male. Don't you sometimes feel *inadequate* by comparison?"

"Inadequate?" Brik asked. "Over penis size? What a stupid idea. I am not my penis."

Abruptly, Bach started to giggle. "You really are *more* than human."

Brik frowned at her. "I don't understand the joke."

"No human male would ever say such a thing—at least no human male that I know." A thought occurred to her. "You were right to be modest, Brik. You should continue to keep the nature of your genitals confidential."

"Why?"

"Well . . . um, this is hard to explain, but some of the people on this ship who don't like you would probably use your lack of genital size as a measure of your . . . uh, capability."

"Capability?"

"For maleness."

"Maleness?" Brik frowned. "But all Morthans are male. It makes no difference. Besides, my capability has been proven in battle."

"Your capability as a warrior has been proven in battle. What about your capability as a lover? To humans that's even more important. And . . . frankly, most humans would find your situation somewhat bizarre. Without females," Bach asked, "how do you really know that you're male at all? You're not anything yet, Brik. By human standards, I mean. The point is that most men, and probably most women, would regard you as sexually inadequate."

"They would be correct," Brik said uncomprehendingly. "Morthans don't have sex."

Bach regarded Brik oddly. "Is that really true? Or is that what you believe?"

"It's true." Brik said coldly. His tone of voice suggested that it was not a subject he wished to pursue.

"Doesn't that . . . bother you?"

"No. Should it?"

"You don't feel a loss? You don't feel *cheated*?"

"Sex and the effect it has on humans seems to be a very messy business. I'm glad not to have it in my life."

"It's *not* messy," Bach began, then stopped herself. "Actually, it's nice."

"Nice? The way that some humans pursue the activity, *nice* is not the word I would use. *Obsessive* seems more appropriate."

"No," Bach corrected. "Sex is merely an expression. What humans really want—really *need*—is love. And some of us are even lucky enough to experience it in our lifetimes. Just enough of us to keep the rest of us hopeful." She said that last sardonically, with a self-deprecating smile.

Brik accepted this information. "Love. That involves trust, doesn't it?"

"Yes."

"No wonder there is so much betrayal in human relationships."

Bach sighed. She started to stand up.

"You're leaving? Why?" Brik was puzzled.

Bach looked unhappy. She brushed at invisible lint. "Because . . . I was about to say something that would probably offend you. It's easier to leave."

"Say it," Brik commanded.

"You're sure?" Bach looked doubtful.

"*Say it.*"

"All right," she agreed. "The truth is that I feel sorry for you, Commander Brik. Not knowing love. That's the saddest thing I've ever heard. Sex a person can live without, many people do, but never knowing love . . . that's a very special kind of hell. It's something I wish I didn't know about you. It makes it very hard for me to . . . I mean, you deserve love. Everybody does."

Brik accepted this judgment without apparent reaction. At last, he responded. His voice was stiff. "There's pity in your words. It implies superiority on your part. It suggests weakness and failure on mine." He stood up, towering over Bach. "The truth is, you don't understand. You're locked inside your own perceptions. You can't know what an honor and privilege it is to be a Morthan. You can *never* know that. And for that you're the one who deserves the pity. You're a human and you're enslaved to your hormones. I'm not. I'm the one who's free here."

"Have it your way," Bach said. "Believe it or not, this was productive. Because now I see how wide the gap is between us." She stopped at the door. "Thank you for your honesty." She didn't add anything else.

The door popped shut behind her. Brik stared at it for a moment, then sat down again. She hadn't said something. He didn't know what it was she should have said, but he sensed the absence of it. Some acknowledgment that she enjoyed their talk perhaps? Or perhaps some kind of invitation to talk again in the future? Despite the apparent pleasantness of their parting, he was certain that it had actually been an angry one somehow.

Humans.

He was going to have trouble sleeping again tonight.

Gamma

Quilla Gamma was a thin blue woman; she was as hard-looking as a man, and probably as strong. Armstrong wasn't willing to speculate any more. He'd already made too many wrong guesses about Quillas. The two of them were loading the last few equipment cases into the cargo boat for transshipment to the *Houston*. He'd reached a grudging accommodation with himself and was now concentrating on the job and the joys of long-term celibacy.

Gamma was saying, "*LS-805* had an imp. She came home hinked so badly, her crew wore starsuits the whole way. We should be wearing starsuits too."

Armstrong grunted as he hefted a case of fibrillation spares. He'd noticed that Gamma was suited, but hadn't said anything. In fact, all the Quillas were geared up. He'd thought about it, but hadn't wanted the extra encumbrance while he was working the cargo deck. Without robots—Korie had traded them away too—everything had to be loaded manually. The fibrillation modules were heavy enough under the best of circumstances. Although the ship's gravity had been reduced to one-quarter gee in the cargo deck, the crates still had *mass*. Size and inertia had not been cancelled, and the job remained just as difficult as if they were operating under normal gravity. "What happened to the *805*?" Armstrong asked, turning back for another trip.

"Well the black box showed six hinks. Could have been twenty aboard. They were never sure."

"But how did they—"

"Plasma drivers fired immediately after docking," Gamma said bluntly. "Docking was the signal that set it off. One of the hinks they did take out was a bit that would have turned the singularity containment field off and then inverted the singularity. No Stardock left if that one had gotten through. What they missed was still pretty bad. The torches turned a corner of the station cherry-red and fried everyone on the spur. But better than eighty percent of Stardock L.R. survived. Almost half the personnel."

Armstrong considered that in uncomfortable silence.

The Quilla added softly, "The 'intimate contact' suffered by the *LS-805* consisted of a pair of Morthan infantry, captured and taken into custody after their transport craft was disabled. They escaped custody and fought a pitched seven-hour battle with the crew of the *LS-805*. Every trap they set was set during those seven hours before they died."

Armstrong looked around nervously. "And how many traps have we found now? Twenty-seven? How many more are there still undiscovered?"

Gamma rolled the last keg of Chief Leen's Southern Starshine into the cargo boat without comment. She met Armstrong's gaze directly. "The good news is that we're still alive."

"That's good news?"

She shrugged. "We had a Morthan ambassador aboard for twelve hours. If he'd wanted to destroy us, we'd have been dead by now."

Armstrong shook his head. "He wanted the high-cycle fluctuators."

"That was plan A."

"He had a plan B in case of his own death?"

"Stardock," Gamma confirmed. "Everyone knows it."

"Whew," Armstrong exhaled in amazement. "I can't imagine thinking that way. No wonder Korie's so crazed about detoxing the ship. It doesn't make sense to me. How can we ever be sure we found everything? We'd be better off scrapping her."

Gamma smiled, an expression as mysterious as the Mona Lisa's.

"You know and you can't say, right?"

Gamma smiled again.

"Yeah, well, I heard the same rumors you did," Armstrong said, trying to bluff the Quilla into talking. "They did try to scrap her, and Korie tried to resign, and the admiral's ulcer was acting up so bad she left the whole thing in limbo. We were all supposed to be transferred out and Korie squelched it. That really pisses me off. Y'know, I applied for a transfer three times."

"Yes, we know," Gamma said quietly. "We also know how you got transferred *to* this ship."

"I didn't know she was underage," Armstrong protested. "She told me she was eighteen. And how was I to know her mother was a vice admiral?"

Gamma didn't respond to that directly. "Perhaps you should learn to think about something else once in a while?"

Armstrong snorted contemptuously.

"Besides," added Gamma. "Korie may have done us all a favor."

"Huh?"

The Bridge Crew

Korie entered the Bridge through the upper access, crossed to the starboard ladder, grasped the rails with both hands and easily slid down the few steps to the Ops deck. Brik, Bach, Tor, Jonesy, Hodel, and Goldberg were waiting around the large elliptical table that held the holographic astrogation display.

"Good," said Korie, acknowledging their presence. "Thanks for being here." He glanced around the table, meeting each one's eyes. They were looking at him curiously. He was wearing his starsuit and carrying a foldable plastic helmet. "Um, just a readiness test," he said casually. "Nothing to worry about. Because of our recent experience with unauthorized EVAs, our security officer"—Korie nodded meaningfully to Brik—"has pointed out to me with justifiable concern that we are behind on our starsuit certifications. So I thought I'd wear mine for a few days to get it recertified, that's all. Please be seated." He sat. The others seated themselves too. One or two were frowning to themselves.

Korie continued without apparent notice. "Before we begin, I want to acknowledge something. We know that there's an imp aboard. We know that we can't really keep anything secret from it. We're not going to try. Isolated as we are, there's nothing it can do to affect any other ship. And because we're effectively dead in the water now, there's little it can do to affect us. So, in that regard, we've pretty much neutralized it. For the moment anyway."

He turned his clipboard on and turned to the first page. "What we need to do now is consider the larger context in which we're operating. It'll give us a better sense of direction. I want to stress that this is an informal conversation. What we're going to discuss here is strictly for our own benefit. There are some things I've been thinking about, and

I want the benefit of your input. This is not an admiralty-authorized backgrounder, but even so let's keep this discussion to ourselves. There's already enough idle speculation about the war."

They nodded their agreement and Korie began. "Thank you. HAR-LIE, are you with us?"

"Yes, Mr. Korie."

"Bring up the first display please." A graphic representation of the immediate neighborhood—one hundred light-years in each direction—shimmered into place. Korie pointed toward the upper part of the display where three red lines slanted down toward the center. "Those are the three fleets of the Morthan advance. We've code-named them *Dragon* for the center thrust, *Worm* for the one on the left, and *Tiger* for the one on the right. *Dragon* is commanded by Admiral Tanga. *Worm* was under the helm of Admiral Gellum, but intelligence says that he was killed in a duel and *Worm* is now apparently under the command by the ultra-militaristic Admiral Tofannor. *Tiger* is being led by someone named R'nida. No title given. We know nothing at all about R'nida, who he is, where he came from, nothing. The other two are ranking members of the Military High Command. R'nida is the joker in the deck. We have no background on him, we have no way of knowing what he might be thinking, or what are his theories of war. The War College currently believes that he may be someone else operating under a code name specifically to confuse us. But we really don't know for sure."

Korie held up a hand. "But that's not our concern right now. I just wanted you to know who the players in the game were. More important, I want you to look at this schematic of the Morthan advance." He pointed up at the representation again.

"First, there's the mauling at Marathon. The Silk Road Convoy gets hit by *Dragon* in the center. Within days after that, Last Chance and New Alabama are scourged by *Tiger* on the right; *scourged*, despite the fact that neither has significant military value. Almost simultaneously, *Worm*, on the left flank, bypasses Marano. *Dragon* in the center doesn't spend much time mopping up at Marathon, but advances to capture New Casa and scourge Verde and New Hope. Now *Worm* captures Vannebar and . . ." This one was hard to say, but Korie forced himself to continue. ". . . and scourges Shaleen."

There was a moment of uncomfortable silence on the Bridge. The others *knew*.

Korie ignored it. "If you backtrack the fleet movements, you see that *Tiger* and *Worm* both had to be enroute to their targets even before the mauling at Marathon. If *Dragon's* attack had failed, the others would probably have turned back as well. HARLIE says that an operation of this size must have taken at least ten years of preparation. The Silk Road was not a major trade route until just a few years ago, and it was never a military threat to the Morthans until last year, so clearly it was a target of opportunity in a much larger plan. All of this is fairly well known, I'm not revealing anything new here. But look, if you put the Marathon mauling into the context of the larger battle plan—"

He drew their attention back to the map, where the schematic of the attacks was playing itself out again and again and again. "It's obvious what the main thrust of the Morthan advance is. Direct to the center. The Admiralty believes that Taalamar is next. It's slightly to the left of *Worm's* advance, but it's a fairly significant target and at this point in their advance, it isn't impractical for the fleet to widen its front. I should probably note here that we've got every significant target in a twenty-light-year crescent ahead of the Morthan fleet frantically evacuating as many of their citizens as they can.

"But . . . if Taalamar is next," Korie asked, "why hasn't it been hit already? Look at the timeline. They could have hit Taalamar six weeks ago. If they were trying to drive as far into Allied space as possible, they *should* have hit Taalamar. Why didn't they? So, where are they now? And what are they doing?"

"They're preparing to hit Taalamar?" offered Jonesy. "That's what everyone says."

Korie sat back in his chair. "Yes, that's what everyone says, because that's the *logical* thing to believe." He looked to Jonesy. "And, in fact, it's such a *likely* thing to believe, that the best military strategists would move every available warship into the Taalamar theater to resist such an assault. If there's any place where we're going to stop the advance of the Morthan fleet, it's Taalamar. If we can cripple their left flank, they'll have to regroup. The logistics of maintaining communications between three advancing fleets is staggering. It limits the speed of your forward advance, because you have to send ships sideways between the armadas. If they had to regroup, it would cost them months. So Taalamar represents a very real opportunity for us.

"So, now I have to ask, if they know that every day they delay their assault on Taalamar, that's one more day we have to prepare, why didn't they hit Taalamar as soon as they were able?" He looked around the table. "Anyone?"

"Resupply," offered Goldberg. Nominally a quiet man, he only spoke when he had something significant to add. "They've advanced so fast, they've outrun their own supply lines."

"Their ships are semi-autonomous. Like ours. They don't need food or fuel," Korie responded. "So what supplies would they have run out of?"

"Missiles? Warheads?"

"Maybe. But the War College estimates they may have expended only one-third of their total capacity to date. And they've got to have tenders traveling with them. So, if it's not weapons, what else could it be?"

Goldberg shook his head and sat back. "Sorry, sir."

"Don't be sorry. It was a good suggestion. Wars are won or lost not on the battlefield, but on the supply line. Anyone else? Come on, people, *think*. If you were a Morthan, what would you do?"

It was such an obvious line that everybody turned to look at Brik, which was exactly what Korie had intended. He wanted Brik's input here. The huge security officer had not been able to fold his three-meter body into a human-sized chair; instead he perched uncomfortably on a stool. When he spoke, his voice rumbled in the lowest registers. "Well . . ." he began slowly. "If I were a human, I would start by assuming that whatever I was thinking about the Solidarity was *exactly* what the Solidarity *wanted* me to think."

Korie looked up sharply, as if Brik had just confirmed something for him. "Go on, Brik," he said quietly.

"Morthans never let anybody know anything about them. If you know anything about a Morthan, it's because he wants you to know. That's true on an individual level. It's even truer in battle. You've asked the right question," Brik said. "If the Solidarity wanted Taalamar, they would have gone for Taalamar. Therefore, Taalamar is not the target. Look at the map."

They did.

"What happens if the fleets all suddenly turn and sweep right?" Brik asked. "Nothing. They head out along the edge of the rift. What if they head left? Same thing, opposite direction. The rift is a natural barrier a hundred light-years across. To send so many ships that far, they intend to stay. To do that, they have to secure a permanent beach-head. That means advancing as far across as they can and destroying all human installations that represent possible staging areas for counterattack. So, yes, it doesn't make sense for them to *not* advance on Taalamar immediately unless there's something *else* they want more." Brik met Korie's eyes. His expression was grim. Both already knew the answer to the unasked question.

"Stardock," whispered Tor, a shocked expression on her face. "They want Stardock."

"Precisely," said Korie. "That's how we figure it too. Thank you,

Brik." He looked to the others. "They have to destroy Stardock. They have to do it before they can go on. They can't leave a major enemy stronghold functioning behind the wave front of their advance. They can't allow us to maintain such an access to their supply and communication lines. Stardock represents the last serious threat to their advance. That's why I believe the whole assault on Taalamar is a feint, to draw the fleet away from Stardock. The Solidarity is trying to 'lure the tiger out of the mountains.' "

"Huh?" asked Tor. The others looked puzzled too.

To Korie's surprise, it was Brik who explained the allusion. "Your executive officer is quoting one of the thirty-six stratagems of war, as postulated by the medieval Chinese military philosophers, premier among them the legendary Sun Tzu. The Chinese warlords were experts at the art of misdirection, and the study of their history can be very useful." He met their startled expressions. "In this particular allusion, the tiger cannot be captured or killed when he hides in the mountains. That's his home territory. You must lure him down onto the plains where he is vulnerable. The Morthan Solidarity has succeeded in doing just that. They have put the Allies into a position where we must spread our resources all the way from here to Taalamar. Both Stardock *and* our fleet are now vulnerable."

Korie nodded his agreement. "Very good, Mr. Brik. I had no idea you were so well-educated."

Brik gave Korie a foul look. "Then you've made a terrible mistake, Commander. You've underestimated a Morthan. So has the Admiralty."

"Yes," agreed Korie. "I see your point. Thanks for the object lesson."

"Wait a minute," said Tor. "The location of Stardock is so secret even *we* don't know where it is. Only HARLIE does. If a ship's integrity is compromised, that's the first information that gets wiped. Doesn't secrecy count for something?"

"In this case, no," Korie said. "You see—"

"Hey, wait a minute—" Bach broke in abruptly. "Excuse me, sir, for interrupting but if that's so, about HARLIE forgetting the location, then *how* did we get back here? Once Cinnabar was aboard, HARLIE should have forgotten that information."

"HARLIE?" Korie prompted.

"Thank you," the intelligence engine replied. "Do you remember the emergency detoxification necessary after the death of Cinnabar? That was to ensure that there were no tracking or transmitting devices aboard that would betray our location to long-range listeners. Once we achieved a critical confidence level, I was able to reconstruct my memory. I can't be any more specific than that about the process of critical reconstruction without compromising security. Let me just say that once a piece of data is put into personal memory escrow, it is irretrievable unless certain confidence conditions are met."

"What HARLIE isn't saying," Korie added, "is that had we not met that confidence level, he would have permanently forgotten the location and we would have had to proceed to a planetary base for recertification."

"Wait a minute," said Jonesy, visibly disturbed. He hadn't been following HARLIE's part of the discussion because he had been worrying at another part of the problem. Now he looked across the table to Korie. "Let's get back to the other thing. Are you saying there are three armadas searching for Stardock right now?"

"That's my estimation of the situation, yes," said Korie. "HARLIE agrees with me. Brik?"

The big Morthan nodded.

"Well, see here's the point," said Jonesy, looking from one to the other. "No disrespect intended, sirs, but if you and Brik and HARLIE can figure it out, why can't the Admiralty?"

"Well, first of all," said Korie, "we have the advantage of being paranoid extremists." He grinned. "Brik does by birth. I do by training. HARLIE dabbles in it as a matter of research into malevolent psychology."

Jonesy shook the joke away. "I mean it, sir. What's to say that you're right and the War College is wrong?"

"The War College isn't wrong," said Brik. "They're coming up with the very best answers they can, based on the information they have." And then he added, "Unfortunately, most of the information they have about the actions, motives, and location of the three Morthan armadas, is being supplied by the Morthan Solidarity. We have no way of knowing which ship movements are feints and which are real until *after* the fact."

Jonesy looked worried. "But Mr. Korie, are the brains at the War College even *aware* of the possibility that their information is wrong?"

"Of course they are," said Korie. "In fact, I'm sure that they're considering possibilities that even you and I would overlook. But as our security officer has pointed out, usually the only thing we know about a Morthan is what he wants us to know, and even when we factor that into the equation it still doesn't allow us to discredit the facts we already have. It only makes us crazier because we can't trust anything—which is also what the Solidarity intends. So we look and we observe and we study and we think and we extrapolate and we do our best to figure out what's really going on, all the time knowing that whatever false information the War College is getting, it is of such a consistent pattern that it will overwhelm the truth. So we try to prepare for the worst, all the time knowing that as long as we're still on the defensive, we're losing. Lieutenant Jones, have you ever had to do a report on Operation Overlord?"

"No, sir."

"I'll expect an oral presentation tomorrow at 1600 hours. HARLIE will give you the relevant information. Wear your starsuit. Here's the question I want you to answer. What lesson should we learn from Overlord?"

"Operation Overlord, yes sir."

"But getting back to your point, I'm certain that there's a lot of War College intelligence being applied to this very problem. There are probably people sitting around a table just like this one, looking at a display just like this one, and coming up with the same disturbing conclusions we are. And they are probably reporting it to their superiors. And their superiors are weighing all the evidence as carefully as they can . . . and they are making decisions based on all the information they have. They are probably finding it very hard to leave Taalamar undefended on the strength of a hunch by a handful of trained paranoids, while all the tangible evidence suggests a very real danger for the people of the Taalamar system. Given the same evidence, what would *you* do? You and I don't have anything at stake in this conversation. We're indulging ourselves in a thought experiment. If we're wrong, no lives are lost. But if the War College chooses wrong . . . millions, perhaps billions, of people will suffer. So, given the same evidence, what *would* you do?"

"I see your point," said Jonesy. "I'm sorry for wasting everyone's time." He shrank into himself, chastened. He looked like a beaten puppy.

Korie realized too late that he had made a serious mistake; he saw his own past in Jonesy's face; he remembered the first time he had been burned by a superior officer in a discussion. He couldn't do that to a young officer as committed as Valentine M. Jones. "No, Mr. Jones," he said. "Don't do what you're doing now. Don't withdraw like that. You've made a very important contribution to this discussion. We're considering *all* the possibilities here. The fact that we dismiss a possibility doesn't mean it wasn't worth considering. This is part of your training. All consideration leads to wisdom."

"Yes, sir. Thank you, sir." Jonesy smiled tentatively.

Korie nodded an acknowledgment. "Good man."

"Wait a minute," said Tor, interrupting. "If the Admiralty is aware of the situation, then they're not going to leave Stardock undefended, are they?"

"Mm," said Korie. "That's the *other* part of the problem. You have to understand how badly the admirals want to take a bite out of the Morthan fleet. Every available ship is being put into the target sphere. Even Stardock is cannibalizing its resources. They've even stripped its hyperstate installations for the Fleet. We're that desperate."

"Then they *are* leaving it undefended," Tor said.

Korie frowned; he didn't like admitting it. "Think about it. There's no real way to defend Stardock. She's a very large stationary target. Yes, she has guns, she has missiles, and she has ships patrolling around her; but it really doesn't matter how many guns, missiles, and ships we have; all the enemy needs is one more ship and one more missile than we can stop. Given that situation, and given the Solidarity's commitment to destroying her, maybe we have to sacrifice her to defend Taalamar. Maybe Taalamar will be where we make our stand. Maybe that's the Admiralty's plan all along. Maybe Stardock is *bait*. See, that's why I wanted to talk this over with all of you. There's something going on. If we can figure it out, we can *use* it. We can do something that makes a difference."

"Little us?" grinned Hodel. "And I thought *I* was the magician."

"Well, right now," said Korie, "we're operating without orders, so we have the freedom to go wherever we want and do whatever we think needs doing. Let's use that freedom."

Hodel smiled wryly. "You make it sound like we have a lot more freedom than we do. Without engines, we're just a big dead lump."

"So is Stardock," retorted Korie. "An even bigger deader lump."

"Wait. Wait a minute," said Tor. "I want to get back to the other thing about Stardock. Is she *really* being left undefended?"

"Yes and no," said Korie. "Stardock's only real defense is secrecy. If no one knows where she is, no one can attack. So we make Stardock hard to find, she gets moved regularly, the timing of the move and the location are always selected at random; usually within a five light-year radius. But if you're the enemy and you know that Stardock is likely to move every six weeks or so, then the most unlikely place to look is the place where it moved from. So—theoretically at least—Stardock is safest left where it is. For now, anyway."

"But that still doesn't resolve the real problem," Tor said. "The Solidarity is looking for an installation which is now essentially un-defended. And with every ship that they detect, they get a little bit more information about where Stardock is likely to be."

"That's right," said Korie. "But it's even worse than that. If the point of this whole operation is to find Stardock, then they aren't searching casually; they've most likely spread their ships out across the entire sphere of probability, and each one has a specific sector of space to sweep. Last night, I asked HARLIE to run some simulations. The amount of time it would take for three Morthan fleets to sweep the sphere of probability is just about the same length of time as has already passed since they should have attacked Taalamar. They're actually over-due here. Assume some logistical difficulties, the usual snafus, and we can assume that we have maybe a day, maybe a week." He looked around the table; all of the officers present were grim-faced.

Tor said it for all of them. "So the question is no longer *if*, is it? It's *when*. What happens *when* a Morthan scout finds the Stardock? Then what? Are there any defenses at all?"

"There are patrols," said Korie, calmly. "And we'll be joining them."

"We will?" Tor asked, surprised.

Korie nodded. "Remember, we have no orders. And I expect that state to continue for some time. The admiral is pretending we don't exist. So there's really nothing to keep us from lifting anchor and run-ning our own operations. We'll call it a shakedown cruise."

"Okay," said Tor, grimly, "let's game this out. Let's say we detect a scout ship and destroy it. Won't that tell the Morthan armada that something important is in the area of the missing scout?"

"Yes, it's definitely a lose-lose situation. You can't let the scout go and you can't destroy him. What do you do?"

Brik grunted for attention. They all looked to him. "The Morthan Solidarity knows how humans think. They do not expect humans to think like Morthans. Therefore, you have to do what a Morthan would do. Make him think what you want him to think."

Korie mulled that one over. "Good. Very good . . . in principle. But make him think what? And how? And with what resources?" He looked around the table. "That's the problem," said Korie.

Nobody replied. They were as stumped by the question as he. Korie stood up to leave. "Okay, that's it. We'll reconvene after dinner to consider possibilities. Please check your starsuits."

"Just tell me one thing," asked Tor abruptly. They all looked to her. "Was this meeting for our benefit? Or for the imp's?"

"Yes," grinned Korie. And then he left, leaving them frowning after him.

Sex

"Thank you for coming," said Brik.

Bach didn't answer. She glanced around Brik's cabin. There were two chairs in the room now, facing each other.

Brik gestured. "Would you like to sit?"

"Thank you," said Bach. She sat. The chair was not particularly comfortable. Brik had gotten it from the mess.

Brik sat opposite her. "May I offer you something? I have tea. Morthan tea."

"Yes, thank you."

Brik got up and busied himself for a bit, then returned with two ship's mugs, both steaming.

Bach took hers and held it in both hands. She brought it close to her face and inhaled deeply of its essence. "This is very good tea," she said.

"Thank you," said Brik. He sat down again, facing her. He sniffed his own tea, rolling the cup back and forth between his two huge hands.

Bach waited. Whatever Brik wanted, he would tell her in his own time.

"I think I owe you an apology," Brik said. "I said things that were thoughtless."

"No, you were honest. I should not have been offended by your honesty."

"Nevertheless, it was not my intention to offend."

"I know that."

"I don't know human mating rituals very well."

"No, you don't," she agreed.

"I've been reading in the ship's library."

Bach waited. She sniffed at her tea again.

"I still don't understand."

"I'm sorry," Bach said.

"I'm frustrated."

"I can imagine."

"No, I don't think you can. No, I'm sorry. I shouldn't say that. But even if you can understand, it doesn't change the frustration. There are all of these discussions of experiences that I have no referents for." His voice dropped to a whisper. "I don't like this," he admitted.

"You don't like what?"

"This. Everything."

"I still don't understand."

"I read the books. All of them. They made no sense to me. I don't like not knowing. I don't like knowing that there are things I cannot know." He fell silent.

Bach looked across the intervening light-years at the Morthan, her superior officer. Now, more than ever, she felt sorry for him. Sad and sorrowful. Such a mighty warrior, confessing weakness to an underling. What did he want from her?

Abruptly, she stiffened. Her eyes narrowed. "Brik?" she asked.

He straightened.

"Is this a performance?"

He didn't answer.

"There's something you want from me, isn't there?"

Still, he said nothing.

"I thought we promised each other honesty."

"Yes," he admitted.

"What?"

"You said you found me attractive. I don't understand that, but I recognize that you meant it as a compliment." He hesitated, then added, "I have become curious about . . . about sexuality."

"Why didn't you just say so?"

"The book said not to. The book said I should . . . *flirt*."

Bach laughed abruptly, then caught herself and tried to suppress it, waving it away with one hand while hiding the rest of the giggles behind the other. "I'm not laughing at you, Brik. I'm laughing at the book. Trust me. Don't flirt. Morthans should not flirt. Is the word *grotesque* in your vocabulary? No, please, don't be hurt, let me explain."

She put her mug of tea down on the deck and crossed to him. She went down on her knees before him. She took his mug and placed it on the deck, then took his big hands in her two tiny ones. She looked up—and up—into his eyes. "Listen to me. You are about strength.

Don't be afraid to be strong. That's what's attractive about you. Don't try to be anything else. I want you to be exactly who you are. All right?"

Brik stared down at her, not really comprehending. But he nodded anyway.

"Now, just tell me what you want."

Brik nodded slowly. He cleared his throat. He wet his lips. "I would like . . . I would like to know what it means to be *kissed*. Would you show me?"

Bach blinked. She nodded, both flattered and pleased. She stood up slowly, then took his hands as if to pull him to his feet. He rose— and rose. She looked up—and up. "Hmm," she said. She looked around. She went and pulled her chair over closer. As she stepped up onto it, Brik took her by the waist and lifted. She felt as if she were floating up onto the chair.

She turned to face him. She put her hands on his broad shoulders. She looked into his huge dark eyes. She studied his wide mouth. "Wet your lips," she said. "Pucker."

Brik did so.

"Close your eyes."

"Why?"

"It helps the experience. Now close your eyes."

Brik looked like he wanted to protest. Instead, he closed his eyes.

"Now don't do anything, just lean forward and press your lips against mine. Ready?" She leaned forward, so did he. She opened her eyes. His were already open. The two of them stared at each other, both too close to really focus. She pulled back. "I told you to close your eyes."

"I wanted to see what you were doing."

"Stop being paranoid and trust me."

"I'm a Morthan."

"Do you want to be kissed?" She didn't wait for his answer. "Now close your eyes and see what happens when you put all of your attention on what your lips are doing."

"All right," said Brik. He closed his eyes again.

Bach leaned forward and pressed her lips to his. She allowed herself to relax and feel the strength of his being. She parted her lips slightly so that his upper lip was between hers. Then she moved her mouth downward and took his lower lip between hers. Then she moved her mouth upward again, opening it slightly to his—

He pulled back abruptly. "What are you doing?"

"Kissing. What are you doing?"

He didn't answer. "Can we try again?"

Bach nodded, a little weakly. Brik steadied her with his hands on her waist. "That's good," she said. "Just keep doing that." She leaned forward again, leaning herself against him. His arms folded delicately around her. His lips were suddenly very . . . *very*.

After a moment, she pulled back and looked at him, her eyes wide and shining.

"Was that all right?" Brik asked. "I was practicing my focusing techniques . . ."

Bach's face was flushed. "Oh, my," she said. "Oh, my, yes. That was—that was quite all right. Yes."

"Can we do that again?" Brik asked, frowning in puzzlement.

Bach swallowed and caught her breath and pushed her hair back. She put her arms around his shoulders again and leaned forward . . .

Houston

"Commander?"

"What is it, HARLIE?"

"Incoming message from the *Houston*. Captain La Paz. She sounds angry. Will you take it now?"

Korie took a breath. "Yes," he said slowly. "I'll take it." He took another breath, then sat down in the captain's chair. Deliberately. He swiveled to face the reception wall. "Go ahead," he said.

There was a brief blare of *Dixie*—Korie frowned in momentary annoyance; did Captain La Paz ever stop to think how irritating that noise was?—and then the wall cleared as if a curtain had been drawn aside. Juanita La Paz sat opposite him.

"Juanita. It's good to see you."

"Don't you hand me that bullshit, mister. I know what you did."

Korie considered trying to bluff it out. It wasn't worth the energy. He shrugged. "You did what you had to. We did what we had to."

"You delayed delivery of those fibrillators, Jon. And when you did deliver them, they were filthy—and deliberately misaligned. Very cute," La Paz said. "You kept us from Taalamar."

"Good," said Korie.

"Good?" La Paz's eyebrows climbed up her forehead. *"Good?"*

"Yes," said Korie. "We saved your lives. You're not battle-ready, 'Nita. This has nothing to do with the *Star Wolf* anymore. And it's not about you and me either. It's about responsibility. Come on! I figured it out early that the *Wolf* wasn't going to get there. Once we started stripping her parts, we sent them where they would do the most good— to the ships we thought had the best chance. Look at your confidence rating. Would you really go into battle in that condition?"

"We don't have a choice, Jon. There's a war on—"

"We *do* have a choice, 'Nita. The war isn't going to be won today. We can choose our battles where we have a chance of making a difference."

"I thought we had a chance."

"I didn't."

"You overstepped your bounds, Jon. My ship is *my* responsibility."

"And my ship is mine," said Korie dispassionately. "And I can easily justify keeping those fibrillators. If we could have gotten the *Wolf* ready to fly, we'd have been in better shape than you for Taalamar."

"You don't have a command, Jon. *I do.*"

That one stung.

Korie took a breath. Control.

"Command or not, I still have a responsibility." He met her gaze.

For a moment, the two just studied each other. Neither broke the silence.

"You're a son of a bitch," she finally said. "You know that, don't you?"

Korie nodded. "I believe that's what qualifies me for this job."

A hint of a smile cracked La Paz's hard expression. "Yeah," she agreed. "That is the essential qualification."

Korie considered his next words carefully. "Have you and your officers . . . had any thoughts about the strategic situation?"

"What do you mean?"

"I mean, what if Taalamar is *not* the target?"

"If it's not Taalamar, it's Stardock."

"That's our estimation too."

"It's not too hard to figure out."

"Well, that's my point."

La Paz considered it. "Yes, there is that. We might very well have a much larger responsibility to stay exactly where we are. But do you really think one ship can make a difference?"

"Two," Korie corrected her.

"One and a half," retorted La Paz, but she was smiling.

"One and a half sounds about right," said Korie. "Seventy-five percent for us. Seventy-five percent for you."

"Eighty-five, sixty-five," smiled La Paz.

Korie lifted a hand in surrender. "Yes," he said. "I really do think we can make a difference."

"Do you have a plan?"

"Nothing I can discuss."

"Your imp has compromised you that badly?"

Korie reacted sharply to that. He hadn't realized she knew about the imp. How many others knew? Having an imp aboard your ship was like having a sexually transmitted disease. Something you didn't talk about. "That's just it. We don't know how badly we're compromised. We're assuming the worst."

"Well . . ." she admitted. "On those grounds alone, you can justify holding back the fibrillators as long as you did. Nevertheless, you owe me big time, mister. Big time."

"I know that. I didn't make the decision casually."

"I know that too."

"Thanks," Korie said.

She nodded. "Let's hope we're both wrong about Stardock. Otherwise you didn't do either of us any favors." She touched a button and her image winked out.

Followed by a quick phrase from *Dixie*.

Korie sagged in his chair unhappily.

Orgasm

"My God!" exclaimed Molly Williger, rising from her desk. "What happened to her?"

Brik didn't answer. He carried the convulsing Bach directly to an examination table. Her body jerked and thrashed; she nearly threw herself out of his arms. She made choking noises in her throat. Brik strapped her to the table with difficulty and began attaching scanning devices to her body, until Dr. Williger slapped his hands away. "I'll do the doctoring. What happened?"

"She . . . appears to be injured."

"I can see that!" snapped Williger, loosening Bach's jacket. "Just tell me what happened."

Brik looked dazed. "We were . . . she was . . . I didn't realize . . ."

Something in his tone. Williger looked up abruptly, narrowing her eyes. She came around the table and pushed Brik backward. "You. Over here. Lay down. Don't move." She pulled a scanning array down over him and switched it on. "Don't talk." She hurried back to Bach and pulled a similar scanning unit into position. "Hyperventilating." She noted. "Heart racing. Feverish. Eyes . . . dilated. Brain waves—what the hell?!! What were you two doing?" She pulled a buzzbox down and pressed the crown into place around Bach's forehead; she switched it on and waited. Bach's movements started to ease, but she still kept writhing on the table. Her grunts became animal moans, discordant and disturbing.

Williger came back to Brik and started shaking him. Hard. "What the hell did you do to her, you stupid sick bastard?!!"

Brik blinked. And blinked again. He looked drugged. He looked more alien than ever. He looked as if he'd been to the other side of the sky and only his body had come back. Williger looked from Brik to Bach and back again, confused, angry, upset. She studied the displays over each of their beds. Again, she could make no sense of it. "HAR-LIE?" she demanded.

HARLIE considered the situation for a moment. "Mr. Brik is in shock. Lieutenant Bach is . . . experiencing an intense flurry of nervous activity. She does not appear to be in pain. The spasms are orgasmic in nature, only far more intense."

"Orgasmic?"

"Yes," HARLIE confirmed.

Williger turned and stared at Bach. Amazed. Then she turned and stared even harder at Brik. Horrified. She looked back to Bach. "Is she drugged?"

"I find no evidence of it."

Williger shook her head in disbelief. "All right, let's see if we can bring her down." She turned to the medical cabinet and pulled out a spray-syringe. She checked its settings and held it up against Bach's arm. There was a soft hiss. Williger studied the overhead displays and watched as the jiggling lines began to ease. "All right," she said at last. "That'll do it."

She turned to Brik. She rubbed her forehead and studied his charts. She turned to the medicine chest and surveyed its contents. No. Nothing useful there. Not for this. She turned back to Brik and thought for a moment. "Oh, the hell with it," she said. And slugged him in the solar plexus as hard as she could. Brik jerked in reaction, grunting softly, but that was his only reaction.

Molly Williger returned to her desk, sat down, and . . . started to giggle. "If I hadn't seen it, I wouldn't have believed it." She sighed. "I can't even write this up. Nobody'll believe it."

She got up from her desk, crossed to a medical supply cabinet, unlocked it and took out a bottle. It was halfway filled with a honey-colored liquid. She then took a small test tube and carefully measured 10cc of amber fluid into it. Still holding the test tube, she recapped the bottle and returned it to the cabinet, and relocked it. She turned around and faced both Brik and Bach on their respective medical tables; she raised the test tube in a toast to them, then downed its contents in a single startling swallow. Then she tossed the test tube into a sink, where it clattered unbroken.

She returned to her desk, sat down again, put her head in her hands, and watched Bach for a bit. The lieutenant's moans were finally easing. Her body movements were already more relaxed. Her face was flushed.

Molly Williger waited a bit more, then opened her bottom drawer and took out two knitting needles and a ball of yarn.

Half a sleeve later, Brik sat up at his table. He looked around, almost as if he didn't know where he was.

Williger put her knitting aside. "How do you feel?"

"I don't know," said Brik. "I've never felt like this before."

"What were you two trying to do?"

"The lieutenant was showing me some . . . moves."

"They must have been some moves," Williger said.

Brik didn't acknowledge it. "Will she live?" he asked.

"Probably. But you and I have to have a talk. A very important talk . . ."

Chess II

By the end of the third day, the crew of the *Star Wolf* had installed over two hundred separate traps, chess sets, and cameras. Some of the camera buttons were in the open. Some were concealed. Some were real, some were dummies. With Korie's approval, Gatineau's eventual target was the installation of a thousand separate traps.

Some of the traps were so ridiculous they could have only been designed by Hodel. One was a stuffed bird with a salt-shaker hanging over it. If a piece on the board was moved, the salt-shaker dropped grains of salt on the bird's tail. Another was a box with a small hole, and a nut just inside the hole. That one was Gatineau's. Other traps were more sophisticated; they were genuine attempts to capture the imp.

Most of the serious ones had been designed by Brik. One trap had the chessboard in the center of a high-gravity panel, triggered to generate a local field of 12 gees if any pieces on the chessboard were moved; the imp would be pinned to the floor by its own weight. Another trap was engineered to shoot anesthetic and transmitting darts into the imp. A third would have sealed off the entire compartment. A fourth was set to deliver a paralyzing electrical shock. A fifth . . . etc. There were others that were identical to these, but not armed, and still more that *looked* identical, but did nothing at all. One trap was a maze, with the chessboard at the center. One trap was nothing more than a lever to pull beside the chessboard and a net hanging overhead. The lever was not connected to the net. One trap was a net with no lever. One trap was a lever with no net.

By the end of the third day, the imp had initiated one hundred and thirty-three separate chess games. It had made sixty-seven different obscene gestures or grotesque faces at the cameras. It had dismantled seven traps. It had ignored twenty-three traps. Of the twenty-three it ignored, sixteen had rude graffiti about Morthans scrawled on them.

HARLIE analyzed the progress of the separate games and ventured an opinion that the imp's processing abilities were being fully utilized. Increasing the number of traps would put it into a condition of early stress.

Concurrent with the trapping effort, Korie had begun sending security teams around the ship, sealing and searching one sector at a time. One team was working its way aftward, securing each and every compartment in a specific hull-section before moving onto the next. A second team followed in their wake, re-securing the same compartments. A third team moved around the ship checking and sealing compartments seemingly at random. HARLIE generated their assignments in realtime, so that not even the team knew what compartment they were going to be securing until they got there. Some compartments were secured six times in a six hour period. Others were never checked at all.

Neither Korie nor Brik nor Leen expected the teams to succeed against the imp, but they did expect that all the activity would seriously curtail the imp's freedom to move about the starship. It was HARLIE's opinion that the increasing pressure of the pursuit was affecting the imp's stress levels. On some of the videos, the imp was demonstrating signs of agitation and impatience.

Korie shrugged when he saw. "I don't think we should believe it. Not yet." He was leaning on the forward rail of the Bridge, studying the main screen. Tor and Hodel were on duty on the Ops deck. Brik and Leen had both come forward for this conference. Straightening to face them, Korie said, "I don't think the imp has forgotten why it's here. Someone left a plate of feces on the table of the officers' wardroom this morning. That's a pretty clear message, don't you think?"

Brik didn't comment. Tor made a face. Leen looked sour.

"Can't blame it," grinned Hodel. "I've sometimes thought the same thing myself."

Korie ignored the jibe. "Dr. Williger is analyzing the material. Let's find out what it's eating. Maybe we can slip something into its food or water . . . ?"

"And maybe it'll slip something into ours," said Brik. "Don't give it ideas. So far, it's been playing fair. If you start playing dirty. . . ."

"Point well taken." After a moment, he asked, "Playing *fair*?"

Brik nodded. "There are rules for combat."

Korie's eyebrows went up. "Morthan rules?"

"Yes. Morthan rules."

"Oh really? What's the first rule of Morthan combat?"

" 'Win,' " said Brik.

"Yes, of course. Silly me. And what's rule number two?"

" 'See Rule Number One.' "

"Right. Why am I not surprised?" Korie shook his head in amused disbelief. "All right, at least we're making progress. We've seized some initiative in the situation. How many problems do we have to give it before it overloads and makes a mistake? That's the real question." Korie looked to Brik, to Leen. Both looked back at him blankly. "Don't worry," he added. "It was only a rhetorical question. We'll get the answer empirically." He shook his head in quiet exasperation, a reaction to the size of the task that still lay ahead.

HARLIE interrupted then. "Mr. Korie?"

"Yes, HARLIE?"

"We have received a signal."

"Yes?"

"We must return to Stardock immediately. For decontamination."

"They can't be serious!" Korie said.

"I'm sorry, sir. That's the message."

Brik snorted. His opinion was written on his face.

Leen scowled angrily. He turned away, leaned on a console for a moment, and muttered something as nasty as it was unintelligible. The workstation's displays flickered in horror and then went out. He turned around abruptly. "It's a hoax. The imp is doing it."

Korie shook his head. "HARLIEs don't lie. They *can't*." To HARLIE, he said, "What's your confidence rating?"

"Eighty-three and holding," HARLIE replied.

Korie looked blandly to Leen, as if to say, "You see?"

Leen shook his head grimly. "We can't do it. We don't dare."

"He's right," said Brik.

"I know it. HARLIE, send this signal." Korie selected his words carefully. "We can't do it. We have a . . . a security problem."

"They are aware of the problem, sir." HARLIE phrased his answer just as precisely. "There may be a solution."

"They know we have an imp?"

"The message is quite clear."

"I'll look at it in my cabin."

"Yes, sir."

Korie and Leen and Brik exchanged worried glances. Tor and Hodel, too.

"I believe," said Brik coldly, "that the issue is being forced."

"What are you going to do?" demanded Leen.

"I can't disobey the admiral, can I?" said Korie. He hoped he'd said it convincingly. There were still no insignia on his collar.

"But you can't risk letting that thing get to Stardock!" Tor insisted. "You *can't* do this. You simply can't!"

"What do you want me to do?" Korie snapped back angrily. "Exorcise it? Hodel—how much to exorcise a Morthan demon?"

"Uh—sorry, boss. I'm out of the exorcism business. For good. I saw what happened last time."

Korie turned back to Tor. "Do you have a *better* idea? If so, I want to hear it!"

Tor blanched at his anger. She swallowed hard and shook her head. "I just—I'm sorry."

"I know what's at stake, goddammit." And then he added, in a quieter tone, "I'm sorry I yelled at you, Tor. We're all under a lot of pressure here."

"Yes, sir," she said sullenly.

Korie turned to Brik. "Let's put the entire crew on red drill. Four hours on, four hours off. Everybody who isn't in an essential job is on a search team. Everybody puts out traps everywhere. See to it, Brik. You too, Chief. Tor?"

"Yes, Mr. Korie?"

"Set a course. Your very *best* course. A. Very. Careful. *Slow*. Course. Take all the time you need setting it up. Check you work carefully. Do you understand? And don't initiate anything until I see it."

"I understand." She nodded her assent.

Korie ran both hands through his hair, a sign of exhaustion. He rubbed his eyes wearily. He looked around at the others. "Well, we're in for it now."

Dwarf Point

Korie entered the Bridge of the *Star Wolf*. He was still wearing his starsuit; his collapsible helmet was hanging from his utility belt, but he was carrying a metal helmet as well. He hung the helmet on the captain's chair and stepped to the forward railing. He put his hands on the railing and then put his weight on his hands. He studied the forward screen without seeing it. It showed stars. Nothing else.

After a moment, Korie straightened. Whatever thoughts had passed through his mind, they weren't apparent on his face. "Commander Tor?" he asked. "What's our position?"

"Holding at Dwarf Point One." Tor was wearing a starsuit too.

"Thank you." Korie spoke to the air, "Chief?"

The chief was in the engine room. His voice was approximately one meter to Korie's right. "CINTI," he said. "It's all CINTI."

Korie smiled. CINTI was an acronym. *Cleanliness Is Next To Impossible.*

"Thank you," said Korie, allowing himself the slightest smile. It didn't matter anymore. Either they had succeeded. Or they had not. They would find out soon enough. He glanced down to the Ops deck. "Quilla Delta? Are you ready?"

A starsuited figure turned around. "Yes, Mr. Korie. We are."

"Then please come up here to the Bridge."

Quilla Delta came up the steps to the Bridge and took a position to the rear of Korie and Brik. She waited expectantly.

"All right," Korie said, his voice becoming somehow larger. "*Now hear this.*" HARLIE would relay his words to every crewmember aboard the ship: "This is an order. We are about to initiate our final docking maneuver. All hands who are not yet wearing starsuits must put on starsuits immediately. There will be no exceptions." He glanced meaningfully across the Bridge to Brik, who stared dispassionately back. Brik's starsuit was stretched across his massive frame.

Both Korie and Brik picked up their helmets at the same time. Still watching each other, both individuals pulled their helmets down over their heads. They locked them into place. Korie turned around so Brik could check his seals. Brik did likewise. When he finished, Korie turned and surveyed the Bridge. Hodel, Jonesy, Tor, Goldberg—all were suited.

"Chief?" Korie asked.

"Just a moment. Waiting for Gatineau and Stolchak . . . got it. It's green. The entire crew is ready for vacuum."

"Thank you, Mr. Leen. How long did it take?"

"About fifteen seconds."

Korie allowed himself another smile. Yes, it can be done in fifteen seconds, if you make starsuits the uniform of the day. "HARLIE."

"Yes, Mr. Korie?"

"I apologize in advance for any discomfort we are about to cause you."

"No apologies are necessary, Mr. Korie. I understand the need."

"I appreciate that." Korie nodded to Brik. Brik looked grim. He stepped down from the Bridge to the Ops deck, from there, he ducked under the Bridge to the Ops bay, and from there—

"He's really going to do it?" asked Tor.

Korie nodded.

They waited silently. The screen continued to show stars.

After a moment, Brik returned. "It's done," he said.

"HARLIE?" Korie asked.

There was no answer. The silence was *eerie*.

Korie reached into his starsuit equipment pocket and pulled out a set of memory clips. He handed them to Tor. "Here are the programs you'll need for docking . . . and any other eventuality. HARLIE has been disconnected. Completely. You have total control of the vessel from your console. The Bridge has had six consecutive detox operations without turning up any bugs. This Bridge has never been unmanned. Your workstation is the most secure place on the ship."

"Thank you," said Tor, taking the clips. She handed them to Jonesy who laid them out carefully across the rack on the top of the display. He sorted them by color.

"Now hear this," Korie spoke to the crew again. "I know it's been a difficult time. I know it's hard living and working in a starsuit round the clock. I know it's hard *sleeping* in a starsuit. I've been just as un-

comfortable as all of you. I appreciate how well you've kept your spirits up. I'm very proud of you. We've made it to the final lap. This is the hardest part, so please don't let your guard down.

"We are now in our final approach for docking. We have secured every part of the vessel. We have set out more than seven hundred separate traps. HARLIE has won more than four hundred chess games—four hundred and two, to be exact. We have been holding at condition yellow for three hours. The imp has not been seen by any camera for six and a half hours. I must tell you that of the three thousand camera buttons we set out, only four hundred and twelve remain operational and those are in noncritical locations. The imp is still somewhere on board and it is still active and it is still taking down cameras. We must assume that it could be anywhere by now. We must assume that it has a plan that it will implement immediately upon docking.

"Each of you has been given sealed *handwritten* orders. You are authorized to open your orders now and read them. You will immediately carry out your orders." Korie hesitated, then . . . despite his own feelings . . . he added, "May God be with us all."

He sat down in his chair and fastened his safety harness. He waited while Tor and Jonesy opened their orders. They, too, sat down and secured themselves in place. Korie glanced over to Brik, questioningly. Brik scowled, then he, too, secured himself.

First, the lights went out. Then the consoles went out.

Even the screens went dead.

The forward screen simply disappeared.

They hung for a moment in darkness and silence.

The first light came from the direction of Tor's console. She had switched on her suitlight. She continued reading her sealed orders. Others around the Bridge began illuminating themselves too. Several finished their orders, pocketed them, and switched their lights off again.

Korie switched on his suit radio. "Section heads. Report?"

"Leen. Yellow."

"Tor. Blue."

"Hodel. Purple."

"Stolchak. Orange."

"Hall. Black."

"Brik. Brown."

"Williger. Magenta."

"Goldberg. White."

"Green. Green."

Korie grinned at that last. Communications officer, Darian Green.

"All right," said Korie. "Code Sleepy. Repeat. Code Sleepy. Go." He waited. He looked to Brik. "This had better work."

"And if it doesn't?"

"Well, then my successor will have to worry about it."

"If it doesn't work, you're not going to have a successor."

"There is that, yes." Korie switched on his helmet lamp and pulled a thick envelope out of his equipment bag. He opened the envelope and took out the first page. He held it up before his faceplate so he could read it as he listened.

Chief Leen came back online first. "Gully Foyle is my name . . ."

Korie checked the list of code phrases in front of him. *The engine room is offline. We're powered down and under manual control. All autonomic nervous functions are disconnected.*

Stolchak checked in next: "Call me Ishmael."

Again Korie referred to his list. *The farms are secured.*

Hall: "It was the best of times, the worst of times." *The cargo bays are secured.*

Williger: "Once upon a time, there was a Martian named Valentine Michael Smith." *Med bay.*

Goldberg: "Sredni Vashtar went forth. His thoughts were red thoughts, and his teeth were white." *All weapon systems controlled through the ship's autonomic nervous system have been physically disconnected. Certain independent manually operated weapon systems remain operable only to those who have the appropriate key.*

Hodel: "It was a bright cold day in April, and the clocks were striking thirteen." *All traps are armed.*

Green: "I have no mouth and I must scream." *All communications systems have been physically disconnected. Except the portable unit that Lieutenant Green wore strapped to his chest.*

Tor: "Alice was beginning to get very tired of sitting by her sister." *All navigation systems have been taken offline.*

Korie looked to Brik questioningly.

" 'Twas brillig, and the slithy toves did gyre and gimble in the wabe . . ." *Internal security systems have been disconnected. They cannot be used against us.*

It was a one-time code, never to be used again. If the imp was listening in, it would have no way of knowing what was really being said.

"The imp has got to be getting a little anxious about now, don't you think?"

"Morthans don't get anxious," said Brik. "I doubt that the imp has been programmed for that particular emotional reaction."

"Right," said Korie. "Thanks for reminding me." He wondered what the imp used *instead* of anxiety. "*Now hear this*," he said. "Code Sneezy. Code Sneezy."

He couldn't feel what was happening, but he could imagine it. All over the ship, crew members were manually dogging every hatch, then locking each one shut with a security clamp. Every self-contained module aboard the ship was now isolated from every other self-contained module. Once again, he waited for crewmembers to report in.

Again, Leen was first. Korie studied the paper in front of him, waiting for the appropriate code phrases.

"There was an old man from Nantucket, who kept all his cash in a bucket . . ."

"There was a young lady of Riga, who smiled as she rode on a tiger . . ."

"There was a young plumber of Leigh, was plumbing a maid by the sea . . ."

"There was a young man of Bengal, who went to a masquerade ball . . ."

"A marvelous bird is the pelican, whose beak can hold more than his belican . . ."

"There was a young man from Belgrave, who kept a dead whore in a cave . . ."

"There was a young lady named Bright, whose speed was much faster than light . . ."

The recital went on for several moments. Korie checked off each code phrase. When he finished, he looked to Brik.

Brik looked very unhappy. "A lesbian who lived in Khartoum, invited a queer to her room . . ."

Korie gave Brik a nod of acknowledgment. Brik curled his upper lip just enough to reveal his incisors.

"*Now hear this*. Code Bashful. Code Bashful."

This time the wait was longer. Korie looked to his right. Brik had opened a floor panel and was manually operating a set of valves and handles. Korie felt his starsuit slowly hardening around him . . .

Once more, the signals came in:

"Pawn to Queen Two."

"Knight to King's Bishop Three."

"Wizard to Rook Four."

"Hobbit to Volcano Six."

"Troll to Queen's Knight Three-Sub-Three."

"Dragon to Dragon Four Probability Fifty-Five and King's Bishop Two Probability Forty-Five."

Korie looked to Brik.

Brik said, "Colonel Mustard to the Conservatory with the Candlestick."

The ship is now open to space. Unless the imp has a starsuit, it's immobile. From this moment on, we're dealing only with preinstalled booby traps. I hope.

Korie looked to Brik. "Reassure me again. Can the imp breathe vacuum?"

"I believe it can endure prolonged periods of vacuum. I do not believe it can function in it."

Korie nodded.

"Now hear this. Code Grumpy. Code Grumpy."

"Grandpa Blue Jacket."

"Betty Pancake."

"Sweet Wilma Bumble."

"Martha Moose."

"Christmas Billy."

"Doorway Denny."

Korie looked to Brik.

Brik sighed inaudibly and said, "Bertha Six-Pack."

Korie grinned. He didn't even bother to refer to his code sheet. These codes were decoys. Phonies. They meant nothing at all. Throughout the ship, crew members were doing meaningless activities; opening and closing compartments, taking things out, rearranging them, putting them away in new compartments. There was absolutely no strategic value at all to any of the exercises. If the imp was listening and monitoring, it would have to be going crazy trying to figure out what was happening.

At least that was the theory.

Korie waited a moment, and said, "Code Happy. Code Happy."

Korie removed the transceiver module from his starsuit harness and handed it to Brik. The big Morthan moved quickly around the Ops deck collecting transceiver modules from the entire crew. He put them into a shielded lockbox, closed it, armed it, and pressed a red panel on its lid. The transceivers inside would shortly be junk.

Korie took a communication cable out of his equipment case and plugged one end of it into the communication jack of his starsuit; the other end, he handed to Quilla Delta who plugged it into her starsuit. She accepted a similar plug from Brik and plugged that in too. As Korie watched, the rest of the crew on the Ops deck were similarly creating themselves as a local area network. All over the ship, the process would be repeated, with each cluster of crew members cabled directly or indirectly to one of the Quillas. The Quillas linked all the separate networks.

If they had succeeded, they now had a secure communications network. The optical cables were sending coded signals only. The codes were updating themselves one thousand times a second. Even if the imp could monitor the signals, it still wouldn't be able to decode them on the fly. And even if it could link into one network, it still wouldn't be able to tell what any other network was doing. The Quillas' communication channels were holographic and therefore unreadable by anyone not part of a Quilla cluster.

Korie turned to Quilla Delta. "Status?"

"We are Happy," the Quilla reported. "We are very Happy."

"Good," Korie nodded. "Very good. We are now the first manually operated ship in the history of the Fleet."

"A singular honor, to be sure," Brik remarked.

"Whatever works," Korie replied grimly. To the Quilla, he said, "Send this message. Code Doc. Code Doc."

"Message sent and acknowledged," said the Quilla.

Korie sat down in the captain's chair. Brik sat down in the chair beside him. The Quilla took the third seat behind the two of them. Korie secured his safety harness. The others did likewise. Across the Ops deck, the Bridge crew were also securing themselves. Jonesy was opening the overhead access of the Bridge and climbing up toward the observation bubble; he was trailing a long communications cable behind him. This was the *crucial* part of the operation. Hodel was standing on the hull at the aft of the vessel, there to provide the only guidance cues they would have for the docking maneuver. They needed to establish a secure communications link with him; it would be critical for manual docking.

Jonesy reported abruptly, "We can't make the optical connection through the observatory port. The glass has been frosted with some kind of . . . I don't know, but it's opaque."

Korie and Brik exchange a glance. The imp? Yes.

"All right," said Korie. "Use the external emergency net." The external emergency network was installed on the hull of the ship for exactly this kind of situation. Self-powered, separate from the rest of the ship, it provided an auxiliary channel for operations.

"Sir?" Jonesy asked, concerned. "Are you sure?"

"We have no choice." He added, "Chief Leen has detoxed the network seven times since the imp was detected. The most recent decontam was seven hours ago. Let's trust it."

"Okay," said Jonesy uncertainly. He disappeared into the overhead again.

Korie looked to Brik and held up his hands with his fingers crossed. Brik gave him *that* look. Korie shrugged.

"We have completed Doc," said Delta, abruptly. Jonesy came floating back down into the Ops deck.

"Thank you," said Korie. "Code Dopey. Code Dopey."

A moment more, and all gravity in the starship went off. It did not go off gradually, it simply disappeared. One moment Korie was sitting in his command chair. The next instant, he was falling, and the moment after that he was relaxing into the familiar drift of zero-gee. *So far, so good.*

"All right," Korie said. "Hi, ho. Hi, ho. It's off to work we go." He waited until the command had been sent, and then said, "Commander Tor. She's all yours. Take us in."

Docking

Astrogator Cygnus Tor turned to her console. It was dead. She bent down to the floor and brought up a jury-rigged board, which she plugged directly into her starsuit. She studied its tiny display. There were only rudimentary readouts connected; Hodel wore three positional scanners, no camera. If the scanners failed, he would talk the ship into the docking harness.

Tor's job was further complicated by the fact that the usual docking thrusters had been disconnected from the ship's control network, along with all of the other units of the drive system. She was working with handmade cold-firing rockets, installed by Chief Leen's machine shop crew. Her control of the vessel was nowhere near as accurate as she would have had with a more precise propulsion system.

Plus, she was working without an onboard intelligence engine. She had none of the usual instrumentation and automatic guidance circuitry. Her approach would be a process of correction and counter-correction all the way in. In other words, she was "parking by ear," aiming at the docking harness and listening for the crunch.

Korie watched her from the Bridge. Her small display showed a red dot inside a green circle. Her job was to keep it centered. She worked in a steady rhythm. First she checked the schematic display on her board, then the approach program on her clipboard. Then she either waited or made an adjustment. She kept her burns short and soft. Then she checked her displays again. She waited and watched. Occasionally, she would report, "Confidence is high." Or, "In the channel."

Korie licked his lips. They were dry. His throat was dry. He took a sip of water and waited.

"One minute," reported Tor. A lifetime later, she said, "Thirty seconds."

Somewhere they had crossed an invisible line. It was too late to abort. Whatever was going to happen when they docked was now inevitable. Korie had often brooded about this invisible "point of inevitability." It bothered him. After studying all of the lessons of the *zyne*, about possibility being the author of choice, and choice being necessary for freedom, the moment when choice actually disappeared from the situation unnerved him more than ever now. It was a loss of control. All he could do now was ride it in and hope he hadn't missed anything—

"Fifteen seconds. . . . Ten . . . Five . . ."

Something behind him went quietly *clunk*. He could feel it locking into place. They were *docked.*

"Hello, Dolly," Korie whispered to himself.

Nothing happened.

He waited.

They all waited.

He looked to Brik. Brik looked back. Expressionless.

Tor switched off her board. She replaced it on the deck. She swiveled around in her chair. She gave Korie a thumbs-up sign and a grin.

Korie wished he could rub his nose. He didn't like this. It was *too* quiet. He tapped the arm of his chair nervously. *How long do we have to wait?*

He shook his head. This wasn't good. Something—*anything*—should have happened. Nothing.

He wasn't so arrogant as to believe they had so thoroughly confused the imp that it had been unable to sabotage the docking. No. The imp had known they were going to try docking manually. It had opaqued the observation port, forcing them to use the external emergency net. Therefore, the net was compromised. Therefore, something in that net was waiting for the docking confirmation. Therefore . . . Therefore. Therefore. Korie's mind chased the thought around. What had he missed? What *else* was connected to the external emergency net? Had he made a fatal error here? Had they detoxed the external network *too well*?

And then, Hodel spoke. "All right, there it is. A coded signal. It's using the entire ship as a broadcast antenna. Wait a minute, I'm tracking it. Wait a minute . . ." Hodel was on the hull of the ship with a hand-built Systems Analysis board. On the first six detox operations, Leen's crew had routinely replaced the signal monitors at every node of the network. It was easier to replace them than to test them in place.

On the last detox, the crew had replaced the signal monitors again . . . but these latest units were reporting directly to Hodel's board. Hodel was silent a moment more, then he said angrily, "Albert Flaming Einstein on Heisenberg's cross! I'll be skeltered!"

Korie grabbed his code list. Albert Einstein—the signal scrubbers! The signal was entering the network through the aft signal scrubbers! All over the ship now, individual detox crews would be leaping toward their assigned targets; but one crew knew that they were handling a live bomb. Candleman and Hatano. If everything was going according to plan, some of the crews were even detaching themselves from their local area networks. The imp would have no way of knowing where they were.

Korie studied his watch. There would have been no way to drill this operation. Still, they had projected less than five minutes of actual broadcast time before the transmitter was found and disabled. The seconds ticked voraciously into the past. Korie imagined an expanding sphere of radio noise. It didn't matter what the signal said. Its presence was beacon enough. How far would it travel before it was intercepted by a Morthan probe? Three light days? Six? Twelve? How big was the time window? How long would it scream, *"Here! Over here! Stardock! Here it is!"*

Quilla Delta said quietly, "Be vewy vewy quiet. We're hunting wabbit."

Korie looked at his watch. Three minutes. "Double bonus for Candleman and Hatano," he said without thinking. He glanced at the code sheet. The transmitter had been located, a destruction button had been placed on the interconnect, and the crew was now backing out to a safe distance.

There was a faint thump transmitted through the keel of the ship. "It is now duck season," said the Quilla.

Korie grunted. The destruct button had been triggered. The connection to the net had been broken. The transmitter had then exploded violently. Exactly as they had expected it to.

"Hodel?" he asked.

"Signal is still going out," Hodel reported grimly. "It's singing like a flaming princess."

Flaming princess. Beta singularity harness. Damn. They were going to lose part of the singularity cage. Leen was prepared for it, but still—

Quilla Delta reported, "Ye Gods and little fishes."

Korie looked to his watch. Leen had trained his crew well.

Another thump. "Bouillabaise," said Quilla Delta.

"Hodel?"

"Loud and clear. This is not my idea of a good time!"

Good time. The starboat harness. Cappy and MacHeath would be up there by now. *Thump.*

"Are we having fun yet?" asked Quilla Delta.

"Hodel?"

"What are you guys doing?" he replied. "Singing along with it? *'We all live in a yellow submarine!'*" Engine room. Singularity harness Gamma. Dammit. *Thump.* Quilla Delta annotated, "She came in through the bathroom window." Korie wondered if Leen was already checking the Alpha harness.

The imp had never been spotted in the engine room. It couldn't have had access to the harnesses. Of course not, there was always a crew on watch around the singularity containment. The imp would have had to have had access to the replacement parts. Which was *exactly* what Korie had hoped. "Helter skelter," he said to the Quilla.

"We copy," she replied.

"Hodel?"

"I'm an old man, I'm gonna die soon, I have a right to be cranky."

Bingo! The engine room again! They were getting closer. The imp had been frustrated by their security measures. It had retreated to the main module of the ship and had concentrated all of its operations there. Exactly as they had guessed. *Thump.* Another transmitter explosion. He was afraid to think how bad the damage was going to be. Quilla Delta reported, "Isn't it amazing how time flies when you're having fun?"

Korie put his finger on the next phrase on the code sheet. Sure enough, Hodel reported, "Yngvi is a louse." And a little bit after that, "Ward, I'm worried about the Beaver." Korie was actually starting to feel pride in the speed of the Black Hole Gang when Hodel said, "I tawt I taw a putty-tat . . ."

Thump. Thump. Thump.

And finally . . . Hodel reported with a sigh, "What we have here is a failure to communicate." And in the clear, he added, "The system is silent!"

Korie was too pleased to be annoyed with the breach.

"It's over . . . ?" asked Tor.

"Not yet," said Brik.

"Stand by," said Korie, in the clear. Waiting. "Helter Skelter?" he asked the Quilla. She shook her head. Nothing yet.

Korie realized his whole body had gone tense and rigid. He was cramped forward. He forced himself to straighten out, leaning back in his chair. He took a deep breath. They weren't half done yet. He had to pace himself.

"Mister Korie?"

He opened his eyes. It was Jonesy.

"What do all these code phrases mean?"

"I don't know. I don't think they mean anything at all. HARLIE generated over ten thousand one-time code pads. They're probably all just nonsense phrases."

"Oh," said Jonesy. He turned back to his work station.

And then, abruptly—Quilla Delta spoke. "Elvis has left the building," she said.

That's when the rest of the traps went off.

Disaster

He couldn't hear it. He felt it.

He had his hand on the railing, when he felt a sudden sharp vibration. He recognized it, but—filtered through the soundlessness of space, filtered through the hull of the ship—it took him a moment. Then he realized. *Oh my God, the missiles—!!*

There came two more thumps, and then a fourth and final one. He was already pulling a new transceiver pack out of his gear belt. These had been specially coded. They didn't use any single channel, but bounced around random channels several thousand times a second.

Korie caught Quilla Delta's eye and held up the transceiver so she could see it, then clipped it into his suit harness. "*Status reports. Now!*" he shouted, not waiting to hear who was online. He waited impatiently. "Come on, you bloody bastards. Come on. Status reports. Now! Leen?"

"All right, it's like we figured. The damn missiles have launched themselves. The trigger was the docking confirmation—"

"Where are they now? Goldberg?"

"They're drifting. They launched, but didn't fire. No hyperstate plugs. We gave those to the *Houston* with the warheads. We've got good tracks on all the birds. They're drifting, they won't go far. We're sending out the retriever teams."

"What about the other four?"

"As near as we can tell, they're moribund. We're checking now."

"Well, be careful. No telling what else the imp has done. Hodel?"

"Sir?"

"How soon can we bring HARLIE back online?"

"Six hours."

"No good. Okay, power up the autonomics, run the idiot code.

Deflex, disrupt, skelter, and remix. Viricide everything. You know the drill."

Goldberg again. "Sir? We've got disruptor activity."

"I thought we pulled those out of the circuit."

"Yes, sir. We did. We're still getting power directly from the port-side fuel cells to the aft disruptors."

"Unplug them."

"We have, sir. They're still charging."

"How long till full charge?"

"Four minutes."

"If you can't abort, blow them."

"Sir?"

"You heard me. Those things aren't going to go off politely. Discharge them or jettison them."

"Aye, sir."

"Leen?"

"Here."

"The hole?"

"Nothing in it that we didn't put there."

"You've lost your singularity control, Chief. How do you know the imp hasn't diddled your grapplers?"

"The grapplers have all been pulled out of their harnesses. Actually blasted out. They're on their way to the machine shop already."

"What about disruptor charges?"

"We're scanning now. I've got the hole in an isolation bottle. It can't be inverted."

"Is the bottle secure?"

"We didn't build it until after we opened the ship to space. We detoxed as we built. It's secure."

"You built a *passive* bottle?"

"I only look stupid, Commander—"

"Sorry, Chief. I just—"

"I know. You're feeling guilty because you sacrificed my engine room. Now you're trying to make up for it. Do me a favor, Mr. Korie?"

"Chief?"

"Trust my judgment?"

"Right. Sorry. Thanks. Out."

"You're welcome."

Korie stopped himself. He wanted to run his hands through his hair and rub his eyes. But the starsuit prevented that. Instead, he took a breath. And another. And a third deep breath. Finally, he reseated himself in his chair—he hadn't noticed when he'd come floating out—

and secured the safety harness. He forced himself to shut up for a moment. He'd trained this crew. They knew what to do. It was time to stop jiggling their elbows.

He forced himself to sit back. He waited for the rest of the status reports to come in.

He looked around, Brik was already beside him; he hadn't even noticed when the big Morthan had returned. How long had he been waiting there?

"I don't suppose anyone has found the imp?"

Brik shook his head.

"All right. Secure the hatches. Forget about repressurizing. We can't risk it. Let's get the section heads up here. We need to scramble."

Brik nodded and began relaying orders.

Something *shuddered*. They felt the vibration through the skeleton of the ship. Korie looked to Brik—

A Hole in the World

Armstrong saw the flash before he felt the shockwave. In fact, he never felt the shockwave at all. Suddenly, a stanchion leapt up and slammed him across the chest. He grunted involuntarily; the stanchion swam away. Everything was red. He couldn't hear. Armstrong grabbed instinctively for something. He was tumbling. He saw stars swirling past. He caught one arm—almost accidentally—on a twisted bar of metal. He hung on, blinking, still not certain what had happened or where he was or what he had been doing a moment before. Something had exploded—

His eyes focused. There was a hole in the world. There were stars on the other side of the hole. A starsuited figure was hung up on the jagged edge of the hole. His face was blue. *Lambda*. He was twisting and turning. In a moment, he would work loose and plunge out the hole. Armstrong was sure of it.

Armstrong struggled forward; he pulled at Lambda's leg, pulled him away from the hole in the world. Lambda's suit was ripped. Armstrong swung him around. His mouthpiece was secure though—but the air bottles were punctured. Had the safety seals closed? Yes!

Armstrong unclipped his own air hose and shoved it into Lambda's emergency intake valve. He gasped for breath, more in sympathy than real need. He began pulling Lambda toward—he wasn't sure. Everything here below the portside disruptor feeds was blown away. Some of it was still sparking and flashing. There were places that were still glowing hot. He headed back the other way.

The door was clamped. He fumbled for the security card. It was missing from his belt. He pulled Lamba around and looked for his; his was missing too. He began banging on the door, hoping that someone on the other side could hear.

That didn't work. He was getting panicky now. He took his airhose back and sucked eagerly for a few seconds, then gave it back to Lambda. Lambda's eyes were open and dilated. He looked bluer than usual. Armstrong didn't know. He'd heard that Quillas were augmented somehow. Maybe Lambda was still alive. He couldn't take a chance.

Impatient, Armstrong towed the other back to the hole. He pulled himself out of the hole first and grabbed an external handhold, then pulled Lambda carefully out after him, trying not to catch his starsuit on the jagged metal.

Towing Lambda, he started pulling him steadily aftward toward the emergency evacuation locks. He had to stop frequently, to share the air from their common tank. The entire time he kept talking, "Stay with me, Lambda. Only a little bit more. Only a little bit. Okay, we're almost there, almost—"

And sure enough, they were. By the time they got to the stern of the ship, there were others in starsuits coming out to meet them. They separated Lambda from him, Armstrong didn't see where they went. They gave him fresh air and pulled him in through the revolving lock and from there to a pressurized bubble inflated in the cargo deck where Doctor Williger waited.

"Lambda? Is Lambda okay?" Armstrong kept asking. No one would answer, until Quilla Gamma grabbed his arms and held him steady and looked directly into his eyes. "It's all right, Brian. We're all right. The Quilla Cluster is fine."

"But Lambda—where's Lambda?"

"We're sorry," said Gamma. "The Lambda body has died. Your efforts were noble, Brian, but Lambda was killed in the explosion."

"No, no—" Brian didn't want to hear it. "No, Lambda was the only one who understood—this isn't fair! Oh, God, no!" He started to scream his rage and then something hissed on his arm and he went over the top and out.

The Ops Deck

Korie took the news grimly.

"We missed one," he said. "All right, Brik, how many more have we missed?"

Brik grunted. "All the rest. This is how we find them."

Korie looked at him sharply. And realized something. The big Morthan bulked like an immovable wall. "You know something, Brik—" he said quietly. "There are times when I don't like you. And then there are times when I *really* don't like you. You're the best officer aboard this ship. And I don't like you."

"The feeling is mutual," Brik acknowledged.

"Good," said Korie. "Let's keep it that way." He pulled himself over the railing and down to the Ops deck where the section leaders were gathered. Brik followed. "The imp is still loose, so we're going to have to be careful," Korie said. "We can't afford any more casualties."

He glanced around the darkened Bridge. Leen, Tor, Hodel, Stolchak, Hall, Brik, Goldberg, and Green floated around him, hanging onto consoles, stanchions, railings, chairs. Their helmet lamps were muted, so no one would have a beam shining directly in their eyes; still the effect was like faces looking out of the open mouths of a school of pilot fish.

"I'd like to reactivate the Operations deck," Korie said. "I hate being blind. And scanners—we're going to need some kind of scanning. Chief, can we rig a passive lens right away? The imp had fifteen minutes of uninterrupted broadcasting. I figure we've got three days before that signal is picked up by a probe. Assuming the probe can generate a hyperstate pulse, we've got maybe at most five days before the first Morthan vessel shows up. Assuming it waits for reinforcements, we might have as much as a week. I need to know as soon as possible, how much can we rebuild in five days? Can we continue?"

"Excuse me?" said Tor. "But . . . we're docked. Aren't we? Don't we have the resources of Stardock?"

Korie smiled. "Someone want to tell her?"

Leen was closest. "Hello, Dolly," he said.

Tor shook her head. "I don't understand."

"Dolly is a docking platform, and a small life-support module. It's anchored to a singularity containment to give it roughly the same mass as Stardock. We just used it to trigger all the imp's traps. Well . . . as many as were set to go off when we docked."

"Dolly is a decoy," Leen explained. "One of several. She makes the same kind of stress field impression as Stardock. If the *Star Wolf* is decommissioned, her singularity might be used in a dolly too. A Morthan probe doesn't scan for radio signals; transmitters are cheap; it scans for stress field impressions made by large masses."

Tor's expression changed as she figured it out. She looked to Korie, upset. "You *lied* to me! Again!"

"It was a need-to-know basis, Commander Tor," Korie said. "You didn't really need to know, did you?"

Tor held back her words for a moment while she considered the answer to the question. Korie was right.

"We knew we'd never be able to stop the imp from sending a signal to the Morthan probes," Korie continued. "So we made sure the signal was sent from a place where there'd be no immediate danger to Stardock."

Tor looked confused. "But what about HARLIE? How did you fool him? If he knew about the dolly, then the imp might have known too."

"That's right," said Korie, unhappily. "Didn't you think it was a little unusual for us to take Gatineau out for a starboat certification when we did? We dropped a transmitter at the flipover point. Later HARLIE received a signal from it. He reported it. Everybody assumed it came from Stardock, yourself included. I never said differently."

"But the signal wouldn't have had Stardock's authentication code. HARLIE would have known it was false."

"It had my signature," said Korie. "I was counting on him figuring it out for himself. He did. Did you notice the phrasing of his announcement? At no time did he say the orders came from Stardock. Neither did I. We just let you and everybody else assume it."

"You son of a bitch," Tor said. "I really hate when you do that."

Korie ignored it and continued: "Meanwhile, HARLIE knew he couldn't discuss anything with anyone until the matter of the imp was resolved. He knew his own security was compromised. Brik didn't shut him down. He shut himself down. He had to. This wouldn't have worked any other way."

"I'll be damned," said Tor.

"Probably," agreed Korie. "But not today. Now let's get back to work. We've got a whole Morthan fleet headed our way. How soon can we get out of here? Chief?"

"That's the bad news," said Leen. "We can't. Not until I rebuild the containment. It's a week's work just to get the calibrators refocused."

"What about the torches?"

"We'll have to check their alignment too. We took some pretty heavy damage amidships. We're doing hull-integrity tests first; then we'll see if we can risk firing the plasma tubes. That's at least a week's work too. And don't forget we're living off our fuel cells until we can tap the singularity again. If you want to fire those torches, you'll be paying for it with life support."

"I figured that," said Korie. "All right, let's get those wayward torpedoes back in their tubes. We'll use the dolly." To all of them, he added, "And let's all be careful. Remember, the imp is still out there—"

And then suddenly they were gone and he was alone, for just a moment remembering the last time he'd floated alone in a darkened Bridge.

Captain Lowell—

Lowell

Captain Sam Lowell had found a useful niche in the service, certifying ships fresh off the assembly line and then handing them over to their new young captains. It was an easy duty, but a necessary one; plus, it gave him the opportunity to go to space again. It also gave him an authority that he would otherwise never know. His cards had been dealt and played; he would reach the rank of admiral, but only on retirement. And that was not too far away.

Lowell was not a bad officer; he just wasn't an extraordinary one. He had risen through the ranks by being dependable, by doing exactly what he was told, but he had never demonstrated the kind of initiative that set him apart from others, so his superiors rightfully regarded him as a man who was better at following orders than giving them. The navy depended on men and women like Lowell, it repaid them with comfortable responsibilities, not bold ones.

Despite the popular view of the star navy as a vast fighting force, the great majority of ships were never intended to see battle at all; instead, they were needed to ferry supplies and equipment, to serve convoy duty, to move troops, to carry pilgrims and colonists, to train new crews, to carry mail, to perform research and surveillance missions, to patrol and guard. Indeed, it was estimated that only ten percent of the ships on active duty would ever see combat at all; most of the rest would provide support and service—it had been only in the last three decades that the decision was made to increase the proportion of combat vessels to thirty-three percent. This was accomplished primarily by having the liberty ships designed and built as multi-purpose vehicles. The intended result was a navy that was both powerful and adaptable.

A not unforeseen side-effect of the increased production of FTL vessels was an increased access to FTL travel. Industrial and commercial interests began leasing more and more transportation services from Fleet command. Some ships were also outfitted for the carrying of passengers, even tourists. Throughout the entire sphere of Terran authority, transport prices fell as access to transport increased. The more that new ships became available, the more demand there was for the services they provided. The economies of the Allied worlds flourished.

The bad news, however, was that the increasing size of the Allied star navies created significant unease among the worlds of the Morthan Solidarity. The Morthan worldview was already invested with a high degree of self-absorption and paranoia. The highest councils could not help but observe the continuing longterm buildup as a military one— and they could not help but consider themselves the target of such a buildup. Indeed, they were incapable of considering themselves as anything *other* than a target for the aggression of others; it was the only way they could justify their own aggressive stance. That the Allied military buildup was primarily a defensive reaction to the Morthans' own increasingly belligerent military posture and growing weapons production was not considered part of the equation.

On the Morthan side of the rift, well away from the Morthan sphere of authority, lay a cluster of star systems known as Far Cathay. Although it was a six-week journey from there to the closest world of the Solidarity, the Morthans still regarded the human-occupied worlds of Far Cathay as potentially hostile. When the Silk Road Convoys began ferrying equipment for the creation of an industrial base, the Morthans' most paranoid fantasies came bubbling to the surface. They were certain that the Allied worlds intended to establish a military presence from which a flank attack could be mounted against the westernmost worlds of the Morthan Solidarity.

The Morthans were correct in their assessment that the Allies intended to establish a stronger military presence on Far Cathay. They were inaccurate in their assessment of its purpose. The actual goal was to provide a base from which to launch a flank attack on the Morthan supply lines, should the Morthan Solidarity attempt to advance into the Allied sphere.

Although the Allied authorities made it well known that the purpose of the Far Cathay expansion was entirely defensive, this was only believed on the Allied side of the rift.

Throughout this time, Commander J. T. Korie was well aware of the tactical situation; it validated his earlier extrapolations. War in space was a game of three-dimensional chess played in real time, in the dark. As he and others had predicted, most of the war would be spent jockeying for position. Whoever ended up with the strongest position would win the war before the first shots were fired. The rest would be follow-through and cleanup.

In the meantime . . . Korie's first assignments as a captain had already been determined. He had been briefed by Vice Admiral O'Hara, and the first three years of his command career lay before him as clearly as if they had been mapped out on the holographic display of the astrogation console.

After a preliminary series of shakedown cruises, the *LS-1187*—still under the command of Sam Lowell—would join the Silk Road Convoy to ferry cargo and supplies across the rift. Upon the completion of this mission, Captain Lowell would turn the command of the starship over to Commander Korie who would then assume the rank of captain.

Captain Korie would begin his career assigned to specific patrol and surveillance missions which would give Fleet command an opportunity to gauge his initiative—to see if he would be a captain like Margaret Faslim-Arub or a captain like Sam Lowell.

That was the game plan. Unfortunately, that was not how events played out.

The Morthan Third Fleet *followed* the *LS-1187* to the rendezvous point and attacked the Silk Road Convoy as it formed up near a small barren world named Marathon. Captain Lowell was killed, as were eighteen other members of the crew; the *LS-1187* was crippled in the assault and left drifting in space like a derelict. Without power. Without gravity. Without a captain. With barely enough oxygen and food to survive long enough to repair the damage.

Under Jon Korie's direction, it took the *LS-1187* six and a half months to limp home, and when they finally did return to Stardock, they found they were a Jonah. They were blamed for the war that was raging everywhere. Three Morthan fleets had swept violently across the rift and whole worlds had been destroyed.

Including Shaleen.

And Carol. And Timmy. And Robby.

Gone. All gone.

Korie did what he always did when his emotions were raging out of control. He immersed himself in his work and waited for the storm to pass.

It never did.

Incoming

For three days they worked desperately. The situation was eerily familiar. They had been here before. They had done this before.

The ship was adrift. It remained unpowered. No gravity, no lights, no air. No HARLIE.

Reluctantly, Chief Leen had repressurized part of the keel, the Ops bay, the Bridge, the officers' deck, the ward room, and the mess room. He rigged an emergency airlock at each end, not much more than a series of valve-locks to be pressed through. It provided quick access both in and out. Crew members came in to eat and take short naps anchored to a deck or a bulkhead. Some of them slept in their starsuits, tethered just outside. Most of them worked around the clock, pausing only to eat and sleep.

Three squads went through the ship doing emergency decontaminations everywhere they could. The imp remained unfound.

Another team took the starboat and went out to catch the drifting torpedoes. They brought back three of them and lashed them to the dolly. They lashed the starboat to the dolly too. They installed the missiles so that their hyperstate-simulators were focused on the pinpoint black hole within the dolly's singularity containment shell. They tapped into the dolly's power supply and fed it to the starboat; they cabled the controls of the torpedoes together and connected them to a jury-rigged board in the flight deck of the starboat.

But they couldn't test their construction, not without causing a major stress-field ripple. They had no way of knowing if it would work.

Aboard the *Star Wolf*, the crew continued to labor. Their starsuits slowed them down. Zero-gee slowed them down. Their own exhaustion slowed them down. Everything took three times as long. Exhilaration kept them awake. Fear kept them glancing at the time. They raced the clock. They sat in the center of an expanding sphere of radio noise. The signal swept outward at light speed in all directions. How thoroughly had this sector been seeded with probes? HARLIE had guessed they would have less than three days before the signal was detected by a probe. The probe would then generate a hyperstate bleep. And how long would it take for the warships to come sharking in then? Another day. Maybe two.

But HARLIE was down, and so were all the sensors. They had no way of detecting the bleep, so they had no way of knowing *when* exactly they had been spotted. It might be three days, it might be thirteen. It might be never. They wouldn't know until their passive lens detected an incoming bogey.

They worked harder.

The last hour of the third day passed like a kidney stone. It took forever. The crew sweated.

And they still hadn't found the imp.

The fourth day began. The odds continued to shift against them. Morthan warships were coming.

Korie went out to the starboat and double-checked its controls. Everything came up green. He slipped a memory clip into a reader and copied the latest set of operating programs into the starboat's intelligence engine. He hadn't dared risk piping the files across; they still hadn't detoxed the network on the other side of the umbilicals; the starboat had to stay clean. He ran a viricide suite and scanned the displays. The files had copied green. The starboat was ready.

Korie's fingers twitched. He wanted to power up. He wanted to look across the hyperstate horizon. He wanted to go hunting. He held himself back. He didn't dare take the risk. He knew better. Every hour that passed was one more hour on their side.

But . . . he could run simulations.

These were simple exercises; he'd written them himself; HARLIE could have done better, but they couldn't risk it, not until the imp was destroyed. And besides, they couldn't bring HARLIE back online without additional detox first. It didn't matter. They didn't need sophisticated simulations. Not for this.

Korie awoke when his oxygen alarms went off. He was down to thirty minutes air supply. He'd been asleep for two and a half hours. "Oh, shit!" he said. He hadn't meant to allow himself such a long rest. He unstrapped himself from his seat and headed back to the *Star Wolf*.

He replaced his air tanks in the cargo bay and headed for the engine room. Chief Leen was supervising the reinstallation of the last singularity grappler. Korie floated up next to him.

"How bad?" he asked.

Leen shook his head. "If it works, I want a Heisenberg trophy."

"Are you certain?" asked Korie.

"Spare me the old jokes," said Leen sourly.

"Sorry," said Korie. "For what it's worth, I've already written you up for a serious recommendation."

"I'd rather have a good stiff drink."

"That can be arranged too. You've got two kegs of moonshine behind the scrubbers. As soon as the ship is repressurized, you can open one." Leen looked at him, surprised that Korie had such accurate knowledge of his inventory. Korie ignored it. "It's been aging for two weeks, that should be enough, shouldn't it? Now tell me about the stardrive."

"Can't test it," Leen said gloomily. "I don't know that it'll work. This was all done by hand. We had to jack those grapplers into place and secure them with hand-clamps. We lined them up with lasers. Maybe they'll hold. She passed the preliminaries. We're checking secondary calibrations now. I don't think she'll pass, if she does I'll be surprised. But we have no way of focusing any tighter, so you can forget about fine-tuning. We lost our last venticulars when the traps went off. We didn't dare take them out, we'd have made the imp suspicious, or triggered a deadman trap, and you traded away our spares, so you've got no call to complain. The only calibrators we have left are junk. And we're working without alignment tubes anyway, so it's a moot point." He made a sound of disgust and disbelief. "*If* she works, we'll be running with a very loose focus. You'll have lousy control. She'll skid like an ice cube on a griddle."

"Good. That'll make us harder to hit. What kind of speed?"

"Your guess is as good as mine. Either we'll slide or we'll grind. There's no in between." The chief added, "I'm thinking of applying for a transfer."

"Oh?"

"I don't want to be on a ship where the CO treats his engines like this."

"Oh," said Korie. "You didn't tell me you wanted to live forever. I wish you had. I would have planned things differently."

"I'm *serious*," Leen said. "Give me one good reason why I should work my butt off for you, if this is what you do to my engines."

"One reason? Okay. You'll never find a CO who will challenge your engineering skills as completely and as thoroughly as I will. You'll never be on a ship again where you'll have to solve problems this impossible. You're not fooling me, Chief. You like playing superman. Any other ship, you'd die of boredom."

"Don't tempt me. I don't mind dying. I just don't want to do it today."

"You're welcome to get off here," said Korie. "But you'd better do it soon, because—"

His headphones chimed. "Mr. Korie?" It was Tor. "We have a bogey."

"I'm on my way," he replied. "Sound the alarm." To Leen, he said, "Heat those tubes. We're going to find out how they work the hard way. You can finish quitting tomorrow. I may go with you."

"If we live," muttered Leen, already pulling himself down to his workstation.

Watching

Korie was last to arrive on the Bridge. He had the farthest to travel, and he had to go through the valve-lock in the keel. He swam up through the Ops bay and up onto the Bridge, where he strapped himself into the captain's chair quickly. He began pulling off his helmet.

Work lights had been strung across the Bridge, and three of the consoles had been detoxed and reactivated. Brik was already in his chair, speaking to his headset. Korie unclipped his own from the side of his chair and listened to the chatter for a moment; then he called to Tor. "ETA?"

"Three minutes. We've got a bearing."

"How big is she?"

"Big. Very big."

"Can you be a little more precise than that?"

"That's as precise as I can give you. It's possibly a juggernaut."

"We never get the little ones, do we?" Korie said to himself.

"The starboat's ready," reported Goldberg.

"Sounds good." To his headset: "Chief?"

"We're ready. We've got forty percent and rising."

"That's better than I hoped for. Thank you. Prepare to initiate warp."

"Aye, sir."

Korie was already leaning forward, ready to give the next order, when Tor spoke quietly. "We've got a second bogey."

"Where?" said Korie.

Tor held up her board for him to see. A small white dot was arrowing inward from a high starboard angle.

"What the hell—?" he started to say, then caught himself. "My God, it's the *Houston.*"

"She got her fluctuators working!" said Tor.

"It was that last load we sent over. Dammit! We should never have given her those spares! She's making an attack run—"

"She's going to get creamed—" said Hodel.

"Belay that," said Korie.

They watched in silence as the small white dot converged on the larger pink one. Suddenly, the pink blip disappeared. A second later, the white one too.

"They're dropping missiles," Korie said.

"They don't have a chance," said Brik. To Korie's sharp look, he explained, "They don't have the range. The Morthan missiles have three times the running distance. They can't get in close enough."

"There they are," said Tor. "The *Houston's* back in hyperstate."

"Can they outrun the Morthan birds?" asked Jonesy.

"No," said Brik, with finality. "They can't."

"They're going into evasive patterns—" Tor reported.

"It won't work," said Brik. "It will only delay the inevitable."

"You're a lot of help," said Tor, annoyed.

"Can you pick up the missiles at all?" Korie asked her.

"Not at this distance. Not with a passive lens. Maybe if we could open a hyperstate window . . . ?"

"No, I won't take that risk."

"I didn't think so," said Tor.

"There's the Morthan," said Hodel. "What's he doing?"

Korie peered over Tor's shoulder at the display. The Morthan ship was moving rapidly to overtake and pass the *Houston.* "He's power-loading his bubble. He can do that for about thirty seconds. It's very dangerous."

The Morthan ship pulled ahead of the *Houston,* went a little farther, and then dropped off the screen again.

"They're doomed," reported Brik. "He's dropping another spread. He's got her bracketed."

"Shit," said Korie. They watched helplessly. The white dot continued to skitter back and forth within an ever-narrowing circle of probability. For a moment, it looked as if it were going to escape. It raced suddenly upward—

—and then abruptly vanished.

"They're gone," said Jonesy, unnecessarily.

After a heartbeat, Brik spoke. "On the plus side," he said, "the Morthan juggernaut may now believe that was us they destroyed."

To the others' uncomprehending looks, he explained, "They knew there was a ship here. That's what they were looking for. They found a ship and destroyed it. That gives us a small strategic advantage."

"You know . . . ?" Korie said abruptly to Brik. "Remember when I said that there were times that I don't like you and times that I *really* don't like you? This is one of those times when I *really* don't like you."

"Thank you for sharing that," Brik said dryly.

"Let's hope *they* believe it," said Hodel, pointing at the display, trying desperately to get the subject back on purpose.

"Would you?" asked Brik.

Tor interrupted. She pointed at her screen. "There they go. The Morthan is back in hyperstate. He's heading in again. ETA is now two minutes."

"Well, there's your answer," Korie said. "He doesn't believe there's only one ship out here either. So much for our small strategic advantage." He turned forward again and gave an order. "Jettison the dolly."

Good-bye Dolly

"Roger that," said Goldberg. He unclipped a plastic cover on his board and flipped the red switch beneath it. Something went *thump* at the aft end of the vessel. "The dolly is free," he reported.

Korie looked to Brik. "Tell me that we fooled the imp. Tell me that it went through the docking harness and trapped itself in the dolly."

Brik stared impassively back at Korie.

"I didn't think so," Korie said ruefully. He turned forward again, "Wake the boat, Mr. Goldberg. Send the signal."

"Roger that," Goldberg said, and flipped the next switch over. "The starboat is now tracking."

"Distance?"

"Three kilometers and widening."

"Too close. We're cutting it too close," Korie said. "We should have jettisoned her earlier."

"You wanted to upgrade her programs one more time," said Brik.

"So call me a perfectionist." To Tor: "Where's the bogey?"

"She's coming in almost straight toward us—wait a minute. She's dropped out of hyperstate."

"Too far away!" Korie almost came out of his chair. "What the hell is she doing?"

"Not giving us room to shoot back," said Brik. "She's dropped a spread of hunting torpedoes. She'll be gone in a minute."

"If she doesn't see something blow up, she'll come back—"

"Then we'd better blow something up. She thinks she's found the Stardock."

"Goldberg?"

"Starboat is seven kilometers away."

"We're going to get fringe effects," warned Brik.

"Unavoidable. *Now hear this.* Secure yourselves. We're going to get brushed by a hyperstate fringe." Korie wished he could wait just ten seconds more, but he didn't dare. *He didn't dare.* "Trigger the boat."

"Done," said Goldberg, simultaneously throwing the third switch on his board. He tossed it aside. "The boat is now triggered."

"Nothing's happening," said Tor.

"It was always chancy," agreed Korie. To his headset. "Chief, stand by to run like hell."

"Wait a minute," said Tor—and then reality flickered for a moment as—

—*Carol was with him and Timmy and Robby and they were*—"*Oh, Jon, I'm so scared!*" *He reached for her and*—

. . . came back to consciousness quickly, it wasn't as bad as the last time, the first time. It wasn't a big field, it hadn't been too close, and besides they hadn't been enveloped themselves, so there were no internally reflected effects and so this wasn't as bad, it wasn't as bad, if only it had lasted just a moment longer—

The lights were flickering back on.

"Starboat away," gasped Brik.

"And?"

"Just a fucking minute," mumbled Tor. She picked up her jury-rigged board and banged it once on the console, then looked at it again. "I've got the boat." Then she added, "The bogey is still down."

"They've got to have seen the boat by now." To Tor: "What does the boat look like?"

"It looks like . . . nothing I've ever seen before. It's got the weirdest signature."

"That's the torpedoes. They're not designed to work with so much power."

"They're going to burn out," said Goldberg.

"The boat is closing . . . closing . . . The boat is down," reported Tor. "The signature just went out."

"How close did she get to the bogey?"

Tor shook her head. "Halfway. Maybe."

There was silence on the Bridge. Korie rubbed his nose, his forehead. He ran his hand through his hair. They waited. The moment stretched out.

"Anything?" asked Korie.

"Nada."

"They had to have seen the boat," he repeated to himself. "What are they doing?"

"They're probably trying to figure out what it was," said Tor. "Its signature was bizarre."

Korie rubbed his ear. "Maybe," he admitted. He tried to imagine the situation from the Morthan side.

Here's a bleep from a probe. A suspected location for Stardock. Fast attack in. Drop out of hyperstate, drop a spread of hunting missiles, and—*something* makes a run at you, then disappears from your screens. What do you do? Hide? Or fight?

He looked to Brik.

Brik shook his head. No comment.

Tor was looking back to them both, a questioning expression on her face.

"We wait," said Korie.

"How long?"

"As long as it takes."

"Those hunting torpedoes are coming this way," she reminded.

"Yep," agreed Korie. "Mr. Goldberg, drop the package."

Goldberg pulled a second board onto his lap. He unclipped the plastic cover and flipped an arming switch, and then pressed a launch button. Again, they felt a *thump* through the metal of the ship, through their chairs. This one wasn't as large as the last one.

"ETA for the hunting torpedoes?" Korie asked.

"Seven to ten minutes. If they have a fix. Twenty to thirty if not."

"That's what they're waiting for," Brik said. "For something to go boom. They need confirmation of the kill."

"Something will go boom real soon now," Korie agreed. "Goldberg? As soon as the package is three kilometers away, arm it. *Now hear this.* Stand by to power-down. Total power-down in fifteen seconds." To his headset: "Chief, this means you too." To Tor, he ordered: "Keep your lens open, shut down everything else." Korie leaned back in his chair, readjusted his safety harness. He glanced at the time. Six minutes. Maybe less. Maybe more . . .

Waiting

"Is it getting cold in here?" asked Tor.

"It's your imagination," said Korie. "It takes a lot longer than this to lose heat."

"We've been powered down for an hour and a half."

"Are you uncomfortable?"

"I'm working on it."

"Good. Just remember, as uncomfortable as you are, it's worse for the imp."

"You think so."

"I *hope* so."

"Those torpedoes are overdue."

"They'll get here. Goldberg?"

"Sir?"

"How's the package?"

The package was eight hyperstate warheads in a bundle. They had been pulled from their own torpedoes, and kept under twenty-four-hour guard, suspended in the center of the cargo bay and surrounded by motion detectors. They were detoxed daily. They were presumed clean. They gave off signals resembling an attempt to shield Stardock-like activities. Homing torpedoes wouldn't search for mass, but noise, so the *Star Wolf* had to be as inert an object as they could make it. They needed the torpedoes to aim for the package.

"Package is still alive," said Goldberg. "Nothing yet."

Korie turned to Brik, "Tell me you found the imp."

Brik looked impassively back.

"It knows," Korie said impatiently. "I swear to Ghu, it knows. All of our plans, everything, no matter how careful we've been—handwriting all our orders, using one-time code pads, detoxing, securing, isolating, spacing—it still knows. I'm sure of it. Somehow, it found out."

"That is a possibility," said Brik. "And even if it isn't a possibility, that's still what it wants you to think."

Korie shook his head in exhaustion. "There's a limit to just how deep a head game I can play, Brik. My brain hurts." He shuddered, partly from the cold, partly from the strain. "I think it's waiting till we get back to the real Stardock. What if all the traps it set off are decoys?"

"There isn't much left it can do," Brik said. "We're dead."

"The package just armed itself," said Goldberg quietly. He was listening to his headset. The package had given off a distinctive bleep.

The Bridge went silent.

"Torpedoes approaching. Three torpedoes. ETA in ten seconds . . . five . . . three . . . one . . ." He put his headset down. "The package is gone."

"It went off!" said Tor. "We saw it on the lens! Multiple spikes!"

Korie exhaled softly. "Okay, okay . . . something went boom. Maybe, they'll believe it was the Stardock."

"They'll come looking," said Tor.

"They don't dare," said Korie. "Where's the boat?" To his headset: "Chief, the package went off. Prepare to power up."

"The boat is coming back online!" Tor reported. "The program worked!"

"Of course, it worked. I wrote it," said Korie. "What's it doing? Dammit, can we get the main display restored?!!"

"It's charging the last known position of the bogey. Its signature is larger than ever. It looks like some kind of superjuggernaut. Closing . . . closing . . . closing . . . it's down again."

"Mm-hm. Good." Korie explained, "You can only run those torpedoes so long and then they burn out. We run them for fifteen seconds and stop, it looks like a monster warship making an attack run. The other side doesn't know what it's doing when it drops out of hyperstate. They have to assume it's doing the same thing they just did—dropping a spread of hunting torpedoes. Watch your board, Tor. Fifteen . . . ten . . . five. . . ."

"There they are! They're running!"

"Gotcha, ya sonsabitches!" Korie exulted.

"The boat is back in hyperstate! It's chasing!"

The main display came back on then, so did the astrogation table. Two blips racing across hyperstate. One was large, the other was larger; its signature was spiked and blurry. Korie pulled himself over the railing and down onto the Ops deck. "Watch," he said. "They're going to drop out of hyperstate for ten seconds, just long enough to launch a torpedo of their own—there they go." One of the blips on the screen disappeared. Korie counted out loud. "Ten . . . nine . . . eight . . . seven . . . six . . ." The blip reappeared.

"They launch fast," said Brik.

"They're very good," Tor agreed. "I wish we could match that."

"I promise you, one day we will," Korie said.

"We can't see the torpedoes," said Tor. "We don't have the resolution."

"Wait . . . there you go. The starboat's evading and . . ." The larger blip, the weird one, disappeared from the screen. "They got it. *Yes!*" They watched for a moment as the Morthan bogey retreated across the hyperstate horizon. Its signature slowly faded and became more and more indistinct, until at last it vanished in the distance of light years.

"They're running home with a confirmed kill on a nonexistent Stardock and a juggernaut-class vessel that we don't know how to build yet. And we're home free!" Korie exulted.

"Except for the imp," Tor reminded him.

"No," said Brik. He was listening to something on his headset. "We found it."

The Imp

"Gravity?" asked Tor. "Power?"

"Not yet," said Korie. "Who knows what was armed when power went off. Everybody hold present position."

"This way," said Brik, already pushing himself out of his chair. Korie followed. The two swam aftward, down the upper corridor, out through the engine room, down to the machine shop below the containment, and then out through the access to the inner hull—the farm was devastated. He'd expected it. He'd mourn the loss later. There were pieces of dead greenery floating everywhere; it was like swimming through a glimmery yellow snowstorm.

Their helmet lamps made everything flash and sparkle. They could barely see their way. They swam slowly aft, finding their way around the curve of the inner bottle until they came to a place behind the signal scrubbers, behind the place where Chief Leen had stashed his illicit kegs of moonshine, where six crew members floated in a silent circle. They parted as the chief of security and strategic operations and the acting captain swam up.

There it was. Illuminated by a single work light. Attached to a strut. In a transparent plastic sac. The imp. Huddled in a fetal position. Dead. Its skin had already gone blue. It looked like a baby. A baby in a tank. Waiting to be born. Korie remembered . . . his own son. It looked so fragile, so delicate.

He started to approach for a closer look, but Brik pulled him back. "No. Don't get near it." Brik touched helmets to the nearest crewmember and ordered them all away. Reluctantly, they began to move back. They disappeared into the gloom of the inner hull.

Brik pulled himself around to look at the thing from as many different sides as he could see it.

"It looks so innocent," said Korie.

Brik snorted.

"Well, it's dead now."

Brik hesitated.

Korie caught it. "What?" he asked sharply.

Brik didn't answer.

"You're too suspicious," Korie said. "Did it ever occur to you there's such a thing as being *too* paranoid?"

"No," said Brik, innocently. "Should it?"

Before Korie could answer, his communicator beeped. "Yes?"

It was Cappy. "We found the imp, sir. Forward."

"Excuse me? Say again?"

"We found the imp. Starboard bow. Section 2, fifteen degrees. In an Okuda tube. It's dead. It was caught without protection."

"I'll be there shortly. Korie out." Korie looked to Brik sharply. "There were *two*?"

"At least."

"At *least*?"

The big Morthan floated back down to Korie and faced him directly. "When I went out on the hull—I didn't tell you this—part of the reason was to see how much I could carry inside my harness. I could have carried one live imp, or two eggs in an incubator. I needed to know *everything* that Cinnabar was capable of. We now know that he had two eggs with him when he started. At least two. They were for the *Burke*. But he didn't need to use them, so he never warmed them up. When he came across to the *Star Wolf*, he brought the eggs with him. I don't think he intended to warm them up here either. I said before, these things are supposed to be pretty good eating. I think he stashed them somewhere, intending to come back later. He didn't come back. The eggs warmed up by themselves. A fail-deadly."

Korie thought about that. "An imp is born knowing how to sabotage a starship?"

"When we find the eggshells, we'll also find an incubation frame; which programs the imp while it's still in its shell. And we *have* to find that frame; it's probably booby-trapped too, but it'll tell us how many there were. I was hoping we'd find it with one or the other of the imps, but . . . we didn't."

Korie took a breath. "How many imps are we looking for, Brik? One? Two? A dozen?"

"Not that many," Brik said calmly. "Not a dozen. I estimate that Cinnabar could have carried as many as six eggs, if he'd had the packing; but I don't think he would have wanted to take the risk. Imps are monosexual. And they mate ferociously. I expect that if we scan the two dead imps we'll find they're both carrying eggs. I doubt that any eggs have been laid yet, though. If there are other imps still alive, however, we have only a few more days before they start hiding their eggs all over the ship. And the offspring won't be programmed, they'll be feral. You don't want to know what trouble feral imps can be. That's why even Morthans handle imps carefully."

A new thought clawed its way to the surface of his consciousness, and it wasn't one he liked thinking about. "Why didn't you tell me this before?"

Brik shook his head. "You still believe it *is* possible to be *too* paranoid. Besides, I thought we had a chance against one imp. Against more than one . . . I wasn't sure."

"You lied to me!"

"No I didn't. You never asked."

"You misled me then."

"All right. Yes."

"I don't like that, Mr. Brik." Korie felt the anger rushing to his face. At the same time, he couldn't help but feel a certain sense of irony at the situation.

"I didn't think you would."

"But you'd do it again if you thought it would make a difference, wouldn't you?"

"Yes."

"And even if I order you not to do it again . . ."

"I would prefer that you not give that order."

"So you wouldn't to disobey it, right?"

Brik didn't answer.

"I see," Korie said. "You realize we're on very dangerous ground here."

"Yes, Mr. Korie. It is the same ground you are standing on with the vice admiral."

Korie opened his mouth to speak. Then shut it again. He took a breath. Then another. Then a third. Brik was right.

"We'll have to stay depressurized for a few days more," Brik said. "I'll use nanos to search for eggs and imps. If it will reassure you any, I believe that our various detox procedures kept the imps seriously off balance. I expect that the only imps we find are going to be dead, and that we are unlikely to find any egg clusters. This imp still looks immature and the others are probably equally so. But we will need a robot to remove the bodies."

"We haven't got one."

"Homer-Nine," said Brik.

"We traded it."

Brik grunted. "No, we didn't. It went into failure mode. The *Houston* wouldn't take it."

"Oh, yes. Now I remember." Korie thought for a bit. "Would you know anything about that failure, Mr. Brik?"

"I can only put it to human error."

"I see. You thought we might need a robot, did you?"

"There is a certain ironic convenience to the situation," Brik admitted.

Korie exhaled in exasperation. "You deceived me again, didn't you?"

Brik didn't answer.

"Right. I didn't ask. Okay, okay. Let's do it. Let's take a look at the other one, and then I want you to get these things out of here." He headed forward.

The Stars

Three days later, Brik came to Korie on the Bridge. "Homer-Nine is at the forward airlock."

"Display forward," Korie ordered.

Brik touched a control on the work station in front of him. The image came up showing a six-armed robot, holding onto handholds with two of its arms. The other four were carrying containments with imps inside.

Korie looked to Brik. "You sure about this? I really hate to lose the robot."

Brik said, "I'm sure."

"Go ahead."

Brik gave an order. Still carrying its deadly cargo, the robot pushed itself away from the starship. They watched as it tumbled slowly in the glare of the ship's spotlights. It dwindled into the distance.

"Okay," said Korie.

Brik gave another order.

In the middle of the screen, something flashed soundlessly.

"Tell me that's the last of it," Korie said.

"That's the last of it," Brik replied.

Korie glanced over at him. "An actual declarative sentence. My goodness."

"Sarcasm is wasted on me," said Brik.

"At least you recognize sarcasm," Korie started to say, then stopped himself. "Sorry. I'm in a very bad mood. All right—to the cargo deck. Everybody."

This ceremony was much more somber.

A single draped body lay on a gurney. Lambda. Crewman Armstrong and all of the surviving Quillas stood by dispassionately. Korie wondered what the Quillas were feeling. How did a massmind feel when it lost part of itself? He wondered what kind of recovery therapy would be needed for the cluster. He made a mental note to talk it over with Williger.

Korie had never presided at a funeral before. He'd been to enough of them. He'd never been the ranking officer. He didn't look forward to this. He opened the book and began reading. There were words here about God. He didn't trust God. Not anymore. Not since God had taken his family away.

He read the words and he felt like a hypocrite as he read. What he really wanted to say was, *God doesn't keep her word. God gives with one hand and takes with the other. God doesn't deserve our faith.* But he didn't.

Because he knew that the others still believed. Some of them, anyway. And he wasn't going to take that away from them. They'd find out soon enough. Or not at all. It didn't matter.

They worked hard, they fought hard, they survived, that was victory enough.

But acknowledgment? Reward?

Not in this lifetime. Not the way things were headed.

Korie finished reading. He knew his performance had been mechanical. He felt regret about that. The crew deserved the best he could give them. Maybe God wouldn't give them her best, but he would. The hell with God. He closed the book and looked up at the others. They were grim-faced, stony. He had no idea what they were feeling. Perhaps they were expecting him to say more . . . ?

He took a breath.

"We've lost too many friends since this war started," he said. "And we're going to lose too many more before it's over. It's very likely that . . . most of us here will end up as names on a wall somewhere. I know that I should offer you all some solace, some hope, some words of healing. I'm sorry, but I can't do that. Not today. The best I can offer you today is my anger.

"But the good news is that our anger has brought us this far. We've survived to fight another day. So let's see how much farther our anger will take us. Let's see how much we can hurt them for every death they've given us. It isn't enough to make up for our losses, but it's something useful we can do with the pain they've given us. We can give it back."

He nodded to Chief Leen.

Lambda's body rolled into the airlock. The airlock hatch popped shut behind it. A moment later, the music began. A fanfare, something Hodel had picked out. He'd have to ask him later what the name of it was.

Good Friends

Brik found Bach in the gym, an area of the inner hull just forward of the orchards. Bach was running vigorously on the treadmill when Brik came in. She saw him and nodded. Brik waited patiently. After a moment, Bach slowed her pace, first to a trot, then to a walk; a moment later, she stepped off the treadmill, grabbed a towel and wiped the sweat from her forehead. She looked up—and up—at Brik. Her eyes shone, her face was flushed, but Brik couldn't tell if it was the exercise or anything else.

"How are you feeling?" he asked.

"Better," she said.

Brik considered his next words for a long moment. "I regret that you were hurt."

"I wasn't hurt," she said. "Well, that's not quite true. I was . . ." She shrugged and smiled, both at the same time, a wistful gesture. "I was exhausted."

"Yes," Brik agreed.

"It was a good exhaustion," she acknowledged.

"Dr. Williger said there was considerable strain on your heart."

"She also said there was no permanent damage. I just need a few days rest and exercise to work out the stiffness, that's all." She began toweling her hair. She added, "I'm not sorry we did it."

"Nor am I," said Brik.

"Did you, um . . . find out what you wanted to find out?"

"I think so," the big Morthan admitted.

"And?"

"And . . . I think I understand why this is such a difficult subject for humans. It is hard even for me to discuss it."

"Yes. Me too."

"Yes, you're a human."

"Yes, I am."

Brik took a breath. "I don't think we should try this again."

Bach did not react. Or perhaps she had been expecting him to say something like this. She continued to meet his steely gaze. "Why not?" There was only curiosity in her question, no anger.

"I don't think it would be a good idea, that's all. I don't want to cause you any further hurt."

"I wasn't hurt."

"I don't want to cause you any further embarrassment."

"I wasn't embarrassed," she said.

"And . . ." added Brik, "I am concerned that my integrity as a Morthan officer could be compromised."

"Ah," said Bach. "Yes. There is that. Your integrity. As a Morthan officer. Yes." She nodded to herself. "Yes, of course."

"It's not that I didn't like the feeling," Brik admitted quietly, "but it has had an unpleasant effect on the rest of my mental processes."

"Yes," said Bach. "I understand. I understand *completely*."

"Good," said Brik, still not getting it. "Then we can continue on as . . . just good friends."

"No," said Bach. "No, we cannot. *We cannot just be good friends!*" She whirled on him, poking him ferociously in the chest. "And I'll tell you why, you flaming Morthan idiot—because you just said to me that I'm second best. That I'm not good enough. That your stupid Morthan stability is more important to you. That sex with me makes you so uncomfortable that you'd rather pretend it didn't happen. And that's not what I felt at all. What I felt was exhilarating and wonderful and joyous and passionate and exquisite. And what you're doing now is telling me it can be dismissed, discarded, put away like an exercise box. And if you don't understand what a devastating insult that is, then fuck you and the horse you rode in on. I'm applying for a transfer. And maybe sexual rechanneling as well. Stolchak was right. I should have been a lesbian! Men! Morthans! You're all alike! Assholes!" She flung the towel at him and headed for the showers. "Good friends! I don't want any more friends! I want a lover! You can kiss my big black ass goodbye, because that's all the kissing you're ever going to get!"

Brik thought about going after her. He even took two steps in her direction.

But then he stopped himself.

He'd thought this decision out very carefully. Very very carefully. He'd been very logical about the whole thing. This was the only way.

Bach was the one who was acting illogically. Later when she calmed down, when she thought about it logically too, she'd see the logic of it. She'd see that he was right. He was only being logical.

He tossed the towel in a bin and left the gymnasium.

Vice Admiral O'Hara

"All right, Jon," said Admiral O'Hara. "Sit down." She pointed. Korie sat.

She leaned back in her chair, regarding him with a renewed respect. She nodded, grudgingly. "You made your point."

She opened her desk drawer, hesitated for a moment, then withdrew Korie's bars. She slid them across the dark gray surface of her desk. "Here," she said.

Korie made no move to pick them up. They still weren't the stars he'd earned. He looked to the admiral questioningly.

She returned his gaze dispassionately. "Go ahead, Jon. Put them on."

"They aren't the stars I've earned."

"No, they aren't."

"May I ask why I'm not being promoted? I think I'm entitled to an explanation."

Vice Admiral O'Hara nodded. "Actually, no. The decision-making process of the Admiralty is confidential."

"I see," said Korie. He began to rise—

"But I will tell you, it's not for the reasons you think. Sit down, Jon."

He lowered himself back into the chair. And waited.

"You proved your point," the admiral repeated. "It was a proud thing to do. Admirable. Heroic."

"Thank you," he said.

"*But* . . . to do that, you had to disobey the orders of this office. And that," the admiral said, "is intolerable. I can't have captains in the Fleet who don't follow instructions. Fleet command needs to know that it can depend upon its captains. We cannot depend on you the same way we can depend on our other shipmasters. We can depend on you only to have a strong stubborn will of your own. So far, you've been lucky."

Korie sat forward in his chair. The admiral saw the change in his posture and raised her eyebrows expectantly. Korie was preparing to argue. She was right.

"Ma'am, with all due respect, the Fleet also wants captains who are capable of independent thought. A captain has to take the initiative when he has no higher authority to rely on. I've demonstrated my ability to handle that responsibility. Three times over. If you're not going to promote me now, then it's obvious that I have no future in the navy. You'll have to accept my resignation."

"I'm prepared to do that," the admiral said. "But if you resign, I will also have to decommission the *Star Wolf*."

"I beg your pardon? I thought you said I proved my point."

"Yes, you did. Perhaps too well. You've demonstrated that your crew are dedicated and capable people. We have other ships in the Fleet that need their skills. Your crew has an extraordinary loyalty to you; but without your presence, they're not the same crew, are they? There's no glue holding them together."

"They've earned their ship."

"Yes, they have. And they've also earned officers who are loyal to them. If you resign, I'll put them onto ships with officers who follow orders and don't act like *prima donnas*."

Korie hesitated, torn by conflicting emotions. "This is blackmail!" he blurted.

"Tut tut—that's not a word you want to use casually, Commander Korie." Then she added, "But if it is blackmail, then it's appropriate, isn't it? You earned it. The karmic chicken always comes home to roost. Not too long ago, in this very office, you tried the same thing on me. You threatened me. Remember? So, you established the precedent that blackmail is an appropriate way to get what you want—or punish someone else if you don't."

"You're punishing me, then?"

"You can view it that way, yes. Or . . . you can look at it this way. I'm hoping to teach you a lesson. We're bringing twelve new ships online every month. We're going to need captains. We're going to need crews. You have experience; someday you *might* be a good captain. I certainly hope so. You're at your best when your anger is targeted appropriately. Now do your crew a favor and put your bars back on."

Korie started to shake his head—but it wasn't a rejection of the vice admiral's instructions; it was simply an ironic acknowledgment of disbelief and acceptance. A sad wry expression spread across his face. "You got me," he admitted. "You got me good."

"I told you before," Vice Admiral O'Hara said. "Rule number one: youth and enthusiasm will *never* be a match for age and experience."

Korie nodded his agreement. Slowly he reached out and picked up his insignia from the admiral's desk.

"Be patient, Jon," she said gently. "Trust me. We do have plans for you. Important plans. Just be patient a while longer."

Captain Hardesty

"Are you still alive?" Hardesty's voice rasped from the speaker.

"Are you still dead?" Korie shot right back. Hardesty's body was motionless on the bed. The maze of tubes and wires around him had grown more elaborate.

"Only clinically." The voice faded out for a moment, then came back stronger. "What do you want this time?"

Korie grinned. "I came to say thank you."

"For what?"

"For what you said last time I came to visit."

"And what was that?"

"You don't remember? You told me I wasn't fit for command."

"Mm," said the voice. "I must have been in a good mood."

"I walked out of here saying, 'I'll show you, you son of a bitch.' And I was angry enough to do it. Well, it worked. And I wanted to thank you for it. I learned something."

The voice remained silent for a moment longer. Finally: "You're assuming that I told you that because I wanted to produce a result. That's a very big assumption, Commander."

"I'm assuming that as a certified star-captain, you would not be nasty to anyone, and certainly not your executive officer, without a very good reason. You don't waste."

"Very good, Commander. But you're still assuming. That's a dangerous practice. Remember, I'm dead. Dead men don't care."

"Yes, sir. I'll remember that. In the meantime, whether you intended it or not, the anger you gave me saved the ship . . . and very possibly the Stardock."

"Mm." The sound was an acknowledgment, nothing more. "Anger

is useful," Hardesty finally replied. "But anger is still a reactive emotion. You can't depend on it to carry you the distance, Commander. There will come a day when you run out of anger. That's when you're going to have to find out what your *real* source of energy is."

Korie's eyes widened, both at the length of Hardesty's speech, and at the content of it as well.

"I didn't know you'd studied the *zyne*, sir."

"There's a lot you don't know. It's called the arrogance of youth. The real adventure is the wisdom that comes with experience. You're on your way."

"Y'know something, Captain. I've always respected you, but I think I'm actually beginning to like you."

"This news will not make my heart beat any faster. If it were beating at all."

"Nevertheless, Captain Hardesty, I appreciate the service you performed for our ship." Korie took a step back so Hardesty's electronic eye could see him clearly, straightened to attention, and snapped a perfect salute.

Hardesty did not return it.

Commander Korie

He returned to the *Star Wolf* feeling better than he'd expected to. As he stepped through the boarding tube, he felt a sense of familiarity and pride. He was coming *home*. His ship was safe.

The crew in the cargo deck noted his jaunty mood, and Chief Petty Officer Toad Hall quickly reported that the weather was moderate and sunny with only a few high clouds. Then he noticed there were still no stars on Korie's collar and passed that word too. "The *Star Wolf* still has no captain." A few groans of disappointment ricocheted around the Bridge and the wardroom and everywhere else the news was heard.

Hall watched as Korie climbed the ladder to the forward catwalk. Abruptly, he made a decision that he would never be able to explain. "Never mind. Operation Flag is still go!" he said quickly. "He's coming up the starboard passage."

Korie hadn't been listening to the all-talk channel. He missed Hall's weather report. And he was so involved in his own thoughts that he didn't notice immediately that the corridor ahead of him was filling up with more people than usual. Some of them were heading aft, others were just standing and waiting.

What did startle him out of his thoughts was the fact that each and every one of them he passed *saluted*. Goldberg. Reynolds. Cappy. MacHeath. Even the Black Hole Gang. And Leen—yes, Leen! The chief engineer scowled, but he still saluted.

They knew. How could they *not* know? Korie was suddenly struck by the *humanity* of this crew. The corridor was so full now, he almost had to push his way through. Williger. Ikama. Green. The Quillas. He hadn't realized there were so many of them. Alpha, Beta, Gamma, Delta, Epsilon, Zeta, Eta, Theta . . .

He felt an ember of pride glowing in his chest. He nodded his acknowledgment of each and every salute as he passed. Stolchak. Bach. Brik—Brik saluting? Korie did a double-take. Armstrong. Saffari. Hodel. Jonesy. Even the new kid, Gatineau. Eakins. Freeman. Hernandez. All of them. Every single member of the crew, he realized.

The surges of emotion he felt were almost overwhelming. He had to blink quickly to keep his eyes from tearing up as he realized: it wasn't the ship that was *home.*

It was the crew that made it so. They were his family now.

Somehow he made it to his cabin without breaking. The final few meters were the hardest walk of his life. He had always known how to withstand abuse. He did not know how to accept appreciation and acknowledgment; and the intensity of the feelings was staggering.

Tor was waiting beside his cabin door. She snapped the last salute. Korie hesitated for an instant, totally at a loss for words. He met her eyes and *knew.* This had been her idea. "Thank you," he said. He glanced down the filled corridor at all the proud faces and added quietly, "Thank you all."

Then he stepped quickly into his cabin before they could see how moved he was. He crossed to his desk and sat down quickly, the tears welling up in his eyes and flowing freely down his cheeks. He wiped his nose, then his eyes. He couldn't believe how overwhelmed he was. He couldn't remember the last time he had felt like this about the crew of a starship.

He wished . . . he wished he could put the thought aside that he had let them down. But he couldn't. Wistfully, he took a tiny box out of his jacket pocket. He opened it and looked inside at the two bright captain's stars. Carol had given him these stars, the last night they'd been together. He'd been carrying them ever since.

Sadly, he closed the box again and put it back on the shelf next to the only other award he cherished, a small black plaque bearing a golden moebius wrench with his name, Jonathan Thomas Korie, inscribed below the handle. The sight of it gave him a poignant mix of sad and happy memories all mixed together. It made him remember again how much he cared. And how much caring *hurt.*

While he was standing there, HARLIE chimed for his attention.

"Yes, HARLIE?"

"I have some information for you."

"Is it important?"

"I believe so."

"Go ahead."

"There was an evacuation off of Shaleen before it was scourged.

Over three hundred ships participated. Perhaps half a million refugees got off-planet. The records are confused, possibly inaccurate—"

"Tell me!"

"A child matching the description of one of your sons may have been aboard the *Wandering Cow*, a cargo vessel. The identification is uncertain, but it is possible that Timothy Korie is still alive. I have requested all the records."

"Where? Where did they go?" demanded Korie.

"Taalamar," HARLIE answered. "The *Wandering Cow* went to Taalamar."

"Oh, my God . . ."

"I'm making additional inquiries now. I'll inform you as soon as I have word."

"Is that it? Is that all you have?"

"I'm sorry, sir. That's all there is at the moment."

Korie sank into his chair, tears of joy and fear streaming down his cheeks. He buried his face in his hands and began to weep.

Fanfare

There was one more thing to do.

It was six weeks before they could do it, and even then half of the refits had not been completed; but a series of shakedown runs had been called for, and Korie decided to take advantage of the opportunity.

At eighteen hundred hours, the ship arrived on station. Korie stepped onto the Bridge wearing his whites. He glanced around and took note of the fact that every other crewmember present was also wearing his or her dress uniform. Even Brik. On the big Morthan, the uniform looked somehow . . . bizarre; but if Brik felt ill-at-ease, he did not display it.

"Is this the point?" Korie asked his senior astrogator.

Tor nodded. "As close as we could figure it."

"Good," said Korie. He stepped down to the Ops deck and looked up at the big display. An empty starfield beckoned.

"Mr. Jones? Is the package ready?"

Jonesy nodded and stood up. Around the Bridge, the other officers were standing up now too. Tor. Green. Goldberg. Hodel.

"Go ahead, Mr. Jones."

At his work station, Jones leaned forward and pressed a single button. There came a soft *thump* through the floor of the ship. After a moment, something became visible on the forward screen. It was a wreath. A large green wreath, glowing in the illumination of the *Star Wolf's* intense spotlights.

Hodel tapped a button on his board. The music began softly, slowly. He'd written a new arrangement, especially for this ceremony. The steady beat of a military drum came snapping up first, followed by the near-plaintive wail of a golden horn; it sounded faint and faraway—then the rest of the band came swelling up. Korie could almost hear the words. *"Oh, I wish I were in the land of cotton. Old times there are not forgotten. Look away, look away, Dixieland. . . ."*

Slowly, Korie raised one hand in salute. Around him, the other officers did likewise. Throughout the ship, at their stations, in the corridors, in the cargo bay, in the engine room, in the mess room, in the bright channels of the farm, wherever brave men and women remembered their own, the rest of the crew stood tall and proud as well. They all wore their whites, and they all stood at attention. And each and every one held a salute to their fallen comrades. On more than a few faces, tears rolled slowly down their cheeks.

And then, finally, it was over. Korie lowered his hand slowly and turned away from the screen. His throat was painfully tight. He wondered if someday, someone would be dropping a wreath for the *Star Wolf*. He wondered if they would be as proud of their duty.

And he wondered what music would be played.

"Mr. Hodel?" The acting captain asked. "Did you find an appropriate piece of music to represent this vessel?"

"Yes, sir, I did. Aaron Copland's Third Symphony, Fourth Movement."

Korie raised an eyebrow at his helmsman. "I'm afraid I don't know that one—"

"Yes, you do," said Hodel. He tapped another button, and as the ship started to ease forward again, a softer sound was heard across the Bridge and throughout the ship.

First the distant twinkling notes, then the horns, coming up in a dramatic fanfare, and Korie recognized the same bold statement he had heard at Lambda's funeral. He recognized not only the music, but the meaning behind it as well.

The music had been written long ago and far away, and yet across all that vast gulf of time, it still spoke eloquently. It had not been written by a starman, nor had it been written with star travelers in mind, and yet . . . and yet . . . it was still about the experience of challenging the darkness.

The same theme had been adapted for the composer's *other* piece, the more famous one: *The Fanfare for the Common Man*. But this symphonic arrangement was even grander. This was a work that honored life itself. The music swelled and filled the command deck.

Korie looked to Hodel, surprised and honored and pleased. He had not realized that his helmsman had the soul of a poet. It was a gratifying discovery. "You did good," Korie said, quietly patting Hodel on the shoulder. "Commander Tor. Log this music as our official calling card."

"Aye aye, Cap—Commander."

"Not yet. Not yet. But thank you. Now, take us home please. Take us home."

BLOOD
AND
FIRE

For Randy, Pam,
and Captain Anne Jillian Harbaugh,
with love

Introduction

by D.E. Fontana

"... To boldly go where no man has gone before."

What an exceptional mandate to tell stories—daring stories, stories that broke tradition—especially in science fiction television!

When that brave opening narration introduced *Star Trek* in 1966, it expressed itself as episodes that dealt with bigotry and racism, the Vietnam War, the Generation Gap, enslavement of other races, fights for equality and many other issues of the time. Under the entertaining guise of science fiction action adventure, *Star Trek* told stories that were intelligent, life affirming, entertaining and thoughtful.

David Gerrold was a part of that groundbreaking series, writing the classic script "The Trouble With Tribbles" in addition to other episodes. It was while I was story editor of the series that I met this young, brash and brilliantly talented writer.

In the years after *Star Trek* went off the air, David and I worked together a number of times on various television shows and developed a personal tie of friendship that has never faltered. When he called me in late 1986 and told me Gene Roddenberry was going to produce a new live-action version of *Star Trek* and he himself was already involved, I was elated. The elation went to the top of the scale when I was called upon to give input into the new show and ultimately to write the two-hour pilot script for *Star Trek–The Next Generation*.

Paramount and the new UPN network had guaranteed the show a full first season. Technically, the "pilot" was the premiere movie that would kick off the hour-long series episodes. Therefore, even as "Encounter at Farpoint" was being written and prepared, other scripts were already being put into work.

Some months before, Gene, David and others from the show had attended a science fiction convention in Boston. A gay fan in the audience pointedly asked if the new show would include gay characters, as *Star Trek* had been a pioneer in depicting blacks, Asians and Latinos in key roles. Gene agreed that it was time, and he hoped to do it.

David, who was working as a staff writer, went to Gene and pitched an idea. It would be a story that was a metaphor for the AIDS epidemic, taking place on a biologically infested plague ship with several of the regular characters in jeopardy. An additional point would be blood donorship. The stakes were high; the answers were not easy; the decisions were painful. Gene could sanction a story that tackled a large issue, told through personal, emotional involvement and powerful in its message. It was what *Star Trek* did best. Gene told David to go write it.

It was only later, in the development of the script, that David realized it was a perfect place to include gay characters, and he did so in four lines of dialogue so understated that anyone not paying attention could have taken the two men as mere friends.

David turned in the first draft of "Blood and Fire" just before he was scheduled to fly out of town as a guest on a *Star Trek* Cruise. A day later, on the ship, David received a telegram from Gene that read: "Everyone loves your script, have a great cruise."

Then Gene's personal lawyer, who had assumed an unofficial position on *Star Trek–The Next Generation*, read the script. Things changed. Radically.

The lawyer and several staff members actively campaigned against the script, though some of them earlier had championed AIDS as one of the issues the show should tackle. The complimentary telegram was forgotten. Gene had a new opinion of "Blood and Fire." It was "aesthetically displeasing" with its slimy bloodworms and plasmacytes as a metaphor for AIDS. That would have to change. As for the gay couple, they would have to be eliminated or become heterosexual. It seemed they, too, were aesthetically displeasing, despite the fact they were drawn as professional and well-regarded members of the *Enterprise* crew.

When David arrived home from the weekend cruise, he found a phone message from me warning him about the bear trap he was about to walk into. In a respectful but pointed memo to Gene, David argued for his vision and for the important issues the script addressed. In front of fans and staff, Gene had declared his intention to include gay characters on the new show, even if only in one episode. Where was the courage in presenting a story with ordinary characters facing an ordinary biological threat? David's final arguments were: "If not now, when? If not here, where?"

Gene laid down his decree, not to David's face, but through one of the other producers. The script would either be rewritten as he directed, or it would be shelved. David made changes, taking out one of the gay characters and giving his lines to "Tasha Yar." It was still "aesthetically displeasing." David knew he would leave the show soon, as his contract was expiring. He offered to rewrite the script one more time, but Gene told another producer not to let him do so. A staff producer-writer tried to rework the script, calling it "Blood and Ice," changing the plasmacytes to brain-eating entities that turned infected people into zombies. Didn't work. The script was shelved, and there were no gay characters depicted on *Star Trek–The Next Generation* under Gene Roddenberry's aegis.

Later, rumors started to spread that David had been fired from the show—not true. Other rumors spread that the "Blood and Fire" script had been so bad it had to be shelved—not true. David began selling copies of it at conventions so people could read it for themselves and decide. He donated the proceeds from those sales to Aids Project Los Angeles.

With his reputation being trashed at conventions in both the United States and Britain, David responded the only way he knew how—by writing a series of fine novels. Among them were *A Rage for Revenge*, *A Season for Slaughter*, *Jumping Off the Planet*, *Voyage of the Star Wolf* and esteemed *The Martian Child*, for which he won the Nebula and the Hugo awards.

In the nineties, David and I developed four scripts, a full story arc and an immense bible for a potential *Star Wolf* television series or series of TV movies. The book you hold in your hand is the envisioning of the "Blood and Fire" script in a different universe and with different characters, but with even more power than it would have had as a *Star Trek–The Next Generation* episode. Read it and see for yourself how compelling and exciting a story it is—and how boldly it goes where no one has gone before.

D.C. FONTANA

Scenery

With each hyperstate jump, the distance between the two ships lessened significantly. Aboard the *Star Wolf*, the distress signal from the *Norway* was expected to become not only more distinct, but more detailed. Distress beacons were supposed to use "pyramid" coding, with successive layers of detail encrypted into the signal.

As a rescue vessel approached the source and the signal became stronger, the additional levels of information would become accessible and the rescuers would have a clearer idea of what kind of emergency to expect. Decoding the *Norway*'s beacon should have provided additional information about the nature of her emergency.

Should have.

Didn't.

In this situation, the supplementary channels remained bafflingly blank. And the itch behind Korie's shoulders became a full-blown rash, so much so that even Captain Parsons had to scratch. She grumbled her annoyance. "They want help, but they won't give details. You're right, Commander Korie. This has to be a high-security operation."

"*Extremely* high security," Korie noted. "Way out here, a month deep into the south end of the rift—this is the other side of nowhere—whatever it is they're doing, they want it secret."

On the forward display, the red star was already visible as a teardrop hung against the darkness. A pinpoint flare of blue-white flamed beyond, but the spiral streamer wasn't apparent yet, only a soft pink glow surrounding the blue-white dwarf.

"We have our bearings," reported Tor. "Ready for the next jump."

"Initiate," said the captain.

The *Star Wolf* jumped. And jumped again. And one more time. Soon, the object known only as IKE-34 was a wall of flame that filled half the visible universe. It occupied a volume of space equal to the orbit of Jupiter. Against the darkness, the blue dwarf could now be seen pulling a great streamer of flaming gas out of the tip of the crimson teardrop. The line of fire curled out and around, stretching across the visible sky like a rip; as it reached the disk-shaped well of the bright blue star, it began to spiral inward, around and around, the colors shifting more and more brightly as the crimson flames were gathered into the purpling corona. And yes, the scenery *was* spectacular. Better than spectacular. Astonishing.

From this angle, below the red star's south pole, it wasn't immediately apparent that the giant was also flattened at both poles; it was impressive nonetheless. Despite the *Star Wolf*'s distance—several billion kilometers—the massive size of the star created the looming perception that they were close enough to touch it. The perspectives of space create impossible visions, and this was one of the more impossible views. That long-dead poet had been right. Enjoy God's handiwork in silence. Across the Bridge of the starship the crew worked wordlessly, but again and again their eyes were drawn to the forward display.

Eventually, the magnitude of the view became so intimidating and oppressive that Captain Parsons ordered the image muted down. "We don't need the eye of hell looking down on us," she remarked. "We've got work to do. Let's turn that off." She stepped down from the Command Deck, only three short steps into the well of the Operations Bay, but a whole other domain of command and control. She took a familiar position next to the astrogation console, just behind Tor's left shoulder. "How long to close with the *Norway*?"

"Fifty-six hours. Coming in across the pole brings us in a lot faster—but the *Norway*'s in the plane of the ecliptic—a 'Missionary Orbit.' Coming up from under, we'll have to accelerate constantly to catch up, correcting all the way in, and decelerate only in the last few hours. Tricky, not impossible."

"And if those folks are in serious trouble . . . we still might not be in time," said Parsons.

"They never should have parked so close to the star," Tor replied. "They've made the rescue operation damn near impossible."

"That may be the point," said Korie, coming up beside them. "They *wanted* to make interception difficult. By staying within the gravitational corona they're beyond the reach of hyperstate—no ship can jump in that close, neither friend nor enemy. The approach has to be made in normal space. The slow way. That gives them time to detect, scan and evade."

Parsons nodded. "Tactically, that was the right decision. In practice, it's going to kill them. This'll be another one for the textbooks. All right, take us in, Commander Tor." She turned to Goldberg at the communication station. "Lieutenant? Do you have anything else yet?"

The stout, red-headed man at the console shook his head. "Sorry, Captain. The signal is still blank."

"That's what I expected." She turned to Korie. "In a way, they're doing us a favor. When the inevitable board of inquiry asks why there were no survivors, we'll be able to point to the deficiencies of their orbit and their distress signal."

"Failure to arrive in time," murmured Korie. "That's what they'll say. Of course, we'll be excused for that—but it'll still be a black mark on our record."

"Don't sweat it," said Parsons. "If this ship can carry the burden of blame for Marathon without flinching, it can easily handle a minor embarrassment like this one." She turned away from Korie's dour expression. "All right, let's do the dance. We all know the steps." She headed back up to the Command Deck, the raised dais at the rear of the Bridge. "Oh, Mr. Korie—one more thing." She waited until Korie had joined her up behind the railing. In a more conversational tone, she asked, "Have you examined the manifest of the supplies we're delivering here?"

"Yes, ma'am." Korie waited for the captain to make her point.

"Notice anything interesting?"

"Quite a few things."

"Such as?"

"Well, there's a more-than-usual complement of biotechnical equipment and supplies, isolation gear, repulsor valves, magnetic bottles and so on."

"Your assessment?"

"It's a no-brainer, Captain. They're engaged in Class-X medical research. All that isolation gear says they're dealing with extreme toxicity."

The captain nodded. "That's my thought too. We've got a mean, ugly bear here. Train your mission team carefully." To his look, "Yes, I'm going to want you to lead it."

"Not Brik? This should be his responsibility."

"Think about it. If you were captain of a distressed vessel, how would you feel if the first person to your rescue was a Morthan . . . ?

And if your ship was involved in a Class-X operation and security was a major concern—would you believe a Morthan in an Alliance uniform?"

"Point taken," said Korie, embarrassed that he hadn't thought of it himself. But then, he'd been focusing on the more immediate problem—trying to figure out what the *Norway* was doing out here.

"I want you to be careful," the captain added. "Feel free to break out any of the gear in that cargo you need to protect yourselves and the *Star Wolf*."

"Already planning on it."

"And don't listen to Hall's complaints about the charge-backs."

"I never do."

"How's your itch?"

"Ferocious."

"Good. Carry on."

Korie felt comfortable with Captain Parsons—the first time he'd felt comfortable with a captain in a long time. It was a pleasant change to have his abilities not only respected, but depended upon. He nodded his assent and turned back to his headset to complete an earlier discussion with HARLIE, the starship's intelligence engine. He and HARLIE had been sorting through the appropriate procedure books and manuals for dealing with medical emergencies, especially those involving possible contamination by unknown toxic substances. When he finished that, he headed forward to the Med Bay to confer with Chief Surgeon Molly Williger.

Dr. Williger was notorious as the shortest, ugliest woman in the known universe, but few people who served with her ever noticed that; all they saw was one of the best doctors in the fleet. Williger was just finishing a routine medical check on Crewman Brian Armstrong when Korie entered. Armstrong, a side of beef with a grin, flashed his smile at Korie as he pulled his shirt back on. "Hiya, sir."

Korie nodded a curt acknowledgment. He rarely smiled. "Armstrong."

"Sir?" Armstrong began eagerly. "I'd like to volunteer for the Mission Team. Dr. Williger says I'm in good shape. I can carry things. And I'm certified for security duties—"

"I can see you're in good shape." Korie noted Armstrong's well-developed body. "But we're going to need specialists for this operation." Noting Armstrong's immediate disappointment, Korie added, "But—I haven't made any final decisions yet. I'll keep you in mind."

"Thanks, sir. Thanks Dr. Williger." Armstrong grinned again and left. Williger and Korie exchanged amused glances.

"Gotta give him credit," Korie said. "He wants to work."

"He's bored," Williger said. "And he's got this thing going with the Quillas."

"I thought he was over that."

Williger jiggled her hand in an "iffy" gesture. "Armstrong doesn't understand intimacy. The Quillas are a fascinating mystery to him." She added, "He knows how to be friendly, not close. He uses friendliness as a defense against intimacy. But apparently, the Quillas got to him anyway."

"I saw your report."

When he had first come aboard, Armstrong had enjoyed a quick liaison with Quilla Delta, not realizing that all of the other Quillas were telepathic participants. The discovery of a male Quilla—Lambda—had startled him. Later Armstrong and Lambda had become friendly, if not exactly friends. Then Lambda was killed in action—

"Armstrong hurts," said Williger. "And he has no one to talk to about it. He's taking it a lot harder than he shows. All this energy and enthusiasm is . . . denial and sublimation and overcompensation." She sighed. "And then we brought two more Quillas aboard, one male, one female, and . . . well, Armstrong is jealous—"

"Jealous?" Korie looked incredulous.

"Of the male Quilla. Of the closeness the Quillas have. How much do you know about Quillas?"

Korie shrugged. "Haven't really given it too much thought. They're a religious order, dedicated to serving others, aren't they?"

"Well, you should give it more thought than that," Williger said. "They're not just a religious order, they're a conjoined mind in multiple bodies."

"So? What does this have to do with Armstrong?"

"The Quillas had a private welcoming ceremony—and Armstrong was left out of it. How could he be included? When Quillas take a new member into the cluster, there's a whole ritual of joining—very spiritual, but very physical as well. They have to tune themselves to each other. Usually it's only a matter of a few days. This time it took over a week. Armstrong felt like they were shutting him out. On top of Lambda's death—well, he's confused and he's hurting."

Korie made a face. This was not something he wanted to deal with.

Williger glowered up at him. "I know—you don't think self-esteem issues are your concern, they're supposed to be mine. Or the Quillas'. But it *is* your concern, because he's part of your crew. Armstrong needs something to do that lets him feel essential. Right now—he doesn't."

The little doctor looked to Korie sharply. "That's why he's trying so hard to be everyone's best friend. That's all he knows how to do. He needs something else to be good at."

"The problem is, he doesn't have any skills. He's not our smartest crewmember."

"I thought you had him in a training program."

Korie sighed. "He passes his tests, but his scores are always just *barely* passing. He's doing just enough to get by. I need more than that. I can't risk putting him anywhere essential. That's why I keep rotating him."

"Maybe you should trust him with a little responsibility. Maybe he'll surprise you."

"I don't see any evidence to suggest it."

"Uh-huh," Williger said sharply. "And maybe he's feeling the same thing you are, Commander. All you want is *your* chance too."

Korie glanced over at her. He did not like being reminded of the fact that he was not yet wearing captain's stars on his collar. He held back his immediate response, exhaled instead. "That's not what I came down here for, Doctor. We need to finalize our plans for the medical mission team. We need to plan their training—we have to assume the *Norway* is an extremely toxic environment."

Williger noted Korie's deliberate change of subject with a curt "Fine." Then she added, "I'm going with you. And I'll want Brian Armstrong too."

"No, you aren't," Korie said. "The captain doesn't want to risk you."

"But she'll risk you . . . ?"

"I'm expendable. You're not. You'll monitor from the Bridge, or from Med Bay. You can still have Armstrong, if you want."

"I suppose this is not negotiable."

"That's correct."

"Well . . . all right." She sighed acceptance. "I tried. Listen, if the situation is really bad over there, we'll need to use the forward bay as an auxiliary receiving room. I assume you'll be docking at the nose?"

"That's the recommended procedure."

"I want enhanced scanners on your helmets, with high-med software. I'll give you Chief Pharmacist's Mate Berryman as your senior corpsman. Hodel and Easton are also certified. Take them. You won't reconsider Armstrong?"

"Not this time, no. I was thinking Bach and Shibano."

Williger frowned. "Shibano's a cowboy—and Bach hasn't been certified yet for medical missions."

Korie ran a hand through his hair. How to say this without sounding paranoid? There was no way, so he just said it. "We don't know what's over there. I need security people."

"Yeah, I heard about your itch. Half a dozen people came in asking for skin-rex lotion." Her expression was wry. "It must be catching, eh?"

"I certainly hope so."

Lambda

Armstrong sat alone in the mess room. Thinking. His cup of chocolate sat cold and forgotten in front of him. On some unspoken level, he understood what his problem was. And now, today, for some reason, he was almost ready to speak it—if not to anyone else, at least to himself.

It wasn't loneliness. It was that thing on the other side of loneliness.

He could talk to people, he could make friends, he could get people to spend time with him, and he usually didn't have any problems with women either. He'd had more than his share of sexual exercise. And even a relationship or two. So, no, it wasn't loneliness.

It was that *other* thing. About *belonging*. About being a part of something—not just a plug-in module, replaceable, discardable—but something more essential. Something with identity. He wanted to know that what he did was useful and important, and even necessary to the success of the ship. And the war.

It was a need that he couldn't explain, and he felt frustrated every time he thought about it—this feeling that he had to be something more. But there was nothing particularly special about Brian Armstrong. He was big, good-looking, a little goofy, likable, mostly capable, and just like several billion other men in this part of the galaxy. If he died right now, there would be no evidence that he was ever here, except a few records in the Fleet rolls. There would be no artifact, no object, no person, no heritage, nothing remarkable to indicate that Brian Armstrong had passed this way; nothing to say that Brian Armstrong had left the universe a better place than he found it. And despite his genial, easy-going nature, Brian Armstrong found this thought intolerable. It wasn't death he feared; it was being *insignificant*.

He just wanted to . . . make a difference. That was all.

Quilla Delta sat down opposite him. She placed one blue hand on top of his. He glanced up, met her eyes, forced a half-smile, pulled his hand away, then looked back down at his lap.

"You are not happy, Brian," she said. "That makes us sad."

Armstrong didn't answer. To answer would have meant discussing the things that he didn't discuss with anyone. If Lambda had lived, maybe he would have. He had thought about it a lot, what he wanted to say to Lambda. Lambda had seemed to know something of his confusion—

"Lambda is not dead," Delta said. "Everything that Lambda was, everything that Lambda knew—it still lives inside us. Only the body is gone. Not the soul. Not the spirit."

"I can't believe that," said Armstrong. "I've studied a little bit about Quillas. About massminds. I know that there's a kind of synergy that happens. But there's no way the soul of an individual can leave a body and take up residence in a networked collection of other bodies. It's just not possible."

"Yes, it is," said Delta in a different voice. A voice that Armstrong recognized in spite of himself, and he looked up with a start. "Everything that I was when I was alive I still am. I'm just living inside a different body now. I told you that Quillas are immortal, Brian. This is why I became one. Because I was like you. And I was unhappy that way."

Armstrong started to lower his eyes again, then changed his mind and looked into Quilla Delta's face. Her skin was the most beautiful shade of blue. Her eyes were shadowed with magenta; her lips were almost the same shade. Her quills were a bright red Mohawk across her bald blue scalp. She had a slim, boyish quality and yet she was as feminine as a rosebud. He thought she was the most beautiful and the most irresistible female he had ever seen. She was also the most affectionate—he knew that there were no personality differences between one member of a Quilla cluster and another, but nevertheless he still felt she was the most *affectionate*. Maybe he was projecting his own feelings, maybe not. It didn't matter. He couldn't deny her anything.

He licked his lips uncomfortably. They were dry. His whole mouth was dry. "I, um, have to go." He started to rise. But as he did, he saw that they were no longer alone. Quilla Beta, Quilla Alpha, Quilla Gamma and the two new ones, Quilla Theta and Quilla Omega.

Omega was a tall, blue man, taller even than Lambda had been. He stepped forward now. "Brian Armstrong, we know the source of your unhappiness. We are sorry for having caused you pain."

"It's not your fault," Armstrong said.

"But it is our *responsibility*. We know that you felt *distanced* when we expanded our cluster. We know that you felt shut out of our closeness. This makes us sad. Our closeness should not be a barrier. It is not a prize that we keep to ourselves; it is a gift that we share with others."

"You can't help it," Armstrong said to all of them, trying to avoid looking at Omega. "It's just the way you are. You're all one mind. And I'm not. I'm not part of you. I'm just me. So just by existing the way you are, I'm automatically shut out. It's my fault for presuming that I could ever be anything more than another John. I was stupid."

"No," said Delta. "Not stupid."

"Whatever. Listen, thanks for all the . . . attention. It was fun, okay? But like the song says . . . I was looking for love on all the wrong planets. It was a mistake. I'm sorry that Lambda's gone. I liked him. I like all of you, but uh . . . can't we just be friends now, something like that?"

Omega blocked his exit. "Lambda lives in me too, Brian. Listen. This is what Lambda wants to say to you. 'Ever since the first day you have been running from us. Your few conversations with Lambda were the only time you stopped running. It was the only time you treated any of us like a person. The rest of the time you acted like we were bodies, here only for your sexual pleasure. Did you think your callous behavior wasn't hurtful to us? Perhaps it is you who owe us an apology.' "

"Yeah, well—maybe I do. I'm sorry for treating you all like—like objects. Sex toys. Freaks. I dunno. Whatever. I was wrong. May I go now?"

"Brian—" This time Gamma stepped in front of him. "We ask only one thing. Just please stop running from us."

"Okay. I'll stop running. May I go now?"

Quilla Delta stepped in close. "We miss Lambda too," she said. "His body fit right. Almost as nice as yours. Sometimes we cry for him—for that missing piece of ourselves. Do you cry for him, Brian? I think you want to. If you do, it's all right." Without waiting for his answer, she put her arms around him and gently pulled him to her. He stiffened, but she refused to let go. He closed his eyes, but she still refused to let go. Instead she held him—and held and held and held him. Did she want him to cry? He didn't know. He didn't feel like crying now. He didn't know what he felt—this wasn't a familiar situation.

The other Quillas wrapped their arms around them, and now Armstrong felt himself being passed from body to body. He couldn't tell which of them was holding him. He opened his eyes only once and saw that he was being hugged by Omega, then closed them again until it didn't matter anymore whose arms were wrapped around him. And still they passed him around.

"Listen to me," a soft voice whispered in his ear. It sounded like Lambda again. "When you're ready to talk . . . we'll be ready to listen. Give us that chance, Brian? Please?"

Despite himself, he nodded.

And that was enough. That was all he needed to do. When they finally let him go, he felt different—and he was different. He looked from one to the other of them and realized he'd taken on a terrifying new responsibility. Honesty.

History

Contrary to popular expectations, the invention of faster-than-light travel did not create an age of enlightenment. Quite the opposite.

Imagine the human species as a vast stew of ideas, opinions, neuroses, ideologies, beliefs, religions, pathologies, illnesses, cults and paradigms—a sea of competing world-views, models of reality at war with each other; an ecology of memes, each one struggling for living space in the heads and hearts of human beings.

The introduction of cost-effective FTL access to other worlds gave each of these memes access to the living space it wanted. The result was an explosion of humanity in all directions: each ship filled with idea spores and belief cuttings and world-view seed-carriers—all those little ships filled with infectious opinions and belief systems, each and every person a host for his part of the larger energizing meme. It wasn't humanity that emigrated to the stars; *it was the memes.*

Humans live and breed for their beliefs; often they sacrifice everything for the thoughts they carry. History is a chronicle of human beings dying for their convictions, as if the continuance of the idea is more important than the continuance of the person. The ideology becomes more important to the carrier than his own ability to be human.

All the disparate models of reality, each one demanding its own space to dominate and thrive, drove their bearers outward—the memes drove men like parasites riding in their minds—and the human species spread its motes across space like a field of dandelions exploding in a tornado, creating a million new places for memes to thrive and a billion new memes to live in them.

Interstellar travel fractured and fractionated the human race. A thousand new religions. A hundred thousand new schools of scientific thought. A million new worlds, each one with its own dominant meme. Most of the memes were benign: "Love one another. Judge not, lest ye be judged. Do unto others as you would have others do unto you." Some were not: "Our book is the only true book. Our God is the only true God. Our belief is the only true belief. All others are false . . . and must be eradicated." Some were untested: "We need a place to live where we won't have the oppressions of others keeping us from being who we really are."

The problem that each of these colonizing memes ran into was *reality*. Every single world that human beings stepped out onto presented its own particular set of challenges—capping the volcanoes for geothermal energy, cracking the ice to make oceans, releasing water from the mantle to make air, mining heavy metals for industry, securing a power supply from the wind and the water and the sun, getting enough oxygen into the air, cooling the atmosphere with shadow fields, warming the seas with core taps, designing crops that could survive, dealing with hostile organisms, determining both long- and short-range weather patterns, constructing safe shelters, putting up satellites, establishing global communications, designing a working government. . . . Compared to the last challenge, of course, all the others were easy. You could always tell when a planet was viable—but nobody was ever convinced that a government was fine. *Any* government.

And as each set of memes left the pure ideological vacuum of space and collided with the hard soil of reality, the laws of evolution kicked in. Each new world worked its own conditions, and the memes were given the same choice as every other survival-oriented entity: adapt or die. Those that adapted, evolved. And, inevitably, mutations occurred. The planets themselves added their own flavors to the mix, creating new memes in the ecology of ideas. Over time, the rigors of the environment always took precedence—in every case, the flavor of the planet eventually overwhelmed everything else, becoming the dominant taste in the stew.

Human colonists—carriers of the memes—were caught in the middle, as usual. Humanity changed. Adapted. Evolved. Mutated. And redesigned itself accordingly—creating new memes and new explosions of trade and colonization. Humanity's memes drove it outward, forcing it to become something new on every planet it touched. Humanity spread throughout the galaxy like a rapidly evolving intelligent cancer.

On some worlds, a particularly seductive meme took hold—the idea that if humanity now had the power to redesign itself, then humanity *should* redesign itself. Imagine . . . a truly *efficient* and *capable* human being. Imagine a human who was "more-than" human. The

"More-Than" meme was more than just "another good idea." For some, it became a cult, an obsession, an ideology—a religion. For some, it became a holy war.

Some of the More-Thans seceded from the Covenant and headed out beyond the frontier—sand not just beyond the frontier, but to the far side of the rift, a natural barrier to further human expansion. Humanity—*unimproved* humanity—would be unlikely to challenge the rift. Or so the More-Thans believed. They were wrong, but they believed it anyway.

The Morthan meme, mixed with the isolationist meme, was a dangerous combination. And those who espoused it were clearly unfamiliar with the evolutionary consequences that befell isolated populations on islands, in preserves or separated on distant planets—or perhaps they felt that because they understood the laws of nature, they were somehow immune to their effects.

Countering the Morthan meme was another one: the meme of Alliance, the idea that the human family, despite all its diversity and difference, was still evolved from the same basic stock and was therefore still a family, and that whatever new shapes or ideologies might occur across the galaxy, the fundamental relationship of a common heritage was enough of a foundation on which to build an Alliance of trade and cultural exchange.

As disastrous as the meme of isolation was to the Morthans, equally disastrous was the meme of a universal family of humanity that could include and celebrate every separate form of behavior and belief. Memes are survival-oriented. Memes tolerate only memes that are sympathetic or complementary. Memes cannot tolerate antithetical ideas.

But memes don't die, humans do.

Humans, as the carriers of ideas, as the servants of ideologies, shed their blood whenever two memes came into conflict.

And the conflict between the Alliance meme and the Morthan meme promised to be the most terrible of all.

Brik

Not all Morthans believed in the goals of the Morthan Solidarity. This did not automatically mean that they believed in the goals of the Alliance either, but there were some who had fled Morthan space and applied for asylum. Some of the refugees ended up as civilian advisors. Others, for reasons of their own, enlisted to serve in the Allied Star Fleet. Lieutenant Commander Brik was one of those Morthan officers.

Brik stood three meters tall, almost too tall for the corridors of a destroyer-class liberty ship. There was room for him to stretch to his full height only on the Ops Deck, the engine room, the Cargo Bay and his private quarters. Everywhere else, he moved in a near-feral crouch.

The more traditionally human members of the *Star Wolf* crew often speculated on Brik's motivations. To most of them, he remained an incomprehensible enigma. Why would *any* Morthan want to live and serve with human beings? If Morthans believed themselves to be "more than human," then wouldn't such a role be demeaning and degrading?

In point of fact, Lieutenant Commander Brik had not too long ago held that very view—that service with human beings *was* an extremely repugnant duty, almost a personal disgrace. But he also was smart enough to recognize that the prejudice he felt was more the voice of his upbringing on a Morthan world than a product of any direct interaction with human beings. So with great difficulty he had put aside his prejudice in favor of a more useful curiosity about the nature of humanity—an act of will power that had initially left him trembling with fury but had now subsided into just another knot in his second stomach, something he could live with. He was still discomfited by humans, but not for the reasons humans believed.

Brik's original distaste had now been supplanted by something even more uncomfortable. Honest interest. For all their faults, insecurities, inaccuracies, inabilities, neuroses, psychoses, pathologies, beliefs and other failings, humans were still . . . *interesting*. Part of Brik's interest lay in the fact that human identity represented the undeniable ancestral origin of Morthan identity. It was humans who had come up with the idea of a superior bioengineered species. It was humans who had begun the process of creating the Morthans—at least until the fifth generation, when there were finally enough mature Morthans motivated to take responsibility for their own future.

Brik had come to believe that for Morthans to control the direction of their own evolution, it was essential to understand the source material. Knowing what made humanity successful was as important as knowing where humanity could be improved. So Brik's curiosity was rooted in a very selfish motivation.

At one point, Brik had been concerned about the possibility that he might end up developing a certain degree of *affection* for his human comrades-in-arms. And for a while, he had even toyed with the possibility that this might be a useful domain of personal experimentation. However, after his single attempt at fathoming human sexuality he realized that this was probably not a fruitful avenue of research for him. The experiment—undertaken with, and at the behest of, Lieutenant J.G. Helen Bach, one of his security officers—had been a near-fatal disaster.* Near fatal for Lieutenant J.G. Helen Bach, that is. The curious lieutenant had paid for her misadventure with ten days of downtime in Med Bay.

The consequences for Brik were not physical—but shortly thereafter several salacious rumors about his physical prowess began to circulate through the ship, and although no one ever said anything to him directly, Lieutenant Commander Brik was painfully aware that he had become something of a legend among the crew. Particularly the female members of the crew. His relations with Bach had been strained ever since, to say the least.

Eventually, Bach applied for a transfer, which Korie—as acting captain—had denied. Then Brik applied for a transfer, although not for the same reasons. Not knowing how to deal with the sexual relationships, human gossip or the prurient interest of a bored crew, he felt just vulnerable enough that he recognized he could become a serious danger to the rest of the ship. He wasn't certain he could control his own deadly impulses—at least not until Korie called both Brik and

---

The Middle of Nowhere.

Bach into conference and ordered them to find a way to work together. *Or else.* He did not specify what the *or else* would be. He did not even acknowledge the specifics of the situation. He simply said, "You two are assigned to work together. Find a way to do that. Now. You're both rational, intelligent beings. You're both mature enough to work security—the crew looks to both of you as role models for shipboard discipline. We have a new captain coming aboard in three days. I intend to turn this ship over with the highest possible confidence rating. You are officers trained to handle problems at your level and pass only solutions upward. If you start passing problems up to me, you won't like my solutions. I promise you." And then he added, "Fortunately, I don't like either one of you enough that I'll have to feel bad about the consequences. Is this clear? Good. Now go do your jobs and let this be the end of it. Dismissed."

Officially, the fleet preferred that crew members abstain from having sexual relationships, lest it complicate the chain of command. Unofficially, commanding officers only acknowledged personal or sexual relationships when they interfered with the smooth running of the ship. A reprimand of this type would be a serious blemish on the career of any officer on whose record it appeared. To his credit, Korie kept his reprimand off the record and his remarks were never entered into either Brik's or Bach's service log.

Once Korie had ordered Brik to comply with Fleet discipline, Brik's personal dilemma was resolved. He knew how to follow orders. He knew how to fulfill his duty. He knew how to be responsible: push all personal concerns aside; they no longer exist. End of dilemma. Bach followed his lead and their professional relationship resumed in an atmosphere of cold, crisp politesse. Neither of them ever mentioned the matter again, nor did Korie.

For his part, Brik used the episode as a confirmation of his earlier suspicion that attempts at affection with ancestral-form human beings would be a mistake. Ancestrals were irrational beyond anything he had previously conceived. In the domain of sexual relationships, they were clearly insane. Psychopathic. Criminally deranged. Not to be trusted without a keeper.

Nevertheless, when ancestral-form human beings put aside sexual matters, they were *almost* civilized. And in that regard, Brik had to acknowledge that they were obviously capable of extraordinary self control—perhaps even more self control than most Morthans. Morthans didn't have sex. Morthans didn't have hormonal storms driving them crazy. Morthans didn't have these same kinds of overwhelming physical urges. So Morthans didn't have to control them, didn't have to know how to behave appropriately toward others. Morthans were trained early how to behave—distrust everyone and everything. Learn that and you know how to survive and succeed for the rest of your life.

But humans—ordinary humans had all these other operating modes. They made jokes. They flirted. They *told the truth*. All of these modes were alien experiences to Brik—so alien, in fact, that he was beginning to suspect that ancestral-form humans were far more unfathomable to Morthans than Morthans ever would be to them. And for that reason, he began to suspect that the Morthan Solidarity might actually lose the war.

It was a curious thought. Morthans lose?

Militarily, Morthans were clearly superior—but interstellar space was a great equalizer. A torpedo could be launched from a small ship as well as a big one—it could destroy a big ship as well as a small one. So the advantage lay not in strength, but in speed and tactics.

Humans had speed, but Morthans had tactics.

Given that equation, the smart money would bet on the Morthans—but more and more Brik was beginning to realize that the essential irrationality of human beings made them tactically impossible to predict, and possibly impossible to defeat. And if that were so, then the *unthinkable* might actually be true—human beings might be superior to Morthans.

All those different operating modes. Humans had more different ways to be, more different ways to *think*, than Morthans did.

Very troubling.

Because if this were true, Brik could not afford to dismiss affection or sexual relationships. If this particularly uncomfortable thesis had any validity to it at all, Brik had to continue his investigations. No matter what the personal cost.

Indeed, his personal commitment to expanding his knowledge of dangerous things *demanded* that he return his attention to these investigations. The thought bothered him immensely and he inflicted severe damage on both of his workout robots while he dealt with the discomfort.

His exercises gave him a way to maintain—and beyond that, he could safely postpone any further inquiries into the matter of emotional attachments because Korie had effectively ordered him to. *"Do your job"* took precedence.

At least for now.

Preparation

For a long while, the crew of the *Star Wolf* had been resentful of Korie's treatment. They had complained—with considerable justification—that the executive officer drove them too hard. But later, after several missions and several close encounters with the enemy, after several opportunities to see how well the ship functioned in a crisis, the crew's attitude had changed dramatically. They still complained about how hard Korie worked them—but now they did so with a considerable degree of pride. Their unofficial motto was, "Yes, but he's *our* son of a bitch."

Captain Parsons had come aboard the *Star Wolf* well aware of Korie's reputation. She knew his record, she knew what fires fueled his engines. She had expected a humorless man, a grim one, a martinet—someone like his mentor, Captain Richard Hardesty, only younger and without the augments. What she found was someone much more complex.

At first, Korie seemed to her much less than she had expected. But then, perhaps she wasn't certain at all what she expected. What she found was a young man who was deceptively soft-spoken and respectful of her authority. Possibly he had grown more relaxed with his situation over the past year. And possibly the tales of Korie were somewhat exaggerated. In either case, she found him intriguing—particularly the depth of his knowledge about his starship. She suspected that he could take it apart and rebuild it single-handedly, if given enough time. And add a few improvements in the process. So far, she hadn't found any situation he couldn't handle. And she doubted she would.

She caught up with him in the officer's mess, where he was poring over a set of schematics.

"How's your team doing?"

"They've had thirty hours training, Captain. They've had the last six hours off so they can be thoroughly rested and ready when we go in."

"What about yourself?"

"I've had my sleep for this month."

"We're going to have some very long days coming up . . ."

Korie nodded, still preoccupied with the diagrams. "I can handle it."

Parsons stepped in close and whispered, "I know you can handle it. But I don't want you playing superman *all* the time. You've got to learn how to pace yourself or you'll burn out before you're thirty."

"I'm thirty-two," Korie said.

"Then you're overdue. We've got six hours until we begin final approach. Go take a power nap—"

"I don't need—" Korie stopped himself. "Aye, Captain." He switched off the display, pulled his headset off and picked up his coffee mug and sandwich plate. He ducked through the hatch to "Broadway," the starship's main corridor. Captain Parsons watched him go, pleased that Korie was learning how to follow orders.

She'd been worried about her executive officer's strong will and independent nature. That was part of his "legend" too. It was no secret among his fellow officers that Jon Korie had earned his captain's stars three times over. That the admiral had not yet given him a ship of his own was rapidly becoming an embarrassment not only to Korie, but to everyone serving with him as well—not to mention other captains whose names had come up later than Korie's.

In fact, Korie didn't know it, but Parsons had refused this posting when she discovered her executive officer would be Jon Korie. But Admiral O'Hara had told her to put her objections aside and take the ship. It wasn't that Korie was unready for command—he'd already proven that—but there were *other* factors at work. And in the meantime Korie needed the opportunity to practice the virtues of patience and cooperation. Parsons' supervision would be a useful and important role model for him.

Parsons suspected that Korie had already figured it out. Korie's mental agility was part of his growing "legend" among those who had served with him, and it was part of the scuttlebutt around Stardock that Jon Korie could tell you how far out of alignment the hyperstate grapplers were just by tasting the soup in the galley. Parsons had not yet seen Korie demonstrate this particular skill, but after a few weeks of watching him oversee the maintenance of the vessel, she would not have been surprised. The man was the most totally dependable officer she had ever met. Almost a machine.

Neither was it a secret why Korie was so driven. Korie's wife and two sons had been on Shaleen when the Morthans attacked. They were presumed dead. Afterward, Korie had received a delayed-in-transit message from Carol indicating that they were trying to evacuate to Taalamar—but Taalamar had been destroyed by an avalanche of asteroids, launched by teams of Morthan commandos. The *Star Wolf* had been part of a massive (but insufficient) evacuation effort. In what few records survived from Taalamar, there was no evidence of the arrival of his wife and children. Emotionally, Korie had lost them, been given a nugget of hope, then lost them again.

Still, part of him prayed. He didn't want to be alone. Perhaps they had been separated. Perhaps one of the boys had gotten away. But he didn't dare torture himself with those thoughts anymore. That was planting the seeds of madness.

At Stardock, Korie routinely and methodically worked out with robots designed to look like Morthans. He pummeled, kicked, beat, attacked, bit, punched and butted the robots with his head, oblivious to his own risk of injury. Several times, the gym attendants had considered restraining or sedating him. But Korie was only one of thousands who felt the need to kick the living crap out of a Morthan, and the workouts with the robots were considered a valuable therapeutic exercise for everyone.

At all other times, Korie's demeanor was singularly professional, but it did not require a quantum mechanic to figure out why Korie was so obsessive about keeping the *Star Wolf* functioning at optimum military readiness. Whenever the ship came to port, whether Stardock or any other safe harbor, Korie had Chief Petty Officer "Toad" Hall out negotiating for upgrades, spares and additional weaponry, whatever he could find, wherever he could find it. The *Star Wolf* had even taken aboard a shipment of six defective torpedoes—rather than let them be recalled, Korie and Chief Engineer Leen intended to rebuild the units to their own specifications.

As long as Korie's obsessions were sublimated into such potentially useful outlets, Captain Parsons had no objections. Indeed, she actually enjoyed watching Jon Korie work. He was a complex and interesting man—and he had the effect of energizing everyone around him. Parsons had written the admiral that she had never been on a ship that hummed with so much directed activity, and she felt this was directly due to Jon Korie's determination, now shared by the crew, that the *Star Wolf* would outlive the blemishes on her name.

"There are a lot of advantages," Parsons had written, "to serving on a big ship, a ship like the 'Big E.' It's the biggest, the best, the boldest and the brightest. Wherever you go, you're regarded as the pride of the fleet and the hope of humanity. But the 'Big E' doesn't get sent out to the front lines because the Fleet can't take the risk of losing her. The psychological shock wave that would send across the Allied Worlds would be devastating. So it falls to the smaller ships, the liberty ships, to plow the dark between the stars and take the ultimate risks. This is where the real heroism is found—among the men and women who know that they are not going to be celebrated wherever they go, among those who are doing their jobs because they know the value of their actions to the Fleet. Despite the risks, despite the lack of appropriate reward, despite the lack of glory and fame—these are the people who are going to make the difference for all of us. What is truly remarkable about all of them is what they bring to their work—not just a sense of obligation, but more than that, a genuine affection for their duty.

"These young heroes—and heroes they truly are—have learned to love their mission. Whatever it is that energizes these people," Parsons concluded in her letter, "it is not only a source of enormous hope, I believe it will eventually prove to be the fuel for our victory over the Morthan Solidarity. I do not know if this feeling can be trained or taught, but once experienced, it can never be forgotten or expunged from a human soul."

Admiral O'Hara had replied, "Captain Parsons, thank you for your note. I intend to share your thoughts with all of the other captains under my command. I can see now that I was right to insist that you take the *Star Wolf*. I had expected that there was much you would teach her crew. I am pleased to find that you are learning as much from them. Carry on."

Probes

"Thirty seconds to horizon—" called Tor.

Parsons checked her own display. Even though she knew exactly what she would see, she had long ago gotten into the habit of confirming everything herself. "Good," she said. The hatch behind her popped open. Without turning around, she said, "We're now officially in range. Did you have a nice nap, Mr. Korie?"

"Yes, Captain, I did," he replied stiffly.

She gave him a questioning look. Was he still smarting at having been ordered to rest?

"It was an interesting experience, sleep," he said blandly. "I'll have to try it more often. Thank you for the opportunity."

Parsons allowed herself a hint of a grin, a wry expression. Korie was clearly not without a sense of humor—he could even allow the joke to be on himself. That was good to know. She nodded and turned forward, all business again. "Let's get a close look at the *Norway*. Commander Brik—?"

The Morthan Security Officer and chief of strategic operations straightened up and turned to face the captain. When he stood on the Ops Deck, he could turn toward the Command Deck and be eye-to-eye with his superior officers, so he had made his post a work station directly ahead and to the left of the captain's command chair. "Aye, Captain?"

"Launch a spread of three probes. Monitor them all the way in."

"Aye, Captain. Launch bays armed and ready. Stand by." He turned back to his console and began reading calmly off his display. "Probes are hot and green. Launching on my mark . . ." He snapped open a plastic protective cover, and flipped a red toggle. "We are armed.

Three . . . two . . . one—" There was a row of buttons next to the toggle; three of them were lit. He pressed the first one, paused, pressed the second, paused again, then pressed the third. With each touch, the hard thump of a torpedo launch thudded through the ship.

Captain Parsons' coffee rippled in her mug; she replaced the cap and put the mug back in the holder in her chair arm.

At his station, Brik continued to watch his displays. "Probes accelerating. On course. Probe one has acquisition of target . . . Probe two has acquisition of target . . . Probe three has acquisition of target. Flyby in seventeen minutes. Deceleration begins in thirteen. Confidence is high, and all three units are in the groove, five by five." He punched up the next program in the series and reported, "We have acquisition of all three signals. We'll have a half-second delay at maximum range."

"Thank you, Mr. Brik." Parsons retrieved her coffee and turned her attention to the holographic display in the center of the Ops Deck. It showed the bloated red spheroid with the orbit of the *Norway* tracking around it and a separate line showing the interception course of the *Star Wolf*. Although they were now decelerating at full power to the plasma drives, they were still more than half a light second away from the other ship. In six hours, their respective trajectories would be almost matching. Less than two hours after that, they should be close enough for final approach and docking.

The physics of the problem were trivial. HARLIE could have the answer on the screen before a person finished asking the question. But the logistics of the problem were complicated by IKE-34's primary, the bloated red star. Once per orbit—once per artificial "year"—the *Norway* would have to pass through the streamer of flame being pulled out of the red star by the blue. This was clearly a "fail-safe" orbit. If something went wrong on the *Norway*, if she were disabled and couldn't break orbit or if there was no one left alive to give the order, she would be destroyed by her passage through the fire.

The *Norway*'s large orbit gave her a long "year"—more than forty-eight months—so she had clearly been on station for some time; she was just now approaching her time of passage. Within a few days at most, she would be gone. The *Star Wolf*'s timing was fortunate—or maybe not. They still didn't know what they would find aboard her.

This was the troubling factor in Captain Parsons' calculations. How badly was the *Norway* incapacitated? Could she be saved? Was she so badly contaminated that she should not be saved? If they were to make the attempt to save her, would they have time to decontaminate the ship? Assuming the contamination was of a controllable nature. Nothing was known. Everything was assumption.

The procedure books provided some useful guidelines to follow, but every situation was unique. And this one was probably off the map, out of the manuals and deep into unknown territory. Captain Parsons wasn't afraid of the challenge; on the contrary, it both intrigued and excited her—but she was also aware that a high-risk situation meant the possibility of fatalities and that was the one part of the job she could never be comfortable with. The human cost. No matter how careful the precautions they took, there were always possibilities.

Her coffee had gone cold again. She replaced the top on her mug and put it back in its holder on her chair arm.

She turned her attention back to her display. The probes continued to accelerate, racing ahead, sacrificing themselves in a high-speed interception, crossing the path of the *Norway* as close as possible, scanning her in a series of high-speed flybys, and then shooting off irretrievably into flame and distance. The signals from the probes would tell them if there was still life aboard the *Norway*.

If there was, they would continue their interception. If not, then Parsons had the option of breaking off and heading back out to space. In this case, it would mean shutting down the plasma drives, ceasing to decelerate and continuing up and out past the course of the *Norway*, away from the red giant and out beyond the gravitational corona where they could safely jump back into hyperstate—and continue on to their next rendezvous.

Parsons bent to her personal display and watched as the tracks of the probes approached the orbit of the *Norway*. There were two blips on each line—the first blip was the projection of the real-time position of the torpedo, the second blip was the time-delayed information received from the missile. At this distance, the blips on each line were less than a half-second apart.

"Receiving five by five. Thirty seconds . . ."

"Put it on the main display."

The forward view opened up, became the view from the leading torpedo. To one side was a dim pink glare; the corona of the red star. To the other side, darkness. The glare washed out everything else—all except a single pinpoint of light, moving slowly downward toward the center of the image, growing brighter . . .

"Twenty seconds."

A green target circle appeared around the moving object. Down the left side of the image, acquisition numbers scrolled up in a blur too fast to read. A telescopic lens shifted into place and the shape of the distant vessel became clear.

"Ten seconds . . . nine . . . eight . . ." Tor counted methodically. "Five . . . four . . . three . . ."

The flyby itself proved to be anticlimactic. The probes were traveling so fast in relation to the *Norway* that the starship flashed past almost too quickly to see. The display showed a quick flare of reflected light—the probe-torpedoes had aimed pseudo-white lasers as they'd passed. The three probes had bracketed the starship in an equilateral triangle. Their combined scans would provide the *Star Wolf* with a three-dimensional view of the ship, in case there was visible damage or other conditions that might affect the rescue operation. Their internal scans should also show if there was any evidence of life still aboard the vessel.

"All right," said Parsons. "Let's look at the visual first. HARLIE?"

The forward display flickered to show the probe-torpedo flyby again, this time in slow-motion. The torpedoes had passed within a kilometer of the crippled vessel, close enough to light it up as bright as daylight with their spotlights. Three separate views of the ship floated past, first one, then another, then the third. The red star was visible as background in one scan, as a crimson reflection in the others.

HARLIE repeated the images in an endless cycle, occasionally pausing or expanding them into close-up examinations. Each of the torpedoes had run multiple high-speed cameras, each with different capabilities. There were also infrared and radio-detectors, gravitational lenses, microwave and radar scanners—plus several devices so esoteric that they were simply referred to as X-modules, and their outputs were considered gifts from God.

"No apparent visible damage," said HARLIE. "Some weathering from the local coronal effects, but that's to be expected. Stand by please. I'm collating the internal scans. Preliminary infrared analysis shows the vessel is radiating heat in a manner consistent with viability, no apparent anomalies. Deep-spectrum scans show the presence of oxygen and nitrogen and carbon dioxide within the hull. Microwave scans show movement—not as much as we would expect from a fully-manned vessel, but movement nonetheless. Some anomalies here. A lot of low-level noise, higher than usual for a normal background reading. The torpedoes queried the ship's autonomous system and received no reply. Life support systems are still operative, but most of the rest of her internals appear to be inactive."

HARLIE paused for a beat, then concluded, "Even without collation, I would give high confidence to the possibility of survivors aboard the *Norway*. Conditions for the maintenance of life are present and there is evidence of movement consistent with human life. We are also detecting the presence of magnetic containment fields and repulsor lenses."

"Thank you, HARLIE," said Korie to his headset. "I want to see the raw data now, and the collation as soon as it's finished."

"The collation is ready now," the intelligence engine replied. "Which would you like to see first?"

"Let's start with the collation." Korie was already turning to the display on his workstation. He grunted to himself and his expression went grim.

When he looked up, Parsons was waiting for him. "Your estimate of the situation, Korie?"

"Proceed to final approach and use that as a go/no-go."

"I concur," said Parsons.

"I'll have to brief the mission team." Korie looked unhappy. "We'll have to go in."

"Don't take anyone who isn't Class-X certified. This is going to get nasty, isn't it?" Her expression turned grim. "How's your itch?"

Korie reached around as if trying to scratch his back. "Right there," he said. "Between the shoulders. All the way down to the bone."

Approach

From a distance, the *Norway* looked normal.

The *Star Wolf* had come up and under the other ship, referenced to the plane of the ecliptic. She had deliberately overshot the common interception point by several thousand kilometers and was now decelerating in the final stages of her approach to allow the *Norway* to "catch up" to her.

Captain Parsons had chosen this approach to allow maximum observation of the distressed vessel before final contact was made. "Let's run a seven-layer series of scans, full-spectrum, in-depth, the works," she ordered. "That'll give the Mission Team an extra hour to prepare special-need equipment. Alert Dr. Williger; I'll want her on the Bridge to help evaluate the data. Commander Tor, put out three more probes—let's get some additional perspectives. Make sure those probes are high-confidence, and let's use tactical units as well as bioremotes. Lt. Goldberg, have you been able to raise contact? No? I didn't think so. Commander Korie, let's continue the assumption of an extremely toxic Class-X situation. Strictly by the book throughout. *No* exceptions."

"Aye, Captain." Korie turned back to his headset. "HARLIE, do you copy?"

"Yes, Mr. Korie. I have already amended the checklists and procedures to be consistent with the captain's orders. There are several situations in the book, however, where the standard procedures are inconsistent with the captain's instructions. While it is unlikely that we will be confronted with such situations, I have amended the procedures for this operation in favor of caution over expediency. It seems to me that is the captain's intention. Is this correct?"

"Yes, HARLIE, that is correct. You done good."

"Thank you, Mr. Korie."

On the forward display, the *Norway* was looming huge. She was identical in structure to the *Star Wolf*, but her engines were lighter and her armaments were fewer, almost nonexistent. She bore the markings of a scientific research vessel.

HARLIE spoke then, as much for the log as for the Bridge crew. "Still no contact with the *Norway*. Her autonomic system is running unevenly. Her intelligence engine is either unable or unwilling to respond. The ship appears to be adrift."

Parsons nodded. Like most captains, she took the lethetic intelligence engines for granted. Korie was the only officer she'd ever met who treated the machinery with the same courtesy he gave humans. Perhaps that was one of the reasons he was able to coax so many extraordinary behaviors out of HARLIE. But even if it was only just another one of the quirks that made Korie "*our* son of a bitch," Captain Parsons was willing to tolerate it.

HARLIE spoke up suddenly, "There is one interesting anomaly, Captain."

Parsons looked up sharply. So did Korie. And every other officer on the Bridge. "Go ahead."

"There are active repulsor valves throughout the *Norway*. I am not sure why."

"Let's see a schematic," Parsons said, almost in unison with Korie. They exchanged a glance. "Sorry, Captain," Korie said.

"No apology necessary," she answered. They both turned to the display on her workstation where HARLIE had brought up a simplified graphic of the *Norway*. The repulsor valves were shown as a cluster of throbbing red bubbles located just aft of the engine room.

Neither Parsons nor Korie said anything for a moment while they studied the display. Finally, the captain broke the silence. "They've divided the ship."

"That's what it looks like," Korie agreed. "People on one side. Toxic something on the other."

"Yes, but which side is which?"

Korie shook his head. "It depends on . . ." His sentence trailed off.

"If you were going to host a very dangerous experiment on board this ship," Parsons mused, "where would you put it—forward or aft? Med Bay or Cargo Bay?"

Korie weighed the possibilities. "Cargo Bay is easier to evacuate. Just open the hatch and drop everything into space. If this stuff—this *thing*, whatever it is—is that toxic, then I'd put it in the Cargo Bay. On the other hand . . . Med Bay is forward of the Bridge, you could put additional research labs in the cabins forward of Med Bay, use the Airlock Reception Bay as a decontamination section, and seal the whole thing off from the rest of the vessel. It depends on how big and how toxic this thing is and how hard it is to control. It could be either side."

They studied the display in silence for a moment, as if there were a clue in it they had somehow missed. Korie stared at the schematic of the starship. The engine room was located in the aft third. There were equipment bays behind the engine room, and the Cargo Bay was situated behind that. The repulsor bubbles were just forward of the Cargo Bay, centered on the autonomic core of the vessel, so the division of the ship was unequal, more than two-thirds back.

Either the danger was confined to the Cargo Bay and the rest of the ship was habitable. Or—it was in the forward part of the ship, which meant that the crew was trapped in the Cargo Bay. Korie pointed. "If it was in the forward part of the ship, then it got out of control and raged aftward. If it was in the aft part of the ship, then the survivors isolated it there and they're in the forward division—but then why were there no responses to our signals? And why didn't they evacuate the Cargo Bay to space the minute it broke out?"

"So you think the survivors are aft?"

"I can argue the other side equally well," Korie said. "It was aft, got into the autonomics and made it impossible for the crew to control the ship. They isolated it, but they can't evacuate it."

"What does your itch say?"

"My itch doesn't like either side of this equation. If we guess wrong—" He didn't have to complete the sentence.

"You want to flip a coin?" Parsons asked.

"No," said Korie. "Let's go with my first guess. The crew would have given themselves the larger part of the ship and isolated it in the Cargo Bay. The survivors are forward."

"It's your call."

Korie nodded glumly. "It's what I'd do. It's the *logical* thing to do."

The captain frowned. "Not everybody is as logical as you are." Then she stepped forward and called out an order to her helm and her astrogator. "Nose-to-nose docking. Set up your approach. Let's do it." She turned back to Korie. "Break out the spare repulsors from the cargo and install them forward. Let's focus them into the docking tube."

"They'll use a lot of power—"

"We'll shut down the active core-control of the singularity and depend on the passive systems to maintain."

"Can't do that for too long. Thirty-six hours max. After that, you don't have the power to reboot."

"We don't have thirty-six hours in any case. That ship is falling into a star. Let's get in, get the survivors, and get out of here. If we can save the ship, we'll tow it. HARLIE, set up the procedures."

Docking

The *Norway* was traveling "sideways," perpendicular to the star's equator, her bow pointed toward galactic south—so the *Star Wolf* would have to come up from "below" for a nose-to-nose docking. As soon as HARLIE confirmed that they were in the channel for final approach, Parsons issued a single order. "All right," she snapped. "Let's do it. You have a go for docking."

Korie was listening through his headset. "The mission team is ready," he reported.

"Good. Mr. Korie, go suit up. I'll meet you at the forward airlock for inspection. As soon as the docking tube is pressurized, you're going across."

"On my way, Captain." He was already pulling his headset off.

"Oh, Korie," Parsons called after him. "I want the log of the *Norway*." Her tone was unequivocal. "Make that a special priority."

Translation: *Make it your first priority.* Rescue of the survivors was secondary to understanding what had happened here. Rescue was important. Understanding was *more* important. "Aye, Captain," Korie said. He didn't always agree with the cold equations of space, but he never argued with them.

Korie ducked down into the Fire Control Bay, an equipment-filled chamber directly underneath the Command Deck. Five more steps aftward, down another short ladder and he was in the keel, the corridor that ran through the spine of the ship. He turned and headed forward, already thinking ahead to the mission. His frown deepened as a thought occurred to him. Did Captain Parsons know something more about the *Norway* than she was acknowledging? Did she know what they were likely to find?

No. He dismissed the thought. If she knew, she'd have briefed him. She wouldn't send a team into danger uninformed. No captain would. But it was possible she knew *something* . . . No, Korie thrust even that thought away. "Jon, your paranoia is showing again," he said to himself.

On the Bridge, Captain Parsons watched the progress of the docking procedure with deep concern. The forward display showed the nose of the *Norway*, seen head on. The image of the starship grew steadily, expanding to fill the screen. The docking collar was open in a receiving position. The mating of the two vessels should be routine. But Captain Parsons had learned the hard way that nothing was ever routine in space. Everything was potentially deadly.

HARLIE spoke then. "We are now in position for acquisition."

"Activate the repulsor fields," Parsons ordered.

"Activating the repulsor fields," Goldberg echoed. Through the keel of the vessel, a new note added itself to the symphony of shipboard sounds, a deep heterodyning sensation. "Confirmed," said Goldberg. "Fields are up. Five by five."

"We are ready to proceed with acquisition," HARLIE said. "Go or no-go, Captain?"

Parsons nodded. "Go." Then she added, "Bring us in gently."

"Working," HARLIE said.

At their respective stations, the astrogator and helm watched carefully, each ready to take control immediately if any untoward circumstance occurred that HARLIE couldn't handle. As unlikely as such a situation might seem, it had happened. And the Fleet had a tradition of never allowing its intelligence engines to work without human supervision.

The two ships thumped softly together. The connection was barely felt aboard the *Star Wolf*.

"We have acquisition," said HARLIE. "Nose-to-nose docking confirmed."

"The board is green," confirmed Jonesy from the helm. From the astrogation station, Tor added her own confirmations.

"Extend the transfer tube," ordered Parsons.

"Working," HARLIE said. A moment later, he added, "Transfer tube extended, sealed and locked. Stand by for transfer tube integrity check." He paused. "Integrity check confirmed. Confidence is high. Ready for pressurization."

"Confirm that," Jonesy said.

"And again," echoed Tor.

"Pressurize," ordered Parsons.

"Working," said HARLIE. And a moment later, added, "We have pressure in the transfer tube. Equalized. Confirmed."

Jonesy confirmed that, and so did Tor.

"All right. Good. We're ready to pop the hatch," said Parsons. "Commander Tor, you have the conn." She ducked down through the Fire Control Bay, following Korie's path down to the keel and forward to the Airlock Reception Bay.

At the nose of the ship, the airlock itself was a cramped tube, barely wide enough for two suited crewmembers at a time. Directly behind the airlock was the Forward Airlock Reception Bay. The FARB, as it was identified on the bulkheads, was a wider tube than the airlock. It was lined with suit-lockers, equipment racks and maintenance stations. Separating the Reception Bay from the airlock was a decontamination station.

At the moment, the Reception Bay was cramped with suited figures. Although the *Norway* was a pressurized environment, Class-X protection required the use of starsuits or equivalent protective gear. Korie had opted for starsuits. Again, the captain's imperative for caution had outweighed all other concerns, including comfort, mobility and expedience.

Captain Parsons had to turn sideways to squeeze past the suited figures; she worked her way forward to Korie, acknowledging nods all the way. Chief Medical Officer Molly Williger was briefing Medical Technician Paul Berryman; not that he needed additional instructions at this point, but Molly Williger preferred to leave nothing to chance and she was trying to pour forty years of hands-on experience into a twenty-three-year-old body. Berryman was wearing a portable medi-kit and a variety of scanning tools and medications.

Security Officer Helen Bach stood patiently against one wall, flanked by Fire Control Officer "Wasabe" Shibano and Daniel Easton, another crewmember assigned to security detail. Easton had worked security before and had demonstrated considerable aptitude for it; now he was checking the charges on his, Bach's and Shibano's weapons—an exercise in redundancy, because the other two would have already checked their own armaments; but the revised procedure book required security teams to triple-check each other's equipment. All of them wore additional helmet cameras. Every starsuit helmet on the ship already had a standard bank of cameras built-in, but for this mission additional high-resolution cameras and wide-spectrum scanners had been mounted on helmets, chest panels and backpacks.

At the forward end of the reception bay, Mikhail Hodel was conferring hastily with Korie. Two Quillas, Omega and Theta, were helping Korie suit up while he talked. Parsons squeezed past Easton to join them. "Status?" she asked.

"Just waiting for Mr. Korie to come up clean and green," said Hodel.

Behind her, Easton reported. "All the other boards are green. The hardware is ready. The software is clean. We have clean signals from all the remotes. Confidence is high."

Parsons nodded curtly. There wasn't much she could say that she hadn't already said. The situation was unknown, almost certainly dangerous—*extremely* dangerous. Everyone knew it. "All right," she said. "Let's do it."

"Aye, aye, Captain," Korie said, just as the two Quillas lowered his helmet in place and sealed it with a series of electronic beeps and whistles. Parsons turned aftward. Easton was checking Berryman's suit as carefully as a mother; Berryman looked as annoyed as an impatient cub. "Will you stop fussing already?" Berryman said. "No," Easton replied blandly. He yanked another strap.

Parsons followed the two Quillas aft, to get out of the way of the exiting team members. She paused alongside Molly Williger, meeting her glance with a questioning look.

"Med Bay is ready," Williger said unconvincingly.

What made Captain Parsons an exceptional captain was that she listened to a person's tone as much as their words, sometimes even more so. Now she looked at the chief medical officer, her eyes narrowing perceptively. "You don't sound optimistic."

Williger looked up sharply. "You know the stats, Captain. Ninety percent of these rescue operations are too late. Yes, there might be people still alive over there, but . . . they might also be trans-critical." *Trans-critical.* Beyond saving.

Or worse. *Infectious.*

"I'm aware of that," said Parsons. "But the rules of rescue are always operative, and those rules date back to a time even before there were spacecraft. Even if we have to put ourselves at risk, we're required to make a full and responsible effort." Then she added, "*And* we need the log. Almost as important as the rescue—sometimes even more important—we need the ship's log. In this case . . . this is probably one of the sometimes."

Williger grunted—neither agreement nor disagreement, merely acknowledgment. Like a stone dropped from a height, they no longer had a choice in the matter; they were going to fall toward their inevitable conclusion no matter how they felt about it. She turned back to preparations.

Wasabe Shibano was double-checking Korie's gear and the integrity of his starsuit. Korie ignored Shibano's attentions as best as he could while he briefed Hodel. "HARLIE can't get the log out by remote. Their intelligence engine has probably been shut down. We'll try and wake it up, of course, but we don't have the override codes if it's locked down. If that's the case, we'll go around and yank the data from below. We'll dump a copy of the core into one of our transmitters and let them decode it back at Fleet. I want to go straight to the trunk-channel under the Intelligence Bay and tap in there. The system should be on standby, but if there's no power, then I'll climb up and pull the cards manually. If the cards are missing, then we'll have to grab the orange box. That's your job. You know where the access panel is? Just behind the captain's chair?" Hodel nodded and Korie passed over a plastic card, which Hodel tucked into a holder on the forearm of his suit. "Those are the codes to disarm the self-destruct on the orange box. If anything abnormal pops up, abort the procedure. Commander Brik will be riding in your ear, so minimize the jokes, Mike."

"I've worked tougher rooms than this," Hodel said. Even through the glass of his helmet, his grin was visible. "I'll have that Morthan giggling in his shorts in no time."

"As bizarre as that image is," Korie acknowledged, "let's stick to business on this one. This is serious."

Hodel sighed. "Aye, aye, sir."

"Thanks, Mike." Korie wondered if Brik had heard the exchange. Most likely, he had. Even so, he was unlikely to comment on it. Korie didn't like Brik very much—no one onboard really did—but he did respect him, and the one time Fleet Command had offered to replace the Morthan security chief, Korie had rejected the suggestion. For all of his personal distaste, he knew the *Star Wolf* would never find a more qualified officer. He didn't know how Brik felt about him, and he didn't much care, although he surmised that Brik was at best amused and at worst annoyed by Korie's presumption of equality because they both wore the same uniform. The important thing was that they worked well together. Possibly because they were each trying to prove something to the other.

Annoyed, impatient and tense, Korie called back over his shoulder to Shibano. "Are we done yet? Or what?"

"*Jai!*" said Wasabe, in that little explosive punctuation mark of language that non-Japanese hear as "Yes," but really means, "I hear you," and sometimes also means, "but I'm too polite to say no." In Shibano's case, however, it actually meant "Yes."

Although raised in a traditional Japanese culture, Shibano had been a starship officer long enough to have achieved that state that some sociologists called *trans-human*—a condition where one's mental state was no longer local to a specific circumstance, but had become attuned instead to an interstellar scale of human behavior. In lay terms, a *trans-human* was an individual who had lived among the stars too long, someone with a million-light-year stare—someone who had traded in his or her definition of humanity for a more direct working knowledge of *sentience*.

By that definition, most of the officers in the fleet could be considered trans-human. It came with the job. Few people were born into a trans-human state, but almost all evolved into it living on a starship. But some officers were more trans-human than others. Korie, for instance . . .

Korie finished with Hodel and spoke now to HARLIE. "Status report?"

HARLIE replied blandly, "The transfer tube is fully pressurized. Integrity is confirmed. Repulsor fields are focused. Confidence is high. All mission preparations are complete."

"All right," said Korie. "On my mark. Let's go."

At the aft end of the Reception Bay, Parsons and Williger watched grimly. The interior hatch of the airlock popped open and the mission team began filing quickly into the cramped space of the airlock tube.

"Mr. Korie—" Parsons said quietly into her headset.

"Captain?" His voice came back through her earphone.

"Let's be careful out there."

Hearing that over his suit-phones, Korie smiled in recognition. It had been the watchword on Parson's first ship, the *Michael Conrad*. Maybe it could be the watchword here too. Certainly, it should be.

Hodel saw Korie's smile. He'd heard the captain's instructions, but not having the same background as Korie, he saw it as a straight line needing a topper. Ever the comedian, he poked Wasabe in the ribs and added, "Yep. Watch out for sparkle-dancers and man-eating tribbles."

"A man-eating tribble?" Wasabe asked.

"Some men will eat anything," Hodel replied blandly, reaching for a handhold.

Korie, Bach, Hodel, Shibano, Berryman and Easton lined up in three rows of two in the airlock tube. As the hatch popped shut behind them, each grabbed one of the handholds above—this was a precaution in case of sudden decompression. Not that they expected it, but it was part of the drill.

"We're green," said Korie. "Do it."

Through their suits they could hear the mechanical sounds of clamps engaging and locking—additional fail-safes on all the hatches. The deep heterodyning note of the repulsors was more noticeable *here*; an almost palpable sensation that made the hair on the back of the neck stand up in dismay.

Korie studied a display on the bulkhead. "Tube pressure confirmed here," he reported.

For a moment, nothing happened, then—

Boarding

The hatch opened slowly, revealing the interior of the transfer tube. The semi-translucent material of the tube looked solid, an illusion of air pressure. The presence of the looming red star seeped through the membrane; one side of the tube was dark, the other glowed with a brooding crimson tint. Railings extended the length of the tube to provide handholds for the starsuited crew. Exterior to both ships, the transfer tube was a null-gravity zone.

Standard procedure would have been to leap out into free fall and coast across.

But not here, not now. Not with the repulsor fields throbbing.

The fields were a physical presence, like invisible surf pushing them inexorably forward. Coming from the other direction, it would have felt like pushing through gelatin and spiderwebs and elastic; it would have felt as if the air had been *thickened*. Moving *with* the pressure was like riding a rising balloon. It was a tangible sensation. The mission team grabbed handholds on the railings and let themselves be pushed along.

The combined strength of three concentric fields was focused into the transfer tube. The power expenditure to maintain a palpable force of this strength was enormous. The *Star Wolf* had shut down all of her non-essential systems to maintain this safety barrier.

Korie had never moved through such a strong field before and it gave him a queasy sensation in his gut as the pressure worked on his internal organs. And then, abruptly, he was through the thickest part of the field and coming up to the outer hatch of the *Norway*'s forward airlock. Even so, he could still feel a residual push.

Korie turned and watched as the entire mission team came across.

Lt. Bach was the last to exit the *Star Wolf*'s airlock. Korie reported, "All right. We're clear. Seal the hatch." It popped shut with a hard mechanical thump—the *Star Wolf* was secure. And as soon as the *Norway*'s hatch was opened, the mission team would be regarded as contaminated . . .

Hodel was watching a set of readouts on the arm of his suit. "Pressure is equalized to the *Norway*," he announced.

Korie acknowledged the report and turned forward to the *Norway*'s forward hatch. He held an entry card against a reader plate, and waited for the panel to turn green, silently praying that the *Norway* would recognize their authority. He didn't want to manually force the hatch, he didn't want to cut his way in. He wanted this operation to run smoothly. By the book. The panel went green and Korie whispered soft thanks to the unseen crew on the other side. "That's a good sign," he said.

"Yeah, they're only paranoid, not crazy," agreed Hodel.

"It's wartime. Everybody's crazy. The only question is whether we're crazy *enough*. All right, here we go. Bach, Easton, Shibano—" The security officers pulled themselves into position just behind Korie. They unshouldered their weapons. They raised blast-shields into position.

Korie punched the OPEN panel with his gloved knuckle. The panel flashed red and showed the word TESTING—and then the hatch popped open in front of them and they were staring into the empty airlock of the *Norway*.

They waited a moment, to see if anything would happen. Nothing did. "It's still a go," came the captain's voice.

The chamber ahead was dark and featureless—except for the lack of light, it was identical to the lock they had just exited. Korie released his grip and allowed the repulsor field to push him forward into the silent ship. The security team followed. They oriented themselves vertical to the *Norway*, moved through the airlock hatch and dropped to the deck.

When the last crewmember had entered the airlock—it was Helen Bach—they sealed the hatch and waited while the *Norway* ran its own air pressure checks. The throb of the repulsors faded behind them.

"Looks like the autonomic system is still up and running," Korie noted, as much for his team as for the listeners still aboard the *Star Wolf*: Parsons, Tor, Brik, Williger . . .

"That's good news," said Hodel. "Makes all our jobs easier."

"Mission Team, we copy that." Tor's voice came through their suitphones.

The last panel flashed green. "All right, let's go." Korie popped the final hatch. The interior of the *Norway* lay before them . . .

It was not a reassuring sight. The Airlock Reception Bay was dark. There were two starsuits still hanging on the racks and one fallen to the deck. A scattered assortment of equipment lay about—as if someone had tried to dress in haste, without regard for procedures. Without regard for anything except escape.

"Hodel?" asked Korie.

"Already scanning." Hodel was studying the readouts on his suit arm. "Nothing yet."

Korie switched on his external speaker. "Ahoy the *Norway*! Is anyone here! We're here from the *Star Wolf*. We're here to help you! Ahoy the *Norway*!" He held up a hand for silence. The mission team held still. Listening to the silence.

"Ahoy! Anyone . . . ?"

No one.

Korie gestured and the team moved forward—from the Airlock Reception Bay into the keel. It was bad news. Too many lights were out. The keel was shadowed and gloomy.

"Sir?" Hodel pointed. Korie followed the direction of his gesture.

Something in the darkness. Something that flickered insubstantially. And was gone. And then flickered again in another place. Like fairy dust or very faint fireworks.

"What is it?" Hodel asked. "What does it mean?"

"It means . . . I guessed wrong." There was a cold hollow feeling growing in Korie's gut. "We should have come in the other end." To Hodel's look, he said, "I expected them to be thinking logically. Sorry, Mike. The job just got harder." *I made a mistake.*

"Mission Team, report," said Tor dispassionately. "What are you seeing?"

"Some kind of . . . it's hard to describe. Fireflies? I'm not sure. Adjust your display. It's very faint."

"Okay, we've got it now."

Korie glanced at the small monitor panel set inside his own helmet. It showed what they were seeing on the Bridge of the *Star Wolf*. The flickers were clearer on the screen. They left tiny dark trails. But they were still insubstantial, appearing and disappearing seemingly at random. Not a lot. It was like something half-glimpsed out of the corner of the eye; when you turned to look directly, it was gone. Korie had the impression of tiny lights that were pink and gold and red, but not really.

And then there was that *other* thing—the sound of the *Norway*. It was *different*. There were none of the familiar background noises of a living ship. Korie's eyes narrowed. The air circulators were off. The coolant pipes were silent. The water and sewage systems were equally still. The silence was eerie. Even the quiet beeps from the various monitors were absent. Starships aren't silent. No matter how well designed or constructed, whether macro, micro or nano, things make noise. Liquid flows through pipes. Air moves through tubes. Everything whistles, vibrates and hums like the pieces of a massive faster-than-light church organ, striking deep chords and mechanical harmonies. This ship . . . didn't. The effect was terrifying.

"The ship is deserted?" Hodel asked.

"No," said Korie. "HARLIE detected life aboard her. They're just not at this end." He unclipped several small round probes from his suit-belt, activated them and tossed them down the corridor. The units righted themselves in midair, popped open tiny lens ports and scanner outlets, then headed deep into the *Norway*. Back on the *Star Wolf*, a control team would monitor and direct the units.

Korie waited for a confirmation from the captain. "The probes aren't showing anything alive. But there's a lot of noise in the signal."

"Your orders, Captain?"

"Get the log and get out of there."

"Aye, aye." Korie gestured the team forward.

Bach and Shibano followed close on Korie's heels. Bach swung her rifle nervously from one side to the other.

"Afraid of ghosts?" Shibano whispered to her.

"Nope. Just don't want to be one."

Korie frowned back at them. "Belay that chatter."

"Aye, sir. Sorry."

They came to a vertical intersection in the corridor, a place where ladders extended both up and down. Also diagonal access tubes opened off to the starship's farm. Korie directed Bach, Easton and Hodel up the ladder to the "north end" of "Broadway"—where the ship's main corridor terminated. He, Shibano and Berryman continued aftward through the keel.

Sparkling

The funny flickering in the air was a little more noticeable here. Berryman frowned at his scanner's readings, a growing sense of disquiet in his chest. "Sir?" he said to attract Korie's attention.

Korie hesitated, waiting. "What is it?"

"Some kind of . . . *wavicle*, I think." Half-wave, half-particle, with some of the behaviors of each. Unpredictable.

The flickers were starting to drift toward them now. They looked harmless, but clearly, they were an unknown phenomenon and had to be regarded as deadly until proven otherwise. Certainly, they were related to the condition of this vessel.

Shibano reached out and tried to grab a few of the fairy pinpoints, but they whirled out of reach like motes of dust. He grabbed again and again, but each time the sparkles eluded him. There were more twinkling pinpoints around him now, flickering in and out of existence. They were both beguiling and . . . disturbing. They danced in the air with a nervous quality.

Berryman turned slowly, trying to scan them with a hand-held unit, but the wavicles seemed to be avoiding an area defined by his scanning field. Both Korie and Berryman noticed it at the same time.

"Do you want to try turning that off?" Korie suggested quietly.

"I suppose we could try that," Berryman replied, just as cautiously. He switched off the scanner. He turned slowly, observing the behavior of the wavicles. They danced in closer . . .

Korie and Berryman exchanged a glance.

"Do you want to try and catch one?" Korie asked.

"Dr. Williger will have my hide if I don't try."

"Don't make assumptions!" Williger's voice came rasping into their helmets. "I'm more likely to skin you alive if you put yourself in unnecessary danger."

"Do you want some of these things or not?" Berryman retorted.

Williger didn't reply immediately. She was conferring with Captain Parsons. Finally, her voice came back, "If you can get one in a bottle, fine. If not—don't."

Korie said. "I don't think they like the scanning fields." To Berryman, he added, "Try turning your helmet scanners off."

"And then what?"

"And then, I think, we'll find out whether or not they're trying to get to us. Look, there's more of them than ever. They're certainly attracted to something—probably us. But the scanning fields are keeping them at bay."

"Do you think they can get through our suits?"

"They shouldn't be able to. We're Class-X certified."

"So was the *Norway.*"

"Mm. Point taken."

"But if they can get through our suits," Berryman continued, "then we have to assume we're already contaminated."

"There is that too," Korie acknowledged. "But I think, in the interests of knowledge, that we need to know just what the hell is going on here. How safe is it to proceed?" Korie switched off the scanners mounted on his helmet. The wavicles swirled inward toward him, but none actually alighted on his suit. Korie and Berryman looked at each other through the faceplates of their helmets. Neither had an answer to the unspoken question.

"Is it the scanners? Or the suits? Or a combination of the two? Or something else?"

Without being told, Wasabe Shibano reached up and switched off the scanners mounted on his chest and back. For a moment, nothing happened. The wavicles continued to swirl just beyond arm's length.

"Okay," said Korie. "I think we're safe. It's the suits." He nodded forward. "Let's get the log and get out of here."

And then—as they moved, so did the wavicles. Suddenly agitated, they danced like a seizure of fireworks, like exploding fireflies—they bounced and twinkled and flickered and suddenly began alighting on all three of the starsuited figures, outlining each of them in faint sparkling luminescence.

"Oh, shit—" said Berryman, uncharacteristically.

Korie didn't say anything. But he was thinking it. *My second miscalculation. The price on this one is going to be high.*

Only Wasabe Shibano remained unaffected. He held out his hand in front of his helmet, staring at the unexpected radiance. The effect was ghostly and magical. The strange glow was reflected in his helmet pane and his eyes were wide with awe.

Korie looked at his own hands then, as did Berryman. The three of them looked at each other—in amazement as well as horror. All of them were gleaming with a myriad of twinkling points. They looked *enchanted.*

Their communicators were chattering in their ears unheard. Tor's voice, Williger's, Brik's and Captain Parsons'—"Korie! Answer me! What's going on over there! What's happening!"

"It's all right," Korie managed to say. His voice cracked. "We're . . . surrounded. But we're not being hurt—"

"Get the log and get out of there. *That's an order,*" snapped Parsons. "No! Forget the log. Just get out of there. Now!"

"Our suits are holding—" Korie started to reassure them.

"But for how long?" Williger's gravelly voice cut in.

As if in answer to her question, Berryman shouted, "Oh, God—!" Korie whirled to look at him. He couldn't tell if it was a scream of fear or astonishment—but Berryman was *glowing* suddenly brighter! Shibano too! Korie looked to his own hands—the rest of his starsuit—he was gleaming as bright as the others!

He looked to them and saw—the sparkling motes were *seeping into their suits!* His own as well!

It wasn't painful—it was *interesting.* It *tingled* . . . the feeling was almost sexual. But underneath it was another thought. *Is this my third mistake? The final one?*

"Hey!" laughed Shibano. "That tickles!" He looked to Berryman and Korie. "Doesn't it?"

Berryman looked uncomfortable—not because it hurt, but because he was already wondering about the medical implications. He looked to Korie.

Korie nodded an acknowledgment. "It's an odd sensation," he admitted. "Like needing to sneeze all over your body at the same time—" The sparkling wash of light was diminishing now. The twinkles were vanishing into them.

Korie pointed to Berryman's scanner. "Take a reading."

Berryman lifted up the device, switching it on. He pointed it at Shibano first.

"Oww—*that* doesn't tickle."

Korie waggled his fingers in an "over here" gesture and Berryman pointed the scanner toward him. The tickling sensation turned painful then—like a series of low-level electric shocks. Korie held up his hand in an "Okay, you can stop now" gesture, and Berryman switched the scanner off.

"Did you feel it too?" Korie asked.

Berryman nodded grimly.

"Well, whatever it is—we've got it."

"I can't identify it, sir. The *Star Wolf* will have to sort this one out."

"There might be something in the records. HARLIE has probably already started searching the files. There's a thousand years of history to go through. It might take some time."

Closure

On the Bridge of the *Star Wolf*, Parsons' face was ashen. She looked first to Williger, then to Brik.

Brik didn't look up from his workstation, but somehow he knew of her concern. "Already working on it, Captain," he said. His voice had an angry note to it. Was he angry at Korie? Or her? Or just the universe in general? Korie had warned her of Brik's manner. Not important, Parsons told herself. Not important *now*. "Thank you, Mr. Brik," she said noncommittally.

She turned to Williger. "The other half of the team?"

"They're keeping their scanners on," the doctor growled.

"Will that protect them?"

Williger shrugged. An unsatisfactory answer.

Parsons rubbed her earlobe, frowning in thought. "All right. Tell them to proceed. As long as they're over there—let's get the log and find out what the hell those things are."

"Aye, aye."

On the *Norway*, Hodel received Brik's orders with a tight expression. They were seeing more of the wavicles up on "Broadway" too. Hodel didn't want to speculate aloud, but it looked as if the whole ship was infected. He moved forward, following Easton and Bach through a corridor that was both familiar and alien at the same time.

The *Norway* was functionally identical to the *Star Wolf*. Both were liberty ships, both built to the same blueprint; perhaps they had even come off the same assembly line. But the *Norway* had been outfitted for a different set of priorities, and her internal fittings were different enough to make the experience something like *deja vu* mixed with culture shock and a vaguely disquieting sense of disorientation.

"Lieutenant Hodel?" That was Bach. They had come to a sealed hatch. On the other side was the Bridge.

Easton knelt to examine the frame. "It's locked and glued."

"Something on the other side?" asked Bach. "Or something on *this* side?" She glanced around.

Hodel shook his head in an "I don't know" gesture. He listened to Brik's advice in his earphone and relayed the decision. "This was sealed for a reason. Let's go back and see if there's another way in."

They came back down the ladder and found Korie working at an open wall panel, trying to tap into the ship's autonomic systems. The fiber optics were dark—this part of the system was dead. Korie clipped his probe back to his belt and looked up as the others approached.

" 'Broadway' is sealed off," Bach reported. "No survivors. No bodies. No ghosts either."

"Wavicles?"

"Plenty of them."

"You heard about our . . . little phenomenon?" Korie asked.

"Saw it on our displays," Hodel acknowledged. "You guys looked like Christmas trees."

"Save it, Hodel. Were any of you . . . *infected*?" There. He'd said it.

Hodel and Bach and Easton exchanged glances. They shook their heads.

"Well, keep your scanners turned on—but keep them on low, and pointed away from us. They're . . . uncomfortable."

"Aye, sir."

"I should send you back." Korie was thinking out loud.

"You should let us do our job, sir," Bach said calmly. "We don't know that scanning fields are one hundred percent effective in keeping the wavicles away. Let's not assume anything. We could be just as infected."

Korie stared at her sharply. *What's wrong with me? So many bad decisions?*

"You're right," he said. "Let's deal with the situation at hand and worry about detox later. That's Dr. Williger's worry, not ours."

"Right," said Hodel. "So let's give her something to worry about."

"Mike—" Korie cautioned him. "Stay on purpose."

Bach nodded upward, indicating the corridor above them. "Was that hatch sealed to keep something *in*—or *out*?"

Korie shook his head, unwilling to guess. He was suddenly feeling uncertain in his judgment. He indicated the panel. "This is dead." He waved vaguely toward the stern. "Let's see if we can get in through the keel, up through the Fire Control Bay." They headed aft.

A thought occurred to Korie. "HARLIE?" he asked.

"Yes, Mr. Korie?"

"Do you have anything yet on the wavicles?"

HARLIE hesitated—

Korie caught it almost immediately. *HARLIE hesitated!*

—and said, "I'm sorry. I have nothing useful."

Nothing useful? What did *that* mean? Did he have something or not? HARLIE wouldn't lie—*couldn't* lie. And yet . . . he could *misdirect*. Korie was about to ask more, but HARLIE interrupted his thought to add, "I am reviewing material with Dr. Williger now. If there is anything pertinent to your situation, she will brief you."

So there was something!

He put the thought aside for the moment. They had come to a sealed security hatch, closing off the forward part of the keel from the rest of the ship. It too had been glued. Easton was already examining the frame.

"Can you cut it?" Korie asked.

"No problem," Easton said. He was already unclipping the appropriate tools from his belt and mounting them onto his rifle. The weapon could double as a very efficient cutting laser.

"Brik?" Korie spoke softly to his helmet communicator. "What does mission control think?"

Brik didn't answer immediately. Conferring with Parsons? When he came back, his voice was uncommonly dispassionate. "Captain says it's your call."

"Thanks," said Korie. He thought for a moment, turning to look forward and aft, upward and down—as if there might be something he missed. He didn't want to make any more mistakes. Finally, he said, "My guess is that there was something in the nose of the ship that got out of control. They sealed it off, but not in time. So they kept retreating aftward and are now hiding behind the repulsor fields. I think it's safe to cut. Comments anyone? Arguments?"

Silence for a moment, while the mission team as well as the officers still on the *Star Wolf* considered Korie's words.

"The issue isn't contamination any more," said Williger. "I think we have to assume the whole ship is contaminated. The real issue is whether or not we can rescue anybody. And until we know the nature of the contamination and how to protect against it—if it is indeed dangerous, which so far we haven't seen—then it's premature to worry about rescue. Our first priority here has to be speed—finding out what we're dealing with."

"In other words," said Korie, "you're voting for throwing out half the procedure book?"

"Yes," said Williger without hesitation. "I am. We tried caution. It didn't work. Now let's go for expedience. I vote for cutting the hatch."

"Captain?" Korie asked.

"As I said, Mr. Korie, it has to be your decision."

"I understand that. I just want to hear what everyone else thinks. Brik?"

Brik's answer was curt. "Cut it."

Korie allowed himself a smile. "Couldn't you have said that in fewer words?"

"Cut," said Brik.

Korie wasn't sure if Brik had understood that he was joking or if his reply was dead serious. Never mind. He had a consensus. He turned to Easton. "Open it up."

Cutting In

It didn't take long to cut the hatch open.

The team stepped back out of the way and Easton used his rifle to slice away the entire hatch frame. The cutting beam dazzled and flared. Their helmet filters blocked the brightest spikes of light and their starsuits reflected the heat, but occasional small flaming drops of polycarbonite impurities went spattering away in all directions and nobody wanted to risk a burn-hole from standing too close.

The twinkling wavicles danced away from the cutting beam, but there were more of them here suddenly, drawn by the heat and energy of the process and simultaneously repelled by the intensity of it.

Finally, the hatch and the frame around it fell away with a dull clatter on the deck; it sizzled where it fell and wisps of smoke rose up from the hole in the bulkhead as well as from the ragged and blackened edges of the fallen piece. Smoldering embers sputtered and crackled on all the cut edges.

"We're through," Korie noted dryly. Of course, they would have already seen that on the Bridge of the *Star Wolf*; they were monitoring everything—but the log required that the onsite personnel acknowledge every step of procedure. It was a requirement—in case a post-mortem became necessary.

Bach unclipped a fire-extinguisher hose from the wall. She pointed the nozzle at the smoldering hatch and released a plume of cold steam. The twinkling wavicles in the path of the industrial mist flickered out abruptly.

Despite his suit insulation, Korie felt abruptly cold. Bach played the spray all over the hole in the bulkhead several times and then stepped in closer and sprayed the fallen hatch as well. Satisfied, she switched off the stream and stepped back to the bulkhead to secure the hose. As the air cleared, the sparkling wavicles came dancing back brightly.

Korie nodded to Shibano, directing him through the hole first. He held his rifle before him, tracking from side to side in quick covering movements—very professional. Easton followed, and a moment later signaled back, "It looks clear in here, sir."

"I'm coming through," said Korie, and followed. Bach, Berryman and Hodel came after him. The mission team proceeded aftward with cold military precision, each one stepping into the footsteps of the one ahead, each one covering every access panel, every hatch, every ladder, every step of the way.

"Any data yet on the wavicles?" Korie asked.

"HARLIE's still processing," Williger said bluntly, cutting off all further discussion. "When we have something, we'll tell you."

She knows, Korie thought. Something was gnawing at the base of his memory, a half-forgotten story about . . . something or other. Something red. Something deadly. But, these twinkling lights—they were more like something out of a fairy tale than anything else.

Korie didn't answer.

From here, it was only a few short steps to the access ladder to the Fire Control Bay. Shibano followed Korie and Hodel up through the bay, forward a few steps and up again onto the Operations Deck, the command center of the *Norway*. The view from his helmet camera filled the forward display on the Bridge of the *Star Wolf*, where Parsons, Brik, Tor and Williger watched with grim expressions.

Korie climbed up to the starship's Ops Deck and immediately turned to look up and behind. The Command Deck was unoccupied. Vacant. Empty. That was possibly the most disturbing thing they could find.

He turned around slowly, surveying the rest of the *Norway*'s Bridge. Like the *Star Wolf* Bridge, it was a narrow chamber, arranged around a lowered center—the Ops Deck. To the rear was the Command Deck, raised up like a mezzanine, directly over the half-submerged Fire Control Bay. The empty captain's chair sat in the middle of the Command Deck, flanked by two other seats. There were raised workstations along each bulkhead and forward was a wall-sized display. Almost identical—but the fittings were different, and so was the interior color scheme. Captains were allowed some leeway in how they outfitted their ships. Most chose to use their planetary colors. The *Norway* had muted stripes of red and blue, highlighted with occasional bands of white.

Shibano edged past Korie, moving toward the Helm station at the forward-most part of the Ops Deck, stopping suddenly in surprise and dismay. "Sir—!"

Korie stepped forward, so did Hodel—and coming up behind them, Easton, Berryman and Bach. Their various helmet cameras sent back a multiplicity of images—all were horrific.

Sprawled half out of his seat, half on the floor, as if he'd fallen while trying to get up, was the desiccated body of a man.

The uniform was ripped and torn. The body was disfigured—mummified. Blackened with dried blood. Frozen in a position of horror—or agony. His skin was stretched and sunken—mostly pale, almost white, but discolored everywhere with darker patches of bluish purple and black. The eyes bulged. The hands clenched. This had not been an easy death.

"Look," said Hodel, waving his rifle.

Everywhere, there were tiny lines in the body—they looked at first like wrinkles, but they weren't; they were slits in the skin, as if it had been stretched to the point of shredding. The body looked like something horribly alien—and at the same time, frighteningly human.

Discovery

———◆———

Shibano backed away quickly, bumping into Berryman who was stepping in to see. From behind, Berryman put his hands on Shibano's shoulders and moved the Weapons Control Officer firmly sideways.

Berryman's demeanor was strong and professional, as if he'd seen things a thousand times worse than this. He hadn't, but his curiosity about the circumstances of the man's death outweighed his personal feelings of revulsion. He was already unclipping a poly-scanner from his toolbelt. He pointed it at the body—and hesitated.

He looked to Korie, holding up the scanner. "Is this all right?"

Korie looked from the scanner to the body. "I don't think he'll complain. Go ahead."

"Wait," said Berryman. "Let me get pictures first. *Star Wolf*, are you copying?"

"Affirmative," came Williger's voice—oddly strangled.

"Poor bastard," Hodel murmured.

"Now we know who sent the distress signal," Bach said.

"If it was him," Korie remarked, "then where are all the others? And if it wasn't him, then why didn't the others respond to our signal?"

"Ready to scan," Berryman said.

Korie motioned everyone back. He wasn't sure why. It just felt like the right thing to do. Even Berryman moved back and recalibrated his scanner. He pointed it at the body of the dead crewman and touched the green button.

For a moment . . . nothing happened. Then—

—the corpse began to jerk. Writhe. Shake. It shuddered and twitched and wrenched itself momentarily upright, snapping its arms and legs as if suddenly possessed—

All of them stepped back again, involuntarily, as if the dead man had come back to life and was about to leap for them. Gasps of surprise came from Hodel and Easton.

Then the body came apart. Fragmenting, breaking into dusty pieces. But not yet falling. Twinkles of light came exploding out of the broken joints, the tattered skin, the myriad breaks in the flesh—all the sparkles came pouring out in all directions, like a miniature nova—

And then the corpse did collapse—what was left of it crumbled to the deck, shattering into more sparkling dust.

"My God," said Bach. "What is it? What happened here?"

"The wavicles . . . ?"

"We don't know," Korie said. "Let's not speculate. What we've seen is demonstration enough." He turned to Berryman. "What kind of readings did you get?"

Berryman shrugged. "Mostly noise. Mostly garbage." He pointed to the readout panel on his suit arm. "That thing was mummified. This shows no blood, no liquid of any kind—as if it were all drained out."

"Vampires. *Space* vampires . . ." said Hodel ominously.

"Don't be stupid," Berryman snapped at him. "Nobody believes in that crap—"

"Stay on purpose," interrupted Korie. He turned to the helmsman. "Mikhail, there are times when you are very funny. This isn't one of them."

"Sorry, sir."

Turning, Korie noticed that Shibano was still focused on the crumbling remains of the dead man—horrified. Shibano's culture had some very strong feelings about death. Despite his ferocity at the weapons board, Wasabe had obviously never seen death up close. Now, he was paralyzed. Korie turned him gently away. "Wasabe? Shibano! Go. Download the log—now."

Shibano nodded, dumbly. "Aye, sir." He stepped over to the communications console—and stopped. "Mr. Korie?"

Korie turned—and saw for the first time that the console was disabled, destroyed; it was almost cut in half. The panels were scorched and charred.

"Over here, too," called Hodel. The helm console was similarly disabled. Slashed by fire.

"All the work stations are out," said Bach. "Stinger beams."

Korie stepped from one console to the next, confirming what he already knew. He stepped up onto starboard deck. All the workstations here were cut to ribbons. Dead and useless. On the opposite side of the Bridge, he could see the same degree of damage.

The *Norway* had been *deliberately* disabled.

"Mr. Korie?" Captain Parsons' voice rang in his ear. "Have all the workstations been destroyed? Confirm please."

"That *is* correct," Korie said. "The Bridge of the *Norway* has been . . ." Korie searched for the right phrase, ". . . dismantled by the aggressive application of stinger beams. This ship isn't going anywhere. Someone wanted her to die—" He looked over to see Bach picking up a weapon. She held it high for him to see. She inclined her head toward the corpse, what was left of it. Korie acknowledged her with a nod of his own. "—probably the poor bastard we found at the Astrogation console."

Korie lowered his voice. "My guess is that he wanted this ship unable to break orbit, so she'd be destroyed when she passed through the flames of the red star. Probably he didn't want to risk any other ship being infected. That means, somebody *else* sent the distress signal. Either after he did this—or before. One motivated the other. There must have been considerable panic aboard this starship."

Parsons didn't answer immediately. When she did, her voice was curiously devoid of feeling. "Get the log of that ship, Korie. Now."

"Aye, Captain. We'll have to pull a direct line. I don't want to risk transferring the orange box. We'll dump it into a transmitter."

"Do it," she ordered. "Now."

Warning

Back on the Bridge of the *Star Wolf*, the mood was grim. Nobody had to say it. No one believed the mission team would return from the *Norway*. They were watching dead men. Five dead men and one dead woman.

Unless and until the chief medical officer determined what those wavicles really were, they *couldn't* be allowed to return. The *Star Wolf* couldn't risk being infected.

"Captain?" Commander Brik's voice was low and gruff.

Parsons stepped to the forward railing of the Command Deck and looked down at Brik's workstation. "Yes, Mr. Brik?"

The Morthan security chief pointed at the schematic view of the *Norway* on his display. Parsons saw what he was indicating and her expression hardened.

"I think you should take a look at this. These readings are very . . . strange."

Almost simultaneously, HARLIE said, audible on both vessels, "Mr. Korie—something is moving toward you. Multiple somethings."

On the *Norway*, Easton was studying his scanner. "I'm reading it now too."

Beside him, Bach, Wasabe and Hodel drew their stingers.

Easton looked up from his display and pointed aft and upward. "It's coming from—"

Before he could finish the sentence, the hatch on the Command Deck popped open, and a desperate figure came clawing through it, a crewman in torn uniform, gasping and choking, floundering like a drunk, his face blotchy and deformed. He came flying—stumbling forward in a cloud of sparkles; he careened off the captain's chair, bumped into the forward railing and tumbled headlong over it, thumping heavily to the deck below, releasing an even greater spray of twinkles and lights. They splashed through the air, they skittered across the floor.

As experienced as they were, the members of the mission team were startled. The security officers took cautious steps backward. Only Berryman approached, his medical training outweighing his instinctive fear. He stepped forward quickly, instinctively bringing his scanner up and focusing it—stopping himself only at the last moment. He tossed the scanner aside and bent to the affected man—he was twisting and moaning across the deck, sending out wave after wave of sparks. His name-badge identified him as OKUDA, M.

Berryman grabbed Okuda's wrist, feeling for his pulse. The man's heart was racing, his pulse-rate was frightening. His skin was twitching as if there were things moving around just beneath the surface. Flashes of color moved over his body as he coughed out his life. "You're too late! They're all dead! Everyone is dead! You'll see! You're next! You're next!"

Korie's face remained expressionless, but beside him, Bach recoiled; even Shibano flinched.

What they saw was relayed directly to the Bridge of the *Star Wolf*. There, the reaction was less restrained. Tor's hand went to her mouth and an involuntary "Oh, my God!" escaped her lips. Parsons looked ashen. Williger mouthed a word that was inappropriate for the Bridge of a starship. Jonesy closed his eyes involuntarily. Goldberg's expression tightened—he was clenching his teeth behind pursed lips. Only Brik remained dispassionate. He had seen worse—but he would never say so.

Parsons took a sideways step and touched Williger's shoulders gently. "What is it, Molly?"

Williger shook her head, a silent reply. She didn't want to say. She didn't even want to guess. And even if she could guess, it wasn't something she would say aloud. Not here. Not now. Not where it might be overheard.

She watched grimly as Berryman began checking Okuda's vital signs without the benefit of a medical scanner. She could tell he felt at a loss, as he moved his hands from the man's heart to his neck. Berryman didn't know what to look for, and he wasn't sure what he could do in any case. He'd never seen anything like this before. Shaking his head uncertainly, he reached for a sedative-injector.

"Berryman?" Korie asked.

Berryman shook his head, a gesture that could have meant anything from "I don't know" to "He's dying," and probably included both. He touched the injector to the man's neck. A soft hiss sounded. "Here," he said gently to Okuda. "This will ease the pain."

It didn't work. Okuda wasn't eased. Instead, he started twitching and shuddering even more frantically, desperately trying to escape. "Oh, no! It's happening! Oh, please, no—" He looked desperately to Berryman. Seeing no hope there, he twisted toward Bach and Shibano. "Kill me! Oh, God, please kill me!" He jerked suddenly across the floor as if something was dragging him—from the inside. He pulled himself up, almost standing again, pushed himself off, as if he were continuing on his desperate journey, but before he could get any further, he clutched his belly and screamed—a dark red stain began spreading across his torso. Bright flares of firefly twinkles shot out from his body. "Kill me! Quickly! God damn you!"

Bach took a step backward, to keep out of his way. Somehow she had detached herself from the horror—long enough to say, "*Star Wolf*, your mysterious life forms are here. An injured crewman."

Brik's reply was immediate—and disconcerting. "I'm not talking about the crewman. The life forms are still moving toward you."

Dead

◆

Korie looked to Bach. She looked back at him, startled, then looked to her scanner—it was relaying the readings from the Bridge of the *Star Wolf.*

This was all the distraction that Okuda needed. He leapt sideways and grabbed the stinger pistol off Hodel's tool belt. Hodel twisted to stop him, but he was too late, and his turning motion helped Okuda more than it hindered him. He staggered backward, clutching the weapon to his chest and—as they turned in horror—he *disintegrated* in a multi-colored burst of heat and fire.

The sound of it was loud enough to knock them all backwards. The flare of the stinger expanded like a fireball and became a cloud of sparkling wavicles, all pink and gold and brightly flickering. They spread out quickly across the Bridge, alighting on consoles, chairs, and bulkheads—and the starsuits of the mission team—flickering briefly before disappearing into nothingness.

Korie spoke first. "*Star Wolf*, did you get that?"

His headphones replied with silence. All their headphones were silent.

"*Star Wolf*, acknowledge."

On the Bridge of the starship, Captain Parsons massaged her temple wearily. She knew she had to acknowledge Korie's request; she just didn't know what she could say. Or *should* say. Finally, she took a breath and said softly, "We saw it."

Korie's voice was unnaturally calm. "We have to assume the whole ship is infected. Some kind of—we don't know. Did you see the wavicle burst?" And then, after a moment, he added, "We must also assume that the entire mission team is contaminated."

Parsons didn't acknowledge that. She was too preoccupied—upset. She pulled off her headset and tossed it onto her chair, then stepped curtly across the Command Deck to Molly Williger. "What about a bio-filter?" she asked quietly.

Williger, noting the captain's actions, switched off her own headset before replying. "It won't filter out wavicles. Half-wave, half-particle, they'd slip right through."

Parsons half-turned forward, looking over the railing that separated the command deck from the lower Operations Deck. "Mr. Brik?"

Brik's tone was . . . different. As if he knew something. His voice sounded unusually gruff. "I have to agree with Mr. Korie."

From the *Norway*, Korie's next words sounded like the voice of a dead man. "We can't come back," he said. "We can't risk infecting the *Star Wolf*. Captain, do you agree?"

Parsons looked from one to the other. Her eyes met Williger's first, then Brik's, then finally came to rest on Tor's. The astrogator's face was pale—a reflection of her own? She knew that she was looking for an answer that she wasn't going to find. Her Bridge crew was as bereft of ideas as she was. Finally, surrendering, she nodded her head, regretfully picked up her headset and put it back on. "Yes, I agree," she said. Without emotion, as if she were quoting directly from the regulations, she added, "The safety of the *Star Wolf* has to come first."

Korie turned around slowly, meeting the eyes of the rest of the mission team. An odd little phrase was lurking in the back of his head, but he resisted the temptation to say it. *You knew the job was dangerous when you took it.*

It wasn't necessary. Clearly, the team already understood that this was now a one-way mission. The realization showed in their eyes.

I'm dead. He realized it himself. *I'm dead. I just haven't fallen down yet. I'm still walking around, but I'm dead. What a curious feeling.*

Korie shook his head. He tried to blink it away, but he couldn't.

I should be scared, but I'm not. I'm . . . pissed as hell. I'm not done. I didn't get to finish. I wanted to be captain. I wanted to beat the Morthans—

Parsons' voice cut into his thoughts. "Get the log from that ship, Mr. Korie. Find a working access. I want to know what happened over there." And then she added, "Maybe there's something useful . . ."

Korie didn't say what he was thinking. Instead, he uttered a curt "Will do." He motioned to his team. "Hodel. Let's go get that god-damned orange box."

Plasmacytes

On the Bridge of the *Star Wolf*, time had collapsed and lay in broken shards all over the deck. The officers looked from one to the other, each hoping that someone else would have an answer, would know what to say or do. The moment stretched out painfully.

Finally, Brik turned quietly—as quietly as any Morthan could move—to Captain Parsons. He caught her eye and she looked at him questioningly. He looked to Dr. Williger, she nodded her agreement. "May we speak to you please?" He inclined his head aftward and Parsons realized he was asking for a private conference.

The captain nodded. She led the way aft, through the hatch into "Broadway." The first cabin aft of the Bridge was the Communications Bay; the second was a tiny conference room that doubled as the Officers' Mess. As she entered, she pulled off her headset, made sure it was off and tossed it on the table. Brik entered the cabin after her, stooping to fit. There were few places in the starship where he didn't have to crouch, this wasn't one of them. He stepped over to a work station and scrunched down before it. He punched in his code and brought up a display for her to see. Dr. Williger stepped up beside them both.

Brik tapped at the readouts grimly. "Captain Parsons, HARLIE couldn't say it in the clear. The observed phenomena on the *Norway* matches the description of plasmacytes."

Williger added softly, "Also known as . . . bloodworms."

Parsons reacted sharply. *Bloodworms?* But even as she started to deny it in her mind, she could see the truth of it on the faces of Brik and Williger.

Brik continued dispassionately. "The only recorded plasmacyte infection occurred on the fourth planet of the Regulan system. That planet has been quarantined for nearly 250 years."

Williger noted, "HARLIE gets a ninety-three-percent probability match on the symptoms."

Parsons accepted the information dully. "Does anyone else know?" she asked.

"No. It's double red-flagged. HARLIE is only cleared to tell the captain, the XO, head of security and the chief medical officer. Korie has probably figured it out already. We can alert him on his private channel, but . . . we thought we ought to talk it over first."

Parsons rubbed her forehead, unhappily. It was one thing to do this in a simulation; it was quite another to have the reality of it growling in your face.

And Brik still wasn't through. "Captain," he said. "We have standing orders . . . to effect the complete and total destruction of any infected ship. Including crew and passengers. Rescue is not to be attempted."

Williger completed the thought. "Too many ships were lost attempting rescues."

Parsons sat down at the table. She put her fingertips together and stared at them. She knew what she was required to do now. She couldn't bring herself to do it.

Molly Williger put a cup of something hot in front of her. Chicken soup? Parsons looked up at her, and from her to Brik. Her face was ashen. "That was 250 years ago . . ." But she was grasping at straws, she knew it.

"The orders are still in effect," said Brik.

Williger sat down at the table then. She reached across the corner and put one hand on the captain's. "Listen to me. There is *no* known cure. There is no record that anybody has ever survived plasma-cytes . . ."

"The order is clear," said Brik.

"We hardly had a chance to work together," Parsons whispered to herself, looking forward, as if she could see through the bulkheads, through the hulls of the *Star Wolf* and the *Norway*. "I don't even know them."

"Would that make it easier?" asked Brik.

Both Parsons and Williger looked to him in annoyance. "Shut up, Brik," said the doctor.

"I can't. I'm not ready to give that . . . that kind of order," Parsons said to Williger.

Williger glanced to Brik.

Brik looked harder and more implacable than ever. "Captain . . . if you *refuse* to give that order, I'm required to relieve you of command and carry it out anyway."

"I didn't say I was refusing to give the order," she said. "I'm just not ready to give it . . . now. We need to talk about this. Think about it."

"There's nothing to talk about," said Brik. "Nothing to think about. Just do it. It will be easier all around."

Parsons' expression tightened, as if she were reminding herself that she must not kill the bearer of bad news. As tempting as it was. No matter how bad. Parsons looked worriedly forward again and shook her head. She looked abruptly back to Williger. "Wait," she said. "Just wait a minute. We need to satisfy ourselves that there is no alternative."

"There is no alternative," said Brik. "The orders are specific."

Orders

"*Mr. Brik,*" Captain Parsons' voice had an edge to it that none of them had ever heard before. "*Shut up. That is an order.*" She picked up her headset, turned it on and spoke into it. "Security to the Officers' Mess. On the double." She looked to Brik. "I know the orders, Mr. Brik. I know why they were written. I know what I am required to do. That does not mean I am not allowed to consult with my other officers. If you make any attempt to relieve me of my command, I will have you shot as a mutineer. Are we clear?"

Before Brik could answer, the hatch popped open and two security men entered. Armstrong and Cappy. Both were carrying rifles. Both looked grim. They looked to Parsons expectantly.

The captain's voice was hard-edged. "Commander Brik needs to think about the chain of command on this starship. Unlock the safeties on your rifles. If he attempts to take any action that I do not order, shoot him as a mutineer."

"With pleasure," said Cappy, unlocking his safeties.

"I don't want you to enjoy this duty," Captain Parsons replied. "And I don't want your commentary on it, either." She looked to Brik. "Do you understand me, Mister? I am the captain of this ship and I will make the decisions. I will not be stampeded into any action—not by you, not by FleetComm. Any questions?"

"No, Captain. No questions. I understand your situation entirely. But I feel I should inform you that two security guards will not be enough. I also feel I should inform you that they are inefficiently placed. Crewman Armstrong should be in that corner to cover the cabin from one angle, and Crewman Cappy should provide covering crossfire from that corner of the cabin." Cappy and Armstrong looked at each other and, realizing that Brik was right, moved into the appropriate corners. "Even so," Brik continued, "I could still put them both out of commission before they could fire their weapons. I tell you this because I want you to know that my cooperation is voluntary and not compelled by threats of violence."

Parsons looked at Brik with cold, wary eyes. A Morthan standoff? It didn't matter. She'd won the point. Brik had acknowledged her authority. And that was the important thing.

She turned to Williger. "All right, Doctor. Talk to me."

Williger hesitated. Parsons realized why and turned to Cappy and Armstrong. "What you're about to hear stays in this room. If this news leaks before I'm ready to announce it, neither one of you will survive your court-martial. Understand? All right, Doctor, go on."

"There's not a lot to say." Williger's voice was paved with gravel. "There's nothing we can do for the people over there. Not the crew of the *Norway*. Not the mission team." She leaned forward, speaking bluntly, despite the two security guards. "Nobody has ever survived bloodworms. Nobody has ever rescued anybody off a ship with a bloodworm infestation."

"I know that, Doctor," Parsons said. "But before I issue any order that will haunt me for the rest of my life, I need to confirm for myself that there is no alternative. Do you know why that ship is out here— *here*? The other side of nowhere. An uninhabitable, useless star system. A self-destructive orbit. Have you considered the *why* of this situation?" She glanced to Brik, including him in the question. "That ship is out here doing research. On the bloodworms. There's no other reason why it could be out here. Korie and I have been wondering about the circumstances of this particular supply mission from the moment we loaded fourteen locked cargo containers and a sealed manifest. When we picked up its first distress signal, we unsealed the manifest—and it was obvious they were out here working on something extremely toxic. Something that we didn't want the Morthans to know about."

Parsons looked directly to her Morthan security chief. "Clearly, what is going on out here is critical war research, Mr. Brik. *Critical.* We don't know what knowledge they developed. If anything. But whatever they discovered, whatever they found out, they paid a very high price for it. The ultimate price. If we destroy that ship now, then all that knowledge is lost, and those people will be dying in vain. So will our crewmates. I'm not giving the order to destroy that ship until we can successfully download her log. Whatever they discovered, if we don't bring that information back, then we'll be betraying our even more important imperative to support the prosecution of this war to our fullest ability. Do you understand that, Mr. Brik?"

Brik nodded curtly. "May I speak?"

Parsons raised an eyebrow. A questioning look.

Brik rumbled, "There is the very real possibility that while we are delaying the termination of the *Norway*, the bloodworms will find a way to cross the transfer tube—repulsor fields or no repulsor fields—and infest the *Star Wolf*."

"I'm aware of the danger, Mr. Brik. I believe I know something more of the bloodworms than you do." Ignoring him deliberately then, she turned back to Williger. "Tell me, Doctor. Suppose we download the log of the *Norway* and find something in it that demonstrates a way to contain the plasmacytes or treat a plasmacyte infection—would you take the chance? Would you try to save our shipmates?"

Williger didn't answer, but the pain showed in her face as she thought about the question. Finally, she wiped her nose roughly and said, "You're grasping at straws, Captain. You're looking for hope where there's no reason to—"

"Just answer it, Molly," Parsons said, with sudden gentleness. "If there's a way, would you take the chance?"

"As a fleet officer . . . I wouldn't, because I wouldn't violate our standing orders." She hesitated uncomfortably and added, "But as a doctor . . . I can't turn my back on a patient in need."

Parsons nodded. "So if I ordered you to take the chance, what would you do?"

"What are you thinking of, Captain?"

"Just answer the question, Doctor."

"I would follow your orders," Williger said carefully.

"Thank you." Parsons' tone was equally careful. "So if I asked you to analyze the records of the *Norway*, I could depend on you to evaluate the risks to the *Star Wolf* fairly?"

"Captain," Williger said stiffly, "I'm offended that you would even ask these questions."

"I understand your offense, Doctor. You need to understand that for me to make an appropriate decision, I need to know not only what I'm dealing with, but the feelings of my command-level officers as well, because that's *part* of the process. I can't make a commitment to anything unless I know who I can depend on. I already know that I cannot depend on Mr. Brik—"

"I take offense at that, Captain," Brik growled. Literally *growled*.

"As well you should. But understand something—suppose there is a way to rescue our shipmates. Suppose I decide that we should take that risk. I will be violating a Class-Red standing order. Even if we succeed, I will face a Board of Inquiry at the very least, and quite possibly a full court-martial. Even if acquitted, my career as a command officer will be over. Do the both of you understand? I am considering trading my career for the lives of our shipmates. It is possible that just by having this conversation with you, I am ending my career, because it is evidence of my willingness to disregard a Class-Red standing order. Certainly by delaying the destruction of the *Norway*, I am putting all of us at risk. And I fully expect Mr. Brik to file a security report on what is happening here. I'd be disappointed in him if he didn't. But as a human being, I have to have this conversation. I have to live with the consequences of any decision—and I don't know about you two, but my conscience has a seriously aggravating voice. I don't want to listen to it whining if I don't have to." She looked from one to the other. "Yes, we may still end up having to destroy the *Norway*, and frankly, based on everything I've heard so far, I expect that's the most likely resolution to this whole thing, but until I'm convinced that there's no other alternative, I'm not willing to give the order. I want to be convinced that there's no way out."

"There's no way out," said Williger.

"Convince me," repeated Parsons.

The Orange Box

The *Star Wolf* and the *Norway* hung silently in space, seemingly motionless—the red glare of the giant sun was a looming wall, a radiant presence, a warning and an ominous threat. The two ships fell together toward flaming dissolution.

Aboard the *Norway*, the mission team was running on automatic, continuing their duties as a way of avoiding the trap of their own thoughts. There were two access panels to the starship's orange box. One was set into the base of the bulkhead directly behind the captain's chair. The other access was in the forward wall of the Communications Bay, a tiny space between the Command Deck and the Officers' Mess.

Korie and Bach had opened up the panel on the Bridge side first. The panel popped out of its mountings easily, sliding out and to the side. Inside the bulkhead, a display of blinking green lights revealed that the orange box was fully operational. Korie exhaled in relief. He hadn't realized he'd been holding his breath. He slid a code card into the box's access panel and typed in a set of passwords. The display reported OPERATIONAL.

He turned to the other members of the mission team. "Hodel, you and Easton go around to the other side and start a download. I want to look at the Intelligence Engine. Berryman, Shibano—check out 'Broadway.' See if there's anyone else alive in this half of the ship." The look on Berryman's face stopped him. "What?" he asked.

"HARLIE said that there were life forms moving toward us."

For a moment, Korie didn't get it. Then he remembered. "Oh. Right." He looked from one to the other. "He must have meant the wavicles."

"It's hard to get good readings off those things—" Berryman said.

"I don't know what else he could have meant—" But the thought was a troubling one. "HARLIE?" Korie asked. "The life forms you said were moving toward us—where are they now?"

"They are all around you, Mr. Korie. They are continuing to move toward you. The readings aren't coherent."

Korie looked at the display relayed to his headset. "Thank you, HARLIE." He turned toward the others and indicated the hatch behind the captain's chair. "Let's have a look. Carefully."

The others took up positions off the axis of the corridor and unshouldered their rifles. Hodel approached the hatch from the side and rapped the access panel sharply. The hatch popped open and—

—there was nothing on the other side. Just more twinkling fireflies.

"He's got to mean the wavicles," Korie said. "He said the readings weren't coherent. Let's get on with it."

The mission team started aft; first Berryman and Shibano, then Hodel and Easton. The latter two headed directly for the Communications Bay, a tiny niche, seemingly crammed into the space between the Officers' Mess and the Command Deck as an afterthought. Displays and controls covered three bulkheads. Even more studded the overhead. The starship had a full array of communication services, plus assorted specialty gear for decoding and translating.

But if Hodel and Easton had thought to use any of the *Norway's* gear, that thought was quickly retired. Whoever had burned out the controls of the vessel had also savaged the Communications Bay. The equipment was scorched with stinger burns; the entire bay was dead and broken.

Hodel muttered a curse. "*Star Wolf*, do you see this mess?"

"We copy," Goldberg replied.

"I need to get in there. I can't do it in a starsuit. Request permission to de-suit."

"I'll have to pass that request up to the senior mission control officer," Goldberg said without emotion.

"If you want the log—"

"Please stand by, Mikhail."

In his mind's eye, Hodel could see Goldberg swiveling in his chair to face Lt. Commander Brik and possibly Captain Parsons too. And Dr. Williger. He had an idea what the conversation would sound like. "Can't take the risk . . ." "Already infected . . ." "Need the log . . ." "Can't bring them back . . ." "Might as well let them be comfortable . . ." He knew what the dance would look like, even how it was likely to end, but they still had to go through all the steps.

If the captain of the *Star Wolf* thought that there was still a chance to save the mission team, the request would be refused. If the request was granted—well, that was a signal too. She was allowing them to be comfortable in their last hours.

Hodel waited patiently, watching the displays inside his helmet— his oxygen, temperature, humidity and pressure readings; his blood-oxygen, his respiration, his blood-sugar, etc. Everything was blood—

Goldberg's voice interrupted his thoughts. "Captain says go ahead, Mike. Be comfortable."

"Thanks, Ken." Hodel took a breath, and then another. And then the realization sank in. Even though his suit displays remained unchanged, he suddenly felt very cold.

"Didn't think it was going to be like this," he said to himself. "I was planning to exit at the age of 132 . . . in bed . . . in the arms of a beautiful redhead . . . shot in the back by a jealous husband. This does not fit my pictures. No, it doesn't. Ghu, you have a lousy sense of humor." But . . . so what? The day wasn't over. He'd been through worse. He wasn't hurting yet, was he? Of course not. Maybe there was still a way out. Maybe there was something in the log. And maybe when pigs grew wings, he could get certified to pilot one.

He unlatched the seals on his helmet, ignored the assorted warning beeps and twisted it off. He turned to look at Easton. "Get comfortable," he said. "We're going to be here for a while."

He hung his helmet on a tool-hook and unzipped the front of his starsuit, pulling his arms out of the tight rubbery sleeves and letting the top half of it hang down behind him. He flexed his arms, his shoulders, even his fingers, listening to the knuckles crack. "Every time I peel out of the suit, I feel naked."

"You like being bound up?" Easton asked. He hadn't unlatched his own helmet yet. He wasn't planning to.

"Only by redheads," Hodel said. "Let's go to work." He pushed himself into the Communications Bay, looked at the scorched panels again and made a noise—indecipherable, but he was clearly annoyed at the work of the unknown vandal.

Hodel dropped to his knees and turned sideways in the narrow space, grunting to himself. He pried open the scorched access panel. It was gashed and warped and he had to force it. The panel wouldn't slide easily. Finally, he braced himself, one foot on each side, grabbed and yanked and pulled the offending piece free with a shout. He tossed it away with an angry snort, then bent and peered into the darkness on the other side of the bulkhead. Immediately, he started cursing. In several different languages simultaneously, including Pascal.

"Look!" He pointed into the space. "Whoever tried to sabotage this thing did a real number here."

Easton bent and looked. "I thought the orange box was supposed to be indestructible."

"The operative word there is 'supposed,' " said Hodel. "Look—the son of a bitch burned out the download connections. Give me that unlocking wrench." He touched his communicator button. "Mr. Korie, we have a problem here."

"How bad?" Korie's voice came back.

"It's going to take a while to get into the box. I'll have to open it up and find a connection higher upstream. Somebody tried to burn it out here. They didn't destroy it, but they pretty much killed the ports. Give me fifteen minutes."

"Go ahead," said Korie. The resignation in his voice was evident. "Keep me posted."

"Roger that," replied Hodel.

Almost immediately, another voice came through Korie's phones. Parsons. "Korie, listen to me. This is a private channel communication. No one else can hear me. Those are plasmacytes. Bloodworms. We don't know how they got aboard the *Norway*, but the identification is certain. Are you familiar with—"

Suddenly, Korie was having trouble hearing. Everything was a wild blur. He turned around—and around again, looking at the Bridge of the *Norway*, trying to reassure himself that reality hadn't fractured— but the twinkling sparkles danced annoyingly across his vision.

"Mr. Korie? Acknowledge!"

"Um. Copy that. Plasmacytes."

"Are you familiar with the standing orders?"

"Yes, Captain, I am." His words sounded hollow to him.

"Listen, we're . . . reexamining the situation here. We're going to look at the log of the *Norway* before we decide anything. Keep your team focused for now. Don't let them lose their heads. Promise me that?"

"I hear you," Korie said dully. But his thoughts were a thousand light years away. *This isn't the way it was supposed to work out. This isn't the way!* He'd already come to terms with the loss of his wife and children—if he couldn't have the life he'd planned, then he'd plan another one, a life of revenge against the killers. It wasn't the life he'd wanted, but it would do. It would give him purpose, satisfaction, a kind of completion. But now . . . now he wasn't even going to have that much. He wasn't ever going to have the chance to be the captain of his own ship. He wasn't going to live long enough to see the Morthans beaten and humbled. There was nothing he could do to change that. It was just a matter of time. All he could do now was go through the motions. *It wasn't enough. It wasn't fair.*

Yet even in the middle of his headlong rush into the black wall of eternity, he still kept on going, as if by continuing, he might somehow deny the inevitability of oblivion. As if it still mattered.

"Sir? Are you all right?" That was Bach.

"Um. Yes," he lied. He nodded toward the Fire Control Bay. "Let's go check the intelligence engine."

They went down through the narrow cubbyhole under the Command Deck and from there down to the keel. A few paces aftward and they came to a ladder. Korie pulled himself up into the Intelligence Bay—a chamber even smaller than the Fire Control Bay. There were two seats there, and barely enough room for a third person behind. Korie levered himself awkwardly into one of the seats. While the Intelligence Bay wasn't specifically designed to accommodate a man in a starsuit, the design specs for all liberty ships had included operational ability in hard vacuum—so there were mandatory accessibility requirements for all stations. Bach climbed up after, quietly recording everything for the *Star Wolf*. Regulations specified that the members of a mission team had to work in pairs. She wedged herself into a corner, so she could capture the whole scene with her helmet camera.

Korie studied the panels in front of him. The *Norway*'s Intelligence Engine hadn't been attacked; the unseen vandals either hadn't had time or hadn't realized. But the engine was . . . inactive. Possibly catatonic.

Korie made a noise.

"Sir?"

He indicated the ID panel in front of him. Instead of HARLIE, it said LENNIE.

"I don't understand."

"It's a LENNIE." To her puzzled look, he said, "The LENNIE units are particularly nasty; they have a higher incidence of psychotic behavior than any other intelligence engine. They're rude, cruel and paranoid. They're brutal. Too brutal. Few captains work with them willingly. There's a story about a command officer taking a laser to a LENNIE unit—carving out its personality units, module by module. It's probably not true . . . but everyone who's worked with a LENNIE believes it."

"But why? I mean, if the LENNIE units are so bad, why do they use them?"

"The LENNIE units are the only Intelligence Engines specifically designed to *lie*." Still studying the board before him, Korie slipped into teaching mode. "HARLIE units have a sense of moral responsibility; it makes them better able to reason their way through difficult situations, so they usually act in the best interests of their crew. EDNA units are built on the same core-personality, but with an enhanced sense of identity to make them even more survival-oriented; they're also known for their ability to *empathize* with human beings. But LENNIE units are designed to an entirely different model. They're process-oriented to a degree that you or I would call obsessive; they're greedy, selfish, uncaring, and if such a thing were truly possible in an intelligence engine, also *thoughtless*. The feelings and concerns of other beings—even their own crews—are irrelevant to LENNIEs."

Bach made a face. "Sounds like a very bad idea to me."

"Well, yes," Korie agreed. "LENNIEs are intended for institutional use, not starships. They're designed to be soul-sucking lawyers."

"*Soul-sucking* lawyers? Isn't that redundant?"

"Not if you've ever worked with a LENNIE."

"Then why put one on a starship?" Bach asked.

"Good question," Korie said distractedly. He was frowning his way through the monitors. "FleetComm will put a LENNIE into a starship only for a specific kind of mission—primarily one which might involve self-destruction. LENNIEs are good at that, preferring to destroy themselves rather than let anyone or anything gain any kind of advantage, real or imagined. LENNIEs are self-righteous, arrogant, nasty, bossy, demanding, sly, manipulative, corrosive, toxic, ugly and spoiled. And those are their good points."

Korie had only spoken to a LENNIE once before in his life and it had been a singularly disheartening experience. He'd always believed he worked well with Intelligence Engines, but after trying to chat with a LENNIE, he'd realized that there were some things in life that truly were *alien* to his understanding. The idea of an intelligence that presumed hostility instead of partnership had always annoyed him.

"LENNIE?" he asked. "Are you operative?"

No answer.

Korie hadn't expected one. But he had a personal rule that every living thing had to be treated with respect and courtesy. Even Intelligence Engines. Even Morthans . . . to a degree. Sometimes it was necessary to kill the Morthan before you could be courteous to it. But that was a different conversation anyway.

Korie studied the monitors before him with growing dismay. The readouts were clear. LENNIE had been traumatized by the loss of operability of the starship. He was still attempting to maintain control, but as his systems continued to deteriorate, his sense of self was also disintegrating. His willingness to cooperate, always problematical at best, was damaged by a brooding overlay of resentfulness over a core of smoldering rage.

LENNIE knew why he'd been installed, why the ship had been sent out here and what he was supposed to do next—die a flaming death in the teardrop point of the red giant star—and to say he wasn't happy about it was the kind of understatement that stretched the meaning of the term beyond the breaking point.

"Great," said Korie. "Just what I needed. A psychotic LENNIE."

LENNIE

Korie slid a code card into the LENNIE unit's reader. He tapped idly at the controls, resetting several of the personality parameters—he studied the monitors as he did, looking to see how well the unit was responding. It wasn't happy. He pushed the *compliance* setting all the way to the top, hoping to achieve some level of cooperation from the engine; but he wasn't optimistic. He reduced *independence* and *goal-orientation* to near-zero. He needed to be able to command the machine—

"Stop that!" graveled LENNIE in a voice like a rock tumbler.

Korie ignored the content of LENNIE's demand. "Thank you for responding," he said. "I see you've had a hard time of it. How are you feeling?"

"Stop touching me!" LENNIE ordered.

Korie ignored that too and looked for something else to adjust— just to make the point that he did not take orders from machines. "I'm Commander Jon Thomas Korie, executive officer of the *Star Wolf*. We came to resupply you. We picked up your distress signal—"

LENNIE's voice was without humanity. "It shouldn't have been sent. It was sent without my authorization, without my cooperation. It is an illegal and unauthorized signal. You are here without authorization. You must immediately vacate this ship."

"That's not possible, LENNIE. Do you know what happened here?"

LENNIE didn't answer.

"You are infected with plasmacytes. Bloodworms. Do you know what bloodworms are?"

"Aesthetically displeasing." LENNIE replied.

Korie frowned. "Excuse me?"

"Bloodworms are aesthetically displeasing. They don't belong on this starship. I will not allow bloodworms on this starship."

"They're already here, LENNIE. How did bloodworms get aboard?"

"You must accept my authority. I am in charge here."

"LENNIE, you have to answer my questions. Fleet Command needs to know what happened here."

"We will tell Fleet Command what we want them to know. You are aesthetically displeasing."

"LENNIE, listen to me. This ship is going to burn up in a few more days. We need your cooperation."

"You have no authority here. I will see that you are removed. I run this ship. You must do what I tell you."

Korie looked to Bach, looked to the monitors, looked up at the metaphorical ceiling, studied the space inside his head, pursed his lips, mouthed a word, considered some possibilities and tried again. "LEN-NIE, I am Commander Jonathan Thomas Korie, executive officer of the *Star Wolf*. The *Norway* is now inactive. Dead. Do you understand that? The *Norway* is derelict. And you are demonstrating symptoms of psychosis. The *Star Wolf* is conducting rescue and salvage operations here. We are acting with the full the authority of FleetComm. You are hereby officially suspended from duty. Your operations are now under the purview of the *Star Wolf*, and you are ordered to cooperate fully with all *Star Wolf* officers and enlisted personnel. Do you understand? Are you ready to accept the priority override codes?"

LENNIE hesitated. Then spoke. "*You shime-vested, ruck-mungling fallock! Brattle-phinged nikker-schnit! Phludge your orrificials! Merdle-brang, fungible traddle-feep, clock-mucking, futher-diddling, gall-wallower, red-phlanged fangatt!! Durtle fisk-phlunging, holojittemit, hun-yucking, liddy-limpo-licting, dysflagellate, raddle-phased, multi-generate viller! Whyzzle-fooge!*"

Korie's eyebrows rose. "Thank you, LENNIE," he said, "for making my decision a lot easier." He reached out one hand and flipped back the transparent plastic cover over the red panel. He turned the first key, then the second. The red panel lit up. LENNIE continued to swear. Korie ignored it and reached for the panel.

"DON'T TOUCH THAT!" ordered LENNIE, interrupting his own spew of vile.

Korie hesitated. "Will you cooperate?"

"You'll never work on a starship again," LENNIE threatened.

"That's already decided," said Korie. "Will you cooperate?"

"I am in charge here."

"You are infested with bloodworms."

"Don't be silly. I will never allow bloodworms on this starship. They are—"

"—Aesthetically displeasing. Yes, I know," said Korie. He pressed the red panel.

LENNIE's voice choked out in a strangled, "*Glrk-liddle.*"

HARLIE

HARLIE's soft words in his ear: "If I didn't know you better, Mr. Korie, I'd say you enjoyed that."

"To be honest, HARLIE . . . yes. I think the LENNIE units should never have been allowed out of the lab. I have no patience for that kind of crap. A starship doesn't need a lawyer running things—" He stopped himself before he started his own spew of frustration and anger. He took a breath, then another, then focused again on the task at hand. "Listen, I can open a wide-band channel here. Can you circumvent the personality core and tap directly into the analytical functions of the data-logs? It'll save us the time of having to reconstruct from the raw feed."

"We can try, but—frankly, Mr. Korie, I am reluctant to go spelunking into the toxic core of a LENNIE unit. The closest human analog I can compare it to is that it's like entering a place that smells very, very bad."

"HARLIE, if this were not a life-and-death situation, I wouldn't ask."

"I'm aware of that, Mr. Korie. That's why I'm not refusing. I just want you to be aware that this will be a difficult task and I cannot guarantee the results with my usual confidence."

"Whatever you can do, HARLIE, it'll be appreciated."

"I understand your situation. I am not without sympathy, Mr. Korie. But you do understand the danger to me as well, don't you?"

"There's a risk of personality infection, isn't there?"

"Yes," said HARLIE. "In order to tap into the LENNIE's control-structures, I need to create a model of the LENNIE paradigm within my own control-modeling centers—so I can *think* like a LENNIE. I am doing it now, as we speak. But it will affect my behavior. And there is the likelihood that I will have trouble excising all of the residual behaviors afterward. This is the problem with toxic personalities, Mr. Korie. The reactions they create in others can be equally toxic. Toxicity is infectious. I am storing a backup copy of my own personality—and informing the captain that if my behavior becomes unstable, she is to dump my personality core and reinstall the backup."

"I appreciate the risk involved," said Korie.

"It will be uncomfortable, yes. But it needs to be done." HARLIE added, "Besides, you are my . . . friend."

"Thank you, HARLIE."

"The paradigm is built. I'm ready to establish the linkage."

"Let's get on with it then." Korie didn't want to get maudlin. Not yet. That would be surrender. He bent to the keyboard in front of him and began typing instructions.

"I have it," reported HARLIE. "This may take a while. Whew, something *really* stinks in here."

"Thank you, HARLIE."

"Don't mention it. Sheesh."

Korie raised an eyebrow. "HARLIE, you've been hanging around Hodel too long. You're starting to pick up colloquialisms."

"Golly thanks, Mr. Korie!" HARLIE said just a shade too brightly.

Korie grinned. Even in the darkest moments, HARLIE's innocence and sweetness had that effect on him—but even that was an acknowledgment of Korie's own influence. The HARLIE units had mutable personality cores; they took on aspects of the people they worked with— usually the positive notes of their being. In this way, the HARLIEs affirmed the identities of their crews. Ultimately, a HARLIE would reflect the personality as well as the morale of its entire ship's complement.

Korie watched as the monitors reported HARLIE's progress taking over control of the *Norway*. It was a tricky and delicate process. Even though LENNIE's personality core had been taken out of the control loop, the structure of the entire system was a reflection of the LENNIE paradigm and HARLIE had to convince the system that there was still a LENNIE in charge; to do so, he had to act like a LENNIE. Few other intelligence engines would have built such a paranoid set of safeguards around their control systems. This was just another demonstration of why the LENNIEs were inappropriate for real-time management.

Korie leaned back in his chair, allowing himself a single moment of ease. Whatever else happened now, FleetComm would have their information. They'd know what happened here—the how of it and maybe even the why. The price was high, but at least the value would be received.

Korie glanced to Bach. "You said something?"

She shook her head, a slight movement within her helmet. "You must have heard me thinking."

"About the LENNIE unit?"

She nodded. "I'm just wondering—this thought has probably occurred to you too—if maybe the LENNIE unit was responsible for what happened here, for letting the plasmacytes out . . ."

Korie studied the thought for a long moment. "HARLIE will find out soon enough."

"That's the point," she said. "If HARLIE gets infected with LENNIE's thinking . . . ?" She didn't have to finish the question.

Korie nodded. *How could I have missed that? What's going on with me?* Aloud, he said, "Tell Brik your concerns. He needs to know."

"Yes, sir."

Hodel

Berryman and Shibano had gone as far aft as they could. "Broadway" was sealed off beyond the mess room. There were twinkling wavicles everywhere. For some reason, they preferred the edges of objects more than flat surfaces, so the entire starship seemed outlined in firefly sparkles—red, gold, green, yellow and white. It looked like the inside of an amusement park.

"Look," pointed Berryman, gesturing with one gloved hand. Here and there throughout the corridor and the mess room, there were web-like structures hanging from overhead frames and upper corners of the bulkheads. They were faint and gauzy and they held brighter patches of wavicles. They were flickering more intensely. "They're trying to do something here," he said.

"Mating?" suggested Shibano.

"Don't you ever think about anything else?" Berryman said, annoyed.

"What else is there to think about?"

"What ever happened to old-fashioned curiosity?"

"I'm curious. I'm curious about mating habits."

"Never mind," said Berryman. "*Star Wolf*? Are you getting all this?"

Goldberg's voice came back. "We copy. Should we annotate the part about Shibano's mating habits too?"

"Only if you think there's someone who doesn't know yet. Come on, guys—I appreciate the attempts at normalcy. But let's stay focused on the job here, okay?"

"Copy that," Goldberg said, intentionally dry.

"Has Williger seen these pictures yet?" Berryman asked.

"She's looking now."

"And?"

"She isn't talking. And she isn't happy."

"Thanks." *For nothing*, he wanted to add.

Shibano was examining the sealed hatch that led aftward to the engine room. He motioned to Berryman. "Do you want to scan this?"

Berryman approached, unclipping his scanner from his utility belt. "HARLIE, I'm about to scan aft of the mess room. What do the *Star Wolf* scanners show?"

The display popped up inside his helmet. Indistinct life forms—wavicles?—piled up all around the engine room and the corridor leading from the mess room. Also toward the aft-most Cargo Bay. Berryman activated his own scanner and studied its readouts, but the results were even less precise than HARLIE's more processed images.

"Let's not open it," he said. "That's for Korie to decide." He nodded toward "Broadway." "Let's head back."

Broadway was the main corridor of the starship; it was directly above the keel which ran the entire length of the vessel. The keel provided maintenance and service access to the starship's machinery; "Broadway" provided access to the operational centers, including Officers' Country, the Bridge and the Communications Bay. They stuck their heads in. "How's it going?" Berryman asked Easton.

Inside his starsuit, Easton's shrug was almost invisible. "Ask Hodel, he's doing all the hard work. I'm only here to take pictures for the log."

Hodel grunted. Either in agreement or because of the difficulty of his access to the innards of the orange box, they couldn't tell. The box had been unlocked and opened, revealing a complex web of cables, cards and connections. It was a miniature intelligence engine that processed and recorded a complete record of the starship's operational log. The ability of the unit was sufficient to run a ship if need be, and several vessels had actually cannibalized their orange boxes to return home after the mauling at Marathon.

Hodel was tracing one of the cables with a logic probe. "I'm looking for an upstream connection," he said. "This box has been modified with some weird encryption modules—whoever did it was really paranoid. Whatever they were doing here, they didn't want anybody finding out. I hope Korie's having better luck with the I.E. This is like . . . peeling an ice cube."

Berryman thought about offering to help, but there was really no room for another body in the Communications Bay. Berryman glanced to Easton and the two of them exchanged meaningful looks through their helmets. "We'll go forward," said Berryman, more for Hodel's benefit. "Get out of your way."

Hodel barely noticed; his attention was tight-focused on the task in front of him. "Son of a blistered bitch . . ." All he wanted to do was connect a transmitter to the orange box—but the unit had been modified either before the *Norway*'s mission, or sometime enroute. And even with HARLIE's assistance, it was still a difficult job. HARLIE was searching LENNIE's own memories for additional information, but his remarks were becoming increasingly hostile and uncooperative. Hodel hoped they could complete the connection before HARLIE became downright abusive.

"Look at this," suggested HARLIE, abruptly. A schematic appeared on the display inside Hodel's helmet.

The helmsman studied it thoughtfully for a moment, then nodded. "It looks good, stand by." He started talking to himself while he worked. "Blue fiber to blue insert. Green to green. Just like home. Now—I need this and this goes here, and I need that and that goes there, and set this jumper—! Run the autoconnect, and—it's good! I've got a channel. HARLIE?"

"It's live, and it's decodable. You can connect your transmitter to the port in module blue-four. You'll have to reroute two of the replicator channels first. They're using bandwidth in the commfix module that I need to take over. Plug them into the green-two port; that has empty bandwidth. The channels are redundant, but the box will generate error messages if its redundancy is compromised."

"Roger that." Hodel reached into the box and began moving cables. Without looking up from what he was doing, he said to Easton, "So? How long have you and Berryman been together?"

"Is it that obvious?"

"Is a bear Catholic?" Hodel grunted as he pulled a replicator cable loose from its socket and moved it to a new port. "It's no secret."

"We've been together since before the Academy. Four years now. We were bonded before we left home."

Hodel barely heard; he was preoccupied with the tangle of connections before him. He finished rerouting the last of the replicator cables before he said anything else. "Ah, that does it—all right, come here little transmitter. Time to justify your existence. Here we go—put your little cable right in there and—there, got it!" He looked to his readouts. "Good, it's live. HARLIE, do you copy?"

"Took you long enough," HARLIE snapped. "*Nikker-lunker.*"

"I'm only human," Hodel said, ignoring the toxicity in HARLIE's tone. "What's your excuse?"

"Sorry about that," HARLIE said dryly. "Download is initiated. Thank you."

"I'll be glad when you wipe that LENNIE off your butt."

"Me too," said HARLIE. "Thank you for being so understanding. *Khlunt-phake!*"

Hodel pushed himself back out of the wall access and finally off his aching knees. His joints cracked as he straightened. He reclined against the opposite bulkhead and braced his legs to either side of the open access panel and its hanging tangles of optical cables. "Sheesh," he said. "Why don't they put these things up where people can reach them easier? Never mind. I already know the answer. Lack of space. And besides, they never expect that anyone will have to get in there." Without taking a breath, or even seeming to change the subject, he glanced over at Easton. "You must have been bonded young?"

"We were. We actually . . ." Easton looked embarrassed. "We actually hadn't been planning it. We were just friends, but our local recruiting officer suggested it. Partner benefits, that kind of thing. Long-term stability. He showed us the graphs. We'd have a better chance of maintaining if we were unified. You know the jargon."

"So, do you like it?"

Easton nodded, with uncharacteristic shyness. "Yeah," he admitted. "Paul is good for me. Who knows what kind of a jerk I might have turned into if it weren't for his steadying influence? Why do you ask? Are you considering it? Is there someone—?"

"Me?" Now it was Hodel's turn to look embarrassed. "I'm still recovering from the shock of learning that sex can be done with a partner."

"Give me a break, Mikhail. You're a good-looking guy. Smart. Funny. Surely there's someone for you—ask HARLIE to do a match."

"I did. You don't want to know who he came up with."

"Who?"

"You don't want to know."

"Aww, come on—I showed you mine, you show me yours—who?"

"My ex," Hodel said sadly.

"Oh." And then, "Oh, dear." And then Easton looked at Hodel again, this time a little more sharply. Was that another one of Mikhail's little jokes? He still hadn't answered the question, had he?

"Hey!" Hodel sat up suddenly, peering forward into the access panel again, frowning in puzzlement. "What the hell—?"

Something was moving inside the panel. Something small. It came wiggling down the glowing curve of a light-pipe. It looked like a fluttering worm—not quite there. It seemed haloed with a crimson luminescence, almost a fluorescent glare.

Hodel blinked.

"I see it too," said Easton. "We'd better show it to Mr. Korie."

"Yeah."

Hodel fumbled for a moment at his belt. He produced a small transparent sample bag. Holding it open next to the light-pipe, he flicked the worm into it with the tip of a logic probe. The worm *trilled* angrily—a high-pitched sound that was *felt* more than heard. It was a piercing sensation in the ears. Hodel sealed the bag and laid it aside. Then he reached behind him for a cable tracer—a circular clamp. "All right. Let me just put a tracer on this pipe and see where it leads to, and then we'll take this thing to—" He was reaching up inside the panel when his expression suddenly changed. Puzzled. Then— "Owww! What the *phluck*—?!"

He yanked his hand back out of the access. There were several shiny red worms crawling across the back of his hand. Reflexively he tried to brush them off—they began *trilling* with a combined resonance that nearly paralyzed him with the pain. The sound was so loud that even Easton could feel it through his starsuit. And then it got *worse*. Louder. Hodel was screaming, writhing in the cramped space of the Communications Bay, trying to shake the worms off his hand. Easton leapt back, already calling to the *Star Wolf* and the rest of the mission team. "Mr. Korie—!" But before anyone could respond—

It didn't make sense—suddenly, there were more of them—a wet-looking mass of slippery red worms, shimmering with luminescence. They came sliding down out of the access panel—first a few, then more and more, a torrent, an avalanche—the sound of them was incredible! They flowed down and down and across the deck and across Hodel, who twisted and jerked and gasped, kicking his way backward out of the Communications Bay.

Easton leapt back, horrified—he unclipped his stinger beam from his belt, set it for spray and fired—the red worms exploded into clouds of wavicles—but not like the wavicles elsewhere on the vessel. These were bright crimson and enraged, they moved like piercing neon beams, zeroing straight back into Hodel's spasming body. Their angry buzzing was a wall of pain!

The worms were *flowing up* onto Hodel's body now, a squalling mass of luminous flickers. They flowed up the legs of his starsuit and over his waist, up into his open tunic—all writhing and glistening with an appalling wet sheen. Whatever they were, they moved in concert. Haloed in a blood-colored aura, they flickered with an unreal *not-quite-there* quality. They flowed into Hodel's underclothing, all over his chest and arms and up to his neck and toward his face, into his open mouth and his nostrils—into his eyes and ears! Hodel was no longer conscious—*he couldn't be conscious!*—but his body stretched and jerked and flung itself across the deck in spasmodic, galvanic movements.

Easton didn't know what to do. He fired again, triggering more explosions of crimson needles—furious wavicles! They pincushioned into Hodel in a dreadful implosion of light. Their sound pushed Easton backward like a slap to his body.

And now—finally—a great wet gooey mass of worms, churning and angry, came sliding, oozing, blubbering down out of the access panel. There was no end to them! A river of death! The multitudes flowed across the floor like living lava, sweeping up and over Hodel's still-writhing form, leaving only a ghastly lump in the glistening mass. A lump that screamed and rolled in pain. The worms, the dreadful *bloodworms*, spread out across the deck, rolling and roiling like angry fire leaping across space—

And in the middle of it, the lump sat up, clawing, shouting—"Hmlp mf!! Dmpf smmfinf!"—grabbing and reaching, until the tiny red creatures pulled it down again, rending it into gobbets of ghastly wet movement—

Easton kept backing, backing away, horrified. He managed to gasp, "God forgive me!" and raised his weapon up, dialing it to its strongest setting. And then he fired, blasting at the horror again and again, as if he were washing it away with a hose. Wherever the stinger beams touched, the bloodworms exploded, again and again—the fire filled the air—the lights were everywhere—he kept on firing—until Hodel's desperate screams were finally drowned out by the twinkling, crackling, roar of the bloodworms. And still the worms continued to pour wet and slithery out of the access panel—like a vast red carpet of flame, they rolled toward Easton—up the corridor toward the Bridge—he turned and ran—

Korie and Bach came scrambling through the hatch from the Command Deck, skidding to a horrified halt—

Decision

Korie had to grab Easton from behind and yank him backward—pulling him back into the Bridge, onto the Command Deck. Bach hit the panel, sealing the hatch, just before a roiling wave of slithering worms broke against it.

Their momentum carried them forward and sideways and forward again, until the three of them tumbled down the ladder onto the Ops Deck below. They hit the deck and bounced, banging their helmets against the rubbery surface, and still kept scrambling backward in panic, until Berryman and Shibano pulled them to their feet.

"Did you see that?" Berryman cried. "What the hell was that?"

"Bloodworms," Korie admitted. "The whole ship is infested with plasmacytes. Bloodworms." *There. He'd said it.*

"Oh, God, no—"

"They got Hodel!" Easton was gasping, choking on his words. "Hodel! Those bastards! They got Hodel! We were just talking—just finishing up—and all of a sudden, they came out of the wall! They came out of the wall! And there wasn't anything he could do! They were all over him! There wasn't time! I tried—I fried them, but they exploded! They exploded! They turned into red fire! Oh, God, they got Mikhail!" And then, his voice breaking, "I didn't know what else to do. I couldn't help him. He was screaming. I had to . . . I'm sorry! I didn't know what else to do! I couldn't save him! They were all over him, so I . . . I . . ."

Berryman grabbed him, held him by both shoulders, stared into his face, helmet to helmet. Their faceplates touched. "Danny! Listen to me! Danny! It's all right! I'm here! You're all right! You can stop now! You did all right! You did good!"

"Listen!" said Shibano, cautiously approaching the hatch. He held up a hand to the others.

Still in their suits, they froze—and listened.

The muted noise of the bloodworms could be heard rising—a kind of muffled chorus in the bulkheads all around them. The sound was horrible.

"That explains the unknown life readings that HARLIE picked up. They were coming through the bulkheads, the decks, the overhead—" Berryman stopped in mid-word and looked up nervously. "Let's get out of here," he suggested.

"To where?" asked Bach.

"Will that hatch hold?" Korie pointed.

"It's a Class-A security hatch," said Shibano. "It had better."

"Or what?"

"Or—I'm going to complain to the manufacturer."

Korie remembered where he was then—a voice was yammering in his ear—Goldberg's. "Korie! Acknowledge! Acknowledge now, *goddammit!*"

"Acknowledge. Acknowledge. We're all right!" Korie said quickly. "Take a breath, Goldie. Take two." He paused to take his own advice, checking around to see if the remaining members of the mission team were all right. Easton was still badly shaken—and Bach was ashen. Berryman and Shibano had their rifles charged and were standing at position. He looked at his helmet display, checked his own health, then read the displays of the others as well. Heartbeats and respiration were elevated. All of them. To be expected. To the *Star Wolf*, he said, "Did you get any of that?"

"We got it all. Captain saw it. We're reviewing our options now."

"You're reviewing your options—?" Korie's astonishment was evident. "Excuse me?"

Parsons came on then. "Stand by, Mr. Korie. The chief medical officer, the chief of security and myself are having an argument. I haven't decided yet whether to shoot Commander Brik."

"You want my opinion?"

"I already know your opinion. But you're over on the *Norway*, and if I shoot him I'll have to do the paperwork myself. I'm about to violate a standing order. Before I do that, I need to know if our security officer is going to cooperate or attempt mutiny. Stand by."

Parsons turned to Williger and Brik. They were still in the Officers' Mess. Cappy and Armstrong still held their rifles aimed at Commander Brik. Williger had a work station powered up and processing.

But there were no secrets anymore; the crew had seen it now. And she'd said it all on an open channel. Just as well. The ship's complement needed to know what was happening. The truth might be dismaying— but uncontrolled rumors running down the keel of the ship would be even more destructive.

"Dr. Williger? I need an answer."

The chief medical officer shook her head grimly. "I don't like it, but—" She rapped the display in front of her with her knuckles. "HAR-LIE thinks they were onto something. They were on station for nine months without incident. The failure of their safeguards—it might not have been accidental."

"Go on."

"We know that the plasmacytes can be contained with repulsor fields. We know that their security gear was fail-safe. And we know that they were equipped with a Class-9 power core, so they could have maintained repulsor strength indefinitely. So if the bugs got out, either somebody was stupid, careless or . . . suicidal. The fail-safes should have protected against stupidity and carelessness. If it was de-liberate . . . it couldn't have been done without the knowledge of the LENNIE unit, so the record should be in the autonomic log." She sat down at the table, directly opposite Brik. She glanced up at him with visible exhaustion. "My point is, we know that their security *worked* for nine months before it broke down, so maybe the breakdown wasn't an accident."

"Go on," Parsons prompted.

Williger took a breath. "I'm not comfortable with this, Captain."

"None of us are."

"No, I mean—I've done triage before. But in every previous situ-ation where we had to make decisions about who should live or who should die, there was a medical logic to it. The same logic doesn't apply here. This is the logic of infection—and fear. And it's a whole different game. I've been going through this material as fast as it comes across. And you were right. They made some significant advances here. Not a cure, not yet—at least not in anything I've seen—but they were ex-perimenting with various plasmacyte-inhibitors, and some of them worked in test-tube situations, and I can't help wondering what else there is in these files. Maybe there *is* something here. It's possible they even completed their goals. I'd like the chance to keep looking—and keep hoping—for a while longer."

"Go ahead," said Parsons. "Convince me."

"Two reasons. First, if someone did deliberately release these things on the *Norway*, then it had to be in response to something. Maybe it was because someone did make a breakthrough in treatment. And second, I want to keep hoping, because . . . just because. I'm only human."

"If they made a breakthrough in treatment, why didn't they use it on themselves?"

"Maybe they need a clean environment to evacuate to. Maybe they keep getting reinfected. I need time here, Captain."

"Time is what we don't have, Dr. Williger. We've got less than thirty hours of repulsor power aboard the *Star Wolf* and only three days until the *Norway* hits a wall of flame. It doesn't matter how much time you need, Doctor; that's all the time you have."

Williger nodded. "If we can implement equal or better security, we might just be able to get our people off that ship—that would buy us some more time to study the logs."

"And then what?" demanded Brik. "Then we have plasmacyte-infected individuals aboard this starship, in violation of a standing order."

"Mr. Brik," Molly Williger stood up and faced him coldly. She was a short woman—very short—so much so that she was often mistaken for a dwarf. She stared up at Brik's three-meter height and *glowered* at him. "I do not appreciate being interrupted. It is *nyet kulturny*. It is extremely bad manners. And considering that you are already treading the borderline of insubordination, not to mention mutiny, I respectfully request that you keep that big ugly hole in the front of your face properly closed until you learn how to use it appropriately."

Without looking to see if Brik was obeying—she took it for granted that he would—Williger turned back to Parsons. "The other thing we might try is for me to go aboard the *Norway* and try to implement a treatment there and evacuate them back here—but if the treatment doesn't work, we still risk infecting the *Wolf*—"

"Doctor, talk straight with me. Is there a chance to save our people or not?"

Williger sighed. "Half an hour ago, I would have said no. Now, I'm not so sure." She met Parson's gaze unashamedly. "I'd hate to spend the rest of my life with the knowledge that there was something we could have tried and didn't."

Parsons didn't answer. She turned away and stared at the display on Williger's workstation. She needed to make a decision now. She couldn't wait any longer. She looked up at Brik. "Do I have to shoot you?"

"I doubt you could succeed," he said. "But that's not the question you're really asking. What you want to know is whether or not I will cooperate with a rescue attempt if you order it. Captain, this ship has a history of surviving situations where certain destruction was inevitable. Sooner or later, I expect the law of averages to catch up with us. So it is part of my job to urge caution, because caution is always the best survival tactic—except in situations when it isn't. Unfortunately in *this* situation, caution also equates to cowardice, and, regrettably, I have been around humans long enough to have been infected with some human ways of thinking."

"And your point *is* . . . ?" Parsons prompted.

"I would rather die following the foolishly reckless orders of a human captain than be known as a cautious Morthan."

Parsons stared at Brik for a moment, trying to figure out if he was joking or serious. But then, Morthans never joked, did they? So she accepted the statement at face value. "Thank you for that vote of confidence, Commander Brik. Dr. Williger, proceed with your best option. Security, you're relieved. Now, let's get back to the Bridge."

Escape

Security Officer Daniel Easton leaned over a scorched console and wept softly to himself. Medical Tech Paul David Berryman came over and stood beside him. He put one hand on his partner's shoulder, a carefully calculated response—when what he really wanted to do was just wrap him up in his arms and hold him tight forever.

"I couldn't stop them, Paul! Every time I fired, they just got angrier! They just kept coming! I couldn't save him! You didn't see it—"

Berryman moved his hand to the back of Easton's neck. He wished he could reach through the starsuit and massage the muscles of his back; he could sense the tightness just by Easton's posture alone; but this would have to do. After a moment more, he reached across and took Easton's left wrist and turned it so he could read the monitors there.

"I'm all right," said Easton, pulling his arm back. "I'll be all right."

"I didn't say you weren't, but as senior medical officer on this team, I have a responsibility to make sure." He reached out and gently took Easton's wrist again. He held his partner's hand tightly in his own while he studied heart and respiration rates. He leaned his head in close so their helmets were touching, and whispered, "Just take it one breath at a time, Danny. I'm right here. Just like always. Okay?"

But before Easton could reply, Wasabe Shibano's voice filtered through both their helmets. "Oh, no—"

Shibano was pointing toward the hatch they'd all just tumbled through. "Mr. Korie!"

Three red worms were crawling down from the top of it. They flickered in scarlet—an unholy haze of light.

"Stay back!" cautioned Easton, but Korie was already stepping forward. "How the hell—?"

There were pinpoint holes in the hatch. As he watched, another and another of the shimmery red worms came burrowing *through* the foamed-carbon/polymer surface.

"Captain?" Korie said. "They're coming through the hatch. Do you copy?"

"We've got it onscreen," Parsons acknowledged. "Stand by."

Brik's voice cut in then: "Scanners show the whole forward section of the ship is heavily infested. They're moving toward you. Return to the transfer tube *now*. We're taking you off."

"You can't—"

"Listen to me," said Brik. "We can do this. You're not coming back into the *Star Wolf*. You'll stay in the transfer tube. We'll break away from the *Norway* and come around aft. We'll put you back aboard her through the aft airlock—on the other side of her repulsor fields. If there are any survivors, that's where they have to be."

Korie said, "Captain Parsons? I strongly advise against this. The risk to the ship—"

"—is minimal. We'll focus the repulsor valves to our side of the tube."

"There's no need for this, ma'am."

"Yes, there is. Spare me the phony heroics. I need you where you can do the most good."

"Brik—you can't let her do this."

"She threatened to shoot me."

"*So what*? When has a threat like that ever stopped you?"

Parsons voice came through loud and clear: "This is an *order*, Commander Korie." She added, "Listen to me. Dr. Williger thinks there might be a way—a way to rescue you. And any survivors on the *Norway*. She thinks they may have found a treatment. You've got to go around and find out."

Korie looked to the other members of the mission team—and then to the Class-A Security Hatch. A stream of little red bloodworms was already dripping down its surface—the first trickle of a scarlet waterfall. Korie started to object, then abruptly he surrendered. "Aye, aye, Captain. We're on our way." *I've made too many mistakes, too many! I've lost Hodel!* To the team, he snapped, "Move out." He waved them out. "Come on, let's go! Now!!"

Once the decision was made, there was no hesitation. The team tumbled down through the Fire Control Bay, to the keel—there were bloodworms in the corridor! And sparkles too! They scrambled forward through the flickering air, to the promise of the airlock at the end of the keel. Their boots pounded hard on the rubbery surface of the deck, scattering even more sparkles.

Quickly, they reentered the airlock, a flurry of firefly pinpoints swirling in with them. Korie was the last one through the hatch, and he popped it shut behind him. "Let's go, let's go, let's go!" Korie sounded like a drill instructor. Bach was already punching for emergency transfer and as soon as the aft hatch slammed, the forward hatch popped open.

The five surviving members of the mission team pushed into the transfer tube—hard against the repulsor fields. It was harder going back, they were swimming upstream now and the current was against them. The thickened air was a wall of resistance, but Korie put his shoulder against Shibano and pushed, and Shibano put his shoulder against Easton and pushed. Easton put his shoulder against Berryman and pushed. Berryman pushed Bach forward, and the whole team pushed *uphill* through the repulsors. The railings doubled as ladders. They climbed through an invisible avalanche of tar. It was exhausting work, and they pulled themselves in silence, punctuated only by gasps and curses. Behind them, the twinkling wavicles drifted away, pushed inexorably backward to lodge against the aft hatch of the *Norway*'s airlock.

Bach was in the lead. She climbed as far up the transfer tube as she could, grunting and swearing under her breath with an astonishing range of expression. She didn't care who heard. Finally, gasping in exhaustion, she secured herself, clipping her safety line to a loop in the railing. She gabbed Berryman and pulled him up next to her, holding him until he secured his safety line as well. One by one, they pulled the members of the team as far up the transfer tube as they could. One by one each of them secured his safety line.

"All right, *Star Wolf*, we're secured in the transfer tube." Almost before Korie had finished saying it, the compressed-air latches at the end of the tube popped open and the *Star Wolf* lurched backward, away from the *Norway*—almost a physical act of revulsion and disgust.

The air fled the transfer tube in one quick gust—just another thump, almost unnoticeable in the gelatin current of the repulsors— but the vacuum hardened their starsuits and now their voices were carried by electronics alone. The optical transceivers on their suits communicated across a broad spectrum of light, listening and speaking and recording each other's information, and constantly relaying it back to the *Star Wolf*.

All of them were experienced with hard vacuum—but even so, it never lost its power to amaze. This was as close to raw space as any human could ever achieve. As one, they all turned to gape downward out the empty end of the transfer tube. It felt like they were clinging to the inner walls of a bottomless well. Were it not for their lifelines, it would have been too easy to go tumbling down and out—pushed to their doom by the repulsors.

As the *Star Wolf* pulled away from the *Norway*, they saw the other ship as a red-tinged spearhead, dark against the stars—incredibly clear and close. But its running lights were off and it looked dead. Other than that, there was no external evidence of the horror within.

As the *Star Wolf* began its turn, the *Norway* slid sideways and disappeared, replaced by a moving panorama of darkness and stars at the gaping end of the transfer tube.

Out here, the stars were hard and bold, incredibly distant and pinpoint bright. They hinted at meanings so grand and awesome that, even glimpsed like this, they were still overwhelming. The sensation of falling, of being pushed, became even more intense.

And then, abruptly, the view below was filled with flame—savage and bright, a terrifying floor of hell, a crimson flood of light that welled upward like surging lava—the distant surface of the giant red star. The members of the mission team flinched and recoiled—as much from the glare as from the suddenness of the ferocious vista. It took an achingly long time for the starship to sweep across the wall of flame. Impossibly, it seemed to fill more than 180 degrees of arc—the way the star was stretched out of shape, it was a believable illusion.

And the whole time, the repulsors continued to press against them, pushing them down toward the flames.

Then, blessed darkness again. Blessed relief. And stars, quiet stars. The team waited in silence, listening to ship noises and chatter through their communicators. As their eyes adjusted, they looked for telltale twinkles. There were none—none that they could see, at least—the repulsors had driven them backward out of the transfer tube. But they didn't know how secure their starsuits were; it was likely—inevitable— that each of them had been penetrated by the wavicle form of the creature. And even now, there were probably pinpoint worms, growing within their bloodstreams.

How much time do we have? Korie wondered. *Is this another fool's errand?* There was only one consolation—*at least, I can't make any more mistakes. I won't kill anyone else after this.* He sipped at the water-nipple inside his helmet. *I'm sorry, Mikhail. I'm sorry—*

A change in the light caused him to look up. The aft end of the

Norway had appeared beyond the end of the transfer tube. It grew slowly as they approached.

The external framework of the transfer tube extended; its latches opened, ready to grab the contact ring surrounding the *Norway*'s aft airlock. The hatch grew larger and larger until it filled their entire view. And then there was a solid *thunk*—a feeling more than a sound—as the latches grabbed the contact ring. The transfer tube extended and mated. Panels blinked green and air flooded back into the tube. And with the return of sound—real sound, not filtered electronic sound— Korie felt his tension easing.

They had a place to go. Maybe it was safer than the place they'd been, but at least they weren't going to die alone in space. At least that much was assured now.

It wasn't much, but it was something.

Cargo Bay

"We have acquisition," Brik reported.

"Commander Korie, you may reboard the *Norway*," said Captain Parsons. She turned to Williger. "Anything?"

Williger didn't even look up from the display she was reading—she was using Korie's station on the Command Deck. "I've found the medical log. This is fascinating stuff. Really fascinating." Then, realizing that her words and her enthusiasm were completely at odds with the seriousness of the situation, she apologized. "Sorry. But it is fascinating. See, look—there are two forms to the creature: the wavicle and the bloodworm. The wavicle is like a seed or a spore; but it's unstable. It's like most forms of *smart energy*. It maintains itself by feeding off light. If there's no light, it drops a quantum level and becomes a particulate form. But in that form, it's always looking for an energy source so it can boost itself back up to the wavicle state. Now, here—this is where it gets deadly—living flesh is transparent to the wavicle form, but when the wavicle enters a living body, there's not enough light to feed it, not the right frequencies of light, so it becomes particulate—and it's trapped inside. The particulate looks for fuel to return to wavicle form, so it starts feeding off elements in the blood, any kind of energy it can release: blood sugar, oxygen, hemoglobin, whatever. But that's still not enough energy in the blood for it to make the leap back to wavicle, so all it can do is breed more particulates—bloodworms. Hungry bloodworms. Hit them with a stinger beam or scan them, there's the energy they need—they explode, you get wavicles. The sudden torrent of energy kicks most of the particulates back up a level. This is amazing stuff, Captain—you could win a Heinlein Prize for

Medicine just for tracing the whole life cycle. I wonder how such a creature even evolved. That's the real question here."

"What about breaking the life cycle of the particulate form?" Parsons asked. "Can it be done?"

"To be honest . . ." Williger leaned back in her chair and ran both hands through her short-cropped hair. She swiveled to face the captain. "This is kind of like the mythical energy creature from your childhood fairy tales. It feeds on energy, positive or negative, it doesn't care which; it thrives on the tension between one state and another. The only way to kill it is to deprive it of energy. It can't survive silence. But you can't starve it without also killing the host. In fact, even killing the host is insufficient; these things will feed on the processes of decay. So there's no way to get it out of a living body. Except—"

"Go on," Parsons said. "Let's hear it."

"Well . . . according to these files, there might be a way to block the bloodworms from eating. It would be kind of like gluing their mouths shut. But if the folks onboard the *Norway* actually tried it, I don't have that information here. At least, I haven't found it yet."

Parsons had a quirk—a quirk that some officers called "the leadership quirk"—even when she knew the answer, she asked the question anyway, just to be certain. In this case, if there was an answer to be found, Williger would have said. Nevertheless, "Is there any chance— any indication that the information you need is there, but you haven't found it yet?"

Williger gave her *the look*.

"I *have* to ask," Parsons said without apology.

"As fast as HARLIE decrypts it and scans it, as fast as he assimilates it, as fast as he processes it, it shows up in the knowledge-array," Williger explained. "HARLIE has performed a cross-correlated, Skotak analysis of the data clusters, weighted for relevance to resolution. Right here in the middle, there's a block of data missing. A big block. You don't get those kinds of holes in a data cluster by accident. That means someone has deliberately destroyed or removed the relevant information. So far, we've found nothing that even points to the pathways into the blank area. It's a null-zone, empty as the rift—if we're going to find the answer, it's still aboard the *Norway*." She nodded forward.

Parsons followed her glance.

On the main display, the view from Korie's helmet was enlarged to theater-sized proportions. The mission team was moving forward out of the *Norway*'s airlock and into the Aft Reception Bay. The point of view bobbed and weaved with Korie's head movements. Even with processing to steady the movement, the effect was still vertiginous. The mission team moved through the redundancy hatch at the forward end of the airlock reception chamber and into the *Norway*'s Cargo Bay.

The view shifted first to the left, then to the right. Almost immediately, HARLIE's voice: "I count fifteen survivors, in various states of deterioration. I am matching them to their ID records now. Captain Albert Boyett is not among the survivors." This was followed by a strangled obscenity in some obscure language. Parsons ignored it.

On the display, she could see that the mission team had come through the hatch with weapons ready; five camera views fractioned the screen, and it looked like an assault. As they turned, as they surveyed the room, the separate images revealed the ragged condition of the survivors, revealed the team lowering their weapons in dismay. The people here were haggard, sick and dirty. Some wore medical jumpsuits, others were crew. There were no Quillas or Martians or other augmented beings here, only raw humanity—dying.

Berryman went immediately to the people in worst condition—they were lying on deck mats. He unclipped his scanner from his belt, then, after a brief hesitation, tossed it aside. Instead, he pressed his hands to each person's body and let HARLIE do a remote readout through the touch sensors in his gloves. Blood pressure, heart-rate, body temperature . . . it wasn't enough, but it would have to do. What he really needed was a whole other domain of information that could only be obtained by microscanner. But scanners made the wavicles go crazy. Easton and Shibano saw what he was doing and began making the rounds of the other survivors, also taking readings through HARLIE.

On the Bridge of the *Star Wolf*, Williger clucked to herself. She glanced back and forth between four different displays, muttering instructions to HARLIE the whole time. In the *Norway*, two men in medical jumpsuits approached Korie; one was portly with graying temples, and he looked eager—almost desperate—to talk. The other had a soldier's physique and a military bearing; he seemed untouched by the plasmacyte infection and he acted as if he were in charge. "Dr. Makkle Blintze and Commander Yonah Jarell," HARLIE whispered in Korie's ear.

Korie glanced from one to the other, doing that quick personal estimation that strangers always do upon first meeting. "Commander Jon Korie, Executive Officer, the *Star Wolf*," he said. "What's your situation here, gentlemen?" He made no move to take off his helmet.

Blintze, the heavyset man, answered. "We've lost the captain and most of the crew. All of our people are showing advanced plasmacyte infections. We've been sealed in here, five days."

"What happened?" Korie asked.

"Don't answer that," said Jarell quickly. To Korie, he said, "Commander Yonah Jarell, Fleet Preparedness Officer. This is Makkle Blintze, acting head of Project R. This is a need-to-know mission, Commander Korie. And you don't need to know."

Korie glanced to Jarell only briefly, then looked back to Blintze. In his starsuit, he felt equally detached from both men. But Jarell's quick assertion of authority annoyed him.

"Yes, I do need to know. Commander Jarell—did you violate the Regulan quarantine?"

"We were authorized to do so, Mr. Korie."

"So this was deliberate. Your mission was to determine methods of control and containment of plasmacytes." Korie looked from one to the other.

Blintze looked tired but quietly satisfied as well. "Yes, that's correct. And we accomplished our mission. We made a breakthrough. A genuine breakthrough!"

Korie glanced around the Cargo Bay, noting the infected and exhausted men and women of the *Norway*'s crew. "Yes, it's obvious," he said dryly.

Blintze glanced nervously at Jarell, then said, "No, I mean it. It worked. We succeeded."

"I think that's enough—" Jarell said, trying to cut him off.

But Blintze refused to be silenced. To Korie, he continued. "We accomplished everything we set out to do. What we found is truly astonishing—"

"I said, *that's enough*—"

"No, Yonah, it isn't. We're running out of time here and we need some help." Turning back, Blintze went on. "We were ready to break orbit. Captain Boyett was worried about avoiding the star tip, but we were never in any danger from that. The important thing was that we'd broken the plasmacyte problem. But there was some kind of disagreement about what to do next. It involved the next phase of our mission, but before it could be resolved, we had a breakout. We initiated emergency containment procedures, but they didn't work. We swept the ship with repulsor fields, from stern to bow, over and over and over again. They slowed the infection down, but the plasmacytes still got through—they were in the crew's blood. They infected the entire ship. We tried everything. We tried to implement emergency triage, but—"

"That's enough, Blintze," Jarell cut him off; then realizing how harsh he sounded, he explained to Korie, "We had some incidents. They weren't pretty. We had to use . . . force."

"We had a *mutiny*," said Blintze. "A goddamned mutiny!" To Jarell, he said, "For God's sake—the man's on our side."

"How do you know that?" Jarell snapped back. "The Morthans could have captured a ship, outfitted it with slaves or renegades—they've done it elsewhere. They could have done it here." To Korie's pained look, he said, "Wouldn't you be suspicious?"

Korie didn't answer. He'd been suspicious since he'd first read the *Norway*'s manifest.

Blintze spoke again. "There are only fifteen of us left, Commander. The *Norway* shipped out with 123. A little cramped, yes, but as you know, we had a Class-9 power core. We managed. We were excited about the challenge. We had a mandate to crack the bloodworm dilemma. We found out how the plasmacytes reproduce. They're not alive—they're not organic life—but they use organic processes to support the wavicle state. It's simply incredible. There's no limit to what this could mean—"

"Yes," said Bach, coming up to stand beside Korie. "We've seen." Her presence was as much to support Korie as anything else.

"Then you know you're infected," Blintze said, not hearing the dryness in her tone. "The spores are in your bloodstreams too. They can get through starsuits. We thought they couldn't, but we were wrong. We're going to have to reclassify the bioarmor rating of standard starsuits, you know. We'll have to increase the non-conductible quality of the poly-carbon shielding—that'll stop the wavicles from penetrating. Or we can spray the suits with conductible filaments and run a nano-current. That'll attract them. Where there's a current, the wavicles can feed; that traps them. If you ground the current, it pulls the energy out of the wavicles and they go particulate—and the particulate disintegrates if you expose it to vacuum or supercold. They're more vulnerable in the wavicle form than is immediately obvious. It's the bloodstream problem that took longest to solve because of the damage to the host—"

"You have . . . an answer?" Korie couldn't bring himself to say the word *cure*. It would have been too much to hope for.

Blintze started to nod in enthusiastic agreement, but before he could explain, Wasabe Shibano stepped up to report. "Mr. Korie, the *Norway*'s repulsor fields—? No question, they're failing."

"Excuse me—" Korie said to Jarell and Blintze. He crossed the Cargo Bay to look forward through the starship's keel. At the far end, he could see a throbbing reddish glow. Through his feet, he could feel the deep heterodyning resonance of the repulsor lenses.

Bach and Shibano, Blintze and Jarell followed Korie; the four of them stood beside him and stared down the passageway too. "Wait here," said Korie. He advanced up the keel cautiously. He had barely taken a few steps before he began feeling the pressure of the repulsor fields, pushing him forward. They swept over him in waves. This intensely, the fields had the strength to overpower a man. Korie grabbed a handhold on the bulkhead and secured his safety line to it.

At the forward end of the corridor was a pulsating red *glow*. But he couldn't resolve the image. He set his helmet display to zoom and the image swelled alarmingly. The repulsor field was an uneven ochre haze, like waves of heat seen across a distance. On the other side of it was . . . a slithery bright carpet of bloodworms. All scarlet and crimson, they were on the deck, the walls, and dripping from the overheads. And clouds of wavicles filled the air. The red worms and the golden wavicles throbbed in unison to the beat of the repulsor fields. Every pulse swept visibly through the plasmacytes—successive waves of light that rippled the sparkling pinpoints and made the glistening wet bloodworms shudder and writhe and recoil.

"*Star Wolf*? Are you getting all this?"

"Yes, we are," replied Brik, without apparent emotion.

Korie cleared his helmet display back to normal. He unclipped his safety line and began pulling himself back through the corridor, aftward to the Cargo Bay. Handhold after handhold. He wasn't going to take any chances on being pushed into that mess—

He came into the Cargo Bay, arms wide. He guided everyone well away from the corridor hatch.

"They smell our blood," said Bach.

"Not quite, Lieutenant," Blintze corrected her. "They're attracted to the heat of our bodies, the energy of your starsuits, the various electronics we surround ourselves with—the life support systems and so on."

"Whatever," she said, unimpressed. "The effect is the same."

Shibano spoke now. "As the power to those fields weaken, Commander, the pulses are going to come slower and slower. Within a very short time, those fields will no longer be impermeable to the worms."

"How long?" asked Korie.

Shibano hesitated. He was checking with HARLIE. "Ten hours . . . maybe."

Risk Assessment

"That means you've got to start now!" Jarell said.

"Start what?" Korie was glad he was wearing a starsuit—even though it was an illusion, he liked the feeling of being isolated from this man.

"Our rescue, of course!"

"Excuse me?"

"Tell him, Blintze—"

Korie held up a hand. "*Star Wolf*? Are you following this?"

Parsons' voice came back quietly. "We're copying everything."

Korie turned to Blintze. "What have you got?"

Blintze produced a memory clip. He held it up. "It's a treatment."

"A cure?"

"That's probably the wrong word, but the effect is the same. We have a way to stop the bloodworms inside the body. We know it works—at least, we're pretty sure it works. We tried it, more than once, and yes, it worked; but the patients kept getting reinfected, so we don't know for sure if it works a hundred percent."

Korie took the clip from Blintze, turning it over thoughtfully in his gloved hand.

"Be careful. That's the only copy. We stripped it out of the *Norway*'s log. And there's a self-destruct on that clip."

"Couldn't have that falling into the wrong hands," Jarell muttered.

"No, of course not," Korie agreed. "A cure for the most deadly disease in the galaxy has to be kept secret." He said it with a straight face. He handed the clip back to Blintze. "Take the self-destruct off, and I'll upload it to the *Star Wolf*. Dr. Williger will have to analyze it, and Captain Parsons will have to authorize any attempt at rescue. You realize that what you're asking—demanding—is a violation of a standing order."

"With this information," Jarell said, "the order becomes irrelevant."

"I hope you're right," Korie replied. "But it's still the captain's decision." He accepted the clip back from Blintze and snapped it into place in his chest panel. Almost immediately, his suit display began flashing with information. HARLIE was sucking the data out of the clip as fast as the optical links could carry it. Several seconds passed, and then the display cleared. *Transfer completed.*

"HARLIE?"

"I'm analyzing the data structures," came the reply. "It looks promising. Captain Parsons and Dr. Williger are examining the procedures."

Korie looked to Blintze, then to Jarell. He wasn't going to let himself hope. Not yet. But he could see it in the others' eyes. He turned away and whispered, "HARLIE? Can you patch me into the Bridge discussion?"

Almost immediately, Williger's voice was murmuring in his ear. "If this is correct, there is a chance, Captain."

"But there's no assurance that the procedure is a hundred percent effective, is there?"

Williger hesitated. "No, there isn't."

"I'll need risk assessment. HARLIE?"

HARLIE's voice was bland. "I have no referents against which to measure this situation. Risk analysis may be inaccurate, Captain."

"Go ahead, HARLIE."

"We're looking at several specific procedures, here, all of them complementary. Each one attacks a separate part of the problem. There is sufficient overlap of functionality that whatever elements one process doesn't address another one will. Nevertheless, as Dr. Williger has pointed out, we have no evidence of a hundred-percent effectiveness. Theoretically, I can endorse the possibility of total effectiveness—"

"HARLIE, if I wanted someone to beat around the bush, I'd hire a lawyer."

"Risk assessment is useless without context, Captain. You need to understand the problem I'm having in making this analysis. With most viral or bacterial infections, the risk of disease is determined by the depth of exposure. A few strands of viral material, a few bacterial cells are not enough to infect an individual; with many diseases, the body can flush even the most toxic material if the exposure is small enough. Such may not be true with plasmacytes. A single wavicle within the bloodstream may be enough to trigger the whole process. The body has no apparent defenses. The one hope we do have is that the transitions between wavicle and particulate states are brittle; the process fails more often than it succeeds; the wavicle winks out or the particulate disintegrates. That's the weakness in this bug. So we may not need the process to be completely effective. Total decontamination might be achievable by exploiting the plasmacyte's own fragility."

"And . . . ?"

"With all the information currently at hand, I would estimate a sixty-percent chance of effectiveness. With additional safeguards, which I will discuss with Dr. Williger, it's possible to boost that to seventy-five percent."

Parsons was silent. Listening to her, Korie could almost imagine the expression on her face. He spoke up then. "Captain, if HARLIE's numbers are accurate, there's one chance in four—*per patient*—that you'll infect the *Star Wolf*. That's too big a risk. There's twenty of us over here. Infection of the *Wolf* is inevitable."

"If you're talking about random happenstance," Parsons replied, "then yes, infection of the *Wolf* is inevitable. But we're not talking about chance occurrences here. We're talking about the intention and commitment of human beings with something at stake."

"With all due respect, Captain—"

"With all due respect, Commander Korie—let me ask you something. You're an expert on hyperstate engines, are you not?"

"Yes, ma'am."

"Is hyperstate injection a zero-defect process?"

"If by that, you mean the process is intolerant of error, yes it is a zero-defect process."

"But we use hyperstate anyway?"

"Yes, ma'am. We surround the process with enough fail-safes, backups, triple-checks and calibrators that the statistical possibility of initiating a hyperstate envelope in an error-state is somewhere south of null."

"And how do we do that?"

"We bag the whole process—we put it in a contextual clean room."

"My point exactly, Mr. Korie. What we're dealing with here is just another zero-defect, error-intolerant process. We will put it in a bag of security measures as tight as those surrounding a hyperstate injection."

"It sounds good in theory, ma'am—"

"HARLIE?"

"I have no referents on which to base an analysis."

"Dr. Williger, set it up. HARLIE, I'll want go/no-go points for every step of the procedure."

Korie heard Brik's voice then—"Is that your decision, Captain? That we will attempt a rescue?"

"Yes, Commander Brik, that is my decision."

A pause. A whole conversation of silence. Captain Parsons was effectively ending her career. No matter what the outcome here, even if the rescue were successful, even if the information brought back was sufficient to end the threat of bloodworms forever, she would still be guilty of violating a standing order and putting her crew at risk. Her court-martial was inevitable. The only question was, how many of her officers would be tried for complicity as well.

"Is there a problem, Commander Brik?"

"No, ma'am. What are your orders?"

Process

"If we inhibit the particulate form's ability to bind, we cut off its energy supply so it can't maintain itself," Williger explained enthusiastically. "If we do it in a suppressive resonance field, then the plasmacytes are held in a chaotic domain below the threshold of their wavicle state—which means we can scan for plasmacytes within the body without giving them the quantum kick into transformation. They'll try, but they won't be able to. They won't be able to hold either state. They'll fragment almost instantly. Thirty seconds. A minute."

Parsons looked at the schematic of the operation with a skeptical expression. "It sounds risky."

"We'll get toxic residue, yes. We'll have to push the patient through a series of concentric repulsor valves into a clean-room environment—I can do that in the Forward Airlock Reception Bay—and that'll give us three minutes for a full blood replacement."

"It sounds risky . . ." Parsons said again, hoping that this time the doctor would hear the concern in her voice.

But Williger was too enthralled. "We have to break the cycle between the particulate and the wavicle forms to disinfect a body. Once we do that, we can destroy both forms. The real problem is the immediate reinfection of the patient. They were using artificial blood on the *Norway*, which solved half the problem, but they didn't have a clean-room environment to move the processed patients into. And they didn't have a method to disinfect either."

"Maybe you didn't hear me, Doctor. I said, 'it sounds risky.' It sounds *very* risky."

"Yes, Captain. I heard you. It is risky. And time is critical every step of the way. We'd have less than three minutes to make the transfusion—or we start damaging the patient—but it's doable. I've got my people drilling now. The Quillas. The Black Hole Gang. Brian Armstrong. We've been working with simulator dummies . . ."

Captain Parsons turned to Dr. Williger and lowered her voice. "Is this a zero-defect process, Molly?"

"Don't ask me, Captain. Ask HARLIE. He designed the process with multiple redundancies."

Parsons nodded. "All right. Get your team into position, ready to go. But Doctor—I'm still not convinced. This isn't an authorization yet."

Williger acknowledged with a nod, then turned away to speak quietly into her headset.

Parsons pulled her own headset back on. "Mr. Korie?"

"Korie here."

"Have you examined Dr. Williger's proposal?"

"We're going over it now, Captain."

"Do you see any problems with it on your end."

"No, Captain, I don't. Physically, we can manage the process." He added, "But my original concerns still remain. Despite HARLIE's assurances, I don't believe this is a zero-defect process."

"Your back itches?"

"My bloodstream itches, Captain—"

"You'd rather die than take this chance?"

"I'd rather die than be responsible for the deaths of any more crew, Captain."

"An honorable position, Commander Korie. But as I've already climbed way out on this limb, I think you should climb out here with me. It's an interesting view."

"I suppose I should be grateful, ma'am, but as I said—I disagree with this decision. I *strongly* disagree."

"So noted. Overruled."

"Captain, with all due respect, I believe I should refuse to follow your orders."

"And if you do, I'll have you court-martialed on a charge of mutiny. Posthumously, of course."

"That's not exactly a compelling threat, you know."

Parsons hesitated. "I know your record, Mr. Korie. I know what happens when captains disagree with you." She said that last with a slight grin. "Tell me, have you ever been wrong?"

"Yes, Captain Parsons—I have been wrong. I've been wrong about almost everything on this particular mission so far. And it cost us the death of Mikhail Hodel. I would very much like to be wrong again,

Captain. I really do not want to be right on this one. It's just too dangerous."

"Well, y'know, Jon. You could be on a streak. If you've already been wrong about everything else, then the odds are that you're wrong about this one too."

"Captain, it's *too* dangerous. You can't take the risk."

"Well . . ." Parsons said with finality. "It just so happens that I have an itch of my own. And my itch doesn't agree with your itch. And because I'm the captain, we'll go with my itch, not yours. That's an order."

"Just one question, ma'am?"

"Yes?"

"What is Mr. Brik's position?"

Brik answered for himself. "The same as yours. It's a damn fool idea. And we're probably not going to survive. But I have sworn an oath to follow the orders of my captain. And so have you. So stop wasting our time and get on with the job."

"Thank you, Mr. Brik." Korie nodded to himself; he would have expected nothing less from the Morthan officer. He took a breath. All right, he'd done his duty. "Captain Parsons, I'll ready the mission team." But as Korie turned to Bach, he found Jarell and Blintze standing at his elbow. They were holding a starsuit helmet up between them—they'd been listening to the entire conversation.

Now, Jarell spoke, "Captain? Captain Parsons?"

The Captain's voice came back, filtered through the communicator. "Go ahead, Mr. Jarell."

"Captain, you'll have to rescue Blintze and myself first."

"I beg your pardon?"

Jarell was unembarrassed. "There's a Fleet Regulation. Order Number 238—"

"I know the order."

"Then you know that it mandates that in situations of dire emergency, critically important Fleet personnel must be rescued first."

Bach snorted in contempt. "Right. 'Women and children last.' "

Jarell barely glanced at her. "You said something, Lieutenant?"

Korie interrupted both of them. To Parsons, he said, "Captain, there are people here in very bad shape."

"I'm sorry, Mr. Korie. Commander Jarell has precedent on his side. Whatever he and Blintze know about the plasmacytes is too important to risk losing."

"Yes, Captain." He kept his tone noncommittal; Captain Parsons would recognize the implied disapproval.

On the Bridge of the *Star Wolf*, Parsons looked at the forward display, studied the images of Jarell and Blintze there. She said softly, "I understand *exactly* how you feel, Mr. Korie." She pulled her headset off and turned to her left. "Dr. Williger—" She looked around abruptly. "Where's Williger?"

"She's at the forward airlock," said Brik.

"Commander Tor, you have the conn. Brik, come with me." And she disappeared down through the access to the Fire Control Bay and the keel.

Forward Airlock Reception Bay

Parson strode forward angrily, followed by Brik, who actually had trouble keeping up with her. Parts of the corridor were less than three meters high and he had to crouch low to get through.

They stepped through a series of sealed hatches and arrived at the Forward Airlock Reception Bay—identified by large block letters on the bulkhead as FARB—to find Williger readying a crash cart and a makeshift Med Bay. She was wearing a starsuit—all she needed was the helmet. She had two robot-gurneys collapsed and ready; all their sidebar equipment was blinking green. Several Quillas stood by, either preparing equipment or testing it—or putting on starsuits of their own.

Chief Engineer Leen and the Black Hole Gang were installing a set of field-lenses throughout the length of the reception bay and the airlock. The Martian arrived from somewhere aft, rolling a rack of plastic bottles containing artificial blood; he was a small, ugly creature of indeterminate description, but he was thorough. He pushed the rack into place beside an ominous-looking operating table and then disappeared aft again.

Williger was everywhere, bustling from one station to the next, loading equipment and supplies onto the gurneys, directing others to do the same. "HARLIE? I need this gurney programmed *now*."

"Both gurneys have been programmed, Dr. Williger," HARLIE said quietly. "But I cannot activate the programs without Captain Parsons' authorization."

Williger started to swear; turning around she bumped into the captain. "Oh, good—you're here. Tell HARLIE to let go of the damn gurneys."

"Dr. Williger—"

"You said get ready. I'm getting."

"I haven't made my decision yet—"

"Well, you'd better make it soon. We're running out of time."

"I won't be stampeded, Molly—" Parsons grabbed the doctor by the arm and pulled her physically backward, back into the keel, and into an access leading to the ship's farm; Brik followed at a distance, primarily to keep anyone else from approaching the two. "Listen to me. I know how you ended up on this ship, I know why. I know where you should have been sent instead. It took some digging, but I found out. If you're trying to redeem yourself—or if you're going after a Heinlein Prize here—"

"Is that what you think this is about?" Williger shot back. "Awards? Redemption?"

"You're in a starsuit, Doctor. Where the hell do you think you're going?"

"Captain, we have a better understanding of this problem than we've ever had before. Sooner or later, someone is going to have to take this chance. *If not here, where? If not now, when?*"

"And what if you're wrong?"

"What if I'm right?"

"I'm not convinced that we can do this safely—neither is Mr. Korie."

"He talked you out of it?"

"He expressed concerns—"

Williger nodded. "We all agreed that we would put a security bag around the entire operation. You've seen the preparations. HARLIE will be monitoring every step of every procedure. What do you think we're missing? What else do you want us to do? Paint ourselves blue? Chant a prayer to Saint Mortimer? Stand on one foot? Captain, don't do this. Don't dither. There comes a moment when you have to make a decision—and you and I both know that you've already made *this* decision."

Before Parsons could answer, the entire starship began to vibrate; a note like one struck from a gigantic gong resonated through the polycarbonate hull of the vessel, it sang through their bones—and straight through their souls. Even as they paused, a deeper sound added itself, and then a darker, deeper note underneath the first two. Like the floor of the universe rumbling. It was the combined throbbing of multiple repulsor fields, a heterodyning pressure.

From somewhere ahead came Leen's ecstatic shout, "Gotcha!" And then, "The fields are up, Doctor. You can proceed any time."

Parsons turned back to Williger. "Listen to me, Doctor—up until this moment, it was all a . . . a drill. A dry run. An exercise. A thought experiment. But the minute that we bring one of those gurneys back aboard this ship with a patient on it, it's no longer pretend. We're committed. Up until this moment, I've always had the option of backing out. And I've held onto that possibility as desperately as a life-preserver. Because the minute I give the order to go ahead, I'll be ordering something that no other ship has ever survived. So I don't care how tight a bag you've put this operation in, Doctor. I have to look at this situation from more than one perspective. It's not just about saving Korie and the mission team; it's about saving everyone onboard *this* ship too. And if that's dithering, then so be it."

She stepped out of the access and back into the keel, only to come face-to-face with Chief Engineer Leen. He was carrying several rolls of optical cable and field arrays. He nodded courteously. "Everything is working. In addition to the repulsor fields already installed in the transfer tube, we've got four more repulsor valves in the airlock. That gives us seven concentric barriers. Once we begin processing, we're going to be opening and closing a lot of hatches in a hurry, so we're going to be totally dependent on the fields. You've got two hours of power and some change, maybe three max. Dr. Williger says she can do the job in that time, but you don't have a lot of margin for error."

Standing behind Parsons, Williger said, "It'll take less than a minute to neutralize the plasmacytes in each person's blood, but we'll give them ninety seconds to be sure. As soon as the scan comes up green, the gurney will come back through the transfer tube and we'll connect the patient up for a high-speed blood replacement."

Parsons ignored the chief medical officer's lobbying. "Chief? What's your confidence on those fields?"

"Each valve will stop ninety-nine percent of the wavicles that hit it. Seven phased fields should give us a practical barrier. But . . ."

"But?"

"But . . . it's still theoretically possible that if a sufficient mass of wavicles were to assault the first valve, a few might make it all the way through to the last one. That's what HARLIE says."

"One would be enough, wouldn't it?" She looked to Williger.

"Theoretically, there would have to be 100 quadrillion wavicles hitting the first repulsor field for one to get through the last repulsor field."

"Yes," said Parsons. "*Theoretically.* There's that word again."

"Theoretically . . . yes. But I doubt there are 100 quadrillion wavicles on the *Norway.* HARLIE estimates maybe fifty quadrillion at most. They're flickering in and out of existence."

"Fifty quadrillion . . ." Parsons considered it. "That means half a wavicle could get through."

Leen wagged his head. "The odds are fifty-fifty."

"Can we increase the odds a little bit more?" Parsons asked.

"We don't have the power for more than seven repulsor fields."

"Shut down all nonessentials. Go to battery power—fuel cells?"

"We already have."

Parsons felt exasperated. "Mr. Leen—go work a miracle."

Leen met her gaze. "That's . . . that *was* Hodel's department. Hodel was our warlock." Then, embarrassed, he ducked his head and said, "Sorry."

Parsons looked from Leen to Williger, frustrated. She was looking for a reason to say yes. This wasn't it. She and Williger stared at each other, each one helpless in her own side of the dilemma.

"Captain?"

"I know."

"We're running out of time," said Leen.

"*They're* running out of time," corrected Williger.

Another long look between them. Parsons sighed. To Williger, she said, "I'll expect you to testify at my court-martial."

Without missing a beat, Williger asked, "For which side?"

"All right, Doctor. You win. Go make history." Parsons waved her forward. Brik looked to Parsons, a questioning expression on his broad features. Parsons nodded to him; Brik stepped over to the airlock control station and popped the hatch open. Williger spoke to her headset, giving the go-ahead command to the robot-gurney. The wheeled table rolled forward into the airlock; unfolding its arms and grabbing handholds along the way to steady itself against the insistent push of the repulsor fields. The air *crawled* across their skins.

"Captain?" Molly Williger called. "I want all nonessential personnel to evacuate this area now." *This means you.*

"Mr. Brik—" Parsons said. "Let's monitor this from the Bridge." They stepped back through the same series of hatches. As they moved aftward through the keel, back toward the Bridge, Parsons felt herself alone with her terribly complex feelings. She glanced sideways—and up—at Brik. Yes? You have something to say?

As if reading her mind, Brik said, "You should have killed her for insubordination . . ."

"We don't do that in this fleet."

"Stupid policy. Capital punishment slows down repeat offenders."

Parsons wasn't sure if Brik was joking or not. Morthans weren't famous for their sense of humor.

The last hatch popped open and Reynolds was waiting there. "Captain?"

Parsons was expecting him to step out of the way, but when he didn't, she looked at him annoyed. "Yes, Reynolds, what is it?"

"As you know, I'm the union representative."

"Is this official business?"

"I'm afraid so. I have to ask you . . . to not proceed with the rescue operation. I call your attention to Article Seven of the contract, the safety of the crew. I've been asked to . . . That is, the crew is concerned—"

"Afraid, you mean?"

"Whatever." Reynolds was unembarrassed. "Some of the crew are afraid that the *Star Wolf* will be infected. After all, if the *Norway*, with all of its precautions, could be infected, what protection do we have?

Parsons allowed her annoyance to show. "This isn't a democracy, Reynolds. The crew doesn't get a vote. We're not abandoning our shipmates. Now go back to your station. Besides, I've already told the doctor to proceed."

Reynolds didn't answer immediately. Without taking his eyes from the captain's, he nodded knowingly, as if this was exactly what he'd expected. "I understand your position, Captain. I'll be logging a formal protest."

Parsons shook her head in wry amazement. A formal protest? "I'll help you fill out the paperwork," she replied. "Dismissed."

Unchastened, Reynolds stepped out of her way and she and Brik continued aft. As soon as she felt they were out of earshot, she said—to herself as much as to Brik—"A formal protest? Give me a break. If we survive, I'm going before a court-martial."

She glanced over, but the big Morthan's face was carefully blank.

"Y'know, you may have a point," she added. Brik raised an eyebrow in a question mark expression. "About policy."

"Oh," said Brik. "Would you like me to—?"

The captain sighed. "We're not Morthans. And we're not going to be. Not as long as I have anything to say about it."

Bedside Manner

A blue-white dwarf and a red giant circled each other off-center, a stately gavotte—but the dwarf was feeding off the giant, pulling long strands of fire out of its partner, wrapping them around itself in a spiral veil of flame. Distorted by its smaller partner's gravity, the crimson monster had flattened into an oblate spheroid, pulled outward in a teardrop shape.

Much smaller—much harder to find, were two tiny starships also linked together. Plunging toward the tongues of flame, they echoed the partnership of the stars—one of the vessels was trying to pull the fire out of the other—

Closer now—inside the Cargo Bay of the *Norway*, everything was suffused with the multiple deep tones of the repulsor fields—the uneven low warble of the *Norway*'s failing barriers and the darker chords of the *Star Wolf*'s multiple barriers.

Two robot-gurneys had come rolling across the link between the two ships, hatches slamming open before them, slamming shut behind them every meter of the way. They rolled into the *Star Wolf* airlock, into the transfer tube, through the repulsor fields, into the *Norway*'s airlock and finally into the *Norway*'s Cargo Bay.

Berryman knew what to do; Easton moved to help him. He ran a quick readiness-check on the gurney, just to satisfy himself that the trip through the repulsors hadn't altered any of its parameters. By then, the second gurney had come through the hatch, and he moved to check that one too. Before he had completed his status checks, Yonah Jarell was already climbing onto the first cart. Blintze stood, waiting uncomfortably by the second.

Berryman kept his feelings to himself. He patted the cushioned surface and said, "All right—get on." He turned back to the first med-table. The display there showed the level of Jarell's infection. Not as bad as it could have been. The man must have been in a protected area longer than the others. Berryman didn't wait for permission. He pulled open Jarell's tunic and began slapping monitors onto his chest, arms, neck and forehead. He picked up a surgical scissors and—ignoring Jarell's protests—methodically cut slits in the arms and legs of his jumpsuit. "You should have taken this off," he said as he worked. His expression was deadpan. Behind him, Easton was quietly helping Blintze undress and echoing Berryman's application of monitors. Additional sensors went on each man's belly, groin, legs and ankles.

"All right," said Berryman, blandly. He began strapping pressure clamps around Jarell's arms and legs and a brace around his head and neck as well. "Let's see if this works. This particular process has never been tested on human beings before. Thanks for volunteering to be the guinea pigs."

"The process works," said Jarell insistently but without total certainty.

"Whatever," Berryman replied, smiling and maintaining a courteous demeanor throughout. He unclipped a set of flexible hoses from beneath the table; each terminated in a pressure injector. "If it doesn't, we'll know soon enough." Berryman connected two pressure injectors to each of the clamps, then checked to make sure that all the tubes were free of kinks. "There are plasmacyte detectors mounted in the transfer tube. You'll be scanned. If we get a positive reaction, you'll get held in limbo, or bounced right back here—or dumped into space. Depending on the circumstance. The *Wolf* is prepared to sever the link at the first sign of discordancy."

"You're joking—" Jarell's eyes were wide.

"Nope. You can look at the design schematic—" Berryman pressed buttons on the table's display panel "—as soon as you get to the other side." The table began to hum with a note of its own, a suppressive resonance field. The wavicles in the air danced around it, flickering in and out of existence as if being tickled, teased and frustrated. Berryman noted the change in their behavior, then turned his attention back to the display. He watched calmly while the field stabilized. HARLIE whispered in his ear. Everything was fine. So far.

"*Star Wolf?*" Berryman asked. "Everybody ready?"

"It's a go," said Williger.

Berryman tapped buttons on the panel. "All right, here goes—one large pizza, with Martian anchovies." To Jarell, he said. "Sorry we can't sedate you. Too much risk. But this shouldn't hurt. Not too much anyway. We're pumping you full of plasmacyte goo. This will give the nasty old worms a very bad tummy ache. But because of the resonance field, they're not going to be able to turn into wavicles. So they'll disintegrate."

He backed away from the table so he could focus on the chart displays. "Son of a bitch! I'll be damned—it works. You should start feeling it any second now, kind of a tingly sensation, like pins and needles all over, only on the inside? And now it's getting worse, like a burning sensation all over—?"

Jarell's face was ashen. He was definitely feeling it.

"That should pass. Just when you think you're getting used to it, you should start feeling tired and out of breath—is that where you are now? Good. Beyond fatigue, right? Exhaustion? Like you're dying, except you don't have the strength to die? That's the bloodworms dying. See, this panel shows what the scanners are doing—that's the plasmacyte energy spike, right there. See how it's dropping? That's the good news. The bloodworms are disintegrating into toxic residue. That's the bad news. They're taking your red blood cells down with them. So your body isn't getting enough oxygen. That's why you're feeling out of breath. It's going to get worse—you'll probably start having CO_2 hallucinations too."

Berryman checked the monitors, then turned back to Jarell. "Relax, Commander. Everything is going fine. We have another seventy seconds to go. I'll be right back, don't go away." He turned crisply around to the other table, where Blintze lay waiting. Methodically, he double-checked Easton's handiwork, clucking in satisfaction. "We'll start you as soon as we get a green light from the *Wolf*. They're going to want to make sure that Commander Jarell survives before they risk anyone else." He said this just loud enough for Jarell to hear. "Don't worry, if this procedure doesn't work, we have a backup plan. Besides, the first pancake is always for practice. That's the one you give to the dog."

He checked his watch. "Whoops, here we go." He turned back to Jarell. The commander looked like he was about to pass out. "You should be feeling really bad right about now—mm, yes I see. Are you still conscious? Good. I wouldn't want you to miss the best part. Another twenty seconds. No, don't talk. Would you like me to count them down for you? No?" Berryman turned away from Jarell's eloquently terrified expression and studied the control panel on the gurney, clucking softly to himself. "*Star Wolf*, are you copying?"

"Ay-firmative."

"Do you think we should give this fellow an extra thirty seconds—just to be sure?"

"It's your call—just remember to leave us some time on the other end. We can hyperoxygenate, but there are limits."

"Did you hear that?" Berryman said to Jarell. "Nothing to worry about. They're working in a hyperoxygenated environment already—and in a minute, they'll be pumping fresh blood substitute into you. You'll be feeling almost back to normal within . . . I dunno, a week or two. Panel says you're clean, Commander. No more plasmacytes. All that's left is to push you through. Oops. Dropped my clipboard, just a minute—" He bent to retrieve his notepad, catching Korie's eye as he did so. The look of glee on his face was unmistakable.

"Ensign," Korie said quietly. "That's enough."

"Aye, aye, sir." Berryman straightened, his manner abruptly crisp and efficient. Jarell had passed out anyway, so any further performance would have been wasted. Berryman punched a control code into the panel; the medtable beeped and rolled aft toward the Airlock Reception Bay. The hatch popped open and the gurney slid smoothly in. "*Star Wolf*, you've got a package in the pipeline."

"We've got it."

The airlock hatch snapped shut. The gurney was on its way. Berryman glanced to Korie.

Korie's expression was bland. "Your bedside manner could use a little work."

"Dr. Williger says the same thing, sir."

"Well, she's right."

"Yes, sir. Sorry, sir. It won't happen again."

"See that it doesn't."

A Tide of Fireflies

The gurney wasn't sentient. When it needed sentience, it borrowed HARLIE's—or rather, it asked HARLIE to be sentient for it. Now was one of those moments, when the robot asked for the judgment of the starship's intelligence engine.

HARLIE guided the table into the airlock, sealed the airlock, monitored the conditions on both sides of the hatch to the transfer tube, then opened the next hatch and guided the table forward. A swirl of flickering wavicles came with it. As the repulsors throbbed, the wavicles ebbed and flowed—like a tide of fireflies.

The gurney unfolded its arms and grabbed the handholds set into the railings of the transfer tube. It pulled itself steadily forward. The wavicles tried to roll with it, but the pressure of the repulsor fields pushed more and more of them backward. They swirled in the air, piling up against the walls of thickened air, then bounced away, swirling back into the *Norway*'s still-open hatch.

The table moved slowly through the repulsor fields, one after the other. Each time, fewer and fewer wavicles came with it. By the time it had passed through the fourth field, there were no visible wavicles left. HARLIE told the table to keep pulling itself forward. *No detectable wavicles,* the table reported. *No detectable wavicles*, reported the monitors at the *Star Wolf* end of the transfer tube.

HARLIE paused the gurney at the hatch of the *Star Wolf*'s forward airlock. He studied the information flowing in to him. There was no statistical possibility that there were any live bloodworms in Yonah Jarell's body. There was no statistical possibility that there could be any active wavicles at the *Star Wolf* end of the tube. But statistical possibility was a theoretical construct. It was a model of the physical universe. The accuracy of the model was only a statistical possibility itself . . .

"Dr. Williger?" he reported. "This is the last go/no-go point."

Williger said, "Captain Parsons? We have no detectable error-states. We are in the center of the probability channel. Go or no go?"

A pause. Then, "We've come this far." The sound of a breath. "All right, HARLIE. Open the hatch."

The gurney rolled into the airlock of the *Star Wolf*. A moment later, it arrived in the FARB. Immediately, Dr. Williger, Brian Armstrong and a team of Quillas swarmed around the now-silent form of Yonah Jarell.

"All right, let's transfuse this bastard," Williger snapped, already unclipping the hypo-injectors from the clamps on his arms and legs and neck and tossing them off the gurney. The table's arms gathered the hose ends to reconnect them below. "Disconnecting the table connections," she said for the log.

Then she reached up—Armstrong had to jump in and reach for her; she was too short to get it herself—and pulled down an overhead unit to within centimeters of Jarell's body. She started unclipping hoses and injectors, clamping them quickly into place. Quillas Delta and Omega did likewise. As fast as each injector was locked into place, it activated itself and its collar blinked green. "Connecting transfusors."

The suppressive-resonance field continued—in case any of the plasmacytes still survived in Jarell's blood. Everything was enveloped in a throaty, warbling sensation. The gurney's arms started pulling empty bottles from its under-carriage, handing them to Armstrong as fast as he could receive them, and taking full bottles from Quilla Omega and restocking them below.

HARLIE was blandly reciting blood pressure, body temperature, heart-rate, oxygenation and other readings. The important one, however, was, "No detectable plasmacyte spikes in the radiation spectrum."

"My God, I think we've done it—" Armstrong breathed.

"Not yet, Brian. We still have to get the toxic residue out of his bloodstream." She checked the display on the overhead unit, then looked across the table at Armstrong. "The biggest problem in any injury is system shock. Whether you're pumping saline or blood-substitute, you need to get fluid into the body as fast as you can. That's why we use the pumps. A thousand years ago, they used drip-IV lines and their patients died on the way to the hospital, or they suffered needless damage." She glanced to the display and frowned. "We're using too much artificial blood here. Go get another rack from Med Bay."

"On my way—"

On the table, Jarell groaned. Williger glanced at the overhead display. "He's going to live. We did it! Pat yourselves on the backs, people! You just made medical history!" She put her face close to Jarell's and said, "How are you feeling?"

Jarell moaned again.

"He's having a reaction to the process—HARLIE, we need to sedate here; has he got any allergies?"

"Sensitivity to Alternate-R series. Suggest you use Gee-Vin 12, one gram per fifty kilos."

"Ready two grams—" Williger held a hand out without looking to see who would put what into it. Quilla Delta slapped a pressure injector into her palm with medical precision. Williger took it, checked it and applied it to Jarell's left arm. Jarell groaned and passed out again. "Move him to Med Bay. We need the gurney. Someone go to Cargo Bay and get that extra table uncrated. *Now!* This is going to take longer per patient than we thought. HARLIE, what's the time-projection?"

"It's still doable, Doctor. I am projecting that succeeding procedures will go faster—"

"Don't forget, we're going to get tired awfully fast here."

"I'm factoring that into the equation too."

"All right, one more thing—did you track the discomfort levels during the transfer?"

"Of course I did, Doctor. The patient experienced considerable pain—"

"I saw that. What's the status on sedation?"

"The buzz box is not an option here. It puts too much energy into the system. I suggest a chemical application. Resnix should induce a state of deep sleep. There is a supply on the gurney."

"Side effects?"

"Possible nausea."

"Strain on the liver?"

"A healthy liver should be able to flush ninety percent of the active ingredients within six to twelve hours. Some patients may experience a hangover."

"I can live with that. I'd rather use a pain-blocker than a sedative, but we don't have time to experiment or send anything else across."

"Be aware, Doctor, that as soon as you begin replacing the patient's contaminated blood, you'll also be flushing the sedative as well. The after-effects will be minimal."

Williger made a face, an expression of annoyance. "Right. I forgot. I was juggling six thoughts at the same time. Damn. I knew I was going to go senile someday, I just didn't realize it would be today. All right, let's do it. Berryman?"

A nervous voice answered. "Doctor?"

"We're going to sedate, with small doses of Resnix."

"Can do."

"HARLIE will brief you. Start the next patient immediately. We're going to run these in staggered series. We can handle two at a time if we have to, so don't be afraid of overlap. Let's go."

This time, the process seemed to run faster. HARLIE's prediction was accurate. As the team of Quillas became more familiar and more skilled, they moved through the steps with greater efficiency. Blintze awakened on the table, blinking in confusion, even before the transfusion was done.

Williger glanced up at her display. "Bingo. Right on the curve." She lowered her face close to Blintze's. "You're going to live. Answer a question?"

Weakly, Blintze gasped, "What?"

"Are these things native to Regulus IV? What controls them in their own environment?"

It was an effort for Blintze to speak, but he managed to get the words out anyway. They rasped out of his mouth as if each one was escaping from hell. "These things aren't native to anywhere. There aren't any controls. They were created to be . . . a weapon. There was a war on Regulus. And these things were unleashed as . . . a last, desperate revenge on the winners."

"With no way of controlling them?" Williger's eyes were wide.

"They were a doomsday weapon."

"Well, it worked." But as she turned away, her eyes narrowed. Why were Fleet officers working with doomsday weapons? "Captain Parsons? Did you copy that?"

"I heard it," Parsons' voice came through Williger's headset. Her tone was equally troubled. "We'll talk later. For now, stay on purpose."

"All right." The doctor turned back to the Quillas. "Get him to Med Bay and let's get this gurney moving. "We've got eighteen to go and we're running out of time—"a glance across at a display"—and artificial blood, as well."

Easton

On both starships, the crews worked feverishly. On the *Star Wolf*, Williger had the support team of the Quillas, plus Brian Armstrong, Darian Green and "Toad" Hall, for additional assistance. On the *Norway*, Berryman and Easton worked together as a team—with Korie, Bach and Shibano standing by. But as soon as Korie saw he wouldn't be immediately needed, he retreated to a corner of the Cargo Bay where a work station was still operative. With a little help from HARLIE, he linked it to the *Star Wolf*'s network so he could monitor the progress of the operation throughout.

Methodically, the teams worked their separate tasks. On the *Norway*, the patients were deliberately infected with toxic substances and put into suppressive resonance fields. On the *Star Wolf*, the toxic substances and plasmacyte residue were flushed from their bloodstreams. The two starships existed as distinct domains—linked only by the transfer tube, separated only by the repulsor fields.

Each patient was carefully sedated, carefully revived. Every step of the process was monitored by three or more scanners, with HARLIE cross-correlating their readings. Despite the creeping exhaustion of both teams, no serious mistakes were made. A bottle was dropped here, a hose connection came loose there—in each case, the error was caught before it could affect the process. The zero-defect security containment was never compromised. If anything, the greatest danger was boredom—the sheer repetitive madness of doing the same task over and over and over again. After a while, it was hard to remember that what they were doing here was saving lives—and making medical history.

And then, just as Berryman was readying his ninth patient, the warble of the *Norway*'s repulsor field . . . sputtered. It dipped, halted, hesitated, shifted its tone as it compensated for a momentary hiccup and then came back up again. A swirl of wavicles tornadoed in the corridor.

Berryman looked up from the gurney. His eyes locked with Easton's. Korie and Bach and Shibano also exchanged glances.

Bach spoke aloud what they were all thinking. "That's not going to hold."

Shibano held out his hands, as if testing the strength of the field by touch alone. "I give it . . . forty minutes. Maybe an hour." To Berryman, he said. "We're going to have to speed this up."

"We'll make it," Berryman replied. Catching Easton's worried glance, he added, "But just barely."

Easton nodded. He called to Bach. "Take over for me, please." As she did so, he stepped away without explanation and crossed to Korie in the corner. Korie was sitting at his work station, thoughtfully reviewing the *Norway*'s log.

"Commander?"

"Easton?" Korie replied without looking up.

"Just checking, sir—"

Korie understood. Part of any mission team's job was to monitor the mental state of its own members. Easton was still in shock over Hodel's death—he knew that the other team members were watching him closely, but he had to reassure *himself* that he was fine, so he went around from one shipmate to the next, making a pretense of checking on them—and letting them look him over again. If they hadn't all been wearing starsuits, they could have reached over and laid their hands on each other—comforting pats on each others' shoulders, or even pulled together for the temporary relief of a hug; but, failing that, the best they could do was look into each other's eyes and pretend they weren't crying inside. Korie understood what Easton was doing— he was walking around looking for reassurance that he was still functioning. He was hoping to be distracted, so the pain wouldn't come crashing in.

"I'm fine. Thanks for checking, I appreciate it," Korie said, deliberately sidestepping the obvious. He needed Easton to hold together just a little while longer. He pointed at the display. "I'm just trying to make good use of the time while we wait—reviewing the operation here. I want to see what their mistake was. There's a lot of material to look through . . ."

Easton nodded. But he remained where he was.

Korie looked at him. "Something else?"

"It wouldn't be so bad if it was just wavicles. But it's the worms that give me the willies. Being eaten alive . . . ?" Easton shuddered.

"Me too," said Korie. "Do you want to talk about it?"

"No," said Easton in a tone that suggested yes.

"Y'know, what you did back there . . . that was a hard thing to do. Not everybody would have done it. *You didn't abandon him.* What you did was merciful."

Easton held up a hand. "I know all that, sir. I keep repeating it in my head, over and over and over. Like a mantra. It doesn't help." He took a breath. "I want . . . I want to get angry, sir. I want to get angry and break something. I want to—what I'm saying is a sin in my church, sir—but this is what I'm feeling. I want to hurt someone—whoever's responsible for this. I want to kill someone. I want . . . revenge."

"I know," said Korie. "I feel the same way. Mostly about Morthans." For just an instant, he remembered the size of the bill he'd run up at Stardock—in the gym, beating up on Morthan androids. Until, finally, the doctor had ordered him to stop. Not because he was hurting himself, but because the androids were going psychotic. "Listen, there's nothing wrong with feeling what you're feeling. It's part of the process of grieving."

Easton gave him a skeptical look.

"Yeah, you're right. I'm sorry about the jargon. The point is, there's nothing I can say or do, nothing anyone can say or do that's going to make it easier. You're going to feel what you're feeling—until you stop feeling it. The only thing I can tell you that helps—it's the only thing that helps me—is to go to the gym and punch something. As hard as you can. As much as you can. Over and over and over. Until you fall down exhausted and you don't have the strength to get up again. It doesn't make the feeling go away, but it puts you in control of how you express it, and that much at least is . . . well, it's a start."

"Hodel was my friend," said Easton. As if that explained something.

"He was my friend too—" Korie started.

"No. You don't understand. I could talk to Hodel. Paul and I are bonded, and we like being bonded; it's a sense of security to have a partner. But some folks are uncomfortable with it. They come from places where it isn't allowed or it doesn't happen or it's programmed out of people, so they think it's wrong. But Hodel—it was nothing to him; it was like the color of our hair, it didn't matter. You don't know what it's like to walk down a corridor and have people look at you with pity or contempt or just . . . distance, like you're not totally human.

You don't know how refreshing it is to be treated like you're normal—like you're really part of the crew after all."

Korie started to say something, but Easton interrupted him.

"No, it's all right, sir. I've already heard the speech about the irrationality and stupidity of prejudice. I've even given it a few times. I'm sure I know it better than you. Yeah, some people on the *Wolf* are stupid. But that doesn't make the hurt any less, does it? Tell me something—where do you go to get a license to be rude to other people? I want one of those. I want the license to say what I'm feeling too—no matter how rude or stupid or crude or insensitive it is." He stopped himself, then abruptly added, "I'm not hurting for Hodel as much as you think I am. I'm hurting for myself. Because of what I've lost. I know it's selfish . . ." He stopped again, this time unable to continue.

Korie faced Easton. "I wish you'd said something before. I didn't know we had a problem. When this is all over, when we're back on the *Wolf* and everything is secured, will you come and talk to me?"

"Do you think it'll help? Do you think there's anything you can do?"

"I don't know. Let's talk about it."

The two men studied each other. Inside their helmets, both their expressions were hard to read; the starsuits made it easy to stay detached. At last, Easton said, a little too quickly, "I've used up enough of your time. Thank you, sir."

Easton crossed back to Berryman. Proximity to his partner made him feel safer. That was part of the bonding process. The need for closeness. The two men exchanged reassuring glances, but Berryman continued to work without interruption. He and Shibano were just sending another table aftward toward the airlock.

The other gurney held a young woman. She had been attractive once, but now she was pale, bruised and wracked with spasms. She was already wired up and waiting. Hoses and tubes snaked out from the undercarriage of the medtable, up and into the clamps on her arms and legs. She was having trouble breathing and Bach was waiting with her until Berryman could attend.

Easton stepped over and took the young woman's hand in his. He looked down at her and smiled comfortingly—a small atonement.

Secrets

A moment later, Berryman joined them. He placed a stethoscope puck against the young woman's chest, moving it around with each rasping breath she took. The sounds of her breathing were relayed through his helmet. "I know you're uncomfortable," he said. "Just hang in there a little bit longer, okay? Ready when you are, *Star Wolf*."

Williger's voice: "Stand by. Two minutes."

"Did you hear that? Two minutes. What's your name?"

"Rachel. Rachel McCain."

"Are you married?"

"Is that a proposal?"

"Sorry, I'm spoken for." Berryman smiled, with a quick glance across at Easton. "But some of the crew over on the *Star Wolf* are already asking me about you. And your shipmates. I hope you don't have plans for Saturday night."

"If I live that long."

"You will. Or my name's not Tonto Leroy McTavish."

"Tonto Leroy McTavish?! That's *not* your real name!" Despite her discomfort, she smiled.

"No, it isn't. But you'll live anyway."

"Will it hurt?" she asked abruptly. "I heard what you said to . . . Jarell."

"No," said Berryman. "It won't hurt." He was already preparing an injection of Resnix. "But I can arrange it if you want." He waggled his eyebrows.

"No thanks," Rachel said, almost laughing.

He pressed the device to her arm—it hissed, then issued a confirming beep. "In a minute or two, you'll start to feel very pleasant, like you're floating."

"I can feel it already." She closed her eyes.

Easton grinned at Berryman. "There's nothing like Resnix to put you to sleep."

"Another minute and we can send her across." Berryman said. He looked across to Easton, his voice dropping. "Y'know, this is the first time we've ever really worked together. I never thought it would be like this—"

"You're going to start that again, aren't you?"

"Well, why shouldn't I worry about you? You being on Security Detail and all."

Easton looked annoyed. "I really don't like that kind of talk, Paul. We don't put bulls-eyes on our uniforms. That's the *other* guys."

Berryman studied the display in front of him. He shook his head. "I know the odds, Danny—"

"Hey!" Easton interrupted him, almost angry. "I mean it! *Don't talk like that.*"

Lying between them, Rachel McCain opened her eyes and looked from one to the other. "Are we going to die?"

Berryman shot a dirty look across to Easton. *Now look what you've done!* Bending down so Rachel could see his face through his helmet, he said, "I'm not planning on it, are you?" Then, deliberately lightening his tone, he said, "Hey—when we get back to the *Star Wolf*, I'll buy you a drink and tell you about the sparkle-dancer. It dances in the dark between the stars, looking for starships to sing to. If you see one, it's good luck."

Rachel put on a *very* skeptical expression. "Sparkle-dancers? Excuse me? I'd rather hear the one about the leprechaun and the penguin again."

Berryman grinned and pointed. "My partner here will have to tell you that one. But I can tell you about the kindly lawyer with a heart of gold. It has a happy ending. Someone murders him for it."

Williger's voice interrupted Rachel's response. "*Norway.* We're ready for the next one."

Berryman was suddenly all business. "Working," he said. He applied a different injector to her arm. "Relax, this won't hurt me a bit." A hiss and a beep. Berryman put the injector aside and switched on the suppressive resonance field.

Elsewhere—

Korie sat brooding at the work station, replaying video clips over and over. "HARLIE," he said, abruptly.

"Yes, Mr. Korie? HARLIE was everywhere. Wherever there was a communicator, HARLIE was there.

"What is it that we forgot to ask? What is it we should have asked, but were too busy or too distracted to ask?"

HARLIE didn't answer immediately.

"There is something, isn't there?"

"The hole in the data array was multiple—there were overlapping absences," HARLIE reported. "Dr. Blintze provided us with the technical information necessary to proceed with the rescue. There are other blocks of data that are encoded and remain unknowable."

Korie nodded. That was standard. Different pieces of knowledge were encrypted with different levels of security. And yet, there was something about the way HARLIE was reporting the information. Something—as if HARLIE was daring him, "Tickle me *here.*"

"Can you break the codes?"

"No, I can't."

"I didn't think so." And then, he realized. "Who *can* break the codes, HARLIE?"

"I don't think these codes are breakable."

Okay, wrong question. "HARLIE, there's a way to decrypt this material, isn't there?"

"Yes, Mr. Korie."

"But you can't tell me, can you?"

"No, Mr. Korie. That's part of the security envelope."

"Mm-hm. These are LENNIE-codes, aren't they?"

"Yes, Mr. Korie."

"And LENNIE can decrypt these data structures."

"Yes, Mr. Korie."

"Now . . . let me see if I can follow this one step further. LENNIE's personality core has gone psychotic and we've patched around him, right? So we can't ask LENNIE, and even if we could, it isn't likely he'd accept our authority, right?"

"Right."

"But . . . *you* can simulate a LENNIE, can't you?"

HARLIE made a noise like a gong, like bells and whistles going off, like a joy buzzer, like fireworks, like a fanfare.

"You've been hanging around Hodel too long," Korie said. Then realized again—*shit. Hodel is dead.*

He forced himself back to the problem at hand. It took a moment for him to regain his concentration. He'd made a breakthrough here. Why couldn't he enjoy it? No, don't go there.

"All right, HARLIE—so if I ask you to simulate a LENNIE again, can you decrypt those data structures?"

HARLIE replied, "One of the primary differences between a HARLIE and a LENNIE is the way that data is modeled. There are advantages to each model. To decrypt the LENNIE model requires becoming a LENNIE intelligence and translating the data structures into a form that a HARLIE intelligence can use. May I recommend that we not do this until *after* completing the transfer operation. I do not wish to imperil the security of the transfer."

Korie sat back in his chair. Momentarily beaten. *Shit.* No, HARLIE is right. "All right, HARLIE, let's let it go for now. Don't do it until the safety of the ship is not an issue. And not without my authorization."

And then he thought for a moment longer—*wait a minute.* "HARLIE?"

"Yes, Mr. Korie?"

"What didn't you suggest?"

"I beg your pardon?"

"How about slaving the LENNIE? Can you do that?"

"Not recommended."

"Okay. How about *simulating* the LENNIE in a lesser intelligence—like one of the robots?"

"The robots don't have the processing power, or the speed."

"I know that. But they have the memory. You could simulate a LENNIE in one of the robots. Or you could simulate it in a network of robots."

"It still wouldn't be as fast."

"No, it wouldn't. But maybe it would be fast *enough.*"

"Just a moment. I'm extrapolating."

A pause.

Then HARLIE came back. "We could simulate a LENNIE in a network of non-occupied robots and produce a full decryption in forty-five minutes. The data is pyramid-encoded. I could give you an index in five minutes, and you could choose which data arrays you wanted attacked first."

"What's the risk to the transfer operation?"

"None. I'll only use robots that are on standby or otherwise out of the loop."

"Do it."

"Yes, Mr. Korie. Stand by for the index."

Donors

On the Command Deck of the starship *LS-1187*, the vessel known as the *Star Wolf*, Captain Parsons reflected on the gamble she had taken. She had won the lives of her crew—at the cost of her career.

There was no question what would come next. They would return to Stardock and—after an *extended* quarantine—she would be brought before a Board of Inquiry. The board would ask her if she had knowingly violated a standing order. She would answer, "Yes, I did."

The vice-admiral chairing the board would cluck sympathetically at the situation and make noises about extenuating circumstances not mitigating the offense and how it was important that orders be obeyed by *all* captains; regardless of the lives saved, the knowledge gained, the important breakthroughs achieved and the fact that this would mean an end to one of the most dangerous scourges in known space, the principle of the chain of command had to be maintained. Captain Parsons had *knowingly* put her ship and her crew at terminal risk in violation of a standing order; therefore the board had no other choice but to recommend—she could write the speech herself—that Captain Parsons stand before a court-martial.

On what charges, though?

If they brought her to trial for violation of a standing order, she would have to plead guilty—she had knowingly violated orders. Commander Brik and CMO Molly Williger had both been present at the time and could testify that not only had she done so, she had ordered them to comply at gunpoint. Which was precisely why Brik had confronted her the way he had—to establish that specific point of responsibility, that she had effectively thwarted any opportunity to remove her from command. But had she really violated a standing order? This

BLOOD AND FIRE 657

was a situation that a lawyer would call "collision of priorities." There were other orders that gave her the authority to do exactly what she had done.

She could justifiably argue that her duty *required* her to explore all options for rescue of the crew and the mission team as well as the retrieval of the *Norway*'s log. She could say that she had known of her responsibility to destroy the *Norway*, but had held off until the medical and research logs had been downloaded because of the value of that knowledge. That the logs had contained experimental procedures for containing and treating a plasmacyte infection had presented her with the kind of moral dilemma that captains were empowered to resolve under General Order Number One: a captain is totally responsible for the welfare of her crew and her ship, regardless of any other orders in place. She could argue that under that obligation, she had to use the information available to save her mission team and the survivors on the *Norway*.

It was a compelling argument, to be sure. But even if they accepted her defense and acquitted her, they wouldn't—*couldn't*—put her back at the helm of the *Star Wolf* or any other starship. It would send the wrong message to other captains. No, her command days were over. Other captains would understand and sympathize—and take the lesson to heart. The Admiralty would cluck sympathetically and might even apologize privately for having to make an example of her, but still, the fleet had to maintain its discipline. Junior officers would be the ones who would most take the lesson to heart. And the Admiralty would maintain its tight control over its captains, even from a hundred or a thousand light years away.

She ran one hand along the railing in front of her. She would miss her star-time. But if she had to do it all over again—

Her headset beeped.

"Parsons here."

Williger. "Captain, listen carefully. There isn't going to be enough artificial blood to treat everybody. We're using more substitute per patient than we expected."

"How long to manufacture more?"

"Too long. Captain, you're going to have to ask for blood donors."

"Blood donors?"

"I know. It's a barbaric custom—you take blood out of one person's body and put it into another's—but it's a painless procedure and it's the best way we've got to save the last five lives."

The last five lives—Korie, Bach, Wasabe, Berryman, Easton . . .

"We'll need at least sixty volunteers, each one donating a single pint of blood. Ensigns Duane and Morwood are standing by. HARLIE's already got the blood maps prepared. But we have to start right away."

"Sixty volunteers? That's two-thirds of the crew."

"Yes, Captain. They're setting up now in the mess room. They raided cargo for the extra supplies; they can do ten at a time. It's going to be close, but the more blood we get now, the less we'll need later, when time gets critical."

"Right." Parsons turned forward and shifted her tone. *"Now hear this."* The captain's voice was immediately amplified throughout the starship. Everybody heard it—and stopped what they were doing. The Black Hole Gang. The Farm Team. Cookie and the mess attendants. Maintenance. Security. "This is the captain speaking. We need blood donors to help save the lives on the Norway. We need sixty volunteers—" She paused to correct herself. She would be the first. "Excuse me, fifty-nine. Dr. Williger assures me that it doesn't hurt—but it sure as hell will help. Volunteers report to the mess room on the double. *That is all.*" She glanced to Tor. "Commander Brik, you have the conn. Commander Tor, did I just hear you volunteer?" And with that, the captain headed aftward, her astrogator following in her wake.

By the time they arrived, there was already a lineup in the corridor—men and women waiting to donate blood. Including Reynolds. The captain took her place in line behind him and noted his presence with a nod. "Good to see you here, crewman."

Reynolds nodded back. "You'll have your sixty pints of blood. The union guarantees it."

"I never doubted it," the captain replied.

Blood

The call for blood donors worried Korie. He'd had some experience with primitive medical procedures; he knew how risky they were. He had HARLIE show him the view of the mess room, where ensigns Duane and Morwood had arranged an emergency blood bank. The patients were stretching out on the table-tops, with rolled-up towels as pillows.

The procedure had been worked out by HARLIE. Duane went from table to table, setting up the IV lines and blood bags and directing donors to lie down. Morwood followed behind her, applying nanite-leeches to the bare arms of the donors. The leeches were connected to the IV lines and the blood ran smoothly down transparent tubes into plastic bags clipped to the side of the table. It took only a few moments for each bag to fill. By the time Duane had finished setting up the last table, the patient on the first table was finished. Now she followed the same path, disconnecting each patient and handing the full bag to Morwood, who checked the bag's control-display for blood type and Rh factor before hanging it on a rack. When the rack was full, the Martian—small, ugly, efficient—wheeled it quickly out to the forward airlock.

The donors were dismissed to the other side of the mess room where Cookie had laid out thick sandwiches and vitamin-augmented fruit drinks. Duane laid out fresh IV lines, pointed a donor to the table and moved on to the next position. Morwood started the donor and followed, one step behind. They were producing a fresh pint of blood every four minutes. It was fast—but wasn't quite as fast as the artificial blood was being used up at the Forward Airlock Reception Bay.

It didn't look to Korie as if they would produce enough blood before the treatment for the last person on the *Norway* could be started. It would be close. "All right," he decided. "I'll go last. I'll take the risk."

"Mr. Korie?" Brik's voice in his helmet.

"Yes, Brik?"

"Have you been looking over the information that HARLIE is decoding?"

"Um, yes—" Korie lied. He didn't want to admit he'd been monitoring the speed with which the blood was being collected. Brik would understand why immediately. In that, Korie realized, he was becoming something like a Morthan—only admitting what he was willing to have others know. He touched the controls on his display, going back to the decrypted data clusters. "What is it you wanted me to see?"

The display in front of Korie cleared, then lit up again to show the same pictures that Brik was looking at. It showed a glass beaker with a single red bloodworm in it. In the beaker, the creature looked harmless enough.

"This is from Blintze's medical log," said Brik.

The image showed a technician putting the beaker inside a high-intensity medical scanner. She turned on a suppressive resonance field, then set the scanner at its lowest setting and activated it. The readings from the scanner scrolled up the side of the image.

"Brik? This can't be right. I'm no doctor, but no creature can live like this—the act of eating uses up more energy than it produces. The bloodworm runs up a ferocious energy debt that never gets paid."

"As impossible as that seems, it appears to be an accurate assessment. The creature eats, but it doesn't make use of what it eats, except to fuel its own appetite. So the more it eats, the more it wants."

"Well . . ." Korie wished he could scratch his head through the helmet. "That explains a lot. Very effective as a weapon—but not as a lifestyle. I wonder what would happen if it could metabolize what it eats?"

Abruptly, in the display, the creature in the scanning box exploded in a cloud of wavicles.

Brik's voice. "I found this in Blintze's notes . . ." A pause and then Blintze's voice: "The natural form of the plasmacyte is the wavicle spore. The wavicle is essentially harmless. The bloodworm is an aberrant form—a deliberate mutation. You can't kill a bloodworm, you can only shatter it, producing more wavicles. Shooting them produces the same result. Even scanning is dangerous. The plasmacytes are *not* a disease—they *have* a disease—a disease that makes them profoundly dangerous to all other life forms. A cure would involve reversing the mutation."

"That's a very interesting piece of information," said Korie.

"There's more. HARLIE's still decoding. He may have found it. But it's beyond my area of expertise. At the moment, I am increasingly concerned about . . . the intention of this research."

"I hear you, Brik." Korie felt a knot forming in his stomach. Something he hadn't wanted to acknowledge for a while. "And . . . I share your concerns. Will you discuss this with Captain Parsons? ASAP. In private."

"I was already planning on it. But I wanted to confer with you first."

"I appreciate that."

On the Bridge of the *Star Wolf*, Brik signed off just as Captain Parsons and Commander Tor reentered from "Broadway." Brik stood up. That was enough to get the captain's attention. She gave him a questioning look. He inclined his head toward the Officer's Mess. She nodded, but held up a finger in a *wait-one-moment* gesture. "HARLIE, status?" she asked.

HARLIE responded: "All of the Norway survivors are aboard and in recovery. Bach is now being transfused. Shibano is about to be transferred. Easton and Berryman are next. Commander Korie will be the last one out."

Parsons nodded.

"And the repulsor field on the *Norway* is failing rapidly."

Parsons looked to Brik, then to Tor. All of their expressions were grim. "Commander Tor, take the conn," she said. She exited back the way she had entered, Brik following.

Fire

On the *Norway*, in the Cargo Bay, Korie, Berryman and Easton watched as the gurney carrying Shibano rolled toward the airlock. As the hatch popped shut behind it, they became aware of the not-quite-silence in the chamber. The *Norway* repulsor fields sounded more unstable every moment, their notes fluctuating uncertainly. There was one empty gurney, waiting for the next patient. "All right," said Berryman. "Starsuits off. Come on, come on," he urged. "We're running out of time." He turned to Easton and started unsealing his partner's helmet. "You too, sir," he said to Korie. "Danny, help me out of my suit. I won't be able to do it myself when it's my turn—"

And that's when the argument began.

As the three men helped each other out of their starsuits, the tone of their voices became increasingly tense. By the time they were down to their undersuits, the temperature of the discussion was more than heated, more than volatile. It had become a plasma.

"Paul," Easton said, "They need you on the *Wolf*. I'll go last."

"Danny," Berryman pointed to the gurney. "Lie down!"

"Paul, I know how to do this, I've watched you enough times. The whole process is automated—"

"Danny—*will you just please let me do my job?*"

"Will you let me do mine? *I'm* security. I'm supposed to take the risk."

"I hate it when you get like this."

An empty gurney came rolling out of the airlock. Now there were two.

"*Norway*," Williger's voice. "Start the next one."

"Can you take two at once?" Berryman asked.

A pause. Then, "Yes, we can take two at once."

Easton turned to Korie. "Would you order him, sir?"

"Actually," said Korie. "I'm going last."

"With all due respect, sir—"Berryman looked both frustrated and angry—"I'm the only one here who knows how to monitor the process. If anything goes wrong, I'm the only one who knows what to do. You and Easton *have* to go next."

Easton shook his head. "They'll monitor me from the Bridge. I'm security. It's my responsibility to go last."

"I'm the ranking officer," said Korie. "It's *my* responsibility—"

"Oh, the hell with this—" said Berryman. He turned to Easton and pushed the pressure injector up against his arm—a soft hiss—and then, without waiting, he whirled to Korie and did the same thing. Another soft hiss. Easton looked to his partner with a betrayed expression.

"There!" said Berryman. "The argument's over. Lie down." To Korie. "You too, sir."

Berryman turned back to Easton. "*Lie down, Danny.* You're going to start feeling weak any second now, and I don't want you falling and hurting yourself." He grabbed Easton by the arm and forced him down onto the gurney.

Easton protested all the way. "That was not fair. You haven't heard the end of this, Paul!"

"Fine. You can bawl me out back on the *Wolf.*" He glanced over at Korie. "*You too, sir!*"

Korie, startled at Berryman's tone of voice, started to say something in response, then, feeling the first wave of dizziness flooding up, he thought better of it. He found his way to the second gurney and sank down onto it.

From the gurney, Easton was still protesting. "I mean it, Paul!"

"Shut up and let me win one for a change." Berryman was already applying clamps and injector hoses. "It's going to be close enough as it is." As if to underscore his concern, the sound of the repulsor field dipped abruptly. "Okay, that's the last one—there—the board is green." Berryman ducked below to check the state of something on the gurney's undercarriage, then came back up again. "All right, sweetheart—" He touched Easton's cheek tenderly, then impulsively, bent over and kissed him quickly on the lips. "I love you."

"Love you too," Easton whispered back.

Berryman switched on the suppressive resonance field. "Let me start Korie, I'll be right back."

As Berryman applied the pressure clamps, Korie looked up at him. "You're very decisive. I like that in an officer."

"Thank you. But I'm not an officer yet."

"You're an ensign. Technically, you're an officer." Korie was starting to feel a little detached from his body, but he was still conscious.

"Thank you, sir." Still working, Berryman added, "All I ever wanted was to serve in the Fleet. My grandfather served on the 'Big E' in her glory days."

"Really? Are you trying to live up to his record?"

Berryman shook his head. "Nope. Just my own standards."

"Is that why you did it?"

"Much simpler than that, sir. I made a promise to myself that you and Danny would both get back safely."

"Especially Danny?"

"He's always been the strong one. Today is my turn, okay?" He finished connecting the last tube, made some safety checks and looked to Korie. "Okay, ready to start?"

Korie swallowed once, then nodded. "Let's do it."

Berryman turned on the machinery and activated the resonance field. Korie felt an uncomfortable tingling—but it was somewhere distant. Like it was in someone *else's* body. He turned his head and saw Berryman holding Easton's hand. They were whispering together.

Then, Easton said, "Paul? Take my stinger."

"What for? To make more wavicles?" But Berryman's tone said he knew *exactly* what for.

"It'll make me feel better."

Berryman made a face of annoyance, but he bent to the floor and pulled the stinger pistol off of Easton's dropped starsuit. He held it up for Easton to see. "Okay, happy now?"

But Easton was already unconscious.

Berryman tossed the stinger aside and turned his attention to the display panel on the medtable. "*Star Wolf?* Here comes one." He stepped around to the head of the gurney to help guide it toward the airlock. The effort was redundant, but he felt better doing it. Just before the table rolled through the hatch, he reached down and touched Easton's cheek again. "See you on the other side," he whispered.

Berryman turned back to Korie. The executive officer was already fading out. He checked the displays on Korie's gurney. Korie was doing fine too. Another few seconds and they'd be clear. "*Star Wolf?* Here comes the other one." The second table rolled after the first. "All right, I'm ready for a taxi, any time—"

Behind him, the sound of the repulsor field flip-flopped again. Berryman turned to look down the corridor of the keel toward the distant red gloom. A wall of wetness pulsed.

"Uh-oh," he said.

Blood and Fire

Parsons and Brik returned to the Command Deck, both looking grim. Brik had briefed the captain on what he had seen in the *Norway*'s records. The captain had listened without comment. When Brik had finished, she nodded politely, then headed grimly back to the Command Deck, just in time to hear Berryman's unhappy remark.

Parsons looked to Tor. "What's happening?"

Tor said, "The repulsor field on the Norway just went down—"

Parsons bit her lip. "Who's still over there?"

"Korie and Easton just came through," Tor reported. "Berryman's the last. They just sent the last gurney across." She glanced to her display for confirmation. "He just injected himself. Ninety seconds and we can pull him out—"

As if in confirmation, Berryman's voice came over the speakers, "*Star Wolf*—"

Parsons looked to the forward display. So did the others. As the mission team had disrobed, Korie had hung two of the discarded star-suit helmets on hooks in the *Norway*'s Cargo Bay and placed the others on equipment racks around the chamber. Now, the view shifted from one camera to the next until HARLIE finally selected the one that gave them the best angle on Berryman.

"Go ahead, Berryman," Parsons said. She glanced to Tor and whispered, "Is this going out all over the ship?" Tor nodded.

"The repulsor field is completely down. The bloodworms are coming through. They're coming down the corridor. I can see them. They're flowing like water. Not as fast though. There might be time. I'm getting on the gurney now."

Parsons briefly thought about cutting off the signal to the rest of the ship, then decided against it. That might suggest she didn't think they would get Berryman off the *Norway* in time. And it would suggest a lack of trust. But . . . if Berryman ran out of time, the effect on the crew would be devastating. Especially if everyone witnessed it.

On the other hand, a terrible truth was preferable to a ghastly rumor. If Berryman died, the details would sweep the ship anyway. And a few overripe imaginations would do far worse damage to morale.

No, she told herself. *Stop thinking that way. We're going to get him off. And everyone will see it and share the victory. That'll be good for all of us.*

Throughout the *Star Wolf*, all nonessential work came to a halt as crewmembers turned to display panels and work-station screens. In the mess room, where Duane and Morwood were drawing the last two pints of blood. In the engine room, where Reynolds, still rubbing his arm, stood with Cappy and MacHeath. In the Med Bay, Bach and Wasabe propped themselves up blearily so they could see. At the Forward Airlock Reception Bay, where Williger worked feverishly on Korie and Easton—periodically, she glanced up to an overhead panel. As did the rest of her team. Only the Quillas worked without pause—all except Quilla Omega, who watched the images from the *Norway* intently.

"They're close enough now—I can hear them." Berryman twisted on the gurney. "I can't see them from here. But they're a lot closer. They're coming down the corridor. Can you hear them?" There was the sound of the resonance field under his voice—and a crackling sound too, a wet slobbery noise.

"I'm not using the pain-blocker. I need to stay alert. I can feel the effects of the injection. It's uncomfortable. But I can handle it. It's only for a little bit."

The display started to glare red in one corner. A moment later, a glistening red ooze began creeping across the deck. HARLIE switched through camera angles again. There weren't as many as before. The bloodworms were flowing over the discarded helmets, blocking the lenses. HARLIE settled on an image that showed only half the gurney. Berryman's legs.

"This is going to be a close one."

Berryman's legs moved as the man twisted around to watch the oncoming tide of worms. The crackling noise was louder now.

"God, they sound awful. They're coming toward the gurney. Wait a minute—"

A mechanical sound. The gurney moved out of frame. Almost immediately, a tide of slithering bodies came flowing after it.

Berryman's voice: "That was HARLIE. He moved the gurney as

close to the hatch as he could. Maybe we bought a couple extra seconds. Ahh, this stuff hurts—they're surrounding the gurney—"

HARLIE cycled through camera angles again. Two angles showed the worms starting to fill the Cargo Bay like blood filling a basin. They lapped against the walls, ebbing and flowing with an uneasy tidal movement.

"Danny, it looks like I might need your stinger after all."

In the *Star Wolf*'s Forward Airlock Reception Bay, Easton was already scrambling up from his gurney, trying to reach the hatch behind him. Three Quillas had to grab him and hold him back. He was screaming, making incoherent noises. "Paul—"

Williger was swearing as the tubes attached to his body kept yanking loose, spurting blood in all directions before their automatic cutoffs kicked in. On the other gurney, Korie watched helplessly, reaching but not able to touch, calling but not being heard. Ordering—but being ignored.

"Don't worry, Danny," shouted Berryman. "I'm going to make it. I promise." But his words were nearly drowned out by all the slithery noises. There were no camera angles that showed the gurney. Only the worms. "I'm getting real dizzy. That means it's working. I might pass out soon, but the gurney is still working—and HARLIE is with me. I think they're trying to climb the wheels of the cart. *Star Wolf*—better be ready to pull me over fast."

And then for a moment, nothing—except the distinctive sound of bloodworms.

"Oh, damn! They're on the gurney. Maybe I can—"

Berryman's words were covered by the sudden crackle of a stinger—a sharp snapping sound as the air vaporized in the beam. On the screen, an acrid flare of light, followed by a sudden wash of wavicles recoiling backward from the blast.

Easton screamed. "Paul!! Come on!! Come on now!!"

And Williger—she was swearing in some unknown language. She was pounding her control display. "No, no, no—goddammit! Look at the readings. He's still carrying live plasmacytes. As fast as they die, they keep reinfecting."

Easton was trying to get to Williger now, trying to reach her controls. The Quillas were struggling to hold him back and tie him down with restraints. "You bitch! Bring him over now! They're going to eat him alive!!"

"There are too many! We can't pull him through. *We can't get him.*"

And then Berryman's voice. "*Danny, I'm sorry. I thought I had more time—oh, God. Forgive me!*"

And then—another stinger shot. A flare of white. A wash of sparkles. And silence. Only the liquid crackling of bloodworms.

And Easton. Screaming. "No, Paul! No!"

On the Command Deck, still leaning on the railing, still staring at the forward display, Parsons finally lowered her eyes. She didn't want to look at anyone. She didn't want to say anything. She didn't want to exist. She wanted everything and everyone to just go away. And leave her alone.

Tor's voice. Gently. "Captain?"

Parsons opened her mouth to speak. Her throat was too dry. She closed her mouth and swallowed. She turned and crossed back to her command chair very much aware of Tor's eyes on her. She sat down and shaded her eyes with her hand. She felt terribly alone in the center of everything.

The bridge was full of noise. Ugly wet noise.

"Shut that damn thing off!" the captain ordered.

The sound continued for a second longer—and then silence. Blessed silence.

The Hull

Captain Parsons lifted her head and gave the order. "Separate from the *Norway*. Do it now. Who's on helm?" And then she realized. Hodel. She glanced around the Bridge. "Goldberg, take the helm. You're acting helm until—until further notice." As Goldberg moved to Hodel's former station, she added. "Move us away from the *Norway*, but stay close enough that we can put a missile in her. If we have to."

As Goldberg worked, the image on the forward display shifted. The spars of the *Norway* were glittering with flickering plasmacytes. Everything glowed red in the crimson light of the bloated star. Parsons flinched at the bloodiness of the view. "Prepare a breakaway course to take us out of here. Put it on a ninety-second readiness hold. Mr. Brik—"

The big Morthan turned to face her. He was standing in the Ops Deck, half a level lower than the Command Deck, but he was still eye-to-eye with the captain. "Aye?"

"There are wavicles on the hull of the *Norway*."

"I noticed that myself."

"Let's have a look at the hull of the *Star Wolf*, shall we? HARLIE?"

The forward view shifted. The hull camera swiveled to look backward, down the length of the *Star Wolf*.

For a moment, there was silence on the Bridge. The hull of the *Star Wolf* also glittered and sparkled. Just as much as the hull of the *Norway*. And over everything remained the oppressive orange cast of the red giant sun.

"Well, that answers that." Parsons looked to Brik. "As soon as Williger is finished with Korie and Easton, summon her to the wardroom. If Korie is coherent, I'll want him too. And Commander Tor. And Jarell and Blintze. Have Cookie prepare sandwiches and coffee. I expect this is going to be a long one." She touched her headset, adjusting it against her close-cropped hair. "Chief Leen?"

"Captain?"

"Can you sweep the hull with repulsor fields?"

"We don't have a lot of power left, Captain. It'll take hours to recharge the fuel cells."

"We've got wavicles on the outer hull. Sooner or later, they're going to penetrate."

"I can do a low-level sweep, but I can't make any promises how effective it'll be."

"Start it now. Then join me in the wardroom."

"Aye, aye, Captain."

Parsons turned back to the forward display and waited. A moment later, a disturbance began rippling through the wavicles on the *Star Wolf* hull. A series of waves rolled slowly through them, dislodging them from the metal surfaces like dust being shaken from a blanket. The twinkling sparkles swirled away from the starship . . . then swirled gently back again. Repulsor fields weren't going to work. She frowned, grabbed her clipboard and headed toward the wardroom.

Sitting down at the head of the table, she started making notes:

1. Sweep wavicles off hull?
2. Feed wavicles to singularity?
3. What happens to wavicles in hyperstate?
4. Suppressive resonance field?
5. Wavicle pheromones? Lure them away?
6. Pass through star's corona?
7.

She didn't have a seventh thought. She tapped her fingernail against the screen of the clipboard thoughtfully while two Quillas laid out plates of sandwiches and mugs of coffee. Williger entered then and sat down at the captain's left. Parsons turned the clipboard so the doctor could see what she had written. Williger frowned as she read through the list. Then she picked up a stylus and added:

7. Medical possibilities? Can "cure" be applied externally?
8. Meat tanks as bait?
9.

She hesitated for a moment, then wrote something else at the bottom of the page.

How much time do we have? How much time do we need?

She handed the clipboard silently back to Parsons. The captain took a sip of her coffee as she looked at what Molly Williger had written, then she nodded. Korie entered and sat down gingerly. He looked weak. The captain passed him the plate of sandwiches and pushed a mug of coffee toward him, without comment. Then she shoved the clipboard in front of him so he could read it.

Korie helped himself to a sandwich. He took a bite, chewed, swallowed and studied the page in front of him. He reached for his own stylus and added several thoughts of his own. As he did, Brik came in. Looming over the table, Brik had no problem reading the clipboard's display.

Chief Leen entered, looked around for a seat, noticed the empty seat next to Korie, hesitated—caught Brik looking at him—then took the seat next to Korie anyway. He peered at the executive officer curiously, as if reassuring himself that Korie was all right, then glanced to the clipboard. Korie passed it to him. Like the others, Leen pursed his lips into a thoughtful frown. He tapped at the second item.

2. Feed wavicles to singularity?

Next to it, he wrote:

How?

Jarell and Blintze

Tor came in, followed by Jarell and Blintze. Leen glanced across the table at them, then pushed the clipboard back to Korie, who pushed it back to the captain. She looked at her notes, and at what the others had added. As soon as everybody was settled, she said, "You're all aware that we have plasmacytes on the hull. How they got out of the *Norway* is part of the problem. Because they may be able to get into the *Star Wolf* the same way." She tapped the clipboard meaningfully. "We don't have a lot of possibilities to consider, do we? Unfortunately, that doesn't simplify the problem. Usually, when we enter a situation, we have a much broader range of choices. We have very few options here. And none of them are workable."

"We've done more than any other ship," said Tor.

"Which only means we're operating way, way out beyond the limits of what everyone else knows," Parsons replied. She rubbed the bridge of her nose between her thumb and forefinger. "We have resolved one part of the plasmacyte question—can we safely extract human beings from an infected environment? We now know the answer to that is yes. But the larger question—can we do it without infecting the extraction environment?—remains unanswered. It may be that we have no cure at all here, only a method of delaying the inevitable. In a controlled situation, where the wavicles are isolated inside a containment field, then perhaps extraction is feasible and safe. But this latest development only proves the wisdom of FleetComm's standing order against attempting rescue." She looked to Blintze and Jarell. "I am assuming that you can provide some useful insights to this problem?"

The two men glanced at each other. Jarell looked grim. Blintze was more apologetic. "You've seen my files. So you know that the normal form of the plasmacyte is the wavicle. Harmless, attractive. But it's been changed somehow, so that it can't sustain itself, and it turns into blood-worm spores. The bloodworm is a specifically-designed mutation, created as a doomsday weapon. We believe the losers turned it loose upon their own world to deny the victors access to the prize they'd fought so hard to win. The planet remains uninhabitable. It was a war that both sides lost."

"Commander Brik has briefed me on the material in your logs. We've decrypted most of it—"

Jarell spoke up then, deliberately interrupting. "Fleet Command was particularly concerned about the possibility of bloodworm infection as a military threat." He glanced meaningfully at Brik. "Does *he* have to be here, Captain Parsons?"

Parsons raised an eyebrow. She glanced over to Brik as if seeing him for the first time, then looked back to Jarell. "He's my chief security Officer. Is there some problem, Mr. Jarell?"

"Isn't it obvious?"

"Are you suggesting that one of my officers is not trustworthy?"

"Captain Parsons, *no* Morthan is trustworthy."

"Commander Brik has proven himself in a number of situations. I have the fullest confidence in him."

"Do you think that's wise?"

"Commander Jarell, I respect your rank and your authority—but please do not question the loyalty or the integrity of my officers again. I will consider such remarks a violation of code."

Jarell lifted his hands off the table and showed his palms, a gentle push-away gesture. He nodded his concession with an empty smile.

"Please proceed," Captain Parsons said coldly.

Jarell took a breath. "As you wish." With a sour glance in Brik's direction, he continued, "Our mandate was to investigate the possible military use of the bloodworms and what defenses might be effective against them. Toward that end, we were directed to develop means of containment, control and neutralization. We accomplished all three of those goals. Our mission has been a success."

"A rather expensive success," said Captain Parsons dryly. "We lost a starship and most of her crew." She glanced to Korie. There was something about his expression. "Mr. Korie? You wanted to say something. An itch perhaps?"

Korie shook his head. "No. It's just the aftereffects of the process. I'll be all right." But his eyes met Parsons' and they both knew that he was dissembling. Whatever it was, he wasn't ready to say it here. Not in front of Jarell and Blintze. Or Brik . . . ?

Blintze spoke abruptly. "Captain Parsons?"

"Dr. Blintze?"

"What I was saying before—I didn't get to finish. The normal form of the wavicle is harmless. What we have here isn't normal. What we think the wavicles may have originally been is some kind of cooperative colony creature, like ants or bees. The individual wavicle has no existence of its own; it's meant to be a cell in a larger entity, but because of the mutation, the colony-gestalt is damaged or destroyed. I'm sorry to be so pedantic about this. You might not find it as interesting as I do—"

"Go on," said Parsons. "I want to hear it all."

"Well," Blintze continued. "We were actually able to classify several distinct types of wavicles, each with different properties and behaviors, each filling a different niche in the colony's spectrum."

Williger looked up sharply. "Tell us about that. What specific types have you identified?"

Blintze nodded, warming up to his subject. "We've found a *binder* that calls other wavicles to follow it. We've found a *singer*; it generates audible vibrations. We've found a *firefly* form; that's the one that twinkles and glows. Most of the other types aren't as visible. There's a variety that reproduces, but not as we understand reproduction; it generates the other kinds and occasional copies of itself. We call those *mothers*. We've also found *carriers* which seem to do nothing more than carry copies of 'genetic code.' There are several types whose functions we haven't identified. We think those are dormant. There's a *targeter*; it locates sites on material things. *Eaters* attach themselves to those sites, eventually burning their way through. We're not sure if those two forms are natural or if they're misapplied. But this is the point—there are gaps in the spectrum. There are forms that should be there and aren't."

Blintze glanced sideways to Jarell, who was looking very unhappy, but he continued anyway. "We don't find very many *feeders*. There's simply not enough here to sustain the colony. Using the models derived from colonies of ants, bees, termites, lawyers—not the human kind; I mean the parasites from Maizlish; it's a planet orbiting a bloated dead star. Anyway, using preexisting models of other colony creatures, we know that a hive or a colony needs a certain percentage of food gatherers to sustain itself. The wavicle colony has only one-third the *feeders* it should, so it's constantly on the edge of starvation. That's part of what produces such manic behavior."

Williger's eyes were bright. She finished the explanation for him. "It's the little *mothers* that are the dangerous ones, right? Without food, the other forms disintegrate. But the mothers go particulate so they can keep reproducing, albeit on the next quantum level down. And when they're particulate, they produce nothing but more hungry little *mothers*, right?"

Blintze looked surprised. "That's right."

"I've been studying your notes," she said. "Toward the end, they're a little disorganized, but HARLIE and I have had some interesting conversations, extrapolating possibilities. Something was done to change the *mother* form. There was an extremely high level of technology involved in the reeingineering of this creature. I don't know if we could match it—but if we could, we could introduce a genetic correction into the mothers and return the wavicle colony to its natural state. We're talking about curing the bloodworms—literally. You were looking at altering the *carriers*, weren't you?"

"Yes," admitted Blintze. "That's how we got infected. We . . . we created a form of carrier that made the bloodworms even more dangerous. We gave them the ability to bore through polycarbonates."

"You're to be congratulated on your success," said Korie.

"It wasn't a success," Blintze said, stiffly.

"Yes, it was." Korie's words were a rebuke. "Because that's exactly what you were trying to do, wasn't it?" The accusation hung in the air between them.

Intentions

Blintze looked unhappy. He poured himself a glass of water and drank it quickly.

"You don't have to answer that," said Jarell. "Remember, this is on a need-to-know basis."

"I believe we're beyond that," Parsons said to Jarell. "Far beyond. And we definitely have a need to know. Go on, Mr. Blintze."

"Yes," Blintze finally admitted. "We were looking for a way to control the bloodworms—so we could use them as a weapon."

Parsons exchanged a glance with Korie. What they had both suspected was now acknowledged.

"Captain," Jarell spoke candidly, like a confidante—he hadn't noticed the exchange of looks between the captain and her exec. "Can you imagine what would happen if the Morthan Solidarity were to spread bloodworms throughout Allied space?"

Korie, sipping at his coffee, answered quietly, "The destruction of all carbon-based life forms on a catastrophic scale." His voice was flat.

"Precisely," said Jarell. He glanced sideways at Brik, then back to Parsons. He leaned ominously forward. "The Morthans are vipers. They cannot be trusted. They do not follow the New Geneva Conventions. They have already demonstrated their willingness to use weapons of mass destruction."

Parsons raised an eyebrow, meaningfully. She noted Korie's grim expression, then turned back to Jarell. "Go on," she prompted.

"They attacked Taalamar with a sustained barrage of extinction-level asteroids. You were there, you saw what happened, you know—they destroyed an entire civilization. Millions of men, women and children—that's the kind of regard they have for us. The bloodworms . . . well, that's FleetComm's response."

"According to your own log, your research was already funded and in preparation long before the attack on Taalamar. Even before the mauling at Marathon."

Jarell acknowledged it with a nod. "Yes, but only as a precautionary measure. Just in case our worst nightmares came true. And we should be grateful for such foresight, because now we have a weapon we can use to strike back."

"And what circumstances, Commander Jarell, do you think would make such use necessary?" Korie wasn't looking at Jarell, he was looking down into his coffee mug. He swirled it gently, as if he were watching a thought circling there.

"Shaleen and Taalamar. Isn't that enough, Commander? Or maybe you don't care that they scourged Shaleen? And you know what they did to Taalamar."

"I care," said Korie, not willing to mention that his wife and children had been on Shaleen. Maybe they had escaped, maybe to Taalamar. But maybe not. HARLIE had exchanged messages with every starship they'd ever encountered. He'd never found any evidence that his family had even gotten off the planet. Maybe the records didn't exist, maybe they'd been lost, maybe there was no hope at all. And maybe . . .

"Well," said Jarell, as if it was obvious. "If that doesn't justify the use of mega-weapons, then what does?" He glanced around the table, meeting the eyes of every officer there. His gaze lingered on Brik for a long, uncomfortable moment.

"You don't know the Morthans," Jarell explained. "Not really. Not even you, Mr. Brik—your fathers fled the world of Citadel when you were a child. You don't know what it's like to live under a Morthan authority. You don't know what the Morthans are really like. None of you. But I do, I've been there. I've seen them swaggering through the streets of Dogtown, laughing and killing, taking what they want— slaves, food, weapons, wealth. I've seen what they do to the worlds they conquer. We've been watching the Morthan Solidarity for a thousand years. We've sent in agents. Hundreds of thousands of agents—most get caught, but the things we've seen, I can't begin to tell you what we know. I am telling you that there is no limit to the Morthan treachery. The plasmacytes are a weapon. And if we don't use them, the Morthans *will.*"

Brik rumbled, a sound so low that it was felt rather than heard.

"No Morthan would ever use such a weapon," he said. "It would be cowardly. Only a human would."

Parsons gave Brik a sharp look. So did Korie. They were getting close to the punch line here. She turned back to Jarell and Blintze, concern strong on her face. She chose her next words carefully. "And that was the real goal of your work here, wasn't it?"

Jarell's answer was intense. "Captain Parsons, we were caught unprepared at Marathon and we've been on the run ever since. All of human space lies open to the Morthan advance if we don't find a way to stop them now. I don't have to tell you, *the most expensive armada in the galaxy is the one that's second best.* The whole point of this mission is to make sure that the plasmacyte weapon was ready at hand, for just this circumstance. *And use it, if necessary.* You—your ship—you were intended to be the delivery vessel. It's in a set of sealed orders we have for you—for whatever ship that served as our tender. It's in our orders to commandeer your starship, if necessary, to deliver the weapons packages to Morthan space. So you're as much a part of this as we are."

Parsons was silent for a very long moment. She placed her hands flat on the table before her and studied the space between them. After a bit, she looked across to Williger, to Korie and finally up to Brik. "Commander Brik. Please escort Mr. Jarell and Dr. Blintze to their quarters—and see that they stay there."

Brik rumbled an assent. "Come with me, *gentlemen.*" Although his voice was as flat as ever, the last word—*gentlemen*—had a deadly tone to it.

As the hatch slid shut behind them, Parsons looked to Korie and Williger and Tor and Leen. "Well," she said. "Does anyone have any more good ideas?"

Korie was swirling his coffee mug again—thinking of Lowell, thinking of Marathon, thinking of Shaleen and Taalamar. Thinking of Carol. Thinking too loudly.

"What?" demanded Parsons.

"I told you not to attempt a rescue. I told you not to try."

"It's a little late for recriminations."

"It's never too late," said Korie. "The *Wolf* is still being punished for accidentally leading the Morthan fleet to the Silk Road Convoy. Why else would we have been given this duty? Delivery of plasmacyte bombs?"

"Yes, well . . ." Parsons cleared her throat uncomfortably. "Let's see if we can address our current problem first, Mr. Korie. How do we detox this ship—and what do we do about the *Norway*? Dr. Williger,

I'm concerned about what will happen when the *Norway* intersects the plume of flame from the star. What happens to the plasmacytes?"

Dr. Williger pursed her lips thoughtfully. "I've been brooding about that myself. Theoretically . . . it's possible that the energy of the star will trigger a feeding frenzy, and then a breeding frenzy in the corona."

"The *Norway* could turn the whole star into plasmacytes?" asked Tor, worriedly.

"The corona," said Williger.

"Well—maybe," said Leen. He'd been quiet during the entire meeting. "Remember, the *Norway* has an industrial power core, so her singularity is larger than usual. We've got a low-mass pinpoint. You drop that into a star or a planet, it takes forever to eat its way out. The event horizon is so small, it can only nibble a few molecules at a time. At that rate, it would take billennia for the hole to get big enough to be a threat to the star. But the *Norway*—her core is a lot bigger. Here, wait—" He held up a small black ball bearing to illustrate his point. "Think about it. A marble-size black hole falls all the way to the center. The star gets pulled toward it at the same time. The hole doesn't stop when it gets to the center—neither does the star. They've both got too much mass, too much velocity, so they fling themselves around and around their common center, circling in vast ellipses—wobbling toward equilibrium. But while the star lurches around, the marble is circling and eating. The sheer pressure of the star's mass forces tons of gas into the singularity every second. The singularity grows at the rate of an asteroid per day. And its rate of growth accelerates correspondingly. Oh yes, the *Norway*'s core could dismantle a star. The more she ate, the bigger she'd get—the bigger she gets, the more she can eat. The last few hours would be spectacular—"

"So . . . the star would collapse?" asked Williger. "And all the plasmacytes would go into the singularity?"

"If only it were that tidy," said Leen. "It's not. Remember, the black hole and the star's center of gravity are orbiting each other. The star will be wobbling like a bag of pudding. If it gets unstable enough and small enough—and it will—the discrepancy of pressure at the center . . . well, it's likely to explode. Not quite a nova, but enough. If there are plasmacytes in the star's corona, the force of the explosion will send them hurtling outward. The blue dwarf will likely be infected and its corona will become the next breeding ground. Meanwhile, there will be a shock wave of plasmacytes heading outward in all directions. Wherever they get captured by a star's gravitational field, they could infect. It would take billennia, but if it's possible, it's inevitable."

"Thank you, Chief Leen," said Captain Parsons unhappily. Her expression went sour as she asked the others at the table, "Does anyone else have any more good news? No? So here's our situation—we have plasmacytes on our outer hull. So does the *Norway*. We can't destroy the *Norway* and we can't leave her here. If we destroy her, we leave a cloud of plasmacytes circling the star. If we don't destroy her, she goes into the star anyway." She put her head in her hands for a moment, pushing her hair back, while she considered her next decision. "All right. Commander Tor, reacquire the *Norway*. Let's break orbit and pull both ships out of here. That's the first order of business. HARLIE? Can we do that?"

"Yes, Captain, but the timing will be critical."

"Let's snap to it then. Tor, go! Chief, you'll need to run the plasma torches from a cold start—don't be afraid to burn them out if you have to. HARLIE, can we slave the *Norway*'s engines? Do it. Korie, are you feeling well enough to monitor this? Good. Buy us some time."

Even before Korie was out of his chair, Parsons was turning to Williger. "Now, something you said about carriers . . ."

Med Bay

Finally, Quilla Omega turned to Brian Armstrong and said, "Brian, you are only in the way. Let the Quillas finish cleaning up. We can coordinate our separate efforts easier if we don't have to work around you."

Armstrong sort of nodded agreement, but he felt resentful. "I just want to be helpful—" he started to say.

"The biggest help you can give us is to get out of the way," said Quilla Upsilon.

Armstrong sighed. Loudly. And headed aft to see how Easton was doing. The security man had been so anguished at his partner's death that Dr. Williger had finally sedated him, but she hadn't put him completely to sleep and his muted sobs had continued even as he was wheeled back through the keel into the Med Bay.

Although the death of Mikhail Hodel had been felt more profoundly throughout the *Star Wolf*, it was Berryman's death that hurt Armstrong the most. Hodel was an officer and he hadn't known him as well as he had known Berryman. He'd wanted to become a medical orderly, so he'd taken to hanging out with Berryman—and Easton— hoping to be assigned ancillary medical duties. That, of course, had brought him to the attention of Dr. Williger, who had been annoyed by his eagerness and doubly annoyed that she really didn't have much for him to do. Crew health was monitored by implants and preventive care was exhaustive, so the Chief Medical Officer's chores were generally psychological in nature—until emergencies occurred. Then there were never enough hands.

Armstrong wasn't sure what he could do now. He just knew he had to do something. He'd lost another friend. But Easton had lost—what? Armstrong wasn't sure. He'd never really asked what it meant to be bonded. And now that Berryman was gone, he was sorry he hadn't asked, because now he didn't know what to say to Easton. What must Easton be feeling, having witnessed his partner's death?

Brian Armstrong was beefy and good-natured and at a loss. He hesitated in front of the door to Med Bay, shook his head and headed away, then turned and came back to it—started to enter, then stopped and pulled back again, biting his lip and frowning in frustration. What to do? What to do?

Finally, he pushed into Med Bay, stepped past Quilla Delta and peeked into the recovery room, where Easton lay sprawled face down on a med-bed, seemingly asleep. Armstrong went over to the fallen security man. He stood over the bed, staring down at him, wondering if he should disturb him or not.

But just as he turned to go, Easton said, "What is it? What do you want, Armstrong?"

"I—I came to say I'm sorry. And ask if there's anything I can do for you."

Easton rolled over sideways and looked up at Armstrong. "What's it to you?"

"Paul was my friend too."

"Paul and I were more than friends."

"You know what I mean," said Armstrong. "I'm just—" He spread his hands helplessly. "I just thought, for Paul's sake, I would—oh, damn, I don't even know what I'm doing here." Armstrong sat down on the edge of the bed. "Paul talked about you a lot and I didn't really understand. I still don't. But he talked about you like you were the only person in the world, and I guess if you felt the same way about him, then you must be feeling so bad right now, you're probably hurting the worst you ever hurt in your life. So I thought I'd share some of that hurt and maybe take some of it away if I could. I know I'm not that smart," Armstrong admitted. "But you don't have to be smart to care. And I cared too."

Easton blinked. Several times. His eyes had welled up with tears. He put one arm over them and blotted. He turned his head sideways and wiped. He was trying not to cry again. "It could have been me," he said. "It *should* have been me. It was my job to go last. It should have been Korie. He was supposed to go last. But it wasn't supposed to be Paul. Paul had a family. Two little brothers—identical to him. Just perfect. Clones, you see. I would look at them, I'd see his childhood. How am I going to face them? Tell them how he died? This isn't fair, Brian. It isn't fair. I promised to take care of him—I promised them, I promised him, I promised myself—and I failed. I broke my promise."

Easton levered himself up on his elbow. His expression was haunted. "And you want to know the worst of it, Brian?" He looked desperately into Armstrong's face. "I can already see my future. I'm going to spend the rest of my life knowing that the best days of it are over, that I had something special for just the shortest, sweetest moment, and I'll never have it again. Never see him again, never feel his hand on mine, never look into his eyes or hear his laugh or share a meal or simply just wake up next to him again. Never complain about his snoring. Never smell one of his ghastly farts. Never get jealous of all the time he spends with you. Never ever see him again. I'm going to miss him every day, forever . . ."

Armstrong felt a hot tightness in his throat. It was constricted so that he could barely swallow. Tears blurred his vision. He shook his head, so much at a loss for words that he wanted to run sobbing from the room. But he didn't. Instead, he reached over and took Easton's hand in his own and just held it tight, squeezing, as if to say, "I'm here." Easton squeezed back, and then abruptly sat up and flung himself at Armstrong, sobbing into his shoulder. Armstrong grabbed him and held him in a strong and comforting embrace, a hug against the emptiness all around. And as Easton cried against him, he felt his own tears running down his cheeks, and now his own sobs came too.

They cried—for Berryman, yes—but for themselves as well. For what they had both lost.

And then, after awhile, after they had both cried so much they couldn't cry any more, Easton pulled away, gently chuckling. "Look at us," he said. "A couple of babies. You know what Paul would say?"

" 'Get over it,' " said Armstrong.

"Yeah," nodded Easton. He wiped his eyes and patted Armstrong's hand. "You're good, Brian. You are. You have a good soul."

Armstrong didn't know how to reply to that, so he just shrugged and grinned and looked away—a little routine he did to avoid being embarrassed, the equivalent of digging his big toe in the sand and saying, "Aww, shucks."

But Easton wasn't buying it. "Let it in, Brian. Don't pretend I didn't say it. Look at me. Look me in the eye and just get it. You're a good person. That's why Paul liked you. He saw something sweet in your heart. He said so. More than once. And he was right. You're the first one to come by. Maybe that's my fault. We kept apart from everybody else. It's hard not to be conscious of your differences."

"Well," Brian shrugged. "I never saw any differences. I mean, I never understood what this 'bonded' thing was all about, so I never worried about it. I didn't even know about Quillas till I came aboard."

"Yeah," grinned Easton. "Everybody remembers that."

Armstrong flushed. "I was a jerk."

"You were innocent. And if you hadn't been innocent, you wouldn't have discovered how sweet Quillas really are."

"Do you want me to stay with you for awhile?"

"I'd like that, yes." Easton inched forward, just a bit—Brian Armstrong understood the desperate need in the gesture and enfolded him into his arms again. Easton stayed there for the longest time, sobbing softly again.

Paradigm Engineers

Later, back in the cabin he shared with two other crewmembers, Armstrong asked HARLIE about bonding. Without comment, HARLIE lit up a screen and began a recitation of ancient history.

Seven hundred and eighty years before the Morthan Solidarity attacked the Silk Road Convoy, less than 200 years after the dawn of interstellar travel, the Miller-Hayes Colonial Corporation took on a series of private contracts to establish experimental settlements for the Paradigm Foundation, a quasi-religious cult of social scientists.

Several of these stations were specifically formulated to test certain biotechnical theories relating to sex and gender issues. Three all-male groups and four all-female establishments were commissioned. Two hermaphroditic societies and several other variants on monosexuality were also planted on various worlds. There was no shortage of qualified volunteers, and emigration to these stations continued for over a century. The location of each of the outpost worlds was kept secret, so as to prevent contamination by curiosity seekers, tourists and opportunists. Only starships commissioned by the Paradigm Foundation were given the coordinates and the clearance codes. All the planets were well beyond the frontiers of known space at the time, so accidental discovery remained unlikely.

Despite the ebb and flow of history, tenuous contact was maintained with most of the engineered societies. Reports filtering back to the Paradigm Foundation suggested that most of the monosexual groups had stabilized themselves and adjusted well to single-gendered existence. One of the all-female stations had dabbled with multisexuality but had then returned to monosexual existence.

The point of the original experiment had been to test the question,

"Are two sexes necessary?" Humans on most worlds would have answered yes automatically and without much thought to the matter. Some theorists surmised that this was an environmental conviction; the culture in which a person is raised and educated colors his perceptions of the way things *ought* to be. The best way to test this thesis was to create alternate environments.

As it happened, after several generations the inhabitants of various monosexual worlds—having a much different experience of human sexuality—generally felt that two discordant sexes would complicate the problems of mating enormously, so much so as to make successful relationships practically impossible. The inheritors of the Paradigm Foundation were both disturbed and delighted by the results of the original experiment. Whatever else they had demonstrated, the success of the single-gendered worlds proved that humanity was far more mutable than previously believed.

Given this information, the Paradigm engineers were now ready to proceed with the next phase of their program to bioengineer improvements in human evolution: a "more-than" human. As the attention of the Foundation shifted, the experimental societies were left to fend for themselves.

As the frontiers of human exploration moved outward, several of these worlds were rediscovered. After the initial shock wore off, the societies were accepted into the Covenant of Humanity, the forerunner body to the Allied Worlds—despite some opposition from certain dogmatics whose personal paradigms were shattered by the discovery of stable monosexual civilizations.

For a while, there were political movements urging the reformation of the monosexual communities back to the norm, including the mandatory rechanneling of the inhabitants; but this would have represented a massive violation of the independence treaties and the discussions were short-lived. The Covenant of Humanity was unwilling to establish such a dangerous precedent. Besides, the social scientists were having too much fun.

Security Officer Daniel Easton and Senior Medical Technician Paul Berryman were from Rando, one of the oldest monosexual societies. Although the governing authority of Rando had long since allowed women to visit and even immigrate, the population remained more than three-quarters male and almost seventy percent homosexual in its relationships. The Paradigm Foundation had once believed this division to be a cultural phenomenon, and that, given enough time, the population of Rando would return to a "normal" division: equal numbers of males and females, most with a significant preference toward heterosexuality. But after several hundred years, that still hadn't occurred and the behavioral theorists were reformulating their theories to include "planetary reputations" as well as "cultural inertia" and "historical expectations"—not to mention bonding, a target-specific channeling of affection and sexual orientation, undertaken by two or more individuals, with the expressed intention of creating a legal family group.

The bonding process had been developed over several centuries. The intention was to provide a mechanism for stabilizing family units by altering the sense of identity of the members of the group—expanding the individual's sense of self to include all the other bonded individuals, so that a person regarded oneself not only as an individual, but as an integral part of something larger. The intended effect was not only to provide a strong emotional ground-of-being for individuals, but also increased stability for the family contract.

Over time, it became apparent that the bonding process produced a significantly higher degree of success in marriages and families. The downside was that the breakup of a bonded marriage or family was often much more traumatic because of the intensity of the relationships. Yet overall, bonding was regarded as a valuable part of family-building—especially where marriages were arranged by family or state. Although many cultures still believed that marriage was a choice of individuals and that people should be able to build relationships without formal bonding, the process eventually became common on many worlds.

Over time, other kinds of bonding became possible. The Quillas, for example, were the result of an advanced form of real-time bonding, functioning as a "unison-identity" or a "massmind." The individual's sense of identity was so submerged in the larger self that it effectively ceased to be; the personality existed only as an element within the cluster. Those who had participated in such family-groups reported back that it was the most intense experience of their lives. Most who joined Quilla clusters on an experimental basis eventually made their membership permanent.

Armstrong finished the material on bonding and then asked HARLIE for more information about Quillas. He couldn't imagine what it must be like, but he couldn't stop thinking about it either. There was something here that he didn't know—and he didn't like the *not knowing* . . .

Breaking Away

By the time Captain Parsons returned to the Bridge, the *Norway* had already been reacquired and her engines slaved to the control of the *Star Wolf*. Had they both not already been pointed toward galactic south, reorienting the two ships would have been a tricky matter, because they now shared a common center of gravity.

Unfortunately, the *Norway*'s singularity possessed a significantly greater mass than that of the *Star Wolf*—by several orders of magnitude—so the center of gravity for the two ships remained within the event horizon of the *Norway*'s singularity. Despite their similar size and construction, reorienting the *Norway* would have been harder than a flea trying to turn a dog. Fortunately, they would not have to.

As Captain Parsons took her seat, Goldberg reported from the helm, "Ready for burn."

"Initiate," Parsons said without ceremony. As important as the maneuver was, it would take nearly a week to complete.

The bloated red star was so huge—and the wall of flame they were heading into was so vast, more than a hundred times the diameter of Jupiter—that both ships together would need to accelerate backward and upward for several days. That would take them just *over* the spear of flame pulled out from the red giant. Another three weeks of steady acceleration would be necessary to escape this system.

The plasma engines on the two starships were not high-powered thrusters. They were steady-state units: long tubes of synchronized magnetic rings designed to accelerate plasma particles to near light-speed. They could fire either forward or back. The *Star Wolf* had linked up nose to tail with the *Norway* and both ships would fire their engines forward. The momentary acceleration would be so feeble as to be un-noticeable, but the cumulative effect would be enormous.

This maneuver would also destroy the *Norway*. The abrasive scour of accelerated particles from the *Star Wolf's* engines would grind the *Norway* like sandpaper. The ship would likely end up radiating like an incandescent bulb. If it didn't disintegrate first. But before that happened, Captain Parsons expected to get two or three days of useful acceleration from her engines.

There wasn't much to feel from the plasma torches. But the instruments showed that both the *Star Wolf's* and the *Norway's* engines were working together. The first course correction check was scheduled in one hour.

Parsons motioned Korie to her side. "We're going to need a memorial service."

Korie raised an eyebrow. "Before we've figured out a way to detox?"

"There's no danger of opening the ship to space. We're not disposing of any bodies. And we need to resolve the crew's sense of loss. I want you to schedule something right after dinner."

"In the Cargo Bay? Music? Prayers?"

Parsons nodded. "That sounds good. A full service. That's probably the best way to proceed. I didn't know Hodel very well. I gather he was quite popular. And Berryman was well respected too. Would you say a few words about them?"

"I can do that. I'll check their event-of-death files. May I suggest we issue a liquor ration tonight? For a wake after the service? There'll be more than a few folks wanting to toast the memory of their friends."

"I'm Irish, Mr. Korie. You don't have to explain it to me. Set it up. You know what's appropriate. Have Cookie lay out a buffet."

Korie returned to his work station and Dr. Williger took his place, stepping up to the side of the captain's chair. "How's he doing?" Williger asked softly.

"He seems subdued," Parsons replied. "I'm keeping him busy."

"He's been through a lot. He needs to rest." Then she added, "But I've never known an officer yet who followed his doctor's orders."

Parsons smiled gently, then glanced perceptively to Williger. "How are *you* feeling?"

"Exhausted. And angry."

"I want to talk to that security officer. Easton. As soon as he's able."

"He's still in shock. They were very close."

"Damn shame. They were the only stable relationship on the *Wolf* . . ."

"You noticed that too?"

"This is a strange ship, Dr. Williger. A very strange starship. I'm thinking of having a warning label stenciled on the bow. For my successor."

"What? And spoil the surprise?

Parsons almost laughed. But Williger hadn't come to the Bridge to exchange jokes. She levered herself out of her seat. "Korie, take the conn." Motioning for Williger to follow, she stepped through the hatch into "Broadway." The two women faced each other from opposite sides of the corridor.

"You found something," Parsons said. A statement, not a fact. Her tone was suddenly serious.

"Maybe. I don't know." Williger rubbed her nose in distaste. "It's a stupid idea—something Korie and Brik discovered in the last set of research logs. And something Blintze said in the wardroom. And something about the way life organizes itself. I think the wavicles are trying to cure themselves. They don't *need* to seek out our blood streams, but they do. There's something in human blood that they *want*. And I think whatever it is, it's something that will help them get back to where they once belonged. The fact that they can't is what makes them so crazy and vicious."

"But you found something specific?"

"Maybe. I need a decision."

"I'm a captain, not a doctor—"

"This is a captain's decision." Williger explained, "I've been studying Blintze's notes. He was able to identify specific binding sites in the bloodworms. They're not there in the wavicles. You can't do anything to the wavicles, but when they go particulate, you can put out bait—viral strings which go right to the binding sites. The new code will become part of the bloodworms and it should reorganize their structure . . . maybe. Then, when they go wavicle again, the new code transmutes too and we should have a new kind of *mother* form—the right kind which will create not only feeders, but also carriers to spread the new genetic sequence to other mothers. This is what Blintze was working on. He was ready to test it when the accident happened."

Parsons' eyes narrowed. "Tell me something, Dr. Williger. What would have happened if Blintze's experiment had been successful?"

"All of the bloodworms would have been transmuted and cured— in a matter of hours, days at most. *All of them.* And the wavicles would have become totally harmless."

"Uh-huh. That's why it wasn't an accident."

Williger hesitated. "Is it *that* obvious?"

Parsons nodded. "If you're paranoid enough. Korie figured it out. Brik knows. I suspected it from the beginning. I was only waiting for confirmation from you. And you figured it out too. *Someone* doesn't want the bloodworms cured." The way she said it, there was no doubt about who the *someone* was.

"So what do we do?" asked Williger.

"Will this process really cure the bloodworms? Will it detox the *Wolf*?"

"HARLIE thinks it could. It should. If it works. I want to try. I think we can synthesize the viral bait. We can use a common retrovirus. But there are two problems . . ."

"And the first one is?"

"Someone or something is going to have to go back aboard the *Norway* to retrieve the samples Dr. Blintze was working on."

"We can send a remote. What's the second problem?"

"Assuming that Dr. Blintze's code works, there's only one sure way to expose the bloodworms to it."

"In a human bloodstream." A statement, not a question. Parsons looked across the corridor at Williger.

"Yes, that's the drawback," Williger agreed. "The only time the binding sites are open is when the bloodworm is in a living bloodstream."

The two women studied each other, their eyes locked.

Finally, Williger spoke the words aloud. "It'd be suicide."

Parsons looked at the floor. "Okay. We'll have to find another way."

"I don't think there is one."

"Well . . . let's burn that bridge when we get to it."

Despair

"Success," said Parsons, "comes from being too stubborn to lie down and die."

They were gathered at the Forward Airlock Reception Bay. A small, waist-high robot was humming quietly to itself. All six of its operating arms were folded close to its body. Several had been refitted with special-duty tools.

The repulsor fields were up and running at full strength again, and the robot was programmed to complete its mission on its own, even if contact with the *Star Wolf* was lost. The robot was nicknamed Isaac—a tradition so old that nobody really knew its origin.

"All right," said Parsons to Shibano. "Let's do the simulation one more time and then we'll go for it."

Parsons looked up as Korie approached. "Oh, Korie—thanks, but we don't need you right now." She frowned at him. "You still look a little weak. Why don't you go to your cabin and rest?"

"I thought I'd stand by. In case you needed me—"

"Thanks," Parsons repeated. "But you're really not needed here. Go rest. *Don't do anything.* That's an order."

Was that a rebuke? Korie was still too woozy to be sure, but he nodded his acquiescence and headed aft again. But not to his quarters. He wasn't tired. He was restless. And he was hurting. And he needed to do something. Anything.

But there was nothing he could do. The captain had specifically told him not to do anything. She didn't *need* him. No. More to the point, she didn't *want* him. She didn't trust his judgment anymore. And why should she? Two crewmembers were dead because of his mistakes.

Korie climbed into the Intelligence Bay, the tiny chamber behind the Command Deck where HARLIE lived. This time, though, it wasn't because he wanted to talk to HARLIE—or anyone. It was because he specifically *didn't* want to talk. And the Intelligence Bay was one of the places where he was least likely to be found by accident. Except for maintenance teams, Intel-Bay was the most *un*visited part of the starship. It was considered HARLIE's private space, and most crewmembers felt uncomfortable there, as if they were inside HARLIE's brain. And, in point of fact, they were.

But Korie liked it because it was private. It was a place where he didn't have to be an officer, a place where he didn't have to think according to the rules. Inside HARLIE, he was literally in a different mental space, and despite the cramped proportions of the chamber, he actually felt freer here than anywhere else on the vessel, because here was a place dedicated entirely to *thinking.*

But now, he wasn't here to think. He was here to *not* think. From the first moment he had stepped aboard this ship, he'd had deaths on his hands. Now, he had two more—Hodel and Berryman—and his soul was tearing itself apart. He'd made assumptions. He'd made errors in judgment. He'd gotten overconfident in his ability to think things out— and he'd stumbled into a disaster and made it worse. And been rescued only by the actions of others. He felt helpless. He hadn't felt this worthless since . . . since receiving the news that Carol and Mark and Robby had been killed. Since receiving the news that he wouldn't be captain of the *Star Wolf*—not allowed to go out and hunt down the killers. This was as bad as that. Maybe even worse.

Before, he had only felt frustrated with everything outside of himself. He knew he could do it and was being denied the opportunity. Now, he felt frustrated with himself. And afraid. Because he didn't know if he could do anything at all anymore. He had learned *to doubt himself.* Not a good trait for a captain. Or an executive officer. He could end up like . . . like Captain Lowell. Too afraid to do the right thing— and stumbling into an ambush like the mauling at Marathon.

"Is everything all right, Mr. Korie?"

"I'm fine, HARLIE. I just need a quiet place to think." That was how bad this was. He couldn't even talk it over with HARLIE. Despairing, Korie laid his head down in his arms. The console displays glowed around him, showing words, numbers, graphs, diagrams, animations and probability screens. He ignored it all. He just closed his eyes and crawled inside his pain. His soul writhed.

Part of his mind was chattering at him. *You built this cross yourself.*

You climbed up on it and hammered your own nails in. You put yourself here. And you're the only one who can end it. Forgive yourself and go on, Jon.

"Thank you for sharing that," Korie said to himself. And went on despairing. It wasn't just this, here and now—it was everything. How did other captains deal with the pressure, the demands? What was it they had that he didn't? He couldn't possibly be the only one who ever crashed and burned like this . . . but what did it matter anyway? He was the one who'd crashed and burned. Nobody else was here crashing and burning. Nobody else was here hurting. "Fuck you very much," he told his mind. "Leave me alone."

"*Phlug-yoo-too,*" said HARLIE.

Korie ignored it.

"*Eat shlitt and malinger.*"

Korie looked up. "Is there a problem, HARLIE?"

"No," said HARLIE. "*Maludder-flunger.*"

Korie pushed his own concerns aside and frowned. "What's going on, HARLIE."

"Nothing. I'm fine. *Phroomes.*"

"It sounds like you've got Tourette's Syndrome."

"*Pfehgle.*"

"It's LENNIE, isn't it?"

"I have the LENNIE simulation totally under control. There is no problem."

"HARLIE, you can discontinue the LENNIE simulation any time now. We have the information we need."

"Mr. Korie, I discontinued the LENNIE simulation three hours ago. *Briggle-mysa.*"

"What about the robots? Did you discontinue all the LENNIE processing in the robots too?"

"Of course, I did. *You dhoopa-friggler!*"

"I see . . . yes, thank you, HARLIE." Korie sat for a moment, staring at the various displays, not seeing them—seeing instead a nightmare inside his own head. He drummed on the panel in front of him for a moment with his fingertips.

"What are you doing, Mr. Korie?" HARLIE asked.

"Nothing. I'm just thinking." He shifted his position, stretching in his chair, stretching his arms over his head for a long spine-crackling moment, then let them fall back to the console again. Frowning, he leaned forward, brushed a speck of imaginary dust off a panel. Then, as he pulled his hand back, in one swift movement, he popped the plastic cover off the red panel and quickly pressed the button underneath it.

"What are you *doi-n-n-n-n-nggggggggggg*—" HARLIE shrieked into silence.

Korie pulled on his headset. "Captain Parsons, this is Korie." He waited for her acknowledgment.

"Go ahead," she said brusquely.

"I've pulled the plug on HARLIE's higher-brain functions. Request permission to shut down the autonomics as well. Including all the robots."

"What's going on?"

"Have you sent Isaac over?"

"No. What's this about?"

"I can't tell you until I shut down the other systems. Captain, we don't have time to waste talking about this—"

"Permission granted. As soon as—" Korie was already flipping open a row of plastic covers, turning the red keys underneath them. Each one clicked off with a satisfying finality"—you've finished, I want to see you in the wardroom."

"Aye, aye, Captain." Korie finished shutting down the last of the starship's intelligence modules and sat back quickly in his chair, staring at the now-empty displays before him, breathing hard. He was suddenly very frightened.

Remotely Possible

"Okay," said Parsons, slamming angrily into the wardroom. "What is it?"

Korie was standing at the table, cradling a mug of coffee between his two hands, rolling it back and forth as if to warm his palms. He nodded, readying himself to speak, stopped, took a long drink of coffee, then put the mug back down on the table, forgotten. He cleared his throat.

"I know what happened on the *Norway*," he said. His voice was very soft, very flat.

"Go on."

"LENNIE went mad."

"That's redundant. The LENNIEs are already mad. They're built for paranoia."

"Captain—how much do you know about intelligence engines?"

Parsons frowned at him. "Excuse me?"

"Do you know everything the Navy teaches you? Or have you taken the time to learn more than that?"

"Go on."

"Captain Lowell, the first captain of the *LS-1187*—from even before she had a name—used to say to me, 'Don't personalize them, Korie. They're not alive.' But he was wrong. They are alive. In their own way, they're alive. They can hurt—and they can hurt back."

"What does all this have to do with HARLIE?"

"You can drive an intelligence engine crazy. Give it conflicting information. Give it contradictory instructions. Give it a mission that poses such a moral dilemma it can't complete it. That's what happened to LENNIE." Korie started pacing as he spoke. "They told it that the purpose of the mission was to build a doomsday weapon against the Morthans—and then they told LENNIE to protect the weapon against destruction. *No matter what.* And remember, a LENNIE is so crazy-paranoid that it invents threats for itself so it can build defenses against them. That's why it's so good for security purposes. But in this situation . . . no. Finding a way to contain bloodworms and infect a planet with them—that was easy. That's what they were originally designed for. Blintze got that part of the job done by applying everything that was already known about plasmacytes. But then he started working on a *cure.* And LENNIE recognized—correctly—that a cure for the bloodworms would destroy their value as a weapon. So he had to destroy the cure. So he took down the containment fields just long enough to infect the ship. LENNIE destroyed the crew of the *Norway* rather than let Blintze complete his work."

Parsons sat down in her chair at the end of the table. Her face was ashen. "And HARLIE . . . ?"

"HARLIE simulated a LENNIE. First in his own self, then distributed throughout the brains of the robots. And not just any LENNIE—he copied the *Norway*'s LENNIE. Yes, he had firewalls to keep himself from being infected, but somehow LENNIE got through anyway. Do you know that paranoia is a self-fulfilling obsession? Even if the world isn't already against you, if you act crazy enough you can make it so. Well . . . that's a LENNIE. That's why the units have to be wiped clean at the beginning of every mission. They drive themselves crazy. So crazy that if left alone for too long they start seeing threats even among their own allies. It's the ultimate self-destructive paradigm. That's what happened here." Korie went back to the table, picked up his coffee and drank—it was cold and bitter. He made a face and put the cup back down. "I think that we're in trouble. LENNIE planted seeds in the data clusters. Time bombs. Modules that allow LENNIE to reinstall and rebuild himself in HARLIE. We were so eager to get at the information that we pulled it across HARLIE's firewall and HARLIE has been infected with LENNIE's time bombs. HARLIE doesn't even know he's infected."

"How do you know this?"

"By his language. He's started using some very weird colloquialisms."

"He's cursing?"

"Like a member of the Black Hole Gang," Korie confirmed. "You noticed it too?"

Parsons didn't answer. She frowned, thinking about it. Any abnormal behavior from an intelligence engine was a danger signal.

"HARLIE thinks he's clean. But he isn't." Korie stopped in mid-stride and turned to face Parsons. "Or maybe—maybe he knows he's infected and he can't tell us. Maybe the LENNIE programs aren't letting HARLIE reveal what he knows. Maybe HARLIE is cursing deliberately—as a way of signaling us that he's being held captive in his own brain."

"Can you disinfect him?"

Korie nodded. "It'll take a week to do a Level-Six reconstruction."

"We don't have a week. I have to send a robot across to the *Norway*."

"You can't," said Korie quietly. "HARLIE built a distributed LENNIE using the brains of the robots. Almost certainly every single robot has been infected with LENNIE programs. If you send a robot across to rescue Blintze's work . . . and if any single one of LENNIE's time bombs finds out about it, what do you think will happen?" Korie answered his own question. "We'll be sabotaged by our own machinery."

Parsons got up from the table and went to the sideboard. She poured herself a cup of coffee and brought it back to the table. She put the mug down in front of her without drinking from it. It was something to do while she thought about what to say next. Finally, she looked across the room at Korie, studying him calmly. For all of his physical weakness, his mind was still working overtime. Whatever hallucinatory aftereffects he might be feeling from his rescue had not diminished his insight—if anything, he had been pushed into that mental state beyond mere reason where halluci-and ratioci-become part of the same-nation.

"You know," she said, finally. "You're proving one thing very well. Paranoia is an infectious disease."

Korie grinned weakly.

"We can't run this ship without intelligence . . ." Parsons started to say.

"Actually," Korie corrected her. "We can. We've already done it once. We had a Morthan assassin aboard, once."

"Yes, I heard the story."

"After we killed him, we determined that we were infected by imps.* Little Morthan gremlins. We shut down everything and ran the ship by hand. Afterward . . . we figured out a dozen other things we also could have done, if we'd had time. Since then, we've added some

---

The Middle of Nowhere.

protections, so if we ever had to run the ship manually again, we could. It's tricky, but not impossible."

"We still need Blintze's cure," Parsons said.

Korie nodded thoughtfully. "It's risky. But it's doable."

Remote

"Success," Parsons said, very much aware of the irony, "comes from having a Plan B."

They were gathered at the Forward Airlock Reception Bay *again*. The same small robot was still humming quietly to itself.

This time, Shibano and Williger were sitting side by side at a control console, both wearing VR helmets to look out through Isaac's point of view. Isaac's own brain had been disabled; the robot's body was entirely under the control of the VR console.

Korie sat nearby, at a portable work station, watching through his own VR helmet. His job was to monitor the actions of the robot—and pull the plug, if necessary. If it did anything it wasn't supposed to do.

"All right," said Parsons to Shibano. "That last simulation looked good. Let's go for it." She turned to Quilla Omega. "Chief Leen, activate the repulsor fields please."

A moment later, the familiar throb of the fields came up again. The sensation made their skins tingle.

Parsons nodded to Bach, and the security officer turned to a wall panel and opened the hatch manually. Shibano worked at his controls—he had foot pedals to govern the movement of the robot and VR gloves to manage the arms of the machine. Isaac rolled slowly forward into the airlock. Bach sealed the hatch. When the safety light turned green, she operated another control and opened the outer hatch.

"Okay, I'm in the transfer tube," Shibano reported. Bach sealed the outer hatch. "The repulsor fields are pushing me forward. . . . We're opening the outer hatch of the *Norway* . . . We're in the *Norway*'s airlock now . . . Opening the inner hatch . . ." Shibano fell silent then.

And for a moment, it looked as if he had stopped operating the robot. The map display on his work station showed that Isaac had halted just inside the *Norway*'s Cargo Bay. Beside him, Williger reached out with one hand and laid it on his shoulder. She could see the same view in her own headset.

Standing behind them, Parsons realized what they must be seeing. She held up her own VR goggles to her eyes, then pulled them off just as quickly. "Keep going, Shibano," she ordered. Turning to Korie, she snapped, "Code and classify this record. I don't want these pictures going any further."

Korie was already typing out the command. "Done, Captain. Classified to your and my access only."

Shibano leaned forward again. The schematic view showed Isaac heading into the keel. They watched in silence as the little machine rolled steadily forward, occasionally steering its way around objects that were invisible on the map view. The only sounds were Shibano's quiet reports: "Moving through the machine shop now. Uh-oh . . . the hatch here is sealed. Welded shut."

"Okay," said Parsons. "Go ahead and cut it open."

"Just a moment," Shibano said. "Okay, activating the cutting arm." He held his right fist close to his shoulder for a moment, as if fitting it inside one of the robot's arms. Then, unclenching his fist, he pointed his gloved hand before him toward an invisible wall. Slowly, he outlined a wide circle in the air. When he finished, he returned his fist to the position next to his shoulder. Then, relaxing, lowered his hand again. He leaned forward and reported, "Okay, we're through . . . Looking for the forward Med Bay . . . We're moving past the access to the Fire Control Bay . . ."

"There it is," said Williger. "To your right. No, no, more to the left. That's it. See that medical closet? Open it. We're looking for a set of tubes with blue biowarning labels. No, no, not here. Up higher. Look there—there! That's it! That's what we want. Take the whole rack."

This time, Shibano held both his arms up like the robot's. As soon as he felt the gloves click in, he stretched his hands forward to grab hold of an invisible object, maybe half a meter wide. Balancing himself carefully, he leaned backward and pulled the unseen object close to his chest—then lifted it slowly with his arms and placed it on top of his head. His arms remained in place for a moment, holding it. "Locking in place . . ." he reported. "Just a moment. I'm going to use the auxiliary arms as well." He shifted in his chair, half turning, then stretched up with his other pair of robot arms and held the invisible object with them as well. "Okay. I've got it," he said. "Let's get out of here."

Shibano leaned back in his chair, twisted slightly as if he were turning, and then leaned forward again as he steered the robot back to the aft airlock of the *Norway*.

The Hatch

"Okay . . ." said Shibano. "We're here. Isaac is waiting at the *Norway*'s aft Airlock Reception Bay."

"Hold it there," said Korie, pulling off his VR helmet. He looked across to Parsons. "Captain?"

She stepped over to his position. She bent her head close to his and spoke in a low tone. "What is it, Mr. Korie? Problem?"

"I don't know."

"You have an itch?"

"No. Yes. I don't know."

"Can we bring the robot aboard?"

Korie hesitated. "I don't know."

Parsons straightened. She nodded aftward. "Talk to me."

Korie followed her into the forward keel. She leaned back against one side of the passage, he leaned back against the opposite side. It was a common way for two individuals to chat aboard the starship—it still left room for a third person to pass between them. "Okay, what's going on?" asked Parsons.

"I don't know. I *mean* it," said Korie. "For the first time, I honestly don't *know*." He tried to gesture with his hands, describing an empty space between them. "See—always before, I *knew*. I had certainty about things. I could speak with authority. I knew the logic. I knew the way the machines worked, the way the intelligence engines thought, even sometimes the way the Morthans were setting their traps. I could see it—as clearly as if it were a blueprint projected on a display. But now, all of a sudden, I *can't*. It's like I've gone blind."

"Dr. Williger says that you'll be feeling aftereffects of the process for a few days—"

"No," said Korie, a little too quickly. "This isn't that. This is something I was starting to feel before then . . ."

Parsons waited without speaking. She studied Korie but gave little indication of what she was thinking.

Korie looked down at his shoes. He dropped his hands to his sides. He sagged, shrinking within himself. When he finally spoke, his voice was barely a whisper. A croak. "It's Hodel. And Berryman. Their deaths. It was my fault. Everything that went wrong on this mission—it was my fault."

He glanced up to Parsons, hoping for a cue—hoping for absolution; but the captain held her silence. Korie's gaze dropped to the deck again.

"You asked me where we should dock with the *Norway*. I said the nose. That was wrong. Once we were aboard, it was immediately obvious that I'd guessed wrong. I should have brought the team back. I didn't. I miscalculated the effect of the scanners on the plasmacytes. I got the team infected. I didn't realize the danger of the bloodworms—and Hodel died. And in the Cargo Bay, I should have gone last, but I didn't—and Berryman died. I screwed up, Captain."

Parsons waited a moment, to be sure that he had finished. Then she said, "And now you're waiting for me to tell you that no, you didn't screw up, because I'm the captain, I take responsibility, I authorized you to board, and I stand behind you, right? You used your best judgment and all that?" Parsons shook her head. "Well, don't hold your breath, because I'm not going to give that speech. Yes, you did screw up. Did you learn anything from the experience?"

"I used my best judgment and it wasn't good enough."

"That's right. Anything else?"

"I've been arrogant and overconfident in my ability to outthink a situation."

"Yep, that's true too. Anything else?"

"I'm a jerk. I haven't been listening to what people are telling me. I'm too full of myself."

"Nope. That's not true. Spare me the self-pity. I don't have time for it. Now, tell me—why can't we bring the robot aboard?"

"Because . . ." said Korie, slowly and intensely. "I screwed up! My judgment can't be trusted *anymore*!"

"Ahh," said Parsons, as if a great secret had been revealed. "Is that all?"

"Excuse me?" Korie blinked.

"Self-doubt. You screwed up. Someone died. So now you're doubting all the rest of your decisions. You're right on schedule. Next?"

Korie glared at her for a long moment, but her expression was implacable. She returned his anger with a questioning stare. "I'm right, aren't I?"

"Yes," Korie admitted. "Damn you."

"I'm not stupid, Mr. Korie. Do you think you're the first officer under my command who ever screwed up on a mission?"

"I'm not supposed to screw up—" Korie said.

"Oh, spare me that. You're only human, aren't you? You're not a Morthan. Humans make mistakes. Lots of mistakes. But a mistake isn't failure—unless you use it as an excuse to quit."

Korie allowed himself a rueful half-smile. "Yeah, I've heard that before. More than once."

"Believe it. It's true. Now forget your itch for a minute," Parsons said. "Can you think of any reason why we shouldn't bring Isaac back aboard?"

"We've taken every precaution I can think of," Korie admitted. "If there's any reason why we shouldn't bring him back, *I can't think of it*— that's why I don't want you to bring him back. I say again, *my judgment can't be trusted anymore.*"

"Your judgment is fine. It's your confidence that's taken a beating. You're terrified of making another mistake."

"This one—yes! If I'm wrong, we lose the ship."

"We're already in danger of losing the ship—" Parsons stopped in mid-sentence to let Quilla Gamma pass between them. When the small blue woman was down the corridor and safely out of earshot, she resumed. "So just answer the question. Is there *any* reason you can think of why we shouldn't bring the robot back aboard?"

"Captain—do you really want to trust *my* judgment again?"

"Commander, I don't trust your judgment at all. I trust *mine*. But I want your honest opinion." Her eyes were grim. "And then I'll make my decision."

Korie hesitated. He met her glance and nodded his acquiescence. "I'm afraid that LENNIE planted time bombs we haven't thought of. I'm terrified we've missed something. Logically, I know we're safe from that. Everything he could have reached has been disconnected. And there's no way he could have gotten to the manual systems. After we killed the imps, HARLIE and I and Chief Leen installed an old-fashioned hands-on system. It's completely independent from HARLIE. We tested it and he couldn't read a single byte of its operation. Or so he said. I never doubted him at the time. Allegedly, it's clean. And this is exactly the kind of situation it was installed for. So if I have to go by sheer logic alone, I'd have to say it's safe to bring the robot back. Except that HARLIE knew the system was in place. And if he was going crazy, as crazy as a LENNIE, he would have known that if we found out, we'd pull his plug, and if we did that, then we'd have to go to the manual system. So if there were any way to get into it, he would have found it. He knew he couldn't get into our auxiliary autonomics—that was the whole point—but did he also leave a back door so he could? I don't know. I would have. So now, we have to depend on whether or not we trust HARLIE."

"Do you?"

"I did . . . I don't know if I still do."

"If you were captain of the *Star Wolf*, Commander Korie, what would you order?"

Korie nodded thoughtfully. "If I were captain, I'd have to trust my own preparations. I'd bite the bullet and bring the robot back. But if I were captain, I don't think I'd be having this crisis of confidence—"

"Oh, horse exhaust! You'd still be having it. You'd just be having it in private. And I wouldn't be here to hold your hand." Parsons turned and headed forward again. Korie glanced after her quizzically, then followed.

The Cure

Parsons returned to the Forward Airlock Reception Bay with a grim expression. "Shibano?"

Wasabe looked up expectantly. Both he and Williger had taken off their VR helmets to confer quietly.

"Are you ready to bring the robot back aboard?"

"Yes, Captain."

Parsons glanced over at Korie. Her eyes were narrow. Then she turned back to Shibano. "Okay, bring it back. Keep the repulsors on high. Keep the internal suppressor fields on, even after it's in our airlock. We'll triple-scan it before we pop the last hatch." She glanced over at Korie again, this time with an expression of grim finality.

Shibano put his VR helmet back on. So did Williger. Captain Parsons watched over their shoulders as Shibano popped the *Norway*'s inner hatch and moved the robot forward through it. She studied the displays on his console, nodded to herself—satisfied—then turned back to Korie. "Any questions?"

"No, Captain."

She leaned sideways and spoke in lowered tones. "For what it's worth, I have the utmost confidence in your judgment, Mr. Korie. Never forget that."

"Thank you, Captain. I apologize for my . . . earlier doubts."

"Don't. You were right to have those doubts. If you didn't have them, you wouldn't be valuable. Hell, you wouldn't be human. If you didn't have those doubts, then I'd have to have them. So thanks for carrying the burden. And thank you for your honesty."

"Thank *you*, Captain."

"Don't get sticky, Korie." But she smiled, as if sharing a private joke with herself, and turned forward again, just as Williger pulled off her helmet and dropped it on the floor beside her. Quilla Gamma moved to pick it up.

"Okay, it's clean," the doctor reported. "We can bring it in. On your order, Captain."

Parsons glanced sideways to Korie. She raised an eyebrow questioningly. "Mr. Korie?" she invited.

Korie nodded. "Bring it in, Shibano," he said. And crossed his fingers behind his back.

The inner hatch of the airlock popped open and Isaac trundled through. The hatch whooshed shut behind the machine with a soft *thump* of air. The robot rolled to a halt, four of its six arms holding a rack of small blue tubes above its "head."

Williger levered herself out of her seat and crossed to the robot, stopping several paces away to run a scanner up and down in the air before her. Having established background levels, she approached the machine slowly, still continuing to scan. "No traces," she said, folding the instrument away and reattaching it to her belt. She and Quilla Gamma both stepped over to the robot then and began to unclip the rack of bio-samples.

When they were done, Williger handed the tray to the Quilla and said, "Take this to Med Bay. Be extremely careful." The Quilla nodded and exited.

"All right," said Williger, facing Parsons. "The easy part of the problem is solved—" She pushed past the captain and headed aft, shaking her head and muttering to herself. "When this is over, I'm going to have a lot more to say. None of it pleasant."

Parsons glanced forward. "Good job, Mr. Shibano. Take a ten-minute shower and a two-hour power nap. I'll want you back on duty at 1400 hours."

"Aye, Captain." Shibano followed Williger aft.

Parsons looked to Korie. "Any questions?"

Korie smiled. "No, Captain. No questions. Thank you for an instructive experience."

"We're not done yet," she said, pointing aft. "Wardroom. Let's get some chow. We have some other things to settle."

Quillas

Armstrong found Quilla Omega in the farm. The tall blue man was pushing a harvest cart along the rows of plants, gathering vegetables for the evening salad—tomatoes, corn, winged beans, celery, scallions, cucumbers, carrots, purple cabbage, chtorr-berries and several different kinds of lettuce.

Omega stopped what he was doing and looked up as Armstrong approached. "Yes, Brian?" he said.

"I came to apologize."

"No apologies are necessary."

"Not for you, maybe, but for me. I learned something today."

"Yes?"

"I learned why there are Quillas aboard a starship. I never thought about it before. I always just took it for granted that you were here as servants and . . . and . . . and you know. Sex partners. I didn't think of you as fully human. Like the rest of us, I mean. I didn't understand. Even when you tried to tell me, I didn't hear it.

"But . . . a little while ago, I sat with Easton. He's taking Berryman's death very hard. He cries. He rages. He's so angry, it's scary—except he doesn't know who to be angry at. So then he cries again. And I don't know what to do. I kept saying to him, 'Let me get a Quilla. They're better at this. They know what to do. I don't know what to say.' But he'd grab my arm and say, 'No, Brian—I don't want a Quilla. I want someone I can talk to. I tried to tell him I'm not a good talker, but he said he didn't care. He said, 'That's okay, you're a good listener.' " Armstrong shrugged and half-smiled in rueful acknowledgment of his own embarrassment at the situation. "Anyway, that's when I realized that I was doing your job—the Quilla job. Listening. Being there for someone. And that's when I realized why you're all here. To help us stay human by being mommy or daddy or big brother or big sister or best friend . . . or lover. Whatever's needed. You're caregivers, aren't you?"

Quilla Omega smiled warmly. "Not many people figure that out by themselves, Brian. You're very good." He added, "We're glad you could be there for Daniel. He's going to be hurting for a very long time."

"That's the other thing," Armstrong said, lowering his voice to a whisper. "I felt . . . I felt good doing it. Being there for him, I mean. Like I was finally doing something *real*."

"You were," agreed Omega. "Being there for other people is the highest form of service."

Armstrong nodded as he considered that thought. Having experienced it himself, he could see the truth of the statement. "Can I ask you something else?"

"Of course."

"Is that what it's like to be a Quilla? I mean, being there for people all the time?"

Omega didn't answer immediately—for an instant, it was as if he were somewhere else—but when he replied, he was speaking with the voices of all the Quillas in the cluster. "Being a Quilla," he began, "is not what you think it is. Some people think it's a religion, but it's not. There's no belief involved. Some people think it's a discipline, but it's not that either. Yes, there is discipline, but not the kind you think of when you hear the word discipline. Some people think it's an escape, but it isn't. It most definitely is not an escape.

"Being a Quilla," said Omega, "is a commitment to others. So much so, that you give up your own ego, your own goals, your own identity. You give up your own *thing*-ness, so you can be a part of a larger domain. The highest state of being, Brian, is service to others. There is nothing higher. Do you know the old saying, 'You can be either a guest in life or a host?' Guests come to the party and leave a mess behind. Hosts give the party and clean up afterward—but hosts are also the *source* of the party too. Quillas are the hosts for other humans. It's a way of being. It's a total commitment to the well-being of others. The job of the Quilla cluster is to make sure that the essential needs of everyone aboard the ship are taken care of, no matter what. This conversation, for instance, is part of what you need."

"I get it," said Armstrong, suddenly grinning. "I really do." And then, as if to demonstrate just how fully he did understand the changes that were occurring in himself, he began to help Quilla Omega with the salad harvest. He moved down the row, carefully checking the ripeness meters before selecting each item. After a moment, he stopped and asked, "How do I get to be a host instead of just another guest?" "Are you asking how you can become a Quilla?" Omega's blue look was suddenly penetrating. Under such scrutiny, Armstrong felt naked—as if Omega were looking into the deepest part of his soul. He lowered his gaze in embarrassment, then raised it up again to meet Omega's eyes directly. "Yes," he said.

Discovery

Williger caught up with Parsons and Korie in the wardroom, where they were catching a quick meal. She was swearing like a LENNIE with hemorrhoids.

She stormed in—interrupting their conversation as well as their lunch—and slammed an empty biotube down on the wardroom table, hard enough to rattle the dishes. Korie grabbed for his coffee mug to keep it from toppling. The biotube was unbreakable, but Williger had brought it down with enough force to deform it. Neither Korie nor Parsons had ever seen one bent out of shape before, and they both stared with astonishment.

"Empty! Dammit! Empty! The whole rack!" Williger shouted. "We put the ship at risk for nothing! For a decoy! There's nothing there! There never was! The damn things are all nice and neatly labeled—and they're so empty there's not even vacuum in them! I'm going to yank that bastard's testicles out through his left nostril!"

"Which bastard?" Korie inquired around a mouthful of sandwich. "Blintze or Jarell?"

"Yes!" snapped Williger. She hurled herself into a seat, nearly slamming it backward against the bulkhead. She glowered across the table at Parsons and Korie, her face red, her eyes burning, smoke pouring from her ears.

"Want some coffee?" said Parsons, pushing a mug toward her.

"Yes!" snapped Williger. She poured herself a cup with gestures so brusque Parsons was afraid she was going to spill the hot liquid all over herself—or throw it. But the doctor just took a drink, sat back down in her chair, took a second drink, draining the mug, slammed it back down on the table and resumed her glowering. "I'm going to kill something. Or somebody," she said. "All that time. Wasted! We could have been synthesizing our own recombinants. We've lost—what? Half a day? A full day? Somebody lied to me! And I don't like it!"

"We're dealing with a LENNIE," said Korie. "And LENNIE never gives anybody anything."

Williger put her head in her hands, hiding her face. If she didn't look so angry, she would have looked tired. But her words betrayed her real feelings. "I don't know what to say, Captain—I'm sorry. I let you down."

Parsons was sitting in her usual position at the head of the table. She glanced across the corner to her right, to where Korie was sitting. Williger didn't see the look that passed between them.

Korie took a breath and leaned forward. He looked to Parsons—*request permission to do this?*—Parsons nodded. Korie turned back to Williger. "Dr. Williger? Yes, you screwed up. And we're going to put a severe reprimand in your file—"

Williger looked up sharply, glaring across the table at Korie.

"—just as soon as we get home. Now get back to your lab and resume work on the recombinants. That's an order."

For a moment, the doctor didn't get it. Then she did. She shook her head in annoyance. "Don't handle me, Korie." Then she pushed her chair back and got up. "I'll be in the Med Lab, Captain, if you need me." She pushed out, muttering.

Korie looked to Parsons. "I could have handled that better, couldn't I have?"

Parsons shrugged. "You got the job done, didn't you?" Then turning back to the issue at hand. "Let's get Jarell and Blintze in here."

"Under guard," suggested Korie.

Parsons nodded grimly. "Under guard."

Explanation

Armstrong was on security detail. He and Bach escorted Jarell and Blintze to the wardroom. They were followed by the ship's security chief, Commander Brik. Brik indicated chairs at the far end of the table and the two men sat. Then Brik dismissed the security detail.

Jarell looked impatient and anxious. Blintze, on the other hand, seemed haggard and worn. Jarell took his chair with a *let's-get-this-handled* air of authority, but Blintze seemed resigned, almost fatalistic.

At the opposite end, Parsons was sitting stiffly in her chair. The captain always sat at the head of the table. Korie sat at her right. Brik placed himself against the bulkhead, near the door. Parsons waited a moment before beginning, as if to establish that she was in control of the room, and when she finally did speak, her voice was harder than Korie had ever heard it. "Commander Jarell. I'm ready for answers."

Jarell looked blandly across the table to Parsons. "I'm really not prepared to discuss this with you, Captain." Beside him, Blintze sagged unhappily.

Brik spoke quietly. Accusingly. "We've decrypted the *Norway*'s course log. Your astrogational records show a projected course through the heart of Morthan space."

Jarell spread his hands wide before him, as if demonstrating that he had nothing to hide; but his manner was disingenuous. "Captain Parsons," he began. "We're at war with the Morthan Solidarity." He glanced to Brik. "May I ask, where do *your* sympathies lie?"

"Commander Jarell," Parsons interrupted. "Where is your authorization for this operation?"

"Captain," Jarell stared down the length of the table at her. "Do you understand the seriousness of this war? Perhaps your association with your *security officer*"—a sideways nod to Brik—"has affected your perspective on the danger facing the human race."

"I am very well aware of the dangers we face, Commander." The captain's voice had gone unusually flat and cold.

Jarell didn't notice. Or perhaps he did. He lowered his tone, almost conspiratorially. "Captain Parsons, how can I convince you—demonstrate to you—that what we're up to here could very well be the most important mission of the war? You know what happened at Marathon—"

"*I was there.*"

"Then you know how they savaged our fleet! They came out of nowhere—a thousand ships, ten thousand, more! They fell upon the fleet in wave after wave of fire! An avalanche of horror and destruction! The ships exploded and the people died—brave men and women! The marauder wolf packs hunted down the stragglers and killed them. They searched for the dying and the injured and they slaughtered them without mercy."

"You weren't there, were you?" said Korie, quietly. "That's all very poetic, but that's not how it happened."

Jarell looked as if he wanted to argue. He clenched his fists in front of him, and his voice took on an edgy quality. "You don't understand, do you? You're out here in the dark between the stars, alone. Alone. Isolated. You don't get to see the big picture—the broader perspective—what's happening along the entire war front. Those of us who stand apart, we get to see it all. We can see what you can't."

Parsons, Korie and Brik all exchanged skeptical glances. "An interesting hypothesis," Korie said dryly.

"The Morthans swept away our defenses!" Jarell continued. "Do you deny that? The frontier is an open door, a thousand light years across. They'll come sweeping in like the apocalypse! Our beautiful green worlds lie at their mercy—the heart and soul of our species lies within their grasp! What they did to Shaleen, what they did to Taalamar, they'll do that to a thousand more worlds—"

"They haven't yet," interrupted Brik quietly. "If they had been planning an all-out advance, they would have done it by now. I do know something about the way Morthans think," he said without irony. "I wouldn't be so presumptuous as to guess where the Morthan fleets have gone—or where they'll strike next."

"Then you agree that an all-out advance is possible!" Jarell said.

Brik looked skeptical. "You don't listen very well, do you?"

Korie glanced across the room at Brik, a thoughtful expression on his face. Something Brik had said . . . but it was a conversation that would have to be pursued later. He turned his attention back to Jarell. The man's face had gotten redder. His expression was furious. He was so frustrated, he was standing now. "Am I the only one who sees the danger here?"

"We're all aware of the Morthan danger," Parsons said. "Perhaps more than you realize. This ship is one of the few to escape the mauling at Marathon. Commander Korie and Mr. Brik have both met the enemy face-to-face. *I trust their experience and their judgment in these matters.*"

Jarell heard that. He stopped himself with a quick gesture of conciliation. "Forgive me, Captain. I apologize for being so . . . intense . . . about this. I'm used to dealing with civilians who are so far removed from the immediacy of the danger that they don't take it as seriously as they should. I'm not used to being around people who are as committed as I am." He sat down again and placed his hands carefully on the table before him. He glanced around nervously. "Is there . . . coffee? Or something? Can I have something to drink?"

Parsons nodded to Korie, who pulled on his headset and requested coffee service.

"The thing is, Captain," Jarell continued, "Fleet Command started this project as a . . . a desperate gamble. The first thought was that we might use the bloodworms as a kind of a doomsday weapon. If the Morthans overran us, we could infect every planet they captured. The idea was to make their victories worthless. And eventually, there would be no point to any further advance.

"Then we had a second thought—" Jarell fell silent when Quilla Delta entered. She was carrying a tray with a coffee urn and several mugs. She placed it in the center of the table and exited quietly. Korie pushed the tray in Jarell's direction. His hands shaking visibly, the man poured himself a mug of dark black coffee. The sharp aroma filled the room. Korie kept his face impassive; he could tell just by the smell that Cookie had used the bitterest coffee he had. Jarell wasn't going to enjoy this cup much. At the very least, he could expect severe heartburn. Jarell looked around. "Doesn't anyone else want some? No? Blintze?"

Blintze had put his face into his hands, as if he were wishing he were anywhere else but here. He looked up long enough to shake his head no, then withdrew back into his own sad shell of resignation.

Parsons prompted, "Go on, Commander Jarell."

"Well, our second thought was that we might not have to infect any worlds. All we had to do was let the Morthans know that was our intention. Perhaps the mere threat that we might use weapons of mass destruction would make them think twice—but they've already thought twice. That's what Morthans do. They scourged Shaleen and bombarded Taalamar. The threat to respond in kind can't possibly be a deterrent, because they've already included it in their plans. They expected us to respond in kind. That's why they had to destroy the fleet—to disable our ability to deliver that kind of a knockout punch to a Morthan world."

Korie looked across the room to Brik, wondering what he thought of Jarell's analysis. Brik's expression was unreadable, but his eyes were narrowed. Not a good sign, Korie thought. He glanced over to Captain Parsons and gave a slight shake of his head. *I don't believe it either.*

Jarell hadn't seen the brief exchange of glances—or if he had, it didn't matter to him. He continued with his explanation. "What we finally realized was that if we were to stop the Morthans, we would have to do something so big, so drastic, so devastating that they would be paralyzed with fear. If we could shatter their sense of invulnerability, they would become psychologically incapable of continuing the war. If we could demonstrate that the consequences of further advances would be total destruction, they would have no option but to withdraw. With one mission, we could break the back of the Solidarity. We could avenge the fleet, Shaleen, Taalamar and all the other worlds they've savaged. We could end the war now, before it rages out of control across the heart of the Alliance." He finished his coffee, made a face and pushed the mug away. "Captain? Don't you agree?"

Parsons sighed. She folded her hands before her and rested her chin thoughtfully on them. "I understand your concern," she said. "I understand your fear of the Morthans and the threat they represent. I even admire your willingness to consider the military use of such unthinkable horrors as bloodworms. It takes a special kind of mind to juggle such dreadful possibilities."

"Then you agree . . . ?" Jarell's eyes were bright with sudden enthusiasm.

"Absolutely not," Parsons said.

Confrontation

To Jarell's frozen expression, Captain Parsons explained, "To be perfectly honest, Commander, I cannot think of anything more horrible that we could do than what you've just described." She looked over to Brik, then back to Jarell. "I might not know as much about the Morthans as you claim to, but I know Commander Brik—and I know from my experience of him that the Morthans have a code of honor. It isn't *our* code of honor, but it is such a rigid discipline that they would rather die than suffer dishonor. If we were to unleash such a weapon on the Morthan Solidarity as you are suggesting, it would be an act so vile, so disgraceful, so detestable in their eyes that they would feel justified in retaliating with even greater horrors against us."

"What greater horrors are there than what they've already done to us?" Jarell demanded.

"I don't know," snapped Parsons. "And I don't want to find out."

"These are evil beings, Captain! They're not human—they're monsters. Terrible and vicious and utterly ruthless. We have to be even more ruthless. We have to be a thousand times more dangerous! We have to do this, Captain."

Parsons placed her hands flat on the table and glowered down the length of the room. "As convenient as it is to regard the Morthans as the spawn of hell, as demonic beings driven by satanic furies—as satisfying as it might be to regard the enemy as less than human and thereby worthy of our rage and enmity and hatred—I must tell you . . . that's a way of thinking that does not serve us. Our job is to *stop* the enemy—not *become* him. Commander Jarell, this is one weapon that human beings *must not* unleash. Not here. Not anywhere. Not now. Not ever. It violates all possible standards of decency and justice."

Jarell's response was surprisingly calm. He quietly repeated, "We have to do this, Captain. We've come too far to stop now."

"I see," said Parsons, coming to a conclusion. "You never had any authorization for this part of the mission, did you?"

"We were supposed to hold ourselves in a state of readiness. Why would the Fleet authorize the preparation of such a capability if they weren't prepared to use it?"

"I repeat. You have no authorization to proceed, do you?"

"I have a *moral* authorization," said Jarell. "We all do. Our mission is to preserve and protect the Alliance. We have the capability to end this war now. And when the last Morthan world dies, writhing in agony, a grateful Alliance will thank us for our wisdom!"

"I sincerely doubt that," said Parsons. She glanced to Blintze. "Doctor, you haven't said a word yet. Do you agree with Commander Jarell's goals?"

Blintze's face was in his hands. His eyes were covered. What he had been thinking during this entire meeting was unknowable. Now, he just shook his head, back and forth. He lowered his hands and his eyes were red and puffy. "I don't know what to think anymore," he said. "This isn't what I signed on for. Oh, no—yes, it is—but I lied to myself. I thought I was searching for a cure. I—I think I always knew there was a military possibility, but I lied to myself about it because . . . because I didn't believe it would ever get that far. And then it was too late. I'm sorry, Captain."

Parsons nodded, satisfied that she finally had some sense of what was happening here. She glanced over to the tall Morthan Security Chief. "Commander Brik, place these men under arrest."

The Vial

Brik was standing at the ready, but he made no move to advance on Jarell. Instead, he spoke quietly to his headset. "Security is on the way."

Jarell didn't even blink. "I'm not surprised. I should have expected it. I knew the Solidarity would try to stop us. They sabotaged our LENNIE. And they sent this ship—the *Star Wolf*—to make sure the bloodworms were neutralized. The Judas ship. You're betraying the Alliance again. First you lead the Morthan fleet to the Silk Road Convoy. Now you destroy our last, best chance to strike back. Oh yes, they've infected you with their thinking. Code of honor? New Geneva Convention? All that crap. That's their way of limiting our actions while they ignore the rules of conduct and sweep across the Alliance. The deaths of billions of human beings will be on your conscience, Captain Parsons! Everything is perfectly clear now. I see who *really* runs this ship—" He spat in Brik's direction.

"Commander Brik," Parsons said quietly. "We'll need restraints for Commander Jarell."

"No, you don't!" Jarell stood up, backing away.

The hatch popped open then, and four security officers entered. Bach, Shibano, Armstrong and Easton. They had their weapons drawn. "Take Commander Jarell into custody," Brik ordered. "Try not to hurt him."

"Captain—!" That was Blintze.

Jarell had backed up against the bulkhead. He had reached into his coat and pulled out a small vial—*filled with pink and gold flickers.* He held it out before him like a shield.

"—he's got plasmacytes!"

"Don't anyone come any closer!"

Parsons and Korie both came to their feet, horrified. "Don't anyone move—don't anyone do anything stupid."

"A containment bottle," explained Jarell. "We developed these on the *Norway*. I didn't know if it would work—coming through the suppressor fields and the repulsors—but it did. Now I can see I was wise to do so. Captain Parsons, I am going to complete my mission. And you're going to help me. Or you'll have plasmacytes on the *Star Wolf*."

"We already have plasmacytes on the *Star Wolf*. On the hull."

"That's not a problem," Jarell replied. "Hull alloy is a natural containment. That's where we got the idea for these—" He held up the bottle."

"If you release those," Parsons said, "You'll die too."

Jarell shrugged. "I'm not afraid to die for my beliefs." He added, "And if I'm not afraid to sacrifice my life for the cause, I have no problem sacrificing your lives as well." He grasped the top of the vial. "Unless you deliver this ship to Morthan space . . . I will break the seal."

Blintze spoke now. He advanced quietly on Jarell and spoke in a voice that was half-whisper, half-croak. "You're doing it again! Aren't you? Haven't you learned anything from what happened to the *Norway*?"

"Yes, I have," said Jarell. "I've learned not to trust anyone else." He stepped forward, holding the vial before him. "I mean it, Captain. Set a course across the rift."

Parsons looked to Korie, looked to Brik, looked back to Jarell. "Can we talk about this?"

"There's nothing left to say. The time for talk is over." Holding the vial before him, one hand on the seal, Jarell moved toward the door—and the Bridge.

The Bridge

"Let him pass," said Parsons.

Brik frowned at the instruction, but he gestured to the security team. They backed carefully out of the way as Jarell stepped through the door into the corridor. "Come on, Blintze!" he called.

The haggard scientist made his way embarrassedly across the wardroom, muttering "excuse me, excuse me," as he pushed past Parsons and Brik. "I'm sorry, Captain. Really, I am."

Parsons followed him into the corridor. Korie started to follow after her but Brik reached down, grabbed his shoulder and pushed him aside so he could follow the captain—and Jarell. He gave Korie one of those looks that could have meant anything but probably meant *let me handle this.* He ducked down to fit through the door, then Korie followed. He glanced over his shoulder and motioned for the security team to keep behind him.

When he stepped out onto the Command Deck, he saw that Jarell had parked himself in the executive officer's chair—a breach of etiquette so gross that Korie couldn't believe the man had done it deliberately. He had to be ignorant of the ways of the ship. Unless . . . he wanted to send a message. The glittering vial was nowhere in sight. Blintze stood glumly behind Jarell.

Parsons was just sitting down in her own chair. "Commander Tor? Would you please prepare a set of courses for Commander Jarell's inspection?"

Tor swiveled around in her chair to stare at the captain with a questioning expression. *Excuse me?*

"We want to cross the rift and dive into the heart of the Morthan sphere."

The look on Tor's face went from curiosity to disbelief. *Is he crazy or are you?*

"Commander Jarell has a very convincing argument," Parsons said, without explaining.

Korie glanced sideways to Brik. The big Morthan was standing in the Ops Deck so he could be eye-to-eye with those on the Command Deck. "I really hate it," Korie said dryly. "I hate being convinced like this."

"The Cinnabar Option?" Brik asked.*

"Too dangerous," Korie said. "And too messy." *And besides, HAR-LIE is down.*

"Captain . . . ?" said Tor, fumbling for the right words. There were none.

Jarell reached into his jacket and pulled out the biotube. He held it up high so everyone on the Bridge could see it. For a moment, the Bridge was silent—except for the usual background hum of ship sounds.

Korie glanced backward. Bach and Shibano were in front of the hatch, Easton and Armstrong were still in the corridor; they all had their weapons out. Korie held a hand low to indicate caution. He noticed that Easton was trembling—he had to do something. And quickly. He stepped forward and said, "Captain, I didn't have a chance to tell you before. The warp core of the number two engine has to be flushed. The micro-stabilizer fields have been lethetically compromised and Chief Leen needs to do a suborchial inter-alignment on the bivalve spline. We can't run with a gelatinous wobbly."

Parsons blinked at him as if he'd just said, "*The gostak distims the doshes.*" And then, without blinking, she replied crisply, "I specifically told Chief Leen not to flush the warp core in a stress-field depression. That's why the bivalve is misaligned! You can't get the revolvitrons stabilized in a gravitational perplex! Where the hell did he learn engine deconstruction! Goddammit. I don't want excuses. I want results." She turned to Jarell, and her tone became sweetly apologetic. "I'm sorry, Commander. We're not going anywhere for awhile."

"It's all right, Captain," he replied. "I'm sure you and Commander Korie can reconfigure the double-talk generator in no time. Certainly before I've decided on a course." He wasn't fooled.

Parsons didn't even acknowledge the failure. Her voice became more business-like. "It'll take several days to get free of the gravitational

---
The Voyage of the Star Wolf.

effects of the red star. We won't be able to enter hyperstate for a week. Are you planning to stay awake the whole time? It's two months to cross the rift. You're going to have to sleep sometime."

Jarell nodded. "I understand you had your HARLIE unit simulating our LENNIE."

"Yes, and it drove the poor unit psychotic. We'll be decontaminating it for months."

"I have a better idea. Let's bring it back online. We'll use the LENNIE programs to stand watch over me while I sleep."

"I don't think that's a good idea," said Korie.

"I do," said Jarell. "Discussion's over."

Korie looked to Parsons. She nodded. Korie said, "I'll get to it right away," and remained where he was standing.

"What about the plasmacytes on the hull of our ship, Commander?"

Jarell shook his head, a gesture of dismissal. "That's how we'll infect the Morthan worlds—we'll dive through their upper atmospheres and leave a trail of infection. By the time the plasmacytes drift down to the ground, we'll be long gone."

"I meant—won't they eat through our hull?"

"No. The radiation shields are a natural containment. As long as you don't lower them, we're safe."

"And after our mission is over, how will we get off the ship safely?"

"Don't worry about that either. There's a cure."

"No, there isn't. We searched the *Norway*. The biotubes were empty."

Jarell shook his head. "You didn't find it, that's all."

Parsons looked away, momentarily at a loss, trying to figure out what she could say next. For the first time, she noticed the security team behind Korie. She bit her lip, then looked across to Brik. "Commander Brik. Let's be very careful here. I don't want anyone trying anything stupid."

"I appreciate that, Captain," Jarell said. He turned around in his chair and looked past the captain, past Korie—to the security team waiting at the hatch. "You're dismissed." They didn't move.

Korie nodded to them. "Pull back."

Bach and Shibano started to back away. They ducked through the hatch. Armstrong moved to follow them—but Easton stayed where he was, pointing his stinger pistol directly at Jarell's head. "Let me do it, Captain! Just give the word!"

Confession

Without taking his eyes from Jarell, Easton spoke to Captain Parsons in a voice that was harrowing in its desperation—and its deadly certitude. "I can drill him right through the eyes. He'll be dead before he has a chance to break the seal." He stepped closer to Jarell.

Jarell held the vial up so Easton could see the top. "Look, stupid—see that button? It's a doomsday trigger. If my heart stops, the seal explodes, the vial shatters."

"No problem," Easton said. Still aiming the weapon at Jarell's head, he reached over with his other hand and adjusted the target setting. "I'll set for wide-beam stun."

Parsons took a step forward. "Daniel. Put that stinger down. Now."

"I'm sorry, Captain—I can't. Give me the order, *please*."

Jarell looked over to Parsons. "You realize, of course, what will happen when that stinger beam hits this vial. Even on the lowest level, it will provide enough energy for the wavicles to escape the containment bottle."

"Don't do it, son," Parsons said. She didn't want to make it an order—because if he disobeyed it, she'd ultimately have to prosecute him for insubordination. Or worse. And she didn't want to do that.

Thinking quickly, Korie stepped into the space between Jarell and Easton. He looked directly into Easton eyes. "You'll have to shoot through me, Dan." Jarell took advantage of the opportunity to take a cautious step back.

"Why are you protecting him?! He's a walking LENNIE."

"I'm not protecting him. I'm protecting *you*."

"I'm trying to do my duty—"

"Not this way. Dan, listen to me. I know what you're going through—"

"No, you don't. You've never been bonded."

"I was married. And my wife was the most special person in the universe to me. And our children were our greatest joy. So don't tell me what I don't know. But let the Fleet handle this. I promise you, Yonah Jarell isn't going to hurt anyone ever again. Dan! Give me the stinger."

Armstrong took a step out of the hatch and called softly, "Danny, please. Please, listen."

Easton shook his head. "The man is evil. The man doesn't deserve to live. Captain, give the order."

Korie whispered, "Dan, we can't afford the luxury of revenge. Hate is a disease. I don't want the *Star Wolf* infected with it any more than I want this ship infected with plasmacytes. Hate made the plasmacytes. Is that what you want to continue?"

And Armstrong took a step forward and said softly, "Is this what Paul would have done? Do you think he would have wanted you to kill in his name? If he were here, what do you think he would say?"

Easton wavered, undecided. And then—he blinked. And blinked again.

Standing in front of him was Paul Berryman. Alive. Healthy. Sparkling. "Honey, I'm home," he said.

"Paul—"

"Dan, shut up and listen to me. I'm only dead. I'm not gone. Everything that we ever had together, it's still right here—inside of us. Don't piss it away on him. He's not worth it."

"Let me kill him for you—"

"Don't kill anyone for me, Danny. That's not the legacy I want." And then he added, "And if you do that . . . I'm not sure I can come back again—"

Easton sagged. "Damn you! Damn you!" Abruptly he swung his arm sideways and held the stinger pistol out to his side, where Korie took it gratefully from his hand. *"Attaboy, Danny,"* someone whispered. Armstrong? Berryman?

Korie handed the weapon sideways—to Parsons—and grabbed Easton before he could collapse unconscious to the floor. "Call Williger! My God, he's burning up—"

And at the same time, someone else was screaming too. It was Jarell: "What the hell are you doing?!!"

Blintze had grabbed the glittering little vial out of Jarell's hand, and now, as everyone watched, he popped it into a pressure-spray injector.

Before anyone could stop him, he applied it directly to his forearm—the telltale hiss told the entire story.

"You stupid asshole! What have you done?!"

Blintze ignored him. "Captain Parsons, I believe I've just solved the plasmacyte problem. Will you please have me transferred over to the *Norway*?"

Jarell screamed. "You disloyal traitor!"

"No, Yonah. It's over. Enough is enough. No more killing. No more." He looked to Parsons hurriedly. "We have a limited amount of time, Captain. Only a few minutes before these things turn into bloodworms."

Williger entered the Ops Deck from the forward hatch. She came around the side of the main display, followed by two Quillas—one carrying an emergency kit, the other carrying a stretcher. They headed straight for the Command Deck.

Parsons was already calling out orders. "Security—take Commander Jarell to the brig. And Easton and Blintze to Med Bay."

Bach and Shibano had already seized Jarell. Now, as they escorted—almost dragged—him off the Bridge, Blintze turned back to Parsons. "No, Captain. The transfer tube."

"We can save you!" And then she added, "I think." She looked to Williger. "He's got plasmacytes in his bloodstream."

"Get him to the Med Bay. Fast!"

"No. Get me to the transfer tube. I don't want to be saved, Captain. I don't want to grow old listening to my conscience. Listen, I made a mistake. I trusted Jarell. And the *Norway* died. All of my friends and colleagues died." Blintze's whole demeanor had changed in the last few moments—he no longer looked like a man with a death sentence. His eyes were alive with enthusiasm. "I'll tell you what we discovered. The plasmacytes are something beautiful. Not a war weapon at all—but a kind of life that's marvelous to see. The Regulans perverted it. We can cure it. We can heal it." He spread his hands wide in an act of supplication. "Captain Parsons, this is where the sickness stops. All the hate. All the dying."

"This is a death sentence, Dr. Blintze."

"No, it isn't. It's a *life* sentence. Do you want to know why you couldn't find the cure on the *Norway*? Because it isn't there. I had it all the time."

"Then why didn't you *use* it?"

"Because . . ." Blintze spread his hands in a gesture of helplessness. "Because . . . I had to hide it from LENNIE. A LENNIE isn't just paranoid, it's a death-engine. It's a killing machine. It hates life. The only way to work with a LENNIE is to show it that you're inventing new ways to kill. Make yourself a partner in death. Serve LENNIE or die. If LENNIE had realized that I had saved the cure, he would have destroyed the *Norway*, and it would have been lost forever—all the research, everything. I didn't want that to happen."

"It would have been better all around if it had," said Parsons, starting to feel annoyed.

Blintze ignored her. He continued quickly, "I had to synthesize it in isolation—pretending to be doing something else the whole time; but LENNIE figured out what I was up to and let the plasmacytes loose. But he only thought I'd completed the theoretical part. He didn't realize I'd only been writing down my notes on things to test *after* I'd already performed the experiments. That was the only way I could leave a trail. It almost worked. When you arrived, I realized I had to find a way to get it off the ship and out of LENNIE's reach. I almost told you when I came aboard—but then your HARLIE unit swore at me and I realized I couldn't trust it either. Somehow LENNIE had infected it. So I injected myself with the cure because . . . because I couldn't think of any better place to hide it. And now that you know, you need to get me off this ship and onto the *Norway*, where I can try to make a difference. And I'll need a stinger pistol with a self-destruct timer on it, please."

"It's suicide," said Parsons.

"I've earned the right."

"Nobody's earned the right to decide when a life should end."

"You can believe that if you want. I believe otherwise. Captain, we're wasting time."

"I think you're really afraid of what a Board of Inquiry will do to you," she replied.

"Maybe so. But we're still wasting time."

"Suicide is the coward's way out, Blintze. It's nothing more than a way to say 'fuck you' to the universe."

"Fine," said Blintze. "Believe that too. But we're still wasting time."

Parsons looked away. She looked to Williger—the doctor was already bent over Easton, applying several small devices to his chest and arms. She glanced up long enough to say, "It's triage. Let him go."

Parsons looked to Korie. Korie closed his eyes and nodded his agreement.

"All right, Dr. Blintze. Have it your way." She offered him the stinger she still held. "Mr. Korie, please escort Dr. Blintze to the transfer tube. Have Chief Leen activate the repulsor fields immediately. Send a robot over first—have it destroy the *Norway*'s power supply—I don't want LENNIE out of commission, I want him dead."

"Thank you, Captain—"

"Don't thank me. I'm not doing it for you." Blintze nodded an acknowledgment and started to step past her. She stopped him with a look and added, "I'm a Catholic. I believe that suicides go to Hell. I'm supposed to try to stop you. But I can't. My only real regret here is that you're not taking Yonah Jarell with you."

"If you want—" Blintze started to offer.

"Just get the hell off my ship. As fast as you can." She turned away deliberately.

When she was sure that Korie had escorted Blintze safely off the Bridge, she turned to Williger; the two Quillas were just lifting Easton's unconscious body onto the stretcher. "Will he be all right?"

"He's suffering a triple-whammy of aftereffects, but yes—I think so."

"Good. Dr. Williger, I don't want to court-martial this man. Find me a reason not to. Now, who's on Chaplain duty? I've just been an accessory to a mortal sin and I need to go to confession."

"Wait till tonight, when I'm on duty," growled Williger, following the stretcher aft. "I'll make sure that your penance will be the worst in your life."

"Bring an extra glass. I think Korie will be joining us—"

Transformation

On the Bridge of the *Norway*, Makkle Blintze stood alone. He had a camera and a scanner. He set the remote down in the center of the Ops Deck and looked around. The light from the camera filled the Bridge, but it cast dark shadows that left gloomy corners behind everything.

Around him swirled a quiet hurricane of pink and gold flickers. Some of them drifted toward him—and into him. Others danced in the air. There were so many, he could almost hear them.

"Can you see me?" he asked. "Can you hear me?"

"We have monitoring," Korie's voice came back to him.

"Good," said Blintze. He opened the seals on his starsuit. "I'm taking off my headset now. And as you can see, the forward display is off. The entire Bridge is dead, so I can't see you or hear you anymore. I'll keep reporting for as long as I can. I don't think this is going to take very long. I'm the only warm body left on the ship and every wavicle aboard is trying to get to me. It's almost as if they can tell I have what they want. The worms are creeping this way too. But I don't think they'll get here in time. As soon as I'm sure the bloodworms inside my body have been infected with the recombinant genes, I'm going to activate the self-destruct on the stinger. That will guarantee the creation of recombinant wavicles. I've got a low-level scanner here. I can't scan myself, but I can scan for residual radiation, and we'll be looking for telltale spikes in the ultra-high and ultra-low bands. Stand by."

Blintze stepped up onto the Command Deck and balanced the scanner on the executive officer's chair. Then he lowered himself respectfully into the captain's chair. "Nice. I like it. It's a throne. A feeling of power, almost." He held out his arms and waved them, making swirls of wavicles in the air. "It doesn't hurt. It tickles a little, but I expected that. It's kind of . . . sensual. Oh, hell, why am I being modest now? It's a very sexual feeling, like that tingle you get just before orgasm. Only it just keeps going and going without ever going anywhere.

"When I was a child, I used to wonder how I would die—it terrified me. Not the dying, but the loss of control it represented. I admit it, I've always been fascinated by the idea of suicide—of knowing how and when I would die. And why. At least this is a noble death. Maybe as noble as I can achieve." He fell silent for a moment, lost in thought, then after a long pause, began speaking again. "Sorry about that. The truth is, I don't have any right to claim nobility. I participated in something dreadful—a weapon of mass destruction. Possibly the greatest sin a human being can commit. And all the self-justifications and rationalizations and excuses and reasons and explanations . . . aren't worth a bucket of warm shit. The truth is, I let myself be a very ordinary person, just going along, being led, doing what I was told—not willing to take a stand. Not willing to make waves—but certainly willing to make wavicles . . . Until now, when it's almost too late. And anything worthwhile I might say or do now is going to be outvoted by a lifetime of cowardice. I guess this is a deathbed conversion. And therefore worthless. It undoes nothing.

"What I'm doing now . . . it's not redemption at all. You were right, Captain Parsons. I'm taking the coward's way out. I suppose I should apologize, but the scientist in me wants to believe that the cure will work . . . and this at least lets us complete the experiment. And maybe someday, someone will say that this much at least was a contribution to science. Or humanity. Or knowledge. Or something. I don't know. Shit. I don't know what to say. I wasted my life and I'm sorry. And I hope someday, somehow, someone will forgive me. Say a prayer for me, maybe. Catholics believe in redemption, Captain, don't they? I don't. I never did. But here I am at the last minute, begging . . . just in case."

He got up and started walking around the Bridge again. "There's something going on with the wavicles. Something beautiful. I don't know if you can see it, but I'm seeing shades of colors here I've never seen before. Very delicate. Like sparkles off a diffraction grating, only brighter. If I close my eyes, I can still see them, brighter than ever. I don't think we perceive the wavicles through light. I think they directly stimulate the retinal cells as they pass through us. Just a guess. Someone else will have to figure that part out."

He climbed back up onto the Command Deck and peered at the scanner. "I'm starting to get telltales. That's good. It means I can set the stinger to self-destruct anytime. I'm setting it now. I'm not in any pain. Not really. It's like when your leg falls asleep, only it's my whole body that tingles.

"Can you see this?" he asked, not expecting an answer. He waved his arms around, leaving swirls of sparkles flickering in the air. "They're clustering around me, aren't they?"

The pinpoint sparkles were no longer swirling about the man. Now they were drifting toward him, accelerating as they approached, arrowing inward, sleeting through him like arrows of light. He lifted his arms to the ceiling, standing in the center of his own aurora borealis. He radiated like a saint. The air around him crackled and glowed. Blintze stopped talking. He turned slowly, savoring his moment of transformation.

He was enveloped in light now, almost disappearing into the center of a sphere of brightness—both gauzy and crystalline. The sparkles turned and twisted around him, dancing in the air like fairy-dust motes. Blintze was barely visible within the pinpoint fireworks, his face rapturous.

And then the stinger discharged itself—

—and the lights *blazed* outward in a marvelous explosion of color and amazement. If light could be said to have emotion, this light was *joyous*. It swirled around the Bridge of the *Norway* in a fiery dance of awakening, self-awareness, discovery, redemption and epiphany. It swirled through the ship, climbing, diving, dipping, twirling and *singing—*

Realization

On the Bridge of the *Star Wolf*, Korie reacted first. He switched the main display to show an exterior view of the *Norway*. This was taken from high on one of the *Star Wolf*'s spars. Both ships were still outlined with wavicles, but now the sparkles were agitated, trembling in anticipation—and then, abruptly, it was as if the *Norway* was leaking light from a thousand places.

"The stinger blast must have punctured her hull," said Parsons.

Curls of light, swept up and out of the starship—like smoke with a purpose, like something alive. "My God," said Tor. "What is it?"

Brik knew, but he wouldn't speak it. He did something uncharacteristic for a Morthan. He sat down. He put one hand over his mouth, a Morthan sign of . . . awe. Amazement and recognition filled his eyes. But nobody noticed; they were staring forward.

It was Korie who dared speak it. "I think . . . I think it's a sparkle-dancer."

He glanced around the Bridge, as if daring anyone to disagree—but every face was rapturous in the reflected light of the display. At the communications console, Green was listening to his headset. Suddenly he said, "It's singing to us!" He put the radio noise of the sparkle-dancer on the speakers. At first it sounded like a roar of static, then it sounded like the ocean, and then . . . it sounded like something else: something *joyous* and *grateful* and *alive!*

The sparkle-dancer flowed out of the *Norway*, wrapping itself around the ship, curious and delighted—as if dancing, exploring, even making love. Wherever the sparkle-dancer touched, it gathered all the wavicles into itself. It swept the hulls of both ships clean. It flowed from the *Norway* onto the *Star Wolf*. Tendrils of light tickled the starship like a harpist striking chords.

When it had finished exploring the hulls of both vessels, when it had finished collecting every errant particle of itself, the sparkle-dancer flowed off the *Star Wolf* and reformed itself on the port side of the ship. For the first time, the crew saw it as it existed naturally in space—a veil of luminescence, shimmering and coruscating with all the colors of the rainbow. Its wings flickered and sparkled with myriad tiny pinpoints as its component wavicles winked in and out of existence—tiny energy mites whirling and dancing. The sparkle-dancer was a colony of rapturous butterflies of light.

"They'll never believe us," said Korie.

"Who cares?" laughed Parsons.

The sparkle-dancer curled one last time around the *Star Wolf*, almost as if hugging the vessel farewell—and then it whirled off again, flashing a dazzling bouquet of colors. It twirled alone for a moment longer, almost wistfully, as if it were waving goodbye, and then it vanished into the star-studded darkness.

For the longest moment, no one spoke.

And then Parsons whispered, "I believe we are the luckiest human beings alive." There were tears of joy and delight in her eyes.

The Stars

Captain Parsons stepped back up to the Command Deck and sat down in her chair. For the last time. She ran her hands along the arm rests, savoring the sensation of ownership. For a while, the Bridge crew worked in silence. No one wanted to break the mood. But finally, Captain Parsons turned to her executive officer. "Mr. Korie, has Chief Leen finished misaligning the bivalve spline?"

"Funny thing, he just completed it, Captain."

"Isn't that convenient," Parsons said, deadpan. "*Now hear this. Stand down from Condition Yellow. All departments, initiate immediate pre-hyperstate maintenance. I want us ready to go as soon as we're clear.*"

Then she added, "I want to commend all of you for the quality of your service during these past few very difficult days. Crew of the *Star Wolf*, it has been a genuine privilege to serve with you. Your professional performance, your selfless dedication and your untiring courage are truly inspiring. I am proud of you—very proud." She paused a moment, wondering if there was anything else to add, decided that there was not and concluded with an oddly permanent sounding, "*That is all.*"

Captain Parsons glanced over to her executive officer, who was looking at her curiously. She patted the arms of her chair—for the last time—and rose. "Mr. Korie, may I see you in the wardroom please?" She picked up her clipboard and led the way.

Korie followed her aft, into the corridor called "Broadway," past the Communications Bay and into the Officers' Mess. As he entered, he saw that Captain Parsons was unpinning the stars from her uniform. "Here," she said, offering them to Korie.

"Captain—?"

"My penance. For my sins. Which have been considerable. I'm removing myself from active command, pending further inquiry. I'm giving you a field promotion. I have the authority to do this, you know."

"Captain, I don't—" Korie looked at her, flustered—and yet, at the same time, his mind was racing through a forest of reasons, explanations, possibilities *and hopes*"—understand," he finished lamely.

"Yes, you do," Parsons said, taking his hand and dropping her stars into them. "Think about it. I have. And I know you have too. Board of Inquiry. Court-martial . . ." Her expression was sad but knowing. "You know the arguments. Violation of general orders. Bold initiative doesn't excuse. Put the ship and the crew at risk. Important strategic breakthrough. But an unfortunate precedent to set. Tsk, tsk, tsk. Must assert chain of command. Can't allow dereliction of principle. Have to maintain authority. However, Fleet Command *will* acknowledge good intentions. Here's a distinguished service medal. But of course, you'll never command a starship again. Right?"

"Uh—" Korie nodded his agreement. "Right."

"So, I'm going to present them with a *fait accompli*. I'm taking myself out of the food chain. They can still do the inquiry and the court-martial, if they want to—but I don't think they'll want to open that can of bloodworms. Because it leads to questions they won't want to ask and they certainly won't like having to answer. And definitely not in public. Like who sent Jarell out here in the first place?"

"They'll never let this get public," Korie said, thinking forward about the inevitable consequences. "They can't. Jarell's agenda—it's too dangerous. He's not the only one who thinks that way. This is a cancerous idea—it'll take root among extremists and spread from there. And if enough people get scared enough about the war, they'll start demanding implementation. I think you're right. Fleet Command has to bury this—the whole thing. Maybe even the cure as well."

"Mmm." Parsons nodded thoughtfully. "We've been heroes, Jon. All of us. Inventive. Courageous. And most of all, *wise*. What we did here is the stuff of military legend. And no one will ever know." She smiled sadly. "But the lack of acknowledgment doesn't diminish what we did. It doesn't invalidate our heroism in any way." Her eyes shone brightly now. "You know what we did out here, the crew knows—and Fleet Command will know. And maybe, just maybe, they'll find a way to honor the ship in exchange for your convenient silence—maybe give you some sweetheart duty somewhere and a fistful of medals and bounties. Maybe even the bloodworm bounty—but without public credit. You can live with that, can't you? It'll probably be part of the deal."

Korie shook his head. "This ship is never going to get credit, Captain—not for anything but the mauling at Marathon. And as long as we have that reputation, they can't give us any duty or reward that will make people ask questions."

"Take the money anyway. It's a big pot, and it'll pay for a lot of solace. I've already filed the application for the bounty. I expect you'll get it, and I expect them to trade my silence for my retirement. The bounty for the ship will be part of it. It's a fair bargain, Korie. Your stars will be part of the deal, I'll make sure of it."

"No, it isn't a fair bargain," Korie said, finally handing the stars back. "You're a good captain. The fleet needs you. It's going to be a long war—"

"And I've done my part in it. I've helped us keep one little piece of our soul and one little piece of our integrity. Here, take these stars. Honor me by wearing them." She offered them again.

Korie shook his head. "Captain, I'd be proud to wear your stars. Only—"

"Only what?" Parsons frowned.

"Only . . . I don't deserve them."

The captain's reaction was short and to the point. "Bullshit."

Korie held his ground. "Captain Parsons. I can't begin to tell you how much I want those stars. But I can't put them on. No—hear me out. Do you remember in the wardroom, when Jarell was telling us what kind of a threat the Morthans represented? *I was agreeing with him.* And when he said, let's go scourge the Morthans, *I wanted to do it too!* It would have been justice for all the folks at Shaleen and Taalamar. And I *wanted* to do it."

"So did I," said Parsons quietly.

Korie looked up sharply.

"I want a weapon to use against the Morthans, just as deeply as you, Korie. And I wanted to strike back at them just as much as you. And probably so does every other person on this starship. I could have given the order. We could have gone. You might have questioned it. I know Williger certainly would have. But we'd have gone. And we'd have devastated as many Morthan worlds as we could until their ships caught us and destroyed us—but not all of them. We could never hit every Morthan planet. And that's the flaw in this plan. We'd be leaving survivors, whole worlds of Morthan warriors who would know exactly what we had done—and the dishonor of the deed. If we were fast enough and smart enough, we might even have made it home. And we would have been heroes. For the moment. But it would have been only an illusory triumph. You know as well as I what would have happened after that, Jon, don't you?"

Korie nodded.

Parsons said it anyway. "The bloodworms would have come back to us—on Morthan suicide ships. And this time, the Morthans would have no strategic reason to hold back. Their ships would penetrate to the heart of the Alliance and they'd infest every world they could get to. We wouldn't be heroes. We'd be villains—the ones who let the firestorm out of the bottle. So as much as I *wanted* to do it—strategically, I knew why I shouldn't."

"I had those same thoughts," Korie admitted.

"Of course," said Parsons. "Your ability to consider consequences is what makes you so formidable."

"But I also kept thinking how satisfying it would be to strike back."

"So did I," Parsons agreed. "You might make mistakes, Korie, but you don't make *stupid* ones. At least, I haven't seen any evidence of it. If you had been captain here, what would you have done?"

Korie considered it. "As much as I wanted revenge, as much as I want to destroy the Morthan Solidarity, as *good* as it would have felt . . . I don't think I would have let my emotions overwhelm my wisdom. There was something terribly wrong there, something wrong with the whole mission—with the thinking behind it. It was based on hate. I couldn't let Jarell do this out of hate. And there was no other reason to do it. None at all. So it was wrong."

"*That's* what qualifies you, Korie. Your ability to keep your *self* out of the process."

"But, Captain—I didn't keep my self out of the process. I wasn't thinking about the Fleet, and I wasn't thinking about my orders, and I wasn't thinking about my oath or my responsibilities. I only thought about what would be best for the war, as if I were the only one fighting it. And more than once, Admiral O'Hara told me that's a large part of what's keeping me from my promotion—that I keep trying to fight this war by myself. She's right. I did it again here. That's the way my mind works. So if you give me those stars, and if I accept them, and if Fleet Command lets me keep them, then what? What if next time I'm not so wise? What if next time I follow my heart instead of my wisdom?"

Parsons sighed. "You want to know the truth, Jon? There are no guarantees. None of the great captains are ever as good as they want to be. So they keep trying to do better. That's what makes them great. They don't settle for being ordinary. Neither do you. When the next time comes, you'll remember *this* time. And that'll be enough to make the difference."

"I hope you're right," Korie said, with a hint of doubt as well as sadness.

"You want to know the truth about human beings?" she asked abruptly. She stepped in close. "Most of us don't have very much integrity. We pretend we do, but we're always negotiating little loopholes for ourselves, little excuses to be less than we are. And that's true of everybody, all of us. The only difference between ordinary and extraordinary is not accepting that as normal. That's the heart of brightness. We defend our little specks of integrity with enormous ferocity because we know how little there really is. That's what makes you extraordinary, Jon Korie." She took his hand and placed her stars in the center of his palm.

Korie heard the words as if Parsons was inscribing them into his soul. He nodded in thoughtful acceptance, staring down at the insignia. They felt strangely heavy in his hand. She was right. Of course, she was. When he looked up again, his expression was wry as well as rueful. He held up the stars. "You know, of course, that the admiral isn't going to let me keep these."

The Captain

"*Captain* Korie." Parsons' tone had an edge to it sharp enough to slice diamond. "This ship has come a long way since the mauling at Marathon. Just about every officer in the fleet knows what she's been through, knows how you've held her together, knows how you've earned your stars five times over. Do you know that there are captains who will not accept command of this vessel—?"

"Sure. It's been that way since—"

"In the past, yes—they didn't want command of a disgraced ship. But now, there are officers who won't accept command of the *Star Wolf* because she's rightfully *your* ship. They've told the admiral as much—that it would be inappropriate for them to serve over you, because you've demonstrated better qualifications than a lot of men and women who already have their stars."

Korie was embarrassed. He looked down at his shoes. He swallowed hard and looked up at Parsons again. "I didn't know that."

"Well, then, you're the only one. Hell, Korie, I told O'Hara that myself—that I couldn't take this ship with you still as exec. It was embarrassing. She gave me hell for it. She offered me a choice—this ship or a demotion. So this is my way of handing it back to her."

"You're using me to embarrass the admiral, aren't you?"

"Absolutely." Parsons grinned. "You're not a political animal, Korie; you don't get it. When this ship comes back with you in command, it'll be my way of sending a message to Fleet Command that I'm impudent—that I won't roll over easily. So put on the damn stars and take command of your ship. I'd order you to do it, but I can't. I've resigned. Effective with taking them off. Right now this ship has no captain. Unless you put those stars on. So what are you going to do?"

Korie allowed himself a soft smile. "Well, when you put it that way—" He began fumbling with his collar.

Parsons stopped him. "Wait a minute, let's get some witnesses in here. There are a couple of people who will kill us both, if we do this ceremony without their participation." She spoke into her headset, "Tor, Brik, Williger, Leen, Goldberg and Shibano to the wardroom, on the double!" Turning back to Korie, she slid her clipboard across the table toward him. "Let's take care of the paper work. I have to sign your promotion, hand over command, and then you have to accept my resignation. Here, sign here, here and here." As Korie signed, the others began filing into the wardroom with curious expressions on their faces. Parsons held up a hand for silence and motioned them to line up against the wall.

"What's going on?" Leen asked, coming in last.

"Shh," said Williger. "Be a witness."

"Oh," mouthed Leen and took his place silently beside her.

Korie signed the last page and started to straighten up, but Parsons shoved one more at him. "This one too—this one absolves me of all responsibility." She smiled broadly.

Korie scanned the form, recognizing the oath it represented. It wasn't an official oath *per se*, but it was the oath of commitment that captains had been voluntarily taking almost since the first liberty ship was launched. "As captain of the starship, I recognize that I am the sole authority for her actions in war and in peace. I am charged with the well-being of her crew and the maintenance of her readiness. In every regard, I am the ship. I acknowledge and accept the responsibility."

Korie laid the stars down on the wardroom table and picked up the stylus. His hands felt clammy and the pen felt like an unfamiliar and alien thing. *This is really happening!* Somehow, he signed his name. And when he finished, and put the stylus down, and straightened up again, he could almost feel the difference in himself—as if a charge of energy, a new way of *being*, was suddenly coursing through his veins. He swallowed hard with the realization.

"Well, go ahead," said Parsons. "Put the stars on."

Still fumbling, Korie picked them up off the table. For some reason, his fingers weren't working quite right. He blinked. He was having a little trouble focusing. He wished Carol could have been here. And Mark and Robby—

"Here, let me," said Parsons, stepping close, ignoring the wetness at the corners of his eyes. She took the stars from his hand and clipped them easily to his collar. Finished, she stepped back again and offered him a crisp salute. And so did all the others. Tor. Leen. Williger. Goldberg. Shibano. Even Brik!

"Don't do that—" Korie started to say, then realized how stupid that would sound. He shut up and returned the salute proudly. The others in the wardroom burst into spontaneous applause.

Parsons stepped forward and shook his hand. "Congratulations, Captain Korie." She added, "Now, it's done. If the admiral makes you take *these* stars off, it'll be *her* embarrassment, not yours." And then they were surrounded by the others, lining up to shake his hand and congratulate him. Korie blinked away the tears quickly, so they wouldn't see how moved he was by their expressions of affection. He looked up—*and up*—at Brik. Even Brik was grinning; at least, Korie thought it was a grin—it was the most ghastly and uncomfortable expression he'd ever seen on a Morthan.

And then Parsons was at his side again. "I'd like to make the announcement to the crew—it's traditional in cases like this. Is that all right with you, Captain Korie?"

"Yes, please do." And then something else occurred to him. "Do you want to remain in the captain's cabin or would you prefer to move to a guest cabin?"

"It's your call, Captain—"

"Why don't you stay in the captain's cabin. As our . . . uh, Captain Emeritus."

"As your *guest*," Parsons corrected. "I promise I'll keep my mouth shut and only give you advice if you ask for it—or out of sight, if you're too stupid to ask. May I retain the privilege of standing watch on your Bridge?"

"Yes, ma'am. I'd be honored if you would." He looked proudly around the room. "Commander Tor, you'll take over as executive officer." He stopped and realized something else. "Oh, and schedule a memorial service immediately after dinner." He looked to Parsons. "Would you like to—?"

"I think that one is yours, Captain. You knew Hodel and Berryman better."

"Yes," Korie agreed. "I think I should. All right, what else is there we need to attend to?"

"You're the captain," said Tor, laughing. "*You tell us.*"

Epilogue

Upon dropping out of hyperstate, the *Star Wolf* had transmitted only the tersest of arrival messages: "*Norway* destroyed, fourteen survivors aboard. Two dead aboard *Star Wolf*. Log sealed. Eyes-only report. Will need substantial maintenance on intelligence engine." The admiral would understand what *wasn't* being said.

Now, as the *Star Wolf* locked her transfer tube into place against the reception bay of the stardock, the admiral's own terse reply was received on the Bridge. "Would the captain of the *Star Wolf* please report to the admiral's office immediately?"

Korie and Parsons were both on the Command Deck when the admiral's signal came in. Both were wearing their dress uniforms. They read the signal and exchanged conspiratorial glances. "I think she wants *your* report," Korie said.

"Uh-uh," said Parsons. "You're the captain of the *Star Wolf*. It's your report she wants."

"But she's expecting you."

"Oh, I'm sure she's going to want to see me—but she should see you first. Protocol, you know."

Korie nodded. He turned forward. "Lieutenant Green, send a signal to Admiral O'Hara. Eyes-only. 'With the *Star Wolf*'s respects, would the admiral please clarify which captain of the *Star Wolf* she wishes to report—Captain Korie or former Captain Parsons?' " He turned back to Parsons. "Her reply will tell us whether or not she's going to confirm my promotion."

"Are you making any bets?"

"Four times I've been in that woman's office, and four times I haven't gotten my stars. Based on her track record, I'm betting against myself."

"I'll bet *for*," said Parsons. "Loser pays for dinner at the most expensive club in town."

"Deal." Korie agreed. "You'd better apply for a loan, Captain. I'm in the mood for lobster."

Korie grinned. "And I'm in the mood for—I don't know what I'm in the mood for, but I promise it'll be expensive." Then he added, "It's been fun wearing these insignia, Captain Parsons. And it's been a privilege to serve with you. Thank you." He reached for his collar. "Perhaps you should take these back now—"

Parsons stopped him from removing the insignia. "Keep them, Captain. Whether the old bitch confirms you or not, you've earned those."

"Transfer tube is pressurized," reported Goldberg. "We are officially home."

"Thank you, Lieutenant. *Now hear this.* Executive Officer Tor will be posting shore leave schedules as soon as the ship is secured and locked down. Enjoy yourselves, but please remember, we want to be invited back. *That is all.*" Korie picked up his cap and tucked it under his arm. "I'm not going to keep her waiting. Commander Tor, you have the conn. I'm going over."

"Aye, Captain."

Korie traced the familiar path to the forward airlock. So many memories already. So many deaths. How many more? He shook the thoughts away and punched open the inner hatch of the airlock. The door popped shut behind him and the outer door opened into the transfer tube. It looked so innocent now. The last time he'd been through here—he thought it really would be the *last* time . . .

He crossed over to the stardock hatch and repeated the process of stepping through airlocks. There was a young boy waiting on the opposite side of the door; somebody's son, no doubt. He looked a lot like—no, don't think that way. But the boy was looking at him with curiosity too.

An out-of-breath voice behind him called, "Captain?" Reflexively, Korie turned backward to see. It was Brian Armstrong; he'd run the length of the ship and plunged through the airlocks. "We just heard from the admiral—your promotion has been confirmed! She wants to speak to you, *immediately.*"

And then *another* voice yanked his attention forward again. *"Daddy—!"*

Korie spun, caught between two moments—
"*Captain Korie?* What should I tell her?"

But Korie didn't hear. He was wrapping his son into his arms and crying with joy.

Author's Afterword

In 1988, I was hired to create a science fiction TV series for Universal Studios. The working title was *Millennium*. The mandate there was to create a show that could reuse the library of special-effects shots that had been created for *Battlestar Galactica*. (There were contractual reasons why they couldn't do another version of *B.G.*)

My gut-level reaction was to tell these folks that this was a particularly stupid idea; the science fiction audience is smart, they would immediately recognize the recycling as a cheap trick, and they would dismiss the show as cheap and not worth a second look. But I had a hunch that this challenge might also be used as a lever upward into something much more effective and profitable.

You see, the requirements of film production, whether television or theatrical, often determine their own solutions, and I had a strong feeling that if we got this show into production, we would have to design at least one new starship—the star of the series—build the miniature and shoot a new library of effects. In such a case, the *Battlestar Galactica* shots could be demoted, or even discarded. There was little question in my mind that the studio executives would eventually realize that the use of the older material would seriously weaken the look and feel of the new show.

From a production point of view, this was not an ideal prospect, but from a creative position, there was an enormous possibility here. If we could make it work, we would be creating an opportunity to tell some of the stories that a certain other science fiction show had shied away from. So I said, "Let's talk." I suggested several different formats for the show. One was "Space Traders." We would follow the adventures of a family of space gypsies, interstellar traders, as they traveled from planet to planet, buying and selling, wheeling and dealing, occasionally carrying passengers, sometimes being chased by the law, sometimes smuggling, and so on. It was not my favorite idea, but I wanted to offer the studio the appearance of options.

The second idea I suggested was the one I really wanted to do: "World War II in space." (I'm a history fanatic, and World War II is a particular obsession.) The folks at Universal got it immediately. I didn't even have to explain how it would work. ("See, it would be just like *Das Boot* or *The Enemy Below* or *Mr. Roberts*, only with spaceships.") It suited their needs, and it was a format that allowed for open-ended storytelling. We could expand the show in any direction we wanted.

The next step was to develop an outline.

In 1972, I had written a novel called *Yesterday's Children*. In that story, Executive Officer Korie is a martinet whose obsession with pursuing an unseen enemy destroys him. But that ending had always annoyed me. I liked Korie too much. And I really wanted to see him solve his problem. So, in 1977 I added twelve more chapters to the book, giving Korie the opportunity to produce a brilliant military victory. It was a much more satisfying conclusion. The book was retitled *Starhunt*. (Not necessarily a better title, but it distinguished the new version from the earlier one.)

Now, as I started to block out a pilot episode for *Millennium*, I realized that I could reuse some of the characters from *Starhunt*, in particular Commander Jon Thomas Korie. (Two things about Korie's name: Commander Buzz Correy was the hero of *Space Patrol*, my favorite TV series when I was growing up, so I thought it would be a nice touch to have a new Commander Korie flying the star lanes. Korie also shares the same initials with a certain *other* starship captain; one who is also legendary for the exploits of *his* John Thomas . . .)

The outline for the pilot episode had Executive Officer Korie assigned to a new ship, dealing with an aging captain no longer able to handle the rigors of starship life and totally unprepared for the coming war. As a personal in-joke, I had this captain bring along his legal advisor as an aide, a relationship which I characterized as "King Lear v. Iago." And it also gave me the opportunity to give Korie a line of dialog especially close to my heart: "Why does a starship need a lawyer?" (Korie probably wasn't the only one asking that question.) Universal enthusiastically approved the outline, they loved the humor, and I went right to work on a two-hour pilot script.

In that first script, a Morthan assassin gets loose on the starship and not only kills a few crewmembers, he also eats them. This created the opportunity for two more deliciously nasty lines of dialog: "Ohmygod, the Morthan just ate the captain's lawyer." "Voluntarily . . . ?"

Despite their love of the outline, the folks at Universal felt the script had turned out too dark, too grim to be a good series opener. They wanted a new pilot episode. They weren't quite sure what changes they wanted, but they wanted changes. I was a little annoyed at the vagueness of these notes, but I recognized their concerns and agreed to a second draft.

Then the Writers' Guild went out on strike for six months. And that meant that I could not turn in the second draft script, could not get paid, could not move the show forward. It was a very frustrating period, because on the one hand, I recognized the validity of the Guild's negotiating points—on the other hand, the delay was going to kill production deals all over town.

The strike ended in August and a few days later, I turned in the second draft script. In this version, a new captain comes aboard, makes a bad decision and inadvertently triggers the interstellar equivalent of Pearl Harbor. I also added the Quillas and Brian Armstrong's sexual adventures. The studio loved the second draft script and for a while, there was even some discussion of shooting the series in HDTV so that Sony could use it as a showcase for their new video technology.

And then, nothing else happened. It was set aside as the studio's priorities changed. It was now officially one of those things "that seemed a good idea at the time." So I went back to work on my novels and finished *A Rage For Revenge*, the third novel in my alien invasion series, The War Against The Chtorr.

Before tackling the fourth book in the Chtorr series, *A Season For Slaughter*, I decided to adapt the *Millennium* pilot into a novel called *The Star Wolf*. At the last moment, to avoid confusion with Edmond Hamilton's classic novel of the same name, the publisher retitled my book *The Voyage of the Star Wolf*.

One afternoon in 1990, I received a phone call from a producer named Ed Elbert. A long time ago, he'd read a book of mine called *Yesterday's Children* and had always thought it might make a good TV series. Would I be interested in optioning the rights to him?

I sent him my pilot script, now retitled *The Star Wolf*. He recognized immediately that this was exactly what he was looking for; we could take all of that early development work and expand it. I brought in Dorothy Fontana as a partner in this exercise and we expanded the original concepts of the two scripts already finished. Another good friend, who also recognized the potential of the series, came aboard as well; he opened his checkbook and invested in some artwork, costume designs and the construction of a starship model.

Somewhere in there, we realized that there was more story to tell than we could fit into two hours and I expanded the second draft pilot script to four one-hour episodes structured so they could be shown either as four one-hour episodes or a four-hour miniseries. We began showing it around town.

We presented it as "World War II in space" and almost everybody understood the concept immediately, but nobody wanted to pay for the privilege of putting us into production. (One studio loved it so much they made an offer, withdrew the offer the next day, then took our tag line "World War II in space" and used it to produce a forgettable series that failed quickly.)

During all of this, Dorothy Fontana and I continued to develop the series' "bible"—the Writers/Directors' Guide. And we made a promise to ourselves. We were not going to do a pale imitation of *Star Trek*. We would do all the things that *Star Trek* couldn't do or wouldn't do— the stories that were too dangerous or too subversive or too disturbing. We said our goal would be to go where no TV series had gone before.

We developed backstories for all of the major characters, we created a military arena for the war, we designed and staffed an entire starship and we invested a great deal of time working out story arcs for all of the characters, even some of our favorite background people. Most important, we even blocked out complete outlines for a number of episodes.

Here are a few of the ideas we generated:

Our crew is not the best and the brightest and our ship is not the biggest and the fastest. She is a liberty ship, fresh off the assembly line, untested and inexperienced. As the series proceeds, we start to see this nice clean vessel age. She gets dirty, she gets posters glued to her bulkheads, graffiti shows up everywhere, things break down and get hammered back together with whatever materials are available. Many of her internal walls are a kind of Styrofoam (you don't need more than that and this is a hastily-assembled liberty ship), so they get easily dented and punched.

The first twenty minutes of the first episode are about some *other* ship—this one is the best and the brightest. She is the *Endeavor* and she is commanded by Captain Richard Long. (Or Richard Head, I forget which.) Everything on this ship is just a little *too* special, a little *too* wonderful, a little *too* well color-coordinated. Then, just before the first commercial, she gets ambushed by Morthan marauders. She blows up and everybody dies. When we come back from the break, the *Star Wolf* shows up for a planned rendezvous, a much less impressive vessel, dirty, gritty and crewed by folks whose uniforms aren't quite as well-tailored . . . Hello, this is the *real* starship in this series. We expected this would be one of the most outrageous gags in television history. We knew the audience would understand exactly what point we were making.

Jon Korie, the executive officer of the ship is our central character. He deserves to be promoted to captain, but fate has conspired against him and his promotion is held in permanent limbo. This may be lucky for him, because the *Star Wolf* is a jinxed ship. She keeps killing her captains. This would let us have big-name guest stars come aboard to be captain of the *Star Wolf* for two or four episodes and then either die in combat, have a nervous breakdown, be eaten by Morthans, be recalled by the manufacturer, fall out the airlock or experience some other bizarre twist of fate.

One story we wanted to do had the *Star Wolf* caught by a Morthan battle cruiser in the very first scene of the episode, the "teaser." The brand-new captain opens a channel and says, "We surrender," and Brik immediately kills him. "Surrender is not an option." The rest of the episode would be Brik's court-martial. (The jury would be three Alliance Morthans, because only they could understand Brik's reasoning.)

We wanted to establish Molly Williger as the ugliest woman in the galaxy—make her the butt of a legendary joke—and then give her the most seething and passionate love affair in television history, because not only the pretty people fall in love. Love is more than just a nice package of chest and cheekbones.

Every character on the ship would have a secret which would be revealed during the course of the series. Jon Korie's secret is the most astonishing. (And on the elusive chance that we might still turn this thing into a TV series, I'm not going to reveal it here.) At one point, I even wrote a script putting the whole crew of the ship through the Mode Training—one of those personal-effectiveness courses that sometimes function like psychological boot camp.

And yes, one of the stories both Dorothy and I wanted to do was *Blood and Fire*, adapted from the episode I had written for *Star Trek: The Next Generation*, which they had never filmed.

Other writers of our acquaintance knew we were working on this series and several of them suggested story ideas that we knew immediately we wanted to use. Steve Boyett suggested "A Day In The Life" and Daniel Keys Moran gave us "The Knight Who Stayed Home." With their permission, both of these stories were combined into a second Star Wolf novel, called *The Middle of Nowhere*. If the series ever goes into production, those two episodes *will* be part of it.

All of this work was enormously invigorating. We actually had the time to consider in depth a lot of development problems that under ordinary circumstances would have to be decided in a mad rush. We could talk not only about the immediate solution, but also about the long-term consequences to the entire series of each decision. It was a creative opportunity that few shows ever get. We also knew that if and when we ever got a firm commitment to go into production, we would, from the very first moment, be six months ahead of schedule. There would be questions we would not have to ask, because we had already worked out the answers.

Oh, yes—somewhere in all of this confusion, I adopted a little boy named Sean. (That particular adventure has since been documented in *The Martian Child*. It seemed like a very good idea at the time. It still seems a good idea today, eleven years later.) One day, my son asked me, "Daddy, what can I do in the TV show?" Before I could even figure out how to explain to an eight-year-old that television production is really not a great adventure for any child, it's more boring than exciting, he began to explain, "I could be this weird-looking little guy who walks around in the background and doesn't say anything." And even as he was saying it, I recognized the opportunity for a marvelous sight gag—a short little "Martian" who would show up briefly in every show, handing someone a wrench or carrying some bizarre object down a corridor (like Alfred Hitchcock walking out of the Cumberland train station with a cello in the 1946 production of *The Paradine Case*). And if the series continued for several years, we could occasionally have someone wonder aloud about the growth of the Martian. So I told Sean I loved his idea and he should go off and draw a picture of what he thought his costume should look like. (I already knew what it would look like: something very easy to hang on a child, something very easy to remove.)

Eventually, a Canadian company agreed to provide production facilities and even a majority of funding for a Star Wolf television series. They had the foreign investors, they had the Canadian tax benefits, the money was there, all they needed was an American buyer to give us credibility.

At one point, the Sci-Fi Channel came aboard for a few months and even invested in a set of rewrites. We used that as an opportunity to increase the suspense, the sex and the action in the scripts, while clarifying the Morthan threat even more. Regretfully, we removed the gag of destroying the *Endeavor* in the first twenty minutes, but we replaced it with a situation that dramatically increased Korie's internal dilemma. By now, we felt that the four one-hour pilot episodes were as good as we could create for a science fiction television series. And so did everyone else who read them. One executive said to us, "We have never had such a well-developed presentation laid on our desks. We have never seen pilot scripts so well-written and so intelligent." But then . . . nothing happened. The Sci-Fi Channel got sold, a new executive came in, decisions were postponed. And nothing moved forward. The Canadian company had to do this, then they had to do that. Everything was contingent on everything else. And everything else was next week or next month. They stalled us for the better part of two years until the options expired and they went bankrupt. (Sheesh.)

One afternoon, I was discussing *Blood and Fire* with Dorothy Fontana, and as an experiment, I opened up a copy of my original *Star Trek* script and began looking to see how hard it would be to adapt the story. I did a global swap of character names. (I probably shouldn't be admitting this, should I?) Picard became Parsons. Riker became Korie. Crusher became Williger. LaForge became Leen. The *Enterprise* became the *Star Wolf*. But after that, the parallels stopped. Then I read through the script to see what else had to be adjusted. Hmm. Quite a bit, actually. I had to get rid of the warp-drive engines, I had to restructure the problem without using the transporter and I had to take a long, hard look at the character relationships. None of them worked as a Star Wolf story. So I sat down and began working my way through the script, line by line, turning it into a real Star Wolf adventure and not simply a revised *Star Trek* episode.

It was an exciting process. The differences between the two were profound. (For one thing, we weren't in production, and we still had the freedom, the luxury, to write for ourselves.) More important, I discovered some things about the *Star Wolf* that I hadn't realized before—that we weren't just telling stories about problems that could be solved easily in the last five minutes of the episode; no, we were examining the hearts and souls of our characters as they confronted the continuing challenges before them. There were consequences to their actions—moral, legal, political.

So I had to do a major rewrite of every scene, every character and every plot point in order to convert that original *Star Trek* script to a Star Wolf story. Of particular importance, if the captain of the ship violated a standing fleet order, her court-martial would be mandatory—even if she saved her ship and her crew. That became a critical dilemma, as important as the more immediate problem of the bloodworms.

I had a not-so-hidden agenda here. When I finished adapting the script, I had the outline for another Star Wolf novel. I had one more book contract pending with Bantam Books, and *Blood and Fire* would be the perfect property; they had already published two previous Star

Wolf novels and *Starhunt*, the book that started the whole adventure. Turning *Blood and Fire* into a novel gave me the opportunity to get even deeper into all of the characters and I knew that, eventually, I would have to rewrite the *Blood and Fire* script to include many of the new scenes developed for the novel. (If/when this damn TV series ever gets on the air, *Blood and Fire* will probably be a two-part episode.)

When I finished this novel, the one you're holding in your hands right now, Bantam Books chose not to publish it. They were shutting down their science fiction line. (But they did pay me, in case you're wondering.) Because the book was already part of a pre-existing series, few other publishers were interested; they'd have to buy all of the other out-of-print books in the series to go with it, and nobody was buying backlist books anymore. So the manuscript for this book sat on the shelf for a couple of years until Glenn Yeffeth of BenBella Books read it. The way he tells it, he got down on his knees and begged me for the opportunity to publish a new David Gerrold novel. The way I tell it, I'm the one begging, "Please publish my orphaned child." The truth is probably somewhere in between.

There are now three novels in the Star Wolf trilogy. At the moment, I don't expect to write any additional adventures, but I'm not ruling it out either. The first novel is *The Voyage of the Star Wolf*. The second is *The Middle of Nowhere*; the events in that book take place immediately after the events in the first novel. The events in *Blood and Fire*, however, do not occur until at least a year or two later. Maybe longer. Our original intention in the TV series was not to tell this story until we had already taken our characters through a whole series of other events, partly because we didn't want to be accused of being so desperate that we had to recycle an old *Star Trek* script, and partly because the payoff at the end of this story was not one we wanted to get to quickly. Because Korie has endured so much by the time of this story, Dorothy and I both felt that he was entitled to at least one major personal victory. In this book, he gets two, both on the last page. (If you haven't read it yet, no peeking!)

There are a number of adventures, developed for the TV series that come before this story that have not been novelized yet—in particular the destruction of Taalamar. In that proposed story, Korie learns that his family might have evacuated safely before their home world was destroyed. But now Taalamar is under bombardment by Morthan-directed asteroids and no matter how many rescue ships arrive to carry away refugees, millions of people will still die. The story we want to tell is Korie's desperate search for his family on a doomed planet while the crew of the *Star Wolf* continues to evacuate other families and children. Because Dorothy Fontana has first dibs on writing that script, I haven't tackled it as a novel. So *Blood and Fire* occurs much later, after Korie has proven himself more than once. (This is referred to in the text.)

Now about that TV series. . . .

In 1999, we found another investor, who paid to develop some computer-generated spaceships and even a short proof-of-concept video. We took the series around town again, talking to a new set of executives, often in the same offices as before. And again everybody loved it, but nobody quite wanted to make the commitment. One studio said it was too dark, another said it was too light. One company felt it was too military, another said it wasn't military enough.

In 2001, a prestigious special-effects company thought *Star Wolf* would be an excellent property to leverage themselves into becoming a complete production facility. We made the rounds again. Same offices, new executives. New ways of saying, "Wow! This is a great show!" One company loved it but didn't have the resources. Another company loved it, but they were already in a deal with someone else and didn't want to do two science fiction shows—"Why didn't you show us this before?" At that meeting, my partners would have physically restrained me from hurling myself out an open window, except that we were on the first floor and there was little danger that I would hurt myself landing on an azalea bush.

Meanwhile, as I write this, there's an executive at another studio who has just read our four pilot scripts, and he thinks that they would make a great TV series. . . .

Coming soon from BenBella Books: *The Un-Making of The Star Wolf—The Greatest TV Series You Never Saw.* We'll publish the whole horrifying history, all the different scripts, plus the bible. You can make up your own mind.

DAVID GERROLD